THE

SCOTLAND YA

OF

EDGAR WALLACE

An omnibus of Wallace's most exciting works — over nine hundred pages — two complete novels — seven stories

British Library Cataloguing-in-Publication Data
A catalogue record for this book is available from
the British Library

EDGAR WALLACE

Richard Horatio Edgar Wallace was born in London, England in 1875. He received his early education at St. Peter's School and the Board School, but after a frenetic teens involving a rash engagement and frequently changing employment circumstances, Wallace went into the military. He served in the Royal West Kent Regiment in England and then as part of the Medical Staff Corps stationed in South Africa. However, Wallace disliked army life, finding it too physically testing. Eventually he managed to work his way into the press corps, becoming a war correspondent with the *Daily Mail* in 1898 during the Boer War. It was during this time that Wallace met Rudyard Kipling, a man he greatly admired.

In 1902, Wallace became editor of the *Rand Daily Mail,* earning a handsome salary. However, a dislike of "economising" and a lavish lifestyle saw him constantly in debt. Whilst in the Balkans covering the Russo-Japanese War, Wallace found the inspiration for *The Four Just Men,* published in 1905. This novel is now regarded as the prototype of modern thriller novels. However, by 1908, due to more terrible financial management, Wallace was penniless again, and he and his wife wound up living in a virtual slum in London. A lifeline came in the form of his *Sanders of the River* stories, serialized in a magazine of the day, which (despite being seen to contain pro-imperialist and racist overtones today) were highly popular, and sparked two decades of prolific output from Wallace.

Over the rest of his life, Wallace produced some 173 books and wrote 17 plays. These were largely adventure narratives with elements of crime or mystery, and usually combined a bombastic sensationalism with hammy violence. Arguably his best – and certainly his most successful, sparking as it did a semi-successful stint in Hollywood – work is his 1925 novel *The Gaunt Stranger,* later renamed *The Ringer* for the stage.

Wallace died suddenly in Beverly Hills, California in 1932, aged 57. At the time of his death, he had been earning what would today be considered a multi-million pound salary, yet incredibly, was hugely in debt, with no cash to his name. Sadly, he never got to see his most successful work – the 'gorilla picture' script he had earlier helped pen, which just a year after his death became the 1933 classic, *King Kong.*

BOOKS BY

AGAIN SANDERS
A KING BY NIGHT
EDGAR WALLACE'S MAMMOTH MYSTERY BOOK
GUNMAN'S BLUFF
MR. COMMISSIONER SANDERS
ON THE SPOT
PEOPLE
RED ACES
TERROR KEEP
THE ARRANWAYS MYSTERY
THE BLACK
THE BLACK ABBOT
THE BOOK OF ALL POWER
THE CALENDAR
THE CLEVER ONE
THE COLOSSUS
THE CRIMSON CIRCLE
THE DARK EYES OF LONDON
THE DEVIL MAN
THE DOOR WITH SEVEN LOCKS
THE DOUBLE
THE FACE IN THE NIGHT
THE FEATHERED SERPENT
THE FLYING SQUAD
THE FORGER
THE FOURTH PLAGUE
THE GIRL FROM SCOTLAND YARD
THE GREEN RIBBON
THE INDIA RUBBER MEN
THE JUST MEN OF CORDOVA
THE LAW OF THE THREE JUST MEN
THE MAN AT THE CARLTON
THE MURDER BOOK OF J. G. REEDER
THE NORTHING TRAMP
THE RINGER
THE RINGER RETURNS
THE SILVER KEY
THE SQUEALER
THE TERRIBLE PEOPLE
THE THREE JUST MEN
THE TRAITORS' GATE
THE TWISTER
WHITE FACE

CONTENTS

THE SILVER KEY

ABOUT MR. J. G. REEDER

RED ACES

THE POETICAL POLICEMAN

THE STEALER OF MARBLE

THE INVESTORS

ABOUT THE RINGER

THE MAN WITH THE RED BEARD

THE END OF MR. BASH—THE BRUTAL

THE SWISS HEAD WAITER

THE BLACK

FOREWORD

'HIS BOOK is an anthology chosen from the work of ıe most popular of all mystery writers—Edgar Wal-.ce. It contains his masterpiece of terror and mystery, *'he Black,* the startling tale of modern crime called *'he Silver Key,* and it introduces you to Mr. J. G. :eeder of the Public Prosecutor's office, with his ıutton-chop whiskers, his umbrella—and his Brown-ıg .45.

It displays the skill, the versatility, and the humor ıat have made a legend of Edgar Wallace. His in-ustry, his sales, his reputation have become fabulous. . short time ago every fourth book sold in England ɔre his name. Very nearly the same number still do. ı Germany the *Romane von Edgar Wallace* fill the ookstalls. In America his sales in all editions run close › a quarter of a million copies a year. His name is ımiliar throughout the civilized world. More people ave read his books than those of any other modern uthor. Kings and presidents, busmen and burglars, ave been his admirers. He has had three successful lays running on the London stage at the same time. Ie has turned out books, articles, plays, motion pic-ures, racing and dramatic columns, at an incredible peed. And he has done it all himself. No "ghosts" ave aided him. No hack writers have taken his plots and written them up. What Wallace signed he wrote Not even Dumas exceeded his output.

For the average writer Wallace's methods woul have made hasty, ill-constructed books. Not so fo Wallace. His mind, which forgot nothing once seen o heard, was stocked with the gossip of the police head quarters of half the world. He was familiar with thou sands of cases, hundreds of criminals. He knew th Yard men intimately, and he knew the underworld wit which the Yard men dealt. That is one of the reason why Wallace's Scotland Yard has such an air of reality As with everything he wrote, he knew what he wa talking about.

He had knocked about the world himself. He ha been soldier, newspaper correspondent, journalist. H knew life, and he had what they all had—all thos writers who have enthralled millions: the gift of th born story-teller. And he knew the human mind, wha thrills and interests it, what bores it. Because he dic he was able to write books that are never slow, neve dull, never uninteresting. His own immense energy an love of life shine through every page.

Estimates of the number of his books vary. Twent of the vast pages in the British Museum Catalogue ar covered by his titles. Probably there were close to 15 novels and possibly twenty more volumes of shor stories, and barring his African stories and a fev others, they were all based, in one way or another, o crime. Even Wallace himself had lost track of th exact number, for he was never greatly interested i the business and statistical end of his career. Some times he would dictate a book over a week-end an ship it off to his publishers without a further glance

On one famous occasion he promised a new manuscript to a publisher with whom he was lunching. He had also promised his regular publisher a new manuscript. But so rapidly did he work that the two manuscripts were ready almost at the same time, and through some mischance the first publisher got the original of one manuscript, and the second the carbon. The oversight was not discovered until each had set the book up, whereupon, with true British sportsmanship, they tossed a shilling to see who would have the honour of actually issuing it.

In *Masters of Mystery*,[1] published in England a short time ago, a book which should be in the library of every detective-story fan, Mr. H. Douglas Thomson has a number of interesting remarks on the Wallace collection. He classifies his books into five main groups, (1) *The Four Just Men Series* (*The Law of the Three Just Men—The Four Just Men—The Just Men of Cordova—The Three Just Men*); (2) the police novels, such as *The Crimson Circle, The Ringer, The Squealer, The Terror, The Silver Key*, etc.; (3) the thrillers, such as *The Green Archer, The India Rubber Men, The Black, The Avenger*, etc.; (4) The J. G. Reeder stories, *Red Aces, The Murder Book of J. G. Reeder*, and *Mr. Reeder Returns* (to be published shortly by A. L. Burt Co.); and (5) The *Sanders of the River* stories, which are about African adventure, and do not deal with detection or mystery. Three of the first four groups are represented in the pages that follow. Mr. Thomson points out that Wallace's virtues include straightforward narrative,

[1] *Masters of Mystery: A Study of the Detective Story*, by H. Douglas Thomson, London, 1931; Wm. Collins Sons & Co.

with no padding and no nonsense; a quality of genuin excitement, with no dependence on artifice for the crea tion of atmosphere; humor which is never strained, a witness Mr. J. G. Reeder, an inimitable character; a inside and very expert knowledge of Scotland Yar and police methods and a close familiarity with th lingo of crooks.

Arnold Bennett, however, seemed to feel that Wal lace was wasting his great gifts in merely entertainin the world. "He is content with society as it is," h wrote. "He parades no subversive opinions. He is 'cor rect.' Now, it is very well known that all novelist who have depicted contemporary society, and wh have lived, abound in subversive opinions. Look a Defoe, Swift, and Fielding. Feel their lash. Remem ber the whips and scorpions of Dickens, and the effor of even the Agag footed Thackeray to destroy utterl the popular convention of the romantical hero. An Hardy's terrible rough-hewing of the divinity tha shapes our ends. . . . It may be counted a maxim tha good modern literature is never made out of correc sentiments. If there are exceptions to this rule the must be extremely few. . . . Perhaps I am unfair t Edgar Wallace. Perhaps in earlier years he has chas tised society with intent to be immortal." Perhaps, a Mr. Bennett points out, Wallace should have laid mor stress on sociology and less on entertainment. That however, is hardly a statement to which the million of readers who have found excitement and relaxatio in his books will subscribe.

Other comments on his work are more illuminating Writing in the London *Daily Telegraph,* "A Frien Who has Watched Him" remarks:

"Many fantastic stories were told of Edgar Wallace. It was said that he hired 'ghosts,' that he had a card index of plots, that he dictated simultaneously a novel to a stenographer and a play to a dictaphone while writing a racing article by hand.

"The truth is that he never used a line of anybody else's writing, and once offered £1000 to anybody who could prove that he did. Nor did he try the impossible feat of simultaneously dictating different stories.

"But he really was a phenomenally fast worker—faster even than Scott, who wrote the 300,000 words or so of *Waverley* in six weeks, or Trollope, who wrote about a hundred long novels while doing the work of a civil servant.

"Wallace had two secrets. One was the amazing, almost mechanical, precision of his mind. He never seemed to be at a loss in the steady flow of words; he had the chess player's faculty of seeing a dozen moves ahead; and he could work in incident after incident, thrill after thrill, that would all link up in the end, with the ease of a Capablanca opening a gambit.

"His other secret was the ease of his style. He never tortured his brain for a startling adjective or a far-fetched simile. He wrote just as he talked, and he was one of the best talkers in London, whether in private or on a platform, crisp, broad, and humorous.

"Much of his work was spoken into a dictaphone. In this way he could get through a play in two or three days. His fastest time, I think, was one act in three hours; and thanks to his clarity of thought and gift of natural dialogue, even this needed little revision. He used also to dictate to a very fast typist.

"In his early days publishers and editors gave him

endless amusement. One magazine editor commissioned twelve stories, and wanted the first in a month. Ten days later Wallace dropped in and gossiped, with a parcel under his arm. 'Don't forget that first story,' said the editor as he rose. 'Oh, I nearly forgot,' said Wallace, and he threw down all twelve."

Another writer in *The Morning Post* remarked:

"He was the Elder Dumas of our day. He had a genius for high-speed story-telling, and, like the immortal author of *The Three Musketeers,* never worried about the quest of the *mot juste.*

"Highbrow critics never did him justice, insisting that he was all matter and no manner at all. In point of fact, his stories are full of vivid descriptive passages, which could hardly have been improved by any amount of work with the file, conversation which reveals a personality in half a dozen words, and characterization which is truly creative. He has seen men naked in the years of unsheltered youth and knew the worst and best of them.

"His early struggles to exist had not embittered him, and he was quick to detect the streak of the lovableness which can be found in the basest characters of real life. He was himself the soul of honor—one of 'Nature's gentlemen' from the first—yet he could understand the mentality of the crook in a way which was the envy of the professional sleuth.

"But perhaps the unique feature of his work was its wealth of incident which, in its rapid involutions, recalled the Pharaoh's eggs of our childhood.

"He did not take himself or his novels seriously, having an unflattering sense of humor. He imitated nobody except himself in his novels; there may have been a falling off in freshness and originality in some of the later ones. A century hence, it may well be, when the disgrace of being a popular 'best seller' is forgiven, he will be rediscovered as the Elder Dumas was in the 'nineties and hailed as a *nature* (there is no exact English equivalent for the French term as used by biographers) who is worthy of critical study."

And J. B. Priestley summed up his work in this way:

"He had no pretensions to literature and called himself a journalist, but nevertheless a great many more pretentious writers have always been much further from literature than Wallace was. And as a popular entertainer on an epic scale his name and fame should be with us for generations."

If this is your first introduction to Wallace's great gallery of characters, you will, if you have fallen under his spell, find his best titles still in print and on the shelves of your bookstore. For sheer entertainment you will find them unsurpassed in any of the flood of new books. One of the things that set Edgar Wallace apart was his faculty of combining speed with consummate craftsmanship. Nothing affected the sureness of his skill. In his own field he was and is supreme—the greatest mystery writer of them all.

THE SILVER KEY

As WITH many another widely read writer, there is a certain lack of uniformity in choosing Wallace's greatest novels. *The Dark Eyes of London, The Black* (included in this volume), *The India-Rubber Men,* among others, have been suggested, but among his later novels none has been more popular or more praised than *The Silver Key*. Like all his books, it combines with its blood and excitement and swift action the gift of style and character which has given Wallace the name of the Dickens of crime. Chief Inspector Surefoot Smith, of the C.I.D., Scotland Yard, the book's detective, is an amazing creation, humorous, astute, and wholly without nerves. His adventures with the eccentric millionaire, Mr. Washington Wirth, the petty crook found murdered in a taxi, the suit of evening clothes in a dusty closet, and the mysterious silver key are an epic of crime.

Chief Inspector Smith, who hates science and loves beer, is the antithesis of Philo Vance. Wallace, who knew the Yard intimately, built him out of his close acquaintance with the relentless, imperturbable, and thoroughly human group of detectives that constitute the C.I.D. You will find excitement of a new flavour when you follow with Surefoot Smith the dark and tangled trail that leads through murder and mystery to an astounding climax. *The Silver Key* ranks high not only among Wallace's novels but among all mystery novels.

THE SILVER KEY

CHAPTER I

THEY were all in this business—Dick Allenby, inventor and heir-at-law; Jerry Dornford, man-about-town and wastrel; Mike Hennessey, the theatrical adventurer; Mary Lane, small-part actress; Leo Moran, banker and speculator; Horace Tom Tickler (alas, for him!) was very much in it, though he knew nothing about it. So were Mr. Washington Wirth, who gave parties and loved flattery; old Hervey Lyne and the patient Binny, who pulled his Bath chair and made his breakfast and wrote his letters; and Surefoot Smith.

There came a day when Binny, who was an assiduous reader of newspapers that dealt with the more picturesque aspects of crime, was to find himself the focal point of attention and his evidence read by millions who had never before heard of him—a wonderful experience.

Mr. Washington Wirth's parties were most exclusive affairs and, in a sense, select. The guests were chosen with care, and might not, in the manner of the age, invite the uninvited to accompany them; but they were, as Mary Lane said, "an odd lot." She went because Mike Hennessey asked her, and she rather liked the stout and lethargic Mike. People called him "poor old Mike" because of his bankruptcies, but just now sympathy would be wasted on him. He had found Mr. Washington Wirth, a patron of the theatre and things theatrical, and Mr. Washington Wirth was a very rich man.

He was also a mysterious man. He was generally believed to live in the Midlands and to be associated with industry. His London address was the Kellner Hotel, but he never slept there. His secretary would telephone in advance for the Imperial suite on a certain day, and on the evening of that day, when supper was laid for his twenty or thirty guests, and the specially hired orchestra was tuning up, he would appear, a stout, flaxen-haired man in horn-rimmed spectacles. The uncharitable said his flaxen hair was a wig, which may or may not have been true.

He was perfectly tailored, invariably wore white kid gloves. He spoke in a high, falsetto voice, and had a trick of clicking his heels and kissing the hands of his lady guests which was very Continental.

His guests were hand-picked. He chose—or Mike chose for him—the smaller theatrical fry: chorus girls, small-part ladies, an obscure singer or two.

Once Mike had suggested a brighter kind of party. Mr. Wirth was shocked.

"I want nothing fast," he said.

He loved adulation—and had his fill of it. He was

a generous spender, a giver of expensive presents; people living on the verge of poverty might be excused a little flattering.

You could not gate-crash into one of Mr. Washington Wirth's parties, invitations to which came in the shape of a small oblong badge, not unlike the badge worn by the ladies in the Royal Enclosure at Ascot, on which the name of the invited guest was written. This the recipient wore; it served a double purpose, for it enabled Mr. Wirth to read and address each of his guests by her name.

Mary Lane was well aware that the invitation was no tribute to her own eminence.

"I suppose if I had been a really important guest I shouldn't have been invited?" she said.

Mike smiled good-naturedly.

"You *are* important, Mary—the most important person here, my dear. The old boy was keen to know you."

"Who is he?"

Mike shook his head.

"He's got all the money in the world," he said.

She laughed. Mary Lane was very lovely when she laughed. She was conscious that Washington Wirth, albeit occupied with the cooing attention of two blonde lovelies, was watching her out of the side of his eyes.

"He gives lots of parties, doesn't he?" she asked. "Mr. Allenby told me to-day that they are monthly affairs. He must be rich, of course, or he wouldn't keep our play running. Honestly, Mike, we must be losing a fortune at the Sheridan."

Mike Hennessey took his cigar from his mouth and looked at the ash.

"I'm not losing a fortune," he said. Then, most unexpectedly: "Old Hervey Lyne a friend of yours, Mary?"

She denied the friendship with some vigour.

"No, he's my guardian. Why?"

Mike put back his cigar deliberately.

The band had struck up a waltz. Mr. Wirth was gyrating awkwardly, holding at arm's length a lady from the Jollity who was used to being held more tightly.

"I had an idea you were connected," he said. "Money-lender, wasn't he? That's how he made his stuff. Is Mr. Allenby related to him?"

There was a certain significance in the question, and she flushed.

"Yes—his nephew." She was a little disconcerted. "Why?"

Mike looked past her at the dancers.

"Trying to pretend they enjoy it," he said. "They're all getting gold-mounted vanity bags to-night—you'll get yours."

"But why do you ask about Mr. Lyne?" she persisted.

"Just wondering how well you knew the old man.

No, he's never lent me money. He wants gilt-edged security and I've never had it. Moran's his banker."

Mike was one of those disconcerting men whose speech followed the eccentric course of their thoughts.

He chuckled.

"Funny, that, Mary. Moran's his banker. You don't see the joke, but I do."

She knew Leo Moran slightly. He was by way of being a friend of Dick Allenby's, and he was, she knew, a frequent visitor to the theatre, though he never came back-stage.

When Mike was being cryptic it was a waste of time trying to catch up with him. She looked at her watch.

"Will he be very annoyed if I leave soon? I have promised to go on to the Legation."

He shook his head, took her gently by the arm, and led her up to where Mr. Wirth was being delightfully entertained by three pretty girls who were trying to guess his age.

"My little friend has to go, Mr. Wirth," he said. "She's got a rehearsal in the morning."

"Perfectly understood!" said the host.

When he smiled he had white, even teeth, for which no thanks were due to nature.

"Per-fectly understood. Come again, Miss Mary Lane. I'll be back from abroad in three weeks."

She took his big, limp hand and shook it. Mike escorted her out and helped her into her coat.

"Another hour for me and then I pack up," he said. "He never stays after one. By the way, I'll bring on your gift to the theatre."

She liked Mike—everybody liked Mike. There was hardly an actor or an actress in London who had not agreed to take half-salary from him. He could cry very convincingly when he was ruined, and he was always ruined when hard-hearted people expected him to pay what he owed them.

A lovable soul, entirely dishonest. Nobody knew what he did with the money which he had lost for so many people, but the probability is that it was usefully employed.

"I don't know what's the matter with our play," he said, as he walked with her along the corridor to the elevator. "Maybe it's the title—*Cliffs of Fate*—what does it mean? I've seen the darn' thing forty times and still I don't know what it's about."

She stared at him, aghast.

"But you chose it!" she protested.

He shook his head.

"He did," he jerked his thumb back to Mr. Wirth's suite. "He said it made him feel a better man when he read it. It's never made *me* want to go more regularly to the synagogue!"

He saw Mary depart, fussed over her like a brood hen. He liked Mary because she was real in a world of unreality. The first time he had taken her out to supper, he had offered her a few suggestions on the quickest method by which a young actress might reach stardom, and her name in lights, and she had answered him sanely and yet in a way that did not entirely wound his vanity—and the vanity of a fat man is prodigious.

Thereafter she went into a new category: he had many; she was the only woman in the world he really liked, though, it is said, he loved many. He strolled back to the hectic atmosphere of the supper room—Mr. Wirth was presenting the bags.

He was unusually gay: usually he drank very little, but to-night . . . Well, he had promised to drink a whole bottle of champagne if anybody guessed his age, and one of the three pretty girls had guessed thirty-two.

"Good God!" said Mike, when they told him.

As soon as was expedient, he took his patron aside.

"About time these people went, Mr. Wirth," he said.

Mr. Wirth smiled foolishly; spoke with the refinement which wine brings to some.

"My deah, deah fellah! I'm quate keepable of draving myself to deah old Coventry."

Certainly this was a new Mr. Wirth. Mike Hennessey was troubled. He felt he was in danger of losing a priceless possession. It was as though the owner of a secret gold mine from which he was drawing a rich dividend were hoisting a great flapping flag to mark its site.

"What you want," he said agitatedly, "is something cooling. Just wait here, will you?"

He ran out, saw the head waiter, and came back very soon with a little blue bottle. He measured a tablespoonful of white granules into a wine glass and filled it with water; then he handed this fizzling, hissing potion to the giver of the feast.

"Drink," he said.

Mr. Wirth obeyed. He stopped and gasped between the gulps.

By now the last guest had gone.

"All right?" asked Mike anxiously.

"Quite all right," snapped the other.

He seemed suddenly sober. Mike, at any rate, was deceived. He did not see his friend to his car, because that was against the rules. Mr. Wirth, wrapped in a heavy coat the collar of which was turned up, his opera hat at a rakish angle over his eyes, made his way to the garage near the hotel, had his car brought out, and was getting into it when the watcher sidled up to him.

"Can I have a word with you, mister?"

Mr. Wirth surveyed him glassily, climbed into his seat and shifted his gear.

"Can I have a word——"

The car jerked forward. The little interviewer, who had one foot on the running board, was sent sprawling. He got up and began to run after the car, to the amusement of the garage workers; car and pursuer vanished in the darkness.

CHAPTER II

THE trailer lost his quarry in Oxford Street and wandered disconsolately onward. A sort of homing instinct led him towards Regent's Park. Naylor Terrace was a magnificent little side street leading from the outer circle. It was very silent, its small, but stately, houses were in darkness.

Mr. Tickler—such was his peculiar name—stopped before No. 17 and looked up at the windows. The white blinds were drawn down and the house was lifeless. He stood, with his hands thrust into his pockets, blinking at the green door that he knew so well, at the three worn steps leading down, and the hollow steel railway that masons had fixed into the stonework to allow the easy descent of a Bath chair.

Inside was wealth, immense, incalculable wealth, and a stupid old man on the verge of the grave. Outside were poverty and resentment, the recollection of the rigours of Pentonville Prison, a sense of injustice. Old Lyne slept on the first floor. His bed was between these two high windows. That lower window marked the study where he sat in the daytime. There was a safe in the wall, full of useless old papers. Old Lyne never kept money in the house. All his life he had advertised this habit. A burglar or two had gone to enormous trouble to prove him a liar and had had nothing for their pains.

There he was, sleeping in luxury, the old rat, under featherweight blankets specially woven for him, under a satin coverlet packed tight with rare down, and here was he, Horace Tom Tickler, with a pinch of silver in his pocket.

But, perhaps, he was not there at all? That was an old trick of his to be out when everybody thought he was in, and in when they thought he was out.

He walked up and down the quiet cul-de-sac for nearly an hour, turning over in his mind numerous schemes, mostly impracticable, then he slouched back towards the bright streets and coffee stalls. He took a short cut through the mews to reach Portland Place, and the most astounding luck was with him.

A policeman walking through Baynes Mews heard the sound of a man singing. It was, if his hearing gave a right impression, the voice of one who had gone far in insobriety, and the voice came from a tiny flat, one of the many above the garages that lined each side of the mews. Time was when they were occupied exclusively by coachmen and chauffeurs, but the artistic and aristocratic classes had swamped these humble West End habitations, and more than half of the new population of Baynes

Mews were people who dressed for dinner and came home from parties and night clubs, their arms filled with gala favours, some of which made strange and distressing noises.

There was nothing in the voice to indicate anything more startling than normal inebriety. The policeman would have passed on, but for the fact that he saw a figure sitting on the step of the narrow door which led to the little flat above.

The officer turned his electric lamp on the sitter and saw nothing which paid for illumination. The little man who grinned up at the policeman was, as the officer said to his sergeant later, "nothing to write home about." He was red-faced, unshaven, wretchedly shabby. His collar might have been white a week before; he wore no tie and his linen, even in the uncertain light of the lamp, was uncleanly.

"'Ear him?" He jerked his head upward and grinned. "First time it's ever happened. Soused! What a mug, eh? Gettin' soused. He slipped me tonight, an' I'd never have tailed him—but for this bit of luck. . . . 'Eard him by accident . . . soused!"

"You're a bit soused yourself, aren't you?"

The policeman's tone was unfriendly.

"I've had three whiskies and a glass of beer. Does a man of the world get soused on that, I ask you!"

The voice upstairs had died down to a deep hum.

At the far end of the mews a horse was kicking in his box with maddening irregularity.

"A friend of yours?"

The little man shook his head.

"I don't know. Perhaps; that's what I got to find out. Is he friendly or ain't he."

The policeman made a gesture.

"Get out of this. I can't have you loungin' about. I seem to know your face too. Didn't I see you at Clerkenwell Police Court once?"

This officer prided himself on his memory for faces. It was his practice to say that he could never remember names, but never forgot faces. He thought he was unique and his remark original, and was not conscious of being one of forty million fellow citizens who also remembered faces and forgot names.

The little man rose and fell in by the officer's side.

"That's right." His step was a little unsteady. "I got nine munce for fraud."

He had in truth been convicted of petty larceny and had gone to prison for a month, but thieves have their pride.

Could a man convicted of fraud be arrested under the Prevention of Crimes Act because he sat in the doorway of a mews flat? This was the problem that exercised the mind of the constable. At the end of the mews he looked round for his sergeant, but that authority was not in sight.

A thought occurred to him.

"What you got in your pocket?"

The little man stretched out his arms.

"Search me—go on. You ain't entitled to, but I'll let you."

Another dilemma for the policeman, who was young and not quite sure of his rights and duties.

"Push off. Don't let me see you hanging around here," he ordered.

If the little man argued or refused, he could be arrested for "obstruction," for "insulting behaviour," for almost anything. But he did nothing.

"All right," he said, and walked off.

The policeman was tempted to recall him and discover the identity of the singer. Instead, he watched Mr. Tickler until he was out of sight.

The hour was a quarter to two in the morning. The patrol marched on to the point where his sergeant would meet him. As for Mr. Tickler, he went shuffling down Portland Place, looking in every doorway to find a cigarette end or cigar butt which might have been dropped by returning householders.

What a tale to tell if he could sell the information in the right quarter! Or he could put the "black" upon the singer. Blackmail gets easy money —if there is money to get. He stopped at a stall in Oxford Circus and drank a scalding cup of coffee.

He was not entirely without funds and had a bed to go to and money for bus fare, if the buses were running.

Refreshed, he continued his way down Regent Street and met the one man in the world he would willingly have avoided. Surefoot Smith was standing in the shadow of a recessed shop window, a stocky man, in a tightly buttoned overcoat. His derby hat was, as usual, on the back of his head; his round face, ruddier than Mr. Tickler's, was impassive. But for the periodical puffs of smoke which came from his big briar pipe he might have been a statue carved out of red brick.

"Hey!"

Reluctantly Tickler turned. He had been quick to identify the silent watcher. By straightening his shoulders and adding something of jauntiness to his stride he hoped to prevent the recognition from becoming mutual.

Surefoot Smith was one of the few people in the world who have minds like a well-organized card index. Not the smallest and least important offender who had passed through his hands could hope to reach a blissful oblivion.

"Come here, you."

Tickler came.

"What are you doing now, Tickler? Burglary, or just fetching the beer for the con men? Two a.m.! Got a home?"

"Yes, sir."

"Ah, somewhere in the West End! Gone scientific, maybe. Science is the ruin of the country!"

Rights or no rights, he passed his hands swiftly over Tickler's person; the little man stretched out his arms obediently and smiled. It was not a pretty smile, for his teeth were few and his mouth large and lop-sided. But it was a smile of conscious virtue.

"No jemmy, no chisel, no bit, no gat." Surefoot Smith gave Mr. Tickler absolution.

"No, Mr. Smith; I'm runnin' straight now. I'm going after a job to-morrow."

"Don't waste my time, boy," said Surefoot reproachfully. "Work! You've read about it. What kind of thieving do you do now? Whizzing? No, you're not clever enough."

Tickler said a bold thing. The lees of wine were still sizzling within him.

"I'm a detective," he said.

If Surefoot Smith was revolted he did not betray his emotion.

"Did you say 'defective' or 'detective'?" he asked.

He might have asked further questions, but at that moment a pocket-lamp flashed twice from the roof of the building he was watching. Instantly the roadway seemed to be covered by the figures of overcoated men converging on the building. Surefoot Smith was one of the first to reach the opposite sidewalk.

A loud rapping on the door told Mr. Tickler all he wanted to know. The place was being raided—a spieling club, or maybe worse. He was grateful for the relief and hurried on his way. At Piccadilly Circus he paused and considered matters. He was quite sober now and could review the position calmly; and the more he thought, the more thoroughly he realized that he had allowed opportunity to slip past him.

He turned and walked along Piccadilly, his chin on his chest, dreaming dreams of easy money.

CHAPTER III

MARY LANE looked at the plain gold watch on her wrist and gasped.

"Four o'clock, my dear!"

There were still twenty couples on the dancing floor of the Legation Club. It was a gala night, and they kept late hours at the Legation on these occasions.

"Sorry you've had such a tiring evening."

Dick Allenby didn't look sorry; he certainly did not look tired. There were no shadows under the laughing gray eyes, the tanned face was unlined. Yet he had not seen his bed for twenty-four hours.

"Anyway, you rescued me," he said as he called a waiter. "Think of it! I was alone until you came. When I said Moran had been and gone I was lying. The devil didn't turn up. Jerry Dornford tried to edge in on the party—he's still hoping."

He glanced across to a table on the other side of the room where the immaculately dressed Jerry sat.

"I hardly know him," she said.

Dick smiled.

"He wants to know you better—but he is distinctly a person not to know. Jerry has been out all the night—went away just before supper and has only just come back. Your other party was dull, was it? Funny devil, this man Wirth. It was cheek of Mike Hennessey to invite you there."

"Mike is rather a dear," she protested.

"Mike is a crook—a pleasant crook, but a crook. Whilst he is at large it is disgraceful that there is anybody else in prison!"

They passed out into the street, and as they stood waiting for a cab Dick Allenby saw a familiar figure.

"Why, Mr. Smith, you're out late!"

"Early," said Surefoot Smith. He lifted his hat to the girl. "'Evening, Miss Lane. Shockin' habit, night clubs."

"I'm full of bad habits," she smiled.

Here was another man she liked. Chief Inspector Smith of Scotland Yard was liked by many people and heartily disliked by many more.

The cab drew up. She refused Dick's escort any farther and drove off.

"Nice young lady, that," said Surefoot. "Actresses don't mean anything to me—I've just come from Marlborough Street, where I've been chargin' three of 'em—at least they called themselves actresses."

"A little raid?"

"A mere nothing," said Surefoot sadly. "I expected to find kings and only pulled in prawns."

"Pawns," suggested Dick.

"Small fish anyway," said Surefoot.

That he was called "Surefoot" was no testimony to his gifts as a sleuth. It was his baptismal name. His father had been a bookmaking publican, and a month before his child was born the late Mr. Smith, obsessed with the conviction that Surefoot, the Derby favourite, would not win, had laid that horse to win himself a fortune. If Surefoot had won, the late Mr. Smith would have been a ruined man. Surefoot lost, and in gratitude he had named his infant child after the equine unfortunate.

"I nearly came up to your workshop the other day and had a squint at that gun of yours—air-gun, ain't it?"

"A sort of one," said Dick. "Who told you about it?"

"That feller Dornford. *He's* a bad egg! I can't understand it—your gun. Dornford said you put in a cartridge and fire it, and that charges the gun."

"It compresses the air—yes."

Dick Allenby was not in the mood to discuss inventions.

"You ought to sell it to Chicago," said Mr. Smith, and made a clicking noise with his lips. "Chicago! Six murders a week and nobody pinched!"

Dick laughed. He had only returned from Chicago a month before and he knew something of the problems that the police had to face.

"These ride murders," Surefoot went on. "I mean takin' fellers out into the country in a car and shootin' 'em. Would it be possible here? No!"

"I'm not so sure." Dick shook his head. "Anyway, it is nearly half-past four and I'm not going to talk crime with you. Come up to my flat and we'll have a drink."

Surefoot Smith hesitated.

"All right; there's no sleep for me to-night. There's a cab."

The cab stood in the middle of the road near an island.

Smith whistled.

"Driver's gone away, sir." It was the club linkman who offered the information. "I tried to get it for the lady."

"He's asleep inside," said Smith, and walked across the road, Dick following.

Surefoot peered through the closed window of the cab, but saw nothing.

"He's not there," he said, and looked again.

Then he turned the handle and pulled open the door. Somebody was there—somebody lying on the floor, with his legs on the seat.

"Drunk!" said Smith.

He flashed his lamp on the figure. The face was visible, yet indistinguishable, for he had been shot through the head at close quarters; but Smith saw enough to recognize something which had once been Mr. Horace Tom Tickler and was now just a dead, mangled thing.

"Taken for a ride!" gasped Surefoot. "Good God! What's this—Chicago?"

CHAPTER IV

IN FIVE minutes there were a dozen policemen round the cab, holding back the crowd which had gathered, as crowds will gather at any hour of the day or night in London. Fortunately, a police sergeant had been at Marlborough Street, attending to a drunk, and he was on the spot within a few minutes.

"Shot at close quarters by a very small-bore pistol," was his first verdict after a casual examination.

In a very short time the ambulance arrived, and all that was mortal of Horace Tom Tickler was removed. A police officer started up the engine of the taxi and drove it into the station yard for closer inspection. The number had already been taken. Scotland Yard had sent a swift car to find the owner, a taxi driver named Wells.

Dick Allenby had not been specifically invited to the investigation, but had found himself in conversation with Surefoot Smith at crucial moments of the search, and had drifted with him to the police station.

The man had been shot in the cab; they found a bullet hole through the leather lining. The body,

Smith thought, had sagged forward to the ground and the legs had been lifted in the approved gang style.

"He was probably still alive when he was on the floor. The murderer must have fired a second shot. We have found a bullet in the floorboard of the cab."

"Have you found the driver?" asked Dick.

"He's on his way."

Mr. Wells, the driver, proved to be a very stout and thoroughly alarmed man. His story was a simple one. He had got to the garage where he kept his car a little before two o'clock. The door of the garage was closed. He left the cab outside, which was evidently a practice of his, for the cleaner, who would come on duty at six o'clock and prepare the cab for the day's work. He could leave it outside with impunity, because cabs are very rarely stolen; they are so easily identified and so useless to the average car thief that they are very seldom "knocked off." His garage was in a stable yard off the Marylebone Road.

So far as he was concerned, he had a complete alibi, for, after leaving the cab, he had gone to the nearest police station to deposit an umbrella and a pocketbook which had been left by a previous passenger. A policeman had seen him leave the car, and to this policeman he had brought the lost property, which he had afterwards deposited at the station. It was a very lonely yard, and, unlike such places, was entirely without inhabitants, the garages forming part of a building which was used as a furniture store.

It was seven o'clock, and the West End was alive with market cars, when Dick drove home to his flat at Queen's Gate. It was curious that the only impression left on him was one of relief that Mary had not walked across the road to the cab and opened the door, as she might have done, and made the hideous discovery. The car had been parked outside the club twenty minutes before the discovery; the driver had been seen to leave the taxi and walk towards Air Street.

The earliest discovery that had been made was that the taxi flag was down and a sum of seventeen shillings was registered on the clock. This gave the police approximately the period between the murder being committed and the body being found.

Late that afternoon Surefoot Smith called on Dick Allenby.

"Thought you'd like to know how far we've got," he said. "We found a hundred one-pound notes in this bird's pocket."

"Tickler's?"

"How did you know his name was Tickler?" Surefoot Smith regarded him with suspicion.

Dick did not answer immediately.

"Well, the odd thing is, I recognized him when I saw him. He used to be a servant of my uncle's."

"You didn't tell me that last night."

"I wasn't sure last night; I wasn't sure, in fact, until I saw the body lifted out. I don't know very much about my uncle's business, but I understand this man was fired for stealing, about six or seven years ago."

Surefoot nodded.

"That's right. I'd come to give you that bit of information. I saw old Lyne this morning, but, bless you, Scotland Yard means nothing to him. Your uncle, is he?" He nodded again. "Congratulations!"

"What did he say?" asked Dick, curious.

Surefoot Smith lit his huge pipe.

"If you think he broke down, I am here to put you right. All he could remember about Tickler was that he was a scoundrel, and anyway we knew that. A hundred one-pound notes! If there had only been a fiver amongst them it might have been easy."

He cleared a space on a crowded bench and perched himself upon it.

"I wonder who the fellow was who took him for a ride? American, I'll bet you! That's what's worrying me—science coming into crime!"

Dick laughed.

"According to you, Surefoot, science is responsible for all crime."

Mr. Smith raised his eyebrows inquiringly.

"Well, isn't it? What's science done? It's given us photography to make forgery easy, aëroplanes to get thieves out of the country, motor cars for burglars. What's wireless done? I've had four cases in the West End in the last six months of fellows who used wireless to rob people! What's electricity done? It helps safe-smashers to drill holes in strong rooms! Science!"

Dick thought there was very little evidence of applied science in the taxicab murder, and said so.

"It might have been committed in a horse cab."

"The driver couldn't have left a horse," was the crushing retort. "I'll bet you this is the first of many."

He reached out and put his hand on the oblong steel box that lay on the bench near him.

"That's science, and therefore it's going to be used by criminals. It's a noiseless gun——"

"Was the pistol last night noiseless?" asked Dick.

Surefoot Smith thought a moment, and then:

"Have you got any beer?" he asked.

There were a dozen bottles under one of the benches. Dick had many visitors who required refreshment. Surefoot Smith opened two and drank them in rapid succession. He was a great drinker of beer, had been known to polish off twenty bottles at a sitting without being any the worse for it, claiming, indeed, that beer intensified his powers of reasoning.

"No," he said, and wiped his moustache carefully with a large red handkerchief; "and yet we have seen nobody who heard the shots. Where were they fired? That cab could have been driven somewhere in the country. There are plenty of lonely places where a couple of shots would not be noticed or heard. You can go a long way in a couple of hours. There were rain marks on the windshield and mud on the wheels. There was no rain in London; there has been a lot just outside of London."

He reached mechanically under the bench, took out a third and a fourth bottle and opened them absent-mindedly.

"And how did you find my noble relative?"

"Friend of yours?" asked Surefoot.

Dick shook his head.

"Well, I can tell you what I think of him."

Mr. Smith described Hervey Lyne in a pungent sentence.

"Very likely," agreed Dick Allenby, watching his beer vanish. "I am hardly on speaking terms with him."

Again Surefoot wiped his moustache with great care.

"This fellow Tickler—you had a few words with him, didn't you, about five years ago?"

Dick's eyes narrowed.

"Did Mr. Lyne tell you that?"

"Somebody told me," said Surefoot vaguely.

"I kicked him out of my flat, yes. He brought rather an insulting message from my uncle, and supplemented it with a few remarks of his own."

Surefoot got down from the bench and brushed himself carefully.

"You ought to have told me all this last night," he said reproachfully. "It might have saved me a bit of trouble."

"I also might have saved myself four bottles of beer," said Dick, slightly irritated.

"That's been put to a good use," said Surefoot.

He examined the odd-looking air-gun again, lifted it without difficulty and replaced it.

"That might have done it," he said.

"Are you suggesting I killed this fellow?" Dick Allenby's anger was rising.

Surefoot smiled.

"Don't lose your temper. It's not you I am up against, but science."

"It certainly is a gun," said Dick, controlling his wrath; "but the main idea—I don't know whether you can get it into your thick head——"

"Thank you," murmured Surefoot.

"—is that this should be put to commercial use. By exploding an ordinary cartridge, or nearly an ordinary cartridge, in this breech, I create a tremendous air pressure, which can be just as well used for running a machine as for shooting a jail-bird."

"You knew he'd been in jail?" asked Surefoot, almost apologetically.

"Of course I knew he'd been in jail—two or three times, I should imagine—but I only know of one occasion, when my uncle prosecuted him. If I were you, Surefoot, I'd go to Chicago and learn something of the police methods there——"

"There ain't any," interrupted Surefoot decidedly. "I've studied the subject."

As Surefoot Smith walked towards Hyde Park he observed that all other events in the world had slumped to insignificance by the side of the taxicab murder. Every newspaper bill flamed with the words. One said "Important Clue"; he wasted a penny to discover that the clue was the first news that a hundred pounds had been found in the dead man's pocket, a fact which had not previously been revealed.

The antecedents of Wells had been investigated during the day and he had been given a clean bill by a man whose chief desire was to find the most damning evidence against him.

Smith was due at Scotland Yard for a conference at four o'clock. He hated conferences, where people sat round and smoked and expressed extravagant views on subjects they knew nothing about. But on this occasion, the first time for many years, he arrived promptly and had the satisfaction of finding that his four colleagues were as barren of ideas as he. They knew—and this was no discovery—that there was a possibility that this was a new type of crime which might become prevalent. Desperadoes had before now stolen cars, but had confined their operations to minor out-of-town burglaries.

There was one scrap of news. A policeman patrolling Portland Place from one of the mews behind had identified the body as that of a man to whom he had spoken at a quarter to two, and this tallied with Smith's own knowledge, for it was at two o'clock that he had seen Tickler walking down Regent Street from the direction of Portland Place.

Curiously enough, though a familiar phenomenon to police investigators, the policeman had said nothing about the drunken man in whose voice Tickler had been interested. Nor, in his report, had he given so much as a hint of that part of the conversation which revealed his knowledge of a man against whom he had had a grudge, and who might conceivably have had as deep an animosity towards him.

"This tells me no more than I know," said Surefoot, putting down the report. "Except that it is not true that Tickler ever had nine months; all his sentences were shorter. Who was it killed this poor little hound? He was broke, or nearly broke. I saw him stop to pick up a cigarette from the sidewalk just before he came up to me. Who picked him up in the stolen cab, and why?"

Fat McEwan leaned back in his well-filled chair and blew a trumpet of smoke to the ceiling.

"If there were such things as gangs you could guess it at once," he said despairingly. "But there are no gangs. This man was not even a nose, was he, Surefoot?"

Surefoot shook his head. A "nose" is a police informer, and Tickler had never been that.

"Then why the dickens should he have been killed? Tell me that."

This was a fair summary of an hour's discussion. Surefoot Smith went down to his little office entirely unenlightened. He found a number of letters, and one that had been posted at Westminster and had been delivered that afternoon. The envelope was dirty; his address was scrawled in an illiterate hand. He tore open the envelope, took out a sheet of paper, obviously extracted from a memorandum book of the cheaper kind. In pencil were the words:

> If you want to know who killed poor Mr. Tickler you'd better go and have a talk with Mr. L. Moran.

Smith looked at the letter for a long time, and then:

"Why not?" he asked himself aloud.

There were a great many things about Mr. Moran that he could never quite understand.

CHAPTER V

FAITH needs the garnishing of romance as much as hope requires the support of courage. Mary Lane had faith in her future, courage to brace the hope of ultimate achievement. Otherwise she was without the more important and disastrous illusions which do so much to create rosy prospects and unhappy memories.

She knew that some day she would be accepted by the West End of London as an important actress, that her name would appear in electric lights outside a theatre, and a little larger than her fellow artistes on the day-bill. But she never dreamed vain dreams of sudden fame, though, in the nature of things, fame is as sudden as the transition of a sound sleeper to wakefulness. Some day the slumbering public would open its eyes and be aware of Mary Lane. In the meantime it was oblivious of her existence—all except a few wide-awake writers of dramatic criticism. These very few, having a weakness for discovery, continuously swept the theatrical sky in search of *n*th dimension stars which would one day (here the astronomical analogy became absurd) blaze into the first dimension. Occasionally they "found"; more often than not they made themselves ridiculous, but covered their failure with well-designed fun poked at themselves and their own enthusiasms—which is one of the tricks of their business.

It was only a half-hearted discovery so far as Mary was concerned. She was a brighter speck in the nebula of young actresses. She might be (they said) a very great actress some day, if she overcame her habit of dropping her voice, if she learned how to use her hands, if this, that, and the other.

Mary strove diligently, for she was at the age when dramatic critics seem infallible. She did not dream unprofitably; never lay awake at night, imagining the eruption of an agitated management into the dressing room she shared with two other girls.

"You're understudying Miss Fortescue, aren't you? Get into her clothes quick: she's been taken ill."

She did not visualize newspaper columns acclaiming the young actress who had found fame in a night. She knew that understudy performances, however politely received, are as politely forgotten, and that a girl who grows famous in an evening steps into oblivion between Saturday and Monday.

On the second morning after her appearance at Washington Wirth's party, she had a brief interview with Mr. Hervey Lyne on the subject of her allowance. It was not a pleasant interview. None of her interviews with Mr. Lyne had ever been that.

"If you go on the stage you must expect to starve!" he snarled. "Your fool of a father made me his executor and gave me full authority. A hundred and fifty a year is all that you get until you're twenty-five. And there is nothing more to be said!"

She was very pretty and very angry, but she kept her temper admirably.

"Twenty thousand pounds brings in more than a hundred and fifty a year," she said.

He glared in her direction; she was just a blotch of blue and pink to his myopic vision.

"It is all you will get until you are twenty-five—and then I'll be glad to get rid of you. And another thing, young lady: you're a friend of my nephew, Richard Allenby?"

Her chin went up.

"Yes."

He wagged a skinny forefinger at her.

"He gets nothing from me—whether I'm alive or dead. Understand that!"

She did not trust herself to reply.

Binny showed her out and was incoherently sympathetic.

"Don't worry, miss," he said in his dull voice; "he ain't himself this mornin'."

She said nothing, hardly noticed Binny, who sighed heavily and wagged his head mournfully as he shut the door. He was by way of being a sentimentalist.

Ten minutes later she was talking vehemently over the telephone to Dick Allenby. His sympathy was more acceptable.

People used to say about Hervey Lyne that he was the sort of character that only Dickens could have drawn, which is discouraging to a lesser chronicler. He was eccentric in appearance and habit; naturally so, because he was old and self-willed and had a vivid memory of his past importance.

Everybody who was anybody in the late Victorian age had borrowed money from Hervey Lyne, and most of them had paid it back with considerable interest. Unlike the late "Chippy" Isaacs, as mild and pleasant a gentleman as ever issued money on note of hand, Hervey was harsh, unconscionable, and rude. But he was quick. The swells who drove in broughams and had thousands on their horses, and gave champagne parties to men who wore side whiskers and women who wore flounces and regarded other women who smoked cigarettes as being damned body and soul, were sometimes in difficulties to find ready money, and generally they chose Hervey first because they knew their fate sooner than if they applied to Chippy.

Hervey said "No" or "Yes" and meant "No" or "Yes." You could go into Hervey's parlour in Naylor Terrace and either come out in five minutes with the money you needed or in two minutes with the sure knowledge that if you had stayed two hours you would not have persuaded him.

He gave up lending money when the trustees of the Duke of Crewdon's estate fought him in the Law Courts and lost. Hervey thought they would win, and had the shock of his life. Thereafter he only lent very occasionally, just as a gambler will play cards occasionally (and then for small stakes) to recover something of the old thrill.

His attitude to the world can be briefly defined: the galley of his life floated serenely on a sluggish sea of fools. His clients were fools; he had never felt the least respect for any of them. They were fools to borrow, fools to agree to enormous and staggering rates of interest, fools to repay him.

Dick Allenby was a fool, a pottering inventor and an insolent cub who hadn't the brains to see on which side his bread was buttered. Mary Lane was a fool, a posturing actress who painted her face and kicked her legs about (he invariably employed this inelegant illustration) for a pittance. One was his nephew, and might with tact have inherited a million; the other was the daughter of his sometime partner, and might, had she been a good actress, have enjoyed the same inheritance— would enjoy it yet if he could arouse himself from his surprising lethargy and alter his will.

His servants were complete fools. Old Binny,

bald, stout, perspiring, who pulled his Bath chair into the park and read him to sleep, was a fool. He might have taken a kindlier view of Binny and left him a hundred or so "for his unfailing loyalty and tireless services," but Binny hummed hymn tunes in the house and hummed them a key or so flat.

Not that Binny cared. He was a cheery soul with large eyes and a completely bald head. A bit of a sluggard, whom his thin and whining wife (who was also the cook of 17 Naylor Terrace) found a difficult man to get out of bed in the mornings. Valet, confidential servant, messenger, butler, chair-puller and reader, Binny, alert or sleepy, was worth exactly three times as much wages as he received.

Old Hervey sat propped up in his armchair, glooming at the egg and toast that had been put before him. His thin old face wore an expression of discontent. The thick, tinted glasses which hid the hard blue eyes were staring at the tray, and his mind was far away.

"Has that jackass of a detective called again?"

"No, sir," said Binny. "You mean Mr. Smith?"

"I mean the fool that came to ask questions about that blackguard Tickler," stormed the old man, emphasizing every sentence with a blow on the table that set the cups rattling.

"The man who was found in the cab?"

"You know who I mean," snarled the old man. "I suppose one of his thieving friends killed him.

It's the sort of end a man like that would come to."

Hervey Lyne relapsed into silence, a scowl on his face. He wondered if Binny was robbing him too. There had been a suspicious increase in the grocery bill lately, Binny's explanation that the cost of food had gone up being entirely unacceptable. And Binny was one of those smooth, smug, crawling slaves who wouldn't think twice about robbing an employer. It was about time Binny was changed. He had hinted as much that morning, and Binny had almost moaned his anguish.

"It's going to be a fine day, sir, for your outing."

He stirred the contents of the teapot surreptitiously with a spoon.

"Don't talk," snapped the old man.

There was another long silence, and then:

"What time is that fellow calling?" he asked harshly.

Binny, who was pouring out the tea at a side table, turned his big head and gazed pathetically at his employer.

"What feller, sir? The young lady came at nine——"

Hervey's thin lip curled in silent fury.

"Of course she did, you fool! But the bank manager—didn't you ask him to come——"

"At ten, sir—Mr. Moran——"

"Get the letter—get it!"

Binny placed the cup of tea before his employer,

rummaged through a small heap of papers on an open secretaire, and found what he sought.

"Read it—read it!" snapped the old man. "I can't be bothered."

He never would be bothered again. He could tell light from dark; knew by a pale blur where the window was, could find his way unaided up the seventeen stairs which led to his bedroom;—but no more. He could sign his name, and you would never suspect that a man more than half blind was responsible for that flourish.

" 'Dear Mr. Lyne,' " read Binny in the monotonous voice he adopted for reading aloud, " 'I will give myself the pleasure of calling on you at ten o'clock to-morrow morning. Yours faithfully, Leo Moran.' "

Hervey smiled again.

"Give himself the pleasure, eh?" His thin voice grew shrill. "Does he think I'm asking him here for his amusement? There's the door bell."

Binny shuffled out and came back in a few seconds with the visitor.

"Mr. Moran," he announced.

"Sit down—sit down, Mr. Moran." The old man waved a hand vaguely. "Find him a chair, Binny, and get out—d'ye hear? Get out! And don't listen at the door, damn you!"

The visitor smiled as the door closed on a Binny who was unconcerned, unemotional, unresentful.

"Now, Moran—you're my bank manager."

"Yes, Mr. Lyne. I asked if I could see you a year ago, if you remember——"

"I remember,"—testily. "I don't want to see bank managers: I want them to look after my money. That is your job—you're paid for it, handsomely, I've no doubt. You have brought the account?"

The visitor took an envelope from his pocket, and, opening it, brought out two folded sheets of paper.

"Here——" he began, and his chair creaked as he rose.

"I don't want to see them—just tell me what is my balance."

"Two hundred and twelve thousand, seven hundred and sixty pounds and a few shillings."

"M'm!" The "m'm" was a purr of satisfaction. "That includes the deposit, eh? And you hold stock?"

"The stock held amounts to six hundred and thirty-two thousand pounds."

"I'll tell you why I want you," began Lyne; and then, suspiciously: "Open the door and see if that fellow's listening."

The visitor rose, opened the door, and closed it again.

"There's nobody there," he said.

He was slightly amused, though Mr. Lyne's infirmities prevented him from observing this fact.

"Nobody, eh? Well, Moran, I'll tell you candidly:

I regard myself as a remarkably able man. That is not boastful, it is a fact which you yourself could probably verify. I trust nobody—not even bank managers. My eyesight is not as good as it was, and it is a little difficult to check up accounts. But I have a remarkable memory. I have trained myself to carry figures in my head, and I could have told you to within a few shillings exactly the figures that you gave to me."

He paused, stared through his thick glasses in the direction of the man who sat at the other side of his desk.

"You're not a speculator or a gambler?"

"No, Mr. Lyne, I am not."

A pause.

"H'm! That fool Binny was reading to me a few days ago the story of a bank manager who had absconded, taking with him a very considerable sum. I confess I was uneasy. People have robbed me before——"

"You're not being very polite, Mr. Lyne."

"I'm not trying to be polite," snapped the old man. "I am merely telling you what has happened to me. There was a scoundrelly servant of mine, a fellow called Tickler. The fellow who was killed . . ."

He rambled on, a long, long story about the minor depredations of his dishonest servant, and the man who called himself Moran listened patiently. He was very relieved when he had taken the thin, limp hand in his and the door of No. 17 Naylor Terrace closed behind him.

"Phew!" he said. He had a habit of speaking his thoughts aloud. "I wouldn't go through that again for a lot of money."

Binny, summoned from the deeps by a bell, came in to find the visitor gone.

"What does he look like, Binny? Has he an honest face?"

Binny thought profoundly.

"Just a face," he said vaguely, and the old man snorted.

"Clear those breakfast things away. Who else is coming to see me?"

Binny thought for a long time.

"A man named Bornford, sir."

"A gentleman named Dornford," corrected his master. "He owes me money, therefore he is a gentleman. At what hour?"

"About eight o'clock, sir."

Lyne dismissed him with a gesture.

At three o'clock that afternoon he ambled out of his sitting room, wrapped in his thick Inverness coat and wearing his soft felt hat, allowed himself, growling complaints the while, to be tucked into his Bath chair, and was drawn painfully into the street; more painfully up the gentle slope to the park and into the private gardens, entry to which was exclusively reserved for tenants of Naylor and other terraces. Here he sat under the shade of a tree, while Binny, perched uncomfortably upon a folding stool, read in his monotonous voice the happenings of the day.

Only once the old man interrupted.

"What time is Mr. Dornford calling?"

"At eight o'clock, sir," said Binny.

Lyne nodded, pushed his blue-tinted glasses higher up the thin bridge of his nose, and folded his gloved hands over the rug which protected his knees from errant breezes.

"You be in when he comes, d'ye hear? A tricky fellow—a dangerous fellow. You hear me, Binny?"

"Yes, sir."

"Then why the devil didn't you say so? Go on reading that trash."

Binny obeyed, and continued with great relish the story of London's latest murder. Binny was a great student of crime in the abstract.

CHAPTER VI

ARTHUR JULES barely deserves description because he plays so small a part; but as that small part was big enough to put one man in the shadow of the gallows, he may be catalogued as a plump, sallow-faced young man, who wore a monocle, had perfectly brushed hair, and was invariably dressed as though he were on his way to a wedding reception.

He was a sort of attaché to a South American legation, and a free lance of diplomacy generally. In more suspicious countries he would have been handed his passport with extreme politeness, and his departure from Southampton would have been watched by the bored detective whose business it is to superintend the shipment of oddities.

He was always important and profound, never more so than when he sat at the bay window overlooking St. James's Street, stroking his little black moustache thoughtfully and speaking with just the slightest trace of an accent to Jerry Dornford.

Everybody knew and liked Jerry, whose other name was Gerald. He had all the qualities which endear a wastrel to the moneyed classes. He was, of course, a member of the Snell, as was Jules. He was indeed a member of all the important clubs where gentlemen meet. He paid his subscription, never passed a check which was dishonoured, had never been warned off or posted as a bankrupt. A tall man, with a slight stoop, brownish hair very thin on the top, deep-set eyes that smiled in a worn, tired face.

Jerry had lived very fast. Few of his creditors could keep up with him. He had been a co-respondent, and again a co-respondent, and was single, and lived in a little flat in Half Moon Street, where he gave small parties; very small. He retained his membership of exclusive racing clubs—bookmakers lived in the hope that he would one day settle with them. He had certain very rich relatives who would certainly die, but were not so certain whether they would bequeath their undoubted wealth to this profligate son of Sir George Dornford. On the other hand, why shouldn't they?

He was in desperate need of money now. Jules knew how desperate: they had few secrets from one another. Whenever the little party in Half Moon Street was as many as four, Jules was the third.

"What is this fellow's name?"

"Hervey Lyne."

"Hervey Lyne? Yes, I know him. A very odd man,"—reminiscently. "When my dear father was secretary of legation—that must have been in 'ninety-three—he borrowed money from Lyne. But

I thought he had retired from business. He was a money-lender, wasn't he?"

Jerry's lips twisted in an unpleasant smile.

"Financier," he said laconically. "Yes, he has retired. I owed him three thousand for years; it's four now. There was, of course, a chance that the dowager would leave a packet, but the old devil left it away, to the other side of the family."

"And he is pressing you?"

Jerry's jaw set.

"Yes," he said shortly. "To be exact, he is getting a judgment in bankruptcy, and I can't stop him. I have been dodging Carey Street all my life. Things have looked very black at times, but there has always been something that turned up."

There was a long and gloomy silence. Jules—he had another name, but nobody could remember it—stroked his little black moustache more quickly.

"Two thousand—that would stop the action, eh? Well, why not? Take two thousand, *et voilà!* There is nothing to it. I do not ask you, like the fellow in the story books, to go to the War Office and rob them of their schemes of mobilization. But I *do* want something, for a gentleman who has himself been working on the lines of your friend. To me it seems a very large sum to pay for so small a thing. Naturally I do not say that to my gentleman. If he desires to be extravagant and my friend would benefit—*tiens,* why not?"

Jerry Dornford made a wry face at the street below. When he was asked to work for money he never forgot that he was a gentleman—it was rather a disgusting thing he was now asked to do, but he had contemplated things even more distressful. He had, in fact, found every solution to his difficulty except suicide.

"I am not so sure that it can be done, anyway," he said.

Two men came into the smoke room. He looked up quickly and recognized both, but was interested particularly in one.

"That's fate," he said.

"Who are they?" asked Jules.

He knew the second of the two, who was a member, but the first man, middle-aged, rather rotund, fair-haired, was a stranger to him.

"That's my bank manager. Incidentally, he is Lyne's banker, too, a fellow named Moran—Major Moran, he loves to call himself. A Territorial fellow."

Jules shot a swift glance in the direction of the men who at that moment were seating themselves at the table.

"A great rifle shot. I saw him at Bisley. I was there with one of our generals, watching the shooting."

He turned his black eyes to Jerry.

"Well, my friend?"

Jerry breathed heavily through his nose and shook his head.

"I'll have to think it over," he said. "It's a beastly thing to do."

"More beastly to be a bankrupt, my friend," said Jules in his caressing voice. "Resignation from all clubs . . . Poor old Jerry, eh? You are going into the Mike Hennessey class. You don't want to be that."

"Why Mike Hennessey?" asked Jerry quickly, and the other laughed.

"An association of ideas. You go often to the Sheridan, eh? I do not blame you . . . a very charming girl."

He made a little grimace as though he were about to whistle.

"Association of ideas, eh? Allenby also likes the young lady. Queer how all things fit in, like the pieces of a puzzle. Think it over, my dear Jerry, and ring me up at the Grosvenor."

He snapped his fingers towards a club waiter, scribbled his initials on a bill, and strolled towards the door, Jerry following. They had to pass Moran and his friend; that bluff, jolly-looking man looked up, nodded with careless friendliness, and caught Jerry's sleeve as he was passing.

"I'd like to see you one day this week, if you're not busy, Jerry."

Jerry never forgot he was a member of Snell's

and a gentleman. He never forgot that Mr. Leo Moran was a sort of glorified bank clerk, who had probably had his education at the state's expense; and, knowing all these things, he resented the "Jerry." It added to his irritation that he knew why Mr. Moran wished to see him. It was outrageous that one couldn't lunch in one's club without being dunned by cads of this description.

He pulled his sleeve away from the detaining finger and thumb.

"All right," he said.

He would have been more offensive if this man had not been a guest at the club, and, more importantly, if it were not in Moran's power to make things deucedly uncomfortable for Mr. Gerald Dornford.

He and Jules passed down the stairs together.

"The swine! Who brought that kind of bird into the club? Snell's is getting impossible!"

Jules, who had a weakness for the rococo qualities of Italian opera, was humming a favourite aria of Puccini's. He smiled and shook his head.

"It takes all sorts of people to make a world, my friend," he said sententiously.

He flicked a speck from his immaculate coat sleeve, patted Jerry on the arm as though he were a child, and went swinging up St. James's Street towards his mysterious Legation.

Jerry Dornford stood for a moment, hesitant,

then walked slowly down towards the palace. He was in a jam, a tight jam, and it wasn't going to be so very easy to get out.

He obeyed an impulse, called a cab and drove to near Queen's Gate, where he alighted, paid his fare and walked on.

Dick Allenby lived in a big house that had been converted into flats. There was no attendant on duty at the door, and the elevator that took him up to the fourth floor was automatic. He knocked at the door of Dick's studio—for studio it had once been, before Dick Allenby had converted it into a work-room. There was no answer, and he turned the handle and walked in. The room was empty. Evidently there had been visitors, for half a dozen empty beer bottles stood on a bench, though there was only one used tumbler visible. If he had known something of Surefoot Smith he might have reduced the visiting list to one.

"Are you there, Allenby?" he called.

There was no answer. He walked across to the bench where the odd-looking steel box lay, and lifted it. To his relief he found he could carry it without an effort. Putting it down again, he walked to the door. The key was on the inside; he drew it out and examined it carefully. If he had been an expert at the job he would have carried wax and taken an impression. As it was, his early technical training came to his aid—it had once been intended that he should follow the profession of engineer.

He listened; there was no sound of the lift moving. Dick, he knew, had his sleeping room on the upper floor, and was probably there now. Dornford made a rapid sketch on the back of an envelope—rapid but accurate. He judged the width of the key, made a brief note, and replaced it as the sound of somebody coming down the stairs reached him.

He was standing, examining the empty beer bottles, when Dick came in.

"Hullo, Dornford!" There was no great welcome in the tone. "Did you want to see me?"

Jerry smiled.

"I was bored. I thought I'd come up and see what an inventor looked like. By the way, I saw you at the theatre the other night—nice girl, that. She was damned rude to me the only time I spoke to her."

Dick faced him squarely.

"And I shall be damned rude to you the next time you speak to her," he said.

Jerry Dornford chuckled.

"Like that, eh? By the way, I'm seeing the old man to-night. Shall I give him your love?"

"He'd prefer that you gave him something more substantial," said Dick coldly.

It was a shot at a venture, but it got home. Gerald the imperturbable winced.

It was odd that up to that moment Dick Allenby had never realized how intensely he disliked this man. There was excellent reason why he should hate him, but that was yet to be revealed.

"Why this sudden antagonism? After all, I've no feeling about this girl of yours. She's a jolly little thing; a bad actress, but a good woman. They don't go very far on the London stage——"

"If you're talking about Miss Lane I will bring the conversation to a very abrupt termination," said Dick; and then, bluntly: "Why did you come up here? You are quite right about the antagonism, but it is not very sudden, is it? I don't seem to remember that you and I were ever very great friends."

"We were in the same regiment, old boy—brother officers and all that," said Jerry flippantly. "Good lord! It doesn't seem like twelve years ago——"

Dick opened the door and stood by it.

"I don't want you here. I don't particularly want to know you. If you see my uncle to-night you'd better tell him that: it will be a point in my favour."

Jerry Dornford smiled. His skin was thick, though he was very sensitive on certain unimportant matters.

"I suppose you knew this fellow Tickler who was killed the other night?" he began.

"I don't want even to discuss murders with you," said Dick.

He went out of the room, pulled open the door of

the lift, and shot back the folding iron gate. He was angry with himself afterwards that he had lost his temper, but he never knew the time when Jerry Dornford did not arouse a fury in him. He hated Jerry's views of life, his philosophy, the looseness of his code. He remembered Jerry's extraordinary dexterity with cards, and a ruined subaltern who went gladly to his death rather than face the consequence of a night's play.

As he heard the elevator stop at the bottom floor he opened the window of the workshop to air it—an extravagant gesture, but one which accurately marked his attitude of mind towards his visitor.

CHAPTER VII

THE bank was closed, and Mr. Moran had gone home, when Surefoot Smith called to make his inquiry.

Surefoot knew almost everybody of any importance in London. Indeed, quite a number of people would have had a shock if they had known how very completely informed he was about their private lives. It is true that almost every man and woman in any civilized community has, to himself or herself, a criminal history. They may have broken no laws, yet there is guilt on their conscience; and it is a knowledge of this psychology which is of such invaluable aid to investigating detectives.

The nearest way to Parkview Crescent led him across the open end of Naylor Terrace. Glancing down, he saw a man coming towards him and stopped. Binny he knew to be an inveterate gossip, a great collector of stories and scandals, most of which were ill-founded. At the back of his mind, however, he associated Mr. Lyne's serving man with the banker. Years before, Surefoot Smith had been in control of this division, and his memory was extraordinarily good.

"Good-afternoon, Mr. Smith."

Binny tipped his wide-brimmed bowler hat, and then, after a moment's hesitation:

"May I be so bold to ask, sir, if there is any news?"

"You told me you knew this man Tickler?"

Binny shook his head.

"An acquaintance. He was my predecessor——"

"I'd have that word framed," said Surefoot Smith testily. "You mean he was the fellow who had your job before, don't you?" And, when Binny nodded: "Then why didn't you say so? Didn't you work for Moran?"

Binny smiled.

"I've worked for almost every kind of gentleman," he said. "I was Lord Frenley's valet——"

"I don't want your family history, Binny," said Surefoot Smith. "What sort of a man is Moran? Nice fellow—generous, eh? Free spender?"

Binny considered the matter as though his life depended upon his answer.

"He was a very nice gentleman. I was only with him for six months," he said. "He lives just round the corner, overlooking the park. In fact, you can see his flat from the gardens."

"A quiet sort of man?" asked Surefoot.

"I never heard him make much noise——" began Binny.

"When I say 'quiet'," explained Surefoot Smith

with a pained expression, "I mean, does he gad about? Women, wine, and song—you know the kind of thing I mean. I suppose your mother told you something when you were young?"

"I don't remember my mother," said Binny. "No, sir, I can't say that Mr. Moran was a gadder. He used to have little parties—ladies and gentlemen from the theatre—but he gave that up after he lost his money."

Surefoot's eyes narrowed.

"Lost his money? He's a bank manager, isn't he? Had he any money to lose?"

"It was his own money, sir." Binny was shocked and hastened to correct a wrong impression. "That was why I left him. He had some shares in a bank —not his own bank but another one—and it went bust. I mean to say——"

"Don't try to interpret 'bust' to me. I know the word," said Surefoot. "Gave little theatrical parties —like that fellow What's-his-name? Drinking and all that sort of thing?"

Binny could not help him. He was looking left and right anxiously, as though seeking a means of escape.

"In a hurry?" asked the detective.

"The big picture comes on in ten minutes; I don't want to miss it. It's Mary Pickford in——"

"Oh, her!" said Surefoot, and dismissed the world's sweetheart with a wave of his hand. "Now what about this man Tickler? Did he ever work for Moran?"

Binny considered this and shook his head.

"No, sir, I think he was working for Mr. Lyne when I was with Mr. Moran, but I'm not certain." And then, as a thought struck him: "He's on the wireless to-night."

Surefoot was staggered.

"Who?"

"Mr. Moran. He's talking on economics or something. He often talks on banking and things like that—he's a regular lecturer."

Surefoot Smith was not very much interested in lectures. He asked a few more questions about the unfortunate Tickler and went on his way.

Parkview Crescent was a noble block of buildings which had suffered the indignity in post-war days, as so many other buildings have suffered, of being converted into apartments. Mr. Moran lived on the top flat, and he was at home, his servant told Surefoot when he came to the door. In point of fact he was dressing for dinner. Smith was shown into a large and handsome sitting room, furnished expensively and with some taste. There were two windows which commanded a view of Regent's Park and the Canal, but it was the luxury of the appointments which arrested Surefoot's interest.

He knew the financial position of the average

branch manager; could tell to within a few pounds just what his salary was; and it was rather a shock to find even a twelve-hundred-a-year manager living in an apartment which must have absorbed at least four hundred, and displaying evidence of wealth which men in his position have rarely the opportunity of acquiring.

A Persian carpet covered the floor; the electric fittings had the appearance of silver, and were certainly of the more exquisite kind that are not to be duplicated in a department store. There was a big Knolle couch ("cost a hundred," Smith noted mentally); in an illuminated glass case were a number of beautiful miniatures, and in another, rare ornaments of jade, some of which must have been worth a considerable sum.

Surefoot knew nothing about pictures, but he was satisfied that more than one of those on the wall were genuine Old Masters.

He was examining the cabinet when he heard a step behind him, and turned to meet the owner of the flat. Mr. Leo Moran was half-dressed and wore a silk dressing gown over his shirt and white waistcoat.

"Hullo, Smith! We don't often see you. Sit down and have a drink." He rang the bell. "Beer, isn't it?"

"Beer it is," said Surefoot heartily. "Nice place you've got here, Mr. Moran."

"Not bad," said the other carelessly. He pointed to a picture. "That's a genuine Corot. My father paid three hundred pounds for it, and it's probably worth three thousand to-day."

"Your father was well off, was he, Mr. Moran?"

Moran looked at him quickly.

"He had money. Why do you ask? You don't imagine I could have furnished a flat like this on a thousand a year, do you?" His eyes twinkled. "Or has it occurred to you that this is part of my illicit gains—moneys pinched from the bank?"

"I hope," said Surefoot Smith solemnly, "that such a thought never entered into my head."

"Beer," said Mr. Leo Moran, addressing th servant who had appeared in the doorway. "You've come about something, haven't you? What is it?"

Surefoot pursed his lips thoughtfully.

"I'm making inquiries about this man Tickler——"

"The fellow who was murdered. Do I know him, you mean? Of course I know him! The fellow was a pest. I never went from this house without finding him on the curb outside, wanting to tell me something or sell me something—I have never discovered which."

He had a rapid method of speaking. His voice was not what Smith would have described as a gentleman's. Indeed, Leo Moran was very much of the people. His life had been an adventurous one. He had sailed before the mast, he had worked at a brass founder's in the Midlands, been in a dozen kinds of employment, before he eventually drifted into banking. A rough diamond, with now and again a rough voice; more often, however, a suave one, for he had the poise and presence which authority and wealth bring. Now and again his voice grew harsh, almost common, and in moments he became very much a man of the people. It was in that tone he asked:

"Do you suppose I killed him?"

Surefoot smiled; whether at the absurdity of the question or the appearance of a large bottle of beer and a tumbler, which were carried in at that moment, Moran was undecided.

"You know Miss Lane, don't you?"

"Slightly." Moran's tone was cold.

"Nice girl—here's luck." Surefoot raised his glass and swallowed its contents at a gulp. "Good beer, almost pre-war. Lord! I remember the time when you could get the best ale in the world for fourpence a quart."

He sighed heavily, and tried to squeeze a little more out of the bottle, but failed.

Moran touched the bell again.

"Why do you ask me about Miss Lane?"

"I knew you were interested in theatricals—there's your servant."

"Another bottle of beer for Mr. Smith," said

Moran without turning his head. "What do you mean by theatricals?"

"You used to give parties, didn't you, once upon a time?"

The banker nodded.

"Years ago, in my salad days. Why?"

"I was just wondering," said Smith vaguely.

His host strode up and down the floor, his hands thrust into the silken pockets of his gown.

"What the devil did you come here for, Smith? You're not the sort of man to go barging round making stupid inquiries. Are you connecting me with this absurd murder—the murder of a cheap little gutter rat I scarcely know by sight?"

Surefoot shook his head.

"Is it likely?" he murmured.

Then the beer came, and Moran's fit of annoyance seemed to pass.

"Well, the least you can do is to tell me the strength of it—or aren't you inquiring about the murder at all? Come along, my dear fellow, don't be mysterious!"

Mr. Smith wiped his moustache, got up slowly from the chair, and adjusted his horrible pink tie before an old Venetian mirror.

"I'll tell you the strength of it, man to man," he said. "We had an anonymous letter. That was easy to trace. It was sent by Tickler's landlady, and it appeared that when he was very drunk, which was every day, sometimes twice a day, he used to talk to this good lady about you."

"About me?" said the other quickly. "But he didn't know me!"

"Lots of people talk about people they don't know," began Smith. "It's publicity——"

"Nonsense! I'm not a public man. I'm just a poor little bank manager, who hates banking, and would gladly pay a fortune, if he had one to pay, for the privilege of taking all the books of the bank and burning 'em in Regent's Park, making the clerks drunk, throwing open the vault to the petty thieves of London, and turning the whole damn thing into a night club!"

Gazing at him with open mouth, genuinely staggered by such a confession, Smith saw an expression in that sometime genial face that he had never seen before: a certain harshness; heard in his voice the vibration of a hidden fury.

"They nearly kicked me out once because I speculated," Moran went on. "I'm a gambler; I always have been a gambler. If they'd kicked me out I'd have been ruined at that time. I had to crawl on my hands and knees to the directors to let me stay on. I was managing a branch at Chalk Farm at the time, and I've had to pretend that the Northern & Southern Bank is something holy, that its directors are gods; and every time I've tried to get a bit of money so that I could clear out, the market has gone——!" He snapped his fingers. "I don't really know Tickler. Why he should talk about me I haven't the slightest idea."

Surefoot Smith looked into his hat.

"Do you know Mr. Hervey Lyne?" he asked.

"Yes, he's a client of ours."

"Have you seen him lately?"

A pause, and then:

"No, I haven't seen him for two years."

"Oh!" said Surefoot Smith.

He said "Oh!" because he could think of nothing else to say.

"Well, I'll be getting along. Sorry to bother you, but you know what we are at the Yard."

He offered his huge hand to the banker, but Mr. Moran was so absorbed in his thoughts that he did not see it.

After Moran had closed the door upon his visitor he walked slowly back to his room and sat down on the edge of the bed. He sat there for a long time before he got up, walked across the room to a wall safe hidden behind a picture, opened it, and took out a number of documents, which he examined very carefully. He put these back, and, groping, found a flat leather case which was packed with strangely coloured documents. They were train and steamship tickets; his passport lay handy, and, fastened in his passport by a thick rubber band, twenty banknotes for a hundred pounds each.

He locked the safe again, replaced the picture, and went on with his dressing. He was more than a little perturbed. That casual reference to Hervey Lyne had shaken him.

CHAPTER VIII

AT TEN o'clock that night quite a number of radio sets would be shut off at the item "The Economy of Our Banking System," and would be turned on again at ten-fifteen, when the Jubilee Jazz Band would be relayed from Manchester.

Binny read the programme through and came at last to the ten o'clock item.

"Moran. . . . Is that the fellow who saw me yesterday?" asked the old man.

"Yes, sir," said Binny.

"Banking systems—bah!" snarled old Lyne. "I don't want to hear it. Do you understand, Binny—I don't want to hear it!"

"No, sir," said Binny.

The white, gnarled hands groped along the table till they reached a repeater watch, and pressed a knob.

"Six o'clock. Get me my salad."

"I saw that detective to-day, sir—Mr. Smith."

"Get me my salad!"

Chicken salad was his invariable meal at the close of day. Binny served him, but could do nothing right. If he spoke he was told to be quiet; if he relapsed into silence old Hervey cursed him for his sulkiness.

He had cleared away the meal, put a cup of weak tea before his master, and was leaving him to doze, when Lyne called him back.

"What are Cassari Oils?" he demanded.

It was so long since Binny had read the fluctuations of the oil market that he had no information to give.

"Get a newspaper, you fool!"

Binny went in search of an evening newspaper.

It was his habit to read, morning and night, the movements of industrial shares; a monotonous proceeding, for Mr. Lyne's money was invested in gilt-edged securities which were stately and steadfast and seldom moved except by thirty-seconds. Cassari Oils had been one of his errors. The shares had been part of a trust fund—he had hesitated for a long time before he converted them to a more stable stock. The period of his holding had been two years of torture to him, for they flamed up and down like a paper fire, and never stayed in one place for more than a week at a time.

Binny came back with the newspaper and read the quotation, which was received with a grunt.

"If they'd gone up I'd have sued the bank. That brute Moran advised me to sell."

"Have they gone up, sir?" asked Binny, interested.

"Mind your own business!" snapped the other.

Hervey Lyne used often to sit and wonder and fret himself over those Cassaris. They were founder's shares, not lightly come by, not easy to dispose of. The thought that he might have thrown away a fortune on the advice of a conservative bank manager, and that when he came to hand over his stewardship to Mary Lane he might be liable—which he would not have been—was a nightmare to him. The unease had been renewed that day by something which Binny had read to him from the morning newspaper concerning oil discoveries in Asia Minor.

In the course of the years he had accumulated quite a lot of data concerning the Cassari Oilfield, most of it very depressing to anybody who had money in the concern. He directed Binny to unearth the pamphlets and reports, and promised himself a possibly exasperating evening.

Eight o'clock brought a visitor, a reluctant man, who had rehearsed quite a number of plausible excuses. He had the feeling that he, being the last of the old man's debtors, was in the position of a mouse in the paws of an ancient cat, not to be killed too quickly; and here, to some extent, he was right.

Hervey Lyne received him with a set grin which was a parody of the smile he had used for so many years on such occasions.

"Sit down, Mr. Dornford," he piped. "Binny, go out!"

"Binny's not here, Mr. Lyne."

"He's listening outside the door—he's always listening. Have a look."

Dornford opened the door; there was no sign of the libelled servant.

"Now, now." Again he was his old business-like self, repeating a speech which was part of a formula. "About this money—three thousand seven hundred, I think. You're going to settle to-night?"

"Unfortunately I can't settle to-night, and not for many nights," said Jerry. "In fact, there's no immediate prospect of my settling at all. I've made arrangements to get you four or five hundred on account——"

"From Isaac and Solomon, eh?"

Jerry cursed himself for his stupidity. He knew that the money-lenders exchanged daily a list of proposals which had come to them.

"Well, you're not going to get it, my friend. You've got to find money to settle this account, or it goes into the hands of my collectors to-morrow."

Jerry had expected nothing better than this.

"Suppose I find you two thousand by the end of the week?" he said. "Will you give me a reasonable time to find the remainder?"

To his surprise he was speaking huskily—the imperturbable Jerry, who had faced so many crises with equanimity, was amazingly agitated in this, the most crucial of all.

"If you can find two thousand you can find three thousand seven hundred," boomed the old man. "A week? I wouldn't give you a day—and where are you getting the two thousand from?"

Jerry cleared his throat.

"A friend of mine——"

"That's a lie to begin with, Mr. Gerald Dornford," said the hateful voice. "You have no friends; you've used them all up. I'll tell you what I'll do with you." He leaned over the table, his elbows on the polished mahogany. He was enjoying this moment of his triumph, recovering some of the old values of a life that was now only a memory. "I'll give you till to-morrow night at six o'clock. Your money's here"—he tapped the table vigorously—"or I'll bankrupt you!"

If his sight had been only near to normal he would have seen the look that came into Jerry's face, and would have been frightened to silence. But, if he saw nothing, he sensed the effect of his words.

"You understand, don't you?"

Some of the steel went out of his tone.

"I understand." Jerry's voice was low.

"To-morrow you bring the money, and I will give you your bill. A minute after six o'clock, and it goes to the collector."

"But surely, Mr. Lyne"—Jerry found coherent speech at last—"two thousand pounds on account is not to be sniffed at."

"We shall see," said the old man, nodding. "I've nothing else to say."

Jerry rose; he was shaking with anger.

"I've got something to say, you damned old usurer!" He quivered with rage. "You blood-sucking old brute! You'll bankrupt me, will you?"

Hervey Lyne had come to his feet, his skinny hand pointing to the door.

"Get out!" His voice was little more than a whisper. "Blood-sucker . . . damned old usurer, am I? Binny—BINNY!"

Binny came stumbling up from the kitchen.

"Throw him out—throw him on his head—smash him!" screamed the old man.

Binny looked at the man who was head and shoulders taller than he, and his smile was sickly.

"Better get out, sir," he said under his breath, "and don't take no notice of me."

Then, in a louder, truculent tone:

"Get out of here, will you?" He pulled open the street door noisily. "Out you get!"

He struck his palm with his fist, and all the time his imploring eyes begged the visitor to pardon his lapse of manners.

When he came back the money-lender was lying back, exhausted, in his chair.

"Did you hit him?" he asked weakly.

"Did I hit him, sir? I nearly broke me wrist."

"Did you break *his* wrist or anything else of him?" snarled Hervey, not at all interested in the injuries which might have come to the assailant.

"It'll take two doctors to put him right," said Binny.

The old man's thin lips curled in a sneer.

"I don't believe you touched him, you poor worm!" he said.

"Didn't you hear me——" began Binny, aggrieved.

"Clapping your hands together! Liar and fool, do you think I didn't know that? I may be blind but I've got ears. Did you hit the burglar last night—or when was it? You didn't even hear him."

Binny blinked at him helplessly. Two nights before somebody had smashed a glass at the back of the house and opened a window. Whether the intruder succeeded in entering the kitchen or not it was impossible to say. Old Hervey, a light sleeper, heard the crash and came to the head of the stairs, screaming for Binny, who occupied a subterranean room adjoining the kitchen.

"Did you hit him? Did you hear him?"

"My idea was to bring in the police," began Binny. "There's nothing like the lor in cases like this——"

"Get out!" roared the old man. "The law! Do

you think I wanted a lot of clumsy-footed louts in my house? Get away, you make me sick!"

Binny left hurriedly.

For the greater part of two hours the old man sat, muttering to himself, twisting and untwisting his fingers one in the other; and then, as his repeater struck ten, he turned to the radio set at his side and switched it on. A voice immediately blared at him:

> "Before I discuss the banking systems of this country I would like to say a few words about the history of banking from the earliest times . . ."

Hervey Lyne sat up and listened. His hearing, as he had said, was extraordinarily sensitive.

CHAPTER IX

Dick Allenby never described himself as being engaged, and the telltale finger of Mary Lane bore no ring indicative of her future. He mentioned the fact casually as he sat in her dressing room between the last two acts of "Cliffs of Fate," and he talked to her through a cretonne curtain behind which she was changing her dress.

"I shall be getting a bad name," he said. "Nothing damages the reputation of an inventor more readily than to be recognized by stage-door keepers. He admits me now without question."

"Then you shouldn't come so often," she said, coming through the curtain, and sitting before her dressing table.

"I won't say you're a matter of life and death to me," said Dick, "but very nearly. You're more important than anything in the world."

"Including the Allenby gun?"

"Oh, that!" he said contemptuously. "By the way, a German engineer came in to-day and offered me, on behalf of Eckstein's—they're the big Essen engineers—ten thousand pounds for the patent."

"What was the matter with him?" she asked flippantly.

"That's what I wondered," said Dick, lighting a forbidden cigarette. "No, he wasn't drunk—quite a capable bloke, and terribly discerning. He told me he thought I was one of the greatest inventors of the age."

"Darling, you are," she said.

"I know I am," said Dick complacently. "But it sounded awfully nice in German. Honestly, Mary, I had no idea this thing was worth so much."

"Are you selling it?" She turned her head to ask the question.

Dick hesitated.

"I'm not sure," he said. "But it is this enormous accession of wealth that has brought me to the point of your unadorned engagement finger."

She turned to the mirror, smoothed her face gently with a puff, and shook her head.

"I'm going to be a very successful actress," she said.

"You are a very successful actress," said Dick lazily. "You've extracted a proposal of marriage from a great genius."

She swung round in her chair.

"Do you know what I'm in dread of?" she asked.

"Besides marriage, nothing, I should think."

"No, there's one prospect that terrifies me." She was very serious. "And that is that your uncle should leave me all his money."

He chuckled softly.

"It is a fear that has never disturbed my night's rest—why do you say that?"

She looked at him, biting her lip thoughtfully.

"Once he said something about it, and it struck me quite recently that he loathes you so much that out of sheer pique he might leave it to me, and that would be dreadful."

He stared at her.

"In heaven's name, why?" he asked.

"I should have to marry you," she said.

"Out of sheer pique?" he bantered.

She shook her head.

"No; but it would be dreadful, wouldn't it, Dick?"

"I think you're worrying yourself unnecessarily," he said drily. "The old boy is more likely to leave it to a dogs' home. Do you see much of him?"

She told him of her visit to Naylor Terrace, but that was old news to him.

They were talking when there came a tap at the door. She half-rose, thinking it was the call boy; but when the knock was repeated and she said "Come in," it was Leo Moran who made an appearance.

He favoured Dick with a little grimace.

"Instead of wasting your time here you ought to be sitting at home, tuning in to my epoch-making address."

"Been broadcasting, have you?" smiled Dick. "Do they make you dress up for it?"

"I'm going on to supper."

This time the knock was followed by the sing-song voice of the call boy, and Mary hurried out. She was glad to escape: for some reason she never felt quite at ease in Mr. Moran's presence.

"Have you seen this show?" asked Dick.

Moran nodded.

"For my sins, yes," he said. "It's the most ghastly play in London. I wonder why old Mike keeps it on? He must have a very rich backer."

"Have you ever heard of Washington Wirth?"

Leo Moran's face was a blank.

"Never heard of him, no. What is he—an American?"

"Something unusual," said Dick. "I was reckoning up the other day; he must have lost ten thousand pounds on this play already, and there's no special reason, so far as I know, why he's keeping it running. Mary's the only woman in the cast who's worth looking at, and she's no friend of his."

"Washington Wirth? The name is familiar." Moran looked at the wall above Dick's head. "I've heard something about him or seen his name. By the way, I met an old friend of yours to-night: Surefoot Smith. You were present when that wretched man Tickler was found, weren't you?"

Dick nodded.

"The fool treated me as though I were an accomplice."

"If the fool you are referring to is Surefoot Smith, he treated me as though I were the murderer," said Dick. "Did you give him some beer?"

Leo Moran opened the door and, after looking down the deserted corridor, came back and closed the door quietly.

"I was hoping I should see you here, Dick. I want to ask you a favour."

Dick grinned.

"Nothing would give me greater joy than to refuse a favour to a bank manager," he said.

"Don't be a fool; it has nothing to do with money. Only——"

He stopped, and it seemed as if he were carefully framing his words.

"I may be out of London for a week or two. My leave is due, and I want to get into the country. I wonder if you could collect my letters at the flat and keep them for me till I come back?"

"Why not have them sent on?" said Dick, in surprise.

Leo Moran shook his head impatiently.

"I have a special reason for asking. I'm having nothing sent on at all. My servant is going away on his holiday, and the flat will be in charge of heaven knows whom. If I send you the key, will you keep an eye on the place?"

"When are you going?" asked Dick.

Moran was vague on this point; there was no certainty whether his leave would be granted. Head office was being rather difficult, although he had a most capable assistant and could have handed over at any moment.

"I want to go at once, but these brutes in the City are just being tin-godlike. You'll never know how near human beings can approach divinity until you have had dealings with general managers of banks," he said. "When you approach them you make three genuflections and stand on your head, and even then they hardly notice you! Is it a bet?"

"Surely," said Dick. "You know where to send the key? And I'll take a little cheap advice from you, now you're here."

He told him of the offer he had received for the gun. There was no need to explain what the gun was, for Leo had both seen and tested it.

"I shouldn't take an outright offer. I should prefer to take half on account of a royalty," he said, when Dick had finished. "Are you going to your flat soon?"

"Almost immediately," said the other. "Mary has a supper engagement."

"With Mr. Wirth?" asked Moran with a smile.

"I thought you'd never heard of him?" said Dick.

"His name came to me as I was speaking. He's the fellow who gives these supper parties. I used to give them myself once upon a time, and Dead Sea fruit they are! But if you're going back I'll walk with you, and renew my acquaintance with your remarkable invention."

Leo Moran would have been ever so much more popular but for the fact that there was invariably a hint of sarcasm in his most commonplace remarks. Sometimes Dick, who liked him well enough, thought he had been soured by some big misfortune; for, despite his geniality, there was generally a bite to his remarks. Dick forgave him as they walked along the Strand for all that he had to say concerning Jerry Dornford.

"There's a wastrel!" said Moran. "I can't tell you why I think so, because I'm interviewing him to-morrow on bank business."

Though the evening was warm, a fog had formed, which, as their cab approached the park, increased in density. It was clearing off as they passed through Knightsbridge.

"As a matter of fact," said Dick, "you're making me do something it has been on my conscience to do all the evening, and that is, go home and look at that gun. Like a fool, I charged it before I came out. I was about to make the experiment of trying to shoot a nickel bullet through a steel plate, and like an idiot I left it loaded. It's thicker here."

The fog was very patchy, and was so dense that the cabman had to feel his way along the curb as they approached the house where Dick Allenby had his workshop.

The little lift was in darkness, and even when Dick turned the switch no light came. As he moved he trod on something which crashed under his feet. Immediately there followed a loud and alarming explosion.

"What the devil was that?" asked Moran irritably.

Dick struck a match. He saw on the floor the remains of a small incandescent globe which had evidently been removed from the roof of the lift.

"That's odd. Our janitor is a little careless," he said, and pushed the button that sent the elevator up to the top floor. He took out a key and had another surprise, for a key was already in the lock, so tightly fitted that it could not be turned one way or the other.

He twisted the handle; the door gave.

"There's somebody been playing monkey tricks here," he said.

Turning on the light, he stood stock still, momentarily incapable of speech. The bench on which the gun had stood was empty. The gun was gone!

CHAPTER X

HE RECOVERED his voice at last.

"Well, I'll be . . .!"

Who could have taken it? He was staggered, so staggered that he could not be angry. Pulling back the door, he examined the key, and, with the aid of a pair of powerful pliers, presently extracted it. It was a rough and ready affair, badly filed, but evidently it had fitted, and had done all that its owner had required, for the lock had turned back.

It was when the unknown had tried to relock the door and take away the key that he had failed.

Dick walked to where the gun had been and glared down at the bench. Then he began to laugh.

"The brute!"

"It's a very serious loss to you, isn't it?" asked Moran.

Dick shook his head.

"Not really. All the plans and specifications are in the hands of a model-maker, and fortunately I applied for letters of patent for the main features three days ago."

He stared at Moran.

"The question is, who did it?"

And then his jaw dropped.

"If he doesn't know how to handle that thing, and isn't jolly careful, he'll either kill himself or some innocent passer-by!" he said. "I wonder if he knows how to unload it?"

He pulled out a chair and sat down, and with a gesture invited his visitor to sit.

"I suppose we ought to tell the police. Now, if old man Surefoot is at the Yard . . ."

He consulted an address book and gave a number. After a long parley with a suspicious man at the Scotland Yard exchange, he found himself connected with Smith. In a few words he explained what had happened.

"I'll come up. Is there anything else missing?"

"No—the beer is intact," said Dick.

When he had hung up the receiver he went into his little larder and dragged in a wooden case.

"Surefoot will be glad; he loathes science. Don't make a face like that, my dear chap—Surefoot's clever. I used to think that beer had a deadening effect on people, but Surefoot is an amazing proof of the contrary. You don't like him?"

"I'm not passionately attached to him," said Moran. He looked at his watch. "If you don't mind, I'll leave you alone with your grief. It's hard luck—is it insured?"

"Spoken like a banker!" said Dick. "No, it isn't. Leo, I never realized I was a genius till now—it's like the things that you read about in thrillers! You see what has happened? Our friend came here in the fog, but to make absolutely sure he shouldn't be seen he took out the light in the lift, so that nobody should spot him on his way down. The door is lattice-work, and if the light had been on he could have been seen from any of the floors, supposing somebody was there to see him. I presume he had a car outside; he put the gun into the machine and got away. Probably we passed him."

"Who would know you had the gun?"

Dick thought for a while.

"Mary knew; Jerry Dornford knew—by Jove!"

Leo Moran smiled and shook his head.

"Jerry wouldn't have the energy, anyway; and he wouldn't know where to market——"

He stopped suddenly.

"I saw him the other day at Snell's Club, with that poisonous little devil Jules—the fellow who is supposed to have been concerned in pinching the French mobilization plans."

Dick hesitated, reached for the telephone directory, found the number he wanted, and put in a call. The line was engaged. Five minutes later the exchange called back to him, and he heard Jerry's voice.

"Hullo, Dornford! Got my gun?" asked Dick.

"Your what?" asked Jerry's steady voice.

"Somebody said they saw you walking out of my house with something under your arm this evening."

"I haven't seen your infernal house, and I'm not likely to see it after your beastly rudeness this afternoon!"

Click!

Jerry Dornford had hung up on him.

"I wonder," said Dick, and frowned as he slowly hung up the receiver. "I can't believe he did it, though there's nothing bad I wouldn't believe about him."

"Do you think it was your German friend?" asked Leo.

"Rubbish! Why should he offer me the money? He would have given me a draft right away this afternoon if I had wanted it. No, we'll leave it to old man Surefoot."

"Then you'll leave it to him alone," said Leo, and buttoned up his overcoat.

He went to the door and turned back.

"You'll not go back on your promise, about clearing my letters? It all depends on what happens to-morrow how soon I go, and the first intimation you'll get will be when you receive my key."

"Where are you going?" asked Dick.

Leo shook his head.

"That's the one thing I can't tell you," he said.

Sitting alone, surveying the empty bench, Dick

Allenby began to realize the seriousness of his loss. If he was bewildered by the theft, the last thing in the world he expected, he was by no means shattered.

He tried to get Mary on the phone, but thought better of it. It would be selfish to spoil her night's amusement. Better start again. He was working at his drawing board on a new plan, and had already conceived an improvement on the older model, when Surefoot Smith arrived.

He listened while Dick described the circumstances of his return; examined the key casually, and seemed more interested in the marks that the machine had made, visible against its dusty surroundings, than in anything else.

"No, it's not remarkable," he said when Dick so described the theft. "Dozens of inventions are stolen in the course of a year . . . yes, I mean burgled. I know a company promoter who floated a business to sell cameras, who had his house burgled and the plans of the invention stolen a week before the company was put on the market. I've known other promoters to have police guards in their houses day and night."

He walked round the room and presently related the sum of his discoveries.

"The man who took this was taller than you." He pointed to a bench near the door, the contents of which were in some disorder. "He rested the gun there while he tried to operate the lock, and that bench is higher than this. He wore gloves; he must have handled this cylinder and there's no finger-prints on it. Who has been here lately?"

Dick told him.

"Mr. Gerald Dornford, eh? I shouldn't think he'd have the nerve. We had some trouble with him once; he was running a little game in the West End. I might look him up, but it would be asking for trouble. I hardly think it's worth while putting him under observation," said Surefoot. "Are you going to call up the press and tell them all about it? They'll make a story of it—'Sensational Invention Stolen'."

"I didn't think of doing anything so silly."

"Then you're wise," said Surefoot.

He looked helplessly around; Dick pointed to the beer case under the bench.

"In a way, and without any offence to you, Mr. Allenby, I'm glad to see it go. All these new inventions are coming so thick and fast that you can't keep track of them."

"Which reminds me," said Dick, "that this thing was loaded."

Surefoot was not greatly concerned.

"If somebody gets shot," he said calmly, "we shall find out who did it."

He was less interested in the robbery than in the killing of Tickler.

"It's a puzzle to me. I can't understand it. I

wouldn't mind if it hadn't been in that cab. It's the Americanization of English crime that is worrying me. These Americans have got our motor-car trade, they've got our tool trade; if they come here and corner our murder market there's going to be trouble."

He stopped suddenly, stooped, and picked something from the floor. It was a pearl waistcoat button.

"This sort of thing only happens in stories," he said as he turned it over. "The fellow was in evening dress, and rubbed this off when he was carrying the gun. As a clue it's about as much use as the evidence of the old lady in every murder case who saw a tall, dark man in a big, gray car."

He looked at the button carefully.

"You can buy these at almost any store in London. You don't even have to buy 'em—they give 'em away."

He made a careful scrutiny of the floor but found nothing new.

"Still, I'll put it in my pocket," he said.

"It may have been Leo Moran's," said Dick, remembering. "He wore a white waistcoat. He and I came back together."

Surefoot's nose wrinkled.

"This! It would have been diamonds and sapphires! Ain't he a bank manager? No, this is the button of some poor depositor. I shouldn't be surprised if it was somebody with an overdraft! What do you think of Mr. Moran?"

He was looking at Dick keenly.

"He's a nice fellow; I like him," said Dick.

"There are moments when I don't, but, generally speaking, I do. Who's Corot?" He pronounced it as though it were spelt Corrot.

"Corot?" said Dick. "You mean the painter?"

Smith nodded.

"Oh, he's a very famous landscape artist."

"Expensive?" asked Surefoot.

"Very," said Dick. "His pictures sell for thousands."

Surefoot rubbed his nose irritably.

"That's what I thought. In fact, he said as much. Seen his flat? It looks as though it had been furnished for the Queen of Sheba, the well-known Egyptian. Persian carpet, diamond lamp-shades . . ."

Dick laughed.

"You're talking about Moran's flat? Yes, it's rather beautiful. But he's got money of his own."

"It was his own when he had it, anyway," said Smith darkly, and left on this cryptic note.

He had left Scotland Yard with some reluctance, for there was visiting London at that period one John Kelly, Deputy Chief Commissioner of the Chicago Police and one of America's foremost detectives. "Great John" had been holding an audience of senior officers spellbound with stories of Chicago's gangland. Earlier in the evening Surefoot had discussed the Regent Street murder.

"It sounds like a 'ride'," said Kelly, shaking his head, "but I guess that kind of crime will never be popular in this country. In the first place, you've no big men in your underworld, and if you had, your police force and Government are pull-proof. It reads to me like an 'imitation murder.' I suppose you've got bad men here—I only know one English gangster. They called him London Len. He was a bad egg—bumped off half a dozen men before a rival gang got after him and got him on the run. He was English-born—so far as I've been able to trace he wasn't in the country five years."

London Len was an "inside man"—he got himself into positions of trust, and at the first opportunity cleared the contents of the office safe.

"Quick on the draw and ruthless," said John; "but he certainly wouldn't give a man a hundred pounds and leave it behind when he shot him!"

Now that he was abroad on this foggy night, Surefoot decided to interview a certain forgetful constable, and before he left the Yard he arranged to meet the man at Marylebone Road station. He found the police officer in mufti, waiting in the charge room, rather proud, if anything, that he had recalled the one fact that he should not have forgotten.

Surefoot Smith listened to the story of the little man who had been found sitting on the doorstep of an apartment in Baynes Mews, and of the inebriated songster.

"It's funny I should have forgotten that," began the policeman. "But as I was shaving this morning I thought——"

"It's not funny. If it was, I should be laughing. Am I laughing?"

"No, sir," admitted the police officer.

"It's not funny, it's tragic. If you'd been a rabbit wearing uniform, you would have remembered to tell your superior officer about that incident. A poor, harmless, lop-eared rabbit would have gone straight to his sergeant and said 'So-and-so and so-and-so.' And if a rabbit can do that, why couldn't you?"

The question was unanswerable, partly because the bewildered young constable was not sure whether "rabbit" had any special esoteric meaning.

"And you're taking credit," Surefoot went on inexorably, "for thinking—I repeat, thinking—as you were shaving this morning, that you ought to have told somebody about meeting that man in the mews. Do you use a safety razor, my man?"

"Yes, sir," said the officer.

"Then you couldn't cut your throat, which is a pity," said Surefoot. "Now lead me to this place, and don't speak unless I speak to you. I am not suspending you from duty, because I am not associated with the uniformed branch. There was a time when I was associated," he said carefully, "but in those days police constables had brains."

CHAPTER XI

THE crushed policeman led the way to Baynes Mews and pointed out the door where he had seen the figure of Tickler sitting. The door did not yield to Surefoot's pressure. He took from his pocket some skeleton keys which he had borrowed at the station without authority, and tried them on the door. Presently he so manipulated the key that he succeeded in snapping back the lock. He pushed open the door, sent a ray of light up the dusty stairs, and climbed, breathing stertorously, to the top. He came upon a landing and a barrier of matchwood, in which was a door. He tried this and again had recourse to his skeleton key.

Without a warrant he had no right whatever to invade the privacy of an English home; but Surefoot had never hesitated to break the law in the interests of justice or the satisfaction of his curiosity.

He found he was in a large, bare room, almost unfurnished except for a big, cheap-looking wardrobe, a chair, a table, a large mirror and a square of carpet. At the back of the room, behind the matchboarding partition, was a wash-place. Singularly enough, there was no bed, not even a couch. On the wall was an old print representing the marriage of Queen Victoria. It was in a dusty maple frame and hung groggily. Mr. Smith, who had a tidy mind, tried to straighten the picture, and something fell to the floor. It was a white glove which contained something heavy; it struck the floor with a clump. He picked it up and laid it on the dressing table. The glove was of kid, with three strips of black lace at the back, and it held a key. It was nothing delicate in the way of keys, but a large, old-fashioned door key of a type fashionable before the introduction of patent locks.

What was remarkable about this key was its colour: it had been painted with silver paint.

Surefoot looked at the key thoughtfully. An amateur had painted it—the inside of the business end had not been touched; the steel was bright and evidently the key was often used.

He brought this beneath the one naked electric globe which served to illuminate the room, but found nothing new about it. Putting the key in his pocket, he continued his search, without, however, discovering anything more noteworthy, until he found the cupboard. Its door seemed part of the matchboard lining of the room, to the height of which it rose. There was no handle, and the key-hole was so concealed in the dovetailing that it might have passed unnoticed but for the fact that Surefoot Smith was a very painstaking man.

He thought at first it was a Yale lock, but when he tested it out with the aid of a big clasp-knife which contained half a dozen tools, he found it was a very simple "catch." The cupboard held a complete dress suit, including silk hat and overcoat. On a shelf was a number of plain but exquisitely woven handkerchiefs, socks, folded dress ties, and the like.

He searched the pockets but could find no clue to the ownership of the suit. There was no maker's tab on the inside of the coat, nor concealed in the breast pocket. Even the trousers buttons were not inscribed with the tailor's name.

He examined the dress shirts; they were similarly unidentifiable. He found nothing more except a large bottle of expensive perfume, a monocle attached to a broad silk ribbon, and a locked box. This he forced under the lamp, and found three wigs, perfectly made. One was wrapped in silver tissue, and it was either new or had been newly dressed.

"Bit queer, isn't it?" said Surefoot Smith aloud.

"Yes, sir," said the constable, who had been silent until that moment.

"I was talking to myself," said Surefoot coldly.

He made another round of the room, but without adding to the sum of his knowledge.

He replaced everything where he had found it, except the key and the glove. After all, there might be a perfectly simple explanation of his finds. The man may have been an actor. The fact that Tickler had been sitting on his doorstep, listening to his drunken song, meant little, and would certainly carry no weight with a jury.

On the other hand, if the explanation was so simple, Surefoot Smith was in a position of some embarrassment. Against his name, if the truth be told, were many black marks for unauthorized entry. This might very well be the cause of another.

He went out into the mews, locked the door, and walked silently into Portland Place, followed by the policeman. And Surefoot Smith did not forget that the constable might possibly be a witness at any inquiry before the Commissioner.

"I think that is all, officer," he said, "but I am not blaming you for failing to report. Things like that," he went on, "slip out of a man's mind. For instance, I left my house yesterday and forgot to take my pipe."

The officer murmured his polite surprise. He was a little mollified, and was sufficiently intelligent to understand the reason for this change of attitude.

"I suppose it's all right, sir, going into that place without a warrant?" he said. "I'm asking because I'm a young officer, new to the force——"

Surefoot Smith surveyed him soberly.

"I went," he said, with great deliberation, "because you reported a suspicious circumstance. You told me you had reason to believe that the murderer might be hiding in that loft."

The constable gasped at this atrocious charge, gasped but was speechless.

"So that, if there's any trouble over it," said Surefoot, "we're both in it. And my word's better than yours. Now go home and keep your mouth shut—it won't be hard for you." He could not resist the temptation to gibe. "In fact, I should say you were a pretty good mouth-shutter."

The key and the white glove he locked away in a drawer of his desk at Scotland Yard. There was nothing remarkable about either article. Surefoot Smith would indeed have been glad to sacrifice his finds for one packet of cartridges the bullets of which corresponded to those extracted from the unfortunate Tickler. In his mind, however, he was satisfied that there was some connection between that flat in Baynes Mews and the murder of the little thief. The finding of the dress clothes signified little; it might only mean that some swell, for reasons best known to himself, wanted a place where he could change without going home. Such things happen in the West End of London, and in the east or any other end of any other large city.

The absence of the bed rather puzzled him, but

here again it simply removed one explanation as to why the flat was used. Yet, if he could have foreseen the future, he would have known that he had in his possession a clue more valuable than the science of ballistics could have given to him.

CHAPTER XII

Mary Lane's party was a very dull one. She was one of ten young people, and young people can be very boring. Three of the girls had a giggling secret, and throughout the meal made esoteric references to some happening which none but they understood. The young men were vapid and vacuous, after their kind. She was glad to get away on the excuse of a matinée.

Mary lived in a large block of flats in the Marylebone Road. These three small rooms and a kitchenette were home and independence to her. She seldom received visitors, rarely men visitors, and never in any circumstances invited a guest so late at night. She was staggered when the lift-man told her that "a gentleman had just gone up to her flat."

"No, miss, I've never seen him before. It wasn't Mr. Allenby, but he says he knows you."

He opened the door of the lift and walked along the corridor with her. To her amazement she saw Leo Moran, who had evidently rung the bell of the flat several times, and was returning to the elevator when they met.

"It is unpardonable of me to come so late, Miss

Lane, but when I explain to you that it's rather a vital matter I'm sure you will not be angry with me. Your maid is asleep."

Mary smiled.

"I haven't a maid," she said.

The situation was a little embarrassing: she could hardly ask him into the flat; still less did she find it possible to suggest that the lift-man should be her chaperon. She compromised by asking him in and leaving the front door open.

Moran was nervous; his voice, when he spoke, was husky; the hand that took a large envelope from his inside pocket was unsteady.

"I wouldn't have bothered you at all, but I had rather a disconcerting letter when I got home, from —an agent of mine."

She knew Moran, though she had never regarded him as a friend, and felt a sense of resentment every time he had come unbidden to her dressing room. Since she received her allowance from old Hervey, she had it also through the bank of which Leo Moran was manager.

"I'll be perfectly frank with you, Miss Lane," he said, speaking quickly and nervously. "It's a matter entirely personal to myself, in the sense that I am personally responsible. The one man who could get me out of my trouble is the one man I do not wish to approach—your guardian, Mr. Hervey Lyne."

To say she was astonished is to put it mildly. She had always regarded Moran as a man so perfectly self-possessed that nothing could break through his reserve, and here he was, fidgeting and stammering like a schoolboy.

"If I can help you of course I will," she said, wondering what was coming next.

"It concerns some shares which I purchased on behalf of a client of the bank. Mr. Lyne signed the transfer, but the other people—that is to say, the people to whom the shares were transferred—have just discovered that it is necessary also that your name shall be on the transfer, as they originally were part of the stocks left in trust to you. I might say," he went on quickly, "that the price of this stock is exactly the same, or practically the same, as it was when it was taken over."

"My name—is that all you want? I thought at least it was something valuable," she laughed.

He put the paper down on the table; it was indubitably a stock transfer; she had seen such documents before. He indicated where her name should be signed, and she noticed above it the scrawl of old Lyne.

"Well, that's done."

There was no mistaking his relief.

"You'll think I'm an awful brute to come at this hour of the night. I can't tell you how grateful I am. It simply meant that I had paid out money of the bank's without the necessary authorization. Also, if old Mr. Lyne died to-morrow, this transfer would be practically valueless."

She made a little grimace.

"Is he likely to die to-morrow?"

He shook his head.

"I don't know; he's a pretty old man."

Abruptly he held out his hand.

"Good-night, and thank you again."

She closed the door on him, went back to her kitchenette to make herself a cup of chocolate before she went to bed, and sat for a long time at the kitchen table, sipping the hot decoction and trying to discover something sinister in this midnight visitation. Herein she failed. If Hervey Lyne died to-morrow? By his agitation and hurry one might imagine that the old man was *in extremis*. Yet, the last time she had seen old Hervey, he was very much in possession of his faculties.

She was at breakfast the following morning when Dick Allenby called her up and told her of his loss. She listened incredulously, and thought he was joking, until he told her of the visit of Surefoot Smith.

"My dear—how terrible!" she said.

"Surefoot thought it was providential. Moran thought nothing."

"Was he there?" she asked quickly.

"Yes—why?"

She hesitated. Moran had so evidently wished his

visit to her to be a private matter that it seemed like betraying him.

"Oh, nothing," she said. And then, as an afterthought: "Come round and tell me all about it."

He was there in half an hour, singularly unemotional and cheerful, she thought.

"It really isn't as dramatically important as it sounds," he said. "If it has been stolen, as Surefoot thinks it has, with the idea of pinching the patent, the buyer will be shrewd enough to make a search of the registrations at the various Patent Offices. I had an acknowledgment from Germany this morning that it has been entered there."

He was interrupted by a knock at the outer door and the maid announced a second visitor. It was not usual, she explained apologetically to Dick, that she should receive guests so early, but Mike Hennessey had telephoned, asking whether he might come.

The first thing she noticed when Mike came into the room was his embarrassment at finding Dick Allenby there. A genial soul was Mike, big-faced, heavy-featured, sleepy-eyed, constitutionally lazy and lethargic in his movements. He was never a healthy-looking individual, but now he looked positively ill, and she remarked upon the fact. Mike shook his head.

"Had a bad night," he said. "Good-morning, Mr. Allenby—don't go: I've nothing private; only I wanted to see this young lady about our play. It's coming off."

"Thank heaven for that," said Mary gratefully. "It's the best news I've had for months."

"It's about the worst I've had," he grumbled.

"Has Mr. Wirth withdrawn his support?"

She was nearer the truth than she guessed. Mr. Wirth's weekly check, which had been due on the previous day, had not arrived, and Mike was taking no chances.

"The notice goes up to-night that we finish on Saturday," he said. "I've had the luck to let the theatre—I wish I'd taken a better offer that I had last week."

He was even more nervous than Moran had been; could not keep his hands still or his body either. He got up from the chair, walked to the window, came back and sat down, only to rise again a few moments later.

"Who is this old fellow Wirth? What's his job?" asked Dick.

"I don't know. He's in some sort of business at Coventry," said Mike. "I thought of running up there to-day to see him. The point is this"—he came to that point bluntly—"to-morrow night's Treasury, and I haven't enough money in the bank to pay the artistes. I may get it to-day, in which case there's no fuss. You're the heaviest salary in the cast,

Mary: will you trust me till next week if things go wrong?"

She was staggered at the suggestion. In the case of other productions Mike's solvency had always been a matter of the gravest doubt, but "Cliffs of Fate" had been under more distinguished patronage, and the general impression was that, whatever else happened, the money for its continuance would come in.

"Of course I will, Mike," she said; "but surely Mr. Wirth hasn't——"

"Gone broke? No, I shouldn't think so. He's a queer man," said Mike vaguely.

He did not particularize his patron's queerness, but was satisfied to leave it at that. His departure was almost as abrupt a gesture as any he had performed.

"There's a pretty sick man," said Dick.

"Do you mean he's ill?"

"Mentally. Something's upset him. I should imagine that the failure of old Wirth's check was quite sufficient; but there's something else besides."

He rose.

"Come and lunch," he invited, but she shook her head.

She was lunching at home; her matinée excuse at the overnight party had been on the spur of the moment. She wondered how many would remember it against her.

Dick went on to Scotland Yard, and had to wait half an hour before Surefoot Smith returned. He had no news of any importance. A description of the stolen gun had been circulated.

"But that won't help you very much. It's hardly likely to be pawned or offered for sale in the Caledonian Market," said Surefoot. And then, abruptly: "Do you know Mr. Washington Wirth?"

"I've heard of him."

"Have you ever met him? Great party giver, isn't he?"

Dick smiled.

"He's never given me a party, but I believe he is rather keen on that sort of amusement."

Surefoot nodded.

"I've just been up to the Kellner Hotel. They know nothing about him except that he always pays in cash. He's been using the hotel for three years; orders a suite whenever he feels inclined, leaves the supper and band to the head waiter; but that's the only thing they know about him—that his money is good money, which is all they want to know, I suppose."

"Are you interested in him?" asked Dick, and told the story of Mike Hennessey's agitation.

Surefoot Smith was interested.

"He's got a bank, has he? Well, he may be one of those Midland people. I've never understood what makes the corn and coal merchants go in for theatricals. It's a form of insanity that's been pretty common since the war."

"Mike will tell you all about it," suggested Allenby.

Mr. Smith's lips curled.

"Mike'll tell us a whole lot," he said sarcastically. "That fellow wouldn't tell you his right hand had four fingers, for fear you brought it up in evidence against him. I know Mike!"

"At any rate, he's got a line on Wirth," said Dick. "He's been financing this play."

Since he could find nobody to lunch with, he decided to take that meal at Snell's, which had all the values of a good club except that there were one or two members who were personally objectionable to him. And the most poisonous were the first two he saw at the entrance of the dining room. Gerald Dornford and Jules had their little table in the window. Jules favoured him with a nod, but Jerry kept his eyes steadily averted as Dick passed.

They had, in point of fact, only just sat down when Allenby had arrived, and in his furtive way Jules had been avoiding the one subject which his companion wished to discuss. He spoke of the people who were passing in the street, recognizing every important motor car that passed; he talked of the military conference which was in session just then, of the party to which he had been the night before, of everything but——

"Now what about this gun?" said Jerry.

"The gun?" Jules looked at him blankly, then leaned back in his chair and chuckled. "What a good thing you came to-day! I wanted to see you. That little project of mine must be abandoned."

"What do you mean?" gasped Jerry, turning pale.

"I mean that my principals, or rather the principals of my principals, have decided not to go any farther in the matter. You see, we've discovered that all the salient points of the gun have been protected by patents, especially in those countries where the invention could be best exploited."

Jerry looked at him, dumbfounded.

"Do you mean to say that you don't want it?"

Jules nodded.

"I mean to say that there's no need for you to take any unnecessary risks. Now let us discuss some other way of raising the money——"

"Discuss be damned!" said Jerry savagely. "I've got the gun—I took it last night!"

Jules stroked his smooth chin and looked at his companion thoughtfully.

"That's awkward," he said. "You took it from the workshop, did you? Well, you can hardly put it back. I advise you to drive somewhere out of London and dump it in a deep pond. Or, better still, try the river, somewhere between Temple Lock and Hambleden."

"Do you mean to tell me"—Jerry's husky voice was almost hoarse—"that I've taken this risk for nothing? What is the idea?"

Jules shrugged.

"I'm sorry. My principals——"

"Damn your principals! You gave me a specific promise that if I got the thing you'd give me a couple of thousand."

Jules smiled.

"And now, my dear fellow, I give you a specific assurance that I cannot get two thousand shillings for the gun! It is unfortunate. If you had procured the invention when I first suggested it, the matter would have been all over—and paid for. Now it is too late."

He leaned over and patted the other gently on the arm as though he were a child.

"There is no sense in being foolish about this matter," he said. "Let us find some other way of raising the wind, eh?"

Jerry Dornford was crushed. He knew Hervey Lyne sufficiently well to realize that, had he produced the two thousand pounds, the old man would have grabbed at the money and given him the extra time he had asked. Hervey could never resist the argument of cash.

He could have grabbed the smiling little cad

opposite him and thrown him out of the window. There was murder in his glance when he looked into the round, brown eyes of his companion. But Jerry Dornford never forgot he was a gentleman, and as such was expected to exercise the self-control which is the peculiar and popular attribute of the well-bred man.

"Well, it can't be helped," he said. "Order me a drink; I'm a bit rattled."

Jules played an invisible piano on the edge of the table.

"Our friend Allenby is at the third table on the right. Would it not be a good idea," he suggested, "to go over and say: 'What a little joke I played on you, eh?' "

"Don't be a fool," interrupted Jerry roughly. "He called me up last night and asked me if I'd had it. He's put the matter in the hands of the police. I had a visit from Smith this morning."

"So!" Jules pursed his red lips. "That is a pity Here is your drink."

They sat for a long time over their coffee, saw Dick Allenby leave the club and cross to the opposite side of St. James's Street.

"Clever fellow, that," said Jules, almost with enthusiasm. "He doesn't like me. I forget the name he called me the last time we had a little discussion, but it was terribly offensive. But I like him. I am fond of clever people; there is nothing so amusing as cleverness."

Dick had hardly left the club before a telephone message came through for him, and this he missed. It was Mary Lane, and at that moment she needed Dick's advice very badly. She called his flat again; he had not returned. She tried a third club, where he sometimes called in the afternoon, but again was unsuccessful.

She had been writing out the small checks which her housekeeping necessitated, when the strange message had arrived. It came in the hands of a grubby little boy, who carried an envelope which was covered with uncleanly finger marks.

"An old gentleman told me to bring it here," he said in his shrill Cockney.

An old gentleman? She looked at the superscription; her name and address were scrawled untidily, and although she had not seen Hervey Lyne's handwriting, she knew, or rather guessed, that it was he who had sent the letter.

The boy explained that he had been delivering a parcel at No. 19 Naylor Terrace, and had seen the old gentleman leaning on his stick in the doorway. He wore his dressing gown and had the letter in his hand. He had called the boy, given him half-a-crown (that must have been a wrench for Hervey), and ordered him to deliver the letter at once.

She tore it open. It was written on the back of a

ruled sheet of paper covered with typewritten figures, and the writing was in pencil:

> Bring Moran to me without fail at three o'clock this afternoon. I saw him two days ago, but I'm not satisfied. Bring police officer.

Here was written, above, a word which she deciphered as "Smith."

> Do not let Moran or anybody know about P. O. This is very urgent.

The note was signed "H. L."

The little boy could give her no other information. She would have called up Mr. Lyne's house, but the old man had an insuperable objection to the telephone and had never had one installed. She looked at her watch; it was after two, and for ten minutes she was making a frantic effort to get in touch with Dick.

Surefoot Smith she hardly knew well enough to consult, and she had a woman's distaste for approaching the police direct. She called up Mr. Moran's bank; he had gone home. She tried his club, with no better success. Moran had left his flat that morning, announcing that he had no intention of returning for two or three weeks. He had gone on leave. Curiously enough, the bank did not tell her that: they merely said that Mr. Moran had gone home early—a completely inaccurate piece of information, she discovered, when the first man, who was evidently a clerk, was interrupted and a more authoritative voice spoke:

"This is the chief accountant speaking, Miss Lane. You were asking about Mr. Moran? He has not been to the bank to-day."

"He's gone on leave, hasn't he?"

"I'm not aware of the fact. I know he has applied for leave, but I don't think he's gone—in fact I'm certain. I opened all the letters this morning."

She hung up the telephone, bewildered, and was sitting at the window, cogitating on what else she should do, when to her joy the telephone rang. It was Dick, who had returned to Snell's Club to collect some letters he had forgotten, and had been told of her call.

"That's very odd," was his comment when he heard about the note. "I'll try to get Smith. The best thing you can do, angel, is to meet me outside Baker Street Tube station in a quarter of an hour. I'll try to land Smith at the same moment."

She got to the station a little before three, and had to wait for ten minutes before a taxicab dashed up and Dick jumped out. She saw the bulky figure of Mr. Smith in one corner of the cab, and, getting in, sat by him. Dick gave instructions to the taxi driver and seated himself opposite.

"This is all very mysterious, isn't it?" he said. "Let me see the letter."

She showed it to him, and he turned it over.

"Hullo, this is a bank statement." He whistled. "Phew! What figures! The old boy's certainly let the cat out of the bag."

She had paid no attention to the typewritten statement on the back.

"Over two hundred thousand in cash and umteen hundred thousand in securities. What is the idea—I mean, of sending this note?"

She shook her head.

Smith was examining the letter carefully.

"Is he blind?" he asked.

"Very nearly," said Dick. "He doesn't admit it, but he can't see well enough to distinguish you from me. That's his writing—I had a rude letter from him one day last week. Did you find Moran?"

Mary shook her head.

"Nobody seems to know where he is. He hasn't been to the bank to-day, and he's not at his flat."

Surefoot folded the letter and handed it back to the girl.

"It looks as if he doesn't want to see me yet awhile, and not at all if we don't bring Moran," he said.

They drove into Naylor Crescent, and it was agreed that Surefoot should sit outside in the cab whilst they interviewed the old man. But repeated knockings brought no answer. The houses in Naylor Crescent stand behind deep little areas, and out of one of these next door a head of a servant girl appeared.

"There's nobody in," she said. "Mr. Lyne went out in his chair about an hour ago."

"Where did he go?" asked Dick.

The servant girl could not say; but Mary was better informed.

"They always go to the same place—into the private gardens of the park," she said. "It's only a few minutes' walk."

The cab was no longer necessary; Dick paid it off. They were about to cross the road when a big, open touring car swept past, and Dick had a momentary glimpse of the man at the wheel. It was Jerry Dornford. The car was old and noisy; there was a succession of backfires as it passed. It slowed down a little at one point, then, gathering speed, disappeared from view.

"Any policeman doing his duty will pinch that fellow under the Noises Act," said Smith.

Presently they came in sight of the chair. Binny was sitting on his little collapsible stool, a paper spread open on his knees, a pair of gold-rimmed glasses perched on his thick nose. The gate into the gardens was locked, and it was some time before Dick attracted the servant's attention. Presently

Binny looked up, and, ambling forward, unlocked the gate and admitted them.

"I think he's asleep, sir," he said, "and that's a bit awkward. If I start wheeling him when he's asleep, and he wakes up, he gives me hell! And he's got to be home by three."

Old Hervey Lyne sat, his chin on his breast, his blue-tinted glasses firmly fixed on the high bridge of his nose. His gloved hands were clasped on the rug which was tucked about his legs. Binny folded his paper, put it in his pocket, folded his stool and hung it on a little hook on the Bath chair.

"Do you think you'd better wake him up?"

Mary went nearer.

"Mr. Lyne," she said.

She called again, but there was no answer.

Surefoot Smith, who was standing at some distance, came nearer. He walked round the back of the chair, came to the front, and, leaning over, pulled open the old man's coat. He closed it again; then, to Mary's amazement, Surefoot Smith caught her gently by the arm.

"I think you'd better run away for about an hour, and I'll come and see you at your flat," he said.

His voice was unusually gentle.

She looked at him, and the colour went out of her face.

"Is he dead?" she breathed.

Surefoot Smith nodded; almost impelled her towards the gate. When she was out of hearing:

"He's been shot through the back. I saw the hole in the cape as I came round. Look!" He opened the coat.

Dick saw something that was not pleasant to see.

CHAPTER XIII

THE ambulance had come and gone. Four men sat in the dead man's study. Binny was one; the other, besides Surefoot Smith and Dick Allenby, was the divisional inspector.

Smith turned to the gray-faced servant.

"Tell us just what happened, my boy," he said.

Binny shook his head.

"I don't know . . . awful, ain't it, him going like that——"

"Were there any visitors?"

Binny shook his head again.

"Nobody, so far as I know."

"Where was he at one o'clock?"

"In this room, sir, in the chair where you're sitting," said Binny. "He was writing something—put his hand over it when I came in. I didn't see what it was."

"It was probably a letter to Miss Lane," said the detective. "Does he often write notes?"

Binny shook his head.

"When he does write them do you deliver them?"

Binny shook his head again.

"No, sir, not always. Poor Mr. Lyne was very suspicious. His sight wasn't very good, and he'd got an idea that people was listening at the door or reading his letters. He'd call anybody off the street to take a note when he sent one, which wasn't often."

"What visitors has he had lately?"

"Mr. Dornford came last night, sir. There was a bit of a quarrel—over money, I think."

"A bad quarrel?" asked Smith.

Binny nodded.

"He asked me to throw him out—Mr. Lyne did."

Surefoot jotted down a note.

"And who else?"

Binny looked serious.

"Mr. Moran came two days ago," Smith said.

"That's right, sir. Mr. Moran came to see him about banking business, and Miss Lane came—I think that's the lot. We don't often have people call."

Again Smith scribbled something. He employed a weird kind of shorthand, which was indecipherable to Dick, who, from where he sat, had a view of the notes.

"Tell us what happened to-day. Do you usually go out in the afternoon?"

"Yes, sir, but at lunchtime Mr. Lyne said he wouldn't go out. In fact he told me not to bother about the chair, that he was expecting some visitors at three o'clock. About three o'clock he changed his mind and said he'd go out. I pulled him into the park gardens and sat down and read a case to him——"

"Do you mean a police court case?"

"That's right, sir. He likes reading about money-lenders' actions against people who owe them something. There was a case this morning——"

"Oh, you mean a Law Courts case—any kind of case, in fact?"

Binny nodded.

"Did he say anything in the park?"

"Nothing at all, sir, of any consequence. He'd been sitting there a quarter of an hour and he asked me to turn up the collar of his coat; he was feeling a draught. I sat down and read to him until I thought he was asleep."

"You heard no sound?"

He thought a moment.

"Yes, there was a bit of a noise, from a car that went past."

For a moment both Smith and Dick had forgotten Gerald Dornford's car, and they exchanged a glance.

"You heard nothing like a shot?"

Binny shook his head.

"Nothing more than the motor-car noise," he said.

"Did Mr. Lyne speak at all—groan, move?"

"No, sir."

Surefoot settled his elbows on the table.

"This is the question I want to ask you, Binny: how long before we found Mr. Lyne was dead did you hear him speak?"

Binny considered.

"About ten minutes, sir," he said. "A park keeper came along and said good-afternoon to him, and, when he didn't answer, I thought he was asleep. That's when I stopped reading."

"Now show me the house," said Smith, rising.

Binny led the way, first to the kitchen, from which opened a bedroom.

His wife was away in the country, living with relations, he told Surefoot, but that made little difference to Lyne's comfort, for Binny did most of the work.

"To tell you the truth, sir, my wife drinks," he said apologetically, "and I'm glad to have her out of the house."

The kitchen was none too tidy. Surefoot Smith saw something on the floor, stooped and picked up a triangular piece of glass from under the table beneath the window. He looked up at the window, felt the puttied edge.

"Had a window broken in?"

Binny hesitated.

"Mr. Lyne didn't want to say anything about it. Somebody broke the glass and opened the window a couple of nights ago."

"A burglar?"

"Mr. Lyne thought it was somebody trying to get in. I didn't send for the police, because he wouldn't let me," he hastened to exculpate himself.

They went upstairs to the front room. There was only one large room on each floor, though both could be divided into two by folding doors. The top room had been Lyne's bedroom, but presented no particular features. A divisional inspector and two of his men would conduct a leisurely search through the possessions and papers of the dead man—Surefoot had taken the keys from the old man's pocket. He had already made a casual inspection of the safe, without discovering anything of moment.

They came back to the study. Surefoot Smith stood for a long time, staring out of the window, drumming his fingers on the leather-covered top. When he spoke it was half to himself.

"There's an American going back to New York to-morrow who might tell us something. I've a good mind to bring him down to a consultation."

"Who's that?" asked Dick curiously.

"John Kelly—he's chief of the detective force in Chicago. He might give us an angle, and then again he mightn't. It's worth trying."

He looked at his watch.

"I wonder if there's any news of Moran—I'm

going to look at his flat. I suppose there'll be a servant there?"

"If there isn't," said Dick, "I can help you. He told me he was going away and that he intended sending me the key, so that I could forward any letters that arrived. If you don't mind I'll walk round with you."

The superintendent of the flat gave a surprising piece of information. Mr. Moran had left only an hour before.

"Are you sure?" asked Dick incredulously. "Didn't he leave this morning?"

The man was very emphatic.

"No, sir, he was out all the morning, but he didn't actually leave till about half-past three. You're Mr. Allenby, aren't you?" He addressed Dick. "I've got a letter to post for you."

He went to his little office, came out, opened the post-box, and took out a stamped envelope which contained a few lines, evidently written in a hurry, and the key of the flat.

> I'm just off. Those brutes have turned me down.

"Who are the brutes?" asked Surefoot.

Dick smiled.

"I presume he's referring to his directors. He told me he was going on his holiday whether they agreed or not."

When they entered the flat there was evidence of Moran's hurried departure. They found, for example, a waistcoat hanging from the edge of the bed, in which were his watch and chain, a gold cigarette case, and about ten pounds in cash. He had evidently changed his clothes quickly and had forgotten to empty his pockets. Another peculiar fact, which both Surefoot and Dick remarked, was that the window overlooking the park had been left open.

"Do you notice anything?" asked Surefoot.

Dick nodded, and a little chill went down his spine. From where he stood, by the open window, he commanded a view not only of the private gardens but of the actual spot where old Hervey Lyne had been killed.

Surefoot searched the floor near the window but found nothing. He passed into Moran's elegant bedroom and made a rapid search. He pulled out the wardrobe door, and something fell out. He had time to catch it before it reached the floor. It was a Lee-Enfield rifle; a second lay flat on the wardrobe floor, and, near it, half a dozen long, black cylinders.

Surefoot snapped open the breech and smelt. He had taken the rifle to the window; he placed the block upon the sill and squinted down the barrel. If it had been recently fired then it must have been recently cleaned, for there was no sign of fouling. He tested the other rifle in the same way; and then he took up one of the cylinders.

"What are those?" he said.

Dick looked at them carefully.

"They're silencers," he said. "But Moran is very much interested in rifle-shooting, especially in any new brand of silencer. He has consulted me once or twice, and has frequently urged me to take up the making of silencers. You mustn't forget, Smith, that Mr. Moran is an enthusiastic rifleman. In fact, he's been runner-up for the King's Prize at Bisley, and shooting was about his only recreation."

"And a pretty good recreation too," said Smith dryly.

He searched the wardrobe and the drawers for cartridges, but could find none. The magazines of both rifles were empty. There was no sign of a discharged shell anywhere in the flat.

Smith went back to the window and judged the distance which separated the room from the place of the killing.

"Less than two hundred yards," he suggested, and Dick Allenby agreed.

Moran had not taken his servant. Surefoot got his address from the superintendent and wired him to report at once.

"You'd better go along and see the young lady. She's probably having hysterics by now."

"It's hardly likely," said Dick coldly, "but I'll see her. Where are you going?"

Surefoot smiled mysteriously; though why he should make a mystery of the most obvious move, it was hard to say.

CHAPTER XIV

THE bank premises were closed when he reached them; he rang a bell at the side door and was admitted. The accountant and the chief clerk and two or three other clerks were on duty. He interviewed the accountant in his office.

"I know nothing whatever about Mr. Moran's movements, except that he applied for leave and it was not granted. I know that, because the letter from the head office did not come addressed to him personally, but to 'the manager,' and was opened by me. I got him on the phone and told him; he said nothing except that he wouldn't be down to-day."

"Have you reported this to your head office?" asked Surefoot.

No report had been made. It was not a very extraordinary happening. Bank managers do occasionally decide to stay away from business; and, as it happened, there had been no inquiries by phone from headquarters, and the fact had not been mentioned.

"It will go in, of course, in the daily report," said the accountant. "To tell you the truth, I was under the impression that Mr. Moran had gone up to the City and had interviewed the managing director; so that when I heard he was taking his leave I naturally supposed that he had persuaded the head office to change its mind. Has anything happened to Mr. Moran?" he asked anxiously.

"I hope not, I'm sure," said Smith with spurious solicitude. "Did he bank with you?"

"He had an account at this branch, but carried only a small balance," explained the accountant. "There was a little trouble about speculation a few years back, and naturally, I suppose, Mr. Moran did not run his main account through us, not wishing the directors to know his business. I can tell you for your private information that he banks with the Southern Provincial. I know that, because once, when his account with us was low, he paid in a check on that bank to put it in credit. May I ask, Mr. Smith, what is the reason for this inquiry?"

In a few words Surefoot told him of the murder.

"Yes, we carry Mr. Lyne's account. It is a fairly large one—not as large as it used to be—he is a money-lender and has a lot of money out."

Smith looked at his watch.

"Is it possible to see any of the directors at headquarters?"

The accountant was doubtful, but he put through a telephone call, only to return with the information that all the directors had gone home.

"If Mr. Moran doesn't turn up in the morning——"

"He won't," said Surefoot.

"Well, if he doesn't, I'd be glad if you saw the head office. I really ought not to be giving you any kind of information, either about Mr. Moran or about any of our customers. Just one moment."

He went behind a desk and consulted a clerk. After a while he came back.

"I might tell you this, whether I get into trouble or not, that the late Mr. Lyne drew sixty thousand pounds from the bank yesterday—that is to say, the check came in to us and was cleared last night. It was a bearer check and passed through some bank in the Midlands. I can't give you the exact details, but I've no doubt head office will give you the authorization."

When Surefoot returned to Scotland Yard he found a group of officers in his room. They were saying good-bye to John Kelly, who was leaving at midnight for the United States.

"I'm sorry," he said, when he heard Surefoot's idea. "Nothing would have given me greater pleasure than to have got in on a murder case. I read it in the evening papers. Have there been any developments?"

Surefoot told him what he had learned at the bank, and the American nodded.

"You might do worse than look after a man

called Arthur Ryan," he said. "I know that he's in England—I'll send you some photographs of him taken when I was in Chicago. That was part of his graft, running banking accounts, switching somebody else's money from one to the other. You'd never guess he was that kind of bird."

Surefoot was forced to decline, with regret, the invitation to an informal farewell dinner. The Chief Constable was waiting for him, a little impatiently, for his dinner hour was more formal.

"We'll have to circulate a description of Moran," said the Chief when he had finished, "but it must be done without publicity, or we'll be getting ourselves into all sorts of trouble. The fact that he keeps a couple of rifles in his room means nothing. Even I know him as a rifle shot. So far as we are aware, there is nothing wrong at the bank, and the only circumstance connecting him with the crime is the old man's note. Have you got it?"

Mary had handed the note to the detective, who produced it from his pocket and spread it on the table.

The Chief Constable nodded.

"The fact that he wants to see Moran again—had he seen him before?"

"Two days ago, according to Binny, the servant—not for two years, according to Moran," said Surefoot slowly, and the Chief looked up.

"Moran said he hadn't seen——"

Surefoot nodded.

"That's just what he said. Allenby asked him casually the night before the murder when he had seen Lyne last. He said two years ago. Allenby is absolutely definite. Now, why did he say he hadn't seen him when he had? And why did old Lyne, when he sent that note, say 'Bring Moran' and immediately follow this by asking for a police officer to be in attendance? There's only one explanation—that he'd discovered something about Moran and intended either to confront him or threaten him with police action. Moran applies for urgent leave from the bank, and this isn't granted. He doesn't come to the bank, and I think we'll find, when I make inquiries at their head office, that the directors know nothing about his being away. Moran had the handling of the old man's account, and if there was anything wrong it meant penal servitude for him; probably the only person who could say whether anything was wrong was Lyne himself. He dies—somebody puts a bullet in him—half an hour before Moran leaves London. That's circumstantial, but better circumstantial evidence than most people are hung on. If you want anything clearer than that, lead me to it."

He continued his inquiries throughout the evening, and about a quarter of an hour before the curtain came down—the penultimate curtain, as it proved—on "Cliffs of Fate," he called at the theatre. Mike Hennessey had gone home, as his manager dramatically described, "a broken man."

"He'd set his heart on this play, Mr. Smith——" began the little manager, but Surefoot silenced him.

"Nobody could set their hearts on a lousy play like this," he said. "It doesn't appeal either to the intelligent or the theatrical classes."

He went through the pass door to the stage, and down a long corridor to Mary's dressing room. Dick Allenby, as he had expected, was with her. She looked tired; evidently the old man's death had been a greater shock to her than either Dick or Surefoot Smith could have expected.

"Oh, yes, the play comes off; but things aren't so bad with poor Mike as he expected. His check turned up and he was able to pay the company, and, I hope, himself."

She could tell him nothing about Hervey Lyne, but she was very informative about Leo Moran when he began to question her. He heard the story of his midnight call—it was news to Dick also.

"But, my dear, I don't understand. He wanted you to sign a transfer——"

"Did you notice the ame of the shares?" interrupted Surefoot.

This she had not seen. Surefoot, who knew a great deal about the City and had been in many financial cases, suggested that it must be a foreign stock. It is the rule on certain foreign stock exchanges that shares cannot be transferred by a trustee without the approval and signature of the beneficiaries for whom he is acting.

"There is nothing fishy about that," said Surefoot thoughtfully. "Even if he was a buyer, old Lyne would not have put his name to a transfer unless he had his money's worth."

Surefoot could do little more that night. Lyne's documents were being carefully examined and tabulated, and the place of the murder was roped off and guarded, a precautionary measure justified when, at midnight, the surgeon's report came through.

Hervey Lyne had been killed by a bullet which passed through his heart from behind. Actually no bullet was found in the body, and Surefoot gave orders that at daybreak every inch of the lawn where the murder was committed should be searched for the spent bullet. By nine o'clock he was in the City, awaiting the arrival of the great men of the bank. As he had expected, no leave had been granted to Leo Moran, against whose name there was a black mark in the bank's books.

"He was a very capable manager, and very popular with our clients; otherwise, I doubt if we should have kept him after his speculations. We know nothing against him whatever, except, of course, this act of indiscipline."

"If he's gone away he has simply taken French leave?" asked Surefoot.

"Exactly," said the managing director, "and that is a very serious offense. We believe he is in Devonshire—at least, that is where he said he was going."

Surefoot smiled.

"He's not in Devonshire—I can tell you that," he said. "He left by a specially chartered aëroplane from Croydon at twenty minutes past four yesterday afternoon for Cologne. Another 'plane was waiting to take him to Berlin, and there we have not as yet traced him."

The managing director looked at him open-mouthed. Surefoot thought he turned a little pale.

"In Berlin?"

He could hardly believe it. One could almost see his mind working. Leo Moran's branch carried very heavy accounts, and a branch manager who disappears suddenly, and in suspicious circumstances, might not have gone empty-handed.

"I shouldn't imagine anything is wrong." He was very much perturbed. "Beyond the fact that he speculated—and of course one never knows to what length a gambler will go—he was a very honest, high-principled man. He had, I know, dreams of making a great fortune, but then we have all passed through that stage without doing anything dishonest." He pressed a bell. "Nevertheless, I will have an immediate examination of the books, and will at once send down our two best inspectors. We must replace Mr. Moran immediately."

Surefoot had managed to get a very accurate description of Leo Moran, but could find no photograph of him. He should not be difficult to trace; he was almost completely bald, which fact, however, he could disguise, if he had reason for disguise at all, with a wig.

Surefoot stopped in his reasoning and frowned. A wig! He remembered the three wigs he had found in a cupboard of a room in Baynes Mews; and he recalled, too, the name of Mr. Washington Wirth, who lived in the Midlands. . . . Sixty thousand pounds had gone from Lyne's account on the previous day through a Midland branch bank.

He asked for and secured authority for obtaining complete information regarding any account that was in Moran's branch, and, armed with this, he went back to the bank and interviewed the chief accountant.

"I happen to know the state of Mr. Lyne's account up till a few days ago," he said. "By error he wrote a note to his ward on the back of the statement."

He produced it from his pocket, and the accountant examined it.

"I'll just check this up," he said. "This would not, of course, show the sixty thousand pounds which was debited the day before yesterday."

He was gone a long time, then came back to the little office where the interview was being held, and put the statement on the table. By it was a sheet of paper, on which he had scribbled a number of figures.

"This statement is entirely inaccurate," he said. "It seems to be dated three days ago, but it does not in any way represent Mr. Lyne's account. It shows, for example, over two hundred thousand pounds on deposit account; the actual amount on deposit is less than fifty thousand—forty-eight thousand seven hundred, to be exact. Most of this has been transferred to the current account at some time or other, the actual cash remaining in that account being about five thousand pounds."

Surefoot whistled softly.

"Then you mean that the difference between the real condition of affairs and this statement is about two hundred thousand pounds?"

The accountant nodded.

"The moment I saw it I knew it was wrong. As a matter of fact, I paid a great deal of attention to this particular account, and I have twice suggested to the manager, Mr. Moran, that he should write to Mr. Lyne, pointing out the low state of his balance. As I say, we don't worry very much about money-lenders' balances, because very often they put all their available cash into loans."

"What about these stocks?"

"They're quite all right, with the exception of thirty thousand pounds' worth of Steel Preferred which were sold four months ago on Mr. Lyne's instructions. The money received for that is in another account."

"Did you receive any letter from Lyne, in answer to yours?"

"In answer to the manager's?" corrected the accountant. "No, sir. I wouldn't see it anyway. It would be on Mr. Moran's file, where you'll probably find it."

Smith considered the matter.

"Did Mr. Moran see Lyne last Tuesday, about ten o'clock in the morning?"

The accountant smiled.

"If he did, he didn't tell me. Last Tuesday morning?" He considered. "He didn't come in till about midday. He said he'd had an interview of some kind, but what it was I don't know." And then, very seriously: "There's something radically wrong, isn't there, and Mr. Moran is in it? I will give you and the bank any help I can. As I said before, I know nothing whatever about these transactions. Would you like to see Mr. Lyne's account? Very large sums have been going out in the past eighteen months, generally on bearer checks. That is not unusual with a money-lender's account. It is customary to deposit promissory notes or acceptances against these withdrawals, but I understand that Mr. Lyne has never done this."

He came back with the ledger, which Smith examined with an expert eye. Money had gone in sums of ten, fifteen, twenty thousand, and invariably through a Birmingham bank.

"Only one of these large checks has been made payable to an individual," said the clerk, turning a leaf and pointing to a name. "It was whilst Mr. Moran was on his holiday——"

Smith looked, and his jaw dropped. The name was Washington Wirth.

CHAPTER XV

HE STARED at the entry for a long time.

"Can I get a trunk call through to this bank in Birmingham?" he asked.

Apparently there was some arrangement for facilitating inter-banking calls, for in a few minutes he was connected. The Birmingham bank manager confirmed all that he already knew. He did not know Mr. Washington Wirth, though he had seen him once in his hotel. Apparently, when Mr. Wirth opened his account, he was suffering from some complaint which confined him to bed and made it necessary that the blinds should be drawn. The manager's chief clerk who interviewed him had taken his signature, and that was the last that had been seen of him. He had an arrangement by which he could draw cash against checks at three other branches of the bank, one at the London office, one at Bristol, and a third, which had never been used, at Sheffield. He invariably, twenty-four hours before the check was presented, notified the Birmingham branch by telegraph that he was drawing money; and although huge sums passed through his account, he had very little to his credit at that moment.

Surefoot Smith sent a detective to Birmingham with a number of specimen signatures, and instructions to bring back Wirth's.

Whoever was the giver of these midnight parties was certainly the man to whom large sums of money had been paid out of Hervey Lyne's account—possibly his murderer. He called up Dick and, finding him working at his new model, told him as much of his discoveries as he thought was necessary.

"You're his next of kin and I suppose you ought to know this," he said.

Dick was staggered when he learned the amount of money that was missing.

"You haven't overlooked the possibility of Mr. Wirth being Hervey Lyne himself, have you?"

"I've thought of that," said Surefoot. "The fact that he couldn't move without a Bath chair means nothing; that's one of the oldest fakes in the world. The checks were undoubtedly signed by him; I've seen the last one—in fact I've got it here."

He took it from his pocket. Turning it over, he saw what he had not noticed before—a scrawling pencil mark on the back. The mark was faint; it had evidently been written by one of those patent pencils which occasionally function and occasionally do not. Even so, an attempt had been made, which was partially successful, to rub off the inscription. With the aid of a magnifying glass the detective examined the writing and presently deciphered it.

"Don't send any more Chinese e . . ." Evidently the writing had wandered off the back of the check onto the blotting paper where the old man wrote.

"Now what the devil does that mean?" asked Smith irritably. "There's no doubt about it being his writing. What does 'Chinese' mean? And who took the trouble to rub it off?"

He scratched his head in his exasperation.

"I ought to have asked the clerk if he'd got any Chinese bonds."

Dick lunched with Mary Lane and passed on to her all that the detective had told him. He was telling her about the check with the inscription on the back when he heard an exclamation, and looked at her in amazement. Her eyes and mouth were wide open; she was staring at him.

"Oh!" she said.

Dick smiled.

"Do you know anything about Chinese bonds?"

She shook her head.

"Tell me it all over again, and tell me slowly, because I'm not particularly clever."

He repeated the story about the faked account and the big checks that had been drawn obviously to the credit of Mr. Washington Wirth. Whenever she could not understand she pressed him for explanations, which he was not always able to give. When he had finished she sighed and leaned back in her chair. Her eyes were bright.

"You look terribly mysterious."

She nodded.

"I am mysterious."

"Do you think you know who killed that unfortunate old man?"

She nodded slowly.

"Yes; I wouldn't dare name him, but I really do think I have what the police call a clue. You see, I lived in Mr. Lyne's house when I was a little girl, and there are some things I've never forgotten."

"I'll tell Surefoot——" he began.

"No, no." She was very insistent. "Dick, you mustn't. If you make me look foolish I'll never forgive you. My theory is probably utterly silly. I'll make a few inquiries before I even hint at it."

"In fact, you're going to be a detective, darling," said Dick. "By the way, poor old Lyne's will has been discovered. I am his heir. The will is full of restrictions. For example, if I marry anybody outside my own nationality and religion I lose something, and if I reside out of England I lose something, and if I don't give his dog a good home I lose something more—his dog has been dead sixteen years, by the way—but, generally speaking, he's very generous and gives you about forty thousand pounds free of death duty."

"Really!"

She was staggered at the old man's munificence;

genuinely relieved, too, that in a moment of caprice he had not carried out the threat to disinherit his unpopular nephew.

Surefoot Smith did not know that the will had been found until he got back to his office, and, calling up Dick to congratulate him that afternoon, was annoyed to find that his news was old.

"As you're an interested party you'd better come down to the Yard right away. I've the bank accountant here and he's got something to say that will interest you."

Dick arrived to find the accountant looking rather bored in his shabby surroundings. Evidently the office arrangements at Scotland Yard did not impress him. He certainly shifted frequently in the hard-seated kitchen chair which had been placed at his disposal. On Surefoot's table was a number of typewritten sheets of paper.

"This is the point," said Smith impressively, pushing the sheets for Dick to see them. "This gentleman, Mr.——"

"Smith," said the accountant.

"That's very awkward," said Surefoot gravely. "Have you got any other name, such as Huxley or Montefiore?"

"Just Smith," smiled the accountant.

"Very awkward indeed," said Surefoot. "Most Smiths adopt another name. This is his name," he went on to explain. "Our friend here" (he studiously avoided calling his brother Smith by that name, and never afterwards did he employ it to describe the accountant) "says that the statement that was sent to Miss Lane was not typed at the bank or on any bank typewriter. He proved this conclusively from my point of view by giving me specimens from all the typewriters used at the bank. A very good bit of detective work, though I don't see that it carries us much farther forward, because if, as we believe, Moran has been bilking these funds, he probably typed the statements at home. The blanks or forms are not difficult to get?"

The accountant shook his head.

"Oh, no; they are printed by hundreds of thousands."

"Could anybody outside the bank secure them?"

The accountant thought it was possible.

"It comes to this, then," said Surefoot, "that you're satisfied this statement was not typewritten in your bank?"

"Or by any bank machine," said the accountant. "Every branch office uses a——" he mentioned the name of an American make of machine—"and always the same type face is used, the same coloured ribbon, the same carbons. The ribbon here is purple; we invariably use black. I didn't realize that till I made inquiries. The type face is entirely different."

He suggested the make of machine on which the

statement had been written, and this afterwards proved to be correct.

Surefoot could not remember having seen a typewriter at Moran's flat. He accompanied Dick, after the accountant had gone, to Parkview Crescent, and made a more careful search. They found a portable typewriter, though it was unusable. Remembering the flat in Baynes Mews, Smith was not greatly depressed by his failure to discover the machine. It was possible, and even likely, that if Moran was the tenant of Baynes Mews, he would also have other places of call. In London there might be two or three flats engaged in false names (that in Baynes Mews had been engaged in the name of Whiteley), which Moran used for his own purpose—supposing it was Moran.

"Have you any doubts?" said Dick.

"I'm full of doubts," said Surefoot. "Some of 'em may be set at rest when I find Jerry Dornford. You remember, after we left Naylor Crescent and were going over to see the old man, Dornford passed in a car that was raising a noise like hell? And do you remember he slowed down just about opposite the place where the old man was sitting?"

"Well?" said Dick, when he paused.

"Well," said the other, indignant at his denseness, "didn't he have a gun of yours?"

"Good God! You don't think that Dornford killed him?"

"Why shouldn't he?" asked the other truculently. "He owed Lyne money, and Lyne had threatened to put him into the court unless he paid on the very day of his murder. If you know Dornford's reputation as well as I do, you know that that's the one thing he'd want to avoid. He prides himself upon being a swell, though his father was a horse dealer and his mother—well, I won't talk about her! Bankruptcy means being kicked out of all his clubs. A bird like that would do almost anything to avoid social extinction—is that the right word? Thank you very much."

"Where is he?"

"That's what I'd like to know," said Surefoot, grimly. "He hasn't been seen since we saw him!"

CHAPTER XVI

MR. SUREFOOT SMITH was one of those individuals who never seemed to do any work. He was to be seen at odd hours of the day, and sometimes in odd places of the West End. It seemed that he was able to dispense with sleep, for you were as likely to meet him at four o'clock in the morning as at four o'clock in the afternoon.

He had a villa at Streatham.

"He is the type of man," Dick Allenby once described him, "who was foreordained to live with a married sister."

In addition, he had a room in Panton Street, Haymarket, and not the more fashionable part of Panton Street either. In all probability this was his real home, though the Streatham villa was not such a myth as his colleagues chose to imagine it.

Thieves knew him and respected him; the aristocrats of the underworld, who were his special prey, avoided him with great care, but not always with conspicuous success. He was the terror of the little card-sharping gangs; confidence men hated him, for he had put more of their kind in prison than any two officers of Scotland Yard. He had hanged three men, and bitterly regretted that a fourth had escaped the gallows through the lunacy of a sentimental jury.

His pleasures were few. Beer was more of a necessity than a dissipation; for how can one sneer at a man who consumes large quantities of malted liquor necessary for his well-being and happiness, and find anything commendable in the physical wreck who seeks, through copious potions of Vichy water, to combat the excesses of his youth?

In the privacy of his Panton Street rooms, he worked out his problems in a way peculiar to himself. He invariably wrote on white blotting paper with a pencil, and seldom employed any other medium except when he was called upon to furnish a conventional report to his superiors. He invariably covered both sides of his blotting paper with writing which nobody but he could read. It was a shorthand invented thirty years ago by a freakish schoolmaster, and the only man who had ever learned it thoroughly was Surefoot Smith. He had not only learned it but improved upon it. It was his boast that no human being could decode anything he ever wrote; many had had the opportunity and tried, for after Mr. Smith had finished with his blotting paper it was passed on to junior officers for a more proper use.

He worked out Leo Moran's movements chronologically so far as they could be traced. One portion of the day previous to the murder had been clearly marked. Moran had broadcast a lecture on banking and economics. Surefoot Smith smiled at a whimsical thought. He would not die without honour, if he was the detective who brought about the execution of the first broadcaster.

After his lecture he had gone to the Sheridan Theatre; thence to Dick Allenby's flat. After that, home, where he had found a letter—Surefoot Smith conceded him the truth of this—which sent him in search of Mary Lane.

What had he been doing on the morning of the murder? Possibly the accountant had called him up and told him that his leave was not granted. Mr. Accountant Smith had not said as much, but then, between bank employees there was a certain freemasonry, and one didn't expect, or was a fool if one did, that they would tell everything about their comrades, even if they were comrades suspected of forgery and murder.

Surefoot Smith allowed also the element of self-preservation to enter into the accountant's evidence. He himself might not be free from blame; the success of the forgery might be due in not a little measure to his own negligence. Everybody had something to hide—and possibly the accountant was no exception.

One thing was certain; the aëroplane had been ordered at a moment's notice. That was not the method by which Moran had intended to leave the country.

What was the stock to the transfer of which he had been so anxious to get Mary Lane's signature? Without a very long and careful search it was unlikely that that question would be answered.

Jerry Dornford's disappearance presented a problem of its own. His manservant in Half Moon Street said he was not worrying; Mr. Dornford often went away for days together, but where, the man could not say, because Mr. Dornford was not apparently of a confiding nature. If the servant guessed, he guessed uncharitably. Here was a man also without money, and almost without friends. He had one or two who had country houses, but inquiries of these had produced no result. The servant remembered the names and addresses of a lady or two, but these could throw no light upon the mystery.

Dornford owned an estate in Berkshire. Part of it was farm land, which produced enough income to pay the interest on the mortgage; and if the mortgages did not foreclose it was because a sale would bring only a portion of the money which had been advanced. There had been a house on the property, but this had been sold to a local golf club many years before, and all that remained of Gerald Dornford's possessions was about three hundred acres of pine and heather.

Here was a man who certainly could not afford two or three addresses.

The bullet had not been found, though the turf had been taken up, to the distress of the park authorities, and the ground sifted to the depth of a foot. There was a possibility that it might have passed at such an angle that it fell into the canal or against the opposite bank. It all depended from what angle the shot had been fired. If Surefoot Smith's first theory held ground and the old man had been killed by a bullet fired from a rifle on the upper floor of Parkview Crescent, the bullet should have been found within a few feet of where the chair had stood. If it had been fired from Dornford's car, it could hardly have passed through his body and reached the canal.

He was in constant touch with Binny, but the chair-man could give no further information. He had not heard the whizz of the bullet as it passed him, not even heard its impact, and offered here a perfectly reasonable excuse, that the noise of Dornford's car would, had it coincided with the shot, have deadened all other sound.

It was four o'clock on a Saturday afternoon, and Surefoot Smith, who had spent most of the night on his feet, found himself dozing in his chair, a practice which for some reason he regarded as evidence of approaching senility. He got up, washed his face in the bathroom wash basin, and went out into the

Haymarket, not very certain as to the direction he should take or in what direction he should continue his investigations.

He crossed Piccadilly Circus and was standing aimlessly watching a traffic block at the corner of Shaftesbury Avenue, when somebody bumped into him. His unconscious assailant was moving on with a muttered apology when Surefoot crooked his finger in his overcoat.

"What's the matter with you, Mike?"

There was reason for his surprise.

In twenty-four hours the appearance of Mike Hennessey had changed. The big face had grown flabby; heavy pouches were under his eyes; his unshaven face was a sickly yellow. Was it Surefoot's fancy, or did he turn a shade whiter at the sight of him?

"Hullo!" he stammered. "Well . . . now . . . isn't that curious, meeting you?"

"What's the matter, Mike?" asked Surefoot.

It was his habit to suspect criminal intentions in the most innocent of men, and his very question was accusative.

"Eh? Nothing. I'm sort of walking about in a dream to-day . . . that play coming off and everything."

"I've been phoning you all the morning. Where have you been?"

Mike started.

"Phoning me, Mr. Smith—Surefoot, old boy! I have been out of town. What did you want me for?"

"You weren't at your lodgings, you weren't at the theatre. Why were you keeping out of the way?"

Mike tried to speak, swallowed something, then, huskily:

"Let's go and have a drink somewhere. I've got a lot on my mind, Surefoot, a terrible lot."

There was a brasserie in a side street near the Circus, where beer could not be legally supplied until six o'clock. Nevertheless they made for this spot and the head waiter bustled up with a smile.

"Do you want to have a little private talk, Mr. Smith? You don't need to sit out here; the place is like a morgue. Come into the manager's office."

The manager's office was not a manager's office at all, except by courtesy. It was a very small private room.

"I'll bring you some tea, Mr. Smith. You'll have coffee, won't you, Mr. Hennessey?"

Hennessey, sitting with his eyes shut, nodded.

"What is on your mind?" asked Smith bluntly. "Washington Wirth?"

The closed eyes opened and stared at him.

"Eh? Yes." He blinked at his questioner. "I think . . . well, he won't be in the theatrical business any more, and naturally that's worrying me, because he's been a good friend of mine."

He seemed to find difficulty not only in speaking

but in breathing. His chest puffed up and down, and then:

"Is that what you wanted to see me about?" he asked jerkily.

"That was just what I wanted to see you about. He was a friend of yours?"

"A patron," said Mr. Hennessey quickly. "I looked after him when he was in town. I didn't know very much about him except that he had a lot of stuff—money I mean."

"And you didn't ask him where he got it, Mike?"

"Naturally," said Hennessey, avoiding his eyes.

The head waiter came at that moment with a tray which contained two large bottles of beer, a bottle of gin, cracked ice, and a siphon.

"Tea," he said formally, put it down and left them.

Surefoot Smith was in no sense depressed as he broke the law.

"Now come across, Micky," he said, not unkindly. "I want to hear just who is this fellow Wirth."

Micky licked his dry lips.

"I'd like to know where I am first," he said, doggedly. "Not that I could tell you anything, Surefoot—not anything for certain. What's my position? Suppose I thought he was somebody else, and said, 'Listen—you either help me, or I'm going to ask questions.' "

"Yes, suppose you blackmailed him?" interrupted Smith brutally.

Mike winced at this.

"It wasn't blackmail. I wasn't sure—do you get my meaning? I was putting up a bluff. I wanted to see how far he'd go." And then suddenly he broke down and covered his face with his big, diamond-ringed hands, and began to sob. "Oh, my God! It's awful!" he moaned.

Other men would have been embarrassed; Surefoot Smith was merely interested. He laid his hand on the other's arm.

"Are you in on the murder? That's the question."

Micky's hands dropped with a crash onto the marble-topped table. His ludicrous, tear-stained face was a picture of bewilderment.

"Murder? . . . What do you mean, murder?" He almost squeaked the question.

"The murder of Hervey Lyne. Didn't you know?"

The man did not answer; he was petrified with terror.

"Lyne . . . murdered!" He croaked the words.

It was amazing to believe that he was the one man in London who did not know that a mysterious murder had been committed in Regent's Park on the previous day, because the newspapers were full of it. Yet Surefoot felt that this was a fact.

"Murdered . . . old Lyne murdered!" Hennessey repeated. "My God! You don't mean that?"

"Of course I mean it. What do you think—that I'm trying to make you laugh?"

Mike Hennessey was silent; speech was frozen in him. He could only sit, regarding the detective with round eyes from which all expression had died. Mike had a weakness for weeping, but he also had an unsuspected strength of will. When he spoke at last his voice was completely under control.

"That's shocking. I didn't read the newspapers this morning."

"It was in last night's," said Surefoot.

The other shook his head.

"I haven't read a newspaper since Thursday morning," he said. "Old Lyne! He was Miss Lane's guardian, wasn't he?"

He was fighting for time—time to get the last weakness in him crushed, and to build himself the reserve that would prevent his collapse.

"No, I've read nothing about it. It's curious how you miss things in newspapers, isn't it? I've been so worried over this theatrical business that I've practically taken no interest in anything else in the world."

"What work did you do for Wirth?"

Surefoot's voice was cold. He had dropped his boy-friend manner, was even without interest in the unopened bottle of beer.

"Did you draw money from the bank on his behalf?"

Mike nodded.

"Yes, I've done that for him—big sums of money. Gone to his bank and met him afterwards by appointment."

"Where?" sharply.

"At various places—railway stations; the Kellner Hotel mostly. He generally drew a big sum when he had his parties, and I used to hand it over to him before the guests came. He said he was a merchant in the Midlands, but to tell you the truth, Surefoot, I've always had my doubts about that. Still, he didn't look a crook, and some of the queerest mugs are rolling in money. Why shouldn't he have been? He's not the first jay that put up money for a theatrical production, and not the last, please God!"

"What bank did you draw it from?"

Mike told him. It corresponded with the information which Surefoot already had.

"He generally gave me a letter to take to the bank manager, asking him to cash the check. I've been to Birmingham and Bristol and——"

"That's all right." Smith leaned heavily on the table. "Who was he—Washington Wirth?"

Mike shook his head.

"Honestly I don't know. If I die this minute I don't know. I got in touch with him after my last bankruptcy proceedings had appeared in the newspapers. He wrote to me and said how sorry he was that a clever man like me had got into trouble, and offered to finance me."

"A written note?"

"Typewritten. I've got the letter in my diggings somewhere. He asked me to meet him at the Kellner. That was before the parties started, when he had a smaller suite. I went. The only thing I knew about him was that he wore a wig and that he wasn't what he appeared to be; but I've never pried into his business."

"That's a lie," said Surefoot. "You just told me that you blackmailed him."

"I didn't really. I put a bluff up on him. I knew he wasn't what he pretended to be; I had to guess what he really was."

He was lying: of that Surefoot Smith was perfectly certain.

"Does it occur to you that you're in rather a tight place if this man is ever arrested? I have reason to believe that he has misappropriated money, the property of the late Hervey Lyne, and I have also reason to believe that he killed the old man—and that's murder. You don't want to be mixed up in murder, Mike, do you?"

Michael Hennessey's face was contorted with anguish. He was almost incoherent when he spoke.

"I'd help you if I could, Mr. Smith—but how can

I? I don't know the man—I swear I don't know the man!"

Smith peered into his face.

"Do you know anything about Moran?"

The big mouth dropped.

"The banker?" he stammered.

"Do you know anything about the faked balance sheet which was sent by accident to Miss Lyne?"

For a second Surefoot thought the man was going to faint.

"No—nothing; I know Moran—I know Wirth, too."

He stopped, was silent a little while.

"Suppose I found him—Wirth—what's my position then?"

Surefoot stood up.

"Your position is just the same whether you find him or whether we find him," he said roughly. "You don't seem to know what you've let yourself in for, Mike Hennessey. Here's a man been murdered—two men have been murdered—probably by the same hand. Tickler was killed for knowing too much. It might be safer for you if I put you inside."

A smile dawned on Mike's face.

"Am I a child?" he asked. He had got back his old poise. "How did I get out of the gutter—by taking notice of threats? Don't worry about me, Surefoot——"

"There's a lot more I've got to say to you," interrupted the detective, "but just wait here till I telephone."

A momentary look of alarm came to the man's face.

"Don't worry; I'm not going to pinch you. I shouldn't want any assistance to do that."

There was a telephone booth in the outer room, and he called Scotland Yard urgently.

"Chief Inspector Smith speaking. I want two of the best men on duty to pick me up at Bellini's. I'm with Mike Hennessey, the theatrical man. He's to be under observation day and night from now onwards, and no mistakes must be made. Do you hear?"

They heard and obeyed. A quarter of an hour later, when they strolled out through the narrow side street to Piccadilly Circus, two young men followed them, and when Mike called a cab and drove off, a second cab carried the watchers.

Mike Hennessey was not at the theatre when the curtain rang down finally on "Cliffs of Fate," and although the termination of this drama meant a search for new work, there was not one of the cast who did not breathe a sigh of relief when the muffled strains of the national anthem came through the thick curtains.

Dick was reading the evening newspaper when Mary came into the dressing room. The story of the Lyne murder was splashed over the front page; it included an interview with Binny and a talk with the park-keeper.

> "I knew Mr. Lyne very well by sight," said James Hawkins, who had been a park-keeper for twenty-three years. "He always came into the gardens in the afternoon, and generally had a little nap before he was taken home. I've spoken a word or two with him, but he was not a gentleman who encouraged conversation. Mostly his attendant, Mr. Binny, used to sit and read to him. I saw Mr. Binny reading that afternoon, and went up to him and said: 'What's the good of your wasting your breath? The guv'nor's asleep.' Little did I think that he was dead! This is the second murder that we've had in the park in thirty-five years. . . ."

Dick put down the paper when the girl came in, and prepared to make himself scarce.

"Sit down. I'm not going to change yet; I'm tired."

"Well, have you found your man?" he asked flippantly.

She did not smile.

"I think so," she said.

"Have you read the account?"

"I've read it—every ghastly line of it."

"Well," he challenged her, "is it Binny or the park-keeper?" and then, realizing that flippancy was in the circumstances a little callous, he apologized.

"I don't know how it is, but I can discuss this murder as though it were of somebody I'd never heard of. The poor old man loathed me, and I'm sure, if he could only have made up his mind as to who else would have taken better care of his fortune than I, he would have left the money to him like a shot! By the way, Binny has a theory of his own. I had a talk with him to-day. He favours Jerry Dornford—mainly, I think, because he doesn't like Jerry."

"Has Mr. Smith told you all the clues he has?" she asked.

She had evidently paid no attention to Binny's theory.

"No, I can't say that he has. He's rather stuffy when it comes to his own business."

"Do you think he would tell me?"

He looked at her in amazement.

"My dear Mary——" he began.

"Don't 'dear Mary' me, or I shall be very rude to you," she said. "Do you think he would?"

She was quite serious and he changed his tone.

"If he thought you could help him I'm sure he would," he said. "He has promised to call here to-night and tell me the latest developments. Would you like me to ask him?"

"I'll ask him myself," she said.

Surefoot arrived very late and very ruffled. He was entitled to his annoyance, for at half-past seven that night a penitent young detective had called him on the phone and had confessed failure.

"You missed him?" roared Smith. "Two of you? What's the matter with you?"

"I'm sorry, sir, but he must have known he was being tailed, and he dodged through the Piccadilly Tube. I'd just turned my head and he was gone——"

"Turned your what?" sneered Surefoot. "All right, scour London and pick him up. You know his address. He's got to be found."

He came to the Sheridan, full of bitterness about the new generation of detectives.

"They expect everything to be done for them. They rely on science instead of their eyesight," he fumed.

"Here's a detective for you."

Dick indicated the girl, and to his surprise Surefoot showed no sign of impatience.

"I should say she's got more sense in her little finger than those—gentlemen have in their big, useless bodies."

He looked at her thoughtfully.

"I'm going to ask you something, Mr. Smith," she said. "Would you tell me all you know about this case? I think I may help you."

Again Dick Allenby was amazed that the big man made no jest of the offer. He looked at her owlishly, opened his big mouth, closed it again, rubbed his head (going through his repertory, noted Dick mentally).

"Why shouldn't you?" he said at last. "Do you want him to know?" He jerked his head towards Dick.

She hesitated.

"If you don't mind. If you do we'll turn him out."

She was dressed for the street by the time the detective had arrived, and suggested that they should go to her flat. They went up in the lift together. Her flat was the last in the corridor. She went ahead of them, and stood stock still, showing an alarmed face to the two men.

The door was wide open!

"Did your servant leave it open?" asked Smith.

Surefoot pointed to the lock; the marks of a powerful jemmy showed where the door had been forced. The lock itself was hanging on one screw.

He went ahead, switched on the lights, without result.

"It's been turned off at the fuse box. Where is it?"

She indicated the position, and after a little fumbling there was a click, and light showed along the short passage.

"He fastened the door after he got in, but couldn't fasten it when he left."

Smith picked up two small wooden wedges from the floor

He went out again into the corridor, the end of which was formed by a half-wood, half-glass door leading to the fire escape. He tried this, and, as he expected, found it open. A flight of iron stairs led into the darkness below. He sent for the lift-man, who could give no information at all. On a Saturday night most of the people who lived in the flats, he said, were in the country, where they spent their week-ends, and there had been no strange visitors that he could remember.

Surefoot went ahead down the passage into the flat, saw a door wide open, and entered Mary's bedroom. It was a scene of indescribable confusion; every drawer of every bureau had been taken out and emptied on the bed and roughly sorted. They found the same in the dining room, where the little secretaire desk, which she had locked before she went out, had been broken and its contents piled onto the table.

Mary gazed with dismay upon the scene of destruction, but was agreeably surprised when she found that a small box which had been in her desk drawer, and which had been wrenched open, still contained the articles of jewellery she had left there. They were valued at something over two hundred pounds, she told the detective.

"Then what on earth did they come for?" she asked.

On further inspection Smith found that even the

waste bin in the kitchen had been turned bottom upward and sorted over. One valuable clue he discovered: a small kitchen clock had evidently been knocked off the dresser and had stopped at eleven-fifteen.

"Less than an hour ago—phew!" Surefoot whistled softly. "In a devil of a hurry, too. Now tell me who knows this place—I mean, who has been here before? Forget all your girl friends but tell me the men."

She could enumerate them very briefly.

"Mike Hennessey has been here, has he? Often? I've seen all the rooms, haven't I?"

"Except the bathroom," she said.

He opened the door of this well-appointed little apartment, switched on the light and went in. The intruder had been here too; the wash basin was half-filled with discoloured water.

"Hullo! what's that?"

Smith's eyes narrowed.

Level with the wash basin, and a little to the right of it, the enamelled walls of the bathroom bore a red smear. The detective touched it; it was still moist. He looked at the tessellated floor. There was nothing, but on the edge of the white bath the smear occurred again.

Behind the door was a clothes hook, and here also there was a trace of red.

"He came in here first," said Surefoot slowly.

"He had to wash his hands, and, turning on the tap, his sleeve brushed the wall. There was blood on it; he didn't notice this. He took his coat off and threw it on the edge of the bath. Then he changed his mind and hung it up."

"Blood?"

Mary stared at the gruesome stain.

"Do you think he hurt himself getting in?"

"No, we should have seen it on the floor or in the passage. Besides, the glass door of the corridor wasn't broken—I wonder where he got it?"

Surefoot considered all the possibilities in the shortest space of time.

"It beats me," he said.

Surefoot Smith went into the kitchen to re-examine the clock. He was no believer in coincidences, had seen the stopped clock too often featured in works of fiction to believe implicitly the story it told. But his inspection removed all doubt; the clock had not stopped, but was still ticking; the jolt had merely thrown the pin connecting the hands from its gear, and no clever clue-maker could have done that.

Mary had followed him into the kitchen, and watched him silently whilst he was making the examination.

"Now will you tell me?" she said quietly.

Surefoot Smith gaped at her.

"About——?"

"You said you would tell me what you have discovered about Mr. Lyne's murder."

He perched himself on the edge of the kitchen table, and briefly told her all he knew.

To say that Dick Allenby was surprised was to put it mildly. He regarded every Scotland Yard detective as reticence personified. Surefoot Smith was notoriously "dumb," and here he was talking freely to the girl, and, if he showed any embarrassment at all, it was the presence of Dick himself which provoked the inhibition.

Mary Lane sat, her hands clasped in her lap, her brow knitted.

"Got anything?" asked Surefoot anxiously.

And then he must have caught a glimpse of the astonishment in Dick Allenby's face, for he scowled at him.

"You think I'm being foolish, Mr. Allenby? Get the idea out of your mind; I never am. Every woman has just the kind of mind that every detective should have and hasn't. No science in it—not that I mean to be disrespectful, Miss Lane—just plain common sense. Got it?"

He addressed the girl again. She shook her head.

"Not quite," she said. "I know why they burgled my flat, of course."

Surefoot Smith nodded.

"But you can't quite understand how they came to think it was here?"

Dick interrupted.

"May I be very dense," he asked politely, "and inquire what this is all about? Didn't know *what* was here?"

"The bank statement," said Mary, without looking up, and again Smith nodded, a broad grin on his face.

"I guess that is what they came for, but I can't understand how they knew."

Surefoot chuckled.

"I am the clever fellow that gave it away," he said. "I told Mike Hennessey this afternoon that a bank statement had been sent to you. I didn't tell him that it was in my pocket, and I could have saved him a lot of time and trouble. It's a great pity."

He ran his hand irritably through his hair and slid off the table.

"Those bloodstains now—they look bad," he said, and loafed out of the room, with the other two behind him, into the bathroom. "That's his sleeve—that's his hand, but too blurred to get a print. The man who came here wasn't hurt, and probably wasn't aware that he was blood-stained. Look at the top of that tap."

He pointed; there was a distinct smear of blood on the white-enamelled word "Hot" on one of the taps.

Surefoot Smith took out his pocket torch and

began to examine the passageway. It gave him nothing in the shape of clues; but when he went outside the fireproof door, and inspected the door itself, he found two new traces of blood, one on the iron railings and one just below the glass panel of the door.

"I'll use your phone," he said, and a few minutes later was talking volubly to Scotland Yard.

Every railway station was to be watched; Dover, Harwich, Folkestone, and Southampton were to be warned.

"Not that he'll attempt to get out of the country. It's curious how seldom they do," he explained to the girl.

His offer to send up a man to be on guard outside the door she refused immediately, but he insisted, and in such a tone that she knew it would be a waste of time on her part to press her objection.

On his way home he called at old Lyne's house to interview Binny. That worthy man was in bed when he knocked, and showed considerable and quite understandable reluctance to open the door. No police had been left on the premises; Surefoot had been content to remove all documents to Scotland Yard for a closer scrutiny, and had sealed up the bedroom and the study.

Binny led him down to the kitchen, poked together the dying remnants of the small fire, and dropped wood on it, for the night was a little chilly.

"I wondered who it was knocking—it brought me heart up into me mouth," he apologized, as he ushered the visitor into the tiny room. "I suppose, Mr. Smith"—his voice was very anxious—"the old gentleman didn't leave me anything? I heard you'd found the will—mind you, I'm not going to be disappointed if he didn't. He wasn't the kind of man who worried very much about servants; he used to say he hated having them about the place. Still, you never know——"

"I haven't read the will thoroughly," said Surefoot, "but I don't seem to remember finding your name very prominently displayed."

Binny sighed.

"It's been the dream of my life that somebody would die and leave me a million," he said pathetically. "I was a good servant to him—cooked his food, made his bed, did everything for him."

The detective pushed over a package of cheap cigarettes, and, still sighing, Binny selected one and lit it.

"There's one way you can help me, I think," said Smith. "Do you remember Mr. Moran coming here?"

Binny nodded.

"Do you know what he came about?"

The servant hesitated a moment.

"I don't know, sir. But I have an idea it had something to do with his balance. Mr. Lyne was a very curious old gentleman; he never wanted to see anybody, and when he did he was always a bit unpleasant to 'em."

"Was he unpleasant to Mr. Moran?"

Binny hesitated.

"Well, I don't want to tell tales out of school, Mr. Smith, but from what I heard he did snap a bit at him."

"You listened, eh?"

Binny smiled and shook his head.

"You didn't have to listen, sir." He pointed to the ceiling. "The study's above here. You can't hear what people are saying, but if a gentleman raises his voice as Mr. Lyne did, you can hear him."

"You know Moran?"

Binny nodded.

"Do you know him very well?"

"Very well, sir. I was servant——"

"I remember, yes."

Surefoot Smith bit his lower lip thoughtfully.

"Did he speak to you after his interview with the old man?"

Again Binny hesitated.

"I don't want to get anybody into trouble——"

"The trouble with you, Binny, is that you can't say yes or no. Did you see him?"

"Yes, sir, I did." Binny was evidently nettled.

"I was taking in a letter that had come by post as he went out. And now, Mr. Smith, I'll tell you the truth. He said a queer thing to me—he asked me not to mention the fact that he'd been, and slipped me a quid. Now I've told you all I know. I thought it was funny—but, bless your heart, he wasn't the first man to ask me not to mention the fact that they'd called on Mr. Lyne."

"I suppose not."

On a little table near the wall was a small paper parcel, loosely wrapped. Surefoot Smith was blessed with a keen sense of smell; he could disentangle the most conflicting and elusive odours. But the odour of putty was not one of the difficult ones; to Surefoot Smith, putty had a pungent and unpleasant aroma. He pointed to the parcel.

"Putty?"

Binny looked at him in surprise.

"Yes, sir."

"Have you been mending windows?" Surefoot looked up.

"No, sir, that was done by a glazier. I broke the scullery window this morning. I didn't like to call anybody in, so I did it myself."

"The trouble in this house is that you're always having windows broken," said Surefoot Smith. "Why didn't you report to the police the attempt to break into this house—oh, I remember, Mr. Lyne didn't want it."

When he went outside he made a more careful examination of the premises in the darkness than he had ever done by daylight. He went to the trouble of going to the back of the house, along the narrow mews, and here he saw how easy it was for a burglar to have obtained admission. The back of the house was not protected, as most of its fellows were, by a garage block, and the door and window were approachable for anybody who could either scale the wall or force the door into the back courtyard. Was it a coincidence that this attempt had been made to gain admission into Lyne's house on the night of . . . ?

Surefoot Smith frowned. It must have been the night that Tickler was murdered. Was there any connection between the two events?

He went back to Scotland Yard to receive reports, and found that his inquiries had produced no result. Berlin could tell him no more about Leo Moran, and there was absolutely no news at all of Gerald Dornford.

He opened the safe in a corner of his little room, took out the glove and the silver key, and laid them on the table. That key puzzled him. Was there any special reason why its owner should have gone to the trouble of painting it so elaborately and yet so carelessly? Any plater would have made a better job of it.

The glove told him nothing. He took from the

big drawer of his desk a large sheet of virgin blotting paper and began to work out again the sum of his problem.

Tickler had been killed; old Lyne had been killed, possibly by the same hand, though there was nothing to connect the two murders. Leo Moran was, to all intents and purposes, a fugitive from justice, a man against whom could be made out a prima-facie charge of felony. His disappearance had coincided, not only with the death of Lyne, but with the discovery that Lyne's bank account had been heavily milked.

Was he in Berlin at all? Somebody was very much interested in the recovery of the bank statement, had gone to the trouble of burgling Mary Lane's flat to recover it—who? One man at any rate knew, or thought he knew, that the statement was at Mary's flat, and that man was Michael Hennessey.

Mike's conduct that afternoon had been consistent with guilty knowledge. He knew at any rate who was Washington Wirth. The gentleman called Washington Wirth was a murderer, possibly a murderer twice over.

In disjointed sentences Surefoot wrote down his conclusions as they were reached; crossed out one and substituted another; elaborated some simple proposition in his mysterious shorthand, only to cross through the wriggly lines and begin all over again. He made a little circle that represented Mary, another for Dick Allenby, another for Gerald Dornford, a fourth for Leo Moran. At the bottom of the page he put a fifth circle for Lyne. How were they connected? What was the association between the four top circles and the fifth?

Between them he placed a larger O that stood for Michael Hennessey. Michael touched Washington Wirth, he touched Mary Lane, and possibly Moran. He crossed out this last conclusion and started again.

Gerald Dornford touched Dick Allenby; Smith could draw a straight line from Dick Allenby to the murdered man—a line that missed all and any intermediary.

He got tired after a while, threw down the pencil, and sat back with a groan. He was reaching for the key when the light went out. There was nothing very startling and nothing very unexpected about that: the bulb had been burning yellow for two or three days, and obviously required replacement. Surefoot Smith, in his lordly way, had demanded a fresh globe, and the storekeeper, in his more lordly way, had ignored the request. Without warning, the bulb had ceased to function.

Surefoot was rising to his feet to reach for the bell when something he saw stopped him dead. In the darkness the key was glowing like green fire.

He saw the handle and every ward of it. And now he understood why it had such an odd colour—it had been treated with luminous paint.

He picked it up and turned it over. The under side was dull and hardly showed, for it had not absorbed the rays of the lamp.

Surefoot went out into the corridor and summoned an officer, and a little later a new bulb was discovered and substituted for the old one. He examined the key now with greater interest, jotting down notes upon his already overcrowded blotting sheet.

He was beginning to see daylight, but only dimly. Then the telephone bell buzzed; he answered the call and then, going to the officer on duty at the door, said to him:

"Mr. Allenby is downstairs. When he comes up, show him in."

He looked at his watch; it was twenty minutes past twelve, and he could only wonder what had brought Dick to Scotland Yard at such an hour. Possibly his gun had been recovered.

"I wondered if you were here," said Dick, as he came into the office and closed the door behind him. "I should have telephoned, but I was scared they wouldn't put me through to you."

"What's the trouble?" asked Surefoot curiously.

Dick smiled.

"There isn't any real trouble; only I've been—or rather, Mary has been—called up by Hennessey's housekeeper for information about the gentleman."

"Hasn't he come home?" asked Smith quickly.

"He wasn't expected home," said Dick. "The lady called up from Waterloo Station; she's been there since nine, with a couple of Mike's trunks. He was leaving for the Continent by the Havre train, and had arranged for her to be there to meet him with his baggage. She waited till nearly twelve, got worried, and apparently called up several people who knew Michael, amongst them Mary. Fortunately, I was just leaving the flat when the woman telephoned."

"Have you been to his house?"

Dick shook his head.

"It wasn't necessary," he said. "He had a furnished flat in Doughty Street; he paid his rent and closed up the place to-night. Obviously he was making a get-away in rather a hurry. He didn't start packing till this afternoon."

"After he'd seen me," said Surefoot. He scratched his chin. "That's queer. I can quite understand his wanting to get away—as a matter of fact, he wouldn't have got any farther than Southampton; I had already notified the ports."

"You would have arrested him?" asked Dick, in amazement.

"There's no question of arrest, my friend," said

Surefoot wearily. "It isn't necessary to arrest everybody you want to stop going out of England. Their passports can be out of order, the visa can be on the wrong page, the stamp can be upside down—there are a dozen ways of keeping the money in the country."

"Did Hennessey know this?"

Surefoot did not answer immediately.

"I can't understand it," he said slowly. "Of course he didn't know. That wouldn't have prevented him from catching the train."

There was a knock at the door, and a pleasant-looking man, whom Dick recognized as a chief inspector, came in.

"The Buckinghamshire police have got a case after your own heart, Surefoot," he said. "A regular American gang murder."

Surefoot became instantly alert.

"A gang murder, eh? What kind?"

"They call 'em ride murders, don't they? Somebody has taken this poor devil for a ride, shot him at close quarters, and thrown him out onto the sidewalk."

"Where was this?"

"On the Colnbrook by-pass, this side of Slough. A big car passed, picked up the man lying across the footpath with its lights, and reported to the police. He couldn't have been dead more than half an hour when the police got to him."

"What is his description?" asked Surefoot.

"A big-made man of forty-five," said the other, "wearing a green tie——"

"That was the colour of the tie Mike Hennessey was wearing this afternoon!"

CHAPTER XVII

MIKE HENNESSEY looked very calm, almost majestic in death; most easily recognizable. Surefoot Smith came out of the sinister little building and waited while the police sergeant turned the key.

Dick was waiting at the station. He had had enough of horrors for one night, and had not attempted to join himself in the identification.

"It's Mike all right," said Surefoot. "The murder was committed at ten-seventeen—or thereabouts. The time is fixed by the big car that found the body, and a motorcyclist who lives in this village reported to the police that he saw a small saloon car standing by the side of the road near where the body was found. I make out the two times as being between ten-fifteen and ten-twenty, and, allowing for the fact that the big machine did not overtake any car on the Colnbrook by-pass, that puts the time at ten-seventeen. The murderer's car might have turned round and gone back. It could, of course, have gone right through the village of Colnbrook, avoiding the by-pass, and I should imagine that is what happened. And now, my friend," he said seriously, "you realize that this was the gentleman who called at your young lady's flat? His coat must have been covered with blood without his realizing the fact until, in searching the bathroom, he touched the wall with his sleeve. He took off his coat, washed his hands, and that's that."

"But surely some garage keeper will be able to identify the car if there was so much blood lost? The interior must be like a shambles."

Surefoot nodded.

"Oh, yes, we'll find the car all right. There were three stolen last night that answer the description. I've just been through to the Yard and found that a machine has been discovered abandoned in Sussex Gardens."

A swift police car took them back to Paddington, and Surefoot Smith's surmise was confirmed. The abandoned car was that which the murderer had used. There was grisly evidence enough that the man had met his death in its dark interior—of other evidence there was none.

"We'll test the wheel for fingerprints, but Mr. Wirth will wear gloves."

"That lets out Moran, doesn't it?" said Dick.

Surefoot smiled.

"Where is Moran? In Germany, we say—he's as likely to be in London. You may get to Germany in a few hours and get back in a shorter time. It may not have been Moran that left at all."

"But why?"

Dick Allenby was bewildered, more than a little alarmed for Mary Lane's safety, and said as much. To his consternation, Surefoot agreed.

"I don't think she should stay in that flat. She may have other evidence, and now she's begun to theorize she might be dangerous to our friend."

He accompanied Smith to the police station whither the car had been taken, and found the usual scene of impersonal activity. There were photographers, fingerprint experts, car mechanics examining the speedometer. The owner of the car, who had been found and brought to the station, was a methodical man: he knew exactly the amount of mileage that was on the dial before the car was stolen, and his information helped considerably.

It seemed to Dick Allenby that he had spent the past fortnight examining blood-stained cars in police yards. There was a touch of the familiar in the scene he witnessed: the staring electric globes at the ends of lengths of flex, the peering police detectives searching every inch of the interior.

There was blood on the seat and on the floor; a trace of it on the gear lever. One of the detectives pulled a cushion from the driver's seat.

"Hullo!" he said, and, looking over his shoulder, Dick saw a flat silver cigarette case that was passed to Surefoot's hand.

Smith opened the case. It was empty. There was

an inscription on the inside, easy enough to read in the light of the bulb.

> To Mr. Leo Moran, from his colleagues in the Willesden branch, May 1920.

Surefoot turned it over and over in his hand. It was an old case; there were one or two dents in it, but it was polished bright, and either was frequently used or had been recently cleaned. Surefoot held it gingerly by the help of a sheet of paper, and had it carefully wrapped.

"We might get a fingerprint on that, but I don't think it's likely," he said. "It's a little odd, isn't it—being under the cushion?"

"He might have put it there and forgotten all about it."

Surefoot shook his head.

"It's not his car, it was pinched. As I say, it's odd."

He did not speak again for some time.

"I mentioned the fact that the young lady is supposed to have the bank statement. Mr. Hennessey passed the information on in the course of the ride, or before. The killer settled with Hennessey—by the way, he was supposed to be driving to Southampton to catch his boat. The car stopped at a filling station at the end of the Great West Road; Hennessey got out and telephoned to his flat—presumably to his housekeeper to send on his baggage. The murderer got rid of Hennessey as quickly as he could, rushed back to town, and burgled Miss Lane's flat. Obviously he was somebody who had been there before."

"Like Moran?" suggested Dick.

Surefoot hesitated.

"He'll do as well as anybody else," he said. "He was looking for the bank statement. He couldn't have known that his coat was covered with blood, until he went into the bathroom, and either saw himself in the mirror or a stain on the wall. I'll tell you something more about him: he's lived in America. How's that for scientific deduction?"

"How on earth do you know that?"

"I don't," said the other calmly; "it's deduction —in other words, guesswork. It's a typical gang killing, though—taking a man for a ride and throwing him out of the car after he's been shot. Nobody seems to have heard the pistol go off, but if they did they'd think it was a motorcyclist. They scorch down the by-pass."

He drove home with Dick, and was very voluble.

"Hennessey was in the swindle from the start. He knew who Wirth was, knew that Wirth was forging checks, and took advantage of his knowledge to blackmail the other man." Then, abruptly: "I'm going to show Miss Lane the key and the check."

It was the first time Dick had heard about the key.

By the time Surefoot Smith reached Scotland Yard, all the grisly relics of the murdered man had been collected and laid on his table. There was a notebook, a few odd scraps of paper, about twenty pounds in cash, a watch and chain and a key ring, but nothing that was particularly illuminating—except the absence of any large sum of money. Obviously, Hennessey did not intend to make his jump for the Continent on a capital of twenty pounds. Surefoot guessed that the murderer, profiting by the previous discovery of money in Tickler's pocket, had relieved him of what might have been very incriminating evidence.

He looked over the papers. One was a page torn from a Bradshaw, with pencil markings against certain trains. Surefoot guessed that Hennessey's plan was to make his way to Vienna.

The second paper was the more interesting. It was a sheet torn from a notebook, and contained a number of figures. Surefoot had a remarkable memory, and he recognized at once that the figures represented those balances which had appeared in the statement. Evidently the paper had been handled many times.

Smith was puzzled. Why had Hennessey taken the trouble to jot these notes down in pencil and keep them? Obviously he knew of the bank statement, had possibly concocted it; but here he would have some other data than this scrap of paper. If the bank statement was an invention, as undoubtedly it was, there was no need to keep this note. Either the man would invent the figures on the spur of the moment, or else he had some book record of the defalcations and the amount that should have stood to old Lyne's account.

Early the next morning he telephoned to Mary Lane, who had spent an uneasy night. She was not even stimulated by the knowledge that there was a police officer in the corridor outside her flat, one at the foot of the fire escape, and another patrolling before the house.

"Come round by all means," she said, and was relieved to know that she was seeing him, for she wanted advice very badly.

The morning had brought no news to Surefoot. The inquiries he had made had drawn blank. A search of Mike Hennessey's flat gave him no clue that was of the least value. Of papers or documents there were none; an old bank book told him no more than that three years before, Hennessey had been living from hand to mouth.

He was rather despondent when he came into Mary's flat.

"It almost looks as if science has got to be brought in," he said gloomily, as he produced a small packet from his pocket and laid it on the table. "Maybe you're it!"

He opened the wash-leather wrapper and disclosed the key. Then from his pocketbook he took out a check and laid it on the table. She examined the faint pencil marks carefully and nodded.

"That is Mr. Lyne's handwriting," she said. "I think I told you that when I was a girl I lived in the same house; in fact, I kept house for him in a very inefficient way. He was rather trying to live with."

"In what way?" asked Surefoot.

She hesitated.

"Well, in many ways—domestically, I mean. For example, he had the same tradespeople for over forty years, and never changed them, although he was always quarrelling with them or disputing the amount he owed them."

She looked at the key, turning it over and over in her hand.

"Would you think I was terribly vain if I told you I thought I could find the man who killed Mr. Lyne?"

"I think you would be very silly if you tried to do it on your own," said Smith bluntly. "This fellow isn't one you can monkey about with."

She nodded.

"I realize that. Will you give me a week to make inquiries?"

"Don't you think you'd better tell me now what your suspicions are?"

She shook her head.

"No; I am probably making a fool of myself, and I have a very natural desire to avoid that."

Smith pursed his thick lips.

"You can't keep these——" he began.

"I don't want them," she said quickly. "You mean the check and the key? Would it be asking you too much to give me a replica of the key? If I find the lock it fits I'll telephone you."

He looked at her in surprise.

"Do you think you can find the lock?"

She nodded. Surefoot Smith sighed.

"This is like doing things in books," he said, "and I hate the way they do things in books. It's romantic, and romantic things make me sick. But I'll do this for you, young lady."

Two days later she received a brand-new shining key, and set forth on her investigations, never suspecting that, day and night, she was shadowed by one of three detectives, whose instructions from Surefoot Smith had been short and not especially encouraging.

"Keep this lady in your sight. If you let her out of your sight, your chance of ever being promoted is practically nil."

It was the third day after the murder of Mike Hennessey that Cassari Oils moved. They had hovered between £1.3s. and £1.7s. for five years. They represented £40 shares, for in pre-war days they had been issued at 1,000 francs. The field was situated in Asia Minor, and had produced enough oil to prevent the company from collapsing, but insufficient to bring the shares back to their normal value.

Mary read the flaming headline on the City page: "Sensational Rise of Cassari Oils," and called up Mr. Smith.

"Those were the shares that you transferred to Moran, weren't they?" he asked, interested. "What did they stand at last night? I haven't seen the paper."

The stock had jumped from 25s. to 95s. overnight. When Surefoot Smith put a call through to the City he was staggered to learn that they stood at £30 and were rising every minute.

He drove up to an office in Old Broad Street which supplied him with particulars of financial phenomena, and discovered the reason from an unconcerned stock jobber.

"They struck big oil about three months ago, and they've been sinking new wells. Apparently they found inexhaustible supplies, but managed to keep it quiet until they'd cleared the market of every floating share. The stock is certain to go to a hundred, and I can advise you to have a little flutter. There's no doubt about the oil being there."

Surefoot Smith had never had a flutter in his life, except that he invariably had half-a-crown on some horse in the Derby which he picked with the aid of a pin and a list of probable runners.

"Who is behind this move?" he asked.

The jobber shook his head.

"If I tried to pronounce their names I'd dislocate my jaw," he said. "They are mostly Turks—Effendi this and Pasha that. You'll find them in the Stock Exchange Year-book. They're a pretty solid crowd; millionaires, most of them. Oh, no, there's nothing shady about them; they're as solid as the Bank of England, and this isn't a market rig. They haven't a London office; Jolman & Joyce are their agents."

To the office of Messrs. Jolman & Joyce, Surefoot Smith went. He found the place besieged. He sent in his card and was admitted to the office of Mr. Joyce, the senior partner.

"I can't tell you very much, Mr. Smith, except what the newspapers can tell you. There are not a large number of shares on the market—I've just told a friend of mine who thought of running a bear that he's certain to burn his fingers. The only big holder I know is a man named Moran—Leo Moran."

CHAPTER XVIII

LEO MORAN! It was no news to Surefoot Smith that this man was interested in the stock, apart from the shares he had acquired from Mary. There was a little touch of trickiness about Moran; that was his reputation both in the bank and amongst his friends. From what Surefoot had gathered, and from his own knowledge of the man, he was capable of quixotic and generous actions, but, generally speaking, carried shrewdness a little beyond the line of fairness. Murderer he might be; forger, as Surefoot believed, he certainly was. The constant of his character was an immense self-interest. He was a bachelor, had no family attachments and few interests besides his shooting and the theatre.

This was a supreme gamble, then—Cassari Oils. Before Surefoot Smith left the stockbroker's office he discovered that Moran was, at any rate on paper, a millionaire. On one point he was puzzled: though Moran had bought steadily, and his operations had covered the years of defalcations, he had spent no very large sum, certainly only a small percentage of the moneys he was making. The man probably had other speculative interests, but these for the moment were impossible to trace.

Mr. Smith went home to his rooms off the Haymarket, and was surprised to find a visitor waiting for him on the landing.

"I haven't been here two minutes," said Mary. "I got on to your secretary at Scotland Yard and he told me that you might be at your flat."

He unlocked the door and ushered her into his untidy sitting room.

"Well, have you found anything?"

She shook her head and smiled ruefully.

"Only my limitations, I am afraid," she said, and sat down in the chair he pulled forward for her.

"You're giving it up, eh?"

She hesitated.

"No."

It required an effort of will to say "No," for she had awakened that morning with an intense sense of mental discomfort and a realization of the difficulties which beset her. She had been half-inclined to send a penitent note enclosing the key to Surefoot, but confidence—not much, but some—had come to her with breakfast, and she had decided upon this, what was to her, a bold move.

"I realize what I have undertaken," she confessed. "Being a detective is not an easy job, is it? Especially when you don't know things."

Surefoot smiled.

"The art of being a detective is to know nothing," he said oracularly. "What do you know? If you know anything less than I do, you haven't heard of the murder. On the other hand, it is possible you may know a great deal more."

"You are being sarcastic."

He shook his head.

"I don't know the word, Miss Lane. What is it you want to know?"

She consulted a little notebook she took from her pocket.

"Can you give me a list of all the big checks that were cashed and the dates? I particularly want to know the dates. If my theory is correct, they are made out on the seventeenth of the month."

Surefoot sat back in his chair and stared at her.

"That is a bit scientific," he said, a little resentfully, and she laughed.

"No, it is horribly like a mystery story. But, seriously, I do want to know."

He pulled the telephone towards him and called a number.

"Funnily enough, that is a bit of information I had never thought of getting," he said.

She felt he was a little nettled that he had been remiss in this respect, and she was secretly amused.

"But then, you see, Miss Lane," he went on, "if I had been at the Yard I would probably get it for you—hullo!"

He had got through to the bank. It took some time before the accountant, with whom he eventually got in touch, was able to supply him with the dates.

The checks were made out on the 17th of April, the 17th of February, the 17th of December, the 17th of May in the previous year—Surefoot jotted down a dozen of them. Hanging up the receiver, he pushed the paper across to the girl.

"I thought so!" Her eyes were very bright. "Every one of them on the seventeenth!"

"Marvellous!" said Surefoot. "Now will you tell me what that means?"

She nodded.

"I will tell you in a week's time. I am going to do a lot of private investigation. There is one thing I wanted to speak about, Mr. Smith." Her voice was troubled. "I don't know whether I am imagining things, but I have an idea that I am being very carefully watched. I am sure a man was following me yesterday. I lost sight of him in Oxford Street; I was looking in a shop window in Regent Street and saw him again. Rather an unpleasant-looking man with a fair moustache."

Surefoot Smith smiled.

"That is Detective Sergeant Mason. I don't think he is much of a good looker myself."

"A detective?" she gasped.

Surefoot nodded.

"Naturally, my dear young lady, I am taking great care of you. You might as well know that you are being shadowed, not because you are under suspicion, but because for the moment you are under our protection."

She heaved a sigh.

"You don't know how relieved I am. It was rather getting on my nerves. As a matter of fact, I don't think I should have come to see you at all but for this."

"What about the seventeenth?" asked Surefoot. "Don't you think it would be wise for you to tell me what your suspicions are about?"

She shook her head.

"I am being mysterious and rather weak," she said.

Her mystery certainly irritated Dick Allenby, who could never be sure of finding her at home. He had a talk with Surefoot and sought his help.

"She will be running into all sorts of danger," Dick complained. "This man obviously will stop at nothing. He may still think that she has got the bank statement."

"Have you seen the young lady at all?"

Surefoot opened another bottle of beer dexterously. He was sitting on a bench in Dick's workroom.

"Yes, I have seen her. She wants me to lend her Binny."

"Lend her Binny?" repeated the detective. "What does that mean?"

"Well, he is in my employ now. She says she wants inquiries made about a former servant of Mr. Lyne's who is living in Newcastle under an assumed name. She wants Binny to go and identify the woman. I saw Binny about it and he remembers her. She left soon after you arrived. She was a fairly old woman. Apparently she had a dissolute son who was a pretty bad character. Binny doesn't remember him, but Mary does. The old lady, who must be nearly ninety, is living in the north, and Mary wants him to go up to make sure that she hasn't made a mistake."

Surefoot Smith looked at him glumly.

"She told me nothing about it. Binny's your servant now? I suppose you own the house. What are you going to do with it?"

"Sell it," said Dick promptly. "In fact, I've already had an offer."

There was a knock at the door; the caretaker came in with a telegram for Dick. Surefoot saw him open it, watched him idly, and saw his jaw drop as he read it. Without a word he passed the wire across to Smith. It had been handed in at Sunningdale, and ran:

> Re patent air gun reported stolen from you. Machine answering description circulated has been found at Toyne Copse lying at the bottom of a hole beneath body of a man believed to be G. Dornford of Half Moon Street. Please report immediately Sunningdale police station to identify property.

CHAPTER XIX

HE AND Surefoot went down into Berkshire together. He had no difficulty in recognizing the rusted steel case which had once been a delicate piece of mechanism. He left it to Surefoot Smith to make other and more grisly identification.

Surefoot returned after visiting the place where the body had been found, and he had further and convincing information. Jerry Dornford's car had also been discovered less than a hundred yards from the place where he had died. The car had evidently been driven over the heath land and concealed in a small copse.

"It's Dornford's own property, and I don't think there will be much difficulty in reconstructing the accident which put him out," said Surefoot. "He had an evening newspaper in the car with him; it is dated the day of old man Lyne's murder."

"Poor devil! How was he killed—or was it a natural death?" asked Dick.

Surefoot shook his head.

"An accident. The gun was loaded, wasn't it? Well, you'll be able to take the thing to pieces and tell me if it is still loaded. I should say it wasn't.

Dornford stole the gun: there's no doubt about that. He either got scared or couldn't sell it, and decided to take it into the country and bury it. Very naturally, he chose a bit of land which is his own property. He took a spade with him—we found that. When they found him he was in his shirt sleeves. He had evidently dug the hole and was in the act of pushing in the gun when it went off. The bullet went through his body; we found it in a pine tree that was immediately in the line of fire. In his pocket we found a demand for the payment of a loan, from Stelbey's, who did most of old Lyne's work. We also found a few notes that are going to make it pretty uncomfortable for somebody called Jules, when we can trace him."

"I can help you there," said Dick, who knew and rather disliked that sleek young man.

They came back to town late in the evening, and Surefoot was rather depressed.

"I always thought that Dornford had something to do with the murder, and put him down as a 'possible.' But it's pretty clear that he couldn't have done it, unless there were two bullets in the gun, or unless he understood the mechanism."

Dick went in search of Mary that night to tell her the news. He had never liked Gerald Dornford, but there were moments when he thought that his dislike was not so actively shared by the girl; but here he did her an injustice. A woman's instincts are keener than a man's, and she had placed Jerry in the definite category of men to be avoided.

She did not get back to her flat till late that night, as he discovered after repeated rings, and it was an unusually exhilarated voice that answered him when eventually he reached her.

"I've had a marvellous day, Dick, and I'm going to surprise our friend to-morrow—no, not to-morrow, the next day."

He tried to break the news gently about Jerry, and was surprised and a little annoyed to find his sensation was discounted.

"I read it in the evening newspaper. Poor man!" she said.

Dick Allenby spent a disturbed night. He was getting very worried about the girl and the risks she was taking. When he rang her in the morning she had already gone out, but when he saw Surefoot that gentleman did much to allay his anxiety.

"I've got the cleverest shadower at Scotland Yard following her night and day; you needn't worry." And then, curiously: "She hasn't told you what line she's following? The only thing I can find from my men is that she's chasing round the suburbs of London, and that she's doing a lot of shopping."

"Shopping?" repeated Dick incredulously. "What sort of shopping?"

"Pickles mostly," said Surefoot Smith, "though

she's been after ham, and took over an hour in the City the other day buying tea. She's being scientific."

If the truth be told, Mr. Smith found it increasingly difficult to avoid being very annoyed with his mysterious collaborator. He hated mysteries.

Mary had gone a little outside of her usual orbit of inquiry that day. She left early for Maidstone and spent the greater part of the morning talking with a country bootmaker, an ancient and a prosy gentleman with a poor memory and a defective system of book-keeping. She got back to town about five, feeling tired, but a hot bath and two hours' rest revivified her. She was bright and fresh when she buttoned up her long coat and went out.

It was ten o'clock; the sky was overcast and a sprinkle of rain was falling when she signalled a taxi and drove to King's Cross. She found the disconsolate Binny waiting on the platform. Although the night was warm he wore an overcoat and a muffler, and was a typical picture of misery and loneliness when she came up to him. The detective who had followed her watched them talking, and was slightly amused, for he had been told something about the object of this northward journey of Mr. Lyne's handy man.

If he was amused, Binny was skeptical.

"I don't suppose I'll remember her, miss. People change, especially oldish people. She was only in the house about three weeks after I took on the job."

"But you would recognize her?" insisted the girl.

He hesitated.

"I suppose I would. I must say, miss," he protested, "I don't like these night journeys. I was in a railway accident once, and my nerves have never got over it. What with poor Mr. Lyne's death and all the newspaper reporters coming to see me, I've got in such a state that I don't know whether I'm on my head or my heels."

She cut short his personal plaint with a repetition of her instructions.

"You will go to this house and ask to see Mrs. Morris—that is the name she has taken, possibly because her son has been getting into trouble——"

"Visiting the sins of the parents upon the children I've heard about; visiting the sins of the children on the parents is something new."

"If it is Mrs. Laxby you are to send me a wire, but you must be absolutely sure it *is* Mrs. Laxby. You've got the photograph of her I gave you?"

He nodded miserably.

"I got it. But ain't this a job for the police, miss?"

"Now, Binny," she said severely, "you're to do as you're told. I've got you a nice sleeping car and it will be a very comfortable journey."

"They turn me out at four o'clock in the morning," said Binny; and then, as though he realized he was probably going a little too far with one who had such authority, he added, in a more cheerful tone: "All right, miss, you leave it to me; I'll send you a wire."

She left the platform a few minutes before the train pulled out, and took another taxi. The detective who followed her had no doubt that she was going back to her flat, and contented himself with giving instructions to his driver to follow the cab in front. Taxi-men are not necessarily good detectives, and it was not until the cab he was shadowing had set down an elderly man at a temperance hotel in Bloomsbury that he realized he was on the wrong trail, and doubled back to the flat to pick her up.

She had not returned, and, in a sweat, he began to cast round before reporting his failure to his very unpleasant superior.

It was a quarter-past eleven when he saw the girl walking quickly in the opposite direction to which his cab was moving. He recognized Mary, jumped out of the cab, paid the driver, and followed through the rain on foot.

CHAPTER XX

UNCONSCIOUS of the fact that she had been shadowed, Mary Lane reached her objective. She was in a small paved courtyard which was made faintly malodorous by the presence of an ash can that had not been emptied for a week. She moved cautiously, finding her way forward step by step with the aid of a tiny electric torch which she had taken from her handbag. At the end of the courtyard was a small door, flanked on one side by a window.

For a little while she stood on the doorstep, listening. Her heart was beating faster; she was curiously short of breath. Her early-morning resolution to abandon her ridiculous quest came back with a stronger urge. It was absurd of her, and a little theatrical (she told herself) to continue these excursions into a realm in which she had no place. Police work was, in its most elementary phase, men's work.

The quietness of the night, the sense of complete isolation, the gloom and drabness which the falling rain seemed to emphasize—all these things worked on her nerves.

She took from her bag the replica key that Surefoot had had cut for her, and, finding the keyhole, pushed in the key. The truth or futility of her theory was to be put to the test.

For a moment, as she tried to turn the key, it seemed that she had made a mistake, and she was almost grateful. And then, as she slightly altered its position, she felt it turn and the lock snapped back with a loud click!

She was trembling; her knees seemed suddenly incapable of supporting the weight of her body; her breathing became painfully shallow. Here her experiment should have ended, and she should have gone back the way she came, but the spirit of adventure flickered up feebly and she pushed open the door. It opened without sound, and she peered into the dark interior fearfully. Should she go in? Reason said "No!" but reason might be womanly cowardice—a fear of the dark and the bogies that haunt the dark.

She pushed the door open wider and went in one step. She flashed the lamp around and saw nothing.

Then out of the darkness came a sound that froze her blood—the whimpering of a woman.

Her scalp tingled with terror; she thought she was going to faint. It came from below her feet, and yet from somewhere immediately before her, as though there were two distinct sounds.

The beam of light she cast ahead wobbled so that she could not see what it revealed. She steadied her arm against the wall and saw what looked like a cupboard door. To this she crept and listened.

Yes, the sound came from there and below. It was the entrance to a cellar. She tried the cupboard door; it was locked. And then there came to her an unaccountable fear, greater than any she had experienced before—there was danger, near, very near; a menace beyond her understanding.

She turned and stood, petrified with horror. The door was slowly closing. She leaped forward and caught its edge, but somebody was pressing it, and that somebody was in the room, had been standing behind the opened door all the time she had been there.

As she opened her lips to scream, a big hand closed over her mouth, another hand gripped her shoulder and jerked her back violently, as the door closed with a crash.

"Oh, Miss Lane, how could you!"

The mincing tone, the falsetto voice, the artificial refinement of it were unmistakable. She had heard that voice at Kellner's Hotel when she had met Mr. Washington Wirth. She struggled madly, but the man held her without difficulty.

"May I suggest, my dear young friend, that you keep quiet and save me from the necessity of cutting your darling little throat?"

Behind the spurious courtesy of that hateful voice lay a threat, horribly, significantly sincere. She knew him now: he would kill her with as little compunction as he would slaughter a rabbit. It was not perhaps expedient to carry out his threat immediately, and her only hope of salvation lay with her wits.

With a moan she went limp in his arms, and he was so unprepared for this that he nearly dropped her and dropped with her, for the sudden collapse almost threw him off his balance. Clumsily he laid her down on the stone floor.

She heard his exclamation of anger, and, after a while, the jingle of keys. He was unlocking the cupboard door.

Noiselessly she rose and felt for the door knob. It turned without a sound, and in a second she had flung open the door and was racing across the courtyard. He was too late to stop her, and she was in the deserted side street before he recovered from his surprise. A few minutes later she had reached a main road; ahead of her she saw two policemen, and her first instinct was to fly to them and tell them of her adventure. She hesitated; they would think she was mad, and besides——

"Hullo, Miss Lane! You gave me a fright."

It was the detective who had been following her all the evening, and he did not hide his relief.

"Where on earth did you get to? I'm Stenford from Scotland Yard. Mr. Smith told me that you knew I was trailing you."

She could have fallen on his neck in her gratitude—she was horrified to discover that she was hysterical. She gasped her story; he listened, incredulous.

"Have you got the key?"

She shook her head; she had left it in the door.

"I'll take you home, Miss Lane, and then I'll report to Mr. Smith."

He was a young detective, full of zeal, and he had hardly left her at the door of her flat before he was racing back to conduct a little investigation on his own before reporting the sum of his discovery to Surefoot Smith.

Mary made herself a cup of tea and sat down to steady her nerves before she went to bed. The flat seemed terribly lonely. Odd noises, common to all houses, kept her jumping. She realized that she would not sleep that night except in other and less nerve-wearing surroundings, and was reaching for the telephone when its bell rang sharply—so unexpectedly that she jumped.

It was the voice of Surefoot Smith, urgent and anxious.

"That you, Miss Lane? Listen—and get this quickly! Go to your front door and bolt it! You're not to open the door until I come—I'll be with you in ten minutes."

"But——"

"Do as I tell you!"

She heard the click as he rang off. She was in a

panic. Surefoot would not have been so alarming unless her situation was a perilous one.

She went out into the hall. It was in darkness. She knew that she had left a light burning. Acting on blind impulse, she darted back into the room she had left, slammed the door and shot home a bolt. As she did so a heavy weight was flung against the door, the weight of a man's body. There were no arms in the room—nothing more formidable than a pair of scissors.

Crash!

The door shook; one of the panels bulged. She turned quickly and switched out the light.

"I have a revolver and I'll fire if you don't go away!" she cried.

There was a silence. She flung up the window. She must be a good actress or die.

"Mr. Smith! Is that you? Come up the fire escape!" She screamed the words.

Again the door crashed, and she had an inspiration. She took up the telephone.

"Get the police station—tell them a man named Moran is trying to break into my room—Leo Moran—please remember the name in case anything happens . . ."

She left the receiver off and crept to the door. Stealthy feet were moving along the corridor; the sound became less audible and ceased.

Mary Lane sank down onto the floor, and this

time there was nothing theatrical in her swoon. It was the frantic knocking on the door and the voice of Dick Allenby that brought her, reeling, to her feet. She drew the bolt to admit him and the detective. She had hardly begun to tell her story when she fainted again.

"Better get a nurse," said Surefoot. "Phew! I never expected to find her alive!"

An agitated Dick, engaged in bathing the white face of the girl, was not even interested to ask how Surefoot had learned of the girl's danger. Mr. Smith's officer had found him at his club and the two men had arrived simultaneously.

"I got a phone call from the detective who was shadowing her, giving me the story she had told. I told him to go straight back to her flat and stay there till I came. About half an hour later the simpleton called me up and said he'd searched the place and found nobody. Can you beat that? And then, of course, a trunk call from Birmingham came on the line and cut me off. I got rid of it and called Miss Lane—I should have called the nearest police station, but I worked it out that I'd be at the flat before they could deal with the matter. My officer called you at your club and got you."

Mary had opened her eyes, and a few minutes later was sitting up, very white and shaken, but calm enough to tell her story. Throughout that night Scotland Yard officers combed London and the suburbs for their man. "May be accompanied by a woman," the official warning ran, and there was added a description of the wanted pair.

On the advice of Surefoot, Mary moved into a hotel. It was a quiet hostelry near the Haymarket. Surefoot had an idea that no harm would come to the girl now that Mr. Washington Wirth's secret was out. He might kill her to avoid the embarrassment of identification, but now that she had spoken she was no longer a menace to his security.

"I hope so, at any rate," she said ruefully. "I am a failure as a detective."

Surefoot sniffed.

"I'm a bad man to ask for compliments," he said. "Beyond the fact that you've found our man and proved it, and apart from what I might call the circumstance that you've discovered how the forgeries were wangled, you've been perfectly useless!"

On the night of the girl's adventure Surefoot had cabled to his friend in New York the particulars of the English gangster who was at large in England. He went further and arranged for the New York Police Department to cable the photograph of the man to Scotland Yard. A description would have been sufficient. There was no mistaking. The day the photograph was received, Surefoot had gone to call on the directors of Moran's bank. A very careful audit had been made of the bank accounts, but no further defalcations had been unearthed.

He was leaving when the general manager, who had placed the facts before him, remarked:

"By the way, I suppose you know Moran? Moran's service in the bank was interrupted when he went to America. He was there three or four years. We have reason to believe that he was engaged in some sort of speculative business—he never gave us any particulars about it."

"That's odd," said Surefoot.

He did not explain where the oddness lay.

"He has also a large interest in Cassari Oils, which have had such a sensational rise," said the manager. "I only discovered this a few days ago."

"I have known it for quite a long time," said Surefoot grimly, "and I can tell you something: he has made nearly a million out of the stock."

The man's eyebrows rose.

"So there was no need for him to be dishonest?"

"There never was," said Surefoot cryptically.

In these days Dick Allenby was a busy man. As principal heir to his uncle he had an immense amount of work to do. The late Mr. Lyne had certain interests in France which had to be liquidated. Dick took the afternoon boat express to Paris.

Between Ashford and Dover there had been a

derailment on the day before, and the passenger trains were being worked on a single line. There was very little delay occasioned by this method of working the traffic, except that it necessitated the boat train being brought to a standstill at a little station near Sandling Junction.

The Continental train drew slowly into the station and stopped. There was another train waiting to proceed in the opposite direction. As they were going to move Dick turned his head idly, as passengers will, and scrutinized the other passengers.

The Pullman car was passing at a snail's pace. The long body drew out of view and there came a coupé compartment at the end of the car. A man was sitting in the corner, reading a newspaper. As the trains passed, he put the paper down and turned his head. It was Leo Moran!

CHAPTER XXI

LEO MORAN! . . . It was impossible to do anything. The train was gathering speed and its next stop was Dover. Surefoot must be told. He might get through by telephone to London, but doubted if he had the time without missing the boat. Fortunately, when he arrived at Dover Harbour station and came to the barrier where passports are examined, he recognized a Scotland Yard man who was scrutinizing the departing passengers. To him he explained the urgency of the matter.

"He didn't come through this port," said the detective, shaking his head. "The train you saw was the one connecting with the Boulogne-Folkestone route. I'll get through to Mr. Smith at once. I've had a very full description of Mr. Moran for a long time, and so have the officers at Folkestone—I can't understand how they missed him."

Smith was not in his office when the call came through, but it was relayed to him almost immediately. Officers were sent to meet the train, but on its arrival there was no sign of Moran. Surefoot afterwards learned that it had been held up at South Bromley station, and that a man who had occupied a coupé had alighted, given up his ticket, carrying his own baggage, which consisted of a small expanding suitcase, to a station taxi.

He had evidently acted on the impulse of the moment, according to the Pullman car attendant, for when, late that night, the taxi driver was interviewed, it was learned that Moran had been driven to another station within a few miles of Bromley, and had gone on to London by the electric train.

A call at his flat produced no result. The hall porter had not seen him. Surefoot put a phone call through to Paris and spoke to Dick.

"You've got the keys of this man's flat, haven't you?"

"Good Lord! Yes, I'd forgotten them. They're in my workroom. See the housekeeper. You will find them . . ."

Smith was less anxious to find the keys than to establish the fact that Leo Moran had not returned. He would naturally call at Dick's place to retrieve the keys, and with this idea in his mind Smith put Dick Allenby's apartments under observation. But Moran did not come near. Either he knew that he was being sought and had reason for keeping out of the way, or he had some other establishment in London about which the police knew nothing.

The second inquiry which Surefoot Smith conducted was even more profitless. At the moment, however, he concentrated upon Moran. The register of every hotel in London was carefully scrutinized.

Mary Lane knew nothing about the discovery, and when Surefoot Smith saw her that evening he made no reference at all to the man Dick Allenby had seen. He made it a practice to call once or twice a day, for, although he was satisfied that there was no immediate danger to the girl, and that every reason for menacing her had disappeared now that the murderer of Hervey Lyne was identified, he took no chances. Men who killed as ruthlessly as "Mr. Washington Wirth" were capable of deeper villainies.

Mary's hotel was an old-fashioned block set in the heart of the West End and in one of its most pleasant backwaters. The furnishings were Victorian, its equipment a little primitive. As a reluctant concession to modern progress its ancient proprietor had installed gas fires in its bedrooms—it was the last hotel in London to adopt electricity for lighting.

The servants were old and slow; its proprietor still regarded the telephone as an unwarranted intrusion upon his privacy. There was one instrument, and that part of the office equipment.

It had its advantages, as Mary found. It was quiet; one could sleep at night. Strange guests rarely came; most of its patrons were part of the great shifting family that had made a habit of the hotel for years and years. Her room was pleasant and bright; it was on the street, and had the advantage of a narrow balcony which ran the full length of the building—a theoretical advantage perhaps, for nothing happened in that quiet street which made a balcony view desirable.

Mr. Smith called the next evening, and was unlucky. If he had been a few minutes earlier he would have followed a sturdy figure that mounted the broad stairs and stood patiently whilst the hotel porter unlocked the next door to Mary's bedroom, before ushering Mr. Leo Moran into the room he had engaged. He had not signed himself Leo Moran in the hotel register, but he had good and sufficient reason for that omission. He was plain Mr. John Moore from Birmingham.

He ordered a light meal to be sent up to him, and when that had come and had been cleared away he locked the door of his room, opened a portfolio, and, taking out a number of documents and a writing pad, became immediately absorbed in the task he had set himself.

There was nothing flimsy about this hotel; the walls were thick; otherwise, he might have heard Surefoot Smith offering astounding theories concerning a certain fugitive from justice.

Surefoot's visit was not a very long one, and, following her practice, the girl read for an hour. Her nerves were calmer; she had got over the shock of that ghastly night. She had asked Surefoot to allow her to go back to the flat.

"I'll give you another week here," he said, shaking his head. "I may be wrong, but I have an idea I can liquidate this business in that time."

"But now that I've recognized him, and the police have circulated his name and description, there is no reason why he should do me any harm," she protested. "I am perfectly sure that it was not revenge but self-preservation——"

"You can't be sure of anything where that bird is concerned," interrupted Smith. "You've got to allow for the fact that he's a little mad."

"Is he the man the American detective spoke about?" she asked curiously.

Surefoot Smith nodded.

"Yes, he was in Chicago and New York for a few years, and was associated with some pretty bad gangs. The curious thing is that, even in those days, the stage had a fascination for him. He used to give hectic parties to theatrical people, and even appeared on the stage himself, though he wasn't a very great success. Out of his loot he financed a couple of road companies—it's the same man, all right."

Mary was getting weary of the restrictions imposed upon her; resented the early-to-bed rule which the doctor had prescribed. She lay in bed, very wakeful, heard ten and eleven strike, and was no nearer to sleep than she had been when she lay down.

Some time before midnight she fell into a doze, for she did not remember hearing twelve o'clock strike. She must have been lying, half-asleep, half-awake, for an hour, when something roused her to complete wakefulness. She shivered and pulled the clothes over her shoulders, and at that instant became wide awake.

The French window, which she had lightly fastened, was wide open; a draught of chill air swept through the room, the door of which was half-open. She had locked it from the inside—she remembered that distinctly.

As she stood by the side of the bed a man's figure appeared in the doorway, silhouetted against the dim light in the passage outside. For a second she stood petrified with fear and astonishment. Then she recognized that stocky figure, and the terror of death came to her, and she screamed.

The man stepped backwards and disappeared. She flew to the door, closed it with a crash and turned the key. Switching on the light, she rang the bell urgently and repeatedly; closed and latched the French windows, and sat, quaking, until she heard a knock at the door and the voice of the night porter, the one able-bodied servant of the hotel.

Slipping into a wrap, she opened the door to him and told him what had happened. His expression was one of profound incredulity. He did not say as much, but she realized that he thought she had been dreaming.

"A man, miss? Nobody's passed me. I've been in the hall since ten."

"Is there no other way he could have got out?"

He thought a moment.

"He might have gone by the servants' stairs. I'll find out. Have you lost anything?"

She shook her head.

"I don't know," impatiently. "Will you please call Superintendent Smith at Scotland Yard? Tell him I want to see him—that it's very, very important."

She went back to her room, locked the door, and did not come out again until Surefoot's reassuring voice accompanied his knock. She opened the door to him thankfully, and he stepped in.

Before she could speak, he called back to the porter who had brought him up.

"There's a bad escape of gas somewhere in this house," he said.

"I noticed it, sir."

The porter went prowling along the passage and came back.

"It's coming from the room next door," he said.

CHAPTER XXII

SUREFOOT knelt and brought his face close to the floor. The smell of gas was overpowering. He tried the handle. The door was fastened on the inside. Repeated knockings produced no response. Stepping back, he threw the whole weight of his body against the frame. There was a crash and he fell headlong into the room. The place was so full of gas that he was almost asphyxiated and only staggered out with difficulty. Going into the girl's room, he soaked a towel in water and, clapping it over his face, ran through to the room and flung open the window. Then, turning his attention to the man who lay on the bed, he put his arm round him and dragged him into the passage.

The man was still breathing. One glance he took at the purple face and in his astonishment almost dropped the inanimate figure. Leo Moran!

By this time the hotel was aroused. A doctor, who lived on the same floor, came out in pajamas and an overcoat, and rendered first aid, whilst Surefoot went back into the room.

He switched on the electric light. The gas was still hissing from the burner on the hearth, and he turned this off before he opened the window wider. He saw now that elaborate preparations had been made for this near-tragedy. There was sticking plaster down each side of the window. He found it also over the keyhole, and the space between the bottom of the door leading into the bathroom had been stuffed with a towel. Near the bed was a half-glass of whisky and soda. Evidently Moran had been writing: Surefoot took up a half-finished letter. He saw it was addressed to the general manager of the bank for which he had worked.

> Dear Sir,
>
> I am back in London, and for reasons which I will explain to you, I am living under an assumed name at this hotel. The explanation which I will give I think will satisfy . . .

Here the writing ended in a scrawl, as though Moran had been suddenly overcome.

There was a closely typed foolscap sheet on the table, but this Surefoot did not see immediately.

He looked round the room; the first thing that struck him was that the door of a large cupboard stood wide open, and on the floor of the cupboard, which was empty, were two muddy footprints. They were unmistakably the prints of goloshes. Somebody had been hiding there. Outside it had been raining heavily; the prints were still wet.

He went outside and found that Moran had been

carried into another bedroom, where the doctor and the porter were engaged in applying artificial resuscitation. Returning to Moran's room, he remembered the typewritten sheet which lay on the top of other documents and picked it up. He had not read half a dozen words when his jaw dropped in amazement, and he sat down heavily in a chair: for this typewritten statement was a murder confession:

> I, Leopold Moran, am about to say farewell to life, and, before going, I want to make a full statement concerning the killing of three men. The first of these is a man named Tickler.
>
> In some way he had discovered that I was robbing the bank. He had been blackmailing me for months. He knew that under the name of Mr. Washington Wirth I was giving parties, and traced me back to a room over a garage which I used to change my clothes and have used on other occasions as a hiding place. He came into this room and demanded a thousand pounds. I gave him a hundred in Treasury notes and then persuaded him to let me drive him down to the West End in a cab that was standing in the mews. As he got into the cab I shot him, closed the door and, driving him down into Regent Street, left the cab on the rank.
>
> The next day I had an interview with Hervey Lyne. He was growing suspicious. I had forged his name to large sums of money and when, at his request, I called on him, I knew that the game was up. I had tried to bribe Binny—his servant—into helping me to keep the old man in the dark, but Binny was either too

> honest or too foolish to fall in with my suggestions. Binny is one of the straightest men I have ever met. I think he was a fool to himself, but that is neither here nor there.
>
> I knew Hervey Lyne was in the habit of going into Regent's Park every afternoon and he always chose a spot where I could see him. On the afternoon in question, realizing that I could see my finish, I shot him from the window, with a rifle to which I had fastened a silencer. What made it so easy was that a noisy car was passing at the time. Afterwards I sent a man to Germany under my name and myself stayed in England.
>
> I was afraid of Hennessey, who was also blackmailing me, and I had to silence him. I drove him into the country and killed him on the Colnbrook By-pass. Before he died, he told me that Miss Lane had the bank statement. That night I entered her house and made a search for it, but found nothing.
>
> All the above is true. I am tired of life and I am going out with no regret.

It was signed "Leo Moran."

Surefoot read the confession carefully and then began a search of the room for the goloshes. There was no sign of them.

He found Mary Lane in her room, fully dressed.

"You didn't see the face of the man who tried to get into the room?"

She shook her head.

"Did you recognize him in any other way?"

She thought she had and told him.

As far as he could judge, there was a quarter of an hour between the appearance of the man and the arrival of Surefoot: time enough, if it were Moran, to lock himself in his room. He was reaching this conclusion when he saw something on the floor that glistened. Stooping, he picked up a key. It lay very near to the open window. Going back to Moran's room, he scraped away the plaster that covered the key-hole, put in the key and turned it. There was no doubt now in his mind.

Moran was still unconscious, though the doctor said he was out of danger. Surefoot had sent for two detectives, and, leaving the banker in their charge, he went back to the Yard.

At one o'clock in the morning three Scotland Yard chiefs were called from their beds and hurried to headquarters. To these Surefoot showed the confession.

"It is as clear as daylight," said his immediate chief. "As soon as he is conscious, shoot him into Cannon Row and charge him."

Surefoot said nothing for a moment, but again examined the foolscap sheet.

"It wasn't typewritten in the room, was it?" he asked. "Perhaps there is such a thing as an invisible typewriter, but I've never seen one. And there was no typewriter in the room. And the door was locked on the inside and the key was on the floor in Miss

Lane's room. And the tape over the window was on the outside, not on the inside. That was a little error on somebody's part."

He put his hand in his pocket and took out a small bottle containing an amber liquid.

"That's the whisky that I found in the glass on his writing table—I want it analyzed."

"How was Moran dressed when you found him?" asked one of the chief inspectors.

"He had everything on—including his boots," said Surefoot. "And what is more, he was lying with his feet on the pillow—it is not the position I should choose if I were committing suicide. All very rum and mysterious and scientific, but it doesn't impress *me!*"

The chief inspector sniffed.

"Nothing impresses you, Surefoot, except good beer. What is your suggestion?"

Surefoot thought for a while.

"Moran's been out this evening—the hall porter saw him come in an hour before he was discovered. The whisky and soda was sent up to his room—the whisky in a glass and the bottle unopened—an hour before that, on his instructions. I've been through the documents I found on his table, and if there's one thing more certain than another, it is that he had no intention of committing suicide. He has come back to buy a lot of outstanding shares in Cassari Oils and to open a London office for the company. He didn't want to call attention to the fact that he was back—it might have upset his plans for getting the shares he wanted. I found all that in a letter he has written to a Turk in Constantinople. I took the liberty of opening it. And he was seeing the general manager of the bank to-morrow—that doesn't look like suicide."

"Well?" asked the three men together when he paused.

"He didn't try to commit suicide. Somebody got into his room whilst he was out—it was easy, for there are two empty rooms that open onto the balcony—and after getting in hocussed the whisky and hid himself in the cupboard. When the dope took effect he came out, picked up Moran from the floor and laid him on the bed. He then stuffed up the ventilation of the room and turned on the gas. Then he got out of the window onto the balcony and made the door air-tight and went out through Miss Lane's room—he probably mistook the room for the one through which he had gained admission to Moran's. He must have dropped the key and was coming back for it, when Miss Lane screamed."

"How did he get out of the hotel, without the night porter seeing him?"

Surefoot smiled pityingly.

"There are three ways out, but the easiest is down the service stairs and through the kitchen.

There is a coffee cook on duty, but it would be easy to avoid him."

He underlined with his thumbnail a few lines of the confession.

"Notice what a good character he gives to Binny. That was a silly thing to do—a child in arms would know that only Binny could have written that statement."

"Binny—the servant?"

Surefoot nodded.

"He's got several other names," he said. "One of them is Washington Wirth. There's the murderer!"

CHAPTER XXIII

THE police chief looked at Surefoot in amazement.

"Binny? You mean Lyne's servant?" asked the senior.

"That's what I mean," said Surefoot calmly.

He dived into the inside of his pocket, took out a flat envelope, and produced from this the transcript of the long cable and a blurred photograph.

"This came over the wire," he explained. "It's a picture of the man—English Len was one of his names—who is wanted by the police of New York and Chicago. He worked with three gangs and was lucky to get away with his life. Listen to this."

He put pince-nez on his broad nose and read from one of the cables:

" 'This man speaks with a very common English accent. He is believed to have been a valet, and his modus operandi is to obtain a situation with a wealthy family and to use the opportunity for extensive robberies. On the side he has worked with several booze rackets, is known to be concerned in the killing of Eddie McGean, and is suspected of other killings.' "

He twisted the photograph round so that the inspectors could see it.

"It's not pretty. It was taken at police headquarters in New York. If you don't know Binny, I'll tell you that is the bird! Even his best friend would recognize him."

Chief Inspector Knowles examined the photograph and whistled softly.

"I know him. I saw him the day you had him up at the Yard, questioning him. Why should he kill the old boy?"

"Because he's been forging his name. It was Miss Lane who put us onto the track, though I was a dummy not to see it myself. All these forgeries were committed on the seventeenth of the month, and she knew, having lived with the old man, that that was the date he paid all his tradesmen's bills. He was in the habit of writing messages on the back of his checks, mainly of an insulting nature. The one we deciphered said 'No more Chinese e——.' Miss Lane knew that the old man lived under the impression that tradesmen spent their lives swindling him. It was his belief that nothing but Chinese or imported eggs were sent to him. To keep his egg and butter man up to the scratch, he used to make a note on the back of the check when he paid his bill. That was his practice with all tradesmen—Miss Lane has seen most of them: bootmakers, tailors, provision merchants of all kinds. And do you know what they told her?"

Surefoot leaned forward over the table and spoke slowly, tapping his finger on the desk to emphasize each word.

"They told her that two or three years ago Lyne stopped paying by check—and paid cash! Binny either used to go round and settle, or send the money by postal order. Do you know what that means? It means that Lyne was going blind, and that the checks he was signing for the tradesmen were checks going into Binny's private account. What made it easier for Binny—which is his real name, by the way—was that the old man would never admit his sight was failing, and in his vanity claimed he could read as well as the next man. It was easy for Binny, on the seventeenth of the month, to put checks before his master and pretend they were in settlement of tradesmen's bills, when in reality they were filled in with pencil for the correct amount. I've seen some of them, and under the microscope you can see the pencil marks and the original amounts for which they were drawn. It was easy to rub them out after the signature had been obtained, and to fill them in for the amount Binny happened to require at the time.

"He must have got wind that these investigations were going on, for he went after Miss Lane, and she saved herself by pretending she thought it was Moran. It was that which probably saved her life. When Binny heard her shout out of the window that Moran was trying to break into her room, he thought he'd leave well alone, and quitted. If he'd had any intelligence, he would have known that all her inquiries incriminated, not Moran, but him! But that's the way of 'em—if criminals had any sense they'd never be hanged."

The chief inspector pushed the photographs back across the table.

"Where was the murder committed—the murder of Lyne, I mean?"

Surefoot shook his head.

"That's the one thing that puzzles me. It is possible, of course, that he did the shooting just at the moment Dornford's car passed. The 'confession' that he prepared to throw the crime onto Moran—he was a mug to say so many nice things about Binny—almost suggests that this is the case. All the other crimes in this document were committed by Binny in the way he described."

He went back to the hotel to see Moran. There were other aspects of the case which needed elucidation.

Mike Hennessey's death puzzled him. If the manager was blackmailing Binny, there was motive enough. But what could Mike Hennessey know, except that the servant of the day was the magnificent Washington Wirth by night? And why should he blackmail the man who was providing him with a generous income?

There was a very special reason for killing Hennessey: of that he was sure.

Before he left the Yard, Surefoot tightened the cords of the net about the man he wanted. Binny had not been seen since the night Mary Lane sent him to Newcastle on a fictitious errand so that she could try the key of the pantry door of Hervey Lyne's house.

The illuminated key was a mystery no longer. Sometimes "Mr. Washington Wirth" came back from these little parties of his, a little exhilarated. It was necessary that he should change his clothes in the room above the garage, and once or twice, in changing them, he had left his key behind. Possibly he was a methodical man and was in the habit of putting the key on the table. Its phosphorescent quality was added so that, even if he switched off the light, he would not forget this necessary method of gaining admission to Lyne's house.

On the night of Tickler's murder he had forgotten the key and was compelled to break a window to get into the scullery—this had been Mary's theory. She had recognized the key; as a child she had seen it every day. She had sent Binny to the north to give herself the opportunity of testing out her theory. She had nearly lost her life in doing so, for Binny was no fool: he had left the carriage and gone back ahead of her to his lair.

The detective found Leo Moran conscious, but a very unhappy man, for the after effects of gas poisoning are not pleasant. All that he told Surefoot confirmed what that intelligent officer had already discovered from a perusal of his private correspondence.

Surefoot showed him the "confession" and read portions of it to the astonished man.

"Murder!" said Moran scornfully. "What rubbish! Who has been murdered?"

When Surefoot told him:

"Hervey Lyne? Good God! How perfectly dreadful! When did this happen?"

"The day you went away," said Surefoot.

Moran frowned.

"But I saw him the day I went away, from my window. He was sitting under the tree in the park —when I say 'the tree' I mean the tree he always used as shade. I've seen him there dozens of times. Binny was reading to him."

"What time was this?" asked Surefoot quickly.

Moran thought for a while, then gave an approximate hour.

"That must have been ten minutes before he was

found dead. It was too far away for you to see whether he was talking?"

Moran nodded.

"When I saw him, Binny was reading to him."

Here was unexpected evidence. Moran was probably the only man who had watched that little group in Hervey Lyne's last moments.

"Where was he sitting—Binny, I mean?"

"Where he usually sat," said Leo Moran instantly. "Facing the old man, practically on a level with his feet. I was watching them for some time."

"Did you see Binny walk round to the back of the chair?"

The other hesitated.

"Yes, he did—I remember now. He walked right round the chair. I remember being reminded of how gamblers walk round a chair for luck."

"You saw nothing else—heard nothing?"

Moran stared at him.

"Do you suspect Binny?"

Surefoot nodded.

"It isn't a case of suspicion, it's a case of certainty."

Again the sick man taxed his memory.

"I am almost sure I am right in saying that he went round the chair. I didn't hear anything—you mean a shot? No, I did not hear that, nor did I see Binny behaving suspiciously."

Surefoot skimmed through the "confession" again.

"Do you know Binny?"

"Slightly. He was my servant; I dismissed him for stealing. I lost a number of little trinkets."

Smith put his hand in his pocket and took out the silver cigarette case that had been found under the cushion of the car in which Mike Hennessey had ridden to his death.

The banker stretched out his hand eagerly.

"Good lord, yes! I wouldn't have lost that for a fortune. It's one of the things that were missing. How did you get it?"

In the man's present condition Surefoot decided it was not the moment to tell of the other horror which had been fastened upon him.

"I thought it might be," he said, pocketing the case. "It was obviously an old one, and not the kind of case you would use, and certainly not the kind you would put where I found it. It had been polished up for the occasion, too."

"What was the occasion?" asked Moran curiously, but the detective evaded the question.

Moran spoke quite frankly of his own movements.

"I was a fool to go off so hurriedly," he confessed, "but I was rather piqued with my directors, who had refused me leave. It was very vital I should be in Constantinople whilst the board of the Cassari Company was being reconstructed. I have very heavy interests in that company, which is now one of the richest oil companies in the world. And, by the way, Miss Lane is a rich lady; the shares I bought from her could not be transferred to me under the Turkish law without yet another signature. Legally I have the right to that; morally I haven't; so the stock she transferred, I am transferring back at the price I paid. Which means that she has more money than she can spend in her lifetime." He smiled. "And so have I, for the matter of that," he added.

There was nothing more to be gained from Moran, and Smith left him to sleep off his intolerable headache. Scotland Yard had phoned that Dick Allenby was on his way back from Paris by aëroplane. He reached Croydon at dawn and found a police car waiting to take him to Regent's Park.

As the car drove into Naylor Crescent he saw Surefoot Smith and three plain clothes officers waiting outside the house.

"Sorry to bring you back, but it is necessary that I should make another search of this house, and it is very advisable you should be present."

"Did you find Moran?" asked Dick impatiently. "You got my telephone message?"

Surefoot nodded.

"Did he tell you anything about Binny?"

"Binny's told me quite a lot about himself," said Surefoot grimly. "I haven't interviewed the gentleman, but he left a very illuminating document."

Dick opened the door of the house and they went in. Although it had only been unoccupied for a very short time, it smelt of emptiness and neglect. Hervey Lyne's study had been tidied up after the detective's search. Every corner had been examined, the very floorboards and hearthstone lifted by the police in their vain effort to find a clue. It was unlikely that this apartment would yield any fresh evidence.

They went into the kitchen, where Mary Lane had had her unpleasant adventure. Smith had visited the place an hour or two after Mary's escape, had passed through the cupboard door down a flight of steps to the coal cellar. The truckle bed he had found there on his first visit had been removed.

"The queerest thing about Binny is his wife," said Surefoot. "Why he should attach himself, or allow himself to be attached, to this poor drunkard is beyond my understanding. He must have smuggled her away the night Miss Lane came here, and where she is at the moment I'd rather not inquire."

Dick had already expressed his opinion on this matter. He thought it was probable that the woman was not Binny's wife at all. Hervey Lyne invariably advertised for a man and wife. To gain admission to the establishment Binny would not have been above hiring a woman to suit this purpose. This theory was rather supported by the fact that "Mrs.

Binny" occupied a small, separate room. That she could have been a source of menace to the murderer was unlikely. The evidence of tradesmen had been that she was invariably in a state of fuddle, and that the cooking was done by Binny himself.

CHAPTER XXIV

THE Bath chair in which the old man had been found dead occupied a place under the stairs, and to Dick's surprise the detective gave instructions to have it taken into the front room study. Surefoot had always had an uncomfortable feeling that he had not paid sufficient attention to the chair. What he had learned in the past few days made a further examination essential.

Immediately opposite the door of the study there was an alcove in the wall of the passage, and he saw now that this served a useful purpose. Obviously Lyne was in the habit of getting into the Bath chair in the study. Against the lintel of the door, at the height of the wheel's hub, were several scratches and indentations where the hub had touched the wood. But for the fortuitous circumstance of the alcove being so placed, it would have been difficult either to take the chair into the room or bring it out. Surefoot put a detective into the chair and made the experiment of drawing him into the street. The width of the conveyance was only a few inches less than the width of the front door opening, and again he found marks on the door posts where the hub had touched. Without assistance he drew the chair into the street. The wheels fitted into the little tram-lines which Lyne had had placed for the purpose. The slope was so gentle that it was as easy to pull the laden chair back into the house.

The experiment told him very little. On the day of the murder he had examined every square inch of the vehicle. He ordered it to be put back in the place where it had been found and then continued his search and examination of the house.

"What do you expect to find?" asked Dick.

"Binny," was the terse reply. "This fellow isn't a fool. He has got a hiding place somewhere, and I wish I knew where to look for it." He looked at his watch. "I wonder if I could persuade Miss Lane to come along?"

Dick Allenby took a cab to the hotel, a little doubtful whether, after the excitement of the night, she would be either physically fit or willing to come to this house of gloom.

He found her in her sitting room, showing no evidence of the strain she had experienced. Her first question was about Binny.

"No, we haven't found him," said Dick. His voice was troubled. "I am getting terribly worried about you, Mary. This fellow would stop at nothing."

She shook her head.

"I don't think he'll worry me again," she said. "Mr. Smith is right: Binny will take no risk that does not bring him profit. As long as he thought he could get the bank statement from me, or stop me speaking and telling what I had discovered about the checks, I think I must have been in terrible danger."

"How did he know you were making inquiries?"

"He knew when I sent him up to the north," she said. "That was a crude little plan, wasn't it? I under-rated his intelligence and he must have been following me when I was visiting the tradesmen. I had an idea once that I saw him. It was the day I went to Maidstone."

She showed no reluctance in accompanying Dick back to the house. On the way she told him that she had seen Leo Moran in the night and that he was out of danger. There had been a time when the doctors had been doubtful as to whether he would recover.

They reached the house. Surefoot was in the little courtyard at the back. She followed Dick down the few steps that led to the kitchen. She shuddered as she recalled her midnight visit to this sinister little apartment. Even now, in the light of day, it had an unpleasant atmosphere, due, she admitted to herself, rather to her imagination than to unhappy memory. There was the "cupboard" door wide open now and the little door into which she had fitted the replica of the silver key. The kitchen and the adjoining scullery seemed amazingly small. She realized that this was due to the fact that her earliest recollections of the house belonged to childhood, when small rooms look large and low articles of furniture unusually high.

Surefoot came in as she was looking around and nodded a greeting.

"Remember this, Miss Lane?"

"Yes." She pointed to the inner kitchen, looking very modern with its lining in white glazed brick. "That's new," she said, and walked in.

The place puzzled her: she missed something, and, try as she did, she could not recollect what it was. Some feature of the room, as she remembered it, was missing. She did not mention her doubts, thinking that memory was playing tricks—a way that memory has.

"You know what this is?" asked Smith.

He had found it in the kitchen drawer: a curious-looking instrument rather like a short garden syringe, except that at the end was a rubber cup.

"It is a vacuum pump," explained Smith.

He wetted the edge of the rubber cap, pressed it on the table and, drawing up the piston, lifted the table bodily at one end.

"What's the idea of that? Have you ever seen it before?"

She shook her head.

Surefoot had found some other things: a small

pot of dark green paint and a hardened mass wrapped in oily paper.

"Putty," he explained. "I saw it when I was here before. Do you know what it was used for?"

He beckoned her and she followed him into a dark passage. The lamp that had been switched on gave very little light, but Surefoot took a powerful little torch from his pocket and, walking up to the door, stooped and, sending the bright light along the inside of the thick door panel, said:

"You see that, and that?"

She saw now a deep circular indentation.

"It was filled with putty and painted over. I thought it was a knot-hole until I started picking out the putty."

"What is it?" she asked wonderingly.

"It is the mark made by a spent bullet," said Smith slowly. "The bullet that killed Hervey Lyne. He was shot in this passage."

CHAPTER XXV

"It's all based on deduction so far," said Surefoot, "but it is the kind of deduction that I am willing to bet on, and that is saying a lot for me: I don't waste money. Binny had known for some time that the old man was suspecting him and things were getting desperate. He had to do something and do it pretty quickly. The old man was getting suspicious about his bank account. He could not suspect Binny or he would not have told him to send for Moran. Lyne hated bankers and never had an interview unless he couldn't help it. When Binny found he had sent for his bank manager he was in a hole. There was only one thing he could do and that was to get a confederate to pose as a bank manager and that confederate was——"

"Mike Hennessey!" said Dick.

Surefoot nodded.

"I haven't any doubt about that," he said. "When we searched Hennessey's clothes we found a paper containing the identical figures that were on the statement. This could only mean that Binny had supplied him with the figures and that Mike had had to commit them to memory in case the old man questioned him. Obviously the paper had been continuously handled. It was extremely soiled and had been folded and refolded."

They were in the kitchen, and, providentially, Surefoot had found a big sheet of blotting paper, which he spread on the table, and on which he elaborated his theory as he spoke.

"Moran was never notified and never asked to call. It happened by a coincidence that he was not in his office at the time of the interview. He was, in fact, consulting with the agents of the Cassari Oils. At the time fixed for the appointment Mike came. Hervey Lyne had never seen the bank manager and, even if he had, he would not have recognized him, for he was nearly blind. He must have said something or done something which left the old man unsatisfied. Lyne was very shrewd. One of his hobbies was working out how he could be swindled and it is possible that he had a doubt in his mind whether the man who called on him was Moran.

"We will never know what it was that made suspicion a certainty. It may have been something he overheard in the kitchen: there were times when Binny and his so-called wife had unholy rows—I got this from the servants in the next house. He picked up the first piece of paper he could find—it happened to be the bank statement—and wrote the message to you." He nodded at Mary. "I do not think there is any doubt that he was sure that the man who had called that morning was not Moran, and that he suspected Binny of being the villain of the piece, and that is why he asked that the police should be sent for. Binny got to know this. Whether the old man charged him at the last moment or said something, we shall only know if Binny tells the truth before he is hanged.

"Binny must have made his plans on the spur of the moment. After he dressed the old man to take him out, he stepped behind him and shot him with a magazine pistol—I dug out the bullet from the door. It is possible that he had no intention of taking him out, but after he found there was very little blood and no sign of a wound, he decided to take the risk. The blue glasses Mr. Lyne wore hid his eyes. He was generally half-asleep as he was being pulled into the park. Binny got away with it. He even asked the policeman to hold up the traffic to allow the chair to pass."

Surefoot Smith sighed and shook his head in reluctant admiration.

"Think of it! Him sitting there dead, and Binny as cool as a cucumber, reading the news to the dead man."

"Is there a chance of Binny getting out of England?" asked Dick.

Surefoot scratched his nose thoughtfully.

"Theoretically, no, but this man is a play-actor,

meaning no disrespect to you, Miss Lane. I don't believe in criminals disguising themselves, but this man isn't an ordinary criminal. At the moment he is in London, probably living in a flat which he has rented under another name. He may have two or three of them. He is the sort of man who would be very careful to make all preparations for a get-away. He has got stacks of money, a couple of automatic guns, and the rope ahead of him. He is not going to be taken easily."

"I don't understand him," said Dick, shaking his head. "Why these theatrical parties? Why Mr. Washington Wirth?"

"He had to have some sort of swell name and appearance. I will tell you all about the theatrical parties one of these days. He never got the right people there, with all due respect to you, Miss Lane. He wanted ladies wearing thousands of pounds' worth of diamonds. He worked that racket in Chicago: got a big party and held them up, but he never caught on in London and never attracted the money. And you have got to allow for vanity, too. He liked to be a big noise even among little people, again with all due respect to you, Miss Lane."

He picked up the vacuum pump and looked at it.

"I'd like to know what this is for. I think I will take it along with me."

He slipped it into his pocket. They went out after locking all the doors—Dick and the girl to the hotel, and the indefatigable Mr. Smith to his Haymarket flat.

An hour passed in that house. There was neither sound nor movement, until an oblong strip of glazed brickwork began to open like a door, and Binny, wearing rubber overshoes, came cautiously into the kitchen, gun in hand. He listened, went swiftly and noiselessly into the passage, up the stairs from room to room before he came back to the front door and slipped a bolt in its place. Returning to the kitchen, he laid his gun on the table and passed his hand over his unshaven chin. His unprepossessing face creased in a smile which was not pleasant to see.

"Vanity, eh?" he said.

It was the one thing the detective had said that had infuriated him.

Binny stood by the table, his unshapely head sunk in thought, his fingers playing mechanically with the long-barrelled automatic that lay at his hand.

Vanity! That had hurt him. He hated Surefoot Smith; from the first time he had seen him he had recognized in this slow, ponderous, unintelligent-looking man a menace to his own security and life. And he had offended him beyond all pardon. Whatever anybody could say about this amazing man, his love of the theatre was genuine. Association with its people was the breath of his nostrils. His first defalcations were made for the purpose of financing a play that ran only a week. He himself was no bad actor. He would require all his skill and genius to escape from the net which was being drawn about him. He went back through the narrow door into a room that was smaller than the average prison cell.

It was narrow and long. On the floor was a mattress where he had slept, and at the foot of the "bed" was a small dressing table, beneath which were two suitcases. He took one of these out and unlocked it. On the top lay a flat envelope containing three passports, which he brought into the kitchen. Pulling up a chair to the table, he examined each one carefully. He had made his preparations well. The passports were in names that Surefoot Smith had never heard of, and there was no resemblance to him in the three photographs attached to each passport. Fastened to one by a rubber band was a little packet of railway tickets. One set would take him to the Hook of Holland, another to Italy. He could change his identity three times on the journey.

From a bulging hip pocket he took a thick pad of banknotes: French, English, German. He took another pad from a concealed pocket in his coat, a third and a fourth, until there was a great pile of money on the table.

For a quarter of an hour he sat contemplating this wealth thoughtfully, then, going back into his little hiding place, he carried out a mirror and a small shaving set and began carefully to make his preparations.

Vulgar grease paints, however convincing they might look on the stage, would have no value in the light of day. He poured a little annatto into a saucer, diluted it and sponged his face carefully, using a magnifying mirror to check the effects.

For the greater part of two hours he laboured on his face and head; then stripping to his under-clothes, he began to dress, having first deposited his money in satchels that were attached to his belt, which was passed round his waist. The contents of the two cases he turned out, for he had examined them very carefully the day before. He could not afford to carry any other baggage than the two automatics and half a dozen spare magazines, which he disposed about his person.

He chose the lunch hour, and then only after a long scrutiny of the street from the study window. The servants might see him, but the chances were that they would be preparing or serving the meal either to their employers or to themselves. It was the hour, too, when no tradesmen were delivering, and the only risk was that Surefoot Smith had left somebody to watch the house. That had to be taken

He unbolted the front door, turned the handle and stepped out. As he reached the Outer Circle, he saw something that made him set his jaw. A slat-ternly-looking woman was walking unsteadily on the opposite side of the street. He recognized her as his miserable companion of the past four years, the half-witted drunkard who had shared the kitchen with him. She did not recognize him, and it mattered little even if Surefoot saw her. He had turned her out the previous day with instructions to go back to Wiltshire, where he had found her, and had given her enough money to keep her for a year.

He plodded on, looking back occasionally to see if he were followed. He dared not risk a bus. A taxi would be almost as dangerous. To drive a car in his present disguise would be to attract undesirable attention.

In the Finchley Road there was a block of buildings the ground floor of which was occupied by shops. Above these was a number of apartments occupied by good middle-class tenants. The corner of the block, however, had been reserved for offices, and this had a self-operated elevator.

Binny went into the narrow passage unchallenged, pressed the button, and had himself carried to the third floor. Almost opposite the lift, at an angle of the wall, was a door inscribed: "The New Theatrical Syndicate." He unlocked the door and went in. The office consisted of one medium-sized room and a small cloakroom. It was furnished plainly and had the appearance of being very rarely used. Except for a desk and a table there was no evidence of its business character.

He shot a little bolt in the door, took off the long coat he wore, and sat down in the comfortable chair. In one of the drawers there was a small electric kettle, which he filled in the wash-place. He brewed himself a cup of coffee, and this, with some biscuits he found in a tin box, in the second drawer, comprised his lunch.

The get-away was going to be simple. His real baggage was in the cloakroom at Liverpool Street. Everything was simple, and yet . . .

Binny could have written a book on the psychology of criminals. He was a cold-blooded, reasoning killer, who never made the stupid errors of other criminals. It was a great pity that he had made the appalling mistake of going back to find the key and had attracted the girl's attention. Otherwise, Leo Moran would have been dead and there would be no proof that the confession, which Binny had typed out so industriously, was not true in every detail.

He had planned it all so carefully: he had intended to drop the key just on the inside of the locked door and had put it in his pocket and forgotten it: a little slip that had messed up his artistic plan. Reason, which had determined his every action, told him to slip out of London quietly that night and trust to his native genius for safety. But that something which is part of the mental make-up of criminal minds clamoured for the spectacular. It would be a great stunt to leave London with one crushing exploit which would make him the talk of the world. In his imagination he could see the headlines in the newspapers. "SUREFOOT SMITH LEFT DEAD AND THE MURDERER ESCAPED!" "SUREFOOT SMITH, THE GREAT CATCHER OF MURDERERS, HIMSELF CAUGHT!" The fantastic possibilities took hold of him. His mind began to work not towards safety, but in the direction of pleasing sensationalism, and he did not realize that the charge of vanity which he so resented was being justified with every mental step he took towards vengeance.

CHAPTER XXVI

Dick Allenby and Mary were lunching at the Carlton, and they were talking about things which ordinarily would have absorbed her.

"You are not listening," he accused her, and she started.

"Wasn't I?" She was very penitent. "Darling, I was thinking of something else. Isn't that a terrible confession? I don't suppose any other girl ever listened to a proposal of marriage with her mind on a nasty old kitchen in an unpleasant little house."

He laughed.

"If you could bring that mind of yours from the drab realities to the idyllic possibilities, I should be a very happy man." And then, curiously: "You mean Hervey Lyne's house! What's worrying you?"

"The kitchen," she said promptly. "There was something there, Dick—I can't think what it was—something I missed, and it is worrying me. I have a dim recollection that the poor old man told me he was having the kitchen rebuilt. I remember him saying what a wonderful fellow Binny was, because he was superintending the operations and saving him a lot of money." She fingered her chin. "There was a dresser," she said thoughtfully. "Of course, that's gone. And a horrid little sink of brown earthenware, and——"

She stopped suddenly and stared at him, wide-eyed.

"The larder!" she gasped. "Of course, that's what it was! There was a larder and a door in the wall leading to it. What has happened to the larder?"

He shook his head helplessly.

"I haven't been terribly interested in larders," he began, but she arrested his flippancy.

"Don't you remember, Mr. Smith said, as we were leaving the house, that he was sure Binny had a hiding place somewhere? I am sure that's it—on the right-hand side as you go in."

Dick Allenby laughed.

"On the right-hand side as you go into the kitchen there is a solid brick wall," he said, but she shook her head.

"I am sure there is something behind it. I remember now, when I went into the courtyard to try the key, I noticed that there had been no change in the exterior. There must be a space there. Dick, providence is with us."

She was looking towards the entrance. Surefoot Smith was there, very disconsolate. He caught her eye and nodded. Obviously she was not the person he wanted to see, for he continued his scrutiny of the room. She caught his eye again and beckoned him. He came forward reluctantly.

"You haven't seen the deputy assistant commissioner, have you? I'm lunching with him—he is paying for it. He said half-past one." He looked at his watch. "It is nearly two. We've pinched Binny's wife, by the way; one of our men picked her up on the Outer Circle, but she's got nothing to say."

"I've found the hiding place!" Mary blurted the news, and Surefoot Smith became instantly alert.

"Binny's?" he asked quickly. "In the house, you mean?"

She told him breathlessly of her theory. He slapped his knee.

"You're right, of course—the vacuum pump. I wondered what he used it for. If there was a door—and it was an easy job to make a door on glazed brick—he could not have had handles, could he? The only way he could get it open would be by sticking the vacuum on the surface of the brick to give him a grip. I have got the pump at the Yard, and the commissioner can wait."

He went out of the room, and half an hour later Hervey Lyne's little house was surrounded. Surefoot came into the hall, pistol in hand, went quickly into the kitchen, and examined the white wall. There was no sign of a door. He fastened the vacuum to the smooth surface and pulled, but, to his chagrin, nothing happened. The strength of two detectives failed to move the door. He moved the position of the pump from time to time, and at the fifth attempt he was rewarded. The slightest pull drew a brick from the wall. It ran on a steel guide, and dropped over in front, leaving an oblong aperture which was hollow.

He put his hand inside and felt a steel handle, which he turned and pulled. The door swung open and he was in Binny's hiding place. The disordered heap of clothes on the floor, the shaving mirror thrown down on the bed, told their own tale. There was greater significance, however, in the saucer he found in the sink. It was still yellow with the annatto colouring which Binny had used.

Surefoot Smith looked at it for a long time, and then:

"I think there is going to be serious trouble," he said.

Surefoot Smith hurriedly turned over the clothes and articles which had been emptied from the suitcase, but he found nothing to give him the slightest clue to Binny's intentions. One thing was certain: he had been in his hiding place and had heard all that had happened that morning. Surefoot had the door shut and himself listened to conversation in the kitchen, and although he could not catch every word he was satisfied that Binny had heard enough.

The annatto in the saucer was a very slight and

possibly useless clue. It told him to look for a yellow-faced man, and this might or might not be a useful guide to the searchers.

The fugitive had left nothing else behind. Surefoot searched diligently, crawling over the floor with his eyes glued to the tiled flooring for some sign of crêpe hair. He expected this stage-mad murderer to have attempted some sort of theatrical disguise, but his search failed to reveal anything that left a hint as to what that disguise might be.

The only piece of incriminating evidence which Binny had left behind was the sealed magazine of an automatic pistol, and, since this could not have been overlooked, the detective surmised that the magazine had been left because the man was carrying as many as he conveniently could.

Another discovery which, at an earlier stage, would have been invaluable was a soiled white glove, obviously the fellow of that which Surefoot had found in Mr. Washington Wirth's changing room.

"You never know," said Surefoot as he handed over the glove to his subordinate. "Juries go mad sometimes, and a little thing like that might convince 'em—keep it."

The larder had evidently been used as a sleeping room. Although the bed was on the floor, and the apartment itself was bare, Binny had often found this a convenient retreat. Very little daylight came through the small window near the ceiling, and apparently he kept that closed most of the time; it was covered with a square of oilcloth.

Before he left, Surefoot tried the experiment of having the clothes packed in the suitcase. He found, as he had expected, that there was only sufficient to fill one. He was satisfied, too, that some of the clothes he had found had been recently changed by Binny, and the conclusion he reached was that one of the suitcases had contained the disguise which the murderer wore when he left the house.

He sent his men on missions of inquiry up and down the street, but nobody had seen Binny leave—he had chosen his hour well. Later he widened the circle of inquiry, but again was unsuccessful.

He found Mary Lane and her fiancé waiting patiently in the palm court of the Carlton, and reported his discoveries.

"If only I'd thought of it before!" she said ruefully.

Surefoot Smith's smile was not altogether unpleasant.

"Either you or I or all of us would have been dead," he said grimly. "That bird carries a young arsenal, and your bad memory probably saved us a whole lot of unpleasantness."

"Do you think he was there?"

He nodded.

"There's no doubt about it."

"He'll get away, then?" asked Dick.

Surefoot rubbed his chin irritably.

"I wonder if that would be a good thing or a bad thing?" he said. "He may try to leave to-day—all the ports are being watched, and every single passenger will be under inspection. The only person who can pass on and out to a ship leaving this coast to-night is a baby in arms—and we search even him!"

He drew his chair closer to the table and leaned across, lowering his voice.

"Young lady," he said, and he was very serious, "you know what rats do when they're in a corner—they bite! If this man can't get out of England by walking out or shooting himself out, he's coming back to the cause of all his trouble. I'm one, but you're another. Do you know where I should like to put you?"

She shook her head, for the moment incapable of speech. She was shocked, frightened a little, if she had confessed it. Binny was on her nerves, more than she would admit. She felt her heart beating a little faster, and when she spoke she was oddly breathless.

"Do you really think that?" And then, forcing a smile: "Where would you put me?"

"In Holloway Prison." He was not joking. "It's

the safest place in London for an unmarried woman who's living around in hotels and flats; and if I could find an excuse for putting you there for seven days, I would."

"You're not serious?" said Dick, troubled.

Surefoot nodded.

"I was never more serious in my life. He may get out of the country; I don't think it's possible that he will. If Miss Lane had not remembered the larder, I should not take the precautions I am taking to-day. The doors out of England are locked and barred—unless he's got an ocean-going motor boat somewhere on the East Coast, and I have an idea that he hasn't."

Then, abruptly:

"Where are you staying to-night?"

Mary shook her head.

"I don't know. I think at the hotel."

"You can't stay there." He was emphatic. "I know a place you could stay. It wouldn't have the conveniences of a hotel, but you'd have a decent bed and security." There was a new police station in the northwest of London, which had married quarters above it, and one of these was occupied by a woman whose husband, a detective sergeant, had gone to Canada to bring back a fugitive from justice.

"I know this woman; she's a decent sort, and

she'll give you a bed, if you wouldn't mind sleeping there."

She agreed very meekly. Indeed, she had a sense of relief that he had found such a simple solution.

Surefoot Smith had a queer sixth sense of danger. He had been concerned in many murder cases, had dealt with scores of desperate men who would not have hesitated to kill him if they had had the opportunity. He had known cunning men and a few clever criminals, but Binny was an unusual type. Here was a killer with no regard for human life. Murder to him was not a desperate expedient—it was part of a normal method.

There was a long conference at Scotland Yard, and new and urgent telegrams were sent to all parts of the country, insisting upon the dangerous character of the wanted man. Ordinarily the English police do not carry firearms, but in this case, as the messages warned a score of placid chief constables, it would be an act of suicide to accost the wanted man unless the police officer whose duty it was to arrest him was prepared to shoot.

Scotland Yard has a record of all projected sailings, and neither from Liverpool nor Greenock was there any kind of boat due to leave in the next thirty-six hours.

Binny's avenue of escape must be the Continent. Strong detachments of C. I. D. men were sent to reinforce the watchers at Harwich, Southampton, and the two Channel ports. And yet, when these preparations were completed, Surefoot Smith had a vague feeling of uneasiness and futility. Binny was in London, would be too clever a man even to think of leaving, unless he was ignorant that his hiding place had been discovered. There was no reason why he should not be. It was hardly likely that he had a confederate.

At five o'clock Surefoot made an exasperating discovery: he was strolling in Whitehall when he saw a newspaper placard: "WANTED MURDERER'S SECRET HIDING PLACE." He bought a paper and saw, conspicuously displayed on the front page, a long paragraph headed: "Secret Chamber in Hervey Lyne's House." Surefoot swore softly and read on:

> This afternoon Inspector Smith of Scotland Yard, accompanied by a number of detectives, made a further search of the house of Hervey Lyne—the victim of the Regent's Park Murder. The police remained on the premises for some time. It is understood that in the course of their investigations a little room, which they had previously overlooked, had been discovered and entered, and unmistakable evidence secured that this secret chamber had been used as a hiding place by the servant Binny for whom the police have been searching. . . .

Surefoot Smith read no further. It was a waste of time wondering who had given the information to the press. Possibly some young detective, who had been engaged in the search and who was anxious to pass on this sensational discovery. To bring home this indiscretion was a matter that could be left till later. In the meantime Binny would know if he were to read the newspapers.

Oddly enough, Binny did not see the paragraph, and had already made up his mind as to the course he would pursue.

At eight o'clock that night Surefoot called at Mary Lane's hotel and escorted her to the plain but very comfortable lodgings he had secured for her.

He had a talk with the inspector on duty, but asked for no guard. She was safe. Binny would be a bold man to show himself abroad, and he certainly would not walk into a police station.

At half-past nine that night Surefoot returned to Scotland Yard and read the reports which had come in. The boat train from Liverpool Street had been carefully combed. There was no sign of Binny or anybody who might have been Binny. Every passport had been examined before the train pulled out, and, as an act of precaution, the railway platform had been cleared of friends who had gathered to see off the passengers before the officer in charge had given the station master the "all right."

A similar course was being followed at Waterloo, where the police were watching and searching the trains for Havre. It was too early to hear from the sea ports.

Binny was an expert chauffeur. It was hardly likely that he would get out of London by train if he intended leaving London.

CHAPTER XXVII

THE detective left the Yard a few minutes after eleven, and, turning to his left, walked towards Blackfriars. To Surefoot Smith that long ribbon of pavement which runs without a break from Scotland Yard to Savoy Hill was a garden of thought. At headquarters somebody with a florid mind had christened it his "Boulevard of Cogitation." Summer or winter, rain or fine, Surefoot Smith found here the solution of all his problems. Men had been hanged, swindlers had been sent down to the shades, very commonplace happenings had assumed a sinister importance, and, by contrast, seemingly guilty men and women had had their innocence established in the course of Surefoot Smith's midnight recreation.

There were very few pedestrians at this hour of the night. The courting couples, for some strange reason, chose the better-lighted river side of the road. Cars flashed past occasionally. There was an irregular procession of street cars at long intervals, and once an occasional night hawk shuffled along the curb-side in search of a stray cigarette end.

Near one of the entrances to the Embankment

Gardens a saloon car was drawn up by the curb. Glancing inside, more from habit than curiosity, Surefoot saw the figure of a woman sitting, and continued his stroll.

He paced on, turning over the question of Binny in his mind. The greater problem was solved; the more dangerous and delicate business of effecting the man's arrest had yet to be accomplished. He was uneasy, which was not usual. Surefoot Smith was a great dreamer. He visualized the most fantastic possibilities, and because he allowed his thoughts the fullest and the widest range he was more successful than many of his fellows. For there is this about dreaming, that it throws the commonplace possibilities into sharp relief, and it is on the commonplace possibilities that most detectives rely.

He turned on his tracks at Savoy Hill and walked slowly back towards the Yard. By this time the reports would be coming in from the coast, though it was still a little too early for any but Southampton, where an extra vigilance was being exercised. A German-American liner, which was due at that port that night, was taking in passengers for Hamburg, and this fact had necessitated sending a second batch of watchers to the port.

He saw the car still standing by the side of the road. It was no great distance from the Lost Property Office, and it was likely that the lady had sent her chauffeur in search of something she had left behind her in a cab in the course of the day. As he drew near her, he saw that the woman was standing by the open door of the machine—a middle-aged lady, he gathered by her plumpness.

To his surprise she addressed him in a high-pitched voice.

"I wonder if you could fetch a policeman for me?"

A staggering request to make of one of the recognized heads of Scotland Yard.

"What's wrong?" asked Surefoot Smith.

She stepped aside from the door.

"My chauffeur," she said. "He has come back rather the worse for drink, and I can't get him out of the car."

A drunken chauffeur is an offense to all good policemen. Surefoot opened the door wider and peered in.

He saw nothing, heard nothing, felt nothing. His consciousness of life went out like a snuffed candle.

CHAPTER XXVIII

His head was aching terribly. He tried to move his hands and found movement restricted. He did not realize why for a long time.

The car was moving with great rapidity, far beyond the legalized speed limit. There were no lights. By the whir of the wheels he guessed he was on a newly made road. It was queer that this fact should have appeared so important to him. He could remember nothing, knew nothing, except that he was lying curled up on the floor of a motor car which was moving rapidly and smoothly. Then he stopped thinking again for a long time and was glad of the unconsciousness which obliterated this throbbing head of his.

The car was now bumping over an uneven surface. It was that which roused him to consciousness. He blinked up, tried to raise himself, felt gingerly along his wrists and recognized the shape of the handcuffs—his own; he always carried an unauthorized pair in his coat pocket. Unauthorized, because they were not of the regulation type—they were American handcuffs which were so much easier to put on—a tap on the wrist and the D swung round and was fast.

Somebody had handcuffed him. Somebody had tied his legs together with a silk scarf. He could feel it, but he could not reach the knot. And then he remembered the woman and the car and the drunken chauffeur who was not there.

The car was bumping painfully. It seemed to be passing over a ploughed field or, at best, a cart track. It was the latter he found when the car stopped.

A little while later the door was pulled open; he saw the outlines of the "woman" and knew exactly who "she" was.

There was a little cottage a few yards away; one of those monstrous little boxes of red brick and tiling that have disfigured the countryside since the war. His coat collar was gripped and he was jerked out into the road, falling on his knees.

"Get up, you——" hissed a voice, and what followed was not ladylike.

He was half-dragged and half-pushed towards the cottage; the door was flung open and he was thrust into a dark interior. It smelt of drying mortar and plaster and new wood. He guessed it was unfurnished. He waited a while. The door was locked on the inside and he was again urged forward into a room so completely dark that he knew the window was shuttered. He fell on the floor. It was amazing that he walked at all with his legs bound, as they were, with the silk scarf.

As he lay there, a vat spluttered, there was a tinkle of an oil lamp chimney being taken off, and presently the room was illuminated by the soft glow of a kerosene lamp. The only articles of furniture in the room were two sofas, a chair and a kitchen table. Wooden shutters covered the window, as he had suspected. There were neither hangings nor curtains of any description, and the table was innocent of cloth.

His captor pulled the chair forward, sat down, his hands on his knees, and surveyed him.

Surefoot would never have recognized this yellow-faced old woman with a gray wig and a long fur coat. The wig was now a little askew—it gave Binny a comical but a terrible appearance. He was sensitive to ridicule, took off the wig and hat with one movement, and appeared even more grotesque with his bald head and his yellow face.

"Got you!" said Binny, huskily.

He was grinning, but there was no merriment in that smile.

"Mr. Surefoot Smith is not so sure on his feet after all."

The jest seemed to amuse him, and then, as though conscious of the attitude which the situation demanded, he assumed that affected, mincing tone which had belonged to Mr. Washington Wirth.

"I built this little place a couple of years ago. I thought it might be useful, but I haven't been here for a long time. I am leaving the country. Perhaps you would like to buy it, Mr. Smith? It's an excellent retreat for a professional gentleman who wishes to be quiet, and you are going to be very quiet!"

From his pocket he took an automatic pistol and laid it on the table beside him, and, stooping down, he lifted Surefoot and sat him in a corner of the room. Bending down, he unfastened the sagging silk scarf about his ankles and jerked off the detective's shoes, throwing them into another corner of the room. He hesitated a second, then loosened Surefoot's collar.

"You are not hurt, my dear Mr. Smith," he remarked. "A rubber truncheon applied to the back of the neck does not kill. It is, I admit, very uncomfortable. There was once a copper in Cincinnati who tried that treatment on me. It was two months before I was well enough to shoot him. You didn't know of my little retreat?"

Surefoot's mouth was dry, his head was whizzing, but he was entirely without fear, though he realized his case was a desperate one.

"Oh yes, I did, Binny," he said. "This place is about a hundred yards from the Bath Road near Taplow. You bought the ground four years ago, and paid a hundred and fifty pounds for it."

For a second Binny was thrown off his balance.

"This house was searched last week by my police officers, and is now under the observation of the Buckinghamshire police. You have got another cottage of a similar character in Wiltshire."

"Oh, indeed?"

Binny was completely taken aback. He was rattled too. Surefoot saw this and pushed home his advantage.

"What's the good of being a fool? We have got no evidence against you for murder. The only evidence is that you have forged Hervey Lyne's checks. The worst that can happen to you is a seven stretch."

Again he had put his finger upon the one great doubt which obsessed the man.

"You may get an extra year for this," said Surefoot, "but what's a year? Get me some water. There's a kitchen just behind this room. Let the tap run: the water was rusty when I was here last week. There's a tin cup on the dresser."

The instinct to obey is stronger than the instinct to command. Binny went out and returned with the tin cup and put it to the detective's lips.

"Now take these handcuffs off and we'll have a little talk. Why didn't you bring Mike Hennessey here instead of——" He realized his colossal error as soon as the words were spoken.

Binny stepped back with a snarl.

"Don't want me for murder, eh? You double-crossing busy! I'll show you what I want you for."

Binny's hand moved towards the gun on the table. He took up the pistol and examined it carefully.

"I have always wanted to tell you where you get off, Smith," he began.

"Your wish has come true," said Surefoot coolly. "But you'd better work fast."

"I'll work fast enough," said the other grimly.

He slipped the gun into his pocket, picked up the scarf, and retied his prisoner's ankles.

He then took off his fur coat and relieved himself of his woman's garments. From a theatre trunk he retrieved an old suit, which he put on.

Surefoot Smith watched him interestedly.

"I gather you have some hard work to do?" he said.

"Pretty hard," said the other, and added significantly: "The ground here is fairly soft. You don't get down to clay till you have dug six feet."

If he expected to terrify his captive he was disappointed.

"Why not let me do it?" said Smith. "You are fat and out of condition. Digging my own grave is a hobby of mine."

For a second Binny seemed to be considering this suggestion.

"No, I'll do it," he said, "fat or not fat."

"Why bother?" Surefoot's voice was almost airy. "As soon as I am missing they will search here and in Wiltshire. I gather your object is to leave no trace. You are not sure now whether we could convict you for murder, are you? If you kill a police officer you are certain to be hanged. Every man in Scotland Yard will turn out to find evidence against you. People who were sleeping in their beds will swear that they saw you cosh me."

He libelled the best police force in the world without shame.

"You might get away with Hennessey," Surefoot went on, "and old Lyne and Tickler, but you could not get away with me. They will come along and search this ground, which, if I remember rightly, is grass-grown, and unless you do a little bit of artistic turfing, they will find me and that will be the finish of you."

Binny paused at the door and turned with an ugly grin on his face.

"I used to know a copper who talked like you, but he talked himself into hell, see?"

He went out and closed the door behind him.

Surefoot Smith sat thinking very hard. He made an effort to break the single link that bound the two cuffs together. It was certainly a painful process, probably impossible. By drawing up his legs and separating them at the knees, he could reach the trebly-knotted silk scarf. It was difficult, but he succeeded in loosening one knot, and was at work on the second when he heard the man returning along the bare boards of the passage.

Binny was finding his task more difficult than he had anticipated. His face was wet with perspiration. He groped in the trunk, took out a bottle of whisky and, removing the patent top, took a long drink.

"Is it courage or strength you're looking for?" asked Surefoot.

"You'll see," growled the other, glaring down at the helpless man malignantly.

The butts of two automatics stuck out of his trousers pockets. Surefoot eyed them longingly.

Binny was halfway to the door when a thought struck him, and he turned back and examined the knots of the scarf.

"Oh, you've undone one, have you? We'll see about that."

Again he searched the trunk and found a length of cord. He slipped it round the link of the handcuffs and knotted the cord firmly behind the detective's neck, so that his hands were drawn up almost to his chin.

"You look funny—almost as if you were playing!" remarked Binny. "I shan't keep you long."

He went out of the room on this promise.

Sprawling there helplessly, Surefoot heard the hoot of cars as they passed. He was, he knew, about two hundred yards from the main road, but it was a road along which, day and night, traffic was continually passing.

The possibility that the Buckinghamshire police would search this little cottage was very remote, unless somebody at Scotland Yard had a brain-wave that this was the most likely place to which the prisoner would be taken. But Scotland Yard might not even miss him. He was an erratic man; when he was engaged in an important case he would absent himself from headquarters for days together, leaving his chiefs fuming. The search would not begin until Binny was well out of the country.

He watched the smoky oil lamp burning; the flame had been turned on too high and one side of the glass chimney was smoked.

Binny was out for a get-away; he would leave no traces. Even the murder would not be committed in the house.

Half an hour, an hour passed, and he heard the heavy feet of the man coming for him, and knew that the hour was at hand.

CHAPTER XXIX

SCOTLAND YARD had missed Surefoot Smith in the sense that the negative reports which had been taken to his room had not been read or attended to. The fact that they were negative would have justified the officer on duty accepting the situation, but for the peculiar conscientiousness of a young police officer who reported to the station at Cannon Row, which is part of Scotland Yard, that a blue saloon car, driven by a woman, had disregarded his stop signal at the junction of Westminster Bridge and the Embankment, and had driven on the wrong side of the road. He had called on it to stop, and, when that failed, had taken its number.

Ordinarily the question of a technical offense of this character would have been left over till the morning, but whilst he was making his statement a Member of Parliament came into the station to report the loss of a blue saloon car, which had been taken from the front of his club in Pall Mall. It had been standing on a rank, against all traffic rules, and he had actually been a witness of the theft.

"It was a man dressed as a woman," was his startling conclusion.

"What makes you think that, sir?" asked the inspector in charge.

"As he got in, the top of the car, which has a very low body, knocked his hat off. It was a bald-headed man with a yellow face like somebody suffering from jaundice."

The inspector sat bolt upright. All England was looking for a bald-headed man with a jaundiced face, and in a few moments the wires were humming.

Again it was a traffic policeman who supplied information, and again it was Binny's anxiety to make a quick run out of London that had betrayed him. He had been held up near Heston, where a tram-line crosses the main arterial road. He had narrowly escaped collision with the tram and the car had skidded. The policeman had walked across the road to examine the license of the driver, whose engine had stopped. The policeman distinctly saw a stout woman driver, but before he could ask a question the engine had been restarted and the car had moved on. This must have happened in the second period of Surefoot's unconsciousness.

It was not until an hour and a half after the inquiry had been sent out that the traffic policeman's report was received. By this time a "hurry up" call for Surefoot had failed to locate him. Moreover, he had left on his table at Scotland Yard a half finished sheet of notes.

Now Surefoot never in any circumstances left his notes behind him; and another significant fact was that he had not handed the key of his room to the officer at the door, a practice which he invariably followed, however hurried might be his departure.

His habit of taking a walk was common knowledge. He had been seen walking towards Savoy Hill. The policeman on duty at the foot of the hill had also seen him turn back. Then somebody remembered the blue motor car that had been standing by the side of the road.

By the time these inquiries had been completed, every detective in Scotland Yard had been assembled on the instructions of the hastily summoned chief.

"He may be heading for the coast. What is more likely is that he's on his way to one of those houses of his," said the chief constable. "Get the Buckinghamshire and Salisbury police on the phone, and, to make absolutely sure, send squad cars right away to both places."

One of the first people who had been interrogated was Dick Allenby. It was known that Surefoot was a friend of his, and Surefoot was an inveterate gossiper who loved nothing better than to sit up till three in the morning with a friendly and sympathetic audience. Dick Allenby's arrival at the Yard coincided with the departure of the first squad car for Salisbury.

"We may be chasing moonbeams," said the chief constable; "very likely old Surefoot will turn up in about a quarter of an hour, but I am taking no unnecessary risks."

"But he would never get bluffed," said Dick scornfully.

The chief shook his head.

"I don't know. This fellow has had a pretty hectic experience in America, and it will not be the first person he has taken for a ride in this country."

Of one thing he was sure—that the threat of a revolver would not have induced Surefoot to get into that car.

He looked at his watch; it was half-past one, and he shook his head.

"I wish the night were over," he said.

From that remark Dick sensed all that the other feared.

Surefoot Smith had less than half a minute to do his thinking and to decide on one of the dozen plans—most of them impracticable—that were spinning in his mind.

The door opened slowly and Binny came in. He wiped his forehead on a big handkerchief he took out of his pocket, and sat down.

"You will come a little walk with me, my friend," he said pleasantly.

He took the bottle from the table, swallowed a

generous drink, and wiped his mouth. Stooping, he untied the scarf that bound Surefoot's ankles and jerked him to his feet.

Surefoot Smith rose unsteadily. His head was swimming, but the terrific nature of the moment brought about his instant recovery. Binny was standing by the door, fingering his gun. He had fixed to the end of the barrel an egg-shaped object, the like of which Surefoot had never seen before, and he found himself wondering how Dick Allenby, who was interested in silencers and who had asserted so often that a silencer could not be used on an automatic, because of the back fire, would reconcile this freakish thing with his theories.

Surefoot walked to the table and stood, resting his manacled hands on its deal surface.

"Saying a prayer or something?" mocked Binny.

"You don't want anybody to know I have been here, do you? You don't want to leave any trace, and that's why you don't kill me in this room?"

"That's the idea," said the other cheerfully.

"If you had a few hundred people rushing in this direction and asking questions, that would spoil your plan, wouldn't it?"

Binny's eyes narrowed.

"What's the idea?" he demanded.

He took one step towards his prisoner, when Surefoot lifted the lamp and flung it into the open hamper. There was a crash as the glass reservoir broke, a flicker of light, and then a huge flame shot up towards the ceiling.

Binny stood, paralyzed to inaction, and in the next moment Surefoot had flung himself upon the man. He drove straight at Binny's face with his clenched hands. The man ducked and missed him. Something exploded in the detective's face; he felt the sting of the powder and heard an expelled cartridge "ting" against the wall.

He struck again, striving to bring the steel handcuffs to the man's head. Binny twisted aside, but did not wholly escape the impact of the shock. The gun fell from his hand on to the floor.

The room was now a mass of flames; the fire had licked through the thin plaster of the wall and the laths were burning like paper. The atmosphere was thick with acrid smoke, the heat already intolerable.

Again Surefoot struck and again Binny dodged. Surefoot had kicked the pistol out of reach—kicked it into the mass of flames that were spurting from the bottom of the canvas-covered trunk. The door was open and Binny darted out of the room, trying to close it after him, but Smith's shoulders were in the way. Jerking the door wider, he stumbled into the passage and hurled himself at the murderer.

The only hope was to keep at close quarters. Binny had another pistol, had it half out of his pocket, when Surefoot pinned him against the hot wall, and, bracing his feet, exerted all his strength to crush him there. In this position it was impossible to hit the man. In the half-light he saw Binny reaching out towards the front door and edged him nearer to facilitate his task. As the door was flung open and the air came rushing in, the hum of the fire became a roar; flames were flung out like red and yellow banners whipped by the wind.

Binny was trying to pull himself clear of the hands that held him by the singlet; striving desperately to pull out his second pistol. His breath was coming in shrill whistles; he was frightened, had lost all his old reserve of courage. He wriggled desperately to escape the pressure of the heavy figure that was jammed against him, and at last, by a superhuman effort, he succeeded, and darted through the door, Surefoot behind him. His gun was out now and he fired. The detective hurled himself on his man and brought him down. He was up in a second and was running towards the back of the house.

The flames were coming from the roof. The countryside for a hundred yards was almost as light as day. Surefoot, handcuffed as he was, flew in pursuit; and then suddenly Binny turned, and this time his aim was deliberate. Surefoot Smith knew that there was no hope now. The man who covered him was a dead shot, and was within half a dozen paces of him.

In desperation he sprang forward. His feet touched air, and he was falling, falling . . .

He heard the shot, wondered dimly if this was death, and was brought to the realization that he was still alive by the impact of his body at the bottom of the hole into which he had fallen. He realized at once what had happened: Binny had been busy all that night preparing this hiding place for his crime, but had missed falling into the hole.

He struggled to his feet, bruised and aching, heard a second shot and looked up. There was a third and a fourth. An authoritative voice was challenging somebody. Then he heard his own name called, and shouted. A man's face loomed over the edge of the pit. It was his own sergeant. They brought him up to the top.

"He won't get away," said the detective to whom Surefoot addressed a gasping enquiry.

"Which way did he go, and where is his car?"

He was weary, aching from head to foot, bruised and scratched, but for the moment he had no thought of comfort.

"Feel in my hip pocket; I think he left the key of these handcuffs."

They unlocked the irons and took them off, and he rubbed his bruised wrists.

"Have you found his car?"

Binny's saloon had not been located. The last time Surefoot had seen it, it was at the door of the cottage, but evidently, during one of his absences, the man had taken it to a hiding place. There was a small garage attached to the cottage—a tiny shed—but this was unoccupied.

By the light of the burning house they picked up the tracks. They crossed the grass land to the left of the cottage and must have passed over the very place where Binny had dug the grave. Thereafter they were difficult to trace, but obviously they went straight across the field in the same direction as the man had taken. A quarter of an hour later they picked up unmistakable evidence that the car had been left standing near a small secondary road. The gate was wide open and the tracks of the machine were visible on the soft, wet earth. He had not made for the main road again, but had turned up the road to Cookham, where traffic would be practically non-existent at this hour of the night and the chances of observation nil.

The solitary police officer on duty at Cookham had seen the car pass, but had not observed the driver. He had turned on to the toll bridge, but at this hour of the night the toll gate is left open. The Bourne End police had seen several cars without taking particular notice of them. He could have taken the Oxford Road across the railway crossing, or he could have followed the river to Marlow.

Surefoot Smith rejected the suggestion that he should go home and rest, leaving the chase to the

Flying Squad and the Buckinghamshire police; he rejected it violently and with oaths.

"This fellow can't go far, dressed as he is," he said, "in a singlet and trousers—I pulled most of his shirt off. He is going to hold up somebody, or burgle a house and get a new outfit. You realize what this man is, don't you? He is trained in the gang methods. He will not stop at murder—you are not dealing with an ordinary English criminal."

They were not kept long waiting for proof of this. Deciding upon the Marlow Road as being more likely to offer opportunities for this desperado, they came upon a policeman pushing a bicycle. It was raining heavily, and his helmet and cape were dripping wet.

"A blue car passed here five minutes ago," he said.

The police car sped on. Just outside of Marlow they found the machine they were seeking; it was empty.

At three o'clock in the morning a car passing along the Oxford Road was stopped by a policeman, who stood in the middle of the roadway with outstretched arms. Driving the car was a well to do farmer from Oxford. He was inclined to be truculent at this stop.

"I am sorry to bother you," said the police officer, "but we are searching for an escaped murderer, and I want you to give me a lift to the other side of High Wycombe."

The farmer, rather intrigued, was not at all displeased, probably a little thrilled, to find himself a participant in a man hunt, and the policeman got into the uncomfortable rear seat of the car. It sped on through the Wycombes.

"I will tell you where to drop me," said the officer.

On the other side of High Wycombe there is a fork road which leads to Princess Risborough.

"Turn here," said the officer.

The driver expostulated—he had to get back to Oxford.

"Turn here," said the police officer, and something cold touched the nape of the farmer's neck.

CHAPTER XXX

"Do as you're told." The policeman's voice was peremptory. The gun in his grimy hand was eloquent. The farmer almost jumped out of his seat with astonishment. He was not wanting in courage, but he was unarmed.

"What's your game?" he asked. He was still unsuspicious that the man behind him was anything but a policeman. "You're not allowed to do that sort of thing."

"Get it out of your nut that I'm a copper," said Binny. "The man whose clothes I'm wearing is lying in a ditch with a break in his bean. Drive where I tell you and save a lot of argument."

The driver turned the car in the direction indicated. They went along a new road, a portion of which was under construction. There were red lamps and a watchman's fire. Dimly the farmer realized that the man behind him was the wanted murderer, and the realization chilled him.

They were in a country which even at high noon is a little deserted. It was a silent desert now. All the time Binny was watching left and right for a suitable place for his purpose. Presently they passed by the side of the road a wooden building that had the appearance of a barn, and he ordered the driver to stop and turn back. There was an open gate by the side of the barn, and through this they drove.

"Stop here," said Binny. He pushed open the door of the saloon. "Now get down."

He took the little electric lantern which had been part of the unfortunate policeman's equipment and flashed it onto the door of the barn. It was unsecured by lock or hasp. He pulled open the door with one hand, covering his prisoner with the other.

"Go inside," he said, and followed.

Half an hour later he came out again, wearing the farmer's tweed suit and his high-collared waterproof jacket. He listened for a second at the door before closing it, got into the limousine, and backed onto the road. There was still a considerable danger of his being stopped. A solitary man driving a car would be suspect, no matter whose clothes he was wearing, and the present solution to his difficulty was merely a temporary measure.

If he could find one of those night trucks that run between London and the provinces it would serve him better. These express lorries carried two and often three men. He had to trust to luck.

Detection was certain if he took a direction which led him away from London. In the few hours that remained before the dawn he must work his way back to London. He had three bolt-holes; had the police found them all?

He drove through Aylesbury and worked right. He had an extraordinary knowledge of topography, and was aiming to reach the Great North Road and approach London from that direction.

Passing through a village, a policeman came out of the shadows and held up his hand. For a second Binny hesitated; his first impulse was to drive on, but he was none too certain of the immediate locality, and the chances were that if he did not stop now he would find a "barrage" a few miles farther on.

Binny had studied the police situation very carefully. He knew that the police could close London in a ring by the establishment of these barrage posts, and that he would be liable at any moment to come upon a place where a lorry was drawn up across the road. He knew too of the canvas belts, heavily spiked, which are thrown across the roadway, with disastrous consequences to the non-stop motorist.

He took his foot off the accelerator and brought his car to a standstill

"Let me see your driving license," said the police officer.

Binny stiffened. He had relieved his victim of all

his portable goods, but a driving license was not amongst them. Motorists have a trick of carrying this important document in the pocket attached to the door. If it were not there . . .

He slipped his gun out of his pocket and laid it on the seat by his side before he lifted up the flap of the pocket and began a search. His heart jumped as his fingers touched the familiar shape of the license. He handed it out and the policeman examined it by the light of his lantern.

"Is this Dornby or Domby?" asked the officer.

"Dornby," said Binny promptly.

It was as likely to be that as the other. The officer handed back the license without a word.

"You haven't seen anybody driving a blue saloon, have you—a man dressed in shirt and trousers?"

Binny chuckled.

"Well, I wouldn't be able to tell the colour of the saloon, and I certainly wouldn't see what the driver was wearing. Why? Do you want somebody?"

"There's been a murder committed," said the policeman vaguely. "We only had a vague idea as to why the 'arrest and detain' notice should have been issued. Good-night, Mr. Dornby."

Binny drove on. The policeman had not looked into that yellow face, but the next policeman might. They were pretty slick at Scotland Yard, he decided, and wondered how these isolated police posts should have been notified.

He looked at the license. John Henry Dornby was the name, of Wellfield Farm. He memorized this, put the license in his pocket and went on.

He had now reached a point where he could avoid villages, for he would soon be striking the North Road, where more efficient barrages would be established, especially when he reached the Metropolitan Police area.

He came at last to the long, winding road that runs from London through Doncaster to the north. Left or right? That was the problem.

He debouched onto the highway through a narrow lane with high banks. It was near a turn of the road. He heard the whirr of a motor car, saw the glow of headlamps, and turned sharply to the left.

The car that came round the corner was hugging the left of the road. The driver saw Binny's machine almost too late to avoid a collision. He swerved to the right, the car skidded on the slippery road, turned completely round and, striking a telegraph post with one of its wheels, hung drunkenly over the side of the ditch.

Binny pulled up to avoid a second collision, for the wrecked machine was now immediately in front of him, and only by jamming on his brakes did he bring his own car to a standstill a few inches from the other. He heard the chauffeur shout, the door was jerked open, and a woman scrambled out into the glare of the headlamps.

Binny stared, hardly able to believe his eyes. The woman standing in the downpour was Mary Lane!

CHAPTER XXXI

SECURITY can be very irksome, especially when it is wedded to a lumpy bed in an ill-ventilated room. The sergeant's wife had given her the second best bedroom, which was, by most standards, a comfortable apartment. Mary felt desperately tired when she put out the light, but the moment her head touched the pillow all her weariness and desire for sleep had left her. She lay for half an hour, counting sheep, making up shopping lists, weaving stories, but grew wider and wider awake. At the end of that time she got up, turned on the light, and slipped into her dressing gown.

She thought the mere act of rising would make her sleepy, but she had been mistaken. She was seized with a longing for her own comfortable quarters at the hotel, and began to dress. She could easily make an excuse to the sergeant's wife, who had gone out for the evening and would not be back till after midnight. There was no telephone in the quarters, but Surefoot Smith had made her free of the station, and she knew she had only to go downstairs and see the night inspector and he would put her in touch with the detective.

She felt horribly ungrateful, but, so far as she had been concerned, she had come to this safe retreat without any enthusiasm. The danger from Binny was probably exaggerated—Surefoot himself had told her that the man could have no further interest in her now that the hue and cry was out.

Scribbling a note to her hostess—a note which contained more lame excuses for her eccentricity than were necessary—she put on her coat and went down to the charge room.

The inspector to whom she had been introduced had gone out, visiting the patrols. Evidently he had not impressed upon the sergeant in charge the necessity for keeping a watchful eye upon the visitor, and he received her explanation for her return to the hotel with polite interest, until she mentioned the name of Surefoot Smith. Then he became very attentive.

"He's not at the Yard, miss. As a matter of fact, there's been some trouble there. We've had a special warning to look out for him."

She opened her eyes in astonishment.

"Look out for him?" And then, quickly: "Has he disappeared?"

The sergeant did not forget that reticence is the first duty of a constable, and became evasive.

"Is it something to do with Binny?" she insisted.

"Well, yes." He hesitated before he became more communicative. "He's the man wanted for the murder of the old man in Regent's Park. Yes, they've got an idea at the Yard that Binny's got him away somewhere. Rather a queer idea that a murderer can get away an inspector of the C.I.D., but there you are!"

She sensed, without realizing, the eternal if gentle rivalry between the uniformed and the ununiformed branches of the Metropolitan Police.

"How could an inspector be lured away? It sounds silly, doesn't it? Personally, I believe it's all bunk, but there you are! We're on the lookout for both of them."

She asked him to get her a cab, and again he was reluctant. Sergeants in charge of station houses have no time to find cabs for visitors; but she was evidently a friend of Surefoot Smith's and he stretched a point in her favour, telephoned to a cab rank, and five minutes later she was driving through the rain to Scotland Yard.

She left just as the squad cars were starting out in search of Surefoot, and she interviewed the chief inspector. He offered her very little information and a great deal of fatherly advice about going to bed. He evidently knew nothing whatever of Surefoot's plan to protect her, and was a little embarrassed when she asked if she might stay at Scotland Yard until some news was received.

"I shouldn't worry if I were you, Miss Lane," he said. "We've got police barrages on all the roads for thirty miles round London, and I am very certain that Surefoot will turn up. He's an erratic sort of individual, and I wouldn't be surprised to see him walk in at any moment."

Nevertheless, she was determined to stay, and he had her taken to Surefoot's own room.

It was a quiet room, and now that the first excitement of the night was over, she realized how tired she was and how foolish she had been to leave even an uncomfortable bed.

She sat at the table, resting her head on one palm, found herself nodding, and, after a while, passing into that uneasy stage of semi-consciousness which is nearly sleep.

She woke with a jump as the chief inspector came in.

"Young lady, you go home," he said. "We've found Surefoot; so far as I can make out, he's not very badly hurt."

He told her briefly what had happened.

"Binny has escaped. Surefoot's theory is that he's breaking north. Have you ever noticed that a fugitive from justice invariably turns north? It's a fact—at least, nearly a fact. Now you go home, Miss Lane, and I'll send an officer round to your hotel in the morning with the latest news."

"Is he coming back to London?" she asked. "Mr. Smith, I mean?"

The chief smiled.

"If he had half the intelligence he's supposed to have, he'd get himself admitted to a nursing home. No. We've formed a sort of headquarters barrage this side of Welwyn. Chief Inspector Roose is in charge, and Surefoot is going across for a consultation. He's all right—your friend Mr. Allenby is with him."

He had a cab called and she drove to her hotel. She must have been half-asleep for two hours, she saw as she passed Big Ben and heard two o'clock strike. She was now wider awake than she had been at any period of the night.

The hall porter who admitted her was searching for her letters when she stopped him.

"Is there a place where I can hire a car?" she asked.

He looked at her in astonishment.

"Yes, miss. Do you want one to-night?"

She hesitated. The chief had said that Dick and Surefoot were at Welwyn, but he had not said where. At first she supposed that they had taken up their quarters at the local police station—she was rather hazy as to what a barrage meant. But there would be policemen on the road, stopping cars, and they would direct her to where the two men could be found.

Why she should go at all was not quite clear even to herself. It was a desire to be "in it," to be close to the big events which touched her own life so closely, to see with her own eyes the development of the story in which she had been a character. She could find plenty of excuses, none that she could have stated convincingly.

"Yes, get me a car. Tell them to come round as soon as they can."

He gave her the key of her room and she went upstairs, and presently the porter came up after her, bringing some coffee he had made, for by night he was not only custodian but cook.

Leo Moran had been removed to his own flat, he told her, but mainly he talked, with a certain amount of pride, about the reporters who had been "coming and going" since the discovery of the gassed banker.

She had hardly finished her coffee before the car came, and, dressing herself a little more warmly, she went down and gave the driver instructions.

As the car drew out of the suburbs into the open country, Binny and his flight assumed a new significance. She was not sorry for him. If she was a little frightened, it was not of the man, but at the thought of the vast machinery that her brain had put into motion. The moment she had heard of that scrawled note on the back of the check she had solved the mystery of Binny's defalcations, and when she had heard that all the forgeries were dated the seventeenth of the month—the day that the old man invariably paid his tradesmen's bills—she was sure.

And now, because she had remembered the shape and appearance of the key of a kitchen door, because she had added checks to key, eighteen thousand London policemen were looking for this bald-headed man. That was the frightening thing; not Binny and the menace of him, but the spectacle of these great winding wheels moving to crush a malefactor.

To Mary Lane, Binny was hardly as much an individual as a force. She thought the car was speeding a little dangerously on the wet road. Once she distinctly felt a skid, and gripped the arm rest tightly.

They could not have been more than a few miles from Welwyn when, rounding a turn, she saw a car come into the road ahead, and went cold, for she realized that, at the speed they were travelling, it was almost impossible to avoid it. Her car swerved and turned giddily; she felt a crash, and was thrown violently to her knees as the machine canted over.

She reached up at the door, and by sheer physical strength flung it open and scrambled out onto the wet road. The chauffeur was already standing by the front fender, staring at the car stupidly.

"I'm very sorry, miss," he said huskily. "I'll have to telephone for another car from town. Perhaps this gentleman will take you into Welwyn."

The second car, in avoiding which the accident had occurred, was behind them. Mary walked towards it as the driver got down from his seat. His coat collar was turned up, and she could not see his face.

"Had an accident?" he asked gruffly.

The chauffeur came forward.

"Will you drive us into Welwyn?" he asked. "I've smashed my near front wheel."

"You'd better wait with the car. I'll drive the lady; it's only a couple of miles ahead," said the other. "Go on, miss, jump in; I'll drop you in the town and send back a breakdown gang for the car."

This arrangement apparently suited the chauffeur, and Mary followed the motorist, and, when he opened the door of his car, entered without any misgivings. He walked round the back of the machine, got in by the other door and sat by her side. She could not see his face; his collar was still turned up. As he started the engine and moved on she thought she heard him laugh, and wondered what there was amusing in the situation.

"It's very good of you to take me," she said. "I'm afraid the accident was our fault."

He did not reply for a moment, but at last:

"Accidents will happen," he said sententiously.

They went two or three hundred yards along the road, and then suddenly the car turned left. She knew roughly the position of Welwyn, knew enough at any rate to realize that they were going away from the town.

"Haven't you made a mistake?" she asked.

"No." His reply was short and gruff, but it aroused in her no more than a sense of resentment.

From the second road they turned into a third, a narrow lane which ran roughly parallel with the main road. It skirted some big estate; high trees banked up one side of the lane, and a wire fence cut the estate from the road. The car slowed, and as they came abreast of a white gate, stopped. The driver turned the machine so that the headlamps searched the gate and revealed its flimsy character. Without hesitation, he sent the car jerking forward, crashing one of the lamps and sending the gate into splinters.

Beyond was a fairly smooth gravel road, and up this the car sped.

"Where are we going?"

A cold chill was at the girl's heart; an understanding of her danger set her trembling from head to foot.

Binny did not reply till they had gone a hundred yards. He found an opening between the trees on the right, set the car in that direction, and jolted on for another fifty yards. Then he stopped the machine.

"What is the meaning of this?" she asked.

"You're a very nice young lady, a very sweet

young lady. Charmed to meet you again in such romantic circumstances."

As she heard that mincing, affected voice she almost swooned. Binny! The horror of her discovery came to her with full force, as he went on:

"Friend of Mr. Allenby's—fiancée, aren't you, young lady? And a friend of my dear friend, Surefoot Smith."

She reached out for the door handle and tried to rise, but he threw her back.

"I've had several ideas about you. The first was that nobody would stop me if they saw me driving with a lady. Then it struck me that I was being optimistic. The second thought that occurred to me, my dear, was that you might be of great assistance to me. And the third thought, my sweet young thing, was that, if the worst came to the worst—they can only hang you once, you know, whatever you do. Not that they will hang me," he went on quickly. "I am too clever for them. Now we'll get out and see where we are."

He leaned over her, pushed open the door, and, catching her by the arm, guided her to the ground.

Just before she had left the hotel, the porter had handed her a thick bundle of letters. She had advertised for a maid and had given the hotel as her address; these were some of the replies. She had thrust them into her pocket, and as she stepped from the car she remembered them. She drew one from her pocket and dropped it on the ground.

Binny had retained the lantern he had taken from the policeman, and with the aid of this they found their way through the plantation.

"You and I will find another car."

He chatted pleasantly, and even in her terror she could find time to wonder how he could return to the character of Washington Wirth. It was grotesque, unbelievable, like a bad dream.

"I am a man of infinite resource," he went on, never releasing his grip of her arm. "For hundreds of years they will talk about Binny, just as to-day they talk about Jack Sheppard. And the wonderful thing about it is that I shall end my life quietly, as a respectable member of society. Possibly I shall be a town councillor or a mayor in a colonial town—a pleasing prospect and a part that I could act!"

It was at this point she dropped her third letter. She must husband her trail; the supply of letters was not inexhaustible. She dropped her fourth as they started to cross the corner of a field.

All the time he kept up his incessant babble.

"You need have no qualms, my dear young lady. No harm will come to you—for the moment. Whilst you are alive, I am alive! You are a hostage—that is the word, isn't it?"

She made no reply. The first feeling of panic had worn off. She could only speculate upon what would happen at the last, when this desperate man was in a corner and she was at his mercy.

Before them loomed against the night sky the outlines of a big house. They came to a lawn surrounded by an iron fence, and, walking parallel with this, they reached an open gateway and a paved yard.

Once or twice there had been a lull in his monologue. He had stopped to listen. It was a very still night; the sound of distant rumbling trains, the whine of motor cars passing along the highway came to them distinctly. He was apparently satisfied, for he made no comment. Now, as they passed into a tiled yard, he stopped again and listened, turning his head backwards. As he did so he saw the flash of a lamp—only for the fraction of a second, and then it disappeared. It seemed to come from the plantation they had left. He had left his lights burning—was that it? He moved left and right a few paces, and did not see the light again.

The possibility that there were gamekeepers in the wood now occurred to him. It was obviously a covert of some kind; the lower part of the fence was made of wire netting.

He never once released his hold of the girl. She felt the tenseness of the moment and held her breath. Then, without a word, he guided her into the yard, and now she observed that he used his lamp with greater caution. There were stables here;

two of the half doors were wide open and hung on broken hinges. There was no need to make any further investigation; the house to which the stables were attached was unoccupied.

They came to what was evidently a kitchen door and found a small, weather-stained notice.

"Keys at Messrs. Thurlow, Welwyn."

There was a long casement window at the back of the house. Binny pushed the barrel of his pistol through two panes, groped for the catch, and, finding it, pulled it open.

"Get in——" he began, and at that moment he was caught in a circle of blinding light.

From somewhere in the yard a powerful lamp was turned on him, and a voice he hated said:

"Don't move, Binny!"

It was Surefoot Smith!

For a second he stood, paralyzed, his arm still clasping the girl's. Suddenly he jerked her before him, his arm round her waist.

"If you come anywhere near me I'll shoot," he said, and she felt the cold barrel of a gun glide along her neck.

"What's the good of being silly, Binny?" Surefoot's voice was almost caressing.

They could not see him in the glare of the light that he or somebody held.

"Stand your trial like a man. It's fifty-fifty we've got nothing on you."

"You haven't, eh?" snarled Binny. "That dog doesn't fight, Smith. You take your men and clear them out of this place. Give me an hour, and I'll leave this baby without hurting her. Come any closer and I'll blow her head off—and then you'll have something on me. It won't be fifty-fifty either."

There was a long pause, and the girl heard the low voices of men in conversation.

"All right," said Surefoot at last. "I'll give you an hour, but you'll hand over the girl right away."

Binny laughed harshly.

"Am I a child? I'll leave her when I'm safe. You go back to where you came, and——"

That was all he said. The silent-footed man who had worked round behind him struck swiftly with a rubber truncheon. The girl had only time to swing herself clear before he crumpled and fell.

The chauffeur of the wrecked car had been in luck. Hardly had Binny disappeared before another machine came into sight, and the chauffeur begged a lift into Welwyn. Less than a mile along the road they ran into a police barrage and he told his story. He gave valuable information, for he had seen the lights of Binny's car turn from the road.

"Practically you were never out of sight, from the moment you left the plantation," said Surefoot. "The broken gate gave him away, and he left the lights of his car burning. It was easy, even without the trail of letters you left. Very scientific, but we didn't see them!"

The arrest and conviction of Binny had a demoralizing effect upon Surefoot Smith. On the day this wholesale murderer stood on the trap in Pentonville Prison, Surefoot departed from the rule of a lifetime, refused all beer and drank spirits. As he explained to Dick Allenby some time later:

"If ever there was a day to get soused—that was the day!"

ABOUT MR. J. G. REEDER

THE great English novelist, Hugh Walpole, writing in an English journel, once remarked of Wallace, "He is the wonder man of modern letters. He has touched more hearts than any English author since Dickens." Of his vast gallery of detectives, Surefoot Smith, Carl Rennett, Timothy Jordan, Superintendent Bliss, Inspector Bradley, and all the rest, possibly none has a greater appeal than Mr. J. G. Reeder, of the Public Prosecutor's office, London. Rather small, very mild, but with a savage snarl which he knows how to use on occasion, with mutton-chop whiskers, an old-fashioned square derby, a tightly furled umbrella which no one has ever seen unrolled, even in a driving rainstorm, he is the very picture of a benign old gentleman. But concealed in an inner pocket is a well-oiled Browning automatic which can spit death with a deadly and merciless accuracy. The crooks who knew him gave Mr. Reeder a wide berth; those who didn't, generally found themselves either behind bars, or, if they were foolish enough to use firearms against him, on a slab at the morgue. Mr. Reeder's specialty was bank crimes, and on such occasions as they occurred Scotland Yard was in the habit of seeking his aid. Generally the Yard's faith was justified; Mr. Reeder was fond of pointing out that he was possessed of a criminal mind, and could think very nearly along the same lines as a crook. The difference was that he thought so much faster.

In the pages following are four of his most exciting and ingenious exploits, taken from two books, *Red Aces* and *The Murder Book of J. G. Reeder*. A new book about him, *Mr. Reeder Returns*, will be published by the Crime Club shortly.

CONTENTS

RED ACES

THE POETICAL POLICEMAN

THE STEALER OF MARBLE

THE INVESTORS

RED ACES

CHAPTER I

When a young man is very much in love with a most attractive girl he is apt to endow her with qualities and virtues which no human being has ever possessed. Yet at rare and painful intervals there enter into his soul certain wild suspicions, and in these moments he is inclined to regard the possibility that she may be guilty of the basest treachery and double dealing.

Everybody knew that Kenneth McKay was desperately in love. They knew it at the bank where he spent his days in counting other people's money, and a considerable amount of his lunch hour writing impassioned and ill-spelt letters to Margot Lynn. His taciturn father, brooding over his vanished fortune in his gaunt riverside house at Marlow, may have employed the few moments he gave to the consideration of other people's troubles in consideration of his son's new interest. Probably he did not, for George McKay was entirely self-centred and had little thought but for the folly which had dissipated the money he had accumulated with such care, and the development of fantastical schemes for its recovery.

All day long, summer and winter, he sat in his study, a pack of cards before him, working out averages and what he called "inherent probabilities," or at a small roulette wheel, where, alternately, he spun and recorded the winning numbers.

Kenneth went over to Beaconsfield every morning

on his noisy motor-bicycle and came back every night, sometimes very late, because Margot lived in London. She had a small flat where she could not receive him, but they dined together at the cheaper restaurants and sometimes saw a play. Kenneth was a member of an inexpensive London club which sheltered at least one sympathetic soul. Except Mr. Rufus Machfield, the confidant in question, he had no friends.

"And let me advise you not to make any here," said Rufus.

He was a military-looking man of forty-five, and most people found him rather a bore, for the views which he expressed so vehemently, on all subjects from politics to religion, which are the opposite ends of the ethical pole, he had acquired that morning from the leading article of his favourite daily. Yet he was a genial person and a likeable man.

He had a luxurious flat in Park Lane, a French valet, a couple of hacks which he rode in the park, and no useful occupation.

"The Leffingham Club is cheap," he said, "the food is not bad, and it is near Piccadilly. Against that you have the fact that almost anybody who hasn't been to prison can become a member——"

"The fact that I'm a member——" began Ken.

"You're a gentleman and a public school man," interrupted Mr. Machfield a little sonorously. "You're not rich, I admit——"

"Even I admit that," said Ken, rubbing his untidy hair.

Kenneth was tall, athletic, as good looking as a young man need be, or can be without losing his head about his face. He had called at the Leffingham that evening especially to see Rufus and confide his worries. And his worries were enormous. He looked haggard and ill; Mr. Machfield thought it possible that he had not been sleeping very well. In this surmise he was right.

"It's about Margot . . ." began the young man.

Mr. Machfield smiled.

He had met Margot, had entertained the young people to dinner at his flat, and twice had invited them to a theatre party.

"We've had a row, Rufus. It began a week ago. For a long time her reticence has been bothering me. Why the devil couldn't she tell me what she did for a living? I wouldn't say this to a living soul but you—it is horribly disloyal to her, and yet it isn't. I know that she has no money of her own, and yet she lives at the rate of a thousand a year. She says that she is secretary to a business man, but the office where she works is in her own name. And she isn't there more than a few days a week and then only for a few hours."

Mr. Machfield considered the matter.

"She won't tell you any more than that?"

Kenneth looked round the smoke-room. Except for a servant counting the cigars in a small mahogany cabinet, they were alone. He lowered his voice.

"She'll never tell me any more . . . I've seen the man," he said. "Margot meets him surreptitiously!"

Mr. Machfield looked at him dubiously.

"Oh . . . what sort of a man?"

Kenneth hesitated.

"Well, to tell you the truth, he's elderly. It was

queer how I came to see them at all. I was taking a ride round the country on Sunday morning. Margot told me that she couldn't come to us—I asked her to lunch with us at Marlow—because she was going out of London. I went through Burnham and stopped to explore a little wood. As a matter of fact, I saw two animals fighting—I think they were stoats—and I went after them——"

"Stoats can be dangerous," began Mr. Machfield. "I remember once——"

"Anyway I went after them with my camera. I'm rather keen on wild life photographs. And then I saw two people, a man and a girl, walking slowly away from me. The man had his arm round the girl's shoulder. It rather made a picture—they stood in a patch of sunlight and with the trees as a background—well, it was rather an idyllic sort of picture. I put up my camera. Just as I pressed the button the man looked over his shoulder, and then the girl turned. It was Margot!"

He dabbed his brow with a handkerchief. Rufus was slightly amused to see anybody so agitated over so trifling a matter.

Kenneth swallowed his drink; his hand trembled.

"He was elderly—fifty . . . not bad looking. God! I could have killed them both! Margot was coolness itself, though she changed colour. But she didn't attempt to introduce me or offer any kind of explanation."

"Her father——" began Rufus.

"She has no father—no relations except her mother, who is an invalid and lives in Florence—at least I thought so," snapped Kenneth.

"What did she do?"

The young man heaved a deep sigh.

"Nothing—just said: 'How queer meeting you!' talked about the beautiful day, and when I asked her what it all meant and what this man was to her—he had walked on and left us alone—she flatly refused to say anything. Just turned on her heel and went after him."

"Extraordinary!" said Mr. Machfield. "You have seen her since?"

Kenneth nodded grimly.

"That same night she came to Marlow to see me. She begged me to trust her—she was really wonderful. It was terribly surprising to see her there at all. When I came down into the dining-room and found her there, I was knocked out—the servant didn't say who she was and I kept her waiting."

"Well?" asked his companion, when he paused.

"Well," said Kenneth awkwardly, "one *has* to trust people one loves. She said that he was a relation—she never told me that she had one until then."

"Except her mother who lives in Florence—that costs money, especially an invalid mother," mused Rufus, fingering his long, clean-shaven upper lip. "What is the trouble now? You've quarrelled?"

Kenneth took a letter out of his pocket and passed it across to his friend, and Mr. Machfield opened and read it.

DEAR KENNETH:

I'm not seeing you any more. I'm broken-hearted to tell you this. Please don't try to see me—please!

M.

"When did this come?"

"Last night. Naturally, I went to her flat. She was out. I went to her office—she was out. I was late for the bank and got a terrible roasting from the manager. To make matters worse, there's a fellow dunning me for two hundred pounds—everything comes at once. I borrowed the money for dad. What with one thing and another I'm desperate."

Mr. Machfield rose from his chair.

"Come home and have a meal," he said. "As for the money——"

"No, no, no!" Kenneth McKay was panic stricken. "I don't want to borrow from you—I won't! Gad! I'd like to find that old swine and throttle him! He's at the back of it! He has told her not to have anything more to do with me."

"You don't know his name?"

"No. He may live in the neighbourhood, but I haven't seen him. I'm going to do a little detective work." He added abruptly: "Do you know a man named Reeder—J. G. Reeder?"

Mr. Machfield shook his head.

"He's a detective," explained Kenneth. "He has a big bank practice. He was down at our place to-day—queer-looking devil. If he could be a detective anybody could be!"

Mr. Machfield said he recalled the name.

"He was in that railway robbery, wasn't he? J. G. Reeder—yes. Pretty smart fellow—young?"

"He's as old as—well, he's pretty old. And rather old-fashioned."

"Why do you mention him?" Mr. Machfield was interested.

"I don't know. Talking about detective work brought him into my mind, I suppose."

Rufus snapped his finger to the waiter and paid his bill.

"You'll have to take pot luck—but Lamontaine is a wonderful cook. He didn't know that he was until I made him try."

So they went together to the little flat in Park Lane, and Lamontaine, the pallid, middle-aged valet who spoke English with no trace of a foreign accent, prepared a meal that justified the praise of his master. In the middle of the dinner the subject of Mr. Reeder arose again.

"What brought him to Beaconsfield—is there anything wrong at your bank?"

Rufus saw the young man's face go red.

"Well—there has been money missing; not very large sums. I have my own opinion, but it isn't fair to—well, you know."

He was rather incoherent, and Mr. Machfield did not pursue the enquiry.

"I hate the bank anyway—I mean the work. But I had to do something, and when I left Uppingham the governor put me there—in the bank, I mean. Poor dear, he lost his money at Monte Carlo or somewhere—enormous sums. You wouldn't dream that he was a gambler. I'm not grousing, but it is a little trying sometimes."

Mr. Machfield accompanied him to the door that night and shivered.

"Cold—shouldn't be surprised if we had snow," he said.

In point of fact the snow did not come until a

week later. It started as rain and became snow in the night, and in the morning people who lived in the country looked out upon a white world: trees that bore a new beauty and hedges that showed their heads above sloping drifts.

CHAPTER II

THERE was a car coming from the direction of Beaconsfield. The horseman, sitting motionless in the centre of the snowy road, watched the lights grow brighter and brighter. Presently, in the glare of the headlamps, the driver of the car saw a mounted policeman in the centre of the road, saw the lift of his gloved hand, and stopped the machine. It was not difficult to stop, for the wheels were racing on the surface of the road, which had frozen into the worst qualities of glass. And snow was falling on top of this.

"Anything wrong?"

The driver began to shout the question, and then he saw the huddled figure on the ground. It lay limply like a fallen sack; seemed at first glimpse to have nothing of human shape or substance.

The driver jumped out and went ploughing through the frozen snow.

"I just spotted him when I saw you," said the policeman. "Do you mind turning your car just a little to the right—I want the lamps full on him.'"

He swung himself to the ground and went, heavy footed, to where the man lay.

The second inmate of the car got to the wheel and turned the machine with some difficulty so that the light blazed on the dreadful thing. The policeman's horse strayed to the side of the car and thrust in his nodding head—he alone was unconcerned.

Taking his bridle with a shaking hand, the second man stepped out of the car and joined the other two.

"It is old Wentford," said the policeman.

"Wentford . . . good God!"

The first of the two motorists fell on his knees by the side of the body and peered down into the grinning face.

Old Benny Wentford!

"Good God!" he said again.

He was a middle-aged lawyer, unused to such a horror. Nothing more terrible had disturbed the smooth flow of his life than an occasional quarrel with the secretary of his golf club. Now here was death, violent and hideous—a dead man on a snowy road . . . a man who had telephoned to him two hours before, begging him to leave a party and come to him, though the snow had begun to fall all over again.

"You know Mr. Wentford—he has told me about you."

"Yes, I know him. I've often called at his house—in fact, I called there to-night but it was shut up. He made arrangements with the Chief Constable that I should call . . . h'm!"

The policeman stood over the body, his hands on his hips.

"You stay here—I'll go and 'phone the station," he said.

He hoisted himself into the saddle.

"Er . . . don't you think we'd better go?" Mr. Enward, the lawyer, asked nervously. He had no desire to be left alone in the night with a battered corpse and a clerk whose trembling was almost audible.

"You couldn't turn your car," said the policeman —which was true, for the lane was very narrow.

They heard the jingle and thud of his horse's canter and presently they heard it no more.

"Is he dead, Mr. Enward?" The young man's voice was hollow.

"Yes . . . I think so . . . the policeman said so."

"Oughtn't we to make sure? He may only be . . . injured?"

Mr. Enward had seen the face now in the shadow of an uplifted shoulder. He did not wish to see it again.

"Better leave him alone till a doctor comes . . . it is no use interfering in these things. Wentford . . . good God!"

"He's always been a little bit eccentric, hasn't he?" The clerk was young, and, curiosity being the tonic of youth, he had recovered some of his courage. "Living alone in that tiny cottage with all his money. I was bicycling past it on Sunday—a concrete box: that is what my young lady called it. With all his money ——"

"He is dead, Henry," said Mr. Enward severely, "and a dead person has no property. I don't think it quite—um—seemly to talk of him in—um—his presence."

He felt the occasion called for an emotional display of some kind. He had never grown emotional over clients; least of all could this tetchy old man inspire such. A few words of prayer perhaps would not be out of place. But Mr. Enward was a churchwarden of a highly respectable church and for forty years had had his praying done for him. If he had been a dissenter . . . but he was not. He wished he had a prayer-book.

"He's a long time gone."

The policeman could not have been more than two hundred yards away, but it seemed a very long time since he had left.

"Has he any heirs?" asked the clerk professionally.

Mr. Enward did not answer. Instead, he suggested that the lights of the car should be dimmed. They revealed this Thing too plainly. Henry went back and dimmed the lights. It became terribly dark when the lights were lowered, and eyesight played curious tricks: it seemed that the bundle moved. Mr. Enward had a feeling that the grinning face was lifting to leer slyly at him over the humped shoulder.

"Put on the lights again, Henry," the lawyer's voice quavered. "I can't see what I am doing."

He was doing nothing; on the other hand, he had a creepy feeling that the Thing was behaving oddly. Yet it lay very still, just as it had lain all the time.

"He must have been murdered. I wonder where they went to?" asked Henry hollowly, and a cold shiver vibrated down Mr. Enward's spine.

Murdered! Of course he was murdered. There was blood on the snow, and the murderers were . . .

He glanced backward nervously and almost screamed. A man stood in the shadowy space behind the car: the light of the lamps reflected by the snow just revealed him.

"Who . . . who are you, please?" croaked the lawyer.

He added "please" because there was no sense in being rough with a man who might be a murderer.

The figure moved into the light. He was slightly bent and even more middle-aged than Mr. Enward. He wore a flat-topped felt hat, a long ulster, and large, shapeless gloves. About his neck was an enormous yellow scarf, and Mr. Enward noticed, in a numb, mechanical way, that his shoes were large and square-toed and that he carried a tightly furled umbrella on his arm though the snow was falling heavily.

"I'm afraid my car has broken down a mile up the road."

His voice was gentle and apologetic; obviously he had not seen the bundle. In his agitation Mr. Enward had stepped into the light of the lamps and his black shadow sprawled across the deeper shadow.

"Am I wrong in thinking that you are in the same predicament?" asked the newcomer. "I was unprepared for the—er—condition of the road. It is lamentable that one should have overlooked this possibility."

"Did you pass the policeman?" asked Mr. Enward.

Whoever this stranger was, whatever might be his character and disposition, it was right and fair that he should know there *was* a policeman in the vicinity.

"Policeman?" The square-hatted man was surprised. "No, I passed no policeman. At my rate of progress it was very difficult to pass anything——"

"Going towards you . . . on horseback . . . a mounted policeman," said Mr. Enward rapidly. "He said that he would be back soon. My name is Enward—solicitor—Enward, Caterham and Enward."

He felt it was a moment for confidence.

"Delighted!" murmured the other. "We've met before. My name—er—is Reeder—R, double E, D, E, R."

Mr. Enward took a step forward.

"Not the detective? I thought I'd seen you . . . look!"

He stepped out of the light and the heap on the ground emerged from shadow. The lawyer made a dramatic gesture. Mr. Reeder came forward slowly.

He stooped over the dead man, took an electric torch from his pocket and shone it steadily on the face. For a long time he looked and studied. His melancholy face showed no evidence that he was sickened or pained.

"H'm!" he said, and got up, dusting the snow from his knee. He fumbled in the recesses of his overcoat, produced a pair of eyeglasses, set them crudely on his nose and surveyed the lawyer over their top.

"Very—um—extraordinary. I was on my way to see him."

Enward stared.

"*You* were on your way? So was I! Did you know him?"

Mr. Reeder considered this question.

"I—er—didn't—er—know him. No, I had never met him."

The lawyer felt that his own presence needed some explanation.

"This is my clerk, Mr. Henry Green."

Mr. Reeder bowed slightly.

"What happened was this. . . ."

He gave a very detailed and graphic description.

which began with the recounting of what he had said when the telephone call came through to him at Beaconsfield, and how he was dressed, and what his wife had said when she went to find his boots (her first husband had died through an ill-judged excursion into the night air on as foolish a journey), and how much trouble he had had in starting the car, and how long he had had to wait for Henry.

Mr. Reeder gave the impression that he was not listening. Once he walked out of the blinding light and peered back the way the policeman had gone; once he went over to the body and looked at it again; but most of the time he was wandering down the lane, searching the ground with his hand-lamp, with Mr. Enward following at his heels lest any of the narrative be lost.

"Is he dead . . . I suppose so?" suggested the lawyer.

"I—er—have never seen anybody—er—deader," said Mr. Reeder gently. "I should say, with all reverence and respect, that he was—er—extraordinarily dead."

He looked at his watch.

"At nine-fifteen you met the policeman? He had just discovered the body? It is now nine thirty-five. How did you know that it was nine-fifteen?"

"I heard the church clock at Woburn Green strike the quarter."

Mr. Enward conveyed the impression that the clock struck exclusively for him. Henry halved the glory: he also had heard the clock.

"At Woburn Green—you heard the clock? H'm . . . nine-fifteen!"

The snow was falling thickly now. It fell on the heap and lay in the little folds and creases of his clothes.

"He must have lived somewhere about here?"

Mr. Reeder asked the question with great deference.

"My directions were that his house lay off the main road . . . you would hardly call this a main road . . . fifty yards beyond a notice-board advertising land for sale—desirable building land."

Mr. Enward pointed to the darkness.

"Just there—the notice-board. Curiously enough, I am the—er—solicitor for the vendor."

His natural inclination was to emphasize the desirability of the land, but he thought it was hardly the moment. He returned to the question of Mr. Wentford's house.

"I've only been inside the place once—two years ago, wasn't it, Henry?"

"A year and nine months," said Henry exactly.

His feet were cold, his spine chilled. He felt sick.

"You cannot see it from the lane," Mr. Enward continued. "Rather a small, one-story cottage. He had it specially built for him apparently. It is not exactly . . . a palace."

"Dear me!" said Mr. Reeder, as though this were the most striking news he had heard that evening. "In a house he built himself! I suppose he has, or had, a telephone?"

"He telephoned to *me*," said Mr. Enward; "therefore he must have a telephone."

Mr. Reeder frowned as though he were trying to pick holes in the logic of this statement.

"I will go along and see if it is possible to get through to the police," he suggested.

"The police have already been notified," said the lawyer hastily. "I think we all ought to stay here together till somebody arrives."

The man in the square hat, now absurdly covered with snow, shook his head. He pointed.

"Woburn Green is there. Why not go and arouse the—the—um—local constabulary?"

That idea had not occurred to the lawyer. His instinct urged him to return the way he had come and regain touch with realities in his own prosaic parlour.

"But do you think . . ." he blinked down at the body. "I mean, it's hardly an act of humanity to leave him——"

"He feels nothing. He is probably in heaven," said Mr. Reeder, and added: "Probably. Anyway, the police will know exactly where they can find him." There was a sudden screech from Henry. He was holding out his hand in the light of the lamp.

"Look—blood!" he screamed.

There was blood on his hand certainly.

"Blood—I didn't touch him! You know that, Mr. Enward—I ain't been anear him!"

Alas for our excellent system of secondary education! Henry was reverting to the illiterate stock whence he sprang.

"Not near him I ain't been—blood!"

"Don't squeak, please." Mr. Reeder was firm. "What *have* you touched?"

"Nothing—I only touched myself."

"Then you have touched nothing," said Mr. Reeder with unusual acidity. "Let me look."

The rays of his lamp travelled over the shivering clerk.

"It is on your sleeve—h'm!"

Mr. Enward stared. There was a red, moist patch of something on Henry's sleeve.

"You had better go on to the police station," said Mr. Reeder. "I will come and see you in the morning."

CHAPTER III

Mr. Enward climbed into the driver's seat gratefully, keeping some distance between himself and his shivering clerk. The car was on a declivity and would start without trouble. He turned the wheels straight and took off the brake. The machine skidded and slithered forward, and presently Mr. Reeder, following in its wake, heard the sound of the running engine.

His lamp showed him the notice-board in the field and fifty yards beyond he came to a path so narrow that two men could not walk abreast. It ran off from the road at right angles, and up this he turned, progressing with great difficulty, for he had heavy nails in his shoes. At last he saw a small garden gate on his right, set between two unkempt hedges. The gate was open, and this methodical man stopped to examine it by the light of his lamp.

He expected to find blood and found it: just a smear. No bloodstains on the ground, but then the snow would have obliterated those. It had not obliterated the print of footmarks going up the winding path. They were rather small, and he thought they were recently made. He kept his light upon them until they led him into view of the squat house with its narrow windows and doorways. As he turned he saw a light gleam between curtains. He had a feeling that somebody was looking out at him. In another moment the light had vanished. But there was somebody in the house.

The footsteps led up to the door. Here he paused and knocked. There was no answer, and he knocked again more loudly. The chill wind sent the snowflakes swirling about him. Mr. Reeder, who had a secret sense of humour, smiled. In the remote days of his youth his favourite Christmas card was one which showed a sparkling Father Christmas knocking at the door of a wayside cottage. He pictured himself as a felt-hatted Father Christmas, and the whimsical fancy slightly pleased him.

He knocked a third time and listened, then, when no answer came, he stepped back and walked to the room where he had seen the light and tried to peer between the curtains. He thought he heard a sound—a thud—but it was not in the house. It may have been the wind. He looked round and listened, but the thud was not repeated, and he returned to his ineffectual starings.

There was no sign of a fire. He came back to knock for the fourth time, then tried the other side of the building, and here he made a discovery. A narrow casement window, deeply recessed and made of iron, was swaying to and fro in the wind, and beneath the window was a double set of footmarks, one coming and one going. They went away in the direction of the lane.

He came back to the door, and stood debating with himself what steps he should take. He had seen in the darkness two small white squares at the top of the door, and had thought they were little panes of toughened glass such as one sees in the tops of such doors. But, probably in a gust of wind, one of them became detached and fell at his feet. He stooped and picked it up: it was a playing card—the ace of diamonds. He put his lamp on the second: it was the ace of hearts. They had both apparently been fastened side by side to the door with pins—black pins. Perhaps the owner of the house had put them there. Possibly they had some significance, fulfilled the function of mascots.

No answer came to his knocking, and Mr. Reeder heaved a deep sigh. He hated climbing; he hated more squeezing through narrow windows into unknown places; more especially as there was probably somebody inside who would treat him rudely. Or they may have gone. The footprints, he found, were fresh; they were scarcely obliterated, though the snow was falling heavily. Perhaps the house was empty, and its inmate, whose light he had seen, had got away whilst he was knocking at the door. He would not have heard him jump from the window, the snow was too soft. Unless that thud he had heard——

Mr. Reeder gripped the sill and drew himself up, breathing heavily, though he was a man of considerable strength.

There were only two ways to go into the house: one was feet first, the other head first. He made a reconnaissance with his lamp and saw that beneath the window was a small table, standing in a tiny room which had evidently been used as a cloak cupboard, for there were a number of coats hanging on hooks. It was safe to go in head first, so he wriggled down on to the table, feeling extraordinarily undignified. He was on his feet in a moment, gripped the handle of the door gingerly and opened it. He was in a small hall, from which one door opened. He tried this: it was fast, and yet not fast. It was as though somebody was leaning against it on the other side. A quick jerk of his shoulder, and it flew open. Somebody tried to dash past him, but Mr. Reeder was expecting that and worse. He gripped the fugitive . . .

"I'm extremely sorry," he said in his gentle voice. "It is a lady, isn't it?"

He heard her heavy breathing, a sob . . .

"Is there a light?"

He groped inside the lintel of the door, found a switch, and turned it. Nothing happened for a moment, and then the lights came on suddenly. There was apparently a small light-making machine at the back of the house which operated when any switch was turned.

"Come in here, will you, please?"

He pressed her very gently into the room. Pretty, extraordinarily pretty. He did not remember ever having met a young lady who was quite as pretty as this particular young lady, though she was very white and her hair was in disorder, and on her feet were snow-boots the impression of which he had already seen in the snow.

"Will you sit down, please?"

He closed the door behind him.

"There's nothing to be afraid of. My name is Reeder."

She had been terrified for that moment; now she looked up at him intensely.

"You're the detective?" she shivered. "I'm so frightened. I'm so frightened!"

Then she drooped over the table at which she sat, her face buried in her folded arms.

Mr. Reeder looked round the room. It was pleasantly furnished—not luxuriously so but pleasantly. Evidently a sitting-room. Except that the mantel-board had fallen or had been dragged on the floor, there was no sign of disorder. The hearth was littered with broken china pots and vases; the board itself was still held in position at one end by some attachment to the mantelpiece. That and the blue hearth-rug before the fire, which was curiously stained. And there were other little splodges of darkness on the surface of the carpet, and a flower-pot was knocked down near the door.

He saw a waste-paper basket and turned over its contents. Covers of little books apparently—there were five of them, but no contents. By the side of the fireplace was a dwarf bookcase. The books were dummies. He pulled one end of the case and it swung out, being hinged at the other end.

"H'm!" said Mr. Reeder, and pushed the shelves back into their original position.

There was a cap on the floor by the table and he picked this up. It was wet. This he examined, thrust into his pocket, and turned his attention to the girl.

"How long have you been here, Miss—— I think you had better tell me your name."

She was looking up at him; he saw her wet her dry lips.

"Half an hour. I don't know . . . it may be longer."

"Miss——?" he asked again.

"Lynn—Margot Lynn."

He pursed his lips thoughtfully.

"Margot Lynn. And you've been here half-an-hour. Who else has been here?"

"Nobody," she said, springing to her feet. "What has happened? Did he—did they fight?"

He put his hand on her shoulder gently, and pressed her down into the chair.

"Did who fight whom?" asked Mr. Reeder. His English was always very good on these occasions.

"Nobody has been here," she said inconsequently.

Mr. Reeder passed the question.

"You came from——?"

"I came from Bourne End station. I walked here. I often come that way. I am Mr. Wentford's secretary."

"You walked here at nine o'clock because you're Mr. Wentford's secretary? That was a very odd thing to do."

She was searching his face fearfully.

"Has anything happened? Are you a police detective? Has anything happened to Mr. Wentford? Tell me, tell me!"

"He was expecting me: you knew that?"

She nodded. Her breath was coming quickly. He thought she found breathing a painful process.

"He told me—yes. I didn't know what it was about. He wanted his lawyer here too. I think he was in some kind of trouble."

"When did you see him last?"

She hesitated.

"I spoke to him on the telephone—once, from London. I haven't seen him for two days."

"And the person who was here?" asked Mr. Reeder after a pause.

"There was nobody here! I swear there was nobody here!" She was frantic in her desire to convince him. "I've been here half-an-hour—waiting for him. I let myself in—I have a key. There it is."

She fumbled with trembling hands in her bag and produced a ring with two keys, one larger than the other.

"He wasn't here when I came in. I—I think he must have gone to town. He is very—peculiar."

Mr. J. G. Reeder put his hand in his pocket, took out two playing cards and laid them on the table.

"Why did he have those pinned to his door?"

She looked at him round-eyed.

"Pinned to his door?"

"The outer door," said Mr. Reeder, "or, as he would call it, the street door."

She shook her head.

"I've never seen them before. He is not the kind of man to put up things like that. He is very retiring and hates drawing attention to himself."

"He was very retiring," repeated Mr. Reeder, "and hated drawing attention to himself."

CHAPTER IV

Something in his tone emphasized the tense he used. She shrank back.

"Was?" Her voice was a whisper. "He's not dead . . . oh, my God! he's not dead?"

Mr. Reeder smoothed his chin.

"Yes, I'm afraid—um—he is dead."

She clutched the edge of the table for support. Mr. Reeder had never seen such horror, such despair in a human face before.

"Was it . . . an accident—or—or——"

"You're trying to say 'murder,'" said Reeder gently. "Yes, I'm very much afraid it was murder."

He caught her in his arms as she fell, and, laying her on the sofa, went in search of water. The taps were frozen, but he found some water in a kettle, and, filling a glass with this, he returned to sprinkle it on her face, having a vague idea that something of the sort was necessary; but he found her sitting up, her face in her hands.

"Lie down, my dear, and keep quiet," said Mr. Reeder, and she obeyed meekly.

He looked round the room. The thing that struck him anew was the revolver which hung on the wall near the right-hand side of the fireplace just above the bookcase. It was placed to the hand of anybody who sat with his back to the window. Behind the armchair was a screen, and, tapping it, Mr. Reeder discovered that it was of sheet iron.

He went outside to look at the door, turning on the hall light. It was a very thick door, and the inside was made of quarter-inch steel plate, screwed firmly to the wood. Leading from the kitchen was the bedroom, evidently Wentford's. The only light here was admitted from an oblong window near the ceiling. There were no other windows, and about the narrow window was a stout steel cage. On the wall by the bed hung a second pistol. He found a third weapon in the kitchen, and, behind a coat hanging in the hall, a fourth.

The cottage was a square box of concrete. The roof, as he afterwards learned, was tiled over sheet iron, and, except for the window through which he had squeezed, there was none by which ingress could be had.

He was puzzled why this man, who evidently feared attack, had left any window so large as that through which he had come. He afterwards found the broken wire which must have set an alarm bell ringing when the window was opened.

There was blood on the mat in the hall, blood in the tiny lobby. He came back to where the girl was lying and sniffed. There was no smell of cordite, and having seen the body, he was not surprised.

"Now, my dear."

She sat up again.

"I am not a police officer; I am a—er—a gentleman called in by your friend, Mr. Wentford—your late friend," he corrected himself, "to do something—I know not what! He called me by 'phone; I gave him my—um—terms, but he offered me no reason why he was sending for me. You, as his secretary, may perhaps——"

She shook her head.

"I don't know. He had never mentioned you before he spoke to me on the telephone."

"I am not a policeman," said Mr. Reeder again, and his voice was very gentle; "therefore, my dear, you need have few qualms about telling me the truth, because these gentlemen, when they come, these very active and intelligent men, will probably discover all that I have seen, even if I did not tell them. Who was the man who went out of this house when I knocked at the door?"

Her face was deathly pale, but she did not flinch. He wondered if she was as pretty when she was not so pale. Mr. Reeder wondered all sorts of queer little things like that; his mind could never stagnate.

"There was nobody—in this house—since I have been here——"

Mr. Reeder did not press her. He sighed, closed his eyes, shook his head, shrugged his shoulders.

"It's a great pity," he said. "Can you tell me anything about Mr. Wentford?"

"No," she said in a low voice. "He was my uncle. I think you ought to know that. He didn't want anybody to know, but that must come out. He has been very good to us—he sent my mother abroad; she is an invalid. I conducted his business." All this very jerkily.

"Have you been here often?"

She shook her head.

"Not often," she said. "We usually met somewhere by appointment, generally in a lonely place where one wouldn't be likely to meet anybody who knew us. He was very shy of strangers, and he didn't like anybody coming here."

"Did he ever entertain friends here?"

"No." She was very emphatic. "I'm sure he didn't. The only person he ever saw was the police patrol, the mounted man who rides this beat. Uncle used to make him coffee every night. I think it was for the company—he told me he felt lonely at nights. The policeman kept an eye on him. There are two—Constable Steele and Constable Verity. My uncle always sent them a turkey at Christmas. Whoever was on duty used to ride up here. I was here late one night, and the constable escorted me to Bourne End."

The telephone was in the bedroom. Mr. Reeder remembered he had promised to 'phone. He got through to a police station and asked a few questions. When he got back, he found the girl by the window, looking between the curtains.

Somebody was coming up the path. They could hear voices, and, looking through the curtain, he saw a string of lanterns and went out to meet a local sergeant and two men. Behind them was Mr. Enward. Reeder wondered what had become of Henry. Possibly he had been lost in the snow. The thought interested him.

"This is Mr. Reeder." Enward's voice was shrill. "Did you telephone?"

"Yes, I telephoned. We have a young lady here—Mr. Wentford's niece."

Enward repeated the words, surprised.

"His niece here? Really? I knew he had a niece. In fact——"

He coughed. It was an indelicate moment to speak of legacies.

"She'll be able to throw a light on this business," said the sergeant, more practical and less delicate.

"She could throw no light on any business," said Mr. Reeder, very firmly for him. "She was not here when the crime was committed—in fact, she arrived some time after. She has a key which admitted her. Miss Lynn acts as her uncle's secretary, all of which facts, I think, gentlemen, you should know."

The sergeant was not quite sure about the propriety of noticing Mr. Reeder. To him he was almost a civilian, a man without authority, and his presence was therefore irregular. Nevertheless, some distant echo of J. G. Reeder's fame had penetrated into Buckinghamshire. The police officer seemed to remember that Mr. Reeder either occupied or was about to occupy a semi-official position remotely or nearly associated with police affairs. If he had been a little clearer on the subject he would also have been more definite in his attitude. Since he was not so sure, it was expedient, until Mr. Reeder's position became established, to ignore his presence—a peculiarly difficult course to follow when an officially absent person is standing at your elbow, murmuring flat contradictions of your vital theories.

"Perhaps you will tell me why *you* are here, sir?" said the sergeant with a certain truculence.

Mr. Reeder felt in his pocket, took out a large leather case and laid it carefully on the table, first dusting the table with the side of his hand. This he unfolded, and took out, with exasperating deliberation, a thick pad of telegrams. He fixed his glasses and examined the telegrams one by one, reading each through. At last he shook one clear and handed it to the officer. It ran:

Wish to consult with you to-night on very important matter. Call me Woburn Green 971. Very urgent. WENTFORD.

"You're a private detective, Mr. Reeder?"

"More intimate than private," murmured that gentleman. "In these days of publicity one has little more than the privacy of a gold-fish in his crystal habitation."

The sergeant saw something in the waste-paper basket and pulled it out. It was a small loose-leafed book. There was another, indeed many. He piled five on the table; but they were merely the covers and nothing more.

"Diaries," said Mr. Reeder gently. "You will observe that each one is dingier than the other."

"But how do you know they're diaries?" demanded the police officer testily.

"Because the word 'diary' is printed on the inside covers," said Mr. Reeder, more gently than ever.

This proved to be the case, though the printing had been overlooked. Mr. Reeder had not overlooked it; he had not even overlooked the two scraps of burnt paper on the hearth, all that remained of those diaries.

"There is a safe let into the wall behind that bookcase." He pointed. "It may or may not be full of clues. I should imagine it is not. But I shouldn't touch it if I were you, sergeant," he said hastily, "not without gloves. Those detestable fellows from Scotland Yard will be here eventually, and they'll be ever so rude if they photograph a finger-print and find it is yours."

Gaylor of the Yard came at half-past two. He had been brought out of his bed through a blinding snow-storm and along a road that was thoroughly vile.

The young lady had gone home. Mr. Reeder was sitting meditatively before the fire which he had made up, smoking the cheapest kind of cigarette.

"Is the body here?"

Mr. Reeder shook his head.

"Have they found that mounted policeman, Verity?"

Again Mr. Reeder signalled a negative.

"They found his horse. He was discovered on the Beaconsfield Road. It had bloodstains on the saddle."

"Bloodstains?" said the startled officer.

"Stains of blood," explained Mr. Reeder.

He was staring into the fire, the cigarette drooping limply from his mouth, on his face an air of unsettled melancholy; he did not even turn his head to address Inspector Gaylor.

"The young lady has gone home, as I said. The local constabulary gave you particulars of the lady, of course. She acted as secretary to the late Mr. Wentford, and he appears to have been very fond of her, since he has left two-thirds of his fortune to the young lady and one-third to his sister. There is no money in the house as far as can be ascertained, but he banks with the Great Central Bank, Beaconsfield branch." Reeder fumbled in his pocket. "Here are the two aces."

"The two what?" asked the puzzled inspector.

"The two aces." Mr. Reeder passed the playing cards over his shoulder, his eyes still upon the fire. "The ace of diamonds, and I believe the ace of hearts—I am not very well acquainted with either."

"Where did you get these?"

The other explained, and he heard Gaylor's exasperated chuckle.

"What's this, a magazine story murder?" he asked contemptuously.

"I seldom read magazine stories," said Mr. Reeder between yawns, "but these cards were put up after the murder."

The detective examined the aces interestedly.

"Why are you so sure of that—why shouldn't they have been put up before?"

J. G. groaned at his scepticism, and, reaching out, took a pack of cards from a little table.

"You will find the two aces missing from this pack. You would have also found that two cards had been stuck together. Blood does that. No finger-prints. I should imagine the cards were sorted over after the untimely demise of Mr. Wentford, and the two significant aces extracted and exhibited."

The inspector made a very careful search of the bedroom and came back to find Mr. Reeder nodding himself to sleep.

"What did they do to the girl—these local blokes?" asked Gaylor coarsely.

Reeder's right shoulder came up in a lazy shrug.

"They escorted her to the station and took a statement from her. The inspector was kind enough to furnish me with a copy—you will find it on this table. They also examined her hands and her clothes, but it was quite unnecessary. There is corroborative evidence that she arrived at Bourne End station at twelve minutes past eight as she says she did—the murder was committed at forty minutes past seven, a few minutes before or after."

"How the dickens do you know that?" asked the astonished officer. "Is there any proof?"

Mr. Reeder shook his head.

"A romantic surmise." He sighed heavily. "You have to realize, my dear Gaylor, that I have a criminal mind. I see the worst in people and the worst in every human action. It is very tragic. There are moments when——" He sighed again. "Forty minutes past seven," he said simply. "That is my romantic surmise. The doctor will probably confirm my view. The body lay here," he pointed to the hearthrug, "until—well, quite a considerable time."

Gaylor was skimming two closely written sheets of foolscap. Suddenly he stopped.

"You're wrong," he said. "Listen to this statement made at the station by Miss Lynn. 'I rang up my uncle from the station, telling him I might be late because of the snowy road. He answered "Come as soon as you can." He spoke in a very low tone; I thought he sounded agitated!' That knocks your theory about the time a little bit skew-wiff, eh?"

Mr. Reeder looked round and blinked open his eyes.

"Yes, doesn't it? It must have been terribly embarrassing."

"What was embarrassing?" asked the puzzled police officer.

"Everything," mumbled Mr. Reeder, his chin falling on his breast.

CHAPTER V

("THE trouble about Reeder," said Gaylor to the superintendent in the course of a long telephone conversation, "is that you feel he does know something which he shouldn't know. I've never seen him in a case where he hasn't given me the impression that he was the guilty party—he knew so much about the crime."

"Humour him," said the superintendent. "He'll be in the Public Prosecutor's Department one of these days. He never was in a case that he didn't make himself an accessory by pinching half the clues.")

At five o'clock the detective shook the sleeper awake.

"You'd better go home, old man," he said. "We'll leave an officer in charge here."

Mr. Reeder rose with a groan, splashed some soda-water from a syphon into a glass and drank it.

"I must stay, I'm afraid, unless you have any very great objection."

"What's the idea of waiting?" asked Gaylor in surprise.

Mr. Reeder looked from side to side as though he were seeking an answer.

"I have a theory—an absurd one, of course—but I believe the murderers will come back. And honestly I don't think your policeman would be of much use, unless you were inclined to give the poor fellow the lethal weapon necessary to defend himself."

Gaylor sat down squarely before him, his large gloved hands on his knees.

"Tell papa," he said.

Mr. Reeder looked at him pathetically.

"There is nothing to tell, my dear Mr. Gaylor; merely suspicion, bred, as I said, in my peculiarly morbid mind, having perhaps no foundation in fact. Those two cards, for example—that was a stupid piece of bravado. But it has happened before. You remember the Teignmouth case, and the Lavender Hill case, with the man with the slashed chest? I think they must get these ideas out of books," he said, bending over to stir the embers of the fire. "The craze for that kind of literature must necessarily produce its reaction."

Gaylor took the cards from his pockets and examined them.

"A bit of tomfoolery," was his verdict.

Mr. Reeder sighed and shook his head at the fire.

"Murderers as a rule have no sense of humour. They are excitable people, frightened people, but they are never comic people."

He walked to the door and pulled it open. Snow had ceased to fall. He came back.

"Where is the policeman you propose leaving on duty?" he asked.

"I'll find one," said Gaylor. "There are half-a-dozen within call. A whistle will bring one along."

Mr. Reeder looked at him thoughtfully.

"I don't think I should. Let us wait until daylight —or perhaps you wish to go? I don't think anybody would harm you. I rather fancy they would be glad to see the back of you."

"Harm me?" said Gaylor indignantly, but Reeder took no notice of the interruption.

"My own idea is that I should brew a dish of tea, and possibly fry a few eggs. I am a little hungry."

Gaylor walked to the door and frowned out into the darkness. He had worked with Reeder before, and was too wise a man to reject the advice summarily. Besides, if Reeder was entering or had entered the Public Prosecutor's Department, he would occupy a rank equivalent to superintendent.

"I'm all for eggs," said Gaylor, and bolted the outer door.

The older man disappeared into the kitchen and came back with a kettle, which he placed upon the fire, went out again and returned with a frying-pan.

"Do you ever take your hat off?" asked Gaylor curiously.

Mr. Reeder did not turn his head, but shook the pan gently to ensure an even distribution of the boiling fat.

"Very rarely," he said. "On Christmas Days sometimes."

And then Gaylor asked a fatuous question; at least, it sounded fatuous to him, and yet subconsciously he felt that the other might supply an immediate and dramatic answer.

"Who killed Wentford?"

"Two men, possibly three," said Mr. Reeder instantly; "but I rather think two. Neither was a professional burglar. One at any rate thought more of the killing than of any profit he might have got out of it. Neither found anything worth taking, and even if they had opened the safe they would have discovered nothing of value. The young lady, Miss Margot Lynn, could, I think, have saved them a lot of trouble in their search for treasure—I may be mistaken here, but I rarely fall into error. Miss Margot is——"

He stopped, looked round quickly.

"What is it?" asked Gaylor, but Reeder put his finger to his lips.

He rose, moving across the room to the door which led to the tiny lobby through which he had made his entrance. He stood with one hand on the knob, and Gaylor saw that in the other was a Browning pistol. Slowly he turned the handle. The door was locked from the inside.

In two strides Reeder was at the front door, turned the key and pulled it open. Then, to the inspector's amazement, he saw his companion take one step and fall sprawling on his face in the snow. He ran to his assistance. Something caught him by the ankle and flung him forward.

Reeder was on his feet and assisted the other to rise.

"A little wire fastened between the door posts," he explained.

A bright beam shot out from his electric torch as he turned the corner of the house. There was nobody in sight, but the window, which he had fastened, was open, and there were new footprints in the snow leading away into the darkness.

"Well, I'm damned!" said Gaylor.

J. G. Reeder said nothing. He was smiling when

he came back into the room, having stopped to break the wire with a kick.

"Do you think somebody was in the lobby?"

"I know somebody was in the lobby," he said. "Dear me! How foolish of us not to have had a policeman posted outside the door! You notice that a pane of glass has been cut? Our friend must have been listening there."

"Was there only one?"

"Only one," said Mr. Reeder gravely. "But was he the one who came that way before—I don't think so."

He took the frying-pan from the hearth where he had put it and resumed his frying of eggs, served them on two plates and brewed the tea. It was just as though death had not lurked in that lobby a few minutes before.

"No, they won't come back; there is no longer a reason for our staying. There were two, but only one came into the house. The roads are very heavy, and they may have a long way to travel, and they would not risk being anywhere near at daybreak. At six o'clock the agricultural labourer of whom the poet Gray wrote so charmingly will be on his way to work, and they won't risk meeting him either."

They had a solemn breakfast, Gaylor plying the other with questions, which in the main he did not answer.

"You think that Miss Lynn is in this—in the murder, I mean?"

Reeder shook his head.

"No, no," he said. "I'm afraid it isn't as easy as that."

Daylight had come greyly when, having installed a cold policeman in the house, they plodded down the lane. Reeder's car had been retrieved in the night, and a more powerful machine, fitted with chain-wheels, was waiting to take them to Beaconsfield. They did not reach that place for two hours, for on their way they came upon a little knot of policemen and farm labourers looking sombrely at the body of Constable Verity. He lay under some bushes a few yards from the road, and he was dead.

"Shot," said a police officer. "The divisional surgeon has just seen him."

Stiff and cold, with his booted legs stretched wide, his overcoat turned up and his snow-covered cap drawn over his eyes, was the officer who had ridden out from the station courtyard so unsuspectingly the night before. His horse had already been found; the bloodstains that had puzzled and alarmed the police were now accounted for.

Gaylor and Reeder drove on into Beaconsfield. Gaylor was a depressed and silent man; Mr. Reeder was silent but not depressed.

As they came out into the main road he turned to his companion, and asked:

"I wonder why they didn't bring their own aces?"

CHAPTER VI

THE most accurate account of the double tragedy appeared in a late edition of the *Evening Post-Courier*.

At some hour between eight and ten James Verity, a member of the Mounted Branch of the Buckinghamshire Constabulary, and Walter Wentford, an eccentric, and, it is believed, a rich recluse, were done to death in or in the vicinity of a lonely cottage in the neighbourhood of Beaconsfield. At a quarter past nine Constable Verity was patrolling the road and came upon a body which was afterwards identified as that of the late Mr. Wentford, who lived in a small cottage some hundred yards from the spot where the body was found. Mr. Wentford had been brutally bludgeoned, and was dead when the discovery was made. Simultaneously with the discovery there appeared upon the scene Mr. Walter Enward, a well-known Beaconsfield solicitor, and his clerk, who, at Mr. Wentford's request, were on their way to visit him. It is believed Mr. Wentford intended making a will, though no documents were found in the house to support this supposition.

Leaving Mr. Enward to watch the body, Constable Verity rode toward Beaconsfield to summon assistance. He was never seen alive after that moment.

The dead man's niece, who also acted as his secretary, Miss Margot Lynn, had been summoned from London, and she, arriving at the cottage a few minutes after the body had been taken away by the unknown murderers, discovered the place in disorder, though she did not at that time suspect a tragedy.

The mystery was still further complicated in the earlier hours of the dawn, when a cow-boy, on his way to work, discovered the dead body of Constable Verity on the Beaconsfield side of the lane where Mr. Wentford's body was found. He had been shot through the heart at close range. No sound of the shot had been heard, but it may be explained that there are very few houses in the neighbourhood, and snow was falling heavily. A carter in the employment of a neighbouring farmer thought he had heard a shot fired much earlier in the evening, but this may be accounted for by the fact that snow was falling so thickly on the railway line, which is situated a mile away, that fog signals were being used.

Chief Detective-Inspector Gaylor has been called in by the Buckinghamshire police, and he is being assisted by Mr. J. G. Reeder, of the Public Prosecutor's Department.

The time-table, so far as can be ascertained, is as follows:

7.0. Constable Verity left police station on patrol.

9.14. Constable Verity discovers the dead body of Mr. Wentford.

9.15. Mr. Enward and his clerk drive up by motor-car, and are stopped by the constable, who rides into Beaconsfield for assistance.

6.45 A. M. The body of Constable Verity is found shot dead 120 yards north of where the body of Mr. Wentford was found.

Mr. Kingfether, the sub-manager of the Beaconsfield branch of the Great Central Bank, read this account and was rightly agitated. He got to the bank very early that morning, for he had a letter to write, and his managerial office gave him the privacy he required. He was a serious man, with serious-looking spectacles on a pale, plump face. He had a little black moustache and his cheeks and chin were invariably blue, for he had what barbers call a "strong beard."

The newspapers arrived as he was writing. They were pushed under the closed outer door of the bank, and, being at the moment stuck for the alternative to an often-reiterated term of endearment, he rose and brought the newspapers into the office, put a new coal on the fire and sat down to glance through them. There were two papers, one financial and one human.

He read the latter first, and there was the murder in detail, though it had only occurred the night before. The discovery of the constable's body was not described, because it had not been discovered when the paper went to press.

He read and re-read, his mind in a whirl, and then he took the telephone and called Mr. Enward. That gentleman was also in his office that snowy morning, though the hour was eight.

"Good-morning, Kingfether . . . Yes, yes, it's true. . . . I was practically a witness—they've found the poor policeman . . . dead . . . yes, murdered . . . yes, shot. . . . I was the last person to speak to him. Dreadful, dreadful, dreadful! That such horrors can be—I say that such horrors can be. . . . I said that such . . . What's the matter with your 'phone? He banks with you? Really? Really? I'll come over and talk with you . . ."

Mr. Kingfether hung up the telephone and wiped his face with his handkerchief. It was a face that became moist on the least provocation. Presently he folded the newspaper and looked at his unfinished letter. He was on the eighth page and the last words he had written were:

. . . can hardly live the day through without seeing your darling face, my own . . .

It was obvious that he was not writing to his general manager, or to a client who had overdrawn his account.

He added "beloved" mechanically, though he had used the word a dozen times before. Then he unfolded the paper and read of the murder again.

A knock at the side door: he went out to admit Enward. The lawyer was more important than usual. Participation in public affairs has this effect. And a news agency had telephoned to ask whether they could send a photographer, and Mr. Enward, shivering at the telephone in his pyjamas, had said "Yes" and had been photographed at his breakfast table at 7.30 A.M., poising a cup of tea and looking excessively grave. He would presently appear in one hundred and fifty newspapers above the caption "Lawyer Who Discovered His Own Client Murdered."

"It is a terrible business," said Mr. Enward, throwing off his coat. "He banked with you? I'm in charge of affairs, Kingfether, though heaven knows I am ignorant about 'em! I don't know how he stands . . . what is his credit here?"

Mr. Kingfether considered.

"I'll get the ledger from the safe," he said.

He locked the centre drawer of his desk, because his letter to Ena Burlsem was there and other documents, but Mr. Enward saw nothing offensive in the act of caution; rather was it commendable.

"Here is his account." Kingfether laid the big ledger on the desk and opened it where his thumb marked a page. "Credit three thousand four hundred pounds."

Mr. Enward fixed his glasses and looked.

"Has he anything on deposit? Securities—no? Did he come often to the bank?"

"Never," said Kingfether. "He used the account to pay bills. When he wanted ready money he posted a bearer cheque and I posted back the money. He has, of course, sent people here to cash cheques."

"That six hundred pounds withdrawn five days ago." Mr. Enward pointed to the item.

"It is strange that you should point that out—it was paid over the counter four days ago. I didn't see the person who called for it—I was out. My clerk McKay cashed the cheque. Who is that?"

There was a gentle tapping at the door. Mr. Kingfether went out of the room and came back with the caller.

"How fortunate to find you here!" said J. G. Reeder. He was spruce and lively. A barber had shaved him, somebody had cleaned his boots. "The account of the late Mr. Wentford?" He nodded to the book.

It was generally known that J. G. Reeder acted for the Great Central Bank, and the manager did not question his title to ask questions. Mr. Enward was not so sure.

"This is rather a serious matter, Mr. Reeder,"

he said, consciously grave. "I am not so sure that we can take you into our confidence——"

"Hadn't you better see the police and ask them if they are prepared to take you into *their* confidence?" asked Mr. Reeder, with a sudden ferocity which made the lawyer recoil.

Once more the manager explained the account.

"Six hundred pounds—h'm!" Mr. Reeder frowned. "A large sum—who was the drawer?"

"My clerk McKay said it was a lady—heavily veiled."

Reeder stared at him.

"Your clerk McKay? Of course—a fair young man. How stupid of me! Kenneth—or is it Karl—Kenneth, is it? H'm! Heavily veiled lady. Have you the number of the notes?"

Kingfether was taken aback by the question. He searched for a book that held the information, and Mr. Reeder copied them down, an easy task since the tens and the fives ran consecutively.

"When does your clerk arrive?"

Kenneth was supposed to arrive at nine. As a rule he was late. He was late that morning.

Mr. Reeder saw the young man through a window in the manager's office and thought that he did not look well. His eyes were tired; he had shaved himself carelessly, for his chin bore a strip of sticking plaster. Perhaps that accounted for the spots on the soiled cuff of his shirt, thought Mr. Reeder, when he confronted the young man.

"No, I will see him alone," said Reeder.

"He is rather an insolent pup," warned Mr. Kingfether.

"I have tamed lions," said Mr. Reeder.

When Kenneth came in:

"Close the door, please, and sit down. You know me, my boy?"

"Yes, sir," said Kenneth.

"That is blood on your shirt cuff, isn't it? . . . cut your chin, did you? You haven't been home all night?"

Kenneth did not answer at once.

"No, sir. I haven't changed my shirt, if that is what you mean."

Mr. Reeder smiled.

"Exactly."

He fixed the young man with a long, searching glance.

"Why did you go to the house of the late Mr. Wentford last night between the hours of eight-thirty and nine-thirty?"

He saw the youth go deathly white.

"I didn't know he was dead—I didn't even know his name until this morning. I went there because . . . well, I was blackguard enough to spy on somebody . . . follow them from London and sneak into the house——"

"The young lady, Margot Lynn. You're in love with her? Engaged to her, perhaps?"

"I'm in love with her—I'm not engaged to her. We are no longer . . . friends," said Kenneth in a low voice. "She told you I had been there, I suppose?" And then, as a light broke on him: "Or did you find my cap? It had my name in it."

Mr. Reeder nodded

"You came down on the same train as Miss Lynn?

Good. Then you will be able to prove that you left Bourne End station——"

"No, I shan't," said Kenneth. 'I slipped out of the train on to the line. Naturally I didn't want her to see me. I got out through the level crossing. There was nobody about—it was snowing heavily."

"Very awkward." Mr. Reeder pursed his lips. "You thought there was some sort of friendship between Mr. Wentford and the young lady?"

Kenneth made a gesture of despair.

"I don't know what I thought—I was just a jealous fool."

A very long silence, broken by a coal falling from the fire on to the iron bottom of the fender.

"You paid out six hundred pounds the other day to a lady on Mr. Wentford's cheque?"

"I didn't know that Wentford was——" began Ken, but Mr. Reeder brushed aside that aspect of the situation. "Yes, a veiled lady. She came by car. It was a large sum of money, but the day before Mr. Kingfether had told me to honour any cheque of Mr. Wentford's, no matter to whom money was paid."

"Will you tell me something about your quarrel with the young lady?" Mr. Reeder asked. "It is, I realize, a delicate subject."

Kenneth hesitated, then told his story as he had told it to Mr. Machfield.

"Miss Lynn called on you that night—did she ask you to destroy the photograph you had taken?"

The young man was surprised at this query.

"No—I had forgotten all about the photograph till the other day. I must have sent the pack to be developed or put them aside to send them. Would the picture of Mr. Wentford be any good to you?"

J. G. Reeder shook his head. He asked very little more. He was, it seemed, the easiest man in the world to satisfy. Before he left he saw the sub-manager alone.

"Did you tell Mr. McKay that he was to honour any cheque of Mr. Wentford's, no matter to whom the money was paid?"

The answer came instantly.

"Of course not! Naturally I should expect him to be sure that the person who presented a cheque had authority. And another curious thing which I have not mentioned. I lunch at the inn opposite and I usually have a seat in the window, where I can see these premises, but I have no recollection of any car drawing up to the bank."

"H'm!" was all that Mr. Reeder said.

He made a few enquiries in Beaconsfield and the neighbourhood and went on to Wentford's house, where Gaylor had arranged to meet him. The inspector was pacing up and down the snowy terrace before the house and he was in very good spirits.

"I think I've got the man," he said. "Do you know anybody named McKay?"

Mr. Reeder looked at him slyly.

"I know a dozen," he said.

"Come inside and I'll show you something."

Reeder followed him into the room. The carpet had been taken up, the furniture moved. Evidently a very thorough search had been in progress. Gaylor swung back the bookcase: the safe door was ajar.

"We got keys from the maker—quick work! They were down here by eight-thirty."

He stooped down and pulled out three bundles. The first was made up of bills, the second of used cheques, the third was a thick bundle of French bank notes, each to the value of 1,000 francs.

"That is surprise No. 1," began the detective, flourishing the money. "French money——"

"I am afraid it doesn't surprise me," said Mr. Reeder apologetically. "You see, I've been examining the gentleman's bank book. By the way, here are the numbers of notes drawn from Mr. Wentford's account." He handed over a slip of paper.

"Six hundred pounds is a lot of money," said Gaylor. "I'll 'phone these through. Well, what else did you find in the bank book?"

"I observed," said Mr. Reeder, "though I did not emphasize the fact, that all the money he paid in was in French bank notes. Number two is——?"

The inspector extracted a sheet of headed paper from one heap. Written in pencil was what was evidently a memorandum from somebody who signed himself "D. H. Hartford."

I have found that the man who is employing a private detective to find you is George McKay of Sennett House, Marlow. I don't know what his intentions are, but they're not pleasant. There is nothing to worry about: he is employing one of the most incompetent private detectives in the business.

"Extraordinary!" said Mr. Reeder, and coughed.

"The first thing to do is to find Hartford——" began Gaylor.

"He is in Australia," Mr. Reeder interrupted. "At the time that letter was written his office address was 327, Lambs Buildings. He became bankrupt and left the country hurriedly."

"How do you know?" asked Gaylor, astonished.

"Because I—um—was the incompetent private detective engaged to find Mr. Lynn, or, as he called himself, Mr. Wentford. And I did not find him," said Mr. Reeder.

"Why did McKay wish to find this man?"

"He owed him money. I know no more than that. The search fell off because—um—Mr. McKay owed me money. One has to live."

"Then you knew about Wentford?"

Mr. Reeder took counsel with himself.

"Um—yes. I recognized him last night—I once had a photograph of him. I thought it was very odd. I also—er—drove over to Marlow and made enquiries. Mr. McKay—Mr. George McKay did not leave his house last night, and at the moment the murder was committed was entertaining the—um—vicar to dinner."

"You're a killjoy," he said, and Mr. Reeder sighed heavily.

"I'm going to have these developed." He held up a little film pack. "I found them in the old man's bedroom. I don't suppose they'll tell us anything."

"I fancy they will be very instructive," said Mr. Reeder, "especially if you are interested in natural history. There will also be a picture of Mr. Wentford or Lynn, with his arm about the shoulder of his niece."

Gaylor sat down.

"Are you pulling my leg?" he demanded.

"Heaven forbid!" answered Mr. Reeder piously.

Gaylor got up and stood squarely before him.

"What do you know about these murders, Reeder?" he challenged.

Mr. Reeder spread his hands wide. His glasses, set askew, slipped a little farther down his nose; he was not a very imposing figure.

"I am a queer man, Mr. Gaylor; I am cursed, as you are aware, with a peculiarly evil mind. I am also intensely curious—I have always been. I am curious about criminals and chickens—I have perhaps the finest Wyandottes in London, but that is by the way. It would be cruel to give you my theories. The blood on the policeman's horse: that is interesting. And Henry—I suppose Mr. Enward's clerk has another name—the blood on his coat, though he did not go near the body of the late Mr. Wentford, that is interesting. Poor Henry is suffering from a severe chill and is in bed, but his mother, an admirable and hardworking woman, permitted me to see him. Then the two aces pinned to the door, all very, very, very interesting indeed! Mr. Gaylor, if you will permit me to interview old George McKay I will undertake to tell you who committed these murders."

"The girl told you something—the girl Lynn?"

"The girl has told me nothing. She also may be very informative. I purpose spending a night or two in her flat—um—not, I hope, without a chaperon."

Gaylor looked at him, amazed. Mr. Reeder was blushing.

CHAPTER VII

THE last page of the letter which Mr. Eric Kingfether had begun with such ease in the early part of the morning was extremely difficult to compose. It had become necessary to say certain things; it was vital that he should not put his communication into writing.

In desperation he decided to make a break with practice. He would go to town. It was impossible to leave before the bank closed, but he could go immediately afterwards, though there was urgent work which should have kept him on the bank premises until six, and some private work of serious importance that should have occupied him until midnight. When the bank closed he handed over the key of the safe to Kenneth.

"I've been called to town. Balance up the books and put them in the safe. I'll be back by six; I'd like you to wait for me."

Kenneth McKay did not receive the suggestion favourably. He also wished to get away.

"Well, you can't!" said the other sharply. "The bank inspector will be in to-morrow to check the Wentford account. It will probably be required as evidence."

Mr. Kingfether got out his little car and drove to London. He parked his machine in a Bloomsbury square and made his way on foot to a big mansion block behind Gower Street. The elevator man who took him up grinned a welcome.

"The young lady's in, sir," he said.

The "young lady" herself opened the door to his ring.

"Look who's here!" she said in surprise, and stood aside to let him in.

She was dressed in an old kimono and did not look as attractive as usual.

"In another half-hour I'd have been out," she said. "I didn't get up till after lunch. These late nights are surely hell!"

She led the way to a sitting-room that was hazy with cigarette smoke. It was a large room, its floor covered with a soft carpet that had once cost a lot of money but was now mottled with stains. Before the fire was a big divan, and on this she had been reclining. The furnishing and appointments of the room were of that style which is believed to be oriental by quite a large number of people. The whole room was halfway to blowsiness. It had a stale, sweet scent. Before the fire, in a shallow basket lined with red silk, a Pekingese dog opened his weary eyes to survey the newcomer, and instantly closed them again.

"Well, my dear, what brings you up to town? I told you to snatch a few hours' sleep—round about one you looked like a boiled owl, and that's not the state to be in when you're chasing money."

She was dark and good looking by certain standards. Her figure was robust, and nature had given generously to the amplification of her visible charms. The red of her full lips was a natural red; the clear skin was of fine texture; her face was scarcely powdered.

For a very long time they talked, head to head. She was an excellent listener; her sympathy had a s ncere note. At half-past five:

"Now off you pop and don't worry. The governor will be seeing you to-night—talk it over with him. I think you'd better, in case anything turns up . . . you know what I mean."

He took a letter out of his pocket and gave it to her with an air of embarrassment.

"I wrote it, or rather started it, this morning . . . I couldn't finish it. I mean every word I say."

She kissed him loudly.

"You're a darling!" she said.

Mr. Kingfether came back to his office to find only a junior in charge. McKay, despite instructions to the contrary, had gone, and the sub-manager sat down to a rough examination of important books in no condition to do justice to his task. He possessed one of those slow-starting tempers that gathers momentum from its own weight. A little grievance and a long brooding brought him to a condition of senseless and unrestrainable fury.

He was in this state when Kenneth McKay returned.

"I asked you to stay in, didn't I?" He glowered at his subordinate.

"Did you? Well, I stayed in until I finished my work. Then the bank inspector came."

Mr. Kingfether's face went white.

"What did he want? Redman didn't tell me he called."

"Well, he did." Kenneth passed into the outer office.

Kingfether sat scribbling oddly on his blotting-pad for a moment, and then for the first time saw the letter that had been placed on the mantelpiece. It was marked "Urgent. Confidential. Deliver by hand," and was from the head office.

He took it up with a shaking hand, and, after a long hesitation, tore the seal. There was a little mirror on the wall above the fireplace, and he caught sight of his face and could hardly believe that that ghost of a man was himself.

There was no need to read the letter twice through. Already he knew every word, every comma. He stood blinking at his reflection, and then went into the outer office. He found Kenneth collecting some personal belongings from his desk.

"I suppose the inspector came about the Wentford cheque?" he said.

The young man looked round at him.

"Wentford cheque? I don't know what you're talking about. You don't mean the cheque I cashed for the woman?"

It required an effort on the manager's part to affirm this.

"What was wrong with it?"

"It was forged, that is all."

"Forged?" Kenneth frowned at him.

"Yes . . . didn't the inspector say anything? He left a letter for me, didn't he?"

Kenneth shook his head.

"No. He was surprised to find that you weren't here. I told him you had gone up to the head office.

I'm getting a bit sick of lying about you. What is the yarn about this cheque?"

Again it required a painful effort on the manager's part to speak.

"It was forged. You've to report to head office to-morrow morning . . . some of the banknotes have been traced to you . . . the cheque was out of your office book."

It was out, yet he felt no relief.

McKay was looking at him open-mouthed.

"You mean the cheque that was changed by that woman?"

The word "woman" irritated Mr. Kingfether.

"A lady was supposed to have called, a veiled lady——"

"What do you mean by 'supposed'?" demanded Kenneth. "You say that the notes were traced to me—I issued them: is that what you mean?"

"You have them—some of them—in your private possession; that's all."

Incredulity showed in Kenneth's face.

"*I?* You mean that I stole them?"

Kingfether had reached the limit of endurance. "How the hell do I know what you did?" he almost shouted. "Head office have written to say that some of the notes you paid over the counter have been traced through a moneylender named Stuart to you."

The young man's face changed suddenly.

"Stuart . . . oh!" was all that he said. A moment later he went blundering out of the side door, leaving Mr. Kingfether to continue his aimless scribblings on his blotting-pad.

Kenneth reached Marlow just before the dinner hour, and he came into the study where old George McKay was usually to be found, working out his eternal combinations. To Kenneth's amazement, his father greeted him with a smile. Instead of the cards, his table was covered with packages of documents and the paraphernalia of correspondence.

"Hullo, son—we've had a stroke of luck. The arbitrators have decided in my favour. I knew jolly well I hadn't parted with my rights in the dyeing process when I sold out, and the company has to pay close on a hundred thousand back royalties."

Kenneth knew of this wrangle between his father and his late company that had gone on through the years, but he had never paid very much attention to it.

"That means a steady income for years, and this time I'm going to look after things—here!"

He pointed to the grate. The fireplace was filled with half-burnt playing cards.

"They've asked me to rejoin the board as chairman. What is the matter, Kenny?"

Kenneth was sitting on the opposite side of the table, and his father had seen his face.

Briefly he told his story, and George McKay listened without comment until he had finished.

"Wentford, eh? He is going to be a curse to me to the end of my days."

Kenneth gasped his amazement.

"Did you know him?"

Old George nodded.

"I knew him all right!" he said grimly. "Reeder was here this morning——"

"About me?" asked the other quickly.

"About me," said his father. "I rather gathered that he suspected me of the murder."

Kenneth came to his feet, horrified.

"You? But he's mad! Why should you——"

Mr. McKay smiled dourly.

"There was quite a good reason why I should murder him," he said calmly; "such a good reason that I have been expecting the police all the afternoon."

Then abruptly he changed the subject.

"Tell me about these banknotes. Of course I knew that you had borrowed the money from Stuart, my boy. I was a selfish old fellow to let you do it—how did the money come to you?"

Kenneth's story was a surprising one.

"I had it a couple of days ago," he said. "I came down to breakfast and found a letter. It was not registered and the address was hand-printed. I opened it, never dreaming what it contained. Just then I was terribly rattled over Stuart—I thought head office might get to know about my borrowing money. And when I found inside the letter twenty ten-pound notes you could have knocked me out."

"Was there any letter?"

"None. Not even 'from a friend.'"

"Who knew about your being in debt?"

One name came instantly to Kenneth's mind.

"You told your Margot, did you . . . Wentford's niece? His real name was Lynn, by the way. Could she have sent it?"

"It was not she who drew the money, I'll swear! I should have known her. And though she was veiled, I could recognize her again if I met her. Kingfether's line is that no woman came; he is suggesting that the cheque was cashed by me. He even says that the cheque was out of a book which I keep in my drawer for the use of customers who come to the bank without their cheque books."

George McKay fingered his chin, his keen eyes on his son.

"If you were in any kind of trouble you'd tell me the truth, my boy, wouldn't you? All this worry has come through me. You're telling me the truth now, aren't you?"

"Yes, father."

The older man smiled.

"Fathers have the privilege of asking, 'Are you a thief?' without having their heads punched! And most young people do stupid things—and most old people too! Lordy! I once carried a quarter of a million bank at baccarat! Nobody would believe that, but it's true. Come and eat, then go along and see your Margot."

"Father, who killed that man Wentford?"

There was a twinkle in McKay's eyes when he answered:

"J. G. Reeder, I should think. He knows more about it than any honest man should know!"

CHAPTER VIII

WHEN her visitor was gone, Ena opened the letter he had left with her, read a few lines of it, then threw letter and envelope into the fire. Funny, the sameness of men . . . they all wrote the same sort of stuff . . . raw stuff dressed up poetically . . . yet they thought they were being different from all other men. She did not resent these stereotypes of passion, nor did she feel sorry for those who used them. They were just normal experiences. She sat clasping her knees, her eyes alternately on the fire and the sleeping dog. Then she got up, dressed quickly, and, going into Gower Street, found a cab.

She was set down at a house in a fashionable Mayfair street, and a liveried footman admitted her and told her there was company. There usually was in the early evening. She found twenty men and women sitting round a green table, watching a croupier with a large green shade over his eyes. He was turning up cards in two rows, and big monies, staked in compartments marked on the green table, went into the croupier's well or was pushed, with additions, to the fortunate winner.

The usual crowd, she noted. One pretty girl looked up and smiled, then turned her eyes quickly and significantly to the young man by her side.

Ena found the governor in his room. He was smoking alone and reading the evening newspaper when she came in.

"Shut the door," he ordered. "What is wrong?"

"Nothing much. Only Fethers is a bit worried." She told him why.

Mr. Machfield smiled.

"Don't *you* worry, my pet," he said kindly. "There has been a murder down his way—did he tell you anything about that? I've just been reading about it. I should be surprised if old Reeder didn't get to the bottom of it—clever fellow, Reeder."

He picked up his newspaper from the floor and his cigar from the ash-tray where he had laid it.

"Rather a coincidence, wasn't it, Ena? Feathers pickin' on that account—Wentford's?"

She looked at him thoughtfully.

"Was it a coincidence?" she asked. "That is what is worrying me. Did he pick on this poor man's account because he knew that he was going to be dead in a few days? I got a horrible creepy feeling when he was sitting beside me. I kept looking at his hands and wondering if there was blood on them!"

"Shuh!" said Mr. Machfield contemptuously. "That rabbit!"

He opened a panel in the wall—it was nothing more romantic than a serving hatch when it was built—and glanced at the gamesters.

"They're playing for marbles!" he said in fine scorn. "But they never do play high in the afternoon. Look at Lamontaine: he's bored sick!"

And certainly the croupier did not look happy. He closed the panel.

"I suppose you'll be raided one of these days?" she said.

"Sure!" he answered easily. "But I've got another couple of houses ready for starting."

"What do you think about Feathers? Will he squeal when they find him out?"

"Like a stuck pig," said Mr. Machfield. "He'll go down for nine months and get religion. That's the kind of fellow who gives the prison chaplain an interest in life. Ena, I've got a little job for you."

She was alert, suspicious.

"Nothing much. I'll tell you all about it. Shall I open a bottle?"

"Yes, if it's milk," she said. "What's the little job and how much does it carry?"

"Would you faint if I said a thousand?" he asked, and opened the hatch again, looking through and closing it.

"Who are you expecting?" she asked. ". . . all right, don't be rude. No, thousands never make me faint. Especially when they're talked about——"

"Now listen."

Mr. Machfield was too good a talker to be brief. He led from a preamble to sections, into sub-sections. . . .

"One minute."

He interrupted his explanation to lift the hatch. She saw him bringing it down; then unexpectedly he raised it again. Was it the effect of odd lighting, or had his face changed colour? He dropped the hatch softly and gaped round at her.

"Who let him in? That doorman has 'shopped' me——"

"Who is it?" she asked.

He beckoned her to his side, lifting the panel an inch.

"Stoop!" he hissed. "Look . . . that fellow with the side whiskers."

"Oh—is he anybody?" She did not recognize the visitor. Possibly he was a bailiff; he looked hopelessly suburban, like the people who serve writs. They always wear ready-to-wear ties and coloured handkerchiefs that stick out of their breast pockets.

"Reeder . . . J. G. Reeder!"

She wanted to raise the hatch and look, but he would not allow this.

"Go out and see what you can do . . . wait a bit."

He lifted a house telephone and pressed a knob.

"Who was that fellow . . . the old fellow with side whiskers? . . . Got a car . . . what name . . . Reeder?"

He put down the 'phone unsteadily. Mr. Machfield gave small membership cards to the right people. They were issued with the greatest care and after elaborate enquiries had been made as to the antecedents of the man or woman so honoured.

"Go and get acquainted . . . he doesn't know you. Go round through the buffet room and pretend you've just come in."

When she reached the gaming room, Ena found Mr. Reeder was sitting opposite the croupier. How he got that favoured chair was a mystery. His umbrella was between his knees. In front of him was a pile of Treasury notes. He was "punting" gravely, seemingly absorbed in the game.

"Faites vos jeux, messieurs et mesdames," said the croupier mechanically.

"What does he mean by that?" asked Mr. Reeder of his nearest neighbour.

"He means 'Make your bet,'" said the girl, who had drawn up a chair by his side.

Mr. Reeder made ten coups and won six pounds. With this he got up from the table and recovered his hat from beneath his chair.

"I always think that the time to—um—stop playing cards is when you're winning." He imparted this truth to the young lady, who had withdrawn from the table at the same time.

"What a marvellous mind you have!" she said enthusiastically.

Mr. Reeder winced.

"I'm afraid I have," he said.

She shepherded him into the buffet room; he seemed quite willing to be refreshed at the expense of the house.

"A cup of tea, thank you, and a little seed cake."

Ena was puzzled. Had the whole breed of busies undergone this shattering deterioration?

"I prefer seed to fruit cake," he was saying. "Curiously enough, chickens are the same. I had a hen once—we called her Curly Toes—who *could* eat fruit and preferred it . . ."

She listened—she was a good listener. He offered to see her home.

"No—if you could drop me at the corner of Bruton Street and Berkeley Square—I don't live far from there," she said modestly.

"Dear me!" said Mr. Reeder, as he signalled to a

cab. "Do you live in a mews, too? So many people do."

This was disconcerting.

"Perhaps you will come and see me one day—I am Mrs. Coleforth-Ebling, and my 'phone number—do write this down——"

"My memory is very excellent," murmured Mr. Reeder.

The cab drove up at that moment and he opened the door.

"Ena Burslem—I will remember that—907, Gower Mansions."

He waved his hand in farewell as he got into the cab.

"I'll be seeing you again, my dear—toodle-oo!"

Mr. Reeder could on occasions be outrageously frivolous. "Toodle-oo!" was the high-water mark of his frivolity. It was not remarkable that Ena was both alarmed and puzzled. Brighter intellects than hers had been shaken in a vain effort to reconcile Mr. Reeder's appearance and manner with Mr. Reeder's reputation.

She went back into the house and told Mr. Machfield what had happened.

"That man's clever," said Machfield admiringly. "If I were the man who had killed Wentworth or whatever his name is, I'd be shaking in my shoes. I'll walk round to the Leffingham and see if I can pick up a young game-fish. And you'd better dine with me, Ena—I'll give you the rest of the dope on that business I was discussing."

The Leffingham Club was quite useful to Mr. Machfield. It was a kind of potting shed where likely young shoots could be nurtured before being bedded out in the gardens of chance. Even Kenneth McKay had had his uses.

When Mr. Reeder reached Scotland Yard, where they had arranged to meet, he found Inspector Gaylor charged with news.

"We've had a bit of luck!" he said. "Do you remember those banknotes? You took their numbers . . . you remember? They were paid out on Wentford's account!"

"Oh, yes, yes, yes," said Mr. Reeder. "To the veiled lady——"

"Veiled grandmother!" said Gaylor. "We have traced two hundred pounds' worth to a moneylender. They were paid by Kenneth McKay, the bank clerk who cashed the cheque—and here is the cheque!"

He took it from a folder on his desk.

"The signature is a bad forgery; the cheque itself was not torn from Wentford's cheque-book but from a book kept at the bank under McKay's charge!"

"Astounding!" said Mr. Reeder.

"Isn't it?" Mr. Gaylor was smiling. "So simple! I had the whole theory of the murders given to me to-night. McKay forged and uttered the note, and to cover up his crime killed Wentford."

"And you instantly arrested him?"

"Am I a child in arms?" asked Gaylor reproachfully. "No, I questioned the lad. He doesn't deny that he paid the moneylender, but says that the money came to him from some anonymous source. It arrived at his house by registered post. Poor young devil, he's rattled to blazes! What are we waiting for now?"

"A Gentleman Who Wants to Open a Box," said Mr. Reeder mysteriously.

("Reeder releases his mysteries as a miser pays his dentist," said Gaylor to the superintendent. "He knows I know all about the case—I admit he is very good and passes on most of the information he gets, but the old devil *will* keep back the connecting links!")

"Humour him," said the superintendent.

CHAPTER IX

MARGOT LYNN had spent a wretched and a weary day. The little city office which she occupied, and where she had conducted most of her uncle's business, had become a place of bad dreams.

She had never been very fond of her tyrannical relative, who, if he had paid her well, had extracted the last ounce of service from her. He was an inveterate speculator, and had made considerable monies from his operations on the Stock Exchange. It was she who had bought and sold on his telephoned instructions, she who put his money into a London bank. Over her head all the time he had held one weapon: she had an invalid mother in Italy dependent on his charity.

All day long, people had been calling at the office. A detective had been there for two hours, taking a new statement; reporters had called in battalions, but these she had not seen. Mr. Reeder had supplied her with an outer guard, a hard-faced woman who held the pressmen at bay. But the police now knew everything there was to know about "Wentford's" private affairs—except one thing. She was keeping faith with the dead in this respect, though every time she thought of her reservation her heart sank.

She finished up her work and went home, leaving the building by a back door to avoid the patient reporters. They were waiting for her at her flat, but the hard-faced Mrs. Grible swept them away.

Once safely in the flat, a difficulty arose. How could she tactfully and delicately dismiss the guard which Mr. Reeder had provided? She offered the woman tea, and Mrs. Grible, who said very little, embarrassed her by making it.

"I'm greatly obliged to you and Mr. Reeder," she said after the little meal. "I don't think I ought to take up any more of your time——"

"I'm staying until Mr. Reeder comes," said the lady.

Very meekly the girl accepted the situation.

Mr. Reeder did not come until ten o'clock. Margot was half dead with weariness, and would have given her legacy to have undressed and gone to bed.

For his part, he was in the liveliest mood, an astounding circumstance remembering that he had had practically no sleep for thirty-six hours. In an indefinable way he communicated to her some of his own vitality. She found herself suddenly very wide awake.

"You have seen the police, of course?" Mr. Reeder sat on a chair facing her, leaning on the handle of his umbrella, his hat carefully deposited on the floor by his side. "And you have told them everything? It is very wise. The key, now—did you tell them about the key?"

She went very red. She was (thought Mr. Reeder) almost as pretty when she was red as when she was white.

"The key?" She could fence, a little desperately, with the question, although she knew just what he meant.

"At the cottage last night you showed me two keys—one the key of the house, the other, from its shape and make, the key of a safe deposit."

Margot nodded.

"Yes. I suppose I should have told them that. But Mr. Wentford——"

"Asked you never to tell. That is why he had two keys, one for you and one for himself."

"He hated paying taxes——" she began.

"Did he ever come up to town?"

"Only on very wet days and foggy days. I have never been to the safe deposit, Mr. Reeder. Anything that is there he placed himself. I only had the key in case of accidents."

"What was he afraid of—did he ever tell you?"

She shook her head.

"He was terribly afraid of something. He did all his own housework and cooking—he would never have anybody in. A gardener used to come every few days and look after the electric light plant, and Mr. Wentford used to pay him through the window. He was afraid of bombs—you've seen the cage round the window in his bedroom? He had that put there for fear somebody should throw in a bomb whilst he was asleep. I can't tell you what precautions he took. Except myself and the policeman, and once Mr. Enward the lawyer, nobody has ever entered that house. His linen was put outside the door every week and left at the door. He had an apparatus for testing milk and he analysed every drop that was left at the house before he drank it—he practically lived on milk. It wasn't so bad when I first went to him—I was sixteen then—but it got worse and worse as the years went on."

"He had two telephones in the house," said Mr. Reeder. "That was rather extravagant."

"He was afraid of being cut off. The second one was connected by underground wires—it cost him an awful lot of money." She heaved a deep, relieved sigh. "Now I've told everything, and my conscience is clear. Shall I get the keys?"

"They are for Mr. Gaylor," said Mr. Reeder hastily. "I think you had better keep them and give them to nobody else. Not even to the person who calls to-night."

"Who is calling to-night?" she asked.

Mr. Reeder avoided the question. He looked at Mrs. Grible, grim and silent.

"Would you mind—er—waiting outside?"

The obedient woman melted from the room.

"There is one point we ought to clear up, my dear young friend," said Mr. Reeder in a hushed voice. "How long had you been in your uncle's house when Mr. Kenneth McKay appeared?"

If he had struck her she could not have wilted as she did. Her face went the colour of chalk, and she dropped into a chair.

"He came through the window into the little lobby—I know all about that—but how long after you arrived?"

She tried to speak twice before she succeeded.

"A few minutes," she said, not raising her eyes.

Then suddenly she sprang up.

"He knew nothing about the murder—he was

stupidly jealous and followed me . . . and then I explained to him, and he believed me. . . . I looked through the window and saw you and told him to go . . . that is the truth, I swear it is!"

He patted her gently on the shoulder.

"I know it is the truth, my dear—be calm, I beg of you. That is all I wanted to know."

He called Mrs. Grible by name. As she came in, they heard the bell of the front door ring. It was followed by a gentle rat-tat.

"Who would that be?" asked Margot. She was still trembling.

"It may be a reporter—it may not be." Mr. Reeder rose. "If it is some stranger to see you on urgent business, perhaps you would be kind enough to mention the fact that you are quite alone."

He looked helplessly round.

"That——" He pointed to a door.

"Is the drawing-room," she said, hardly noticing his embarrassment.

"Very excellent." He was relieved. Opening the door, he waved Mrs. Grible to precede him. "If it should be reporters we will deal with them," he said, and closed the door behind him.

There was a second ring of the bell as Margot hurried to the door. Standing outside was a girl. She was elegantly dressed, was a little older than Margot, and unusually pretty.

"Can I see you, Miss Lynn? It is rather important."

Margot hesitated.

"Come in, please," she said at last.

The girl followed her into the sitting-room.

"All alone?" she said lightly.

Margot nodded.

"You're a great pal of Kenneth's, aren't you?"

She saw the colour come into Margot's face, and laughed.

"Of course you are—and you've had an awful row?"

"I have had no awful row," said Margot quietly.

"He's a jealous boy—they all are, my dear. I always say there is no better proof that a man is gone on you. He's a darling boy, and he's in terrible trouble."

"Trouble—what kind of trouble?" asked Margot quickly.

"Police trouble——"

The girl swayed and caught at the back of a chair.

"Don't get upset." Ena was enjoying her part. "He'll be able to explain everything——"

"But he said he believed me . . ." She was on the point of betraying the presence of the hidden Mr. Reeder, but checked herself in time.

"Who said so?" asked Ena curiously. "A copper—policeman, I mean? Don't take any notice of that kind of trash. They'd lie to save a car fare! We know that Kenneth didn't forge the cheque——"

Margot's eyes opened wide in amazement.

"Forge a cheque—what do you mean? I don't understand what you are talking about."

For a moment Ena was nonplussed. If this girl did not know about the forgery, what was agitating her? The solution of this minor mystery came in a flash. It was the murder! Kenneth was in it! She went cold at the thought.

"Oh, my God! I didn't think of that!" she gasped.

"Tell me about this forgery——" began Margot, and then her visitor remembered her errand.

"I want you to come along and see Kenneth. He's waiting for you at my flat—naturally he can't come here. He'll tell you everything."

Margot was bewildered.

"Of course I'll come, but——"

"Don't 'but,' my dear—just slip into your things and come along. Kenneth told me to ask you to bring all the keys you have—he said they can prove his innocence——"

"Dear, dear, dear!" said a gentle voice and Ena flung round, to face the man who had come into the room.

She was trapped and knew it. That old devil!

"The key of the larder now, would that be of any use to you?" asked Mr. Reeder in his jocular mood. "Or the key of Wormwood Scrubbs?"

"Hullo, Reeder!" The girl was coolness itself. "I thought you were alone, young lady. I did not know you were entertaining Mr. and Mrs. Reeder."

Such an outrageous statement made Mr. Reeder blush, but it did not confuse him. Nor did Mrs. Grible seem particularly distressed.

"This lady is Mrs. Grible, of my department," he said gravely.

"She must have some use," said Ena. She picked up her coat which she had taken off. "I'll 'phone you later, Miss Lynn."

"The cells at Bow Street police station are hygienically equipped, but they have no telephones," said Mr. Reeder, and for the first time in many years Ena lost her nerve.

"What's the idea—cells?" she demanded loudly. "You've got nothing on me——"

"We shall see—will you step this way?" He opened the door of the drawing-room. "I should like to have a few words with you."

He heard a knock at the outer door and looked at Margot.

"I shall be on hand," he said.

She went to the door—and fell back at the sight of her visitor. It was Kenneth McKay. He looked at her gravely, and without a word took her into his arms and kissed her. He had never kissed her that way before.

"Can I see you?"

She nodded and took him back to her room. The other three had disappeared.

"It is only right that you should know, darling, that I'm in terrible trouble. I've just come from home, and I suppose the police are after me. They may be after my father, too. He knew Wentford—hated him. I didn't dream that——"

"Ken—what about you? Why do the police want you?"

He looked at her steadily.

"It is about a forged cheque. Some of the money has been traced to me. Darling, I've come to ask you something, and I want you to tell me the truth. Kingfether as good as told me I was a liar when I said I'd cashed it for a veiled woman. I don't mind really what he says—he's a crook, that fellow! Money has been missing from the bank—they sent old Reeder down weeks ago——"

"How did they trace money to you?" she interrupted. "And what do you want me to tell you?"

"You knew that I owed money—I told you." She nodded. "And how worried I was about it. I can't remember whether I told you how much I owed——"

She shook her head.

"You didn't," she said, and he drew a long breath.

"Then it wasn't you," he said.

He described the arrival of the letter containing the banknotes.

"Two hundred pounds, and of course I wanted the money badly."

"Who else knew that you were short of money?" she asked.

"Oh, everybody." He was in despair. "I blabbed about it—Kingfether said that he never ordered me to cash any cheque that came, and that the story of a veiled woman who arrived by car from London when he was out at lunch was all moonshine—hullo!"

He saw the door of the drawing-room opening and gasped at the sight of Mr. Reeder.

"It wasn't moonshine, my young friend," said Mr. Reeder. "In fact, I—er—have interviewed a garage keeper who filled up the tank of the lady's car, and incidentally saw the lady."

He turned to the room and beckoned Ena. Kenneth stared at her.

"Well?" she said defiantly. "Do you think you'll know me again?"

"I know you now!" he said huskily. "You're the woman who cashed the cheque!"

"That's a damned lie!" she screamed.

"S-sh!" said Mr. Reeder, shocked.

"I've never seen him before!" she added, and Margot gasped.

"But you told me——"

"I've never seen him before," insisted the woman.

"You'll see him again," said Mr. Reeder gently. "You on one side—the wrong side—of the witness box, and he on the other!"

Then she lost her head.

"If there was a swindle, he was in it!" she said, speaking rapidly. "You don't suppose any clerk would pay out six hundred pounds to somebody he had never seen before unless he had his instructions and got his corner! How did I know the cheque was forged? It seemed all right to me."

"May it continue to seem all right," said Mr. Reeder piously. "May you be consoled through the long period of your incarceration with the—er—comfort of a good conscience. I think you will get three years—but if your previous convictions influence the judge, I fancy you will get five!"

Ena collapsed.

"You can't charge me," she whimpered. "I didn't forge anything."

"There is a crime called 'uttering'," said Mr. Reeder. "'Uttering—knowing to be forged.' Will you take the young lady's arm, Mrs. Grible? I will take the other—probably we shall meet a policeman *en route*. And did I say anything about 'conspiracy?' That is also an offence. Mind that mat, Mrs. Grible."

CHAPTER X

THERE was some rather heavy play at Mr. Machfield's private establishment—heavier than usual, and this gave the proprietor of the house cause for uneasiness. If Mr. Reeder had reported his visit that afternoon to the police, and they thought the moment expedient, there would be a raid to-night, and in preparation for this all the doors leading to the mews at the back were unfastened, and a very powerful car was waiting with its engine running. Mr. Machfield might or might not use that method of escape. On the other hand, he could follow his invariable practice, which was to appear amongst those present as a guest: a fairly simple matter, because he was not registered as the proprietor of the house, and he could trust his servants.

Certainly the car would have its uses, if everything went right and there was no untoward incident. Just lately, however, there had been one or two little hitches in the smooth running of his affairs, and, being superstitious, he expected more.

He looked at his watch; his appointment with Ena was at midnight, but she had promised to 'phone through before then. At a quarter to nine, as he stood watching the players, there came a newcomer at the tail of three others. He was in evening dress, as were the majority of people round the board, and he looked strangely out of place in those surroundings, though his blue chin was newly shaved and his black hair was glossy with pomade, and in the lapel of his coat he wore a dazzling gardenia.

Mr. Machfield watched him wander aimlessly around the table, and then caught his eye and indicated that he wished to see him. Soon afterwards he walked out of the room and Mr. Kingfether followed.

"You're rather silly to come to-night, K," said Mr. Machfield. "There's just a chance of a raid—Reeder was here this afternoon."

The manager's jaw dropped.

"Is he here now?" he asked, and Mr. Machfield smiled at the foolishness of the question.

"No, and he won't be coming to-night, unless he arrives with a flying squad. We'll keep that bird out, at any rate."

"Where is Ena?" asked Kingfether.

"She'll be in later," lied Machfield. "She had a bit of a headache, and I advised her not to come."

The bank manager helped himself to a whisky from a decanter on the sideboard.

"I'm very fond of that girl," said Kingfether.

"Who isn't?" asked the other.

"To me"—there was a tremor in the younger man's voice—"she is something outside of all my experience. Do you think she's fond of me, Machfield?"

"I am sure she is," said the other heartily; "but she's a woman of the world, you know, my boy, and women of the world do not carry their hearts on their sleeves."

He might have added, that, in the case of Ena she carried the business equivalent of that organ up her sleeve, ready for exhibition to any susceptible man, young or old.

"Do you think she'd marry me, Machfield?"

Mr. Machfield did not laugh. He had played cards a great deal and had learned to school his countenance. Ena had two husbands, and had not gone through the formality of freeing herself from either. Both were officially abroad, the foreign country being that stretch of desolate moorland which lies between Ashburton and Tavistock. Here, in the gaunt convict establishment of Princeton, they laboured for the good of their souls, but with little profit to the tax-payers who supported them, and even supplied them with tobacco.

"Why shouldn't she? But mind, she's an expensive kind of girl, K," said Machfield very seriously. "She costs a lot of money to dress, and you'd have to find it from somewhere—five hundred a year doesn't go far with a girl who buys her dresses in Paris."

Kingfether strode up and down the apartment, his hands in his pockets, his head on his chest, a look of gloom on a face that was never touched with brightness.

"I realize that," he said, "but if she loved me she'd help to make both ends meet. I've got to cut out this business of the bank; I've had a fright, and I can't take the risk again. In fact, I thought of leaving the bank and setting up a general agency in London."

Mr. Machfield knew what a general agency was when it was run by an inexperienced man. An office to which nobody came except bill collectors. He didn't, however, wish to discourage his client; for the matter of that, Kingfether gave him little opportunity for comment.

"There is going to be hell's own trouble about that cheque," he said. "I had a letter from head office—I have to report to the general manager in the morning and take McKay with me. That is the usual course."

Such details were distasteful to Mr. Machfield. He needed all the spare room in his mind for other matters much more weighty than the routine of the Great Central Bank, but he was more than interested in the fate of McKay.

Kingfether came back to Ena, because Ena filled his horizon.

"The first time I ever met her," he said, "I knew she was the one woman in the world for me. I know she's had a rough time and that she's had a battle to live. But who am I to judge?"

"Who, indeed?" murmured Mr. Machfield, with considerable truth. And then, pursuing his thought, "What will happen to Mr. Kenneth McKay?"

Only for a moment did the manager look uncomfortable.

"He is not my concern," he said loudly. "There is no doubt at all that the signature on the cheque ——"

"Oh, yes, yes," said the other impatiently. "We don't want to discuss that, do we? I mean, not between friends. You paid me the money you owed me, and there was an end to it so far as I am concerned. I took a bit of a risk myself, sending Ena down—I mean, letting Ena go," he corrected, when he saw the look on the other's face. "What about young McKay?"

The manager shrugged his shoulders.

"I don't know and I really don't care. When I got back to the bank this afternoon he'd gone, though I'd left instructions that he was to stay until I returned. Of course, I can't report it, because I did wrong to go away myself, and it was rather awkward that one of our bank inspectors called when I was out. I shall have to work all night to make up arrears. McKay might have helped me. In fact, I told him——"

"Oh, he came back, did he?"

"For five minutes, just before six o'clock. He just looked in and went out again. That is how I knew the inspector had called. I had to tell this pup about the cheque and the banknotes. By the way, that is a mystery to me how the notes came into his hands at all—I suppose there is no mistake about them? If he was in the habit of coming here he might have got them from the table. He doesn't come here, does he?"

"Not often." Mr. Machfield might have added that nobody came to that place unless they had a certain amount of surplus wealth, or the means by which easy money could be acquired.

There were quite a number of his clients who were in almost exactly the same position as Mr. Kingfether—people in positions of trust, men who had the handling of other people's money. It was no business of Machfield's how that money was obtained, so long as it was judiciously spent. It was his boast that his game was straight; as indeed it was—up to a point. He had allowed himself throughout life a certain margin of dishonesty, which covered both bad luck and bad investments. Twice in his life he had gone out for big coups. Once he had failed, the other time he had succeeded but had made no money.

He was not *persona grata* in all the countries of the world. If he had arrived at Monte Carlo he would have left by very nearly the next train, or else the obliging police would have placed a motor-car at his disposal to take him across to Nice, a resort which isn't so particular as to the character of her temporary visitors.

"I'm sorry for McKay in a way, although he is such an impossible swine, but it's a case of his life or mine, Machfield. Either he goes down or I go down—and I'm not going down."

Nothing wearied Mr. Machfield worse than heroics. And yet he should have been hardened to them, for he had lived in an atmosphere of hectic drama, and once had seen a victim of his lying dead by his own hand across the green board of his gaming table. But it was years ago.

"You'd better slide back to the room," he said. "I'll come in a little later. Don't play high: I've still got some of your papers, dear boy."

When he returned to the room, the manager had found a seat at the table and was punting modestly and with some success. The croupier asked a question with a flick of his eyelids, and almost imperceptibly Machfield shook his head, which meant that that night, at any rate, Kingfether would pay for his losses in cash, that neither his I.O.U.'s nor cheques would be accepted.

From time to time the players got up from the tables, strolled into the buffet, had a drink and departed. But there was always a steady stream of newcomers to take their places. Mr. Machfield went back to his study, for he was expecting a telephone message. It came at a quarter past ten. A woman's voice said: "Ena says everything is O.K."

He hung up the telephone with a smile. Ena was a safe bet: you could always trust that girl, and he did not question her ability to keep her visitor occupied for at least two hours. After that he would do a little questioning himself. But it must be he, and not that other fool.

There was no sign of raiders. He had special scouts posted at every street corner approaching the house, and a man on the roof (no sinecure this on a night of rain and sleet) to take and transmit their signals in case of danger. If there were a raid he was prepared for it. More likely the police, following their invariable custom, would postpone the visitation until later in the week. And by that time, if all went well, the house would be closed and the keys in the hands of the agents.

Kingfether was winning; there was a big pile of Treasury and five-pound notes before him. He looked animated, and for once in his life pleased. The bank was winning too; there was a big box recessed into the table, and this was full of paper money and every few minutes the pile was augmented.

A dull evening! Mr. Machfield would be glad when

the time came for his loud-speaking gramophone to play the National Anthem. He always closed down on this patriotic note: it left the most unlucky of players with the comforting sense that at least they had their country left to them.

He was looking at the long folding door of the room as it opened slowly. It was second nature in him to watch that opening door, and until this moment he had never been shocked or startled by what it revealed. Now, however, he stood dumbfounded, for there was Mr. Reeder, without his hat, and even without his umbrella.

Nobody noticed him except the proprietor, and he was frozen to the spot. With an apologetic smile Mr. Reeder came tiptoeing across to him.

"Do you very much mind?" he asked in an urgent whisper. "I find time hanging rather heavily upon my hands."

Machfield licked his dry lips.

"Come here, will you?"

He went back to his study, Reeder behind him.

"Now, Mr. Reeder, what's the idea of your coming here? How did you get in? I gave strict instructions to the man on the door——"

"I told him a lie," said Mr. Reeder in a hushed tone, as though the enormity of his offence had temporarily overcome him. "I said that you had particularly asked me to come to-night. That was very wrong, and I am sorry. The truth is, Mr. Machfield, even the most illustrious of men have their little weaknesses; even the cleverest and most law-abiding their criminal instincts, and although I am neither illustrious nor clever, I have the frailties of my—er—humanity. Not, I would add, that it is criminal to play cards for money—far from it. I, as you probably know, or you may have heard, have a curiously distorted mind. I find my secret pleasures in such places as these."

Mr. Machfield was relieved, immensely relieved. He knew detectives who gambled, but somehow he had never associated Mr. J. G. Reeder with this peculiar weakness.

"Why, certainly, we're glad to see you, Mr. Reeder," he said heartily.

He was so glad indeed that he would have been happy to have given this odd-looking man the money wherewith to play.

"You'll have a drink on the house—not," he added quickly, "that I am in any position to offer you a drink. I am a guest the same as yourself, but I know the proprietor would be annoyed if you came and went without having one."

"I never drink. A little barley water perhaps."

There was, unfortunately, no barley water in the establishment, but this, as Machfield explained, would be remedied in the future—even now if he wished. Mr. Reeder, however, would not hear of putting "the house" to trouble. He was anxious to join the company, and again by some extraordinary quality of good luck, he managed to insinuate himself so that he sat opposite the croupier. Somebody rose from their chair as he approached, and Mr. Reeder took the vacant seat.

He might have taken a chair on the opposite side of the table, for at the sight of him a pallid Kingfether had whipped out his handkerchief and covered the lower part of his face as though he were suffering from a bad cold.

Stealthily he rose from his seat and melted into the fringe of people standing behind the players.

"Don't let me drive you away, Mr. Kingfether," said Reeder's voice, and everybody heard him.

The manager dropped back till he stood against the wall, a limp, helpless figure, and there he remained through the scene that followed.

Mr. Reeder had produced a bundle of Treasury notes which he counted with great care. It was not a big bundle. Mr. Machfield, watching, guessed he was in the ten-pound line of business, and certainly there was no more than that on the table.

One by one those little notes of Reeder's disappeared, until there was nothing left, and then a surprising thing happened. Mr. Reeder put his hand in his pocket, groped painfully and produced something which he covered with his hand. The croupier had raised his cards ready to deal—the game was *trente-et-quarante*—when the interruption came.

"Excuse me." J. G. Reeder's voice was gentle but everybody at the table heard it. "You can't play with that pack: there are two cards missing."

The croupier raised his head. The green shade strapped to his glossy head threw a shadow which hid the top half of his face.

He stared blandly at the interrupter—the dispassionate and detached stare which only a professional croupier can give.

"*Pardon?*" he said, puzzled. "I do not understand m'sieur. The pack is complete. It is never questioned——"

"There are two cards without which I understand you cannot play your game," said Mr. Reeder, and suddenly lifted his hand.

On the table before him were two playing cards, the ace of diamonds and the ace of hearts. The croupier looked down at them, and then, with an oath, pushed back his chair and dropped his hand to his hip.

"Don't move—I beg of you!"

There was an automatic pistol in Mr. Reeder's hand, and its muzzle was directed towards the croupier's white waistcoat.

"Ladies and gentlemen, there is nothing to be alarmed about. Stand back from the table against the wall, and do not come between me and Monsieur Lamontaine!"

He himself stepped backward.

"Over there!" he signalled to Machfield.

"Look here, Reeder——"

"Over there!" snarled J. G. Reeder. "Stand up by your friend. Ladies and gentlemen"—he addressed the company again without taking his eyes from the croupier—"there will be a few moments of acute unpleasantness. Your names and addresses will be taken, but I will use my best endeavours to avoid police court proceedings, because we are after something much more important than naughty people who play cards for money."

And then the guests saw strange men standing in the doorway. They came from all directions—from Mr. Machfield's study, from the hall below, from the roof above. They handcuffed Lamontaine and took away the two guns he carried, one in each hip pocket—Machfield was unarmed.

"What will the charge be?"

"Mr. Gaylor will tell you that at the police station. But I think the question is unnecessary. Honestly, don't you, Mr. Machfield?"

Machfield said nothing.

CHAPTER XI

Mr. Reeder kept what he called a case-book, in which he inscribed a passionless account of all the cases in which he was engaged. Some of these cases had no value except to the technician, and would not interest anyone except perhaps the psycho-pathologist. Under the heading "Two Aces" appeared this account, written in his own handwriting:

In the year 1919 [wrote Mr. Reeder] there arrived at the Hotel Majestic in Nice a man who described himself in the hotel register as Rufus Machfield. He had a number of other names, but it is only necessary that Machfield should be used to identify this particular character. The man had a reputation as a cardsharp, and, in the pursuit of his nefarious calling, had "worked" the ships plying between England and New York. He had also been convicted on two occasions as a professional gambler in Germany.

He was of Danish origin, but at the time was a naturalized Englishman, with a permanent address in Colvin Gardens, Bayswater. At the Majestic Hotel he had met with Charles or Walter Lynn, an adventurer who had also "operated" the ships on the North Atlantic. On one of these trips Lynn had become acquainted with Mr. George McKay, a prosperous woollen merchant of Bradford. There is no evidence that they ever played cards together, and Mr. McKay does not recall that they did. But the friendship was of value to Lynn because Mr. McKay was in the habit of coming to Nice every year, and was in residence at the time Lynn and Machfield met. McKay was known as a resolute and successful gambler, and before now had figured in sensational play.

The two men, Lynn and Machfield, conferred together and decided upon a scheme to rob McKay at the tables. Gambling in Nice is not confined to the recognized establishments. There was at the time a number of *Cercles Privés* where play was even higher than at the public rooms, and the most reputable of these was "Le Signe" which, if it was not recognized, was winked at by the French authorities.

In order to swindle McKay, a patron of this club, it was necessary to secure the co-operation and help of an official. Lynn's choice fell upon a young croupier named Lamontaine, and he in turn was to suborn two other croupiers, both of whom it was intended should receive a very generous share of the money.

Lamontaine proved to be a singularly pliable tool. He had married a young wife and had got into debt, and was fearful that this should come to the ears of the club authorities. An interview was arranged in Lyons; the scheme was put before the croupier by Lynn, and he agreed to come in, taking a half share for himself and his two fellow croupiers, the other half being equally divided between Lynn and Machfield. Lynn apparently demurred at the division, but Machfield was satisfied with his quarter share; the more so as he knew Mr. McKay had been winning very heavily, and providing he had the right kind of betting, there would be a big killing.

The game to be played was baccarat, for McKay could never resist the temptation of taking a bank, especially a big bank. It was very necessary that arrangements should be hurried on before the merchant left the South of France, and a fortnight after the preliminaries, Lamontaine reported that everything was in trim, that he had secured the co-operation of his comrades, and it was decided that the coup should be brought off on the Friday night.

It was arranged that Lynn should be the player, that after play was finished the conspirators should meet again at Lyons, when the loot was to be divided.

The cards were to be stacked so that the bank won every third coup. It was arranged that the signal for the conspirators to begin their betting was to be the dealing of two aces, the ace of diamonds and the ace of hearts. Somebody would draw a six to these, and the banker would have a "natural"—which means, I understand, that he would win.

Thereafter the betting was to be done by Lynn, and the first was a banco call—which meant, as the cards lay, that the bank would be swept into their pockets. They knew Mr. McKay would bid for the bank, but they would bid higher, and Lynn then took the bank with a capital of a million francs. Fourteen times the bank won, and had now reached enormous proportions, so much so that every other table in the room was deserted, and the table where this high play was going on was surrounded by curious watchers.

There were fourteen winning coups for the bank, and the amount gathered up at the finish by Lynn was something in the neighbourhood of £400,000. Lamontaine states that it was more, but Machfield is satisfied that it was in that region. The money was taken to the hotel, and the following night Lynn left for Lyons. He was to be joined the next day by Machfield, and on the Sunday they were to meet the croupier in Paris and pay him his share.

The night that Lynn left, however, one of the officials of the rooms made a statement to his *chef.* He had lost his nerve and he betrayed his comrades. Lamontaine, with the other croupier, was arrested on a charge of conspiracy, and Machfield only got away from the South of France by the skin of his teeth. He journeyed on to Lyons and arrived there in the early hours of the following afternoon. He hoped that no news of the arrests would have got into the papers and scared his partner, and certainly he did not wire warning Lynn. When he got to the hotel he asked for his friend, but was told that he had not arrived, nor had he made reservation of the rooms which had been agreed upon.

From that moment he disappeared from human ken, and neither Machfield nor any of his friends were able to trace him. It was no accident: it was a deliberate double-cross. Machfield played the game as far as he was able, and when Lamontaine was released from prison and came to Paris, a broken man, for his young wife had died while he was in gaol, he helped the croupier as well as he could, and together they came to England to establish gaming-houses, but primarily to find Lynn and force him to disgorge.

There was another person on the track of Lynn. McKay, who had been robbed, as he knew after the French court proceedings, employed me to trace him, but for certain reasons I was unable to justify his confidence.

I do not know in what year or month Lamontaine and Machfield located their man. It is certain that "Mr. Wentford," as he called himself, lived in increasing fear of their vengeance. When they did locate him he proved to be an impossible man to reach. I have no doubt that the house was carefully reconnoitred, his habits studied, and that attempts were made to get at him. But those attempts failed. It is highly probable, though no proof of this exists, that he was well informed as to his enemy's movements, for so far as can be gathered from the statement of his niece and checked by the admissions of Machfield, Lynn never left his house except on the days when Machfield and Lamontaine were in Paris—they frequently went to that city over the weekend.

It was Lamontaine who formed the diabolical plan which was eventually to lead to Wentford's death. He knew that the only man admitted to the house was the mounted policeman who patrolled that part of the country, so he studied police methods, even got information as to the times on which the beat was patrolled, and on the night of the murder, soon after it was dark, he travelled down to Beaconsfield by car through the storm, accompanied by Machfield.

Lamontaine at some time or other had been on the French stage (he spoke perfect English) and I have no doubt was in a position to make himself up sufficiently well to deceive Wentford into opening the door. At seven o'clock Constable Verity left the station and proceeded on his patrol. At seven-thirty he was ruthlessly murdered by a man who stepped out of his concealment and shot him point-blank through the heart.

The body was taken into a field and laid out, the two murderers hoping that the snow would cover it. Lamontaine was already wearing the uniform of a police constable, and, mounting the horse, he rode on to Wentford's house. The old man saw him through the window, and, suspecting nothing, got down and opened the door.

He may not have realized that anything was wrong until he was back in his parlour, for it was there that he was struck down. The two men intended leaving him in the cottage, but a complication arose whilst they were searching the place, or endeavouring to open the safe behind the bookcase. The telephone rang, and they heard Margot Lynn say that she was coming on but was delayed. One of them answered in a disguised voice.

The thing to do now was to remove the body. Lifting it out, they laid it over the horse's saddle, and, guiding the nervous animal down to the road, led it towards Beaconsfield. Here a second complication arose: the lights of Mr. Enward's car were seen coming towards them. The body was dropped by the side of the road, and the constable took his place on the horse's back. The animal was smothered with the blood of the murdered man, and the clerk of Mr. Enward, the lawyer, taking the bridle quite innocently, must have rubbed his sleeve along the shoulder, for it was afterwards discovered that his coat was stained. That gave me my first clue, and I was able, owing to my peculiar mind, to reconstruct the crime as it had been committed.

The two men joined one another again in the vicinity of the cottage. They were not able to make any further attempt that night. One of them, however, heard that the girl knew where the money was cashed. I am afraid I was responsible for this, and it was intended that she should be taken away, with the key of the safe deposit. . . .

Machfield had already become acquainted with the straitened circumstances of young McKay, the son of his victim, and probably to hit at his father, who he must have known was still hunting for him, used an opportunity which was offered by chance, to ruin him, as he believed.

Two hundred pounds, representing a portion of the money obtained from the bank by a fraudulent manager (3 years Penal Servitude; Central Criminal Court) through the instrumentality of his woman friend (5 years P.S., C.C.C.) was sent anonymously to the younger McKay by Machfield, and was traced to the young man.

After this came a note, also in Mr. Reeder's hand:

Rufus John Machfield and Antonio Lamontaine (sentence: death, C.C.C.) executed at Wandsworth Prison, April 17th. Executioner Ellis.

Mr. Reeder was a stickler for facts.

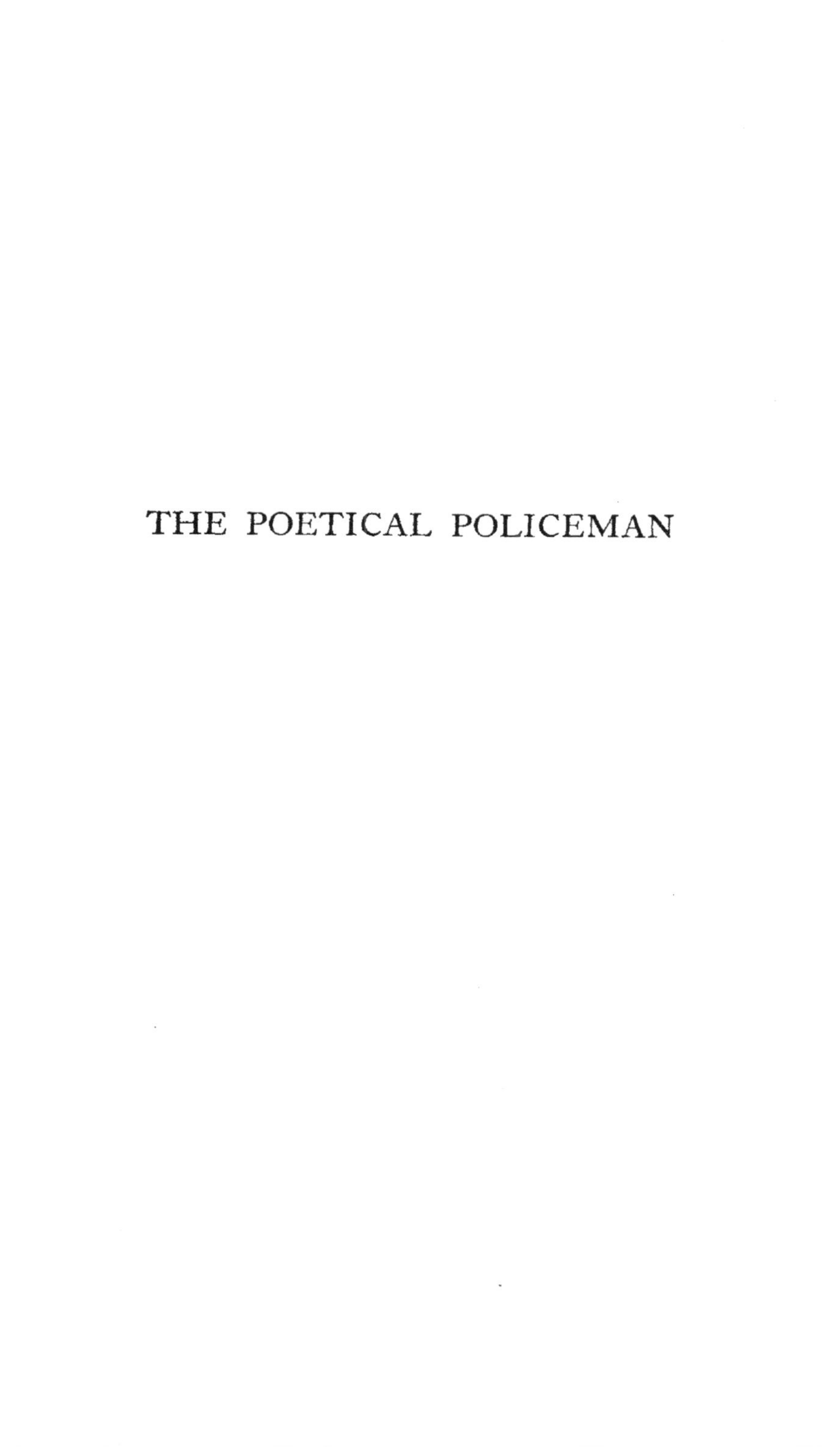

THE POETICAL POLICEMAN

The Poetical Policeman

THE day Mr. Reeder arrived at the Public Prosecutor's office was indeed a day of fate for Mr. Lambton Green, branch manager of the London Scottish and Midland Bank.

That branch of the bank which Mr. Green controlled was situate at the corner of Pell Street and Firling Avenue on the "country side" of Ealing. It is a fairly large building and, unlike most suburban branch offices, the whole of the premises were devoted to banking business, for the bank carried very heavy deposits, the Lunar Traction Company, with three thousand people on its payroll, the Associated Novelties Corporation, with its enormous turnover, and the Laraphone Company being only three of the L.S.M.'s customers.

On Wednesday afternoons, in preparation for the pay days of these corporations, large sums in currency were brought from the head office and deposited in the steel and concrete strong-room, which was immediately beneath Mr. Green's private office, but admission to which was gained through a steel door in the general office. This door was observable from the street, and to assist observation there was a shaded lamp fixed to the wall immediately above, which threw a powerful beam of light upon the door. Further security was ensured by the employment of a night watchman, Arthur Malling, an army pensioner.

The bank lay on a restricted police beat which had been so arranged that the constable on patrol passed the bank every forty minutes. It was his practice to look through the window and exchange signals with the night watchman, his orders being to wait until Malling appeared.

On the night of October 17th Police-Constable Burnett stopped as usual before the wide peep-hole and glanced into the bank. The first thing he noticed was that the lamp above the strong-room door had been extinguished. The night watchman was not visible, and, his suspicions aroused, the officer did not wait for the man to put in an appearance as he would ordinarily have done, but passed the window to the door, which, to his alarm, he found ajar. Pushing it open, he entered the bank, calling Malling by name. There was no answer.

Permeating the air was a faint, sweet scent which he could not locate. The general offices were empty and, entering the manager's room in which a light burnt, he saw a figure stretched upon the ground. It was the night watchman. His wrists were handcuffed, two straps had been tightly buckled about his knees and ankles.

The explanation for the strange and sickly aroma was now clear. Above the head of the prostrate man was suspended, by a wire hooked to the picture-rail, an old tin can, the bottom of which was perforated so that there fell an incessant trickle of some volatile liquid upon the thick cotton pad which covered Malling's face.

Burnett, who had been wounded in the war, had instantly recognised the smell of chloroform and, dragging the unconscious man into the outer office, snatched the pad from his face and, leaving him only long enough to telephone to the police station, sought vainly to bring him to consciousness.

The police reserves arrived within a few minutes, and with them the divisional surgeon who, fortunately, had been at the station when the alarm came through. Every effort to restore the unfortunate man to life proved unavailing.

"He was probably dead when he was found," was the police doctor's verdict. "What those scratches are on his right palm is a mystery."

He pulled open the clenched fist and showed half a dozen little scratches. They were recent, for there was a smear of blood on the palm.

Burnett was sent at once to arouse Mr. Green, the manager, who lived in Firling Avenue, at the corner of which the bank stood; a street of semi-detached villas of a pattern familiar enough to the Londoner. As the officer walked through the little front garden to the door he saw a light through the panels, and he had hardly knocked before the door was opened and Mr. Lambton Green appeared, fully dressed and, to the officer's discerning eye, in a state of considerable agitation. Constable Burnett saw on a hall chair a big bag, a travelling rug and an umbrella.

The little manager listened, pale as death, while Burnett told him of his discovery.

"The bank robbed? Impossible!" he almost shrieked. "My God! this is awful!"

He was so near the point of collapse that Burnett had to assist him into the street.

"I—I was going away on a holiday," he said incoherently, as he walked up the dark thoroughfare toward the bank premises. "The fact is—I was leaving the bank. I left a note—explaining to the directors."

Into a circle of suspicious men the manager tottered. He unlocked the drawer of his desk, looked and crumbled up.

"They're not here!" he said wildly. "I left them here—my keys—with the note!"

And then he swooned. When the dazed man recovered he found himself in a police cell and, later in the day, he drooped before a police magistrate, supported by two constables, and listened, like a man in a dream, to a charge of causing the death of Arthur Malling, and further, of converting to his own use the sum of £100,000.

It was on the morning of the first remand that Mr. John G. Reeder, with some reluctance for he was suspicious of all Government departments, transferred himself from his own office on Lower Regent Street to a somewhat gloomy bureau on the top floor of the building which housed the Public Prosecutor. In making this change he advanced only one stipulation: that he should be connected by private telephone wire with his old bureau.

He did not demand this—he never demanded anything. He asked, nervously and apologetically. There was a certain wistful helplessness about John G. Reeder that made people feel sorry for him, that caused even the Public Prosecutor a few uneasy moments of doubt as to whether he had been quite wise in substituting this weak-appearing man of middle age for Inspector Holford—bluff, capable, and heavily mysterious.

Mr. Reeder was something over fifty, a long-faced gentleman with sandy-grey hair and a slither of side whiskers that mercifully distracted attention from his large outstanding ears. He wore halfway down his nose a pair of steel-rimmed pince-nez, through which nobody had ever seen him look—they were invariably removed when he was reading. A high and flat-crowned bowler hat matched and yet did not match a frock-coat tightly buttoned across his sparse chest. His boots were square-toed, his cravat—of the broad, chest-protector pattern—was ready-made and buckled into place behind a Gladstonian collar. The neatest appendage to Mr. Reeder was an umbrella rolled so tightly that it might be mistaken for a frivolous walking cane. Rain or shine, he carried this article hooked to his arm, and within living memory it had never been unfurled.

Inspector Holford (promoted now to the responsibilities of Superintendent) met him in the office to hand over his duties, and a more tangible quantity in the shape of old furniture and fixings.

"Glad to know you, Mr. Reeder. I haven't had the pleasure of meeting you before, but I've heard a lot about you. You've been doing Bank of England work, haven't you?"

Mr. Reeder whispered that he had had that honour, and sighed as though he regretted the drastic sweep of fate that had torn him from the obscurity of his labours. Mr. Holford's scrutiny was full of misgivings.

"Well," he said awkwardly, "this job is different, though I'm told that you are one of the best informed men in London, and if that is the case this will be easy work. Still, we've never had an outsider—I mean, so to speak, a private detective—in this office before, and naturally the Yard is a bit——"

"I quite understand," murmured Mr. Reeder, hanging up his immaculate umbrella. "It is very natural. Mr. Bolond expected the appointment. His wife is annoyed—very properly. But she has no reason to be. She is an ambitious woman. She has a third interest in a West End dancing club that might be raided one of these days."

Holford was staggered. Here was news that was little more than a whispered rumour at Scotland Yard.

"How the devil do you know that?" he blurted.

Mr. Reeder's smile was one of self-depreciation.

"One picks up odd scraps of information," he said apologetically. "I—I see wrong in everything. That is my curious perversion—I have a criminal mind!"

Holford drew a long breath.

"Well—there is nothing much doing. That Ealing case is pretty clear. Green is an ex-convict, who got a job at the bank during the war and worked up to manager. He has done seven years for conversion."

"Embezzlement and conversion," murmured Mr. Reeder. "I—er—I'm afraid I was the principal witness against him: bank crimes were rather—er—a hobby of mine. Yes, he got into difficulties with money-lenders. Very foolish—extremely foolish. And he doesn't admit his error." Mr. Reeder sighed heavily. "Poor fellow! With his life at stake one may forgive and indeed condone his pitiful prevarications."

The inspector stared at the new man in amazement.

"I don't know that there is much 'poor fellow' about him. He has cached £100,000 and told the weakest yarn that I've ever read—you'll find copies of the police reports here, if you'd like to read them. The scratches on Malling's hand are curious—they've found several on the other hand. They are not deep enough to suggest a struggle. As to the yarn that Green tells——"

Mr. J. G. Reeder nodded sadly.

"It was not an ingenious story," he said, almost with regret. "If I remember rightly, his story was something like this: he had been recognised by a man who served in Dartmoor with him, and this fellow wrote a blackmailing letter telling him to pay or clear out. Sooner than return to a life of crime, Green wrote out all the facts to his directors, put the letter in the drawer of his desk with his keys, and left a note for his head cashier on the desk itself, intending to leave London and try to make a fresh start where he was unknown."

"There were no letters in or on the desk, and no keys," said the inspector decisively. "The only true part of the yarn was that he had done time."

"Imprisonment," suggested Mr. Reeder plaintively. He had a horror of slang. "Yes, that was true."

Left alone in his office, he spent a very considerable time at his private telephone, communing with the young person who was still a young person, although the passage of time had dealt unkindly with her. For the rest of the morning he was reading the depositions which his predecessor had put on the desk.

It was late in the afternoon when the Public Prosecutor strolled into his room and glanced at the big pile of manuscript through which his subordinate was wading.

"What are you reading—the Green business?" he asked, with a note of satisfaction in his voice. "I'm glad that is interesting you—though it seems a fairly straightforward case. I have had a letter from the president of the man's bank, who for some reason seems to think Green was telling the truth."

Mr. Reeder looked up with that pained expression of his which he invariably wore when he was puzzled.

"Here is the evidence of Policeman Burnett," he said. "Perhaps you can enlighten me, sir. Policeman Burnett stated in his evidence—let me read it:

"Some time before I reached the bank premises I saw a man standing at the corner of the street, immediately outside the bank. I saw him distinctly in the light of a passing mail van. I did not attach any importance to his presence, and I did not see him again. It was possible for this man to have gone round the block and come to 120 Firling Avenue without being seen by me. Immediately after I saw him, my foot struck against a piece of iron on the sidewalk. I put my lamp on the object and found it was an old horseshoe; I had seen children playing with this particular shoe earlier in the evening. When I looked again towards the corner, the man had disappeared. He would have seen the light of my lamp. I saw no other person, and so far as I can remember, there was no light showing in Green's house when I passed it."

Mr. Reeder looked up.

"Well?" said the Prosecutor. "There's nothing remarkable about that. It was probably Green, who dodged round the block and came in at the back of the constable."

Mr. Reeder scratched his chin.

"Yes," he said thoughtfully, "ye-es." He shifted uncomfortably in his chair. "Would it be considered indecorous if I made a few inquiries, independent of the police?" he asked nervously. "I should not like them to think that a mere dilettante was interfering with their lawful functions."

"By all means," said the Prosecutor heartily.

"Go down and see the officer in charge of the case: I'll give you a note to him—it is by no means unusual for my officer to conduct a separate investigation, though I am afraid you will discover very little. The ground has been well covered by Scotland Yard."

"It would be permissible to see the man?" hesitated Reeder.

"Green? Why, of course! I will send you up the necessary order."

The light was fading from a grey, blustering sky, and rain was falling fitfully, when Mr. Reeder, with his furled umbrella hooked to his arm, his coat collar turned up, stepped through the dark gateway of Brixton Prison and was led to the cell where a distracted man sat, his head upon his hands, his pale eyes gazing into vacancy.

"It's true; it's true! Every word." Green almost sobbed the words.

A pallid man, inclined to be bald, with a limp yellow moustache, going grey. Reeder, with his extraordinary memory for faces, recognised him the moment he saw him, though it was some time before the recognition was mutual.

"Yes, Mr. Reeder, I remember you now. You were the gentleman who caught me before. But I've been as straight as a die. I've never taken a farthing that didn't belong to me. What my poor girl will think——"

"Are you married?" asked Mr. Reeder sympathetically.

"No, but I was going to be—rather late in life. She's nearly thirty years younger than me, and the best girl that ever . . ."

Reeder listened to the rhapsody that followed, the melancholy deepening in his face.

"She hasn't been into the court, thank God, but she knows the truth. A friend of mine told me that she has been absolutely knocked out."

"Poor soul!" Mr. Reeder shook his head.

"It happened on her birthday, too," the man went on bitterly.

"Did she know you were going away?"

"Yes, I told her the night before. I'm not going to bring her into the case. If we'd been properly engaged it would be different; but she's married and is divorcing her husband, but the decree hasn't been made absolute yet. That's why I never went about with her or saw much of her. And of course, nobody knew about our engagement, although we lived in the same street."

"Firling Avenue?" asked Reeder, and the bank manager nodded despondently.

"She was married when she was seventeen to a brute. It was pretty galling for me, having to keep quiet about it—I mean, for nobody to know about our engagement. All sorts of rotten people were making up to her, and I had just to grind my teeth and say nothing. Impossible people! Why, that fool Burnett, who arrested me, he was sweet on her; used to write her poetry—you wouldn't think it possible in a policeman, would you?"

The outrageous incongruity of a poetical policeman did not seem to shock the detective.

"There is poetry in every soul, Mr. Green," he said gently, "and a policeman is a man."

Though he dismissed the eccentricity of the constable so lightly, the poetical policeman filled his mind all the way home to his house in the Brockley Road, and occupied his thoughts for the rest of his waking time.

It was a quarter to eight o'clock in the morning and the world seemed entirely populated by milkmen and whistling newspaper boys, when Mr. J. G. Reeder came into Firling Avenue.

He stopped only for a second outside the bank, which had long since ceased to be an object of local awe and fearfulness, and pursued his way down the broad avenue. On either side of the thoroughfare ran a row of pretty villas—pretty although they bore a strong family resemblance to one another; each house with its little fore-court, sometimes laid out simply as a grass plot, sometimes decorated with flower-beds. Green's house was the eighteenth in the road on the right-hand side. Here he had lived with a cook-housekeeper, and apparently gardening was not his hobby, for the fore-court was covered with grass that had been allowed to grow at its will.

Bcfore the twenty-sixth house in the road

Mr. Reeder paused and gazed with mild interest at the blue blinds which covered every window. Evidently Miss Magda Grayne was a lover of flowers, for geraniums filled the window-boxes and were set at intervals along the tiny border under the bow window. In the centre of the grass plot was a circular flower-bed with one flowerless rose tree, the leaves of which were drooping and brown.

As he raised his eyes to the upper window, the blind went up slowly, and he was dimly conscious that there was a figure behind the white lace curtains. Mr. Reeder walked hurriedly away, as one caught in an immodest act, and resumed his peregrinations until he came to the big nursery gardener's which formed the corner lot at the far end of the road.

Here he stood for some time in contemplation, his arm resting on the iron railings, his eyes staring blankly at the vista of greenhouses. He remained in this attitude so long that one of the nurserymen, not unnaturally thinking that a stranger was seeking a way into the gardens, came over with the laborious gait of the man who wrings his living from the soil, and asked if he was wanting anybody.

"Several people," sighed Mr. Reeder; "several people!"

Leaving the resentful man to puzzle out his impertinence, he slowly retraced his steps. At No. 412 he stopped again, opened the little iron gate and passed up the path to the front door. A small girl answered his knock and ushered him into the parlour.

The room was not well furnished; it was scarcely furnished at all. A strip of almost new linoleum covered the passage; the furniture of the parlour itself was made up of wicker chairs, a square of art carpet and a table. He heard the sound of feet above his head, feet on bare boards, and then presently the door opened and a girl came in.

She was pretty in a heavy way, but on her face he saw the marks of sorrow. It was pale and haggard; the eyes looked as though she had been recently weeping.

"Miss Magda Grayne?" he asked, rising as she came in.

She nodded.

"Are you from the police?" she asked quickly.

"Not exactly the police," he corrected carefully. "I hold an—er—an appointment in the office of the Public Prosecutor, which is analogous to, but distinct from, a position in the Metropolitan Police Force."

She frowned, and then:

"I wondered if anybody would come to see me," she said. "Mr. Green sent you?"

"Mr. Green told me of your existence: he did not send me."

There came to her face in that second a look which almost startled him. Only for a fleeting space of time, the expression had dawned and passed almost before the untrained eye could detect its passage.

"I was expecting somebody to come," she said. Then: "What made him do it?" she asked.

"You think he is guilty?"

"The police think so." She drew a long sigh. "I wish to God I had never seen—this place!"

He did not answer; his eyes were roving

round the apartment. On a bamboo table was an old vase which had been clumsily filled with golden chrysanthemums, of a peculiarly beautiful variety. Not all, for amidst them flowered a large Michaelmas daisy that had the forlorn appearance of a parvenu that had strayed by mistake into noble company.

"You're fond of flowers?" he murmured.

She looked at the vase indifferently.

"Yes, I like flowers," she said. "The girl put them in there." Then: "Do you think they will hang him?"

The brutality of the question, put without hesitation, pained Reeder.

"It is a very serious charge," he said. And then: "Have you a photograph of Mr. Green?"

She frowned.

"Yes; do you want it?"

He nodded.

She had hardly left the room before he was at the bamboo table and had lifted out the flowers. As he had seen through the glass, they were roughly tied with a piece of string. He examined the ends, and here again his first observation had been correct: none of these flowers had been cut; they had been plucked bodily from their stalks. Beneath the string was the paper which had been first wrapped about the stalks. It was a page torn from a note-book; he could see the red lines, but the pencilled writing was indecipherable.

As her foot sounded on the stairs, he replaced the flowers in the vase, and when she came in he was looking through the window into the street.

"Thank you," he said, as he took the photograph from her.

It bore an affectionate inscription on the back.

"You're married, he tells me, madam?"

"Yes, I am married, and practically divorced," she said shortly.

"Have you been living here long?"

"About three months," she answered. "It was his wish that I should live here."

He looked at the photograph again.

"Do you know Constable Burnett?"

He saw a dull flush come to her face and die away again.

"Yes, I know the sloppy fool!" she said viciously. And then, realising that she had been surprised into an expression which was not altogether ladylike, she went on, in a softer tone: "Mr. Burnett is rather sentimental, and I don't like sentimental people, especially—well, you understand, Mr. ——"

"Reeder," murmured that gentleman.

"You understand, Mr. Reeder, that when a girl is engaged and in my position, those kind of attentions are not very welcome."

Reeder was looking at her keenly. Of her sorrow and distress there could be no doubt. On the subject of the human emotions, and the ravages they make upon the human countenance, Mr. Reeder was almost as great an authority as Mantegazza.

"On your birthday," he said. "How very sad! You were born on the seventeenth of October. You are English, of course?"

"Yes, I'm English," she said shortly. "I was

born in Walworth—in Wallington. I once lived in Walworth."

"How old are you?"

"Twenty-three," she answered.

Mr. Reeder took off his glasses and polished them on a large silk handkerchief.

"The whole thing is inexpressibly sad," he said. "I am glad to have had the opportunity of speaking with you, young lady. I sympathise with you very deeply."

And in this unsatisfactory way he took his departure.

She closed the door on him, saw him stop in the middle of the path and pick up something from a border bed, and wondered, frowning, why this middle-aged man had picked up the horseshoe she had thrown through the window the night before. Into Mr. Reeder's tail pocket went this piece of rusted steel and then he continued his thoughtful way to the nursery gardens, for he had a few questions to ask.

The men of Section 10 were parading for duty when Mr. Reeder came timidly into the charge room and produced his credentials to the inspector in charge.

"Oh, yes, Mr. Reeder," said that officer affably. "We have had a note from the P.P.'s office, and I think I had the pleasure of working with you on that big slush* case a few years ago. Now what can I do for you? . . . Burnett? Yes, he's here."

He called the man's name and a young and good-looking officer stepped from the ranks.

"He's the man who discovered the murder—he's marked for promotion," said the inspector. "Burnett, this gentleman is from the Public Prosecutor's office and he wants a little talk with you. Better use my office, Mr. Reeder."

The young policeman saluted and followed the shuffling figure into the privacy of the inspector's office. He was a confident young man: already his name and portrait had appeared in the newspapers, the hint of promotion had become almost an accomplished fact, and before his eyes was the prospect of a supreme achievement.

*Slush = forged Bank of England notes.

"They tell me that you are something of a poet, officer," said Mr. Reeder.

Burnett blushed.

"Why, yes, sir. I write a bit," he confessed.

"Love poems, yes?" asked the other gently. "One finds time in the night—er—for such fancies. And there is no inspiration like—er—love, officer."

Burnett's face was crimson.

"I've done a bit of writing in the night, sir," he said, "though I've never neglected my duty."

"Naturally," murmured Mr. Reeder. "You have a poetical mind. It was a poetical thought to pluck flowers in the middle of the night——"

"The nurseryman told me I could take any flowers I wanted," Burnett interrupted hastily. "I did nothing wrong."

Reeder inclined his head in agreement.

"That I know. You picked the flowers in the dark—by the way, you inadvertently included a Michaelmas daisy with your chrysanthemums—tied up your little poem to them and left them on the doorstep with—er—a horseshoe. I wondered what had become of that horseshoe."

"I threw them up on to her—to the lady's window-sill," corrected the uncomfortable young man. "As a matter of fact, the idea didn't occur to me until I had passed the house——"

Mr. Reeder's face was thrust forward.

"This is what I want to confirm," he said softly. "The idea of leaving the flowers did not occur to you until you had passed her house? The horseshoe suggested the thought? Then you went back, picked the flowers, tied them up with the little poem you had already written, and tossed them up to her window—we need not mention the lady's name."

Constable Burnett's face was a study.

"I don't know how you guessed that, but it is a fact. If I've done anything wrong——"

"It is never wrong to be in love," said Mr. J. G. Reeder soberly. "Love is a very beautiful experience—I have frequently read about it."

Miss Magda Grayne had dressed to go out for the afternoon and was putting on her hat, when she saw the queer man who had called so early that morning walking up the tesselated path. Behind him she recognised a detective engaged in the case. The servant was out; nobody could be admitted except by herself. She walked quickly behind the dressing-table into the bay of the window and glanced up and down the road. Yes, there was the taxicab which usually accompanies such visitations, and, standing by the driver, another man, obviously a "busy."

She pulled up the overlay of her bed, took out the flat pad of bank-notes that she found, and thrust them into her handbag, then, stepping on tiptoe, she went out to the landing, into the unfurnished back room, and, opening the window, dropped to the flat roof of the kitchen. In another minute she was in the garden and through the back gate. A narrow passage divided the two lines of villas that backed on one another. She was in High Street and had boarded a car before Mr. Reeder grew tired of knocking. To the best of his knowledge Mr. Reeder never saw her again.

* * * * * *

At the Public Prosecutor's request, he called at his chief's house after dinner and told his surprising story.

"Green, who had the unusual experience of being promoted to his position over the heads of his seniors, for special services he rendered during the war, was undoubtedly an ex-convict, and he spoke the truth when he said that he had received a letter from a man who had served a period of imprisonment with him. The name of this blackmailer is, or rather was, Arthur George Crater, whose other name was Malling!"

"Not the night watchman?" said the Public Prosecutor, in amazement.

Mr. Reeder nodded.

"Yes, sir, it was Arthur Malling. His daughter, Miss Magda Crater, was, as she very truly said, born at Walworth on the 17th of October, 1900. She said Wallington after, but Walworth first. One observes that when people adopt false family names, they seldom change their given names, and the 'Magda' was easy to identify.

"Evidently Malling had planned this robbery of the bank very carefully. He had brought his daughter, under a false name, to Ealing, and had managed to get her introduced to Mr. Green. Magda's job was to worm her way into Green's confidence and learn all that she could. Possibly it was part of her duty to secure casts of the keys. Whether Malling recognised in the manager an old prison acquaintance, or whether he obtained the facts from the girl, we shall never know. But when the information came to him, he saw, in all probability, an opportunity of robbing the bank and of throwing suspicion upon the manager.

"The girl's rôle was that of a woman who was to be divorced, and I must confess this puzzled me until I realised that in no circumstances would Malling wish his daughter's name to be associated with the bank manager.

"The night of the seventeenth was chosen for the raid. Malling's plan to get rid of the manager had succeeded. He saw the letter on the table in Green's private office, read it, secured the keys—although he had in all probability a duplicate set—and at a favourable moment cleared as much portable money from the bank vaults as he could carry, hurried them round to the house in Firling Avenue, where they were buried in the central bed of the front garden, under a rose bush—I rather imagined there was something interfering with the nutrition of that unfortunate bush the first time I saw it. I can only hope that the tree is not altogether dead, and I have given instructions that it shall be replanted and well fertilised."

"Yes, yes," said the Prosecutor, who was not at all interested in horticulture.

"In planting the tree, as he did in some haste, Malling scratched his hand. Roses have thorns—I went to Ealing to find the rose bush that had scratched his hand. Hurrying back to the bank, he waited, knowing that Constable Burnett was due at a certain time. He had prepared the can of chloroform, the handcuffs and straps were waiting for him, and he stood at the corner of the street until he saw the flash of Burnett's lamp; then, running into the bank and leaving the door ajar, he strapped himself, fastened the handcuffs and lay down, expecting that the policeman would arrive, find the open door and rescue him before much harm was done.

"But Constable Burnett had had some pleasant exchanges with the daughter. Doubtless she had received instructions from her father to be as pleasant to him as possible. Burnett was a poetical young man, knew it was her birthday, and as he walked along the street his foot struck an old horseshoe, and the idea occurred to him that he should return, attach the horseshoe to some flowers, which the nurseryman had given him permission to pick, and leave his little bouquet, so to speak, at his lady's feet—a poetical idea, and one worthy of the finest traditions of the Metropolitan Police Force. This he did, but it took some time; and all the while this young man was philandering—Arthur Crater was dying!

"In a few seconds after lying down he must have passed from consciousness . . . the chloroform still dripped, and when the policeman eventually reached the bank, ten minutes after he was due, the man was dead!"

The Public Prosecutor sat back in his padded chair and frowned at his new subordinate.

"How on earth did you piece together all this?" he asked in wonder.

Mr. Reeder shook his head sadly.

"I have that perversion," he said. "It is a terrible misfortune, but it is true. I see evil in everything . . . in dying rose bushes, in horseshoes—in poetry even. I have the mind of a criminal. It is deplorable!"

THE STEALER OF MARBLE

The Stealer of Marble

MARGARET BELMAN'S chiefest claim to Mr. Reeder's notice was that she lived in the Brockley Road, some few doors from his own establishment. He did not know her name, being wholly incurious about law-abiding folk, but he was aware that she was pretty, that her complexion was that pink and white which is seldom seen away from a magazine cover. She dressed well, and if there was one thing that he noted about her more than any other, it was that she walked and carried herself with a certain grace that was especially pleasing to a man of æsthetic predilections.

He had, on occasions, walked behind her and before her, and had ridden on the same street car with her to Westminster Bridge. She invariably descended at the corner of the

Embankment, and was as invariably met by a good-looking young man and walked away with him. The presence of that young man was a source of passive satisfaction to Mr. Reeder, for no particular reason, unless it was that he had a tidy mind, and preferred a rose when it had a background of fern and grew uneasy at the sight of a saucerless cup.

It did not occur to him that he was an object of interest and curiosity to Miss Belman.

"That was Mr. Reeder—he has something to do with the police, I think," she said.

"Mr. J. G. Reeder?"

Roy Master looked back with interest at the middle-aged man scampering fearfully across the road, his unusual hat on the back of his head, his umbrella over his shoulder like a cavalryman's sword.

"Good Lord! I never dreamt he was like that."

"Who is he?" she asked, distracted from her own problem.

"Reeder? He's in the Public Prosecutor's Department, a sort of a detective—there was a case the other week where he gave evidence. He used to be with the Bank of England——"

Suddenly she stopped, and he looked at her in surprise.

"What's the matter?" he asked.

"I don't want you to go any farther, Roy," she said. "Mr. Telfer saw me with you yesterday, and he's quite unpleasant about it."

"Telfer?" said the young man indignantly. "That little worm! What did he say?"

"Nothing very much," she replied, but from her tone he gathered that the "nothing very much" had been a little disturbing.

"I am leaving Telfers'," she said unexpectedly. "It is a good job, and I shall never get another like it—I mean, so far as the pay is concerned."

Roy Master did not attempt to conceal his satisfaction.

"I'm jolly glad," he said vigorously. "I can't imagine how you've endured that boudoir atmosphere so long. What did he say?" he asked again, and, before she could answer: "Anyway, Telfers are shaky. There are all sorts of queer rumours about them in the city."

"But I thought it was a very rich corporation!" she said in astonishment.

He shook his head.

"It was—but they have been doing lunatic things—what can you expect when a half-witted weakling like Sidney Telfer is at the head of affairs? They underwrote three concerns last year that no brokerage business would have touched with a barge-pole, and they had to take up the shares. One was a lost treasure company to raise a Spanish galleon that sank three hundred years ago! But what really did happen yesterday morning?"

"I will tell you to-night," she said, and made her hasty adieux.

Mr. Sidney Telfer had arrived when she went into a room which, in its luxurious appointments, its soft carpet and dainty etceteras, was not wholly undeserving of Roy Master's description.

The head of Telfers Consolidated seldom visited his main office on Threadneedle Street.

The atmosphere of the place, he said, depressed him; it was all so horrid and sordid and rough. The founder of the firm, his grandfather, had died ten years before Sidney had been born, leaving the business to a son, a chronic invalid, who had died a few weeks after Sidney first saw the light. In the hands of trustees the business had flourished, despite the spasmodic interferences of his eccentric mother, whose peculiarities culminated in a will which relieved him of most of that restraint which is wisely laid upon a boy of sixteen.

The room, with its stained-glass windows and luxurious furnishings, fitted Mr. Telfer perfectly, for he was exquisitely arrayed. He was tall and so painfully thin that the abnormal smallness of his head was not at first apparent. As the girl came into the room he was sniffing delicately at a fine cambric handkerchief, and she thought that he was paler than she had ever seen him—and more repellent.

He followed her movements with a dull stare, and she had placed his letters on his table before he spoke.

"I say, Miss Belman, you won't mention a word about what I said to you last night?"

"Mr. Telfer," she answered quietly, "I am hardly likely to discuss such a matter."

"I'd marry you and all that, only . . . clause in my mother's will," he said disjointedly. "That could be got over—in time."

She stood by the table, her hands resting on the edge.

"I would not marry you, Mr. Telfer, even if there were no clause in your mother's will; the suggestion that I should run away with you to America——"

"South America," he corrected her gravely. "Not the United States; there was never any suggestion of the United States."

She could have smiled, for she was not as angry with this rather vacant young man as his startling proposition entitled her to be.

"The point is," he went on anxiously, "you'll keep it to yourself? I've been worried dreadfully all night. I told you to send me a note saying what you thought of my idea—well, don't!"

This time she did smile, but before she could answer him he went on, speaking rapidly in a high treble that sometimes rose to a falsetto squeak:

"You're a perfectly beautiful girl, and I'm crazy about you, but . . . there's a tragedy in my life . . . really. Perfectly ghastly tragedy. An' everything's at sixes an' sevens. If I'd had any sense I'd have brought in a feller to look after things. I'm beginning to see that now."

For the second time in twenty-four hours this young man, who had almost been tongue-tied and had never deigned to notice her, had poured forth a torrent of confidences, and in one had, with frantic insistence, set forth a plan which had amazed and shocked her. Abruptly he finished, wiped his weak eyes, and in his normal voice:

"Get Billingham on the 'phone; I want him."

She wondered, as her busy fingers flew over the keys of her typewriter, to what extent his agitation and wild eloquence was due to the rumoured "shakiness" of Telfers Consolidated.

Mr. Billingham came, a sober little man, bald and taciturn, and went in his secretive way into his employer's room. There was no hint in his appearance or his manner that he contemplated a great crime. He was stout to a point of podginess; apart from his habitual frown, his round face, unlined by the years, was marked by an expression of benevolence.

Yet Mr. Stephen Billingham, managing director of the Telfer Consolidated Trust, went into the office of the London and Central Bank late that afternoon and, presenting a bearer check for one hundred and fifty thousand pounds, which was duly honoured, was driven to the Crédit Lilloise. He had telephoned particulars of his errand, and there were waiting for him seventeen packets, each containing a million francs, and a smaller packet of a hundred and forty-six *mille* notes. The franc stood at 74.55 and he received the eighteen packages in exchange for a check on the Crédit Lilloise for £80,000 and the 150 thousand-pound notes which he had drawn on the London and Central.

Of Billingham's movements thenceforth little was known. He was seen by an acquaintance driving through Cheapside in a taxicab which was traced as far as Charing Cross—and there he disappeared. Neither the airways nor the waterways had known him, the police theory being that he had left by an evening train that had carried an excursion party via Havre to Paris.

"This is the biggest steal we have had in years," said the Assistant Director of Public Prosecutions. "If you can slip in sideways on the inquiry, Mr. Reeder, I should be glad. Don't step on the toes of the city police—they are quite amiable people where murder is concerned, but a little touchy where money is in question. Go along and see Sidney Telfer."

Fortunately, the prostrated Sidney was discoverable outside the city area. Mr. Reeder went into the outer office and saw a familiar face.

"Pardon me, I think I know you, young lady," he said, and she smiled as she opened the little wooden gate to admit him.

"You are Mr. Reeder—we live in the same road," she said, and then quickly: "Have you come about Mr. Billingham?"

"Yes." His voice was hushed, as though he were speaking of a dead friend. "I wanted to see Mr. Telfer, but perhaps you could give me a little information."

The only news she had was that Sidney Telfer had been in the office since seven o'clock and was at the moment in such a state of collapse that she had sent for the doctor.

"I doubt if he is in a condition to see you," she said.

"I will take all responsibility," said Mr. Reeder soothingly. "Is Mr. Telfer—er—a friend of yours, Miss——?"

"Belman is my name." He had seen the quick flush that came to her cheek: it could mean one of two things. "No, I am an employee, that is all."

Her tone told him all he wanted to know.

Mr. J. G. Reeder was something of an authority on office friendships.

"Bothered you a little, has he?" he murmured, and she shot a suspicious look at him. What did he know, and what bearing had Mr. Telfer's mad proposal on the present disaster? She was entirely in the dark as to the true state of affairs; it was, she felt, a moment for frankness.

"Wanted you to run away! Dear me!" Mr. Reeder was shocked. "He is married?"

"Oh, no—he's not married," said the girl shortly. "Poor man, I'm sorry for him now. I'm afraid that the loss is a very heavy one—who would suspect Mr. Billingham?"

"Ah! who indeed!" sighed the lugubrious Reeder, and took off his glasses to wipe them; almost she suspected tears. "I think I will go in now—that is the door?"

Sidney jerked up his face and glared at the intruder. He had been sitting with his head on his arms for the greater part of an hour.

"I say . . . what do you want?" he asked

feebly. "I say . . . I can't see anybody . . . Public Prosecutor's Department?" He almost screamed the words. "What's the use of prosecuting him if you don't get the money back?"

Mr. Reeder let him work down before he began to ply his very judicious questions.

"I don't know much about it," said the despondent young man. "I'm only a sort of figurehead. Billingham brought the checks for me to sign and I signed 'em. I never gave him instructions; he got his orders. I don't know very much about it. He told me, actually told me, that the business was in a bad way—half a million or something was wanted by next week. . . . Oh, my God! And then he took the whole of our cash."

Sidney Telfer sobbed his woe into his sleeve like a child. Mr. Reeder waited before he asked a question in his gentlest manner.

"No, I wasn't here: I went down to Brighton for the week-end. And the police dug me out of bed at four in the morning. We're bankrupt. I'll have to sell my car and resign from my club—one has to resign when one is bankrupt."

There was little more to learn from the broken man, and Mr. Reeder returned to his chief with a report that added nothing to the sum of knowledge. In a week the theft of Mr. Billingham passed from scare lines to paragraphs in most of the papers—Billingham had made a perfect getaway.

In the bright lexicon of Mr. J. G. Reeder there was no such word as holiday. Even the Public Prosecutor's office has its slack time, when juniors and sub-officials and even the Director himself can go away on vacation, leaving the office open and a subordinate in charge. But to Mr. J. G. Reeder the very idea of wasting time was repugnant, and it was his practice to brighten the dull patches of occupation by finding a seat in a magistrate's court and listening, absorbed, to cases which bored even the court reporter.

John Smith, charged with being drunk and using insulting language to Police Officer Thomas Brown; Mary Jane Haggitt, charged with obstructing the police in the execution of their duty; Henry Robinson, arraigned for being a suspected person, having in his possession housebreaking tools, to wit, one cold chisel and a screwdriver; Arthur Moses, charged with driving a motor car to the common danger—all these were fascinating figures of romance and legend to the lean man who sat between the press and railed dock, his square-crowned hat by his side, his umbrella gripped between his knees, and on his melancholy face an expression of startled wonder.

On one raw and foggy morning, Mr. Reeder, self-released from his duties, chose the Marylebone Police Court for his recreation. Two drunks, a shop theft, and an embezzlement had claimed his rapt attention, when Mrs. Jackson was escorted to the dock and a rubicund policeman stepped to the witness stand, and, swearing by his Deity that he would tell the truth and nothing but the truth, related his peculiar story.

"P.C. Perryman No. 9717 L. Division," he introduced himself conventionally. "I was on duty in the Edgware Road early this morning at 2.30 a.m. when I saw the prisoner carrying a large suit-case. On seeing me she turned round and walked rapidly in the opposite direction. Her movements being suspicious, I followed and, overtaking her, asked her whose property she was carrying. She told me it was her own and that she was going to catch a train. She said that the case contained her clothes. As the case was a valuable one of crocodile leather I asked her to show me the inside. She refused. She also refused to give me her name and I asked her to accompany me to the station."

There followed a detective sergeant.

"I saw the prisoner at the station and in her presence opened the case. It contained a considerable quantity of small stone chips——"

"Stone chips?" interrupted the incredulous magistrate. "You mean small pieces of stone—what kind of stone?"

"Marble, your worship. She said that she wanted to make a little path in her garden and that she had taken them from the yard of a monument mason in the Euston Road. She made a frank statement to the effect that she had broken open a gate into the yard and filled the suit-case without the mason's knowledge."

The magistrate leant back in his chair and scrutinised the charge sheet with a frown.

"There is no address against her name," he said.

"She gave an address, but it was false, your worship—she refuses to offer any further information."

Mr. J. G. Reeder had screwed round in his seat and was staring open-mouthed at the prisoner. She was tall, broad-shouldered, and stoutly built. The hand that rested on the rail of the dock was twice the size of any woman's hand he had ever seen. The face was modelled largely, but though there was something in her appearance which was almost repellent, she was handsome in her large way. Deep-set brown eyes, a nose that was large and masterful, a well-shaped mouth and two chins—these in profile were not attractive to one who had his views on beauty in women, but Mr. J. G.

Reeder, being a fair man, admitted that she was a fine-looking woman. When she spoke it was in a voice as deep as a man's, sonorous and powerful.

"I admit it was a fool thing to do. But the idea occurred to me just as I was going to bed and I acted on the impulse of the moment. I could well afford to buy the stone—I had over fifty pounds in my pocketbook when I was arrested."

"Is that true?" and, when the officer answered, the magistrate turned his suspicious eyes to the woman. "You are giving us a lot of trouble because you will not tell your name and address. I can understand that you do not wish your friends to know of your stupid theft, but unless you give me the information, I shall be compelled to remand you in custody for a week."

She was well, if plainly, dressed. On one large finger flashed a diamond which Mr. Reeder mentally priced in the region of two hundred pounds. "Mrs. Jackson" was shaking her head as he looked.

"I can't give you my address," she said, and the magistrate nodded curtly.

"Remanded for inquiry," he said, and added, as she walked out of the dock: "I should like a report from the prison doctor on the state of her mind."

Mr. J. G. Reeder rose quickly from his chair and followed the woman and the officer in charge of the case through the little door that leads to the cells.

"Mrs. Jackson" had disappeared by the time he reached the corridor, but the detective-sergeant was stooping over the large and handsome suit-case that he had shown in court and was now laying on a form.

Most of the outdoor men of the C.I.D. knew Mr. J. G. Reeder, and Sergeant Mills grinned a cheerful welcome.

"What do you think of that one, Mr. Reeder? It is certainly a new line on me! Never heard of a tombstone artist being burgled before."

He opened the top of the case, and Mr.

Reeder ran his fingers through the marble chips.

"The case and the loot weighs over a hundred pounds," said the officer. "She must have the strength of a navvy to carry it. The poor officer who carried it to the station was hot and melting when he arrived."

Mr. J. G. was inspecting the case. It was a handsome article, the hinges and locks being of oxidised silver. No maker's name was visible on the inside, or owner's initials on its glossy lid. The lining had once been of silk, but now hung in shreds and was white with marble dust.

"Yes," said Mr. Reeder absently, "very interesting—most interesting. Is it permissible to ask whether, when she was searched, any—er—document——?" The sergeant shook his head. "Or unusual possession?"

"Only these."

By the side of the case was a pair of large gloves. These also were soiled, and their surfaces cut in a hundred places.

"These have been used frequently for the same purpose," murmured Mr. J. G. "She evidently makes—er—a collection of marble shavings. Nothing in her pocketbook?"

"Only the bank-notes: they have the stamp of the Central Bank on their backs. We should be able to trace 'em easily."

Mr. Reeder returned to his office and, locking the door, produced a worn pack of cards from a drawer and played patience—which was his method of thinking intensively. Late in the afternoon his telephone bell rang, and he recognised the voice of Sergeant Mills.

"Can I come along and see you? Yes, it is about the bank-notes."

Ten minutes later the sergeant presented himself.

"The notes were issued three months ago to Mr. Telfer," said the officer without preliminary, "and they were given by him to his housekeeper, Mrs. Welford."

"Oh, indeed?" said Mr. Reeder softly, and added, after reflection: "Dear me!"

He pulled hard at his lip.

"And is 'Mrs. Jackson' that lady?" he asked.

"Yes. Telfer—poor little devil—nearly went

mad when I told him she was under remand—dashed up to Holloway in a taxi to identify her. The magistrate has granted bail, and she'll be bound over to-morrow. Telfer was bleating like a child—said she was mad. Gosh! that fellow is scared of her—when I took him into the waiting-room at Holloway Prison she gave him one look and he wilted. By the way, we have had a hint about Billingham that may interest you. Do you know that he and Telfer's secretary were very good friends?"

"Really?" Mr. Reeder was indeed interested. "Very good friends? Well, well!"

"The Yard has put Miss Belman under general observation: there may be nothing to it, but in cases like Billingham's it is very often a matter of *cherchez la femme!*"

Mr. Reeder had given his lip a rest and was now gently massaging his nose.

"Dear me!" he said. "That is a French expression, is it not?"

He was not in court when the marble stealer was sternly admonished by the magistrate and discharged. All that interested Mr. J. G. Reeder was to learn that the woman had paid the mason and had carried away her marble chips in triumph to the pretty little detached residence in the Outer Circle of Regent's Park. He had spent the morning at Somerset House, examining copies of wills and the like; his afternoon he gave up to the tracing of Mrs. Rebecca Alamby Mary Welford.

She was the relict of Professor John Welford of the University of Edinburgh, and had been left a widow after two years of marriage. She had then entered the service of Mrs. Telfer, the mother of Sidney, and had sole charge of the boy from his fourth year. When Mrs. Telfer died she had made the woman sole guardian of her youthful charge. So that Rebecca Welford had been by turns nurse and guardian, and was now in control of the young man's establishment.

The house occupied Mr. Reeder's attention to a considerable degree. It was a red-brick modern dwelling consisting of two floors and having a frontage on the Circle and a side road. Behind and beside the house was a large garden which, at this season of the year, was bare of flowers. They were probably in snug quarters for the winter, for there was a long green-house behind the garden.

He was leaning over the wooden palings, eyeing the grounds through the screen of box hedge that overlapped the fence with a melancholy stare, when he saw a door open and the big woman come out. She was bare-armed and wore an apron. In one hand she carried a dust box, which she emptied into a concealed ash-bin, in the other was a long broom.

Mr. Reeder moved swiftly out of sight. Presently the door slammed and he peeped again. There was no evidence of a marble path. All the walks were of rolled gravel.

He went to a neighbouring telephone booth, and called his office.

"I may be away all day," he said.

There was no sign of Mr. Sidney Telfer, though the detective knew that he was in the house.

Telfer's Trust was in the hands of the liquidators, and the first meeting of creditors had been called. Sidney had, by all accounts, been confined to his bed, and from that safe refuge had written a note to his secretary asking that "all papers relating to my private affairs" should be burnt. He had scrawled a postscript: "Can I possibly see you on business before I go?" The word "go" had been scratched out and "retire" substituted. Mr. Reeder had seen that letter—indeed, all correspondence between Sidney and the office came to him by arrangement with the liquidators. And that was partly why Mr. J. G. Reeder was so interested in 904, The Circle.

It was dusk when a big car drew up at the gate of the house. Before the driver could descend from his seat, the door of 904 opened, and Sidney Telfer almost ran out. He carried a suit-case in each hand, and Mr. Reeder recognised that nearest him as the grip in which the housekeeper had carried the stolen marble.

Reaching over, the chauffeur opened the

door of the machine and, flinging in the bags, Sidney followed hastily. The door closed, and the car went out of sight round the curve of The Circle.

Mr. Reeder crossed the road and took up a position very near the front gate, waiting.

Dusk came and the veil of a Regent's Park fog. The house was in darkness, no flash of light except a faint glimmer that burnt in the hall, no sound. The woman was still there—Mrs. Sidney Telfer, nurse, companion, guardian and wife. Mrs. Sidney Telfer, the hidden director of Telfers Consolidated, a masterful woman who, not content with marrying a weakling twenty years her junior, had applied her masterful but ill-equipped mind to the domination of a business she did not understand, and which she was destined to plunge into ruin. Mr. Reeder had made good use of his time at the Records Office: a copy of the marriage certificate was almost as easy to secure as a copy of the will.

He glanced round anxiously. The fog was clearing, which was exactly what he did not wish it to do, for he had certain acts to perform which required as thick a cloaking as possible.

And then a surprising thing happened. A cab came slowly along the road and stopped at the gate.

"I think this is the place, miss," said the cabman, and a girl stepped down to the pavement.

It was Miss Margaret Belman.

Reeder waited until she had paid the fare and the cab had gone, and then, as she walked toward the gate, he stepped from the shadow.

"Oh!—Mr. Reeder, how you frightened me!" she gasped. "I am going to see Mr. Telfer—he is dangerously ill—no, it was his housekeeper who wrote asking me to come at seven."

"Did she now! Well, I will ring the bell for you."

She told him that that was unnecessary—she had the key which had come with the note.

"She is alone in the house with Mr. Telfer, who refuses to allow a trained nurse near him," said Margaret, "and——"

"Will you be good enough to lower your voice, young lady?" urged Mr. Reeder in an impressive whisper. "Forgive the impertinence, but if our friend is ill——"

She was at first startled by his urgency.

"He couldn't hear me," she said, but spoke in a lower tone.

"He may—sick people are very sensitive to the human voice. Tell me, how did this letter come?"

"From Mr. Telfer? By district messenger an hour ago."

Nobody had been to the house or left it—except Sidney. And Sidney, in his blind fear, would carry out any instructions which his wife gave to him.

"And did it contain a passage like this?" Mr. Reeder considered a moment. " 'Bring this letter with you'?"

"No," said the girl in surprise, "but Mrs. Welford telephoned just before the letter arrived and told me to wait for it. And she asked me to bring the letter with me because she didn't wish Mr. Telford's private correspondence to be left lying around. But why do you ask me this, Mr. Reeder—is anything wrong?"

He did not answer immediately. Pushing open the gate, he walked noiselessly along the grass plot that ran parallel with the path.

"Open the door, I will come in with you," he whispered and, when she hesitated: "Do as I tell you, please."

The hand that put the key into the lock trembled, but at last the key turned and the door swung open. A small night-light burnt on the table of the wide panelled hall. On the left, near the foot of the stairs, only the lower steps of which were visible, Reeder saw a narrow door which stood open, and, taking a step forward, saw that it was a tiny telephone-room.

And then a voice spoke from the upper landing, a deep, booming voice that he knew.

"Is that Miss Belman?"

Margaret, her heart beating faster, went to the foot of the stairs and looked up.

"Yes, Mrs. Welford."

"You brought the letter with you?"

"Yes."

Mr. Reeder crept along the wall until he could have touched the girl.

"Good," said the deep voice. "Will you call the doctor—Circle 743—and tell him that Mr. Telfer has had a relapse—you will find the booth in the hall: shut the door behind you, the bell worries him."

Margaret looked at the detective and he nodded.

The woman upstairs wished to gain time for something—what?

The girl passed him: he heard the thud of the padded door close, and there was a click that made him spin round. The first thing he noticed was that there was no handle to the door, the second that the keyhole was covered by a steel disc, which he discovered later was felt-lined. He heard the girl speaking faintly, and put his ear to the keyhole.

"The instrument is disconnected—I can't open the door."

Without a second's hesitation, he flew up the stairs, umbrella in hand, and as he reached the landing he heard a door close with a crash. Instantly he located the sound. It came from a room on the left immediately over the hall. The door was locked.

"Open this door," he commanded, and there came to him the sound of a deep laugh.

Mr. Reeder tugged at the stout handle of his umbrella. There was a flicker of steel as he dropped the lower end, and in his hand appeared six inches of knife blade.

The first stab at the panel sliced through the thin wood as though it were paper. In a second there was a jagged gap through which the black muzzle of an automatic was thrust.

"Put down that jug or I will blow your features into comparative chaos!" said Mr. Reeder pedantically.

The room was brightly lit, and he could see plainly. Mrs. Welford stood by the side of a big square funnel, the narrow end of which ran into the floor. In her hand was a huge enamelled iron jug, and ranged about her were six others. In one corner of the room was a wide circular tank, and beyond, at half its height, depended a large copper pipe.

The woman's face turned to him was blank, expressionless.

"He wanted to run away with her," she said simply, "and after all I have done for him!"

"Open the door."

Mrs. Welford set down the jug and ran her huge hand across her forehead.

"Sidney is my own darling," she said. "I've nursed him, and taught him, and there was a million—all in gold—in the ship. But they robbed him."

She was talking of one of the ill-fated enterprises of Telfers Consolidated Trust—that sunken treasure ship to recover which the money of the company had been poured out like water. And she was mad. He had guessed the weakness of this domineering woman from the first.

"Open the door; we will talk it over. I'm perfectly sure that the treasure ship scheme was a sound one."

"Are you?" she asked eagerly, and the next

minute the door was open and Mr. J. G. Reeder was in that room of death.

"First of all, let me have the key of the telephone-room—you are quite wrong about that young lady: she is my wife."

The woman stared at him blankly.

"Your wife?" A slow smile transfigured the face. "Why—I was silly. Here is the key."

He persuaded her to come downstairs with him, and when the frightened girl was released, he whispered a few words to her, and she flew out of the house.

"Shall we go into the drawing-room?" he asked, and Mrs. Welford led the way.

"And now will you tell me how you knew—about the jugs?" he asked gently.

She was sitting on the edge of a sofa, her hands clasped on her knees, her deep-set eyes staring at the carpet.

"John—that was my first husband—told me. He was a professor of chemistry and natural science, and also about the electric furnace. It is so easy to make if you have power—we use nothing but electricity in this house for heating and everything. And then I saw my poor darling being ruined through me, and I found how much money there was in the bank, and I told Billingham to draw it and bring it to me without Sidney knowing. He came here in the evening. I sent Sidney away—to Brighton, I think. I did everything—put the new lock on the telephone box and fixed the shaft from the roof to the little room—it was easy to disperse everything with all the doors open and an electric fan working on the floor——"

She was telling him about the improvised furnace in the green-house when the police arrived with the divisional surgeon, and she went away with them, weeping because there would be nobody to press Sidney's ties or put out his shirts.

Mr. Reeder took the inspector up to the little room and showed him its contents.

"This funnel leads to the telephone box——" he began.

"But the jugs are empty," interrupted the officer.

Mr. J. G. Reeder struck a match and, waiting until it burnt freely, lowered it into the jug. Half an inch lower than the rim the light went out.

"Carbon monoxide," he said, "which is made by steeping marble chips in hydrochloric acid —you will find the mixture in the tank. The gas is colourless and odourless—and heavy. You can pour it out of a jug like water. She could have bought the marble, but was afraid of arousing suspicion. Billingham was killed that way. She got him to go to the telephone box, probably closed the door on him herself, and then killed him painlessly."

"What did she do with the body?" asked the horrified officer.

"Come out into the hot-house," said Mr. Reeder, "and pray do not expect to see horrors: an electric furnace will dissolve a diamond to its original elements."

* * * * *

Mr. Reeder went home that night in a state of mental perturbation, and for an hour paced the floor of his large study in Brockley Road.

Over and over in his mind he turned one vital problem: did he owe an apology to Margaret Belman for saying that she was his wife?

THE INVESTORS

The Investors

THERE are seven million people in Greater London and each one of those seven millions is in theory and practice equal under the law and commonly precious to the community. So that, if one is wilfully wronged, another must be punished; and if one dies of premeditated violence, his slayer must hang by the neck until he be dead.

It is rather difficult for the sharpest law-eyes to keep tag of seven million people, at least one million of whom never keep still and are generally unattached to any particular domicile. It is equally difficult to place an odd twenty thousand or so who have domiciles but no human association. These include tramps, aged maiden ladies in affluent circumstances, peripatetic members of the criminal classes, and other friendless individuals.

Sometimes uneasy inquiries come through to headquarters. Mainly they are most timid and deferential. Mr. X. has not seen his neighbour, Mr. Y., for a week. No, he doesn't know Mr. Y. Nobody does. A little old man who had no friends and spent his fine days pottering in a garden overlooked by his more gregarious neighbour. And now Mr. Y. potters no more. His milk has not been taken in; his blinds are drawn. Come a sergeant of police and a constable who break a window and climb through, and Mr. Y. is dead somewhere—dead of starvation or a fit or suicide. Should this be the case, all is plain sailing. But suppose the house empty and Mr. Y. disappeared. Here the situation becomes difficult and delicate.

Miss Elver went away to Switzerland. She was a middle-aged spinster who had the appearance of being comfortably circumstanced. She went away, locked up her house, and never came back. Switzerland looked for her; the myrmidons of Mussolini, that hatefully efficient man, searched North Italy from Domodossola to Montecatini. And the search did not yield a thin-faced maiden lady with a slight squint.

And then Mr. Charles Boyson Middlekirk, an eccentric and overpowering old man who quarrelled with his neighbours about their noisy children, he too went away. He told nobody where he was going. He lived alone with his three cats and was not on speaking terms with anybody else. He did not return to his grimy house.

He too was well off and reputedly a miser. So was Mrs. Athbell Marting, a dour widow who lived with her drudge of a niece. This lady was in the habit of disappearing without any preliminary announcement of her intention. The niece was allowed to order from the local tradesmen just sufficient food to keep body and soul together, and when Mrs. Marting returned (as she invariably did) the bills were settled with a great deal of grumbling on the part of the payer, and that was that. It was believed that Mrs. Marting went to Boulogne or to Paris or even to Brussels. But one day she went out and never came back. Six months later her niece advertised for her, choosing the cheapest papers—having an eye to the day of reckoning.

"Queer sort of thing," said the Public Prosecutor, who had before him the dossiers of four people (three women and a man) who had so vanished in three months.

He frowned, pressed a bell, and Mr. Reeder came in. Mr. Reeder took the chair that was indicated, looked owlishly over his glasses, and shook his head as though he understood the reason for his summons and denied his understanding in advance.

"What do you make of these disappearances?" asked his chief.

"You cannot make any positive of a negative," said Mr. Reeder carefully. "London is a large place full of strange, mad people who live such—um—commonplace lives that the wonder is that more of them do not disappear in order to do something different from what they are accustomed to doing."

"Have you seen these particulars?"

Mr. Reeder nodded.

"I have copies of them," he said. "Mr. Salter very kindly——"

The Public Prosecutor rubbed his head in perplexity.

"I see nothing in these cases—nothing in common, I mean. Four is a fairly low average for a big city——"

"Twenty-seven in twelve months," interrupted his detective apologetically.

"Twenty-seven—are you sure?" The great official was astounded.

Mr. Reeder nodded again.

"They were all people with a little money; all were drawing a fairly large income, which was paid to them in bank-notes on the first of every month—nineteen of them were, at any rate. I have yet to verify eight—and they were all most reticent as to where their revenues came from. None of them had any personal friends or relatives who were on terms of friendship, except Mrs. Marting. Beyond these points of resemblance there was nothing to connect one with the other."

The Prosecutor looked at him sharply, but Mr. Reeder was never sarcastic. Not obviously so, at any rate.

"There is another point which I omitted to mention," he went on. "After their disappearance no further money came for them. It came for Mrs. Marting when she was away on her jaunts, but it ceased when she went away on her final journey."

"But twenty-seven—are you sure?"

Mr. Reeder reeled off the list, giving name, address, and date of disappearance.

"What do you think has happened to them?"

Mr. Reeder considered for a moment, staring glumly at the carpet.

"I should imagine that they were murdered," he said, almost cheerfully, and the Prosecutor half rose from his chair.

"You are in your gayest mood this morning, Mr. Reeder," he said sardonically. "Why on earth should they be murdered?"

Mr. Reeder did not explain. The interview

took place in the late afternoon, and he was anxious to be gone, for he had a tacit appointment to meet a young lady of exceeding charm who at five minutes after five would be waiting on the corner of Westminster Bridge and Thames Embankment for the Lee car.

The sentimental qualities of Mr. Reeder were entirely unknown. There are those who say that his sorrow over those whom fate and ill-fortune brought into his punitive hands was the veriest hypocrisy. There were others who believed that he was genuinely pained to see a fellow-creature sent behind bars through his efforts and evidence.

His housekeeper, who thought he was a woman-hater, told her friends in confidence that he was a complete stranger to the tender emotions which enlighten and glorify humanity. In the ten years which she had sacrificed to his service he had displayed neither emotion nor tenderness except to inquire whether her sciatica was better or to express a wish that she should take a holiday by the sea. She was a woman beyond middle age, but there is no period of life wherein a woman gives up hoping for the best. Though the most perfect of servants in all respects, she secretly despised him, called him, to her intimates, a frump, and suspected him of living apart from an ill-treated wife. This lady was a widow (as she had told him when he first engaged her) and she had seen better—far better—days.

Her visible attitude toward Mr. Reeder was one of respect and awe. She excused the queer character of his callers and his low acquaintances. She forgave him his square-toed shoes and high, flat-crowned hat, and even admired the ready-made Ascot cravat he wore and which was fastened behind the collar with a little buckle, the prongs of which invariably punctured his fingers when he fastened it. But there is a limit to all hero-worship, and when she discovered that Mr. Reeder was in the habit of waiting to escort a young lady to town every day, and frequently found it convenient to escort her home, the limit was reached.

Mrs. Hambleton told her friends—and they agreed—that there was no fool like an old fool, and that marriages between the old and the young invariably end in the divorce court (December *v.* May and July). She used to leave copies of a favourite Sunday newspaper on his table, where he could not fail to see the flaring headlines:

OLD MAN'S WEDDING ROMANCE
WIFE'S PERFIDY BRINGS GREY HAIR IN SORROW
TO THE LAW COURTS.

Whether Mr. Reeder perused these human documents she did not know. He never referred to the tragedies of ill-assorted unions, and went on meeting Miss Belman every morning at nine o'clock and at five-five in the afternoons whenever his business permitted.

He so rarely discussed his own business or introduced the subject that was exercising his mind that it was remarkable he should make even an oblique reference to his work. Possibly he would not have done so if Miss Margaret Belman had not introduced (unwillingly) a leader of conversation which traced indirectly to the disappearances.

They had been talking of holidays: Margaret was going to Cromer for a fortnight.

"I shall leave on the second. My monthly dividends (doesn't that sound grand?) are due on the first——"

"Eh?"

Reeder slued round. Dividends in most companies are paid at half-yearly intervals.

"Dividends, Miss Margaret?"

She flushed a little at his surprise and then laughed.

"You didn't realise that I was a woman of property?" she bantered him. "I receive ten pounds a month—my father left me a little house property when he died. I sold the cottages two years ago for a thousand pounds and found a wonderful investment."

Mr. Reeder made a rapid calculation.

"You are drawing something like 12½ per cent.," he said. "That is indeed a wonderful investment. What is the name of the company?"

She hesitated.

"I'm afraid I can't tell you that. You see—well, it's rather secret. It is to do with a South

American syndicate that supplies arms to—what do you call them—insurgents! I know it is rather dreadful to make money that way—I mean out of arms and things, but it pays terribly well and I can't afford to miss the opportunity."

Reeder frowned.

"But why is it such a terrible secret?" he asked. "Quite a number of respectable people make money out of armament concerns."

Again she showed reluctance to explain her meaning.

"We are pledged—the shareholders, I mean—not to divulge our connection with the company," she said. "That is one of the agreements I had to sign. And the money comes regularly. I have had nearly £300 of my thousand back in dividends already."

"Humph!" said Mr. Reeder, wise enough not to press his question. There was another day to-morrow.

But the opportunity to which he looked forward on the following morning was denied to him. Somebody played a grim "joke" on him

—the kind of joke to which he was accustomed, for there were men who had good reason to hate him, and never a year passed but one or the other sought to repay him for his unkindly attentions.

"Your name is Reeder, ain't it?"

Mr. Reeder, tightly grasping his umbrella with both hands, looked over his spectacles at the shabby man who stood at the bottom of the steps. He was on the point of leaving his house in the Brockley Road for his office in Whitehall, and since he was a methodical man and worked to a time table, he resented in his mild way this interruption which had already cost him fifteen seconds of valuable time.

"You're the fellow who shopped Ike Walker, ain't you?"

Mr. Reeder had indeed "shopped" many men. He was by profession a shopper, which, translated from the argot, means a man who procures the arrest of an evildoer. Ike Walker he knew very well indeed. He was a clever, a too clever, forger of bills of exchange, and was at that precise moment almost permanently employed as orderly in the convict prison at Dartmoor, and might account himself fortunate if he held this easy job for the rest of his twelve years' sentence.

His interrogator was a little hard-faced man wearing a suit that had evidently been originally intended for somebody of greather girth and more commanding height. His trousers were turned up noticeably; his waistcoat was full of folds and tucks which only an amateur tailor would have dared, and only one superior to the criticism of his fellows would have worn. His hard, bright eyes were fixed on Mr. Reeder, but there was no menace in them so far as the detective could read.

"Yes, I was instrumental in arresting Ike Walker," said Mr. Reeder, almost gently.

The man put his hand in his pocket and brought out a crumpled packet enclosed in green oiled silk. Mr. Reeder unfolded the covering and found a soiled and crumpled envelope.

"That's from Ike," said the man. "He sent it out of stir by a gent who was discharged yesterday."

Mr. Reeder was not shocked by this revelation. He knew that prison rules were made to be broken, and that worse things have happened in the best regulated jails than this item of a smuggled letter. He opened the envelope, keeping his eyes on the man's face, took out the crumpled sheet and read the five or six lines of writing.

DEAR REEDER:

Here is a bit of a riddle for you.

What other people have got, you can have. I haven't got it, but it is coming to you. It's red-hot when you get it, but you're cold when it goes away.

Your loving friend,

IKE WALKER

(doing a twelve stretch because you went on the witness stand and told a lot of lies).

Mr. Reeder looked up and their eyes met.

"Your friend is a little mad, one thinks?" he asked politely.

"He ain't a friend of mine. A gent asked me to bring it," said the messenger.

"On the contrary," said Mr. Reeder pleasantly, "he gave it to you in Dartmoor Prison yesterday. Your name is Mills; you have eight convictions for burglary, and will have your ninth before the year is out. You were released two days ago—I saw you reporting at Scotland Yard."

The man was for the moment alarmed and in two minds to bolt. Mr. Reeder glanced along Brockley Road, saw a slim figure, that was standing at the corner, cross to a waiting tram-car, and, seeing his opportunity vanish, readjusted his time table.

"Come inside, Mr. Mills."

"I don't want to come inside," said Mr. Mills, now thoroughly agitated. "He asked me to give this to you and I've give it. There's nothing else——"

Mr. Reeder crooked his finger.

"Come, birdie!" he said, with great amiability. "And please don't annoy me! I am quite capable of sending you back to your friend Mr. Walker. I am really a most unpleasant man if I am upset."

The messenger followed meekly, wiped his boots with great vigour on the mat and tiptoed up the carpeted stairs to the big study where Mr. Reeder did most of his thinking.

"Sit down, Mills."

With his own hands Mr. Reeder placed a chair for his uncomfortable visitor, and then, pulling another up to his big writing table, he spread the letter before him, adjusted his glasses, read, his lips moving, and then leaned back in his chair.

"I give it up," he said. "Read me this riddle."

"I don't know what's in the letter——" began the man.

"Read me this riddle."

As he handed the letter across the table, the man betrayed himself, for he rose and pushed back his chair with a startled, horrified expression that told Mr. Reeder quite a lot. He laid the letter down on his desk, took a large tumbler from the sideboard, inverted it and covered the scrawled paper. Then:

"Wait," he said, "and don't move till I come back."

And there was an unaccustomed venom in his tone that made the visitor shudder.

Reeder passed out of the room to the bathroom, pulled up his sleeves with a quick jerk of his arm and, turning the faucet, let hot water run over his hands before he reached for a small bottle on a shelf, poured a liberal portion into the water and let his hands soak. This done, for three minutes he scrubbed his fingers with a nail-brush, dried them, and, removing his coat and waistcoat carefully, hung them over the edge of the bath. He went back to his uncomfortable guest in his shirt-sleeves.

"Our friend Walker is employed in the hospital," he stated rather than asked. "What have you had there—scarlet fever or something worse?"

He glanced down at the letter under the glass.

"Scarlet fever, of course," he said, "and the letter has been systematically infected. Walker is almost clever."

The wood of a fire was laid in the grate. He carried the letter and the blotting-paper to the hearth, lit the kindling and thrust paper and letter into the flames.

"Almost clever," he said musingly. "Of course, he is one of the orderlies in the hospital. It was scarlet fever, I think you said?"

The gaping man nodded.

"Of a virulent type, of course. How very fascinating!"

He thrust his hands in his pockets and looked down benevolently at the wretched emissary of the vengeful Walker.

"You may go now, Mills," he said gently. "I rather think that you are infected. That ridiculous piece of oiled silk is quite inadequate—which means 'quite useless'—as a protection against wandering germs. You will have scarlet fever in three days, and will probably be dead at the end of the week. I will send you a wreath."

He opened the door, pointed to the stairway and the man slunk out.

Mr. Reeder watched him through the window, saw him cross the street and disappear round the corner into the Lewisham High Road, and then, going up to his bedroom, he put on a newer frock-coat and waistcoat, drew on his hands a pair of fabric gloves and went forth to his labours.

He did not expect to meet Mr. Mills again, never dreaming that the gentleman from Dartmoor was planning a "bust" which would bring them again into contact. For Mr. Reeder the incident was closed.

That day news of another disappearance had come through from police headquarters, and Mr. Reeder was waiting at ten minutes before five at the rendezvous for the girl who, he instinctively knew, could give him a thread of the clue. He was determined that this time his inquiries should bear fruit; but it was not until they had reached the end of Brockley Road, and he was walking slowly up toward the girl's boarding-house, that she gave him a hint.

"Why are you so persistent, Mr. Reeder?" she asked, a little impatiently. "Do you wish to invest money? Because, if you do, I'm sorry

I can't help you. That is another agreement we made, that we would not introduce new shareholders."

Mr. Reeder stopped, took off his hat and rubbed the back of his head (his housekeeper, watching him from an upper window, was perfectly certain he was proposing and had been rejected).

"I am going to tell you something, Miss Belman, and I hope—er—that I shall not alarm you."

And very briefly he told the story of the disappearances and the queer coincidence which marked every case—the receipt of a dividend on the first of every month. As he proceeded, the colour left the girl's face.

"You are serious, of course?" she said, serious enough herself. "You wouldn't tell me that unless—— The company is the Mexico City Investment Syndicate. They have offices in Portugal Street."

"How did you come to hear of them?" asked Mr. Reeder.

"I had a letter from their manager, Mr. De

Silvo. He told me that a friend had mentioned my name, and gave full particulars of the investment."

"Have you that letter?"

She shook her head.

"No; I was particularly asked to bring it with me when I went to see them. Although, in point of fact, I never did see them," smiled the girl. "I wrote to their lawyers—will you wait? I have their letter."

Mr. Reeder waited at the gate while the girl went into the house and returned presently with a small portfolio, from which she took a quarto sheet. It was headed with the name of a legal firm, Bracher & Bracher, and was the usual formal type of letter one expects from a lawyer.

DEAR MADAM:

Re Mexico City Investment Syndicate: We act as lawyers to this syndicate, and so far as we know it is a reputable concern. We feel that it is only due to us that we should say that we do not advise investments in any concern which offers such large profits, for usually there is a corresponding risk. We know, however, that this syndicate has paid 12½ per cent. and sometimes as much as 20 per cent., and we have had no complaints about them. We cannot, of course, as lawyers, guarantee the financial soundness of any of our clients, and can only repeat that, in so far as we have been able to ascertain, the syndicate conducts a genuine business and enjoys a very sound financial backing.

Yours faithfully,
BRACHER & BRACHER.

"You say you never saw De Silvo?"

She shook her head.

"No; I saw Mr. Bracher, but when I went to the office of the syndicate, which is in the same building, I found only a clerk in attendance. Mr. De Silvo had been called out of town. I had to leave the letter because the lower portion was an application for shares in the syndicate. The capital could be withdrawn at three days' notice, and I must say that this last clause decided me; and when I had a letter from Mr. De Silvo accepting my investment, I sent him the money."

Mr. Reeder nodded.

"And you've received your dividends regularly ever since?" he said.

"Every month," said the girl triumphantly.

"And really I think you're wrong in connecting the company with these disappearances."

Mr. Reeder did not reply. That afternoon he made it his business to call at 179 Portugal Street. It was a two-story building of an old-fashioned type. A wide flagged hall led into the building; a set of old-fashioned stairs ran up to the "top floor," which was occupied by a China merchant; and from the hall led three doors. That on the left bore the legend "Bracher & Bracher, Solicitors," and immediately facing was the office of the Mexican syndicate. At the far end of the passage was a door which exhibited the name "John Baston," but as to Mr. Baston's business there was no indication.

Mr. Reeder knocked gently at the door of the syndicate and a voice bade him come in. A young man, wearing glasses, was sitting at a typewriting table, a pair of dictaphone receivers in his ears, and he was typing rapidly.

"No, sir, Mr. De Silvo is not in. He only comes in about twice a week," said the clerk. "Will you give me your name?"

"It is not important," said Reeder gently, and went out, closing the door behind him.

He was more fortunate in his call upon Bracher & Bracher, for Mr. Joseph Bracher was in his office: a tall, florid gentleman who wore a large rose in his buttonhole. The firm of Bracher & Bracher was evidently a prosperous one, for there were half a dozen clerks in the outer office, and Mr. Bracher's private sanctum, with its big partner desk, was a model of shabby comfort.

"Sit down, Mr. Reeder," said the lawyer, glancing at the card.

In a few words Mr. Reeder stated his business, and Mr. Bracher smiled.

"It is fortunate you came to-day," he said. "If it were to-morrow we should not be able to give you any information. The truth is, we have had to ask Mr. De Silvo to find other lawyers. No, no, there is nothing wrong, except that they constantly refer their clients to us, and we feel that we are becoming in the nature of sponsors for their clients, and that, of course, is very undesirable."

"Have you a record of the people who have written to you from time to time asking your advice?"

Mr. Bracher shook his head.

"It is a curious thing to confess, but we haven't," he said; "and that is one of the reasons why we have decided to give up this client. Three weeks ago, the letter-book in which we kept copies of all letters sent to people who applied for a reference most unaccountably disappeared. It was put in the safe overnight, and in the morning, although there was no sign of tampering with the lock, it had vanished. The circumstances were so mysterious, and my brother and I were so deeply concerned, that we applied to the syndicate to give us a list of their clients, and that request was never complied with."

Mr. Reeder sought inspiration in the ceiling.

"Who is John Baston?" he asked, and the lawyer laughed.

"There again I am ignorant. I believe he is a very wealthy financier, but, so far as I know, he only comes to his office for three months in the year, and I have never seen him."

Mr. Reeder offered him his flabby hand and walked back along Portugal Street, his chin on his breast, his hands behind him dragging his umbrella, so that he bore a ludicrous resemblance to some strange tailed animal.

That night he waited again for the girl, but she did not appear, and although he remained at the rendezvous until half-past five he did not see her. This was not very unusual, for sometimes she had to work late, and he went home without any feeling of apprehension. He finished his own frugal dinner and then walked across to the boarding-house. Miss Belman had not arrived, the landlady told him, and he returned to his study and telephoned first to the office where she was employed and then to the private address of her employer.

"She left at half-past four," was the surprising news. "Somebody telephoned to her and she asked me if she might go early."

"Oh!" said Mr. Reeder blankly.

He did not go to bed that night, but sat up

in a small room at Scotland Yard, reading the brief reports which came in from the various divisions. And with the morning came the sickening realisation that Margaret Belman's name must be added to those who had disappeared in such extraordinary circumstances.

He dozed in the big Windsor chair. At eight o'clock he returned to his own house and shaved and bathed, and when the Public Prosecutor arrived at his office he found Mr. Reeder waiting for him in the corridor. It was a changed Mr. Reeder, and the change was not due entirely to lack of sleep. His voice was sharper; he had lost some of that atmosphere of apology which usually enveloped him.

In a few words he told of Margaret Belman's disappearance.

"Do you connect De Silvo with this?" asked his chief.

"Yes, I think I do," said the other quietly, and then: "There is only one hope, and it is a very slender one—a very slender one indeed!"

He did not tell the Public Prosecutor in

what that hope consisted, but walked down to the offices of the Mexico City Investment Syndicate.

Mr. De Silvo was not in. He would have been very much surprised if he had been. He crossed the hallway to see the lawyer, and this time he found Mr. Ernest Bracher present with his brother.

When Reeder spoke to the point, it was very much to the point.

"I am leaving a police officer in Portugal Street to arrest De Silvo the moment he puts in an appearance. I feel that you, as his lawyers, should know this," he said.

"But why on earth——?" began Mr. Joseph Bracher, in a tone of astonishment.

"I don't know what charge I shall bring against him, but it will certainly be a very serious one," said Reeder. "For the moment I have not confided to Scotland Yard the basis for my suspicions, but your client has got to tell a very plausible story and produce indisputable proof of his innocence to have any hope of escape."

"I am quite in the dark," said the lawyer, mystified. "What has he been doing? Is his syndicate a fraud?"

"I know nothing more fraudulent," said the other shortly. "To-morrow I intend to obtain the necessary authority to search his papers and to search the room and papers of Mr. John Baston. I have an idea that I shall find something in that room of considerable interest to me."

It was eight o'clock that night before he left Scotland Yard, and he was turning toward the familiar corner, when he saw a car come from Westminster Bridge toward Scotland Yard. Somebody leaned out of the window and signalled him, and the car turned. It was a two-seater coupé and the driver was Mr. Joseph Bracher.

"We've found De Silvo," he said breathlessly as he brought the car to a standstill at the curb and jumped out.

He was very agitated and his face was pale. Mr. Reeder could have sworn that his teeth were chattering.

"There's something wrong—very badly wrong," he went on. "My brother has been trying to get the truth from him—my God! if he has done these terrible things I shall never forgive myself."

"Where is he?" asked Mr. Reeder.

"He came just before dinner to our house at Dulwich. My brother and I are bachelors and we live there alone now, and he has been to dinner before. My brother questioned him and he made certain admissions which are almost incredible. The man must be mad."

"What did he say?"

"I can't tell you. Ernest is detaining him until you come."

Mr. Reeder stepped into the car and in a few minutes they were flying across Westminster Bridge toward Camberwell. Lane House, an old-fashioned Georgian residence, lay at the end of a countrified road which was, he found, a cul de sac. The house stood in grounds of considerable size, he noted as they passed up the drive and stopped before the porch. Mr. Bracher alighted and opened the door, and

Reeder passed into a cosily furnished hall. One door was ajar.

"Is that Mr. Reeder?" He recognised the voice of Ernest Bracher, and walked into the room.

The younger Mr. Bracher was standing with his back to the empty fireplace; there was nobody else in the room.

"De Silvo's gone upstairs to lie down," explained the lawyer. "This is a dreadful business, Mr. Reeder."

He held out his hand and Reeder crossed the room to take it. As he put his foot on the square Persian rug before the fireplace, he realised his danger and tried to spring back, but his balance was lost. He felt himself falling through the cavity which the carpet hid, lashed out and caught for a moment the edge of the trap, but as the lawyer came round and raised his foot to stamp upon the clutching fingers, Reeder released his hold and dropped.

The shock of the fall took away his breath, and for a second he sprawled, half lying, half sitting, on the floor of the cellar into which he had fallen. Looking up, he saw the older of the two leaning over. The square aperture was diminishing in size. There was evidently a sliding panel which covered the hole in normal times.

"We'll deal wth you later, Reeder," said Joseph Bracher with a smile. "We've had quite a lot of clever people here——"

Something cracked in the cellar. The bullet seared the lawyer's cheek, smashed a glass chandelier to fragments, and he stepped back with a yell of fear. In another second the trap was closed and Reeder was alone in a small brick-lined cellar. Not entirely alone, for the automatic pistol he held in his hand was a very pleasant companion in that moment of crisis.

From his hip pocket he took a flat electric hand-lamp, switched on the current and surveyed his prison. The walls and floor were damp; that was the first thing he noticed. In one corner was a small flight of brick steps leading to a locked steel door, and then:

"Mr. Reeder."

He spun round and turned his lamp upon the

speaker. It was Margaret Belman, who had risen from a heap of sacks where she had been sleeping.

"I'm afraid I've got you into very bad trouble," she said, and he marvelled at her calm.

"How long have you been here?"

"Since last night," she answered. "Mr. Bracher telephoned me to see him and he picked me up in his car. They kept me in the other room until to-night, but an hour ago they brought me here."

"Which is the other room?"

She pointed to the steel door. She offered no further details of her capture, and it was not a moment to discuss their misfortune. Reeder went up the steps and tried the door; it was fastened from the other side, and opened inward, he discovered. There was no sign of a keyhole. He asked her where the door led and she told him that it was to an underground kitchen and coal-cellar. She had hoped to escape, because only a barred window stood between her and freedom in the "little room" where she was kept.

"But the window was very thick," she said, "and of course I could do nothing with the bars."

Reeder made another inspection of the cellar, then sent the light of his lamp up at the ceiling. He saw nothing there except a steel pulley fastened to a beam that crossed the entire width of the cellar.

"Now what on earth is he going to do?" he asked thoughtfully, and as though his enemies had heard the question and were determined to leave him in no doubt as to their plans, there came the sound of gurgling water, and in a second he was ankle-deep.

He put the light on to the place whence the water was coming. There were three circular holes in the wall, from each of which was gushing a solid stream.

"What is it?" she asked in a terrified whisper.

"Get on to the steps and stay there," he ordered peremptorily, and made investigation to see if it was possible to staunch the flow. He saw at a glance that this was impossible. And now the mystery of the disappearances was a mystery no longer.

The water came up with incredible rapidity, first to his knees, then to his thighs, and he joined her on the steps.

There was no possible escape for them. He guessed the water would come up only so far as would make it impossible for them to reach the beam across the roof or the pulley, the dreadful purpose of which he could guess. The dead must be got out of this charnel house in some way or other. Strong swimmer as he was, he knew that in the hours ahead it would be impossible to keep afloat.

He slipped off his coat and vest and unbuttoned his collar.

"You had better take off your skirt," he said in a matter-of-fact tone. "Can you swim?"

"Yes," she answered in a low voice.

He did not ask her the real question which was in his mind: for how long could she swim?

There was a long silence; the water crept higher; and then:

"Are you very much afraid?" he asked, and took her hand in his.

"No, I don't think I am," she said. "It is wonderful having you with me—why are they doing this?"

He said nothing, but carried the soft hand to his lips and kissed it.

The water was now reaching the top step. Reeder stood with his back to the iron door, waiting. And then he felt something touch the door from the other side. There was a faint click, as though a bolt had been slipped back. He put her gently aside and held his palms to the door. There was no doubt now: somebody was fumbling on the other side. He went down a step and presently he felt the door yield and come toward him, and there was a momentary gleam of light. In another second he had wrenched the door open and sprung through.

"Hands up!"

Whoever it was had dropped his lamp, and now Mr. Reeder focussed the light of his own torch and nearly dropped.

For the man in the passage was Mills, the ex-convict who had brought the tainted letter from Dartmoor!

"All right, guv'nor, it's a cop," growled the man.

And then the whole explanation flashed upon the detective. In an instant he had gripped the girl by the hand and dragged her through the narrow passage, into which the water was now steadily overrunning.

"Which way did you get in, Mills?" he demanded authoritatively.

"Through the window."

"Show me—quick!"

The convict led the way to what was evidently the window through which the girl had looked with such longing. The bars had been removed; the window sash itself lifted from its rusty hinges; and in another second the three were standing on the grass, with the stars twinkling above them.

"Mills," said Mr. Reeder, and his voice shook, "you came here to 'bust' this house."

"That's right," growled Mills. "I tell you

it's a cop. I'm not going to give you any trouble."

"Skip!" hissed Mr. Reeder. "And skip quick! Now, young lady, we'll go for a little walk."

A few seconds later a patrolling constable was smitten dumb by the apparition of a middle-aged man in shirt and trousers, and a lady who was inadequately attired in a silk petticoat.

* * * * *

"The Mexican company was Bracher & Bracher," explained Reeder to his chief. "There was no John Baston. His room was a passage-way by which the Brachers could get from one room to the other. The clerk in the Mexican syndicate's office was, of course, blind; I spotted that the moment I saw him. There are any number of blind typists employed in the City of London. A blind clerk was necessary if the identity of De Silvo with the Brachers was to be kept a secret.

"Bracher & Bracher had been going badly

for years. It will probably be found that they have made away with clients' money; and they hit upon this scheme of inducing foolish investors to put money into their syndicate on the promise of large dividends. Their victims were well chosen, and Joseph—who was the brains of the organisation—conducted the most rigorous investigation to make sure that these unfortunate people had no intimate friends. If they had any suspicion about an applicant, Brachers would write a letter deprecating the idea of an investment and suggesting that the too-shrewd dupe should find another and a safer method than the Mexican syndicate afforded.

"After they had paid one or two years' dividends the wretched investor was lured to the house at Dulwich and there scientifically killed. You will probably find an unofficial cemetery in their grounds. So far as I can make out, they have stolen more than a hundred and twenty thousand pounds in the past two years by this method."

"It is incredible," said the Prosecutor, "incredible!"

Mr. Reeder shrugged.

"Is there anything more incredible than the Burke and Hare murders? There are Burkes and Hares in every branch of society and in every period of history."

"Why did they delay their execution of Miss Belman?"

Mr. Reeder coughed.

"They wanted to make a clean sweep, but did not wish to kill her until they had me in their hands. I rather suspect"—he coughed again—"that they thought I had an especial interest in the young lady."

"And have you?" asked the Public Prosecutor.

Mr. Reeder did not reply.

ABOUT THE RINGER

"In the list of admirable murderers," says the New York *Sun, "The Ringer* stands first." His real name was Henry Arthur Milton, but Scotland Yard knew him best by another name—the Ringer—and knew him as the best wanted man in Europe. Like the Three Just Men, although for different reasons, he took it upon himself to deal out his own private vengeance on certain monsters who were beyond the reach of the law. Swift and silent, with strange sources of information, he glides like a panther in and out of the careers of many people who would have preferred not to know him. Because he did not stop at murder, when he thought murder was indicated, the Ringer was earnestly wanted by Superintendent Bliss of the C.I.D., although Bliss owed many a tip to the Ringer's kindly interest in the Yard's problems.

In the field of philosophic criminology, of which Wallace was so fond, the Ringer stands high. His popularity is deserved. Never more than in these stories of his blood-curdling exploits did Wallace's genius for packing a novel into the space of a short story, for writing without a word too many, an unnecessary pause, show to better advantage. And in the person of this Galahad of hi-jackers, as *Time* calls him, Wallace created probably his best-known character. On the stage, the screen, and in books millions of people have enjoyed him.

On the following pages are three of the best stories of his exploits. You will find many more in *The Ringer* and *The Ringer Returns,* two books which should be in every detective-story library.

CONTENTS

THE MAN WITH THE RED BEARD

THE END OF MR. BASH—THE BRUTAL

THE SWISS HEAD WAITER

THE MAN WITH THE RED BEARD

THE MAN WITH THE RED BEARD

To THE average reader the name of Miska Guild is associated with slight and possibly amusing eccentricities. For example, he once went down Regent Street at eleven o'clock at night at sixty miles an hour, crippled two unfortunate pedestrians, and smashed a lamp standard and his car. The charge that he was drunk failed, because indisputably he was sober when he was dragged out of the wreckage, himself unhurt.

Nevertheless, an unsympathetic magistrate convicted, despite the conflict of medical evidence. Miska Guild went to the Sessions with the best advocates that money could buy and had the conviction quashed.

The inner theatrical set knew him as a giver of freakish dinner parties; had an idea that he gave other parties even more freakish but less descriptive. Once he went to Paris, and the French police most obligingly hushed up a lurid incident as best they could.

They could not quite hush up the death of the

pretty chorus-girl who was found on the pavement outside the hotel, having fallen from a fifth-floor window, but they were very helpful in explaining that she had mistaken the French windows for the door of her sitting-room. Nobody at the inquiry asked how she managed to climb the balcony.

The only person who evinced a passionate interest in the proceedings was one Henry Arthur Milton, a fugitive from justice, who was staying at the hotel—not as Henry Arthur Milton, certainly not as "The Ringer," by which title he was known; indeed, he bore no name by which the English police could identify him as the best-wanted man in Europe.

Mr. Guild paid heavily for all the trouble he had caused divers police officials and came back to London and to his magnificent flat in Carlton House Terrace quite unabashed, even though some of the theatrical celebrities with whom he was acquainted cut him dead whenever they met him; even though the most unpleasant rumours surrounded his Paris trip.

He was a man of thirty, reputedly a millionaire three times over. It is certain that he was very rich, and had the queerest ideas about what was and what was not the most amusing method of passing time. Had the Paris incident occurred in London neither his two nor his three millions would have availed him, nor all the advocacy of the greatest lawyers averted the most unpleasant consequences.

One bright November morning, when the sun rose in a clear blue sky and the leafless trees of Green Park had a peculiar splendour of their own, the second footman brought his breakfast to his bedside, and on the tray there was a registered letter. The postmark was Paris, the envelope was marked "Urgent and confidential; not to be opened by the secretary."

Miska Guild sat up in bed, pushed back his long, yellowish hair from his eyes, bleared for a moment at the envelope and tore it open with a groan. There was a single sheet of paper, closely typewritten. It bore no address and began without a conventional preamble:

On October 18 you went to Paris, accompanied by a small party. In that party was a girl called Ethel Seddings, who was quite unaware of your character. She committed suicide in order to escape from you. I am called The Ringer; my name is Henry Arthur Milton, and Scotland Yard will furnish you with particulars of my past. As you are a man of considerable property and may wish to have time to make arrangements as to its disposal, I will give you a little grace. At the end of a reasonable period I shall come to London and kill you.

That was all the letter contained. Miska read it through; looked at the back of the sheet for further inspiration; read it through again.

"Who the devil is The Ringer?" he asked.

The footman, who was an authority upon such matters, gave him a little inaccurate information. Miska examined the envelope without being enlightened any further, and then with a chuckle he was about to tear the letter into pieces but thought better of it.

"Send it up to Scotland Yard," he commanded his secretary later in the morning, and would have forgotten the unpleasant communication if he had not returned from lunch to find a rather sinister-looking man with a short black beard who introduced himself as Chief Inspector Bliss from Scotland Yard.

"About that letter? Oh, rot! You're not taking that seriously, are you?"

Bliss nodded slowly.

"So seriously that I'm putting on two of my best men to guard you for a month or two."

Miska looked at him incredulously.

"Do you really mean that? But surely . . . my footman tells me he's a criminal: he wouldn't dare come to London?"

Inspector Bliss smiled grimly.

"He dared go into Scotland Yard when it suited him. This is the kind of case that would interest him."

He recounted a few of The Ringer's earlier cases, and Miska Guild became of a sudden a very agitated young man.

"Monstrous . . . a murderer at large, and you can't catch him? I've never heard anything like it! Besides, that business in Paris—it was an accident. The poor, silly dear mistook the window for her sitting-room door——"

"I know all about that, Mr. Guild," said Bliss quietly. "I'd rather we didn't discuss that aspect of the matter. The only thing I can tell you is that, if I know The Ringer—and nobody has better reason for knowing him and his methods—he will try to keep his word. It's up to us to protect you. You're to employ no new servants without consulting me. I want a daily notification telling me where you're going and how you're spending your time. The Ringer is the only criminal in the world, so far as I know, who depends entirely upon his power of disguise. We haven't a photograph of him as himself at Scotland Yard, and I'm one of the few people who have seen him as himself."

Miska jibbed at the prospect of accounting for his movements in advance. He was, he said, a creature of impulse, and was never quite sure where he would be next. Besides which, he was going to Berlin——

"If you leave the country I will not be responsible for your life," said Bliss shortly, and the young man turned pale.

At first he treated the matter as a joke, but as the weeks became a month the sight of the detective sitting by the side of his chauffeur, the unexpected appearance of a Scotland Yard man at his elbow wherever he moved, began to get on his nerves.

And then one night Bliss came to him with the devastating news.

"The Ringer is in England," he said.

Miska's face was ghastly.

"How—how do you know?" he stammered.

But Bliss was not prepared to explain the peculiar qualities of Wally the Nose, or the peculiar behaviour of the man with the red beard.

When Wally the Nose passed through certain streets in Notting Dale he chose daylight for the adventure, and he preferred that a policeman should be in sight. Not that any of the less law-abiding folk of Notting Dale had any personal reason for desiring Wally the least harm, for, as he protested in his pathetic, lisping way, "he never did no harm" to anybody in Notting Dale.

He lived in a back room in Clewson Street, a tiny house rented by a deaf old woman who had had lodgers even more unsavoury than Wally, with his greasy, threadbare clothes, his big, protruding teeth, and his silly, moist face.

He came one night furtively to Inspector Stourbridge at the local police station, having been sent for.

"There's goin' to be a 'bust' at Lowes, the jewellers, in Islington, to-morrer, Mr. Stourbridge; some lads from Nottin' Dale are in it, and Elfus is fencin' the stuff. Is that what you wanted me about?"

He stood, turning his hat in his hands, his ragged coat almost touching the floor, his red eyelids blinking. Stourbridge had known many police informers, but none like Wally.

He hesitated, and then, with a "Wait here," he went into a room that led from the charge room and closed the door behind him.

Chief Inspector Bliss sat at a table, his head on his hand, turning over a thick dossier of documents that lay on the table before him.

"That man I spoke to you about is here, sir—the nose. He's the best we've ever had, and so long as he hasn't got to take any extraordinary risk—or doesn't know he's taking it—he'll be invaluable."

Bliss pulled at his little beard and scowled.

"Does he know why you have brought him here now?" he asked.

Stourbridge grinned.

"No—I put him on to inquire about a jewel burglary—but we knew all about it beforehand."

"Bring him in."

Wally came shuffling into the private room,

blinking from one to the other with an ingratiating grin.

"Yes, sir?" His voice was shrill and nervous.

"This is Mr. Bliss, of Scotland Yard," said Stourbridge, and Wally bobbed his head.

"Heard about you, sir," he said, in his high, piping voice. "You're the bloke that got The Ringer——"

"To be exact, I didn't," said Bliss gruffly, "but you may."

"Me, sir?" Wally's mouth was open wide, his protruding rabbit's teeth suggested to Stourbridge the favourite figure of a popular comic artist. "I don't touch no Ringer, sir, with kind regards to you. If there's any kind of work you want me to do, sir, I'll do it. It's a regular 'obby of mine—I ought to have been in the p'lice. Up in Manchester they'll tell you all about me. I'm the feller that found Spicy Brown when all the Manchester busies was lookin' for him."

"That's why Manchester got a bit too hot for you, eh, Wally?" said Stourbridge.

The man shifted uncomfortably.

"Yes, they was a bit hard on me—the lads, I mean. That's why I come back to London. But I can't help nosing, sir, and that's a fact."

"You can do a little nosing for me," interrupted Bliss.

And thereafter a new and a more brilliant spy

watched the movements of the man with the red beard.

He had arrived in London by a ship which came from India but touched at Marseilles. He had on his passport the name of Tennett. He had travelled third-class. He was by profession an electrical engineer. Yet, despite his seeming poverty, he had taken a small and rather luxurious flat in Kensington.

It was his presence in Carlton House Terrace one evening that had first attracted the attention of Mr. Bliss. He came to see Guild, he said, on the matter of a project connected with Indian water power. The next day he was seen prospecting the house from the park side.

Ordinarily, it would have been a very simple matter to have pulled him in and investigated his credentials; but quite recently there had been what the Press had called a succession of police scandals. Two perfectly innocent men had been arrested in mistake for somebody else, and Scotland Yard was chary of taking any further risks.

Tennett was traced to his flat, and he was apparently a most elusive man, with a habit of taking taxicabs in crowded thoroughfares. What Scotland Yard might not do officially, it could do, and did do, unofficially. Wally the Nose listened with apparent growing discomfort.

"If it's him, he's mustard," he said huskily. "I

don't like messing about with no Ringers. Besides, *he* hasn't got a red beard."

"Oh, shut up!" snarled Bliss. "He could grow one, couldn't he? See what you can find out about him. If you happen to get into his flat and see any papers lying about, they might help you. I'm not suggesting you should do so, but if you did . . ."

Wally nodded wisely.

In three days he furnished a curious report to the detective who was detailed to meet him. The man with the red beard had paid a visit to Croydon aerodrome and had made inquiries about a single-seater taxi to carry him to the Continent. He had spent a lot of his time at an electrical supply company in the East End of London, and had made a number of mysterious purchases which he had carried home with him in a taxicab.

Bliss consulted his superior.

"Pull him in," he suggested. "You can get a warrant to search his flat."

"His flat's been searched. There's nothing there of the slightest importance," reported Bliss.

He called that night at Carlton House Terrace and found Mr. Miska Guild a very changed man. These three months had reduced him to a nervous wreck.

"No news?" he asked apprehensively when the detective came in. "Has that wretched little creature discovered anything? By gad! he's as clever as any of you fellows. I was talking with him last night. He was outside on the Terrace with one of your men. Now, Bliss, I'd better tell you the truth about this girl in Paris——"

"I'd rather you didn't," said Bliss, almost sternly.

He wanted to preserve, at any rate, a simulation of interest in Mr. Guild's fate.

He had hardly left Carlton House Terrace when a taxicab drove in and Wally the Nose almost fell into the arms of the detective.

"Where's Bliss?" he squeaked. "That red-whiskered feller's disappeared . . . left his house, and he's shaved off his beard, Mr. Connor. I didn't recognise him when he come out. When I made inquiries I found he'd gorn for good."

"The chief's just gone," said Connor, worried.

He went into the vestibule and was taken up to the floor on which Mr. Guild had his suite. The butler led him to the dining-room, where there was a 'phone connection, and left Wally the Nose in the hall. He was standing there disconsolately when Mr. Guild came out.

"Hullo! What's the news?" he asked quickly.

Wally the Nose looked left and right.

"He's telephonin' to the boss," he whispered hoarsely, "but I ain't told him about the letter."

He followed Miska into the library and gave that

young man a piece of news that Mr. Guild never repeated.

He was waiting in the hall below when Connor came down.

"It's all right—they arrested old red whiskers at Liverpool Street Station. We had a man watching him as well."

Wally the Nose was pardonably annoyed.

"What's the use of having me and then puttin' a busy on to trail him?" he demanded truculently. "That's what I call double-crossing."

"You hop off to Scotland Yard and see the chief," said Connor, and Wally, grumbling audibly, vanished in the darkness.

The once red-bearded man sat in Inspector Bliss's private room, and he was both indignant and frightened.

"I don't know that there's any law preventing me taking off my beard, is there?" he demanded. "I was just going off to Holland, where I'm seeing a man who's putting money into my power scheme."

Bliss interrupted with a gesture.

"When you came to England you were broke, Mr. Tennett, and yet immediately you reached London you took a very expensive flat, bought yourself a lot of new clothes, and seemingly have plenty of money to travel on the Continent. Will you explain that?"

The man hesitated.

"Well, I'll tell you the truth. When I got to London I was broke, but I got into conversation with a fellow at the station who told me he was interested in engineering. I explained my power scheme to him, and he was interested. He was not the kind of man I should have thought would have had any money, yet he weighed in with two hundred pounds, and told me just what I had to do. It was his idea that I should take the flat. He told me where to go every day and what to do. I didn't want to part with the old beard, but he made me do that in the end, and then gave me three hundred pounds to go to Holland."

Bliss looked at him incredulously.

"Did he also suggest you should call at Carlton House Terrace and interview Mr. Guild?"

Tennett nodded.

"Yes, he did. I tell you, it made me feel that things weren't right. I wasn't quite sure of him, mind you, Mr. Bliss; he was such a miserable-looking devil—a fellow with rabbit's teeth and red eyelids. . . . ."

Bliss came to his feet with a bound, stared across at Stourbridge, who was in the room.

"Wally!" he said.

A taxicab took him to Carlton House Terrace. Connor told him briefly what had happened.

"Did Wally see Mr. Guild?"

"Not that I know," said Connor, shaking his head.

Bliss did not wait for the lift; he flew up the stairs, met the footman in the hall.

"Where's Mr. Guild?"

"In his room, sir."

"Have you seen him lately?"

The man shook his head.

"No, sir; I never go unless he rings for me. He hasn't rung for half an hour."

Bliss turned the handle of the door and walked in. Miska Guild was lying on the hearthrug in the attitude of a man asleep, and when he turned him over on his back and saw his face Bliss knew that the true story of the chorus-girl and her "suicide" would never be told.

THE END OF MR. BASH

THE END OF MR. BASH—THE BRUTAL

"Bash" was really clever. He stood out from all other criminals in this respect. For the ranks of wrongdoers are made up of mental deficients—stupid men who invent nothing but lies. They are what the brilliant Mr. Coe calls in American criminals "jail bugs." The English criminal, because he does not dope, becomes a pitiable and whining creature who demands charity, and the American criminal develops into a potential homicide.

Bash was a constant, but not, in the eyes of the law, an habitual criminal. He had never been charged because he had never been caught. He was an expert safe-breaker and worked alone.

He might have been forgiven, and, indeed, admired by scientific and disinterested students of criminology for his burglaries, for he had none of the nasty habits of part-time burglars, which means that he was never in the blue funk that they were. But Bash earned his name of infamy from a practice which neither police nor public ever forgave.

He was never content to work with the knowledge that there was a watchman sleeping peaceably on the premises he was supposed to guard.

He would first seek out the unfortunate man, and, with a short and flexible life-preserver, beat him to insensibility. The same happened to several unhappy servants. He spared neither man nor woman. He had been suspected of doing worse than bludgeon, but no complaint had been made public.

It was Inspector Mander who suggested that Bash was a name by which one Henry Arthur Milton might be identified. He developed his thesis with great skill but little logic, and Mr. Bliss, on whom the interesting theories were tried, listened with a face that betrayed none of the emotions he felt.

"He has got the same methods as The Ringer; in many ways he has the same identity—nobody knows him——"

"He may be Count Pujoski," suggested Bliss.

"Who is he?" asked Mander, interested.

"I don't know—nobody knows. There isn't such a person," said Bliss calmly. "If the fact that you don't know two people proves that you know one means anything, how much easier it is not to know three!"

Mander pondered this, having no sense of humour.

"I don't see how——" he began.

"Get on with your funny story," said Bliss.

But Mr. Mander had run short of arguments.

"I often wonder why you don't write a pantomime" (Bliss could be foully offensive) "or a children's play! The Ringer! Good God!"

All his contempt was comprehended in that pious ejaculation.

"The only connection I see," said Bliss, "is the possible connection between The Ringer and our bashing friend. The newspapers have got hold of the story of what happened to Colonel Milden's parlourmaid, and that is the sort of thing that will make The Ringer see red. If he isn't too busy putting the world right in other directions and he gives his mind to Mr. Bash, we shall be saved a lot of trouble."

Bliss had discovered by painful experience that The Ringer had extraordinary sources of information; it was pretty certain that he was, in some rôle or other, in the closest touch with the great underworld of London. It was equally certain that none of the men he employed had the least idea of his identity.

There was a reward offered for his capture, and the average criminal would sell his own brother at a price—especially if he were certain that no kick was coming from the associates of the man betrayed.

Who was Bash? At least a dozen men in London must know—the receivers who fenced his stolen property, close confidants who had at some time or other worked with him. But these would never tell.

There were times when Superintendent Bliss sighed for the good old days of the rack and the thumb-screw. What they would not squeak to the police, however, they might very well tell to a "sure-man."

In Penbury Road, Hampstead, was a small detached house with a tiny garden forecourt and a narrow strip of garden behind. Here dwelt Mr. Sanford Hickler, a man of thirty-five, athletic, sandy-haired, slightly bald. He was both arty and crafty, and his house in Hampstead was full of arty and crafty objects—ancient dower chests that might have dated back to the Middle Ages and certainly came from the Midlands.

Mr. Hickler had greeny wallpaper and yellowy candlesticks, and his study was littered with junk that he called "pieces." Some of these pieces he had picked up in Italy, and some he had picked up in Greece; most of them would hardly be picked up at all. And there were a few maternity homes for the *lepidoptera* family hanging on the wall, which were distinguished by the name of tapestry.

Mr. Hickler's hobby was literature. He was a graduate of a famous university, and he knew literature to be something that was no longer manufactured. He studied literature as one studies a dead language or the ruins of Ur. It did not belong to to-day. With the passing of the years his mind had broadened. He had come to the place where the works of the late Mr. Anthony Trollope were literature.

He was sitting one evening reading the sonnets of Shakespeare when there was a knock at the door, and his maid, who was also his cook, came in. She had just put on the brown uniform and the coffee-coloured cap and apron which were the visible evidence of her transition.

"A Mrs. Something or other to see you, sir. She came in a car."

Mr. Hickler put down his sonnets.

"Mrs. Something or other came in a car? What does she want?"

"I don't know, sir—she said it's about books."

"Show her into the drawing-room," he said.

A great many boring people went to see Mr. Hickler about books. He had a local reputation as a poetaster.

"Very good."

He put a slip of paper to mark his place in the volume he had been reading, and went up the short, narrow passage to the tiny room, more arty and crafty than any of the others, since it was furnished with one settle, a spinet, two Medici prints, and a rush carpet. And there he saw a figure that was out of all harmony with the æsthetic surroundings.

The lady was big, squat, and old-fashioned; a

more revolting figure he never hoped to see. Her hair was obviously dyed; a large and fashionable hat sat at a large and unfashionable angle over her spurious locks. Her face was powdered a dead white, and she exhaled a perfume that made Mr. Hickler shudder.

The modishness of her headgear was discounted somewhat by the length of her skirt and the antiquity of her fur coat.

"No, thank you, I won't sit down," she said in a shrill voice. "You're Mr. Hickler? Will you see this for me, please?"

He took the book she offered to him in her large, gloved hand, and saw at a glance that it was a veritable treasure—the very rare Commentaries of Messer Aglapino, the Venetian. Turning the leaves reverently, he peered down at the print, for the lights in his house were so shaded that it hardly seemed worth while to have lights at all.

"Yes, madam, this is a very rare book—probably worth three or four hundred pounds. I envy you your possession."

He handed the book back with a courteous little bow.

"Mrs.——?"

"Mrs. Hubert Verity. You probably know our family. They are Shropshire people. I only wish my nephew was Shropshire in spirit as well as in birth."

She raised her black eyebrows and closed her eyes. Evidently her nephew was not especially popular.

"Won't you sit down?" he asked.

She shook her head.

"I prefer to stand."

Her high-pitched voice was very painful to the sensitive ears of Mr. Hickler.

"I don't know why I should trouble you with my affairs; but I never could stand a miser, and Gordon is a miser. My dear husband was thoroughly deceived by him or he would never have left him thirty thousand pounds, which was quite as much as, if not more than, he left me.

"I've had a lot of misfortune owing to these terrible Stock Exchange people who tell you shares are going up when they're really going down—and well they know it! And when I went to my nephew to-day to ask him for a trifling loan—I must put The Cedars in a state of repair, with dear Alfred coming back from South Africa in the spring—he showed me his pass-book!

"I could have laughed if I wasn't so enraged. I said to him: 'My dear boy, do you imagine that I am a fool? Do you think I don't know you well enough to know that you keep your money fluid, like the miser that you are!' It was a dreadful thing to call one's own nephew, but Gordon Stourven deserves every word. I could tell the Income Tax Commissioners a few things about Gordon."

She tossed her grotesque head and simpered meaningly. And then she looked at the book.

"Three hundred pounds . . . and I want the money very badly. I suppose you wouldn't like to buy it?"

The book was worth five hundred at least, but Mr. Hickler hesitated. His inclination was to buy; his sense of discretion told him to temporise.

"I am not in a position now to buy the book," he said, "but if you would give me the first offer, perhaps I could take your name and address."

She gave the name of her house in Kensington.

"I shall be out of town until next Wednesday week. I go to Paris for my dresses."

She said this importantly, and Mr. Hickler did not laugh.

"I like you: you're businesslike. If Gordon Stourven had half your straight-forwardness life would be ever so much more enjoyable. That man is so mean that he will not have a telephone in his office. I said to him: 'My dear boy, do you imagine I'm coming through this horrible city to Bucklersbury and climb to the top floor of a wretched office building just to see you?' In fact, I offered to pay for the telephone myself. . . ."

Mr. Hickler listened, apparently without interest; and later accompanied the lady as she waddled to her car. She insisted upon leaving the book behind, and for this concession he was grateful.

He waited till the car had disappeared and then he went back to the house, closed the door, and took the volume into his sitting-room, turning the pages idly. Somebody had been looking through it that very day: there was a bookmark—a credit slip from the Guaranty Trust, of that day's date, and it showed the exchange of a draft for 180,000 dollars into English currency.

Mr. Hickler turned the slip over and over. The book had been in the possession of Mr. Gordon Stourven; and here was Mr. Gordon Stourven's name scribbled in pencil on the top of the slip. A man who dabbled in cash finance, obviously, and a wealthy man. It was all very interesting, all very foreign to the art and the craft and the æstheticism in which Mr. Hickler lived his normal life.

The next day business took him to the City, and he drove down in the cheap little car that he permitted himself—the car that has its hundred-thousand duplicates up and down the land. There were two block of offices in Bucklersbury, but the first he entered was the one he sought.

Mr. Gordon Stourven's name was painted in black on one of the many opalescent slides that filled an indicator. He lived on the fifth floor and his number was 979. Mr. Hickler took the elevator, toiled down the long corridor, and after a while stopped before a door on the glass panel of which was "Gordon Stourven," and, in smaller characters at the bottom left-hand corner:

The Vaal Heights Gold Mining Syndicate.
The Leefontein Deeps.
United American Finance Syndicate.

Since the panel also announced that this was the general office, he turned the handle and stepped in.

An L-shaped counter formed a sort of lobby, in which he waited until his tapping on its surface brought a bespectacled and unprepossessing young lady.

"Mr. Stourven's out," she said promptly and hoarsely. "He's gone to lunch with his aunt."

Mr. Hickler smiled faintly.

"I had better wait and see him," he said, and held up a little parcel. "This book is the property of the lady and I wish to return it."

She looked at him for a long time before she decided to lift the flap of the counter and invite him across the linoleum-covered floor to a small inner office. She pulled a chair from the wall.

"You'd better sit down," she said jerkily. "I don't know whether I'm doing right—I've only been at this place for two days. The young lady before me got sacked for pinching—I mean stealing—I mean taking a penny-halfpenny stamp. You wouldn't think anybody would be so mean, would you? But she was

—he told me himself! And he's worth thousands. I'm going myself to-day."

"I'm sorry to hear that," smiled Mr. Hickler.

"I'm only staying to oblige him," explained the bespectacled girl. "He mislaid his keys this morning and the way he went on to me about it was a positive disgrace. Why should I pinch anything out of his old safe?"

Hickler did not encourage conversation. He very badly wished to be alone. Presently his desire was gratified.

There was the safe, embedded in the wall. Curious, he mused, what faith even intelligent people have in five sides of masonry! It was an American safe that grew unfashionable, except among the burglaring classes, twenty years before. He examined it thoughtfully. Two holes drilled, one below and one above the lock . . . even that wasn't necessary. A three-way key adjustment would open that in a quarter of an hour.

He stepped to the door softly and looked through a glass-panelled circle in the opaque glass. The girl was at her desk, writing laboriously, her mouth moving up and down with every figure she wrote. He put his hand in his hip pocket and took out his little cosh—a leather-plaited life-preserver.

The girl could be dealt with very expeditiously; but the danger was too great. Stourven might return at any moment. He took another and a closer scrutiny of the safe and smiled. Then he went to the desk and examined the memoranda and the papers.

The only thing that really interested him was the carbon sheet of a type-written letter—and a letter so badly typewritten that he guessed it was the work of the disgruntled young lady with spectacles. It was addressed to a Broad Street Trust Company and bore that day's date.

> Dear Mr. Lein,—I am prepared to close the deal to-morrow and will meet you at your lawyer's as arranged. I do not agree with you that I have a great bargain. The property must be developed—it seems to have fallen into a pretty bad state of disrepair.
>
> In the circumstances I do not think that £18,700 is a very attractive price. However, I never go back on my word. I quite understand that lawyers require cash payments, and in any circumstances my cheque wouldn't be of much use to you, for I keep a very small balance at the bank.

Mr. Hickler replaced the letter carefully where he had found it. He had not removed his gloves since he left his house. It was a peculiarity of Mr. Hickler that he never removed his gloves except in his own home. People thought it was because he had been nicely brought up, but that was not the reason.

He went into the outer office, still carrying the book.

"By the way, I don't think you should have invited me into Mr. Stourven's private office. If I were you, I shouldn't say you took me there." He smiled benignantly at her.

Yes, he was glad he didn't have to tackle this bespectacled imbecile. She looked like one of those thin-skulled people with whom one might easily have an accident; and she was wiry and vital—the sort of shrimp who, if one didn't get her at the first crack, would scream and raise hell.

On his way downstairs he stopped to inquire at the janitor's office whether there were any offices to let and what were the services. The janitor told him.

"By the way, what time do the cleaners start their operations?" he asked.

This was rather an important matter. The hours the office cleaners arrived and left very often determined an operation.

They came on at midnight, explained the porter. So many of the offices were let to stockbrokers, who in the busy season worked very late. There were two entrances to the building; the other was an automatic lift, which tenants could operate themselves, the general elevator going out of action at 9 p. m.

All this Mr. Hickler learned, and more. There were two offices to let in the basement. The porter very kindly took him down and flattered them to their face.

"No, sir, I go off at six, but we've got a night

man on duty. We have to do that because we've a great deal of property and money in this building. One of our tenants, Mr. Stourven, was asking me that very question this morning. He's only been here a fortnight himself—he came from somewhere down in Moorgate. A very nervous gentleman he is too." The porter smiled at the recollection.

Mr. Hickler, who was paying the closest attention to the accommodation of the offices, explained that he thought of founding a small literary society in the City for clerks who, in the hours so crudely devoted to the mastication of beef-steak pudding, might enrich their souls with an acquaintance with the *soufflés* of Keats.

The porter thought it was a very good idea. He did not know who Keats was, but had a dim notion that he was the gentleman who had found a method of destroying beetles and other noxious friends of the pestologist.

The little car went back to Hampstead at a slow rate, was garaged in the tiny shed at the end of the garden before Mr. Hickler went into his house, stripped his gloves and gave his mind to the evening's occupation.

He was clever, very clever, because he devoted thought to his trade. He applied to a "transaction" such as to-night's the same minute care, the same thought, the same close analysis as he gave to a disputed and obscure line of one of the earlier English poets.

Nobody knew very much about him; nobody guessed why he had called his tiny cottage "The Plume of Feathers." Even the bronze ornament above the knocker on his door, representing, as it did, such a feathery plume, did not explain his eccentricity.

Yet the name of his house was one of the most careless mistakes he ever committed, and if there had been the remotest suspicion attached to him, if Scotland Yard had been even aware of his existence, The Plume of Feathers would have been illuminating—for it is the name of an inn immediately facing Dartmoor Prison, an inn towards which Mr. Hickler had often cast wistful eyes on his way to the prison fields.

He was not Mr. Hickler then; he was just plain James Connor, doing seven years' penal servitude for robbery with assault, to which sentence had been added a flogging, which he never forgot.

He was prison librarian for some time; cultivated his fine taste in *belles lettres* with the grey-backed volumes of the prison library. Only two men in London knew of his connection with that dreadful period of inaction. One of them, as Bliss rightly surmised, was the greatest of the fences—great because he had never betrayed a client and had never been arrested by the police.

Mr. Hickler expected a telephone call concerning the book, but it did not come. At half-past seven he put a small suitcase and a rough, heavy overcoat in the back of his car, and drove by way of Holloway to the Epping Forest road. Here, in seclusion, he made a rapid change of clothes; drove back to Whitechapel, where he garaged the car, and made his way to Bucklersbury on foot.

The only evidence that the activity of the human hive was slackening was discoverable in the fact that one of the two doors which closed each entrance was already shut. He awaited his opportunity, stepped briskly into the deserted passage, found the automatic lift, and went up to the top floor. The corridor here was, except for one lamp, in darkness. There was no light in any of the offices, and that was a great relief.

Mr. Stourven's outer door was, of course, locked, but only for about three minutes. By that time Mr. Hickler was inside and had shot the bolt. He did not attempt to put on the lights, preferring the use of his own hand-lamp.

Both the outer office and the inner office were empty. He made a quick examination of the cupboards, tried the windows—he was free from all possibility of interruption.

Setting his lamp on the floor, he took the remainder of his tools from his pocket and set to work on the safe—the easiest thing he had ever attempted. In twenty-five minutes the key he had inserted some thirty times gripped the wards of the lock. It went back with a snap. He turned the brass handle and pulled open the heavy door of the safe.

He was on his knees, peering into the interior. He had scarcely time to realise that the safe was empty except for thousands of fragments of thin glass before he fell forward, striking his head on the edge of the safe.

Bliss had a letter. It was delivered by a district messenger, and he knew it was from The Ringer before he opened it. It came to him at his private residence.

You will find our friend Bash in office No. 979, Greek House, Bucklersbury. He is, I should imagine, quite dead, so he will not be able to tell you how splendid an actor I am. I went to see him at his artistic little place in Hampstead—my most difficult feat, for I had to keep my knees bent all the time I was talking to him in order to simulate dumpiness. You should try that some time.

I persuaded him to burgle a safe in my office. Inside the safe I smashed, just before I closed the door, a large tube of the deadliest gas known to science. I will call it X.3 and you will probably know what it is. It was then in liquid form, but, of course, volatilised immediately to a terrific volume.

And the moment he opened the door he was dead, I shoul

imagine, but you might make sure. And you had better take a gas mask. You are too good a man to lose.

There was no signature but a postscript.

Or why not send Mander without a gas mask?

THE SWISS HEAD WAITER

THE SWISS HEAD WAITER

THERE was a broad streak of altruism in the composition of Henry Arthur Milton, whose other name was The Ringer. There was, perhaps, as big a streak of sheer impishness. At Scotland Yard they banked on his vanity as being the most likely cause to bring him to ruin, and they pointed out how often he had shown his instant readiness to resent some slight to himself. But Inspector Bliss, who had made a study of the man, could not be prevailed upon to endorse this view.

"He chooses the jobs where his name has been used in vain because they give him a personal interest," he said; "but the personal interest is subsidiary."

It was never quite clear whether the Travelling Circus offended through the careless talk of "Doc" Morane or whether there was an unknown and more vital reason for the events at Arcy-sur-Rhône.

Now, as a rule, systematic breakers of the law are so busy with their own affairs that they do not bother their heads about the operation much less speak slightingly of their own kind. But the Travelling Circus were kings in their sphere, and were superior to the rules which govern lesser crooks. There were three of them: Lijah Hollander, Grab Sitford, and Lee Morane. Li was little and old, a wizened man. Grab was tall and hearty, a bluff, white-haired man, who was, according to his own account, a farmer from Alberta. "Doc" Morane was a tough looker, broad and unprepossessing, ill-mannered. Whether he had ever been anything but a doctor of cards nobody knew or cared.

The Doc was the leader of the gang and had a definite part to play. Little Li Hollander supplied one gentle element, Grab the other; it was the Doc who got rough at the first suggestion of a victim that the game was not straight. Mr. Bliss had expressed the view before that The Ringer controlled the best intelligence department in Europe; apparently he should have included the Western Ocean.

The S. S. *Romantic* was sixteen hours from Southampton and the smoke-room was almost empty, for the hour was midnight and wise passengers had gone early to bed, knowing that they would be awakened at dawn by the donkey engines hoisting passengers' baggage into the tender at Cherbourg. A few of the unwise had spent the evening playing poker, and among these was a newspaper man who had been to New York to study the methods of Transatlantic criminals—he was the crime reporter of an important London newspaper. He was a loser of forty pounds before he realised exactly what he was up against, and then he sat out and watched. When the last flushed victim had gone to bed, he had a few words to say to the terrifying Doc and his pained associates.

"Forty pounds, and you can give it back to-night. I don't mind paying for my experience, but I hate paying in money."

"See here"—began the Doc overpoweringly.

"I'm seeing here all right," said the imperturbable scribe: "that's been my occupation all the evening. I saw you palm four decks and it was cleverly done. Now do you mind doing a bit of see-here? There's a Yard man comes on board at daybreak. I'm the crime reporter of the *Megaphone*, and I can give you more trouble than a menagerie of performing fleas. Forty hard-earned pounds—thanks."

The Doc passed the notes across and, dropping for the moment his rôle of bully-in-chief, ordered the drinks.

"You've got a wrong idea about us, but we bear no malice," he said when the drinks came. "The way you were going on I thought you might be that Ringer guy!" he chuckled amiably. "Listen—if The Ringer worked in the State of New York he'd have been framed years ago. He tried to put a bluff on me once, but I called him. That's a fact—am I right, Grab?"

Grab nodded.

"Surely," he said.

The report of this conversation was the only evidence Bliss had that there was any old grudge between The Ringer and the Circus. Very naturally he could not know of the subsequent conversation on the Col de Midi.

"No, I never met him—we had a sort of 'phone talk. I was staying at the Astoria in London," the Doc went on, his dead-looking face puckered in a smile. "If I'd met him I don't think there would have been any doubt about what'd have happened —eh, Grab?"

The white-haired Grab agreed. He was a living confirmation of all that the Doc asserted, guessed, believed, or theorised.

That was about the whole of the conversation. The Circus left the boat at Cherbourg and travelled south, for this was the season when rich Englishmen leave their native land and go forth in search of the sun. Doc and his friends lingered awhile in Paris, then took separate trains for Nice. Here they stayed in different hotels, packed up a parcel of money which had once been the exclusive property of a bloated Brazilian, missed Monte Carlo—Monte does not countenance competition—and went, by way of Cannes and San Remo, to Milan.

Milan drew blank, but there are four easy routes into Switzerland.

"There's a new place up the Rhône Valley full of money," said Doc. "They threw up two new hotels last fall, and they've opened a new bob run that's dangerous to life and limb. The Anglo-Saxon race are sleeping on billiard tables and parking their cash in the pockets."

A week later. . . .

"Mr. Pilking" came into the Hotel Ristol, stamping his boots to rid them of the snow, for a blizzard was sweeping down the Rhône Valley and the one street of the little village of Arcy-sur-Rhône was a white chasm through which even the sleighs came with difficulty.

He was a big, florid man, red-faced, white-haired, and he wore a ski-ing suit of blue water-proofed cloth. He had left his skis leaning against the porch of the hotel, but he still carried his long ash sticks.

Mr. Pilking stopped at the desk of the concierge to collect his post, and clumped through the wide lounge to his room. His post was not a heavy one; the guests at the hotel knew him as a business man with large Midland and Northern interests; not even on his holidays could he spare himself, he often said—but his post was very light.

Arcy-sur-Rhône is not a fashionable winter resort. It lies on a shelf of rock, a few thousand feet above the Rhône Valley, and is not sufficiently high to ensure snow, but at an elevation which appeals to people whose hearts are affected by higher altitudes. There is generally a big and select party at the Ristol in January, for Arcy has qualities which not even St. Moritz can rival. The view across the Lake of Geneva is superb, the hotel is so comfortable that its high charges are tolerable, and it can add to its attractions the fact that in all its history it had never consciously harboured an undesirable in the more serious sense of the word. The ski-ing was good, the bob run one of the best in Switzerland; it enjoyed more than its share of snow, and the hotel notice-boards were never disfigured with that hoteful notice *Patinage Fermé*.

As to whether or not Mr. Sam Welks was altogether desirable, there were several opinions. He was a stoutish man who wore plus-fours all day, never dressed for dinner, talked loudly on all occasions, and was oracular to an offensive degree. Mr. Pilking saw him out of the corner of his eye as he passed. He was standing with his back to a pillar, his waving hands glittering in the light of the electroliers—for Mr. Welks wore diamond rings without shame.

". . . Gimme London! You can say what you like about scenery and that sort of muck, but where's a better scene than the Embankment on a spring day, eh? You can 'ave your Parises an' Berlins an' Viennas; you can 'ave Venice an' Rome. Take it from me, London's got 'em skinned to death, as the Yankees say. An' New York . . . ! Why, I've made more money in London in a week than some of them so-called millionaires have made in a month o' Sundays! There's more money to be made in dear old London . . ."

He always talked about money. The dark-haired head waiter, who spoke all languages, used to listen and smile quietly to himself, for he knew London as well as any man. The head waiter was new to Arcy-sur-Rhône; he had only been a week in the place, but he knew every guest in the hotel. He had arrived the same day as Mr. Pilking and his two friends who were waiting for him in his ornate sitting-room.

Doc Morane looked up as Grab came clumping into the room.

"Look at Grab!" he said admiringly. "Gee! I've got to go play that she-ing game—I was a whale at it when I was a kid. Maybe, I'll take Sam out and give him a lesson!"

Old Li Hollander, nodding over an out-of-date visitors' list, woke up and poured himself a glass of ice water.

"We're dining with that Sam Welks man to-night, Grab," he said. "I roped him into a game of bowls after lunch, and he wanted to bet a hundred dollars a game. I could have beaten him fifty, but thought I'd give him a sweetener. That man's clever!"

The Doc was helping himself to whisky.

"I like a clever guy," he said, "but I don't like head waiters who remind me of somebody I've seen before."

Grab looked at his leader sharply.

"All head waiters look that way," he said. "Maybe we've seen him somewhere. These birds travel from hotel to hotel according to the season. Do you remember that guy in Seattle, Doc, the feller you had a fight with when you were running around with Louise Poudalski?"

The Doc made a little face. The one person in the world he never wished to be reminded about was Louise Poudalski, and if there was a memory in that episode which grated on him, it was the night in a little Seattle hotel when a German floor waiter had intervened to save Louise from the chastisement which, by the Doc's code—even his drunken code, for he was considerably pickled on that occasion—she deserved. He often used to wonder what had happened to Louise. He had heard about her years ago when he was in New York—she was keeping house for a Chinaman in New Jersey, or was *it* New Orleans?

"Louise," said Li reminiscently, "was one of the prettiest girls——"

"Shut up about Louise," snarled the Doc. "Are we sweetening this Welks man to-night or are we giving him the axe?"

Grab was for sweetening; but then, in matters of strategy, Grab was always wrong. Li thought that Sam Welks was a "oncer."

"These clever fellows always are. Let 'em win, and they stuff the money into their wallet and tell you they know just when to stop, and that the time to give up playing is when you are on the right side. Soak him to-night and maybe you'll get him to-morrow. The right time to watch a weasel is the first time."

Doc Morane agreed, and Li, dusting the cigar ash from his waistcoat and brushing his thin locks, went down in search of the sacrifice.

Mr. Welks was talking. There seldom was a moment when he was not talking; and Li saw, hovering in the background, the new head waiter, a tall, dark man with a heavy black moustache.

Mr. Welks was in a truculent mood. The manager of the hotel, in the politest possible terms and with infinite tact, had suggested that it would be a graceful compliment to the other guests if he conformed to the ridiculous habit of dressing for dinner.

"Swank!" Mr. Welks was saying to his small and youthful audience—the young people of the hotel got quite a lot of amusement out of studying Mr. Welks at first hand in preparation for giving lifelike imitations of him after supper.

"It's what the Socialists call being class-conscious. It's the only thing I have ever agreed with the Socialists about. I have lived in Leytonstone for twenty-three years man and boy, and I have never dressed for dinner except when I have been going out to swell parties—why should I here, when I am out on an 'oliday? It's preposterous! I pay twenty shillings in the pound wherever I go. I am paying seventy-five francs a day for my soot, and if I can't dress as I like I'll find another hotel. I told this manager—I'm John Blunt. What's the idea of it? Why should I get myself up like a blooming waiter?"

Mr. Hollander thought he saw a faint smile on the face of the head waiter, though apparently he was not listening to the conversation.

"That's my view entirely," said Li. "If I want to dress I dress; if I don't want to dress, I don't dress."

"Exactly," said Mr. Welks, kindling towards his supporter.

Li took him by the arm and led him to the bar.

"If there's going to be any fuss I'm with you," he said. "And that gentleman, Mr. Pilking, a very nice man indeed, although an American" (Li was born in Cincinnati) "he holds the same opinion."

They drank together, and Mr. Welks gratefully accepted the invitation, extemporised on the spur of the moment, that he should dine in Mr. Pilking's private room that night.

The Doc and Pilking strolled providentially into the bar to confirm this arrangement, and for an hour the conversation was mainly about Mr. Welks, his building and contractor's business, the money he made during the war, the terrible things that happened to competitors who did not profit by Mr. Welks's example, his distaste of all snobbery and swank, his clever controversies with the Board of Trade, and such other subjects as were, to Mr. Welks, of national interest.

It was after he had drifted off that a curious thing happened which was a little disquieting. The three shared in common a sitting-room, out of which opened on the one side Grab's bedroom and on the other side the Doc's. Li had his bedroom a little farther removed. The Doc went up to his room to make a few necessary preparations for the dinner and the little game which was to follow. He pushed down the lever handle of the sitting-room door, but it did not yield, and at that moment he heard the sound of a chair being overturned. There should have been a light in the sitting-room, but when he stooped to look through the keyhole there was complete darkness.

He went along to the door of his own bedroom

and tried that. This, too, was bolted on the inside. The Doc retraced his footsteps to Pilking's room. Here he had better luck. The door was unfastened, and he entered, switching on the light. The door communicating between the bedroom and the sitting-room was wide open. He went in, turned the switch, and walked to the door, which, to his surprise, he found unbolted. He passed through the door leading to his own bedroom, and here he had a similar experience, the door opening readily.

There was no sign of an intruder, no evidence that anything had been disturbed. If the chair had been overturned it had been set on its feet again. He opened the door of the long cupboard, which might conceal an intruder, but, save for his clothes suspended on hangers, it was empty.

Returning through the sitting-room, he went out into the corridor. As he did so he saw a man come, apparently from the stairs, stand for a moment as if in doubt, and then, catching sight of the Doc, turn swiftly and disappear—not, however, before Doc Morane had recognised the dark-haired head waiter.

Very thoughtfully he returned to his apartment and made another search. Nothing, so far as he could see, had been disturbed. He locked the doors and opened a suitcase which stood on a small pedestal. There must have been over a hundred packs of cards in that case, each fastened with a rubber band and each representing half an hour's intensive arrangement. These had no appearance of having been disturbed. He relocked the grip and went slowly back to his companions, and at the earliest opportunity told them what had happened.

"Somebody was in the room," he said, "and I pretty well know who that somebody was."

Elijah was obviously worried.

"Maybe that waiter is a hotel 'tec," he said. "Up at St. Moritz the Federal people sent a couple of 'tecs into one of the hotels and pinched the Mosser crowd."

Mr. Sam Welks did not go to his host's room that night unprepared for the little game that was to follow. It was Li who had suggested it. "Mr. Pilking was not particularly keen," he said. He didn't like playing for money; one wasn't sure if the people who lost could really afford to lose.

The talkative Sam had bridled at the suggestion—this was over cocktails before dinner.

"Speakin' for meself," he said, "I don't worry about people losin'. If they can't afford to lose they shouldn't play. That foreign-lookin' waiter feller had the nerve to tell me not to play cards with strangers. I told him to mind his own business. I never heard such cheek in my life! If anybody can catch me, good luck to 'em! But they couldn't. I've met some of the cleverest crooks in London, an' they've all had a cut at me."

He chuckled at the thought.

"Bless your life! When a man's knocked about the world as I have it takes a clever feller to best him. See what I mean? It's an instinct with me, knowin' the wrong 'uns. I remember once when I was stayin' at Margate. . . ."

They let him talk, but each of the three was thinking furiously. It was Doc Morane who put their thought into words.

"That waiter was frisking the apartment," he said, "and that means no good to anybody. We'll skin this rabbit and get away to-morrow if he looks like squealing——"

"He'll not squeal," said the saintly Li, who was the psychologist of the party. "He wouldn't admit he'd been had. The most he'll do is to ask for a No. 2 séance, but I'm all for getting while the road's good. This is going to be one large killing!"

The dinner in the little salon was a great success. Grab, who was something of a gourmet, had ordered it with every care.

Under the mellowing influence of '15 Steinberger Cabinet, Mr. Welks grew expansive. He wore his noisiest plus-fours, and, as a further gesture of defiance against the conventions, a soft-collared shirt of purple silk.

"You've got to take me as I am," he said, "as other people have done before. I don't put on side and I don't expect other people to. My 'ome in Leytonstone is Liberty 'All—I don't ask people who their fathers was—were. I could have been a knight if I'd wanted to be, but that kind of thing doesn't appeal to me. Titles—bah!"

The time came when the dinner table was wheeled out into the corridor and a green-covered table was brought into the centre of the room. Again Mr. Pilking made his conventional protest.

"I don't like playing for money. Although I know you two gentlemen, I don't know Mr. Welks, and I've always made a rule never to play with strangers."

He said this probably a hundred times a year, and it never failed to provoke the marked victim.

"Look here, mister," said Welks hotly, "if my money's not good enough for you, you needn't play! If it comes to that, I don't know you. Money talks—hear mine!"

He thrust his hands into his pockets and took out a thick roll of Swiss bills, and from a pocket cunningly placed on the inside of his plus-fours, a thicker wad of Bank of England notes.

"The Swiss are milles—which means a thousand—an' these good old English notes are for a hundred. Now let's see yours!"

With a perfect assumption of hesitancy, Mr.

Pilking produced a goodly pile and his companions followed suit.

For the first quarter of an hour the luck went in the direction of Mr. Welks—which was the usual method of the Travelling Circus.

Unseen by any, Doc Morane "palmed" a new pack. The substitution was made all the easier by the fact that Welks was separating the larger from the smaller notes which represented his inconsiderable winnings.

"Cut," said the Doc, offering the pack.

"Run 'em," replied Mr. Welks professionally.

Something went wrong with the hand. Welks should have held four queens and the Doc four kings. These latter appeared in Doc Morane's hand all right, and the betting began.

Li threw in his hand when the bidding reached six hundred pounds. Grab retired at eight hundred. The Doc brought the bidding to a thousand.

"And two hundred," said Mr. Welks recklessly.

Doc Morane made a rapid calculation. This man was good for a few thousands if he was gentled.

"I'll see you," he said, and nearly collapsed when the triumphant Mr. Welkes laid down four aces.

Li took the pack from the table, and with a lightning movement dropped it to his lap as he slipped a new pack into its place. Li was the cleverest of all broad-men at this trick.

"Run 'em," said the Doc as the pack was offered to him.

This time there could be no mistake. The four knaves came to him, and he knew by Li's nod and Grab's yawn that they each held one ace, king and queen. Mr. Welks drew two cards—which was exactly the number he should have drawn. The Doc knew that he now held two kings and three tens.

They bid up to eight hundred, which was more than any sane man would bet on a "full house."

"I'll see you," growled Doc Morane.

Mr. Welks laid down a small straight flush.

"You'll have to take a cheque," said the Doc when he recovered.

"I'll take the cash you've got and a cheque for the rest," said Welks. He was a picture of fatuous joy. "I'm a business man, old boy, but I know something about poker, eh?"

That ended the party; they were too clever not to accept his invitation to the bar for a celebration. The three went upstairs together and Doc Morane locked the salon door.

"Somebody was in here before dinner, planting new decks of cards," he said. "Did you lamp the head waiter? I'll fix that bird!"

"What are we going to do?" asked Li fretfully. "Do we get or stay?"

"We're not leaving till we get that money and

more," said Grab savagely. "What do you say, Doc?"

Doc Morane nodded.

"Me an' Welks are like brothers," he said significantly. "We're going she-ing on the Midi slopes to-morrow morning, and I'll hook him for to-night. You fellows stay home and fix those cards."

A little railway carried a small and cold party to the ski-ing fields early the next morning. Because the upper stretches of the line were snowed under the party descended on the Col de Midi, which is a razor-backed ridge which mounts steeply up to the precipice face of the Midi Massif.

Mr. Welks was no mean exponent of the art, and led his companions up the snowy slopes. And all the time he sang loudly and untunefully the vulgar song of the moment.

The head waiter had not been in the train. Once or twice the Doc looked round to make sure. He saw a Swiss guide signalling frantically, but nobody seemed coming their way, and when Mr. Welks pulled up after an hour's laborious climb they were alone.

"You're not a good skier, my friend," he said pleasantly.

The Doc wiped his perspiring forehead and growled something.

"A little farther," said Mr. Welks, and went on.

The Doc noticed that he went tenderly along the crest of a snowy cornice, but did not understand why until he had passed and, looking back, saw that they had passed a snowy bridge over a deep chasm.

"Dangerous, eh?" Mr. Welks smiled gleefully. "You can take off your skis."

"Why?" asked the Doc, frowning.

"Because I ask you."

The Doc took off his skis: he invariably did what he was told to when the teller covered him with a Browning pistol.

Mr. Welks lifted the skis and threw them into the chasm.

"On the other side of this ridge is Italy," he said pleasantly. "That is where I am going. What will happen to you I don't know. It is impossible to walk back. Perhaps the head waiter—who is the best detective in Switzerland—will rescue you. He was going to arrest you, anyway. By the way, it was I who planted the cards last night."

"Who are you?" The Doc's white face was whiter yet.

Mr. Welks smiled.

"My wife had a little friend in Seattle—one Louise Poudalski. Remember her?"

Before Doc Morane could reply, The Ringer was flying down the Italian slope, his skis raising snow like steam. . . .

THE BLACK

WHEN *The Black* first appeared, Will Cuppy, that gay and ironic expert on the world's mystery stories, remarked that it was decidedly one of Wallace's major *opera,* with a sane plot, a group of human characters, and a puzzle that gave the reader a chance. Another commentator pointed out that it had the neatest trick ending since O. Henry laid down his pen.

The Black has all that—sane plot, real characters, brilliant ending—but it has more: the intangible quality that has made Edgar Wallace the greatest best-seller of our times. It displays his story-teller's gift in its finest flower. Each page, each sentence, even, leads on to the next with a complete inevitability. The reader is constantly tempted to skim on through the book to untangle the complex, swiftly moving plot, restrained only by the skill and humour of the narrative itself. In other words, *The Black* is a good book.

The Black himself is James Morlake, the most remarkable burglar to be found between the covers of any book. The most dangerous man in England was no match for him, any more than the Flying Squad from Scotland Yard could limit his depredations. Those depredations were not haphazard; they had a purpose, and what that purpose was, and how Morlake moved to its accomplishment, makes up the thrilling story that many Wallace fans have called his masterpiece.

THE BLACK

TO MARNEY

CONTENTS

CHAPTER		PAGE
I.	The Black	1
II.	The Lady of Creith	6
III.	The Head of the Creiths	13
IV.	A Caller at Wold House	17
V.	The Monkey and the Gourd	19
VI.	Hamon Tells His News	21
VII.	Into the Storm	26
VIII.	The Robber	31
IX.	Mr. Hamon Loses Money	34
X.	The Frame-up	38
XI.	Jane Smith	47
XII.	Miss Lydia Hamon	50
XIII.	At Blackheath	55
XIV.	Caught	59
XV.	Joan Makes a Confession	64
XVI.	Mr. Hamon Is Shown Out	68
XVII.	Gentle Julius	70
XVIII.	The Trial	74
XIX.	The Tea Shop	78
XX.	A Caller	82
XXI.	A Volume of Emerson	87

CONTENTS

CHAPTER		PAGE
XXII.	Welcome Home	96
XXIII.	The New Housekeeper	104
XXIV.	Jim Learns Things	110
XXV.	The Cablegram	114
XXVI.	Joan Called Jane	118
XXVII.	Mrs. Cornford's Lodger	124
XXVIII.	Mr. Welling Gives Advice	129
XXIX.	A Love Call	134
XXX.	Sadi	140
XXXI.	Joan Tells the Truth	143
XXXII.	Captain Welling Understands	148
XXXIII.	The Foreign Sailor	156
XXXIV.	The Cord	160
XXXV.	The Letter That Came by Post	165
XXXVI.	The Bannockwaite Bride	175
XXXVII.	The Letter	179
XXXVIII.	A Yachting Trip	185
XXXIX.	The Chapel in the Wood	189
XL.	The Lover	193
XLI.	A Photograph	199
XLII.	Captain Welling: Investigator	204
XLIII.	The Man in the Night	210
XLIV.	Murder	214
XLV.	Wanted	219
XLVI.	Pointed Shoes	221
XLVII.	The Yacht	224

CONTENTS

CHAPTER		PAGE
XLVIII.	Mutiny	230
XLIX.	The Man on the Beach	236
L.	The Play	240
LI.	The Courtyard	244
LII.	The House of Sadi	248
LIII.	The House in the Hollow	253
LIV.	A Visit to the Basha	260
LV.	The Lady from Lisbon	264
LVI.	Captain Welling Adds a Postscript	272
LVII.	The Ride to the Hills	276
LVIII.	At the White House	279
LIX.	The Face at the Window	287
LX.	The Marriage	291
LXI.	The Beggar Husband	295
LXII.	The Escape	302
LXIII.	The End of Sadi	305
LXIV.	A Moorish Woman's Return	310
LXV.	The Reverend Gentleman	313
LXVI.	A Luncheon Party	320
LXVII.	The Return	326
LXVIII.	The End of Hamon	332

CHAPTER I

The Black

JAMES LEXINGTON MORLAKE, gentleman of leisure, Lord of the Manor of Wold and divers other titles which he rarely employed, unlocked the drawer of his elaborate Empire writing-table and gazed abstractedly into its depths. It was lined with steel and there were four distinct bolts. Slowly he put in his hand and took out first a folded square of black silk, then a businesslike automatic pistol, then a roll of fine leather. He unfastened a string that was tied about the middle and unrolled the leather on the writing-table. It was a hold-all of finely-grained sealskin, and in its innumerable pockets and loops was a bewildering variety of tools, grips, ratchets—each small, each of the finest tempered steel.

He examined the diamond-studded edge of a bore, no larger than a cheese tester, then replacing the tool, he rolled up the hold-all and sat back in his chair, his eyes fixed meditatively upon the articles he had exposed.

James Morlake's flat in Bond Street was, perhaps, the most luxurious apartment in that very exclusive thoroughfare. The room in which he sat, with its high ceiling fantastically carved into scrolls and arabesques by the most cunning of Moorish workmen, was wide and long and singular. The walls were of marble, the floor an amazing mosaic covered with the silky rugs of Ispahan. Four hanging lamps, delicate fabrics of silver and silk, shed a subdued light.

With the exception of the desk, incongruously gaudy in the severe and beautiful setting, there was little furniture. A low divan under the curtained window, a small stool, lacquered a vivid green, and another chair was all.

The man who sat at the writing-table might have been forty—he was four years less—or fifty. His was the face of a savant.

eager, alive, mobile. There was a hint of laughter in his eyes, more than a hint of sadness. A picturesque and most presentable person was James Lexington Morlake, reputedly of New York City (though some doubted this) and now of 823 New Bond Street in the County of London and of Wold House in the County of Sussex. His evening coat fitted the broad shoulders perfectly; the white bow at his collar was valet-tied.

He looked up from the table and its sinister display and clapped his hands once. Through the silken curtain that veiled the far end of the room came a soft-footed little Moor, his spotless white fellap and crimson tarboosh giving him a certain vividness against the soft background.

"Mahmet, I shall be going away to-night—I will let you know when I am returning." He spoke in Moorish, which is the purest of the three Arabics. "When, by the favour of God, I return, I shall have work for you."

Mahmet raised his hand in salute, then, stepping forward lightly, kissed each lapel of James Morlake's dress coat before he kissed his own thumb, for Morlake was, by certain standards, holy to the little slave man he had bought in the market-place of Rahbut.

"I am your servant, *haj*," he said. "You will wish to talk with your secretary?"

Morlake nodded, and, with a quick flutter of salaaming hands, Mahmet disappeared. He had never ceased to be amused by this description of Binger. "Secretary" was the delicate euphemism of the Moor who would not say "servant" of any white man.

Mr. Binger appeared, a short, stout man with a very red face and a very flaxen moustache, which he rapidly twirled in moments of embarrassment. Without the evidence of the neatly parted hair and the curl plastered over his forehead, he was obviously "old soldier."

He looked at his employer and then at the kit of tools on the table, and sighed.

"Goin' hout, sir?" he asked dolefully.

He was that unusual type of Cockney, the man who put aspirates where none were intended. Not one Londoner in ten thousand has this trick, ninety per cent. may drop an "h" —only the very few find it.

"I'm going out; I may be away for some days. You know where to find me."

"I *hope* so, sir," said the gloomy Binger. "I hope I shan't find you where I'm always expectin' to find you—in a hawful prison cell."

James Morlake laughed softly.

"You were never designed by providence to be a burglar's valet, Binger," he said, and Mr. Binger shivered.

"Don't use that word, sir, please! It makes me tremble with horrer! It's not for the likes of me to criticise, which I've never done. An' if you hadn't been a burglar I'd have been a corpse. You ran a risk for me and I'm not likely to forget it!"

Which was true. For one night, James Lexington Morlake, in the course of business, had broken into a warehouse of which Binger was caretaker. Morlake took the warehouse *en route* to a bigger objective—there was a bank at the end of the warehouse block—and he had found an almost lifeless Binger who had fallen through a trap and had broken a leg in the most complicated manner it is possible to break a leg. And Morlake had stopped and tended him; carried him to the hospital, though Binger guessed him for what he was, "The Black"—the terror of every bank manager in the kingdom. In this way both men, taking the most amazing risks, came into acquaintance. Not that it was, perhaps, any great risk for James Morlake, for he understood men.

He selected a cigarette from the gold case he took from his pocket, and lit it.

"One of these days, perhaps I'll become a respectable member of society, Binger," he said, a chuckle in his voice.

"I 'ope so, sir, I do most sincerely pray you will," said Binger earnestly. "It's not a nice profession—you're hout all hours of the night . . . it's not healthy! Speaking as a hold soldier, sir, I tell you that honesty is the best policy."

"How the devil did you know that there was an 'h' in 'honesty?' " asked James Morlake admiringly.

"I pronounced it, sir," said Binger.

"That is what I mean—now, Binger, listen to me. I want the car at the corner of Albemarle Street at two o'clock. It is raining a little, so have the hood up. Don't be within a dozen yards of the car when I arrive. Have an Oxford number-plate behind and the Sussex plate under the seat. A vacuum flask with hot coffee and a packet of sandwiches—and. that's all."

Binger, at the parting of the curtains, struggled to express what he felt was improper and even sinful to say.

"Good luck, sir," he said faintly.

"I wish you meant it," said James Morlake as he rose and, catching up the long black coat from the divan, slipped pistol and tools into his pocket. . . .

At the Burlington Street Safe Deposit, the night watchman had a stool on which he might sit in the lone long watches. It was a stool with one leg in the centre, and had this great advantage, that, if its occupant dozed, he fell. Nature, however, evolves qualities to meet every human emergency, and in the course of the years the night watchman, by leaning his elbow on a projecting ledge and stiffening his body against the wall, could enjoy a comfortable condition of coma that approximated to sleep. . . .

"Sorry!" said a gentle voice.

The watchman woke with a start and stumbled to his feet, reaching for the revolver that should have been on the little wooden ledge.

"Your gun is in my pocket and the alarm is disconnected," said the man in black, and the eyes that showed through the taut silk mask that covered his face twinkled humorously. "March!"

The night man, dazed and already searching his mind for excuses that would relieve him of the charge of sleeping on duty, obeyed.

The vaults of the Burlington Street Safe Deposit are underground, and for the use of the watchman there is a small concrete apartment fitted with an electric stove and a folding table. There is also a small safe built into the wall.

"In here," said the man in black. "Face the wall and save my soul from the hideous crime of murder."

Standing with his nose to concrete, the watchman heard the snap of a lock and the jingle of keys. In the safe were kept the pass keys and duplicates, and normally it could not be opened except by the President or Secretary of the company. The stranger seemed to experience no difficulty in dispensing with the help of these officers.

There came the thud of the room door closing, and then the turn of the key. After that, silence, except for the shrill whistle of air through the overhead ventilator. In ten minutes the visitor was back again, and the watchman saw him replace the keys he had taken, close and lock the safe.

"That is all, I think," said the stranger. "I have stolen very little—just enough to pay for my vacation and a new car. One must live."

"I'll get fired over this!" groaned the watchman.

"It depends on the lie you tell," said the mask, standing in the doorway, twirling his automatic alarmingly. "If you say that you were drugged, as the night patrol at the Home Counties Bank said, you may find people sceptical . . ."

"What about the hall-man?" asked the watchman hopefully.

"He is in his box, asleep . . . veritably doped by an ingenious method of my own," said the intruder.

He slammed the door, and again the key turned. It seemed to turn twice, and so it proved, for when the custodian tried the door it opened readily. But The Black had gone.

Three headquarters men were at the safe deposit within a few minutes of the alarm sounding. They found the hall-keeper slowly recovering his senses and the night watchman voluble and imaginative.

"Don't tell me that stuff about drugs," said Chief Inspector Wall irritably. "It may go in the case of the hall-man, but you were asleep, and as soon as he turned a gun on you, you played rabbit. That's your story, and I won't listen to any other."

The hall-man could offer no explanation. He was sitting in

his little office drinking coffee that he had made, and that was all he remembered.

"Keep that coffee-cup for analysis," said Wall. "The man must have been on the premises—it was easy once he doped the hall-keeper."

The upper part of the safe deposit was let out in office suites, the ground floor and basement being the premises of the deposit. A broad passage led from the street to the vault entrance, and was barred half-way down with a heavy steel gate to which the hall-man sitting in his office on the inside alone had the key.

"The thing was simple," said Wall, when he had finished his cross-examination. "Peters left his office and went down to see the night man. In some manner The Black got through—he'll open any lock. After that he had only to watch and wait."

In the early hours of the morning the secretary of the Safe Deposit arrived, and accompanied the police in a more thorough search through the inner vaults.

One little safe was unlocked. It was that which stood in the name of James Morlake, and the safe was entirely empty.

CHAPTER II

The Lady of Creith

STEPHENS, the butler at Creith House, read of the robbery in the morning newspaper, and, being of a communicative nature, he carried the news to his master with his morning coffee. He might have created a greater sensation had he told the guest of the house, but he disliked Mr. Ralph Hamon for many reasons, and added to his dislike was a certain uneasiness of mind. A servant may find pleasure in his prejudices only so long as they are directed toward the uninfluential. So Mr. Ralph Hamon had appeared on his first few visits to the

Earl of Creith. His attitude of deference toward the head of the house, his humility in the presence of the young lady, his eagerness to please, emphasised his inferiority. But his desire to stand well with the folk of Creith House did not extend to the servants. The tips he gave were paltry or were pointedly withheld, but for this Stephens and his staff were prepared, for Mr. Hamon's chauffeur had advertised his meanness in advance.

It was the change in the financier's attitude toward the family that worried Stephens and caused his plump, smooth face to wrinkle in uncomfortable thought.

In the early days he had addressed the Earl as "my lord"—and only servants and tenants and tradesmen "my lord nobility." And Lady Joan had been "your ladyship." Now it was "my dear Creith" and "my dear young lady," more often than not in a tone of good-natured contempt.

Stephens stood at the long window of the banqueting hall, staring across the broad expanse of shaven lawn to the river that traced the northern boundary of the Creith acres. It was a glorious morning in early autumn. The trees held to their deep green, but here and there the russet and gold of autumnal foliage showed on the wooded slopes of No Man's Hill. Sunlight sparkled on the sluggish Avon, the last wraith of mist was curling through the pines that crested the hill, and the tremendous silence of the countryside was broken only by the flurry of wings as a hen pheasant flew clumsily from covert to covert.

"Morning, Stephens."

Stephens turned guiltily as he heard the voice of the man about whom he was at that moment thinking so disrespectfully.

Ralph Hamon had come noiselessly into the panelled hall. He was a fair man of middle height, stockily built, inclined to stoutness. Stephens put his age at forty-five, being inclined, for personal reasons, to discount the visitor's slight baldness. Mr. Hamon's large face was sallow and usually expressionless. His high, bald forehead, his dark, deep-set eyes and the uncompromising line of his hard mouth suggested learning. Stephens was reminded of a hateful schoolmaster he had known in his youth. The baldness was emphasised by the floss-like wisp of hair that grew thinly on the crown, and was especially noticeable when he stooped to pick up a pin from the polished floor.

"That is lucky," he said, as he pushed the pin into the lapel of his well-fitting morning coat. "There's no better way of starting the day than by getting something for nothing, Stephens."

"No, sir," said Stephens. He had a desire to point out that the pin was somebody's property, but he refrained. "There has been another Black robbery, sir," he said.

Hamon snatched the paper from his hand, frowning.

"A Black robbery—where?"

He read and his frown deepened.

"The Burlington this time," he said, speaking to himself. "I wonder——?" He glared at Stephens, and the stout man wilted. "I wonder," said Mr. Hamon again, and then, abruptly: "Lord Creith is not down?"

"No, sir."

"And Lady Joan?"

"Her ladyship is in the park. She went riding an hour ago."

"Humph!"

Mr. Hamon's thick nose wrinkled as he threw down the newspaper. Overnight he had asked Joan Carston to ride with him, and she had made the excuse that her favourite hack had gone lame. Stephens was not a thought reader, but he remembered hastily certain instructions he had received.

"Her ladyship didn't think she would be able to ride, but her horse had got over his lameness this morning."

"Humph!" said Mr. Hamon again.

He took a quill toothpick from his pocket and nibbled at it.

"Lady Joan told me that she had put somebody in one of the cottages on the estate—at least, she didn't tell me, but I heard her mention the fact to Lord Creith. Who is it?"

"I don't know, sir," said Stephens truthfully. "I believe it is a lady and her daughter . . . her ladyship met her in London and gave her the cottage for a holiday."

One corner of Hamon's mouth lifted.

"Being a philanthropist, eh?" he sneered.

Stephens could only wonder at the cool assurance of a man

who, a year before, had almost grovelled to the girl about whom he could now speak with such insolent familiarity.

Hamon walked slowly through the stone-flagged entrance hall into the open. There was no sign of Joan, and he guessed that if he asked Stephens which way Joan had gone, the man would either plead ignorance or lie. Hamon had no illusions as to his popularity.

If the girl was invisible to him, she saw him plainly enough from No Man's Hill, a black against the green of the lawn. She sat astride the old hunter she rode, looking thoughtfully toward the big, rambling house, her young face troubled, the clear grey of her eyes clouded with doubt. A slim, gracious figure, almost boyish in its outlines, she watched the black speck as it moved back to the house, and for a second a faint smile trembled at the corners of the red lips.

"Up, Toby!" She jerked the rein, disturbing the grazing horse, and set his head to the top of the hill. No Man's Hill had been disputed territory for centuries, and its right to be included within the boundaries of the adjoining estates had impoverished at least three generations of two families. The Creiths had fought their claim in the courts since 1735. The Talmers had indulged in litigation for fifty years, and in the end had died embittered and ruined. The owners of Wold House had gone the same way. Would the new owner of the Wold continue the bad work, Joan wondered? Somehow she thought he was too sensible. He had been two years in occupation and had not issued a writ, though his title deeds undoubtedly gave him that disastrous right.

Presently she stopped and, dismounting and letting the horse graze at will, she climbed the last sheer slope and came to the top. Mechanically she looked at the watch on her wrist. It was exactly eight o'clock. And then her eyes sought the bridle path that skirted the foot of the hill.

She need not have examined her watch. The man she was overlooking had ridden out of the copse at exactly this moment, day after day, month after month. A tall man who sat his horse easily and smoked a pipe as he rode.

She took the glasses from the case she carried and focussed

them. The scrutiny was inexcusable; Joan admitted the fault without hesitation. It was he; the lean, æsthetic face, the grey patch at the temples, the open-throated rough shirt. She could have drawn him, and had.

"Joan Carston, you are an unmaidenly and shameless woman," she said sternly. "Is this man anything to you? No! Are you enveloping him in a golden cloud of romance? Yes! Isn't it vulgar curiosity and the desire of youth for mystery that brings you here every morning to spy upon this middle-aged and harmless gentleman? Yes! And aren't you ashamed? No!"

The unconscious object of her interrogations was parallel with her now. In one hand he carried a thin, pliable riding whip with which he smoothed the horse's mane absently. Looking neither to left nor right, he passed on, and she watched him with a puzzled frown until he was out of sight.

Mr. James Lexington Morlake was as great a source of puzzlement to the people of the country as to himself. For two years he had been master of Wold House, and nothing was known of him except that he was apparently a rich man. He most certainly had no friends. The Vicar had called upon him soon after his arrival. He had been canvassed on behalf of local charities, and had responded handsomely, but he had declined every social invitation which would bring him into closer touch with his neighbours. He neither visited nor received. Judicious enquiries were set afoot; cook talked to cook, and parlourmaid to parlourmaid, and in the end he stood disappointingly revealed as a man whose life was exemplary, if a little erratic, for nobody could be certain whether he was at home at Wold or in London. Even to his servants he did not disclose his plan for the day or the week. This eccentricity was common property.

Joan Carston mounted her horse and rode down the hill toward the path the man had followed. When she came to the track she looked to her left in time to see the battered sombrero he wore disappearing in the dip that leads to the river.

"I'm a rash and indelicate female, Toby," she said, addressing the twitching ears of her horse. "I am without reserve or proper pride, but oh! Toby, I'd give two paper pounds sterling—which is all I have in the world—to talk with him and be disillusioned!"

She sent her audience cantering along the road, turning off through the dilapidated gate which led her back to her father's estate. Where the main road skirted Creith Park was a lime-washed barn-like cottage, and to this she rode. A woman standing in the garden waved her hand as the girl approached. She was of middle age, slim and pretty, and she carried herself with a dignity which almost disguised the poverty of her attire.

"Good morning, Lady Joan. We reached here last night and found everything ready for us. It was lovely of you to take such trouble."

"What is work?" said Joan swinging herself to the ground. "Especially when somebody else does it? How is the interesting invalid, Mrs. Cornford?"

Mrs. Cornford smiled.

"I don't know. He doesn't arrive until to-night. You don't mind my having a boarder?"

"No," Joan shook her head. "I wonder you don't stay here permanently. Father said you might. Who is your boarder?"

Mrs. Cornford hesitated.

"He is a young man I am interested in. I ought to tell you that he is, or was, a dipsomaniac."

"Good heavens!" said the startled girl.

"I have tried to help him, and I think I have. He is a gentleman—it is rather tragic to see these cases, but at the Mission, where I help when I can spare the time, we see many. You are sure you won't mind?"

"Not a bit," laughed Joan, and the woman looked at her admiringly.

"You look pretty in riding things," nodded Mrs. Cornford approvingly.

"I look pretty in anything," said Joan calmly. "There is no sense in blinking facts: I *am* pretty! I can't help it any more than you can. I'm going to breakfast with you!"

"Yes, they are expecting me at Creith," said Joan, spreading marmalade thickly on her bread. "At least, our visitor expects me. Father expects nothing but a miracle that will bring him a million without any effort on his part. The miracle has partly materialised."

Mrs. Cornford's eyes spoke her surprise.

"No, we're not rich," said Joan, answering the unspoken question; "we are of the impoverished nobility. If I were a man I should go to America and marry somebody very wealthy and live a cat and dog life until I was well and truly divorced. As I am a girl, I must marry a home-bred millionaire. Which I shall not do."

"But surely . . ." began Mrs. Cornford.

"The house, the estate, our London house, are, or were until a week ago, mortgaged. We are the poorest people in the county."

Joan's cool confession took the other's breath away.

"I'm sorry," she said gently. "It is rather terrible for you."

"It isn't a bit," said Joan. "Besides, everybody here is at poverty's door. Everybody except the mysterious Mr. Morlake, who is popularly credited with being a millionaire. But that is only because he doesn't discuss his mortgages. Everybody else does. We sit round one another's tables and talk foreclosures and interests and the price of corn and cattle disease, but mostly we talk about the loss the country will sustain when the improvident nobility are replaced by the thrifty democracy."

Mrs. Cornford was silent, her grave eyes searching the girl's face. Joan had known her a year. It was an advertisement which Mrs. Cornford had inserted in a London newspaper asking for needlework that had brought Joan to the dingy little suburban street where the woman earned sufficient to keep herself and her daughter by her quick and clever fingers.

"It is not easy to be poor," she said quietly, and Joan looked up.

"You've been rich," she said, nodding her head sagely. "I knew that. One of these days I'm going to ask you to tell me the grisly story—no, I won't! Yes, it's horrible to be poor, but more horrible to be rich—on terms. Do you know Mr. Morlake?"

The elder woman smiled.

"He is a local celebrity, isn't he? I should hardly know him, but he seems to exercise the imagination of the people hereabouts. The girl from the village whom you so kindly sent here to tidy the cottage told me about him. Is he a friend of yours?"

"He is a friend of nobody's," said Joan. "In fact, he is so unfriendly that he must be rich. I used to think that he was going to be my prince charming," she sighed dolefully.

"I wonder if you are really sad?" smiled the woman. "I wonder."

Joan's face was inscrutable.

"You wouldn't imagine that I had a grisly past too, would you?" she asked. "Remember that I am quite old—nearly twenty-three."

"I shouldn't imagine so," said Mrs. Cornford, amusement in her fine eyes.

"Or a terrible secret?"

"No, I shouldn't think that either." Mrs. Cornford shook her head.

Joan sighed again.

"I'll go back to my burden," she said.

The "burden" was walking in the long chestnut avenue when she overtook him.

"I'm glad you've come, Lady Joan," he said with ill-assumed heartiness. "I'm starving!"

Joan Carston wished she had waited an hour or two.

CHAPTER III

The Head of the Creiths

FERDINAND CARSTON, ninth Earl of Creith, was a thin, querulous man, whose dominant desire was a negative one. He did not want to be bothered. He had spent his life avoiding trouble, and his deviations had led him into strange places. His "paper" was held by half a score of moneylenders, his mortgages were on the books of as many banks. He did not wish to be bothered by farm bailiffs and factors, or by tenant farmers. He could not be worried with the choice of his agents, and most of them did not bother to render him accurate accounts. From time to time he attempted to recover his heavy liabilities by daring speculations, and as he could not be troubled with the business of investigating their soundness, he usually returned to the well-worn path that led to the little moneylenders' offices that infest Sackville and Jermyn streets.

And then there came into his orbit a most obliging financier who handsomely accepted the task of settling with troublesome banks and clamouring Shylocks. Lord Creith was grateful. Deuced grateful. He sold the reversionary rights in the Creith estates, and not only discharged at one sweep all his liabilities, but touched real money.

He was in his library, examining with interest Tattersall's Sale Catalogue, when his guest came in unannounced.

"Hullo, Hamon!" he said without any great geniality. "Had breakfast?"

"Joan had breakfast out," said Hamon curtly.

"*Did* she?" asked Creith, looking at him over his glasses and at a loss to continue, yet feeling that something was expected of him he added: "*Did* she?"

Hamon pulled up a chair and seated himself at the opposite side of the writing-table.

"Have you ever thought what will happen when you die?" he asked.

Lord Creith blinked quickly.

"Never thought of it, Hamon, never thought of it. I've been a good churchman, though the tithes are an infernal nuisance —I suppose I'll go up to heaven with the best of 'em."

"I'm not thinking about your spiritual future," said Mr. Hamon. "I'm thinking about Creith."

"The title goes to Joan—it descends that way in our family," said his lordship, biting the end of a pen-holder. "But why bother me about these details, my dear fellow? If Joan wants to preserve the estate she'll marry you, and I've no objection. We've had some devilish queer people in our family before, and I daresay we shall go on having devilish queer people. My great great grandmother had a wooden leg."

Mr. Ralph Hamon overlooked the uncomplimentary reference, and was not prepared to encourage a discussion on the deficiencies of Lord Creith's ancestors.

"If Joan doesn't want to marry me?" he said. "I suppose you've some influence?"

Lord Creith took off his glasses deliberately.

"With Joan? Bless your life, she doesn't take the slightest notice of anything I say! And very properly. I'm about the worst adviser that anybody could have. She'll do what she likes. Her dear and blessed mother was the same. Don't bother me now, my dear good fellow."

"But suppose Joan refuses me point blank?" persisted the other.

Lord Creith's smile was broad and bland.

"Then, my dear boy, you're finished!"

Hamon bit off the end of a cigar deliberately, as Lord Creith looked significantly at the door.

"You *must* have some influence, Creith," he said doggedly. "Talk to her."

The older man leaned back in his chair, obviously bored, as obviously resigned to boredom.

"I'll speak to her," he said. "Oh, by the way, that farm you wanted, you can't have. I find that the mortgage was foreclosed by the Midland Bank a month ago, and the property has been sold to that queer fish, James Lexington Morlake. Though why the dickens he wants it——"

"Morlake!"

Creith looked up in surprise. The sallow face of Mr. Ralph Hamon was puckered, his slit of a mouth was parted in amazement and anger.

"Morlake—no—James Lexington Morlake? Does he live near here? Is he the man you were talking about the other day—you said he was an American. . . ."

He fired the questions in rapid succession, and Lord Creith closed his eyes wearily.

"I don't know who he is . . . though I mentioned his name —what is the matter with you, Hamon?"

"Nothing," said the other harshly, "only——" He turned the subject. "Will you speak to Joan?" he asked curtly, and stalked out of the library.

Joan was in her room when the maid came for her, and short as was the space of time elapsing between the summons and the answering, Lord Creith was again absorbed in his catalogue.

"Oh, Joan . . . yes, I wanted to see you about something. Yes, yes, I remember. Be as civil as you can to Hamon, my dear."

"Has he been complaining?"

"Good Lord, no!" said Lord Creith. "Only he has an idea that he would like to marry you. I don't know how you feel about it?"

"Do you wish me to tell you?" she asked, and his lordship shook his head vigorously.

"I don't think so—not if it's going to bother me. Of course, you know I've sold everything . . . house, land and the place in London?"

"To Mr. Hamon?"

He nodded.

"Everything," he said. "If you don't marry him, there will only be the bit of money I have when I—er—step off, if you forgive the vulgarity."

"I gathered that," she said.

"Of course, your grandmother's money comes to you when you are twenty-four. Happily, I haven't been able to touch that, though I tried very hard—very hard! But those lawyers are cute fellows, deuced cute! Now what about marrying this fellow Hamon?"

She smiled.

"I thought you wouldn't," said her father with satisfaction. "That is all I wanted you for . . . oh, yes, do you know this man Morlake?"

If he had been looking at her he would have been startled

by the pink flush that came to her face. But his eyes were already on the catalogue.

"Why?"

"I mentioned his name to Hamon—never saw a man get more annoyed. What *is* Morlake?"

"A man," she said laconically.

"How interesting!" said his lordship, and returned to his sale list.

CHAPTER IV

A Caller at Wold House

JAMES MORLAKE sat in the shade of the big cedar that grew half way between his house and the river. His lame fox-terrier sprawled at his feet, and a newspaper lay open on his knees. He was not reading; his eyes were fixed on the glassy surface of the stream. A splash, a momentary vision of wet silver as a trout leapt at an incautious fly, brought his head round, and then he saw the man that stood surveying him from the drive.

One glance he gave, and then returned to the placid contemplation of the little river.

Hamon walked slowly forward, his hands thrust into his pockets.

"Well," he said, "it is a long time since I saw you. I didn't know that you were living around here."

Jim Morlake raised his eyes and yawned.

"I should have sent you a card," he said lazily. "One ought to have 'at home' days. If I had known you were coming this morning, I'd have hired the village band and put up a few flags."

Mr. Hamon pulled forward a chair and sat down squarely before the other, and when he spoke, it was with the greatest deliberation.

"I'll buy this house from you—Morlake——"

"*Mister* Morlake," murmured the other. "Let us remember that we are gentlemen."

"I'll buy this house from you and you can go abroad. I'll forgive your threats and your mad fool talk about . . . well, you know—but you will get out of the country in a week."

Morlake laughed softly, and Hamon, who had never seen him laugh, was astounded at the transformation that laughter brought to the sombre face.

"You are a most amusing person," said the tall man. "You drop from the clouds, or spout out from the eternal fires after an absence of years, and immediately start in to rearrange my life! You're getting fat, Hamon, and those bags under your eyes aren't pretty. You ought to see a doctor."

Hamon leant forward.

"Suppose I tell your neighbours who you are!" he asked slowly. "Suppose I go to the police and tell them that *Mister* Morlake"—he laid a sneering emphasis on the title—"is a cheap Yankee crook!"

"Not cheap," murmured Morlake, his amused eyes watching the other.

"Suppose I tell them that I once caught you red-handed robbing the Prescott Bank, and that you blackmailed me into letting you go!"

Morlake's eyes never left the man's face.

"There has been a series of burglaries committed in London," Hamon went on. "They've been worked by a man called The Black—ever heard of him?"

Morlake smiled.

"I never read the newspapers," he drawled. "There is so much in them that is not fit for a country gentleman to read."

"A country gentleman!"

It was Mr. Hamon's turn to be amused. Putting his hand in his pocket, he withdrew a note-case, and, opening its worn flap, he pulled out a tight wad of banknotes.

"That is for your travelling expenses," he said, as Morlake took the money from his hand. "As for your little house and estate, I'll make you an offer to-morrow. Your price——"

"Is a hundred thousand," said Morlake. "I'd take this paltry sum on account if it wasn't for the fact that you've got the number of every note in your pocket-book and a busy detective waiting at the gate to pull me as soon as I pocketed the swag! A hundred thousand is my price, Hamon. Pay me that, in the way I want it paid, and I'll leave you alone. One hundred thousand sterling is the price you pay for a month of quietness!"

He threw the money on to the grass.

"A month—what do you mean, a month?"

Again the big man raised his quiet eyes.

"I mean the month that elapses in this country between trial and execution," he said.

CHAPTER V

The Monkey and the Gourd

Ralph Hamon leapt to his feet as if he had been shot. His face was livid, his thick lips bloodless.

"You're a liar . . . a damned Yankee crook! Hang me? I'll settle with you, Morlake! I know enough about you. . . ."

Morlake raised a hand in mock alarm.

"Don't frighten me! My nerves are not what they were. And be a sensible man. Tell me all about yourself. I hear that you cleared half a million in Varoni Diamonds. Honestly too; which is queer. If you had only waited, Hamon! You wouldn't be going about in fear of your life. Do you know how the natives catch monkeys? They put a plum or a date at the bottom of a narrow-necked gourd. And the monkey puts in his hand and grips the date but can't get his clenched first through the narrow neck. He is too greedy to loose hold of the date and hasn't the strength to smash the gourd. And so he's caught. You're a monkey man, Hamon!"

Hamon had mastered his rage, but his face was deadly white.

"I don't understand you," he said. "You're one of these clever Alecs who like to hear themselves talk. I've warned you. Maybe you're the gourd that is going to get smashed."

"That occurred to me," nodded the other, "but I shall be broken in a good cause. In the meantime, I shall stay at Wold House, rejoicing in my mystery and in the interest I inspire in the country bosom."

"I'll settle that mystery!" roared Hamon. He paused at the edge of the gravel path and raised an admonitory finger. "I give you seven days to clear," he said.

"Shut the gate as you go out," said James Morlake, not troubling to turn his head.

Hamon sprang into the car that he had left on the road and drove homeward in a savage mood; but the shocks of the day were not at an end.

He had to follow the main road before he reached the uneven lane that bordered the Creith estate. It was the Hamon estate now, he reflected with satisfaction. He was master of these broad acres and sleepy farms that nestled in the folds of the downs. But his mastership was incomplete unless there went with his holding the slim, straight girl whose antagonism he sensed, whose unspoken contempt cut like the lash of a whip.

To tame her, humble her, punish her for her insolence, would be a sport more satisfying than any he had followed in his chequered life. As for the man called James Morlake . . . he winced as he thought of that almost exact counterpart to Joan Carston.

He had turned the bonnet of his car into the lane when his eyes rested upon the whitewashed cottage behind the wooden fence, and he stopped the machine. He remembered that a friend of Joan's had been installed here—a woman.

Ralph Hamon was an opportunist. A friend of Joan's might become a friend of his, and if, as he guessed, she was not too well blessed with the goods of this world, he might find a subterranean method of sapping the girl's prejudice against him.

He got down from the machine and walked back to the road and through the gateway. A red brick path flanked by tall dahlias led to the cottage door. He glanced left and right. The occupant was not in the garden, and he knocked. Almost immediately the door opened and the tall figure of a woman confronted him.

Their eyes met, and neither spoke. He was staring at her as if she were a visitant from another world, and she met his gaze unflinchingly.

He tried to speak, but nothing came from his throat but a slurred growl; and then, turning violently, he almost ran down the path; the perspiration rolling down his face, his mouth dry with fear; for Elsa Cornford had that half of his secret which the master of Wold House did not guess.

CHAPTER VI

Hamon Tells His News

"WASN'T that thunder?" asked Lord Creith, and raised his hand to hide a yawn.

Joan sympathised with his boredom, for the dinner had seemed interminable.

"Sounds like it," said Hamon, rousing himself with a start from an unpleasant reverie.

The three people had scarcely spoken through the meal. Once Lord Creith had made a pointed reference to the dullness of the country and the fun that a man of Ralph Hamon's quality could find in town, but the financier had ignored his opportunity.

"It *is* thunder," said Creith with satisfaction. "October is rather late for storms. I remember when I was a boy . . ."

He made a feeble effort to galvanise the little party into an interest which they did not feel, and ended his reminiscence almost before it had begun. And then, unconsciously, he turned the conversation to a channel which made two pairs of eyes turn instantly to his.

"I've been asking Stephens about this fellow Morlake. Queer fish—very queer. Nobody knows the least thing about him. He came from nowhere three years ago, bought up Wold House and settled himself as a country gentleman. He doesn't hunt or dance, refuses every invitation that has been sent to him, and apparently has no friends. A queer devil."

"I should say he was!"

Joan heard Mr. Hamon's loud chuckle of laughter, and looked across at him in surprise.

"Do you know him?"

Mr. Hamon selected a cigarette from the box on the table before he answered.

"Yes, I know him. He is an American crook."

"What!"

Joan tried to suppress the indignation in her voice, but failed, and apparently the man did not notice the implied defence of the master of Wold House.

"Yes," said Mr. Hamon, enjoying the sensation he had created, "he's a crook. What his real name is, I don't know. He is one of the big men of the underworld, a cracksman and a blackmailer!"

"But surely the police know all about him?" said the amazed Creith.

"They may. But a man like Morlake, who has made a lot of money, would be able to keep the police 'straight.' "

Joan had listened speechless.

"How do you know?" she found her voice to demand. Hamon shrugged his shoulders.

"I had an encounter with him a few years ago. He thought that he had found something about me which gave him a pull. He tried to blackmail me, and he had a narrow escape. He won't be so fortunate next time, and the next time"—he opened and closed his hand suggestively—"is near at hand! I've got him like this!"

Joan sat stunned by the news. Why this revelation should so affect her she could not explain, even to herself. She hated Ralph Hamon at that moment—hated him with an intensity out of all proportion to his offence, real or imaginary. It required the exercise of every scrap of self-control to prevent her anger bursting forth, but that she exercised and listened, biting her lip.

"His real name I don't know," Mr. Hamon went on. "The police have had him under observation for years, but they have never been able to collect evidence to convict him."

"But I never knew of this," interrupted Lord Creith, "and I am a magistrate. The county police invariably speak well of him."

"When I said 'police' I meant headquarters," corrected Hamon. "Anyway, they are not the kind of people who would talk."

"I don't believe it!" Joan's pent-up indignation came forth in a rush. "It is an absurd story! Really, Mr. Hamon, I am beginning to suspect you of reading sensational stories!"

Hamon smiled.

"I admit that it sounds unreal," he said, "but there is the truth. I saw the man this morning."

"Mr. Morlake?" asked Joan in surprise, and he nodded.

"He was pretty uncomfortable when he saw me, I can tell you, and to know that he had been recognised. He begged me not to tell anybody——"

"That isn't true. Of course, it isn't true," said Joan scornfully, and Hamon went a dull red. "Mr. Morlake is the last man in the world who would beg anything from you or anybody else. I don't believe he's a thief."

"A friend of yours?" asked Hamon loudly.

"I've never met him," said Joan shortly. "I have seen him ... at a distance, and that is all."

There was an awkward silence, but Ralph Hamon was blessed with a thick skin, and although he had been given the lie direct, he was not particularly disconcerted, not even when, attempting to resume the discussion of Morlake's past, Joan brusquely turned the talk into another direction. When Lord

Creith had gone to his room, she walked out of the house to the lawn, to watch the lightning flickering in the southern sky, and to think free of Hamon's stifling presence, but he followed her.

"It looks as though it will be a stormy night," he said, by way of making conversation, and she agreed, and was turning back to the house when he stopped her. "Where did you find that woman who's living in the gardener's cottage?" he asked.

She raised her brows in astonishment. It was the last question in the world she expected from him.

"You mean Mrs. Cornford? Why—is she a criminal too?" she asked.

He smiled indulgently at the sarcasm.

"Not exactly; only I am interested. I have an idea that I met her years ago. I suppose she knows me, doesn't she?" he asked carelessly.

"She has never mentioned your name, possibly because I have never spoken about you," she said, a little surprised and her curiosity piqued.

"I seem to remember that she was a little wrong in the head. She was in a lunatic asylum for twelve months."

The girl was surprised into laughing.

"Really, Mr. Hamon," she said dryly, "I begin to suspect you of trying to frighten me. Such of my friends as aren't criminals must be lunatics!"

"I didn't know he was a friend of yours," said Hamon quickly.

He went toward her in the darkness.

"I have already told you that Mr. Morlake is not a friend. He's a neighbour, and neighbours, by our convention, are friends until we discover they are otherwise. Shall we go in?"

"One moment."

He caught her by the arm, and gently she freed herself.

"That isn't necessary, Mr. Hamon. What do you want to tell me?"

"Has your father spoken to you?" he asked.

"My father frequently speaks to me," said the girl. "Do you mean about you?"

He nodded.

"About your wanting to marry me?"

"That's it," he said a little huskily.

"Yes, he did speak about it to me," said Joan steadily, "and I told him that, whilst I was very sensible of the compliment you paid me, I have no desire to marry you."

Hamon cleared his voice.

"Did he also mention the fact that I am virtually the owner of Creith?"

"He also mentioned that," said the girl bravely.

"I suppose Creith is very dear to you? Your ancestors have had it for hundreds of years?"

"Very dear, indeed," said Joan, stifling her anger, "but not so dear that I am prepared to sacrifice my life's happiness to retain the title of mistress of Creith. There are worse things than being homeless, Mr. Hamon."

She made a move to go, but again he restrained her.

"Wait," he said. His voice was low and vibrant. "Joan, I am twenty years older than you, but you're the sort of woman I have dreamt about since I was a boy. There isn't a thing I wouldn't do for you, there isn't a service I wouldn't render you. I want you!"

Before she realised what he was doing he had caught her in his arms. She struggled to escape, but he held her in a grip that could not be broken.

"Let me go—how dare you!"

"Listen!" He almost hissed the word. "I love you, Joan! I love you, although you hurt me with your damned contempt. I love your face, your eyes, your dear, slim body. . . ."

She twisted her head aside to avoid his greedy lips. And then, from the hallway, she heard, with a gasp of relief, the voice of her father calling:

"Where are you, Joan?"

Hamon's arms dropped, and she staggered back, breathless and shaken, horror and disgust in her soul.

"I'm sorry," he muttered.

She could not speak; she could only point to the door, and he went in. She herself did not follow for some minutes, and Lord Creith peered at her short-sightedly.

"Anything wrong?" he asked, as he saw her pale face.

"Nothing, Daddy."

He looked round. Hamon had disappeared through the open door of the drawing-room.

"A primitive fellow. I'll kick him out if you say the word, my dear."

Again she shook her head.

"It's not necessary. Yes, he is a little primitive. If he doesn't go to-morrow, will you take me to London?"

"I'm going to London anyway," said his lordship with satisfaction. "Do you wish me to talk to Hamon?" he asked anxiously.

"It isn't necessary," said Joan, and Lord Creith went back to his study relieved, for he hated any kind of bother.

CHAPTER VII

Into the Storm

SHE went straight up to her room, resolved not to risk a further interview with the man in whose eyes, even in the failing light, she had read the very deeps of human passion. She felt physically sick as she recalled those horrible seconds on the lawn, and she searched the drawer of her bureau for the key of the bedroom door, and, finding it, turned the lock—a thing she had never done before in her life. Then she sat down before her mirror, calmly to review a disturbing evening.

Predominant of the emotions which the night had called forth was the shock of the discovery about James Morlake. It could not be true; and yet Hamon would not have framed such an accusation unless it was well based.

She got up from her chair, opened one of the long windows and stepped out on to the stone balcony above the porch. The lightning was flickering whitely in the sky; there came to her ears the low roll and sustained rumble of thunder; but it was not at the sable skies she was looking. Across the park one faint yellow light showed the position of Wold House.

If all that Hamon said were true, did this strangely isolated man know that he was suspected? Ought he to be told? She uttered a little exclamation of impatience. It was madness on her part, sheer, stark lunacy to think about him. She knew him only as a figure that had often come within the focus of her field-glasses, a remarkable, an attractive face around which she had woven all manner of dreams. Nearer at hand, she would be disillusioned; and just at that moment she particularly desired that, even though she hated Hamon for sowing the first seeds of disenchantment.

She had never spoken to Morlake, never been within fifty yards of him, knew no more than servants' gossip could tell her, or than she could imagine for herself. If Hamon had spoken the truth, then he was in danger. If it were not true, then, for his own purpose, the financier was hatching some plot which would lead to Morlake's undoing.

She came back to the room and stared at herself in the mirror.

"I must be disillusioned," she said slowly and deliberately, and knew, as she spoke, that she was deceiving herself.

She went to her bureau, took out a long raincoat and a little hat, and laid them on her bed.

Creith House retired early, but it was not till half-past ten that she heard the front door being locked by Stephens, and the surly voice of Mr. Hamon bid the servant good-night as he came up the stairs on the way to his own room. She listened and heard the thud of Hamon's bedroom door as it closed. A quarter-of-an-hour passed and the house was silent.

Once more she returned to the balcony. The light was burning at Wold House, and she made her sudden resolve. With the coat over her arm, and holding her hat in her hand, she unlocked the door and stole fearfully down the broad stairway to the hall, where a night-light burnt. Stephens had retired; she could hear only the ticking of the big clock in the hall.

The key of the front door hung on the wall, a big and ungainly article, and she put this into her bag before she pulled back the bolts gently, unlocked the door and closed it behind her.

There would be no difficulty in finding her way. The lightning snickered and flashed almost incessantly. With a wildly beating heart she passed down the drive under the shadow of the rustling chestnut trees, through the lodge gates on to the main road.

She was being a fool, a sentimental idiot . . . she was behaving like a romantic school-girl. Reason put out a hundred hands to hold her back. Something which was neither reason nor sentiment, some great instinct more potent than any controlling force of mind or heart, sent her forward eagerly to her strange quest.

Once she shrank into the shelter of a hedge as a car flashed past, and she wondered what the neighbours would think if they had seen Lady Joan Carston hiding from observation at that hour of the night. At any rate, they would never dream that she was on her way to warn an American crook whom she did not know, and had never met, that his arrest was imminent. She reflected on this with a certain amount of grim amusement.

Presently she was walking in the shelter of the high redbrick wall that surrounded Wold House. The wrought-iron gates were closed, and she had to fumble for some time before she found the latch that admitted her. The light she had seen had disappeared; the house was in darkness, and she stood in the shadow of a tree, trying to summon up sufficient courage to go on with her self-appointed mission.

She had taken a step forward when unexpectedly the door of the house opened. A bright light glowed in the passage, and in its rays she saw silhouetted in the doorway the figure of a man, and she drew back again to the cover of the shadow. Behind the man she saw James Morlake. He was talking in a low voice, and, even from where she stood, she felt a little thrill of satisfaction that it was the voice of a gentleman.

But who was the other? In some indefinite way the figure was strangely familiar to Joan. And then:

"Feeling better now?"

"Yes, thanks." She had to guess what the mumbled reply was.

"You will find the cottage on the road. I don't know Mrs. Cornford, but I believe there is a lady staying there."

"Awfully foolish of me to come here, but I went to the station bar . . . and time passed . . . and then this beastly storm came on. I'm afraid I'm rather drunk."

"I'm afraid you are," said Jim Morlake's voice.

Mrs. Cornford's lodger! The dipsomaniac. They came down the steps together, the younger man reeling a little till Jim put out his hand and steadied him.

"Awfully obliged to you, I'm sure—my name is Farringdon—Ferdie Farringdon. . . ."

And then a flicker of lightning showed his face, white, haggard, unshaven. The girl shrank back, wild-eyed, biting her lip to arrest her scream. Gripping a bough of the laurel bush to hold herself erect, she watched them pass into the gloom. She was still standing motionless, frozen, when Jim returned alone.

She watched him go into the house, saw the door close, and still she waited. Great drops of rain were splashing down; the thunder was louder, the lightning more vivid.

She had no longer any thought of warning him. She was absorbed, transfixed by the ghost that had risen from the night. With an effort she stirred herself and ran down the drive.

She tried to open the gate, but to her horror it was steadfast. Morlake must have locked it after he had seen the other on his way. What should she do?

She moved stealthily across the lawn, but here the river barred her further movement. She could get over the wall if she knew where a ladder was to be found.

And then the front door opened again and she drew swiftly into the shadows as somebody came out. It was Morlake: she could not mistake him. He walked quickly down the path, and she heard the clang of the gate as it closed behind him. As soon as the sound of his footsteps had died down, she ran to the gate—it was unlocked, and, with a sigh of thankfulness, she passed through.

Which way had he gone, she wondered. Probably toward the village. It was hardly likely that any business would take him in the direction of Creith House, unless he was going to the cottage to make sure that Farringdon had returned.

She had not gone a dozen yards before she was wet through, for the rain was hissing down with torrential fury. The roar and crash of thunder deafened her, the everlasting flutter of blue lightning brought intervals of blindness between each flash. Up to this moment she had not been afraid, but now the terror of the storm came on her and she broke into a run, and at last came in sight of the lodge gates. She felt in her sodden bag for the key—Yes, it was there.

Quickly she passed up the avenue and had reached the end, when she stopped dead, her eyes wide open in fear. Ahead of her, not a dozen yards away, the lightning revealed the figure of a man in black, standing motionless and in her path. She could not see the face under the brim of the wide sombrero he wore.

"Who are you?" she asked shakily.

Before he could reply, there was a blinding burst of flame, a crash as though giant hands had torn a sheet of steel apart; something lifted her from her feet and flung her violently to the earth.

The man in the path stood paralysed for a second, then, with a cry, he leapt forward, and, lifting the prostrate figure, dragged her from the burning tree. A light had appeared in one of the windows of Creith House, another followed. The household was awake, and the blazing chestnut would bring them into the open.

He looked round and saw a clump of rhododendrons, and lifting the unconscious girl he carried her into the shadow of the cover just as the butler came out of the house to the porch.

Who she was the stranger did not know. Possibly some belated servant returning from the village. He did not trouble to examine his burden, and might have been no wiser if he had, for Joan's face was smeared with the soft loam mud into which she had mercifully fallen.

Evidently nobody intended coming out to fight the flames. He heard a voice from one of the windows demanding that the fire brigade be sent for.

"'Phone, my dear man, 'phone! And don't bother me till the beastly fire is out."

It was at that moment that Joan recovered consciousness. She opened her eyes and stared wildly round. Somebody was supporting her head on his knee. Her face was wet with falling rain; above her were the swaying branches of bushes. How did she get there?

"I think you'll be O. K. now," said a voice, strangely muffled.

She stared up at him, recognising instantly the voice of James Morlake.

"What has happened?" she asked, and then she smelt the pungent perfume of burnt wood and shivered.

The tree under which she had stood had been struck, and by some miracle she had escaped.

"Thank you ever so much——" she began, and at that moment the lawn was made radiant with a sustained glare of lightning.

She was looking into a face that was covered from brow to chin with a black silk mask!

CHAPTER VIII

The Robber

"It is true—true!" she grasped, and he heard the pain in her voice and peered down.

"What is true?—please don't shout or they will hear you."

Trembling helplessly, she tried to regain control of her voice.

"You *are* a burglar!" she said, and heard his smothered exclamation.

"You mean . . . the mask? I'm afraid you saw it. One mask

doesn't make a burglar, you know, any more than one swallow makes a summer! On a wet night like this a man who wishes to keep that school-girl complexion would naturally protect——"

"Please don't be absurd!"

She realised, so keen was her sense of humour, that the dignity of her tone did not exactly accord with her own deplorable situation. She was lying uncomfortably on wet grass, her face. . . . She hoped he could not see her face, and furtively wiped some of the mud away with the slimy corner of her raincoat, which, for some extraordinary reason, she had carried over her arm through the storm.

"Will you help me up, please?"

For answer he stooped and lifted her to her feet without any apparent effort.

"Are you staying at the Hall?" he asked, and there was something so formal and so suggestive of polite small talk about the question that her lips trembled.

"Yes—I am. Are you . . . were you thinking of burgling the Hall?"

She felt rather than heard him laugh.

"You won't believe that I am not a burglar——"

"Are you?"

There was a challenge in the voice.

"Really," said James Morlake after a while, "this situation is verging on the grotesque. . . ."

"Are you?" she asked again, and as she expected, so he replied.

"I am."

She would have been bitterly disappointed if he had said anything else. A burglar he might be, a liar he could not be.

"Well, we've nothing to burgle, Mr——" She stopped suddenly. Did he know that she had recognised him?

"Mr.——?" he suggested. "You said just now 'It is true' —meaning it was true that I am a burglar. Were you expecting a visitation to-night?"

"Yes," she said, having none of his scruples. "Mr. Hamon said that we might be robbed."

It was the lamest of inventions, but the effect upon the man was unexpected.

"Oh! You're a visitor at the Hall. I beg your pardon, I thought you were . . . er . . . well, I didn't exactly know what you were—would you mind looking straight at the house?"

"Why?"

"Please——"

She obeyed naturally and turned her back on him. Somebody was coming out to the smouldering tree. A storm lantern was swaying and the gait of the newcomer suggested a reluctance to investigate at close hand the phenomena of nature.

"It is Peters," she said, and looked round.

She was alone; the masked man was gone.

It was easy to avoid Peters, but as she reached the corridor leading to her room, she suddenly confronted her father.

"Good God! Joan . . . where on earth have *you* been . . . you gave me a fright."

"I went out to see the tree," she said (she had never lied so easily in her life).

"What the deuce do you want to go out into the beastly rain to see trees for?" grumbled Lord Creith. "Let Peters see it! Your face is all muddy. . . ."

She bolted into her room as the door of Hamon's chamber opened and his pyjamaed figure showed.

"Something struck?" asked Hamon.

Lord Creith turned his head.

"One of your trees, my dear fellow," he said with satisfaction. "By Jove! I only just realised that it wasn't my tree!"

And, consoled by the knowledge that there really was nothing to justify any personal worry, his lordship went back to bed, undisturbed by the cannon of the heavens or the lightning which lit up his room at irregular intervals.

Joan's was the only room in Creith Hall that possessed the luxury of an adjoining bathroom, and she was sufficiently feminine, as she stripped off her wet clothes, to be absorbed for the moment in the thoroughness of her soaking to the partial exclusion of all thoughts of her adventure.

She came back to the problem of Mr. Morlake as she sat

in bed nursing her knees and watching through the open window the passage of the storm. The chestnut tree was smoking and the lightning gave her a glimpse of two brass-helmetted men gazing impotently at the ruin. The village fire brigade was, in point of costume, an exact replica of its great metropolitan model. It was only on the minor point of efficiency that it fell short.

Had Morlake recognised her? It was very doubtful. She had never met him, and she guessed that he was so incurious as to the identities of the people of Creith House that he was genuine when he mistook her for a visitor. Who did he think she was? A servant, perhaps.

"Now I think you are thoroughly and completely disillusioned, Joan Carston," she said soberly. "Your wonder-man is a burglar! And you can only be interested in burglars if your mind is morbid and unwholesome and your outlook is hopelessly decadent. Let this be a lesson to you, young woman! Concentrate upon the normalities of life."

So saying, she got out of bed, and, craning her neck, looked across the park toward Wold House. The tiny light was burning. Mr. Morlake had returned home.

Sighing thankfully, she returned to bed, and she was sleeping soundly when James Morlake stepped from the concealment of the rhododendrons and, crossing the lawn, slipped the edge of a small jemmy under the bottom of a window that looked into the dark entrance hall.

CHAPTER IX

Mr. Hamon Loses Money

JOAN came down early, intending to breakfast before Mr. Hamon was up. She had nearly finished her healthy repast when Hamon burst into the room, and he was not pretty to see. He wore his socks, a pair of trousers from which the braces were hanging, and a vividly striped pyjama coat. His unshaven face was dark with anger as he glared round.

"Where's Stephens?" he roared, and then, realising that neither his tone nor appearance was in harmony with the requirements of good breeding, he said in a more subdued voice: "Excuse me, Lady Joan, but I've been robbed."

She had risen to her feet and was looking at him, wide-eyed.

"Has somebody stolen your shoes and coat?" she asked, and he flushed.

"I only just discovered it—the robbery, I mean. Somebody broke into my room last night and took a wallet with three thousand pounds! It was that dog Morlake. I'll fix him! I've given the swine his chance——"

"It is a pity that the robber did not also steal your vocabulary, Mr. Hamon," said the girl coldly.

She was far from feeling the indifference she displayed. Then Morlake had come back after all! She felt a sense of grievance against him—he had deceived her. She examined her mind, after the spluttering Hamon had disappeared, in search of a more sympathetic audience, for some intelligent reason for her grievance. The deception lay in the light which showed in the window of Wold House, she decided, though James Morlake might not have been responsible for its appearance. From the confusing evidence offered by the victim, by Peters, and reflected by Lord Creith, it appeared that, at some hour in the early morning, a person unknown had forced an entrance through one of the windows which flanked the hall door; that he had entered at least two rooms (Joan gasped as the possibility flashed across her mind that hers might have been one, and was unaccountably piqued to learn that the second room was an empty room next to Mr. Hamon's); that he had taken, from underneath the pillow which supported the unconscious head of Ralph Hamon, a leather wallet containing between £3,000 and £4,000 in banknotes, and added the indignity of unloading the revolver which lay on a table by the side of Mr. Hamon's bed; the cartridges were discovered in the grounds.

"My dear good man," said Lord Creith, visibly bored by the fourth recital of Ralph Hamon's loss, "it is a simple matter to convey to the bovine constabulary which is at present tramping over my flower beds that you suspect this Morlake person. As a magistrate, I shall be happy to issue a warrant for his arrest, or, what is more important, the search of his house. If he has stolen your money, it will be discovered in his possession."

"I don't want to do that," said Hamon, sourly. "There is no proof other than my word."

"But I thought you said that the police had him under observation?" Joan ventured to say, though at the thought that she was assisting in the arrest of her burglar she went hot and cold.

"Not exactly under observation," admitted Hamon; "but there are men who know about him—men at headquarters, I mean. My friend, Inspector Marborne, has been shadowing him for years. No, I'm not going to hand the case over to the local police—they'd only bungle it. Besides, a man of Morlake's character is too clever to have the stuff in the house. I'll go over and talk to him."

He looked savagely across at the girl as the sound of her soft laughter came to him.

"I'm so sorry," she said apologetically, "but it does sound silly, doesn't it, for the robbed to argue with the robber? I know such things happen in books, but you don't seriously mean that you will go to him and tell him you suspect him?"

"I think all this talk about our neighbour is romantic nonsense," said Lord Creith, energising himself to take an interest in the matter. "The whole thing is so simple: if he's a burglar, and you know he's a burglar, have him arrested. If he doesn't happen to be a burglar, but is an innocent country gentleman, as we are all agreed he seems to be, then, of course, you're liable to very severe damages in any action at law which he may bring. Anyway, it was foolish of you to carry so much money about with you, my dear man! Three thousand pounds! Great heavens! What are banks for?" he looked at his watch. "I am going up to town in half-an-hour. I won't offer you a lift, because my machine can only hold two people comfortably in ordinary circumstances and one person, uncomfortably, when Joan is travelling. My dear, will you try to keep your baggage down to half-a-dozen trunks and as few hat-boxes as possible?"

"You're going to town?" said the other, disappointed. "I thought you were staying for the rest of the week."

"I told you on Monday I was going to town," said his lordship, who had done nothing of the sort. "There is a sale at Tattersall's to-morrow which I must attend; and Joan has an appointment with her dentist. You may stay on if you wish; don't let me interefere with your plans."

"When will you be back?" asked Hamon.

"In about a month," said Lord Creith.

Ralph Hamon decided that he also would go to the metropolis, and hinted that his own car was big enough to take the whole party. The hint was neither seen nor heeded.

"That's over," said Lord Creith, with a sigh of relief, as the car turned out of the lodge gates to the post road. "Hamon is a very admirable person, but he's inclined to get on one's nerves."

He screwed an eyeglass in his eye as they approached Wold House.

"That is the home of our maligned neighbour, isn't it, Joan? Never seen the fellow: what is he like?"

"Oh, just an ordinary, inoffensive-looking man," said Joan lamely.

"Is he now?" said his lordship, interested. "That is very suspicious. I never like inoffensive-looking men."

At that moment the chauffeur jammed on his brakes. A car was coming out through the gates of Wold House, a long, black machine, the sole occupant of which was Mr. James Morlake. Glancing over his shoulder, he saw the danger and brought his machine perilously close to the ditch on his left as Lord Creith's car shot past.

"Narrow squeak, that," said his lordship comfortably. "Our man was, of course, in the wrong: he should have sounded his horn. So that is Mr. Morlake, eh? I don't agree with your description, my dear. A more offensive-looking person I have never seen. From the scowl on his face he might have been a murderer."

"I was talking of him as a man," said Joan calmly, "not as a motorist."

A savage howl from a siren behind brought the Creith car to the near side of the road, and the snaky black machine shot past them, its driver looking neither to the right nor to the left.

Joan knew the type of car: it was a high-powered Italian machine, and one of the costliest in Europe. Evidently Mr. James Morlake spared no expense in the pursuit of his nefarious calling.

CHAPTER X

The Frame-up

DIVISIONAL INSPECTOR MARBORNE came from his chief's office, closed the door behind him gently, and was whistling to himself as he walked down the stone stairs of police headquarters. Even his friend and associate, a detective sergeant of many years' standing, was deceived.

He followed his superior into the street, and in the comparative quietude of the Thames Embankment, asked eagerly:

"Was it O. K.?"

"It was *not* O. K.," said the other carefully. "It was as near O. K. as makes no difference. In fact, Barney, the Pure Police movement has spread so thoroughly that I was as near to being asked to turn in my coat as ever I've been. The old man said that he had proof that I'd been taking 'quieteners' from Bolson's gambling house in Upper Gloucester Place, and gave me the number of the notes that Big Bennett paid me for tipping off his brother that he was going to be 'pulled in.' I'm booked for retirement, and so are you—the old man said he knew that you were in it."

Sergeant Barney Slone winced, for he had tastes which would make living on a pension a painful proceeding.

"There is one chance, and only one, and I'm going to take it," said the inspector. "I hate depending upon men like Lieber and Colley, but they are our long suits. Bring them up to my apartment for a bit of dinner to-night."

"What are you going to do?"

"I'm going to get The Black," said Inspector Marborne, and his subordinate stopped in his walk and stared at him.

"Get him—how?" he asked incredulously.

But the inspector was not prepared to explain.

"I know him—at least, I think I know him—if I don't, a friend of mine does. It will be the biggest thing I've ever done, Barney."

For more than five years The Black, so called because he wore clothing of funereal hue, had been the bugbear of London. No strong room was invulnerable to the attack of this skilful and single-handed burglar. Banks and safe deposits had been the sole objects of his attention—a fact which had added considerably to the difficulties of the police.

Curiously enough, the extent of The Black's depredations was never known. His hobby was to rifle private boxes and safes where respectable men hid up the items that would seriously challenge their respectability if they were dragged to the light of day. Some men hid money that way, forgoing the interest that might accrue for the sake of having at hand a nest egg against a stormy day when their worst fears were realised. Naturally, these were vague about their losses, often denying that they had lost anything of value. The Black was obviously a student of human nature, and robbed well, and it was a fact that, in the course of five years, though twenty-three burglaries stood to his discredit, there was no definite charge of stealing a definite sum which might pass the scrutiny of a Grand Jury.

At five o'clock that afternoon, Mr. Marborne called at 307 Grosvenor Place, where Ralph Hamon had his London residence. Marborne was a type of policeman to be found in every city of the civilised world. Graft is not the canker of any particular police force: it is a disease which makes its appearance, and will continue to appear, wherever lowly and unscrupulous men rise to positions of authority. Wherever easy money is available, there will be found men ready and willing to take the tempting prizes of dishonesty without any thought of their responsibilities or their treachery to the causes they represent.

Hamon was writing letters when the detective was shown into the drawing-room. He rose and greeted the visitor effusively.

"Come right in, Marborne. I'm glad to see you. You got my letter?"

"Yes, I had it this morning," said Marborne, depositing his hat on the floor and seating himself carefully. "Three thousand pounds you lost, eh? I suppose you've got the numbers of the notes?"

"Yes, I have the numbers, but that won't worry him. You know how easy it is to pass stolen money; and when you're dealing with an expert like The Black, I don't think it's worth while building any hope of catching him through the notes."

Further conversation was interrupted by the arrival of the servant with a large silver tray and the refreshment which was essential to Marborne's comfort.

"You're sure it was The Black?" asked the detective, when his host had carefully closed and locked the door behind the servant.

"Certain."

"Why didn't you report it to the local police?" asked Marborne curiously. "It would have been a simple matter to have got a search-warrant—you were staying with Lord Creith, and he's Chairman of the Quarter Sessions."

Hamon shook his head.

"That isn't the way. I had no evidence but my suspicion. You don't suppose for one minute that we should have found the stuff in Morlake's house, do you? No, that course was suggested by Lord Creith himself, but I didn't proceed with it, because"—he leant forward, and lowered his voice—"that would have spoilt the scheme I spoke to you about a month ago."

The detective pursed his lips dubiously.

"It's going to be a pretty hard job to frame up a charge, and it'll cost you a bit of money, Mr. Hamon. I have been thinking it out, and though I know the very men for the work, it will mean spending money freely."

"Spend to the limit," said Hamon violently, "but get him! He's in London—I suppose you know that?"

The detective nodded.

"Yes, I've 'tailed him up' as far as it's possible. I've got a friend of mine, Sergeant Slone, on the job, but it hasn't been easy. Our code doesn't allow a man to be 'tailed' unless an official report has been made against him to the police, and I've had to get Slone to work in his spare time."

"Any work done for me will be paid for," said Hamon a little impatiently. "Have you got the scheme worked out?"

The inspector nodded.

"There is a house on Blackheath," he said, "owned by a retired Colonial officer. He is a rich man, and has a wonderful collection of antique jewellery. There are only his wife, his daughter and three servants in the house, and I've got a man who could crack it in about five minutes. It wouldn't be so easy to get the jewellery, because that is kept in a safe, but there's no need to worry about touching the stuff. The thing is to get him to the house, and to leave enough evidence to catch your man. The real difficulty is going to be to break down any alibi that he may have. It is useless pulling him in for a burglary at Blackheath if he can prove that at the time he was in his club."

"Can you bring him to Blackheath by any means?" asked the interested Mr. Hamon.

The detective nodded.

"That is what I'm working for," he said, "but it will require a whole lot of manœuvring. Morlake lives in a sort of Oriental flat in Bond Street and has two servants—a Moor named Mahmet—he's travelling a lot in Morocco—and a valet named Binger, who is a pensioner of the 14th Hussars. Binger doesn't live on the premises: he lives with his wife and family in the Blackheath Road—that's why I chose Blackheath. Usually, when Morlake's in town, Binger comes down to Blackheath by one of the all-night cars that run on the southern route. Sergeant Slone has become friendly with Binger, who doesn't know, of course, that Slone is a police officer. Every attempt he has made to get Binger to talk about his boss has been useless so far. I'm perfectly sure he knows a lot more about Morlake than he tells. But he's as dumb as an oyster the moment the conversation turns round to James Morlake."

"How is this going to help you?" asked Hamon.

"It's going to help me a lot," said the inspector deliberately. "Morlake is fond of this man, and when he was ill, about two years ago, he used to go down every day in his car to Blackheath Road and bring him fruit and books, and had his own doctor attending him. Sometimes Binger comes home early, and the next night this happens we'll work the frame-up. Can you get anything of Morlake's—a handkerchief, a pocketbook——?"

Hamon shook his head.

"No," he said shortly. "I have never been into his house."

"That is unfortunate, but it isn't absolutely necessary. I'll have his initials engraved on a pocket-knife—it's easier to prove that you own an article than it is to prove you never owned it! It'll cost a bit—as I say, it's going to be a costly business."

Mr. Hamon took his note-case out, and passed across the table a sum considerably in excess of Marborne's wildest anticipations.

With this money in his pocket, and a corresponding sense of elation in his soul, the detective strolled out to join the waiting Slone. He had reason for gratification, since the plan, if successful, would not only make him a comparatively rich man (supposing Hamon kept his promise), but would wipe out the memory of a number of very ugly incidents that had disfigured his official career, and would inevitably qualify him for promotion if "The Black" were convicted.

Slone was waiting for him on the corner of the street.

"Did he drop?" he asked, and Inspector Marborne frowned.

"I wish you'd get out of that vulgar way of talking, Slone," he said severely. "My friend gave me a little money for expenses, but I don't want you to think that he's the Bank of England. I've got a hundred for you on account, which I'll give you when we get to my flat. You told Colley to be there?"

"He's been waiting all the afternoon," said Slone. "Lieber hasn't turned up—but he's slow, being Dutch. What is the big idea?"

"You'll hear about it," said the other cryptically.

Colley proved to be an undersized, wizened man whose face had been not the least of his misfortunes. For, to the evidence which had been produced against him from time to time in various courts of law, there was added the unflattering testimony of a face in which "criminal" was written so unmistakably that the most sentimental of jury-women was ready to convict him before the evidence was through.

He was waiting on the pavement opposite the detective's lodgings, and followed the two men through the door. In Mr. Marborne's snug sitting-room he took the cigar that was offered him with an ingratiating smile.

"The sergeant said you wanted to see me, Mr. Marborne," he said. "I got a bit of a fright at first, because I thought you wanted me for that Mill Hill job. If I never move out of this room alive, I'm as innocent——"

"Shut up about the Mill Hill job. I know who did it," said Marborne. "I've got some work for you, Colley."

The face of the thief fell.

"I don't mean honest work," said the detective, "so don't get alarmed! Now listen to this, and listen very carefully. There's a friend of mine who wants to have a little joke with somebody. You needn't worry about the joke being on you, because it won't be."

He explained carefully in detail just what was required of Colley, and as he listened, the man, who at first was alarmed, began to see daylight.

"You want me to get in and get out again quick: is that it?"

"Not too quick," corrected Marborne. "I shall want you to make a bit of a fuss. Let 'em see you, you understand?"

Colley pulled a wry face.

"If this fellow's a Colonial, maybe he's got a gun, and if he sees me before I see him, there'll be some one-sided shooting. It's a fine joke, Mr. Marborne, but it don't amuse me as much as a good Chaplin film."

It took an hour of solid talking to persuade Colley that the danger was negligible and the reward so munificent that he need not work again for a year. In the end he was persuaded, and it was arranged that he should be within call for the next week. When the interview was over, Mr. Marborne went forth to what he knew would be the most difficult of his tasks, and with him went a Mr. Lieber, a belated arrival on the scene.

"I may not want you, Lieber, but you can wait around in case I do. You know Morlake?"

Mr. Lieber, who was stout, shook his head, for he needed all his breath to keep pace with the long-striding detective.

"You can't mistake him, and anyway, I'll be with you to point him out."

"Is he a crook?" wheezed Lieber.

"He's a crook, and I want an identification—the same as you got for me in the Crewe case. A handkerchief, a pocket-book, papers—anything. But I may not need you. Here we are—wait on the corner and follow me when I come out."

Binger opened the door to the caller and eyed him suspiciously, for, although Marborne was unknown to the valet, there was a something "official" in his manner which the old soldier instantly recognised.

"I don't know whether Mr. Morlake is hin or whether he's hout," he said. "If you wait a bit I'll see."

He closed the door in his visitor's face and went into the big Oriental room where James Morlake was reading.

"He says his name is Kelly, sir, and maybe it his and maybe it hain't."

"What did he say his business was?" asked Morlake, closing his book.

"He said he'd met you in Morocco some years ago, and had only just found your address."

"Show him in, will you?" said James Morlake, after a moment's thought, and Mr. Marborne, strolling into the big room, took in its beauty with an admiring glance.

"Sit down, Mr. Kelly. I have no chairs, because I have no visitors—perhaps you will sit on the divan."

Marborne seated himself with a little smirk.

"It is a long time since I met you, Mr. Morlake. I suppose you don't remember me dining at your table at the Cecil, in Tangier, some ten years ago?"

"I have a dim recollection," said Morlake, eyeing his visitor carelessly.

"I was travelling for a hardware firm," said Marborne glibly, and all the time he was speaking he was casting his eyes around, trying to find some little article by which his man might be identified on some future and vital occasion. "I don't know whether you trouble to keep chance acquaintances in your mind, but I have a very pleasant recollection of our meeting."

"I remember you now," said Jim Morlake; "though you have altered a little since I saw you last."

Mr. Marborne looked up at the carved ceiling.

"Beautiful bit of work there; they couldn't do it in this country, or any other," he said. "You've got a lovely place. Nobody would imagine, walking on Bond Street, that there was a real Moorish room within half-a-dozen paces."

He had found what he needed: it lay in the shadow at the back of the stationery rack—a small leather folder on which he could see, even at that distance, three initials. It was too small for a pocket-book, and he guessed it to be a little stamp case until, nearer at hand, he saw that it held a clip of flat matches.

Rising from the divan, he strolled across the room until he stood opposite the watchful man, his hands resting on the desk. Presently:

"I have no business whatever to interrupt a busy person like you," he said, "but I thought, as I was in London for a day, I'd give you a call. It was not inconvenient, I hope?"

His fingers had touched the match case and closed over it. To slip the little leather folder into his pocket was unnecessary: it was so small that he could palm it.

"I'm always glad to see my old Moroccan friends," said Jim. "Won't you have a drink, Mr. Kelly?"

"No, thank you," said Kelly. "I won't occupy any more of your time. I was told that you didn't live in town—that you had a house somewhere in Sussex."

"Yes, I have a house in Sussex," said Jim quietly.

By this time the match case was in the detective's pocket.

"If you're ever in Liverpool, look me up—John L. Kelly," said Marborne, as he put out his hand. "You'll find me in the telephone directory—943 Lime Street. I'm very glad indeed to have met you again, Mr. Morlake."

Jim took the hand and watched his visitor as he strolled towards the curtained hallway.

"Oh, by the way," he said, as the man reached the curtain, "you might be good enough to leave my matches behind—I may want them.

Marborne stared and started.

"Your—your matches?" he stammered.

"Yes, they're in your right-hand trousers pocket, Inspector," said Jim, hardly looking up from the book he had opened.

"I have no matches," said Marborne loudly.

"Then you have used them, and I will take the case," said Jim. "And, Inspector, if you give me any trouble, I shall call up headquarters and tell your chief something about the gentleman who runs a receiver's business in Marylebone Lane. You get a rake-off of ten per cent., I am told—I am sure the excellent Commissioner does not know that."

Marborne's face twitched and he changed colour. He opened his mouth to speak, but thought better of it, then, taking the case from his pocket, he flung it on the ground.

"Thank you," said Jim gently.

The man's face was dark with rage, as, stung by the cool contempt of the other, he turned.

"I'll get you one of these days, Morlake," he quavered in his fury. "You'll not get away with it *all* the time!"

"And you won't get away with my matches *any* time," said Jim, and, to Binger, who had appeared in the opening between the curtains: "Show this gentleman out, and see that he doesn't take my umbrella from the hall-stand."

CHAPTER XI

Jane Smith

WHEN the door had closed upon the infuriated policeman, Binger hastened back to his employer.

"That man was a detective," he whispered hoarsely.

"I know that," said Jim, stifling a yawn. "He stole my matches—what other proof was needed, Binger?"

"What did he come here for, sir?" asked Binger in agitation.

"To find out all about me, and apparently to get a light for his cigar. He knows all he'll ever know. Don't worry your head about him, Binger."

"Them fellows are as hartful as monkeys," said the valet.

"Hartfuller," agreed Jim, "but not much. A monkey isn't clever at all: get that into your nut, Binger. He's the most stupid of all the lower animals."

"Are you going out to-night, sir?" after a pause.

"No, I'm staying in to-night. You may go home early to your wife and family—I suppose you have a family?"

"Yes, sir, I've two boys in the Harmy," said Binger proudly.

Jim Morlake nodded.

"I don't think I shall want you for anything more. Tell Mahmet to bring me coffee: I shall be working late to-night."

When the man had gone, he laid down his book and began slowly to pace the big room, his hands clasped behind him, a far-away look in his eyes and a frown upon his handsome face. He heard the thud of the door as Binger went home, and a few seconds later the little Moorish servant came in, bearing a tray with the paraphernalia for coffee-making.

Jim watched him idly, and when the man's task was finished and he had salaamed his way out of the room, he walked to the divan, and stooping, lifted the top that came up like the lid of a box. In the cavity beneath was a small steel safe lying on its back. He fitted a key in the lock and, pulling up the door, took out a large bundle of banknotes. For half an hour he was sorting them into their various denominations. When he had finished, he counted the bundles carefully, enclosed them in various envelopes, on each of which he wrote a different name and address, which he took from a pocket diary which he carried in his waistcoat pocket. This done, he replaced all the envelopes in the safe, closed and locked it and replaced the "lid" of the divan.

He looked at his watch: it was half-past eleven. He did not feel tired; the book he had been reading was very dull, yet no outside amusement attracted him.

He sat down again to consider the problem of Marborne's visit. Marborne, in his simplicity, had imagined that he was unknown, but in truth there was not a detective holding any rank in the headquarters police whose face James Morlake did not know.

Why had he come? Why had he been guilty of so paltry a theft? Jim had not seen the matches go, but he had known they were on the desk and when the detective had walked to the table he had observed the palming. What was the object, he wondered—he could supply half-a-dozen solutions, none of which was wholly convincing to himself.

He got up and passed through a narrow arched doorway into a smaller room, furnished with a bed and a wardrobe. He would go out, he decided, and changed his shoes. He was opening the door of the flat when he saw a letter on the floor. It had evidently been pushed through the slot, and, picking it up, he saw that it had been delivered by hand. It was addressed in pencilled writing to "Mr. Morelake," and it was marked "Urgent."

Tearing open the envelope, he read the few scrawled lines it contained, and reading, he frowned. Presently he folded the letter, put it back in its envelope and slipped it into his pocket.

"Mahmet, did you hear anybody outside?" he asked when the servant had come in response to his signal.

"No, effendi—not since the secretary went. I was in the hall then."

Morlake took the letter from his pocket.

"This was not here when you let Binger out?"

"No—there was nothing."

The letter must have been delivered while he was changing his shoes.

Restoring the scrawled warning to his pocket, he went out on the stone landing. His flat was the only residential apartment in the building, the lower floors being offices, the ground floor a *couturière's* establishment. Usually at this hour of the night the caretaker, the only other person in the building at night, was to be found smoking in the small entrance hall, but to-night he was absent.

As Morlake came into the street, Inspector Marborne, standing in the shadow of a door, tapped his companion on the shoulder.

"There's your man, Lieber," he said.

The pickpocket nodded and walked across the road, following the tall man, who was moving at a leisurely pace toward Piccadilly. As he reached the corner, Morlake stopped and looked left and right irresolutely as though he were undecided which way he should go. At that moment a stout little man, walking rapidly, came into violent collision with him.

"Steady, my friend," said James Morlake, recovering from the shock.

"Excuse me," mumbled the little man, and went on his way at the same furious rate, Jim Morlake looking after him with a glint of amusement in his eyes.

Inspector Marborne was waiting for the thief at the corner of Air Street, and as the little man turned into that deserted thoroughfare, Marbone fell in at his side.

"Well?" he demanded.

"I got something," said Lieber, putting his hand in his pocket. "There's no handkerchief or case in his pocket, but I got a letter."

Impatiently the inspector tore it from his hand and, halting beneath a street standard, examined the prize.

"It is addressed to him all right," he said. "Now, Mr. Morlake, I think I've got you."

He pulled out the letter and read it. Lieber watching him, saw his mouth open in horrified amazement.

Dear Mr. Morlake [the message ran], *Ralph Hamon employs a police officer named Marborne, who is laying a trap for you.*

It was signed "Jane Smith."

"Who the devil is Jane Smith?" gasped Marborne.

This was the identical question that James Morlake was asking himself at that moment.

CHAPTER XII

Miss Lydia Hamon

The detective turned from his examination of the letter to glower at his companion.

"You're a fine thief, Lieber!" he snarled. "Is this all you could get?"

Lieber's puffy face fell.

"Ain't it enough, Mr. Marborne?" he asked, aggrieved. "You said 'Get a letter,' and I got it."

"You got it all right," said the other grimly. "Oh, yes, you got it!"

He stuffed the letter into his pocket and left his gaping agent staring after him.

Little things amuse, but they also distress little minds. The discovery that his association with Hamon was known to "Jane Smith" worried him horribly—it worried him more because he was so deeply committed to the plot that it was impossible to go back. The scheme must be carried through, but first he must make sure of his ground. He hailed a taxi and drove to Grosvenor Place. The servant who admitted him, and who knew him, said that Mr. Hamon was out.

"Will you see Miss Hamon?" asked the man.

"Miss Hamon?—I didn't know there was a Miss Hamon," said Marborne in surprise.

The butler might have explained that the visits of Miss Hamon to London were few and far between, and he could have supplemented the information that, rare as they were, the household of 307 Grosvenor Place would have been delighted if they were even rarer. For Lydia Hamon was that type of young woman (and the type was not exclusively confined to the young) who, having risen to affluence from the borderland of poverty, lived in a state of perpetual fear that their superiority to the rest of the world was not being duly recognised.

"Oh, yes, Mr. Hamon has a sister—she lives in Paris."

Lydia certainly lived in Paris. She had a small apartment on the Bois and a very highly-polished coupé that was driven by a Japanese chauffeur in a rose-red livery. She studied art in a genteel way, knew many old Royalist families and spoke French to her own satisfaction.

Leaving Marborne in the hall, the servant went into the drawing-room, closing the door behind him. It was a little time before he reappeared to beckon the visitor forward.

Lydia Hamon was pretty and thin. Her hair, a dull red, was bobbed in the French manner and bound by a filet of bronze-coloured ribbon. Her arms, otherwise bare, were encircled by bracelets that flashed and glittered in the light of shaded wall brackets. She turned her dark eyes languidly in the direction of the detective as he entered, and the thin eyebrows arched inquiringly. Otherwise, she made no attempt to greet the visitor, nor did she rise from the couch on which she was lying.

Marborne, a susceptible man, was struck dumb by what he regarded as her unearthly beauty. The green evening gown, the dull gold of dainty shoes and silken stockings, the delicate hands that shaded her eyes as though his coming had introduced a new brilliancy into the room, were all parts of the charm which momentarily overwhelmed him.

"You want to see my brother?" she drawled (she actually said "brothah," and the gentility of the intonation took his breath away).

"Yes, miss, I have a little business with him."

She looked at the diamond-studded watch on her wrist.

"He will be back very soon," she said. "I know nothing about business, so I'm afraid I can't help you. Won't you sit down, Mr. Marlow?"

"Marborne," murmured the detective, seating himself gingerly on the edge of a chair. "I haven't had the pleasure of meeting you before, Miss Hamon."

She inclined her head, signifying her regret that this pleasure had not been his.

"I live mostly abroad, in my dear Paris," she said. "Life there is so different, so real! London, with its commercialism and absence of soul, frightens me."

Inspector Marborne, who was not a classy talker, felt it was a moment to suggest that the efficiency of the London police force was such that nobody need be frightened, but happily, before she could lead him again out of his depth, Hamon came in.

"Hullo, Marborne!" he said anxiously. "What is wrong?" He glanced at the reclining figure on the sofa. "You've met my sister? Lydia, this is Mr. Marborne, a friend of mine and an officer of the Metropolitan Police."

"Really?" She raised her eyebrows again, but, to Marborne's disappointment, did not seem particularly impressed.

"We'll go up to my den," said Hamon, and he hustled the detective from the room before the impressionable Marborne could begin taking leave.

Behind the closed doors of Hamon's room, the inspector told his story.

"Let me see the letter," said Hamon.

He studied it under the light of the table lamp, his lips pursed, his eyebrows gathered in a frown.

"Jane Smith? Who the dickens is Jane Smith?" he muttered.

"Is there anybody who knows about—about this matter?" asked Marborne.

"Nobody. I mentioned it to my sister, but to no other soul."

At first astonished, Marborne was a little perturbed.

"I wish you hadn't mentioned it to anybody, Mr. Hamon," he said.

"I haven't," said the other impatiently. "I did no more than tell Lydia that I'd got a scheme for settling with Morlake. One thing I'll swear—that the writing isn't Lydia's, and anyway, she doesn't know the man, and would not write to him if she did. Is this all you've got?"

"It is all that is necessary," said Marborne airily. "I've got the scheme so well fixed that it isn't necessary we should have anything of Morlake's. The envelope will be found—any clue that leads us to Morlake is sufficient."

He did not tell of the visit he had paid, feeling that it was hardly the moment to confess a fresh failure.

"When are you going to do the job?" asked Hamon.

Marborne shrugged.

"It depends entirely upon circumstances. I hope to fix it this week," he said. "You need have no fear. I can get enough evidence to convict him, and once he's pinched, it will be easy to search his flat and his house in Sussex. Why didn't you have him arrested in the country? It would have been an easy matter to have got a search-warrant——"

"Don't ask dam' fool questions," said the other impatiently. "Let me know when you're taking him, and I'll be on hand to furnish the etceteras."

When the detective had gone, Hamon went down to his sister.

"Who is that man?" she asked, yawning undisguisedly. "You always seem to have such queer people at your house, Ralph."

"Why did you come over?" he asked.

"Because I'm short of money. I've bought the loveliest little statuette—a genuine Demetri; and I've been losing a terrible lot at cards. One must keep one's end up, Ralph."

He looked at her without speaking.

"Besides, I've promised to spend a week-end with dear Lady Darlew. She has an awfully nice boy at Eton——"

"Now listen to me, Lydia," interrupted Hamon. "When I started making money, you were serving in a West End bar, earning enough to keep body and soul together, and I'd like you to remember that fact. I'm not made of money, and I'm not going to increase your allowance. You forget these friends of yours who have sons at Eton, and remember that you were serving bad drinks at Lembo's Dive." He saw the fury in her eyes, but went on.

"The time is rapidly approaching when you are going to earn your keep, my girl."

"What do you mean?" she asked. She was no longer the languid child of fashion, but stood before him, her hands on her hips, her voice harsh with anger. "Do you expect me to go back serving drinks whilst you're making tens of thousands? I've helped you, Ralph, and don't forget it! You haven't forgotten Johnny Cornford, I hope, and what I did for you there?"

His face went a shade paler.

"You needn't talk about Johnny Cornford or anybody else," he said roughly; "and don't go up in the air, because I'm talking to you for your good. I shall want your help, I tell you. Marborne's got a big idea of catching Morlake, and if we can't catch him one way he's got to be caught another, and you've got to do it."

"Oh, I have, have I?" she sneered. "And what do I get for it? The same as I got out of the Cornford business—nothing!"

"I got nothing, either," he said quickly.

"That is a lie! Oh, you needn't scowl at me, Ralph: I'm not afraid of you! I heard that tale about Cornford before. Nothing!"

"I got nothing, I tell you," he said loudly. "It was the biggest disappointment I ever had. If the luck hadn't run for me, I'd have been down and out. I never had a penny of Cornford's money."

There was a brief but ominous silence, and then she asked:

"What am I to do with this Morlake? Is he to be jollied along? Has he any money?"

"Stacks of it," said the other tersely, "but it isn't his money I want."

She raised her thin eyebrows.

"You must be pretty well off not to worry about his money," she said; and asked again: "What am I to do?"

"It depends entirely on how well Marborne's plan goes," said her brother. "We needn't discuss it till then."

"What is he like?" she asked. "This Morlake?"

He went out of the room and came back with a photograph, which he handed to her, and she looked at the picture with a calculating eye.

"He's rather nice-looking," she said. "Who is he?"

"I'd give a lot of money to know," snapped Hamon. "Don't ask questions, Lydia. All I want to know from you is: is he the type of man that you could make up to if it paid you good money?"

She looked from the picture to her brother.

"That type, and any type," she said briefly.

CHAPTER XIII

At Blackheath

IT WAS on a Friday night, and a thin film of fog lay over the City, the forerunner of those dense mists which in a month's time would make the town uninhabitable.

Jim Morlake had finished the light dinner which the Moor had served, and was reading the evening newspaper with the air of one who hoped to find something amusing in its pages, but had very little expectation of his hopes being realised. Binger had gone home earlier than usual, with instructions not to return for three days, for that night Morlake intended returning to Wold House, and his suitcase awaited him in the hall. He could have gone earlier, but the fog had been unusually thick that afternoon, and he was waiting for it to disperse. The car was at the door, and, putting down the newspaper, he walked to the window, pulled aside the heavy curtains and looked out.

"I think I will go now, Mahmet," he said, and at that moment the telephone bell rang sharply.

He took up the instrument, and a strange and excited voice called him by name.

"Is that Mr. Morlake? . . . I am speaking from Blackheath. Binger has been knocked down by a motor-bus and has been taken to 12 Cranfield Gardens. Can you come at once?"

"Is he badly hurt?" asked Morlake quickly.

"He is not expected to live," was the answer. "I am Dr. Grainger."

Jim only waited long enough to discover the exact location of Cranfield Gardens, and a few minutes later he was driving at full speed in the direction of Blackheath. The fog in the south of London was thicker than he had anticipated, and progress was slow, but it cleared at New Cross and presently disappeared altogether, and he looked up into an unclouded sky, in which the stars were twinkling frostily.

Lieber, watching the flat, saw the car depart, and, hastening to a public telephone booth, gave a number. It was Marborne who answered him.

"He's gone," said Lieber breathlessly. "Went away at five minutes past ten."

"Is he alone?"

"Yes, driving his own car. And he looked to be in a hurry."

Marborne hung up the telephone receiver, paid the proprietor of the little Greenwich restaurant, in which he had been waiting for an hour for the news, and hurried out to where Slone and Colley were waiting for him.

"There is no time to be lost, Colley. Get into that house just as quickly as you can."

"It's early yet, Mr. Marborne. They won't be in bed," protested Colley.

"The whole house goes to bed at nine," said the other impatiently. "Do you think I haven't made sure of that?"

The car that had been hired for the night carried them to Blackheath, and at the corner of Cranfield Gardens Colley received his instructions.

"You'll get through the pantry window and up to the first

floor. If you like to smash one of the glass cases where the jewellery is kept, you can. Now there will be no risk, Colley. As soon as you've done your work and got the family aroused, get out. You haven't any time to spare."

The burglar slunk away into the darkness, and the uncomfortable Slone interrogated his superior.

"It's crude, inspector. He'll never fall into a trap as open as that," he said. "He'll go straight to his servant's house and he'll find him at home."

"I tell you he will come straight here. I could tell by his voice, when I called him up, that he is worried about Binger."

The two men walked rapidly down Cranfield Gardens and turned into a gateway.

"I can hear the sound of a car coming up the hill," said Marborne suddenly. "Get into the shadow of the steps."

"I don't like it," growled Slone. "It's too easy, I tell you. It can't go right——"

"Shut up!" hissed the other. "Here is the car."

Turning from Blackheath Hill, Jim Morlake stopped the machine and alighted. No. 12 was the fourth house from that end of the street he had entered, a high-fronted, sombre house, showing no sign of light. He had unlatched and passed through the wooden gate before the absence of the red light which usually advertises a doctor's house occurred to him, and he walked back to inspect the gate posts to make sure. Yes, it was No. 12. Hesitating no longer, he walked up the path and mounted the stone steps. As he did so, he heard, from inside the house, a shot and the thump of heavy feet in the hall, and drew back.

And then there came to him instinctively an understanding of his danger, and he flew down the steps. Two strides he took in the direction of the gate, and something struck him. He half turned, dazed and semi-conscious, and again the blow fell and everything went dark.

When he recovered consciousness, he was lying on a hard wooden form, and a man was doing something to his head. He opened his eyes, and in the dim light of the cell in which he lay he saw a bearded figure fixing a bandage.

"Lie down," said the doctor authoritatively, and Jim obeyed.

It *was* a cell: he had recognised the character of the apartment the moment he had opened his eyes. How had he got there, and what had happened? Then he remembered the blow that had struck him down. His head was throbbing painfully; he had an uncomfortable feeling of restriction about his hands, and, looking at them, he saw that they were clipped together with handcuffs.

"Why am I here?" he asked.

"I daresay the inspector will tell you all about it," said the doctor as he pinned the ends of the bandage and stepped back to admire his handiwork.

"Oh, he will, will he?" said Jim dully. "Well, I should very much like him to come and give his explanation. How is Binger?" He smiled faintly. "I suppose the Binger story was a fake? The inspector to whom you refer is Inspector Marborne?"

"You'd better ask him," said the diplomatic doctor. "He will be here in a few minutes."

He went out, and the cell door clanged on James Morlake. With some difficulty he raised himself to a sitting position and took stock of his unhappy state. Mechanically he put his hand in his pocket: it was empty. He tried another with a similar result. His watch and chain had gone, his cigarette-case, everything he had possessed had been taken from him.

He was very much alert now; he even forgot the physical pain he suffered.

There was a click of a lock, the cell door opened, and Marborne came in with a smile of triumph on his face.

"Well, Morlake, we've got you at last!"

"I ought to have given you those matches," said Jim coolly; "and really, if I'd known that you had taken such a fancy to them, Marborne, that you would waylay and rob me, I'd have saved you the trouble."

"I don't know what you mean about matches," said Marborne brusquely. "All I know is that we've caught you with the goods. You know my name?"

"I know your name," nodded Jim. "You're Inspector Marborne."

"I am Inspector Marborne," said the man in his best official manner, "and I shall charge you with burglariously entering No. 12 Cranfield Gardens last night. I shall further charge you with being in possession of a loaded revolver and housebreaking implements. I shall further charge you with breaking and entering the Burlington Safe Deposit on the seventeenth of this month, and still further with breaking and entering the Home Counties Bank on the twelfth of August."

He paused.

"Don't let me interrupt your curious recital," said Jim. "You will also caution me that anything I say may be used in evidence against me. That is your duty, you know, inspector, but you omitted the customary caution."

The detective was scrutinising him keenly.

"You'll be interested to know that I've also arrested your accomplice, Jane Smith," he said, and Jim chuckled.

"I'm delighted! I should very much like to see Jane Smith. And have you arrested our friend Hamon too?"

The detective smiled indulgently.

"None of that, Morlake," he said. "You know I've not arrested Mr. Hamon. What charge could you make against him?"

Jim was silent for a moment, and then:

"Wilful murder," he said quietly; "and I should charge you with being an accomplice after the fact."

CHAPTER XIV

Caught!

For a time the police officer did not recognise the significance of Jim's charge.

"What do you mean?" he asked roughly. "Wilful murder!"

"As to how much you know of the matter I have yet to learn, Marborne," said Jim Morlake quietly. "But on the day I catch Hamon it will go pretty hard with *you!*"

"When you catch Hamon—are you pretending to be a policeman too?" asked the other sarcastically.

"I'm not even pretending to be a policeman. I have never sunk so low," said Jim.

The detective stooped down and pulled him to his feet.

"You're coming out to see a few of the jiggers that were found on you when you were arrested," he said, and pushed him along the corridor to the charge room.

On the station sergeant's desk was a variety of articles. There was a black silk mask, the eyeholes of which, as Jim saw with a professional glance, had been newly cut; an automatic pistol, a complete set of house-breaking tools, a small acetylene blow-lamp, a tiny rubber case containing six phials, and three small skeleton keys.

"Are these supposed to be mine? Where did I carry them—in my waistcoat pocket?" he asked.

"Some were in your coat pocket, some were concealed under the cushion of your car," said the detective. "You admit these are yours, I suppose?"

"I admit nothing. The only thing I can't see, which really belongs to me, is a gold watch and chain, which I presume you have confiscated for personal use. There was also a little money—some sixty-five pounds—which isn't visible. Are those also your personal perquisites, Marborne?'

"I've got the money and the watch in my desk," said the station sergeant. "You don't make your case any better by bringing charges against this officer, Morlake."

"Perhaps I don't," admitted Jim after a moment's thought. He held up his manacled hands.

"These are not exactly necessary, are they, sergeant?"

"I don't think so."

The sergeant took down a key from behind his desk, and unlocking the handcuffs, removed them. In charge of the gaoler, Jim was removed to the cell.

Joan Carston was at breakfast at Lowndes Square, reading the morning newspaper, when Hamon was announced, and with a groan she put down the journal and glanced pathetically across to her father.

"Bless the man! Why does he come at this hour of the morning?" he demanded irritably. "I thought we should be free of him for a month or so?"

He was not in a pleasant frame of mind. The horse he had backed for the long distance handicap at Newmarket had been struck out overnight, and he was not unnaturally annoyed.

"We shall have to see him: let us get it over," said Joan, resigned.

Ralph Hamon's manner was both brisk and cheerful: in fact, the girl had never seen him quite so bright as he was, as he pranced into the dining-room—the description was hers.

"I have some very interesting news for you people this morning," he said, almost jovially, as, without invitation, he pulled out a chair and sat down to the breakfast table. "We've got the devil!"

"Good business," murmured his lordship. "I hope you will fasten the customary chains to his legs and cast him down into his jolly old pit."

"Which particular devil are you talking about, Mr. Hamon?" asked the girl, with a sinking of her heart.

"Morlake. He was caught red-handed last night, burglaring a house at Blackheath."

She jumped to her feet.

"You don't mean that!" she gasped. "Mr. Morlake . . . oh, no, it isn't true!"

"It is delightfully true," said Hamon. (She thought he smacked his lips.) "He was caught red-handed in the act of breaking into the house of a man who has a collection of antique jewellery. Fortunately, two police officers who have had him under observation for some time had shadowed him, and took him just as he was running out of the house, having been disturbed in his work by the owner, a Colonel Paterson."

Lord Creith took off his glasses and stared at the other in amazement.

"You mean James Morlake, our neighbour?" he asked incredulously.

Hamon nodded.

"I mean The Black, the cleverest burglar we've had in this country for years."

Joan had sunk back to her seat: the room seemed to be swimming. Hamon was telling the truth; there was no mistaking the exhilaration in his voice.

"Of course you caught him," she said at last, speaking slowly as though to herself. "You said you would, didn't you?"

"I didn't exactly catch him myself," said Hamon, loth to relinquish the credit, "but I must confess that I was able to give the police a great deal of useful information. And by the way, Lady Joan, my sister is giving herself the pleasure of calling on you to-day."

"Yes?" said Joan absently. "Oh, yes, you have a sister in Paris. I'm afraid I shan't be at home this afternoon."

"I thought you wouldn't be, so I told her to call this morning. You'll like Lydia: she's a good girl, though I'm afraid I've spoilt her a little. But she's one of the best."

"When will Mr. Morlake come for trial?" she asked, dismissing the existence of Lydia Hamon.

"He'll come up this morning for the preliminary hearing, and then I suppose he'll be remanded, and next week he'll be committed for trial. You're interested in him, aren't you? Well, it is only natural that you should be. These rascals have a certain romantic interest, even for the more law-abiding."

"Not every rascal," she answered instantly. "I know some who are the most uninteresting creatures it is possible to meet!"

She had recovered her poise, and Lord Creith, who knew his daughter remarkably well, detected what Mr. Hamon had failed to notice—a certain gentle malignity in her voice, and writhed at the memory of past encounters with his daughter that had left him a little limp.

"Has he any friends? I mean, is there anybody who would bail him?"

"No bail would be allowed," answered Hamon promptly.

"Having got the fellow, it is hardly likely that the police are going to risk his bolting, especially as he put up a tough fight before he was captured."

"Was he hurt?" she asked quickly.

"He got a blow or two," said Hamon, with a careless shrug, and her eyes did not leave his.

"You know a great deal about this: I suppose they 'phoned you up and told you, as you were interested?"

"I only know what I read in the newspapers," said Hamon quickly, and he saw her lip curl.

"It is not in the newspapers," she said. "It happened too late last night to be in the morning Press."

She got up from the table and walked out of the room without another word.

"Joan takes a tremendous interest in this fellow," growled Hamon.

"Why shouldn't she?" demanded Lord Creith, beaming at him. "I think he's immensely interesting. By Jove, I wish I'd known he was a burglar! I'd have gone to him and found an easier way of making money than selling my poor old Creith, lock, stock and barrel. Where will this interesting criminal come up for trial?"

"At Greenwich Police Court," said the other.

"Greenwich!" said Lord Creith, as though Greenwich Police Court were the last place in the world he would have imagined the man would be brought for judgment.

It was near mid-day when a gaoler called his name, and Jim Morlake walked through an open door into the large court and was guided to the steel pen. The court was crowded, and the reporters' bench, designed to hold three uncomfortably, held half-a-dozen young men in agony, whilst an army of Pressmen overflowed into the public benches.

Brief evidence of the arrest was given; a hint was offered that new and more startling charges would be produced at the next hearing, and the police, represented by their official lawyer, asked for a remand—a course which Jim's attorney mechanically opposed, though his opposition was overruled.

"On the question of bail, your worship——" began the defending counsel, but the magistrate shook his head.

"There can be no question of bail," he said.

And here there occurred an unexpected interruption. A tall, lean man stepped, without invitation, to the witness-box and handed his card to the magistrates' clerk.

"This gentleman"—he looked over his glasses at the wondering Jim—"is a neighbour of mine, and I am particularly anxious that he shall have every facility for preparing his defence."

"I am extremely sorry, Lord Creith," said the magistrate, "but in these cases, where the police oppose bail, as I understand they do, we cannot deviate from the rule of the court."

Jim went back to his cell wondering what on earth had induced this distinguished-looking old man, whom he knew by name, and whose home he had once burgled, to come forward and, in order to serve a man he did not know, court the publicity which many of his class so intensely disliked.

CHAPTER XV

Joan Makes a Confession

JOAN read, with as great astonishment, the account of her father's interposition in an evening newspaper, and when he came in to dinner that night she was waiting for him in the hall.

"Really, Daddy, you're a most wonderful person," she said, kissing him. "Did you see him?"

"I saw him," admitted Lord Creith, in whom any demonstration of affection on the part of his daughter produced a sense of discomfort, "and quite a nice-looking fellow he is, Joan." He shook his head. "The police say he's a most dangerous rascal. You'd never dream it to see him. To tell you the truth"—he looked round and lowered his voice—"our friend Hamon is infinitely more criminal-looking! And for heaven's sake, don't repeat my words, Joan. The last time I said something unpleasant about Hamon, you blurted it out in the middle of dinner, and I had to lie myself blue to save my face."

Joan had successfully avoided meeting Miss Lydia Hamon that morning, and was hopeful that so inexcusably rude had she been in her failure to keep an appointment, that the girl would not call upon her. At any other time she would have been curious to see what type of individual a sister of Ralph Hamon would be. To-day one thought and one subject absorbed her.

The two hours before dinner Lord Creith ordinarily devoted to what he described as a siesta, and Joan usually occupied that period in dealing with her correspondence. She was in no heart to write to-day, and less in a mood to entertain visitors, so that Peters's announcement that Lydia Hamon had called wrung from her a sigh of despair.

"Ask her to come up," she said, and braced herself to be polite.

Her first feeling, on seeing the visitor, was one of surprise. Lydia had many accomplishments, not least of which was an exquisite taste in dress, and so fragile and sweet she looked, as she came into the drawing-room, that Joan found it difficult to believe that the girl could claim any relationship with the unprepossessing Mr. Hamon.

"I'm so sorry I have interrupted you," drawled the visitor, with a glance at the writing-table, which Joan had hastily littered with notepaper in preparation for an excuse to cut the interview short. "I called this morning; Ralph said you would be expecting me, but you were out."

Joan murmured her apologies, wondering what was the urgency of the business which brought the girl at this unconventional hour to make her call.

"I am only in London for a few days, and I simply had to see you," said Lydia, as though supplying an answer to the question uppermost in Joan's mind at that moment. "I live in Paris. Do you know Paris very well?"

"I know it a little. It is not my favourite city," said Joan.

"Really!" Those arched eyebrows of Lydia's rose. "I can't understand anybody not loving Paris: it is so delightful to people of taste."

"Then my taste is deficient," said Joan almost good-humouredly.

"No, I didn't mean that." The girl hastened to correct any possibly bad impression. "I think one *lives* there. Do you know the Duc de Montvidier? He is a great friend of ours."

She rattled off the names of a dozen noble Frenchmen without Joan discovering one in whom she might claim to have an interest, let alone an acquaintance.

"Ralph tells me he has bought your place in Sussex," said Lydia, playing with the handle of her parasol and looking past the girl. "It is a beautiful place, isn't it?"

"Yes, it is lovely," said Joan quietly.

"I think it is such a pity," cooed Lydia, "the old place passing out of your possession, which has been in your family for hundreds of years—it must be a great blow to you. I told Ralph that I wondered he had the heart to take possession."

"He hasn't taken possession yet; he doesn't so long as my father is alive," said Joan, beginning to understand the reason for the visit.

"Oh, yes, I know. I wasn't thinking about your father, I was thinking about you more particularly. And I know Ralph thinks about you a great deal."

Lydia looked under her eyelashes at the expressionless face of her hostess.

"Ralph worries very much. He is awfully kind-hearted. Very few people understand him. To the average every-day person, Ralph is just a money-grabbing Englishman with no soul above commerce. In reality, he is tender and kind and the most loyal of friends."

"He ought to make some girl a good husband," said Joan, leaping instantly into the breach.

The reply took Lydia aback. It was so abrupt a declaration of all that she meant to hint, that she lost her place in the narrative she had so well rehearsed.

"That is what I think. Honestly—though perhaps you will think it an impertinence of me to say so—Ralph is a prize worth winning."

"I don't know why you should think it an impertinence," said Joan, "since I am not a competitor for the prize."

A spirit of mischief was in her—the devil which on occasions caused Lord Creith great uneasiness of mind.

"You see, I couldn't very well marry your brother—to put the matter very plainly."

"Why not?" Lydia was betrayed into asking.

"Because I'm already engaged," said Joan. "In fact, the engagement is such a long-standing one that I shouldn't like to break it off."

"Engaged!"

It was evidently news to Lydia, and inwardly she grew angry with her brother that he had not added this information to the important details with which he had furnished her.

"Yes, I'm engaged."

"But you wear no engagement ring?" said Lydia.

"An engagement ring is not necessary when two hearts are in unison," replied Joan smugly.

"My brother doesn't know."

"Then you have some news to tell him," said Joan.

Lydia had risen and was twirling her parasol awkwardly, being at a loss now as to how the interview could be terminated with the least possible delay.

"I'm sure I hope you will be happy," she said tartly, "but I think it is the greatest mistake in the world for a girl of your breeding to marry somebody without money. And of course, if he had any money, he wouldn't have allowed Ralph to have bought your father's estate."

"Such marriages sometimes turn out badly," said Joan sweetly, "but one hopes this particular match—which is a love match into which the sordid question of money has never intruded—will be an exception."

The object of the girl's vsit was now explained. Her chagrin, her confusion, the undisguised annoyance in her face and mien told Joan all that she wanted to know.

"Perhaps you will change your mind," said Lydia, holding out a limp hand. "Ralph is the sort of man who is not easily put off anything he wants. He is a very good friend and a very bad enemy. There is a man who is kicking his heels in a prison cell who knows that!"

She saw the flush dawn in Joan's face, but misunderstood the cause.

"I don't know why people in prison should amuse themselves by kicking their heels," said Joan coldly; "and in all probability Mr. Morlake is quite cheerful."

"You know James Morlake?"

Joan met the dark eyes of Lydia Hamon and held them. "I ought to," she said slowly. "I am engaged to him."

CHAPTER XVI

Mr. Hamon Is Shown Out

THE Earl of Creith came down to dinner in the care-free mood which an afternoon nap, for some mysterious reason, invariably induced, and over the coffee Joan described her interview.

"Good heavens!" said his lordship, for the moment aghast. "What a thing to say!"

"I had to shock her," said Joan in justification.

"Shock her! But, merciful Moses! there were other ways of doing it, Joan. You could have told her that the wine at Creith was corked—as it undoubtedly is—or that the roof leaked—which it does. Why tell her that you're engaged to be married to a—a sort of burglar? You're not, are you?" he asked suspiciously.

"I'm not. I don't even know him."

"H'm!" said her father, puckering his forehead. "Suppose this gets into the papers? 'Peeress Engaged to Burglar,' or 'Earl's Daughter to Wed Notorious American Cracksman on

His Release from Prison,' eh? How do you think *he'd* like it?"

Joan opened her mouth in consternation.

"I never thought of that!" she gasped.

"After all," said the Earl, deriving infinite satisfaction from the knowledge that for once he was master of the situation, "after all, he may have his feelings. Burglars may consider themselves a cut above the new poor——"

"Please don't be absurd, Father! Who would tell him?"

"Anyway, it was a foolish thing to do, because this Hamon man will be coming round and bothering me about it. And nobody knows better than you, Joan, that I hate being bothered."

"You can tell him you know nothing about it—which is true. You can also say that I am my own mistress, which is also true."

The old man gulped down his coffee.

"Perhaps he won't come," he said hopefully, but he had not risen from the table when Ralph Hamon's loud knock announced his arrival.

"I'm not in!" said Lord Creith hastily. "Tell him I'm out, Joan . . ."

He made a hasty and somewhat undignified exit.

She walked into the drawing-room to find a fuming Hamon stalking up and down the carpet. He spun round as she opened the door.

"What is this story that Lydia tells me?" he stormed.

The change in him was remarkable. At the best he was an unpleasant-looking man—now she shuddered to see him. His jaw was out-thrust, his eyes blazed with anger.

"So you know Morelake, do you?—you're Jane Smith!" he pointed an accusing finger at her, and her calm nod seemed to infuriate him.

"Joan, I've told you before—I tell you again that you are the only woman in the world for me. I will have you—and nobody else. I'd kill him and you too rather! If this is true, I'll never leave him till he's dead!"

She did not flinch, and in her quiet disdain the tortured man thought her never so beautiful. Slim and white, a fragile thing of youth, with her child face and the figure that was nearly woman. His hands went out toward her instinctively, but she did not move.

"I know a dozen men who would take you by the collar and throw you out of this house if they knew a half of what you said."

Her voice was steady: she showed no trace of that agitation which he expected.

"If I am misinformed——" he began huskily.

"You are. It was a stupid joke on my part to tell your sister that I was engaged, but I disliked her so; she was so horribly common with her affectations and her talk of the aristocrats she knew—such a feminine edition of you, Mr. Hamon. I could imagine her screaming at me, as you have been screaming. A wretched virago shrieking me down."

She had left the door open as she came in, and Peters, she knew, was in the hall.

"Peters," she called, and the butler came in. "Show Mr. Hamon out; he is not to be admitted either to this house or Creith."

Peters bowed, and, his eyes upon Ralph Hamon, jerked his head to the door.

It was one of the happiest moments of his life.

CHAPTER XVII

Gentle Julius

Colonel Carter, of the Criminal Investigation Bureau, took his cigar from his mouth in order to smile the more comfortably.

"My dear Welling, you are romantic, and because you are romantic you ought to have been a failure. Instead of which, by some mysterious dispensation of providence, you are a very successful detective officer. Romance plays no part in our work; there is nothing romantic about crime. A is a thief, with peculiar but well-known methods; B is a stolid, unimaginative police officer who, called into a case of burglary, larceny, anything you like, finds that the crime has been committed by somebody who employs the methods of A. Perhaps A makes a hobby of forcing kitchen windows, or using chance-found ladders, or is in the habit of taking a meal after the robbery is committed. Anyway, there are characteristics of A. So B arrests him, and generally he is right. You, on the other hand, would find, in the remnants of a stolen meal, proof that the robber was starving and would look for a hungry-looking, left-handed man!"

Julius Welling, Chief of the 8th Bureau, sighed. He was an elderly, white-haired man with a sad face and a trick of rubbing his nose when he was embarrassed.

"You've won through, heaven knows how," mumbled Carter through his cigar. "Maybe it is luck—maybe inspiration."

"You have omitted all the possibilities of genius," said the other gently.

In the service which he had adorned for thirty-five years they christened him "Gentle Julius." His rank was equivalent to a Chief Constable, for every promotion that could come to a successful police officer had been his, and on the rare occasions that he wore a uniform, his decorations ran in three straight rows from buttons to shoulder.

Jackson Carter and he had entered the service on the same day, the former an office man with a peculiar gift for organisation, the other so immersed in his study of men and women that he scarcely noticed the passing of the years that brought him so much honour.

"As I say, you're a romantic old dog," said Carter, on his favourite theme, which was very nearly his only recreation, the baiting of his lifelong friend. "Though I admit—and this is very handsome of me—that your dreamings have sometimes led you to queer results."

Julius Welling smiled with his eyes.

"Where will my present dream lead me to?" he asked.

"To failure," said the other seriously. "We've got The Black—there is no doubt about it. I wish somebody else than Marborne had got him, for I had sharpened the toe of my right boot for him, but there is the luck of the game; Marborne has caught him. We have all the evidence we want. Apart from the fact that he was taken in the act, the burglar's kit and gun we found on him, a whole lot of stuff has been discovered in his flat in Bond Street. A parcel of money marked with the stamp of the Home Counties Bank——"

"I could get that by applying to the Home Counties," murmured Mr. Welling.

"A cash box buried in his garden——"

"Why should he bury a cash box in his garden?" asked the other plaintively. "Only amateur crooks do that sort of thing."

"Well, how did it get there?" asked the exasperated Carter.

Mr. Welling rubbed his nose thoughtfully.

"It may have been planted there to get a conviction," he suggested. "Marborne caught Shellman, the banknote forger, that way."

The chief stared at him.

"Do you mean it was a frame-up?" he asked, and Welling nodded.

"The particular charge on which he was convicted was faked. I've known it for some time. Shellman, of course, was a forger, too clever to be caught. The charge on which he went down for ten years was undoubtedly framed for him, and Marborne did the framing."

"That is news to me," said the other with a frown.

"As to this Morlake man," Mr. Welling advanced his views with characteristic timidity, "doesn't the story he tells sound rather fishy? He says that his servant was ill—the servant lives at Blackheath, remember. He comes to the house and is suddenly bludgeoned. Taken unawares and bludgeoned—and he is supposed to carry a gun! He comes to burgle a house and leaves his car at a corner of the street with all the lights on, when there is a lane not half-a-dozen yards away where the car could be hidden? He is supposed to have broken in at the back of the house, where there is a garden and an easy wall that would get him into open country, and yet he escapes by the front door! He 'shows fight'—how? Never forget that he has a loaded pistol, yet he 'shows fight' to such purpose that Marborne has to take his 'stick' to him. What was his gun doing all this time?"

Colonel Carter shook his head.

"The story of the telephone call is a lie——"

"On the contrary it is true," said old Julius, almost apologetically. "The New Cross exchange heard the message. They were testing junction lines because a subscriber had reported a fault, and the engineers happened to be listening in on this particular junction when the call went through."

Colonel Carter opened his eyes.

"You've been working on this case?" he said. "You're not tailing The Black?"

Gentle Julius shook his head.

"I've been tailing Marborne," he said, more gently than ever. "You see, Jack, the chief holds about the same views as you concerning the inspector, and he put me on to see that he came to no harm. And the man who called up Morlake and told him the tale about the injured servant was the inspector. I want Marborne's coat for my exhibition of ex-officers' uniforms. And, Jack, noth'n's more certain than that I'll have it!"

"And what about Morlake?" asked Carter.

Gentle Julius spread out his lined hands in a gesture of indifference.

"They may convict him or they may not," he said; "but one thing I can tell you, and it is this. James Lexington Morlake *is* The Black, the cleverest bank smasher we've seen in twenty years. I've proof and more than proof of that, Jack."

He pursed his lips and his white brows met in a prodigious scowl.

"Ten years ago," he said, speaking with more than his ordinary deliberation, "the Haslemere police picked up a dying sailor on the Portsmouth Road."

"What on earth are you talking about?" demanded the startled Carter.

"I'm talking about The Black," said Welling, "and why he's

a burglar—get that in your mind, Jack—a dying sailor with his life hammered out of him, and not a line or a word to identify him; a dying sailor that sleeps in a little churchyard in Hindhead, without a name to the stone that is over him. Ain't that enough to turn any man burglar?"

"You love a mystery, don't you, Julius?" asked his irritated friend, when Welling rose.

"Mysteries are my specialty," said Julius gently.

CHAPTER XVIII

The Trial

THE Central Criminal Court was crowded on the second and last day of the trial, when James Lexington Morlake came up the stairs that led into the large and roomy dock. The white court, with its oaken panels, was pleasing to Jim's discriminating eye; the scarlet and crimson of the judge's robes, the velvet and fur of the Sheriffs', the gold and red of the City Marshal—they harmonised perfectly.

The judge carried in his hand a tight bouquet of flowers and laid them on his desk. It was a far cry from the days of those fœtid courts when the judges carried disinfecting herbs, and an act of grim necessity had been translated through the ages into a pretty custom.

A little bob of the white-wigged head as the judge seated himself. He glanced casually at the prisoner, and, settling himself in his padded chair, waited for the concluding evidence of the last police witness.

Once or twice he leant forward to ask a question in a sharp, thin voice, but on the whole he seemed immeasurably bored, and when he concealed a yawn behind his hand, Jim sympathised with him.

"This is my case, my lord," said the prosecuting counsel as the last witness stepped down.

The judge nodded and glanced at Jim.

"Have you any witnesses to call, Morlake?" he asked.

Jim was not represented by counsel, and he had conducted his own cross-examination of the witnesses.

"No, my lord. I should have called the operator at the New Cross exchange, but the police have admitted that a message came through asking me to call at 12 Cranfield Gardens. From the known time that message came through, and the known hour of my arrest, it is clear that I could not have entered the house in the time. The police rely upon the fact that I was supposed to have been in possession of housebreaking tools and a pistol—neither the purchase nor former possession of which they have traced to me.

"The police in their evidence have told the jury that I am an expert burglar, and that I have robbed many banks——"

"They have stated that you are under suspicion, and the night watchman at the Burlington Safe Deposit has recognised your voice—that is all that has been said definitely concerning any previous crime you may have committed," interrupted the judge. "I take it that you are not going to the witness stand to give evidence on your own behalf?"

"That is so, my lord."

"Then this, I understand, is your speech for the defence? Very well."

Jim leant on the edge of the pen, his eyes fixed on the jury.

"Gentlemen, if it is true that I am a clever bank smasher, does it not occur to you that, in attempting to rob a dwelling-house in order to obtain jewellery of great historical but of little intrinsic value, I was acting in a blundering and amateurish fashion? Why should I, if, as is stated, I robbed the Burlington Safe Deposit of a large sum only a week ago? Gentlemen"—he leant forward—"you may accept as a fact that I *did* rob the Burlington!"

There was a stir in the court and a sudden hum of noise. Up in the public gallery a girl who had sat through the two days of trial, following every word with tense interest, began twisting her handkerchief into a tighter ball, her heart beating a little faster.

"You need not and should not make any statement incriminating to yourself," the judge was warning the tall man in the dock.

"Nothing I have said will or can incriminate me," said Jim quietly. "I am merely asking the jury to accept the hypothesis that I am an expert burglar, in order that they may judge the probability of my breaking into the house in Cranfield Gardens. The police have insisted that I am responsible for these burglaries. So far as the laws of evidence would allow them, they have enveloped my life in a cloud of suspicion. Let me clarify the air, and admit that I am The Black, without specifying for which of these many burglaries I am responsible.

"Was the Blackheath robbery typical? Was there anything to gain, any necessity? Is it not more likely that the story of the telephone call was true, and that I was arrested by, let us say, the honest error of that admirable officer Inspector Marborne?"

Here he left the case to the prosecuting counsel and the judge. It was the latter whose speech counted.

"I have not the slightest doubt," said Mr. Justice Lovin, "that the accused James Morlake is a man of criminal antecedents. I have less doubt that he is the burglar who has gained unenviable notoriety as The Black. But the least doubt of all in my mind concerns his guilt in the charge which has been brought against him in this court and in this present case. The police evidence has been most unsatisfactory. I am not satisfied that either Marborne or Slone, who gave evidence, told the whole truth. There was here almost convincing proof of what is called in America a 'frame-up'—in other words, concocted evidence designed to deceive the court and to secure a conviction. I shall therefore direct you to return a verdict of not guilty. I will add . . ." He turned his stern eyes to the prisoner.

"I will add that, if ever James Lexington Morlake is convicted before me on a charge of burglary, I shall send him to penal servitude for life, believing that he is a menace to society, and a man with whom no honest or scrupulous man or woman should consort."

For a second it seemed to the girl in the gallery that Jim Morlake shrank under the terrific denunciation, and his face went a shade paler. In an instant he had recovered, and, standing erect, heard the formal verdict of Not Guilty, and stepped down to freedom.

The people made way for him as he passed, eyeing him curiously. One white-haired man alone intercepted him.

"Glad you got off, Morlake."

Jim smiled faintly.

"Thank you, Mr. Welling—I know you mean it. It was a frame, of course."

"I guess so," nodded Welling gravely, and went toward the gloomy-faced Marborne, who was coming out of the court. "Heard the judge, Marborne, eh? Pretty bad, that?"

"He didn't know what he was talking about, sir," said the detective with an air of injured innocence. "I've never been so insulted in my life."

"And now *I'm* going to insult you," said Welling. "You're suspended from duty; that applies to you, Slone. Attend the C. C.'s office on Wednesday and bring your uniform in a bundle!"

Jim had watched the little scene interestedly, and guessed its significance. Very few people had come out of court, for the next case was a murder charge. The big marble hall was almost deserted as he slowly crossed toward the stairs.

"Excuse me."

He turned and met the eye of the waiting girl. She was plainly dressed and very pretty, and the gloved hand she held out to him trembled slightly.

"I'm so glad, Mr. Morlake! I'm so glad!"

He took her hand with a half smile.

"You were in court both days," he said. "I saw you in the corner of the gallery. I'm glad it is over—the old gentleman did not spare me, did he?"

She shivered.

"No . . . it was dreadful!"

He wondered what he ought to say or do. Her friendliness and sympathy touched him more than he dreamed was possible. He saw that she was lovely, and he wanted to stop and talk to her, but he had an uncomfortable sense of shyness.

"I hope," he said gently, "that you will not think too favourably of me. A distinguished criminal is very thrilling, but a very bad object of admiration."

He saw the smile trembling at the corner of her lips and felt unaccountably *gauche*.

"I'm not hero-worshipping, if that is what you mean," she said quietly. "I'm just being—awfully sorry for you! I don't think you're very sorry for yourself," and he shook his head.

Looking round, he saw that a policeman was eyeing him curiously from the doorway of the court, and in a desire to shield the girl from the consequences of what might well be a folly, he suggested:

"I think I'll go now."

It needed some courage to say what she had to say.

"Won't you come to tea somewhere?" she said, a little breathlessly. "There is a small restaurant in Newgate Street."

He hesitated.

"Yes—thank you," he said.

"You know, you owe me something," she said as they walked downstairs.

"Owe you?" he asked in surprise. "What do I owe you?"

"I once sent you a very important letter," said the girl.

He stared at her.

"You sent me a letter? What is your name?"

"I am Jane Smith," she said.

CHAPTER XIX

The Tea Shop

HALF in amazement, half amused, he stared at her.

"Jane Smith?" he repeated. "Are you the lady who wrote a letter warning me about Hamon?"

She nodded.

"Do you know him? Is he a friend of yours?"

"Oh, no." She shook her head vigorously. "But I have seen him; he sometimes comes to the village where I am staying—to Creith."

"Oh, you live at Creith? I don't remember having seen you there."

She smiled.

"I shouldn't imagine you know a soul in the village," she said drily. "You're not exactly sociable, are you? And anyway," she went on quickly, "you're hardly likely to call on people of our humble circumstances."

The "restaurant" proved to be a tea shop, which, at this hour of the day, was almost deserted, luncheon having been finished and the tea rush not having yet started. She took a seat at a table in the corner, and gave the order for tea in such a businesslike way that Jim Morlake guessed she was not unused to domestic management. He wondered who she was, and how it came about that he had not noticed so strikingly beautiful a girl.

"Have you lived at Creith long?"

"I was born there," said Jane Smith.

He ruminated for a few minutes, and then:

"How did you come to know that Hamon was plotting this frame-up?"

"I didn't know, I just guessed," she said. "A friend of mine lives at Creith House, and she has heard a great deal about Mr. Hamon."

Jim nodded.

"I owe Lord Creith something for his good intentions," he said, speaking half to himself and half to the girl, and smiled faintly. "I don't suppose his lordship would be very pleased if I called in person to thank him. He has a daughter, hasn't he?"

Jane Smith nodded.

"Somebody told me about her—a very pretty and a very wilful young lady, and, if I understand aright, somewhat romantic?"

Jane Smith's lips curled.

"I never heard that Lady Joan was romantic," she said, almost sharply. "I think she is a very practical, intelligent girl—she is certainly pretty, but that is no credit to her."

The tea came, and she busied herself pouring out for him. He watched her thoughtfully until she had finished and handed the cup to him. Suddenly her manner underwent a change.

"Mr. Morlake," she said seriously, "this has been a terrible lesson to you, hasn't it?"

"The trial?" he asked, and nodded. "Yes, it has been rather a lesson. I underrated Hamon, for one thing, and overrated the genius of the unscrupulous Mr. Marborne, for another. It was a very crude and stupid attempt to catch me."

She was looking at him steadily, her unwavering eyes fixed on his.

"You're not going to break the law any more, are you, Mr. Morlake?" she asked quietly. "You've been very—very successful. I mean you must have made a lot of money. It isn't necessary to take any further risks, is it?"

He did not reply. There was something about her that was familiar to him, something he recognised and which yet evaded him. Where had he seen her? Or was it her voice he recognised? Then:

"I know you," he said suddenly. "You were the girl who was knocked out by the storm!"

She went suddenly red.

"Yes," she confessed. "You didn't see my face."

"I remember your voice: it is one of those peculiarly sweet voices that are very difficult to forget."

He was not being complimentary or offensive, but the colour deepened in her face.

"You said you were a visitor, too. How could you be a visitor if you live in the village?"

"Jane Smith" recovered herself instantly.

"I told a lie," she said coolly. "I find lying is the easiest way out of most difficulties. If you must know, Mr. Morlake, I was in service at the Hall."

"A servant?" he said incredulously.

She nodded.

"I am a parlourmaid," she said calmly, "and a very good parlourmaid."

"Of that I am sure," he hastened to say, and then he looked at her hands, and she was thankful that she was wearing her gloves. "So that is how you knew, eh? Well, I'm very much obliged to you, Miss Smith. Are you still at the Hall?"

She shook her head.

"I lost my job," she said mendaciously, and added: "Through being out so late on the night of the storm."

And then, her conscience beginning to prick her, she turned the conversation to safer channels.

"You are not going to be a burglar any more, are you?" To her amazement, he smiled.

"But surely not!" she gasped. "After your terrible escape, and all that the judge said! Oh, Mr. Morlake, you wouldn't be such a fool!"

This time he laughed aloud.

"It is evident to me, young lady, that you do not estimate the joys and thrills of a burglar's life, or you would not ask me so light-heartedly to give up what is something more than a recreation and a means of livelihood. The judge was certainly fierce! But really, I don't take much notice of judges and what they say. The chances are that, by the peculiar system obtaining in England, I shall never go before that judge—there are half-a-dozen who try cases at the Old Bailey, and possibly, on my next appearance, I shall meet a kind and humanitarian soul who will dismiss me with a caution."

His quizzical eye and bantering tone awakened no response in the girl. She was troubled, almost hurt, by his obduracy.

"But isn't there anybody"—she hesitated—"who could persuade you? Somebody who is very dear to you, perhaps? A relation or—a—a girl?"

He shook his head.

"I have no relatives or friends in the world," he said; "and if that sounds pathetic, I beg of you to believe that I feel no particular sorrow that I am so unencumbered. It is very kind of you, Miss Smith"—his voice and his tone softened—"and

I do appreciate the thought that is behind your request. But I must go on in my own way, because my own is the only way to peace of mind. And now I think you have been too long in a criminal's company, and I'm going to send you home. Are you living in London?"

"Yes, I live here—I mean, I have friends here," she said, somewhat confused.

"Then off you go to your friends."

He paid the bill, and they walked out of the shop together. Suddenly, to his surprise, she turned and walked back to the shop again and he followed her.

"There is a man I don't want to see," she said breathlessly, and, looking through the window, he saw Mr. Ralph Hamon striding savagely along the sidewalk, and watched him turn into an office building, his whole attitude betraying the wrath which the acquittal of James Morlake had aroused.

CHAPTER XX

A Caller

RALPH HAMON's business activities were many, his interests varied. The high, narrow-fronted office block in which were housed his various enterprises rejoiced in the name of Morocco Building, for Mr. Hamon's interests were mainly centred in that country. Here were the head offices of the Rifi Concession, the Marakash Lead Mines, Moroccan Explorations, and half-a-dozen other incorporated concerns.

He slammed through the outer office, his face black with anger. The trial he had not attended, deeming it expedient to keep away from the precincts of the court, but the result of the case had come through on the tape machine at his club, and as the words "Not Guilty" were spelt out before his outraged eyes, Mr. Hamon's wrath had flamed to red heat.

It was incredible, monstrous. And yet he had been warned by Marborne that the case was not going so well against his enemy as he could have wished. The discovery by the police (it was not Marborne who had made this) that a call had been put through summoning Morlake to Blackheath, had made all the difference between conviction and acquittal. So satisfied was Hamon, who knew little of the processes of the law, and regarded a man as doomed from the moment a policeman's hand fell upon his shoulder, that a conviction would follow, that he scouted the possibility of Morlake escaping. And now the dreadful fact stared him in the face. Jim Morlake was free. The old struggle was to be continued, the old menace revived.

Mr. Hamon's office had something of the air of a boudoir, with its thick carpet and tapestried furniture. A faint aroma of cedar hung in the air, for he favoured the heavy perfumes of France. Pushing aside the accumulation of correspondence which his clerk brought in, he dismissed him with a curse.

"There are three cables from Sadi, sir," said his secretary, standing at the entrance of the room, ready to make a more hasty retreat.

"Bring them in," growled Hamon.

He read and, with the aid of a book he took from his desk, decoded the messages, and apparently they did not add to his pleasure, for he sat huddled up in his chair, his hands stuffed in his pockets, a scowl on his face, for a quarter of an hour, until, reaching out for the telephone, he gave the number of his house in Grosvenor Place.

"Tell Miss Lydia I want to speak to her," he said, and when, after an exasperating delay, he heard her voice: "Put the connection through to my study," he said in a low voice. "I want to talk to you privately. Morlake has been acquitted."

"Really!" asked the languid voice.

"And cut out that 'reahly'!" he snarled. "This isn't the time for any of your fancy society stuff! Get that connection through."

There was a click, and after a few seconds her voice called him again.

"What is wrong, Ralph? Does it make much difference—Morlake getting off?"

"It makes all the difference in the world," he said. "You've got to get at him, Lydia. I never thought it would be necessary, but it is! And, Lydia, that trip of yours to Carlsbad is off. I may have to go to Tangier, and I shall want you to come with me."

He heard her exclamation of concern, and grinned to himself.

"You said you would never ask me to go back there," she said, almost plaintively. "Ralph, is that necessary? I'll do anything you ask me, but please don't let me go back to that dreadful house."

There was no affectation in her voice now; she was very sincere, very earnest, pleading almost.

"I'll see," he said. "In the meantime, you wait for me; I'll be back in half-an-hour."

He put down the receiver and hastily ran through the smaller pile of correspondence on his desk which called for personal attention, marking a letter here and there, putting a few into his pocket to answer at his leisure. He was on the point of ringing for his clerk, when that harassed individual appeared in the doorway.

"I can't receive anybody," snapped Hamon, seeing the card in the man's hand.

"He says——"

"I don't care what he says; I can't see anybody. Who is it?"

He snatched the card from the clerk's hand, and read:

Captain Julius Welling.
Criminal Investigation Bureau.

Ralph Hamon bit his lip. He had heard of Welling in a vague way. Once or twice Marborne had made an uncomplimentary reference to the Chief of the 8th Bureau, from which he gathered that Welling was both honest and efficient. Why should Welling want to see him, he wondered.

"Show him in," he said curtly, and Julius Welling was ushered into the room.

Hamon was taken aback to find a man much older than he had expected; a mild-looking, white-haired gentleman, with a slight stoop and a deferential manner. He looked less like a policeman than any man Mr. Ralph Hamon had seen.

"Won't you sit down, Captain Welling?" he said. "Can I be of any service to you?"

"I thought I'd just call in," said Julius gently. "I happened to be passing—you're very handily situated here, Mr. Hamon—only a few yards from the Central Criminal Court."

Hamon shifted uncomfortably as this dubious advantage was pointed out to him.

"I suppose you weren't in court for the trial of Morlake?" said Julius, depositing his hat carefully upon the ground and hanging his short umbrella on the edge of the desk.

"No," said the other curtly, "I was not very much interested in the case."

"*Weren't* you now?" said Julius. "I had an idea you were. Now, how did I get that into my head?"

His mournful eyes were fixed upon the other, and Hamon grew uncomfortable under the glance.

"I suppose I was, in a sense," he admitted. "This fellow has been a nuisance to me for years. And of course, as you know, I was able to supply some valuable information to the police."

"Not to the police," said Julius, "but to Inspector Marborne—which I admit, at first glance, looks to be the same thing, but which isn't. A queer man, Mr. Morlake, don't you think?"

"All criminals are queer, I understand," said Hamon, and the other nodded slowly.

"All criminals are queer," he agreed. "Some are queerer than others. And quite a lot of people are queer who aren't criminals; have you noticed that, Mr. Hamon? He has a Moorish servant—Mahmet; and I understand that he speaks Arabic rather well. For the matter of that, you speak the language also; isn't that so?"

"I speak the Moorish Arabic, yes," said Hamon shortly.

"Dear me!" mused Gentle Julius, gazing out of the window. "Isn't that a remarkable coincidence? Both you men have an association with Morocco. You've floated a number of companies with a Moorish end to them, haven't you, Mr. Hamon? Of course you have; I needn't have troubled to ask you that question, because all the information I require is in the Stock Exchange Year-book. The Marakash Company now; that was to exploit some oil wells which existed in the desert of Hari. There was a desert, but there was no oil, if I remember rightly, and you went into liquidation."

"There was oil, but the wells went dry," corrected Hamon.

"And Morlake—was he interested in Moorish finances? He lived there for some time, I understand. Did you meet him?"

"I never met him—I saw him once," said the other, shortly. "I know he lived there. But Tangier is the sink into which all the refuse of Europe flows."

Julius agreed with a nod.

"That is so," he said. "Do you remember the Rifi Diamond Syndicate? I think you floated that about twelve years ago?"

"That also went into liquidation," said Hamon.

"I'm not thinking so much about the company, and what happened to the company, as of the shareholders."

"You needn't think about them at all, because I was the only shareholder," said Hamon roughly. "If you have come in to make enquiries about my companies, Captain Welling, I'd be very glad if you wouldn't beat about the bush, but tell me plainly what you want to know."

"I want to know nothing," Julius put out his hands in a gesture of deprecation. "I have reached the age, Mr. Hamon, when a man loves to gossip. Dear, dear, dear! It doesn't seem so many years ago that I saw the prospectus of the Rifi Diamond Syndicate and heard about the wonderful stones that had been taken out of that mine, about forty-five miles south-west of Tangier. Did you catch many suckers on that?"

The air of the question was so innocent, the bland voice so even, that for a moment Hamon did not realise its offensiveness.

"What do you mean—suckers?" he stormed. "I tell you none of the shares were issued, or, if they were, none were taken up. Not a penny came from the public. And if you doubt my word, you can see the books. An article appeared in one of the London financial papers, attacking the Syndicate and calling into question the *bona-fides* of the vendors, and sooner than have the slightest scandal attaching to my name, I washed my hands of the whole affair."

"And not a share was issued," said Mr. Welling.

Hamon's attitude was tense; he seemed suddenly to have grown old.

"Not a share," he said defiantly.

Julius Welling sighed, gathered up his umbrella and hat, and rose stiffly to his feet.

"Gracious me!" he said in his mild way. "Then the whole thing is an inexplicable mystery! For, if no shares were issued, why is James Morlake on your trail, Hamon? Why for ten years has he been robbing banks? Why is he a burglar?"

Julius walked to the door, opened it and turned for his final shot.

"Ever meet a sailor on the Portsmouth Road, Hamon?" he drawled, and, as the man staggered under the shock: "You don't meet them often nowadays; they go by railroad! It is safer: there's less chance of being clubbed to death on the cars than on the lonely Portsmouth Road. Think that over!"

CHAPTER XXI

A Volume of Emerson

How much did the old man know, he wondered. Had Morlake told him?

His mind went back to a sunny day in Morocco, and to two men who rode on mule back across the desert toward the blue line of the Rifi Hills. He had been one of these; his guest, a man without a name, had been the other; and as they climbed a sandy slope, a young man had come riding toward them at a gallop and had drawn rein to watch them after they had passed. It was the first time Hamon had ever seen James Lexington Morlake.

And he remembered that he had had a wild and insensate impulse to turn upon the man who was looking after them, and shoot him down. It was one of those atavistic urges which come to civilised men whose animal instincts had not wholly atrophied. The watcher stood for danger—Ralph Hamon brought his hand mechanically to his hip where a gun had hung, and then, with an effort, he merged from the tangle of his dreams and went out to the office, to find his bored secretary waiting.

"I am going now," he said gruffly. "Come to my house tomorrow morning: I shall not be at the office all day. Bring any personal letters and cables."

He had forgotten another person who was waiting, until he was nearly home.

"You told me you were coming straight back," said Lydia furiously, for patience did not appear amongst her known virtues. "I have a dinner engagement with Lady Clareborough. I can give you five minutes."

She was resplendent in evening dress, and he looked at her stupidly.

"You can give me five minutes, can you? Well, I guess that'll be long enough," he said. "Lydia, you don't know this man, Morlake?"

"Morlake?" she said wearily. "Haven't we finished with him?"

"The question is, whether he has finished with me," said Hamon.

The hand that brushed back his scant locks trembled slightly.

"That is the question—whether he's finished with me. You've got to get acquainted with that man. I don't care what money you spend; I don't care how you get to know him. You can see him as soon as you like. But I want to patch up some sort of peace with him, and I think you're more likely to do the trick than I am. You're clever, and you've a good invention. He may be the sort of man who'll fall for a woman like you—there are very few men who wouldn't," he said.

She sighed with elaborate patience.

"What do you mean by 'fall for me'? Do you mean that he'd marry me, or fall in love with me, or what?"

"I don't care what he does so long as you can persuade him to cut out this little vendetta of his."

"Won't the law cut it out?" she asked significantly. "I read the account of the trial and the judge's remarks, and it seems to me that you're going to give yourself a lot of trouble. Besides, Ralph, I do not intend jeopardising the position I've won for myself by making up to a convicted burglar—he's as good as convicted. I have my friends to think of."

There was a steely look in his eye as he interrupted her.

"Go to your dinner, my good girl," he said harshly. "I thought you'd got that social bug out of your head."

She opened her mouth to retort, but the suppressed malignity in his glare silenced her.

Lydia Hamon knew when to quit.

Ralph Hamon was a rich man, with the soul of a miser. He was the kind that treasures odd scraps of useless things, in the hope that one day they may come in handy. His wardrobe overflowed with ancient and almost threadbare clothing that he would not give away. It was his practice in his own home to shed himself of the immaculate attire in which he appeared in public, and take a little further wear out of clothing which had already rendered more than its normal service. He never wasted a scrap of paper if writing space was left upon it; and when people wrote to him on double sheets, he invariably tore off that which had not been used and employed it for note-making.

Jim Morlake had vividly illustrated this weakness when he told him the parable of the monkey and the gourd. Not only was it a weakness, but it promised to be fatal. All that was sane in Ralph Hamon told him to make a fire of one scrap of paper that was in his possession; and yet, though he had made up his mind a dozen times, he was physically incapable of applying a match to its corner.

The library where he worked was on the first floor of the house in Grosvenor Place, and looked out upon a dreary courtyard and the roofs of a string of garages. Though he was nc great reader, three of the walls were covered with bookcases filled with conventional volumes. Any student of human nature would have known that the books had been "furnished" without any respect to their literary quality. There was the inevitable twelve volumes of Scott, the usual encyclopædias, the sets of mid-Victorian authors' works. They were bound in harmony with the room, and their exterior satisfied the eye of the financier, even if their contents made no appeal to him.

There was one book, however, which he had often occasion to take down from a narrow section of the bookshelf covered by glass doors. In this protected area was, amongst other works, a volume of Emerson's Essays, a somewhat portly collection flanked by Hazlitt and volumes of Addison's "Spectator." Slipping the room door bolt into its socket and drawing the curtains, Hamon opened the case and took this handsome volume, which was heavier than a book should be, for he had to use both hands to lift it from the shelf and carry it to the table.

Even now it might be mistaken by the uninitiated for an ordinary volume, for the binding was skilfully imitated and even the marbled edge of the leaves had been reproduced. Selecting a key from a bunch which he carried at the end of a long chain in his pocket, Hamon thrust it between the cover and the "pages" and turned it, and, pulling back the cover, he disclosed a shallow box half filled by papers. The book was of solid armoured steel, and was the repository for such papers as Hamon wished to have near him.

One of those he took out and laid on the desk, looking down at the closely written statement it contained. There was nothing in the words he read but was to his disadvantage. There was imprisonment and possibly death in every line. There was not one word that did not damn him, body and soul, for what he was; and yet, when he took out his matchbox and struck a light with trembling fingers, he hesitated, and finally flung the match into the fireplace and replaced the square paper in the box.

There was a knock at the door, and, hastily shutting down the lid, he pushed the "book" back amongst its fellows, and closed the glass door.

"Who is there?" he asked.

"Will you see Mr. Marborne?" asked the servant in a low voice.

"Yes. Ask him to come in."

He slipped back the bolt and went out on to the landing to meet the disgruntled detective.

"Well, you've made a mess of it, Marborne," he said sourly.

"It's made a mess of me, I can tell you, Hamon," said the other. "I have been asked to turn my coat in. I wish I had never troubled with this damned Morlake."

"There's no sense in bleating," said Hamon impatiently. "What do you mean by 'turning in your coat'?"

He took a bottle of whisky and a syphon from a cupboard and deposited them on his desk.

"Welling told me to do it, and I expect I'm finished. And, anyway, I should have been in bad odour after what the judge said about police methods. You've got to find me a job, Hamon."

"Oh, I have, have I?" sneered the other, pausing with a glass in each hand. "I've *got* to find you a job! Now isn't that the coolest bit of nerve!"

"I don't know who's got the nerves, you or me," said the inspector gruffly, "but——"

"Don't let's quarrel." Hamon poured a frugal portion of whisky into the glass and set the syphon sizzling. "I daresay we can find a place for you; I happen to want a man in Tangier to look after some of my interests. It was not I who got you into trouble, my friend, it was Mr. James Lexington Morlake."

"Damn him!" said Marborne, and swallowed the toast and the contents of the glass at a gulp.

"That's pretty good whisky," suggested Hamon.

"I hardly tasted it," was the reply.

Marborne seated himself at the desk. took out his pocket book and found a sheet of paper, which he opened.

"I have made out a list of my expenses in this business," he said. "Here they are."

He handed them across to the other, and Hamon winced as he read the total.

"That's a bit stiff," he said. "I didn't authorise you to incur this expenditure."

"You told me to spend as much as I liked," said the detective.

"Why, that's nearly a thousand!" spluttered Hamon. "What am I—a child in arms?"

"I don't care what you are, you'll settle that," said the man. "There's a cut for Slone."

"You seem to forget that I've paid you money already——" Hamon began, when there was an interruption.

The butler came to the door and whispered something which Marborne could not catch.

"Here?" said Hamon quickly.

"Yes, sir, downstairs."

Hamon turned to his visitor. His anger had departed.

"He's downstairs," he said.

"He—who?" asked the startled detective. "Do you mean Morlake?"

Hamon nodded.

"You'd better stay here. I'll see him. Leave the door ajar. If there's any fuss, come down."

Jim Morlake was waiting in the hall, and Hamon greeted him with the greatest cordiality.

"Come right in, Morlake," he said, opening the door of the drawing-room. "I can't tell you how pleased I am to read that you were acquitted."

Jim did not answer until he was in the room and the door was shut.

"I've decided to drop my nefarious career, Hamon," he said, coming straight to the point.

"I think you're wise," said the other heartily. "Now is there anything I can do——"

"There's one thing you can do, and that is to give me a certain document, signed by the man with whom I saw you in Morocco some twelve years ago."

"Suppose I had it," said the other after a pause, "do you think I should be fool enough to give it to you, to place my—my liberty in your hands?"

"I would give you ample time to get out of the country, and I would agree not to support the charge made in that document. And without my support and my evidence, the case against you would fall to the ground. At any rate, you would have ample time to get to another country."

Hamon laughed harshly.

"I've no intention of leaving England," he said, "and certainly not now, on the eve of my wedding. I am marrying Lady Joan Carston."

"She has my sympathy," said Jim. "Isn't she Lord Creith's daughter?"

Hamon nodded.

"She'll not marry you without knowing something about you."

"She knows everything about me that she should know."

"Then I must tell her a little that she shouldn't," said Jim. "But your matrimonial adventures are entirely beside the point. I've come to give you a chance, and, incidentally, to save myself a lot of trouble and the serious consequences which would follow a certain line of action on my part. I want that document, Hamon."

Again Hamon laughed.

"You're chasing the wind," he said contemptuously. "And as to this precious document, it has no existence. Somebody has been jollying you and playing upon your well-known simple heart. Now listen, Morlake: can't we settle our differences like gentlemen?"

"I could settle *my* differences like a gentleman," said Jim, "because I happen to have been born that way. But you'll never settle yours, except like a cheap, swindling crook who has climbed over ruined homes to his present heights of prosperity. This is your last chance, and possibly mine. Give me that statement, and I will let up on you."

"I'll see you in hell first," said the other savagely. "Even if I had it—which I haven't——"

Jim nodded very slowly and thoughtfully.

"I see. The monkey's hand remains in the gourd; he's too

greedy to let go." He turned to the door and raised a solemn forefinger. "I warned you, Hamon," he said, and went out.

Hamon closed the door on him and went up the carpeted stairs to the library.

"Well, our friend is still truculent," he said, but he spoke to an empty room.

Marborne had gone. Hamon rang the bell for the butler.

"Did you see Mr. Marborne go?" he asked.

"Yes, sir, he went a few seconds ago—in fact, just before you came from the drawing-room. He seemed rather in a hurry."

"That is very strange," said Hamon, and dismissed the servant.

Then he saw the sheet of paper on the desk with its scribbled message.

If you won't pay my bill, perhaps you'll pay a bigger one [it read].

Hamon scratched his chin. What was the meaning of that cryptic message? Written, he noticed, on his best notepaper. Evidently Marborne was piqued about the questioning of his account, and had gone away in a fit of temper. Hamon shrugged his shoulders and sat down at his desk. He had no time to worry about the pettishness of his tools.

Happening to glance round, he noticed that the door of the glass-fronted bookcase was ajar, and he could have sworn that he had closed it. And then, with an oath, he leapt to his feet.

The steel "book" was in its place, but the title was upside down. Somebody had moved it. He pulled it down and tried the lid, and, to his horror, it opened. He had forgotten to lock it.

He turned over the papers with a trembling hand. The fatal statement was gone!

With a howl of rage he leapt to the door and yelled for the butler.

"Which way did Marborne go?" he asked quickly.

"He went to the right, sir, toward Grosvenor Square," said the butler from the bottom of the stair.

"Get me a taxi—quick!"

Hamon went back into his room, replaced the papers that he had tossed from the box, locked it and pushed it between the books. A minute later, a taxicab was taking him to Mr. Marborne's lodgings.

Marborne had not returned, the landlady told him, and had only that moment telephoned through to say that he would not be coming back that night, as he might be leaving for the Continent.

There was only one thing to do, and that was to go straight to Scotland Yard. The man was still a police officer, and would probably report to headquarters sooner or later. He had the good fortune to find Welling, and the old man seemed in no wise surprised at the visit.

"You want to see Marborne, eh? I'm afraid he's not on duty. I'm even more afraid that he will never be on duty again," said Julius. "Is it anything important?"

"Will he come here at all—to report, I mean?" asked Hamon breathlessly.

"He's certain to come," said the old man. "In fact, he has a very pressing engagement with the Chief Commissioner tomorrow morning."

"Has he any friends? Where does Slone live?"

Julius Welling adjusted his glasses and looked keenly at his visitor.

"You're in a great hurry to find him; is anything wrong?" he asked.

"Yes—no. Nothing of great importance to anybody but myself—and Marborne."

"Indeed!" said Julius politely.

He opened a book and found Slone's address, which he wrote on a piece of paper for the visitor.

"I'm greatly obliged to you, Captain Welling. I didn't expect you'd take this trouble," said Hamon.

"We always do what we possibly can for members of the public," said Julius in a hushed voice.

No sooner had his visitor left than he picked up the automatic telephone and switched to the hall.

"A man named Hamon is coming down," he said briskly. "Tell Sergeant Lavington to tail him up and not to lose sight of him. I want to know where he's going, and what the trouble is."

He put down the telephone and rubbed his thin hands gently together, a far-away look in his eyes.

"And I think there *is* trouble," he said, addressing the ceiling; "bad trouble."

CHAPTER XXII

Welcome Home

JIM MORLAKE had never driven quite so slowly as he did on his way home to Wold House. He could well imagine that Sussex society had been shocked to its depths. The vicars and the churchwardens, the squires and squireens, the heads of noble houses who, on the strength of their neighbourship, had offered him their hospitality, the villagers themselves, sticklers for propriety, would regard his arrest and the judge's remarks as something cataclysmic. He maintained a considerable style in the country. His house was a large one; he employed butler and housekeeper, a dozen maids, cooks and the like, and he had never been quite sure of the number of gardeners who were on his pay roll.

He smiled as he thought of the effect his appearance at the Central Criminal Court would have upon these worthy folk. They were well paid and excellently well treated. His butler, and the butler's wife, who was housekeeper, had grown tremulous in their gratitude for the little services which he had rendered them. What they were thinking now, he could not guess, as he had had no communication with Wold House since his arrest. He had instructed the local bank manager to pay their salaries and such monies as were necessary to carry on the household, and in response he had received only one letter, from the gardener, asking whether it was his wish, in view of recent happenings, that the daffodil bulbs should be planted on the edge of the wood as he had ordered.

The gates of Wold House were open; he turned the car into the drive, and the solemn chauffeur, who was waiting for him, touched his cap respectfully and took charge of the machine with a certain grim thoroughness that was ominous.

Jim passed into his sitting-room. The butler bowed him in and opened the door of the sitting-room for him.

"Is everything all right, William?" asked Jim, as he slowly stripped his gloves and overcoat and handed them to the man.

"Everything is in excellent order, sir," said Mr. William Cleaver, and then: "I should like, at your earliest convenience, to have a word with you, Mr. Morlake."

"As soon as you like," said Jim, sensing the coming exodus. "Take my coat out and come back immediately."

The butler was ill at ease when he returned.

"The truth is, sir," he said, "I am going to ask you tc release me from my engagement. And that—er—applies also to Mrs. Cleaver."

"You wish to leave me, eh? Don't you like the job?"

"It is a very excellent situation," said Cleaver precisely, but withal nervously; "only I find the country does not agree with me, sir, and I have been offered an excellent situation in town."

"Very good," said Jim curtly.

He unlocked the drawer of his desk, opened the cash-box and took out some money.

"Here is your salary to date."

"When would it be convenient for me to go?" asked the butler.

"Now," was the laconic reply. "There is a train to your beloved 'town' in an hour, by which time you will be out of this house. You understand, Cleaver?"

"Yes, sir," said the discomfited servant. "There have been other—er—applications, but I have refused to deal with them."

"I see." Jim nodded. "Send in the eager applicants, please."

First came the cook, a stout woman but genteel to her finger-tips, being an earnest Christian and a member of the Established Church.

"I want to give in my notice, sir."

"Why?" asked Jim bluntly.

"Well, the fact is, my niece is ill and I want to go to her."

"You mean you want to leave at once?"

"I don't want to put you to any inconvenience," the woman hastened to state, "and to oblige you——"

"Oblige nothing," said Jim Morlake. "You will leave now. If your niece is ill, she'll probably be dead by the time your month's notice has expired. Here are your wages."

There came a long procession of them: a parlour-maid, slightly tearful, and obviously acting under the instructions of her rigid parents; another, a little self-righteous and inclined to lift her nose at the very thought of serving a criminal; last came the groom and the chauffeur. Each offered a reason why they wanted to leave in a hurry, but only one spoke the truth. Some had relatives ill, some had been offered good situations; one, at least, hinted at an approaching marriage and the desire to devote the time to "getting things together." Neither man nor woman stated in precise language why he or she was leaving Wold House. None, until a little kitchenmaid, smutty of face and squat of figure, stood before the desk, her big hands on her hips.

"Why are you leaving, Jessie?" asked Jim.

"Because you're a burglar," was the blunt reply, and, leaning back in the chair, he shook with silent laughter.

"I think there is two pounds due to you. Here are five. And may I, a real live burglar, salute you as the only honest member of this little community? Don't look at that note as though it would bite you: it hasn't been forged and it hasn't been stolen."

At last they had gone, all of them, their corded trunks loaded upon a wagon which he had had brought up from the village by telephone, and he walked at its tail and, closing the gates behind the final load, returned to his empty house.

To bring down Binger was worse than useless, besides which, he needed him in London; and Mahmet, though an excellent brewer of coffee, would certainly fail in all other branches of the culinary art. He wandered through the deserted house from kitchen to attic. It was spotlessly clean, and would remain so for a day or two.

"There's only one thing for a sensible man to do," he told himself, and that was to go back to London.

But he was too much of a fighter to shirk even the petty challenge which his domestic staff had thrown out to him. He went down to the lower regions and took stock of the larder. He sought bread and butter and tea. He could have got along without either, but he wanted to know just where he stood.

The principal shop in the village was Colter's Store, which supplied most things, from horse feed to mangles. As his car drew up before the shop, he saw through the window an excited young man pointing, and the bearded Mr. Colter emerged from his tiny office at the end of the counter. Jim got down from the car at leisure and strolled into the shop.

"Good morning," he said. "I want you to send some bread up to Wold House, and a couple of pounds of butter. I think I shall also want some eggs."

Mr. Colter pushed his assistant out of his way and confronted his customer from the other side of the counter, and there was a light in Mr. Colter's eyes which spoke eloquently of his righteousness.

"I'm not sending bread or anything else up to your house, Mr. Morlake," he said. "I've kept my hands clean of tainted money all my life, and I'm not going to start truckling with thievery and burglary at my time of life!"

Jim took the cigar from between his lips, and his eyes narrowed.

"Does that mean that you refuse to serve me?"

"That's just what it means," said Mr. Colter, glaring at him through his powerful spectacles. "And I'll tell you something more, Mr. Morlake: that the sooner you take your custom and yourself from Creith, the better we shall like it."

Jim looked round the store.

"You do a fairly big trade here, don't you, Colter?" he asked.

"An honest trade," said Mr. Colter emphatically.

"I mean, this business is worth something to you? I'll buy it from you."

Mr. Colter shook his head, and at that moment his stout partner, who had been a silent audience of the encounter, emerged from the door leading into the parlour.

"We don't want your money; we neither sell nor buy," she said shrilly. "It's quite enough to have burglars living like gentlemen, without their trying to corrupt decent, honest, God-fearing people."

"Oh, I'm glad there's somebody you fear," said Jim, and walked out of the house.

His bank was almost opposite, and bankers have few prejudices.

"Glad to see you got out of your trouble, Mr. Morlake," said the manager briskly. "By the way, the police examined your account—you know that?"

"And failed to find any connection between my various robberies and my unbounded affluence," smiled Jim. "Now listen, friend: the last time I was here, you were trying to induce me to take an interest in village house property. I notice that the store next to Colter's is empty."

The manager nodded.

"It fell in under a mortgage. The owner tried to run a garage, but Creith doesn't lie on the road to anywhere, and he went broke in a month. Do you want to buy?"

"Name a price, and let it be reasonable. Imagine you're negotiating with the Archbishop of Canterbury, and forget that I am an opulent burglar," said Jim.

An hour later, he walked out of a lawyer's office the proprietor of the store.

At ten o'clock that night there arrived from London a young and energetic man.

"I 'phoned the Grocers' Association for you, and they tell me that you're something of a live wire."

"Undoubtedly I am," said the youth immodestly.

"There's a store next to Colter's in the village. I want you to take charge of that to-morrow morning; get in carpenters and painters, and stock it with every article that Colter sells. Mark down all the prices twenty-five per cent. below his. Get a van and beat up the country for custom. If he lowers his price, you lower yours, you understand? But anyway, keep it a standard twenty-five under."

"That'll cost money," said the young man.

"You probably have never heard of me. My name is Morlake, and I am by profession a burglar. My capital is therefore unlimited," said Jim soberly. "If there is any need to bring new capital into the business, just notify me and I'll take my gun and a bag and raise debentures at the nearest bank."

He had biscuits, tea and a large slice of ham for dinner; for supper, he had biscuits and tea without the ham; and in the morning, when he went in search of a breakfast menu, he rejected all other combinations than tea and biscuits. It was a little monotonous, but satisfactory. In his shirt sleeves he swept his room and the hall, made his own bed, and scrubbed down the broad steps at the front of the house. He began to sympathise with the housemaids who had left him.

All day long, strange trolleys had been dashing into the village, and a small army of carpenters and painters from a neighbouring town, men who thought it no disgrace to work for sinners, but rather prided themselves upon the distinction of being in the employ of a gentleman who had figured at the Old Bailey, were working at top speed, to convert the drab and uninhabitable garage into a store. The live wire was tingling. Stocks were arriving every hour. Mr. Colter stood before his door, one hand in the pocket of his apron, the other fingering his beard.

"It will be a nine days' wonder," he said to an audience of his neighbours. "These here-to-day-and-gone-to-morrow people! Why, I've had competition and beat 'em this past thirty years!"

By the afternoon the printing had been delivered, and the neighbouring villages learnt of sensational and permanent reductions in the price of almost every commodity. Mr. Colter went to the police station to seek legal advice, and was referred to a lawyer by the police sergeant, who wasn't quite sure of his ground, and certainly had no knowledge of the legal aspect of this undercutting process. It was the first time in his life he had ever paid a penny to a lawyer, but the occasion demanded extraordinary expenditure, and it did not seem to Mr. Colter that he received value for his money when he was told that he could do nothing.

"To talk about conspiracy is absurd," said the man of law. "There is nothing to prevent this new fellow from giving his goods away."

"But a burglar's money is behind this scandalous business!" wailed Mr. Colter.

"If it was a murderer, it would make no difference," said the lawyer with satisfaction.

Colter, after consultation with his wife, put on his coat and went up to Wold House. He found Jim in the hall, sitting on a stair with an array of silver at his feet which he was polishing.

"Sit down," said Jim politely, and Mr. Colter looked round. "You can sit on the floor, or you can go up one stair higher than me and sit there. I can hear you quite well, and it isn't necessary that I should see your face."

"Now see here, Mr. Morlake, I think this business has gone a bit too far. You know you're taking the bread and butter out of my mouth?"

"I know you denied me those self-same commodities," said Jim, "and others," he added.

"I am going to his lordship to-morrow. I am going to see if the Earl of Creith will allow one of his neighbours to be robbed of his livelihood. Not that you will," said Mr. Colter. "I have friends in this neighbourhood of forty years' standing! I've got the whole community behind me!"

"You watch 'em walk in front of you when the twenty-five per cent. reduction comes into operation!" said Jim.

"It's the most scandalous thing that has ever happened in the history of the world!" screamed the tradesman.

"You have forgotten the Massacre of the Huguenots," said Jim, "and Nero's lion parties, and a few other indelicate happenings."

Mr. Colter went back to the village, drew up a statement of his position, which was printed by a misguided stationer, and distributed it to every house in the village—misguided because the next morning brought a letter from a Horsham lawyer demanding that the name of the printer's legal representative be sent him, as his client intended to commence an action for libel.

Tea and dry biscuits were beginning to pall on Jim, when he found, that same morning, an unexpected cache of eggs. He could not be bothered to light the kitchen fire; he found a stove and a supply of spirit, and this he set up in his somewhat untidy study. He had brewed the tea, and had laid the table with a copy of the morning newspaper, and set about cooking the eggs. He knew little about egg cooking, except that a certain amount of heat, a certain number of eggs and a frying-pan were requisite. The room was grey with smoke and pungent with the odour of a burnt pan when the unexpected visitor arrived.

She came through the open door and stood in the doorway, open-mouthed, watching his primitive essay in cookery.

"Oh, what are you doing?" she asked in consternation, and, running across the room, took the smoking abomination from his hand. "You have put no fat in the pan!" she said. "How can you expect to cook eggs without some kind of grease?"

He was speechless with amazement. The last person he expected to see at Wold House, in this moment of crisis, was Jane Smith. Yet Jane Smith it was, prettier than ever in her plain blue suit, her big white Peter Pan collar, and the little black hat.

"Where the dickens did you come from?"

"I came from the village," she said, wrinkling her nose with an expression of distaste. "Phew! Open the window."

"Why, don't you like eggs?"

"Did these eggs express any wish to be cremated?"

He made no move.

"I suppose you know——"

"I know everything." She blew out the spirit fire and put down the pan, then, taking off her coat and hat, she threw them on the sofa. "I have come to look after you," she said, "you poor American waif!"

CHAPTER XXIII

The New Housekeeper

Obediently he carried down the spirit lamp, cups and saucers and cracked teapot to the kitchen, and stood in awe, watching her as she kindled a fire in the big kitchen range.

"Let me do that for you," he said.

"You ought to have volunteered hours ago," she reproached him, "but if you had, I shouldn't have allowed you. You would only have made a lot of smoke——"

"Fire lighting is an art: I never realised it till now. Does your mother know you're here?" he asked suddenly.

"I hope so," she said. "Mother is in heaven."

"Your father?"

"Father is in London, which is quite a different place. Look in the larder and see if you can find some lard."

"That seems to be the proper place for it," he said.

"Have you any milk?" she asked, when he returned with a large white and bulbous supply.

"We have no milk, but we've lots of preserved milk."

"Haven't you a cow?"

He shook his head.

"I'm not sure whether I have or whether I haven't. I've really never taken an interest in the details of my estate, but I'm under the impression that I am entirely cowless."

"Why do you stay here?" She was sitting on her heels before the crackling fire, looking up at him curiously. "Why didn't you go back to London? You've got a flat, haven't you?"

"I prefer staying here," he said.

"How lordly! I prefer staying here." She mimicked him. "You're going to starve to death here, my good man, and freeze to death too. You ought to know that the people of Creith would never consent to stain their white souls by contact with a gentleman with *your* seamy past! Get some servants from London: they're less particular. They have cinemas in London that educate them in the finger nuances of criminality. Why don't you bring your man down—Binger?"

"Binger?" he said in surprise. "Do you know him?"

"I've spoken with him," she said. "When you were in durance I made a call on him, to see if there was anything I could do. It required a great deal of tact because I wasn't supposed to know that you were under arrest. I asked him where you were, and he said you were 'hout.' "

"Instead of which I was hin!" laughed Jim.

"Hout or hin, he was deliciously diplomatic. And I saw your Moor, and your beautiful room. Did you live in Morocco?"

"For a short time," he said.

She was busy with the eggs for a little while, and he saw she was thinking deeply.

"Of course, you know why this antagonism has sprung up in the village against you? It isn't wholly spontaneous, or due to the purity of Creith's morals. A week ago, Mr. Hamon came down and interviewed most of the leading tradespeople, and I believe he also saw your butler. I know, because my maid, who lives in the village——"

"Your what?" he asked sharply.

"Maid—it is short for maiden aunt," she said, not so much as dropping an eyelid. "My maiden aunt, who lives in the village and who is something of a gossip, told me."

"You were here, then?"

"No, I was in London at the time. She told me when I came back. There are your eggs."

"I couldn't possibly eat three," he protested.

"It is not intended that you should: one is for me," she replied.

She went into the hall and brought down a bag, and extracted a new loaf and a small oblong brick of butter.

"We will dine in the kitchen, because I feel more at home there," she said. "And after breakfast I am going to see what needs doing. I can only stay a few hours every day."

"Are you coming to-morrow?" he said eagerly.

She nodded, and he sighed his relief.

"The curious thing was that I didn't see you come at all,

though I was looking through the window and I had a good view of the drive."

"I didn't arrive by the road," she said. "I discovered a little foot bridge across the river that joins Creith Park and your meadows. Naturally, I still retain a certain amount of self-respect, so I came furtively."

He laughed at that.

"If you're trying to make me believe that you care two cents what the village is thinking of you, you're working on a hopeless job," he said. "What puzzles me is"—he hesitated—"you may be a villager: I daresay you are; in fact, you must be, otherwise you wouldn't know so much about the people. But that you're a member of the downtrodden working classes, I will never believe."

"Go and find the carpet-sweeper," she ordered, "and I will show you that, if I'm not downtrodden, I'm certainly a labourer."

It seemed to him that she had hardly been there ten minutes before she came to the study, dressed ready to go.

"You're not going already!" he gasped in dismay.

"Yes, I am," she nodded, "and you will be good enough to stay where you are and not attempt to follow me. And I also rely upon you that you do not ask any of your village acquaintances—which, I should imagine, are very few by now—who I am or who my relations are. I want to keep the name of Smith unsullied. It is a fairly good name."

"I know of none better," he said enthusiastically. "Good-night, Jane."

He held out a hand, and was unaccountably thrilled to see the faint pink that came to her face.

"There is one favour I'm going to ask you in return for my services, and it is that you call off your campaign of vengeance; in other words, that you leave poor Colter alone. He is acting according to his lights, and it isn't going to give you any great satisfaction to ruin him."

"I've been thinking of that to-day," said Jim a little ruefully, "and wondering exactly what I can do. I don't like to strike my colours and leave the enemy triumphant."

"He's not at all triumphant: the poor man's scared to death. I can tell you all his secret history. He has been speculating in oil shares, at the suggestion of Mr. Hamon (I expect Mr. Hamon has an interest in the company) and the poor man is on the verge of bankruptcy. You have only to open your store and run it for a week, to push him over the edge—plunk! That is vulgar," she added penitently, "but will you think it over, Mr. Morlake? I don't know whether you can afford to withdraw, but I think you can."

An hour after the girl had left, Jim walked down to the village and into Colter's Store. A very humble Mr. Colter hastened to discover his needs.

"I want bread, butter and eggs," said Jim firmly. "I want them delivered every morning, with a quart of milk and such other commodities as I require."

"Yes, sir," said the humble Colter. "This store of yours, Mr. Morlake, is going to ruin me—I've had three farmers here today; they are supposed to be thorough gentlemen and friends of mine, but they're holding up their winter buying until your shop is open. They say that isn't the reason, but I know 'em!"

"The store will never open so long as I have my eggs, butter, bread and milk," said Jim patiently. "Is that understood?"

"Yes, sir," said the fervent storekeeper, and showed him to the door.

That night the young enthusiast was sent back to London after selling his stocks to Colter below cost price; and when Jim came down in the morning and opened the front door, he found Mr. Colter's boy sitting on the steps.

Jane Smith came late that morning, and something in her appearance arrested his attention.

"You've been crying," he said.

"No, I haven't. I've had very little sleep, that is all."

"You've been crying," he repeated.

"If you say that again, I won't stay. You're really annoying, and I never thought you would be that."

This silenced him, but he was worried. Had she got into some kind of scrape through this escapade of hers? He never troubled to believe that she was a housemaid. Probably she was some poor relation of one of the big families in the neighbourhood. There were many little villas and tiny half-acre lots scattered about the countryside.

They were eating a rather dismal lunch together when he asked her plainly:

"Where do you live?"

"Oh, somewhere around," she said vaguely.

"Do you ever speak the truth, young woman?"

"I was the most truthful person in the world until I——" She checked herself suddenly.

"Until you——?" he suggested.

"Until I started lying. It is very easy, Mr. Raffles."

"Oh, by the way"—he remembered suddenly—"two of the housemaids of this establishment came and interviewed me this morning whilst you were making the beds. They want to come back."

"Don't have them," she said hastily. "If you do, I shall go."

And, conscience stricken at her selfishness, she added quickly:

"Yes, get them if you can. I think you ought to get your servants back as soon as you possibly can. They're only following the lead of Cleaver, and most of them will be dying to get back, because there's a whole lot of unemployment in the county. Only—I should like you to let me know before they come."

He helped her to wash up after lunch, and then went upstairs to his study to write some letters, whilst she laid his dinner before she left. The kitchen stairs led into the back hall, and he was more than surprised, when he turned a corner of the stairs, to see a girl standing in the entrance hall. He had left the door wide open, and either he had not heard her ring, or she had not taken the trouble to push the bell. She was very pretty, he saw at a glance, and fashionably dressed, and he wondered if it was a delegation from the women of Sussex demanding his instant withdrawal from the country.

Flashing a smile at him, she came toward him.

"You're Mr. Morlake, I know," she said, as he took her hand. "I've seen your photograph. You don't know me."

"I'm afraid I haven't that advantage," said Jim, and showed her into the drawing-room.

"I simply had to come and see you, Mr. Morlake. This stupid feud of yours with my brother mustn't go on any longer."

"Your brother?" he asked in wonder, and she laughed roguishly.

"Now don't pretend that you don't dislike poor Ralph very intensely."

A light was beginning to show.

"Then you are Miss Hamon?" he said.

"Of course I'm Miss Hamon! I came over from Paris specially to see you. Ralph is terribly worried about this *frightful* quarrel you're carrying on."

"I suppose he is," said Jim subtly. "And you have come all the way from Paris to patch up our feud, have you? Of course you're Lydia Hamon. How stupid of me! I remember you years and years ago, before the days of your brother's prosperity."

Lydia Hamon had not the slightest desire to be remembered years and years ago, and she turned him off that dangerous topic.

"Now tell me, Morlake, isn't it possible for you and Ralph to get together, as you delightful Americans say, and——"

The door opened abruptly, and Jane Smith came in. She was dressed for going home and was pulling on her gloves.

"I thought you were in your study," she began and then her eyes fell upon the visitor.

If the apparition of Lydia Hamon startled her, the effect on Lydia was staggering. She raised a pair of unnecessary lorgnettes and surveyed the girl with a look of horror.

"Surely I'm not mistaken?" she said. "It is Lady Joan Carston!"

"Damn!" said Joan.

CHAPTER XXIV

Jim Learns Things

LADY JOAN CARSTON! Jim could not believe his ears.

"Surely you are mistaken, Miss Hamon?" he said. "This lady is Miss——" He stopped.

"This lady is Lady Joan Carston, and I am delighted to see that you are such good friends. I'm sure my brother's fiancée will be only too happy to help me in my little scheme to make you and Ralph better friends."

"Who is your brother's fiancée?" asked Joan, electrified by this cool claim.

"It is generally understood that you are," smiled Lydia sweetly.

"It may be understood in lunatic asylums, where many people are even under the impression that they are related to Napoleon Bonaparte," said Joan sharply, "but it is certainly not understood either by me or by my father. And we should be the first to know."

Lydia shrugged her shoulders. She was trying to find an explanation of the girl's presence in this house and from her viewpoint only one explanation was possible. And then it began to dawn on her that the house was empty, save for these two people, and her attitude, her manner and her voice became instantly stiffened by the shock.

"I suppose your father is here, Lady Joan?" she asked primly.

"My father is not at Creith," replied the girl, who saw what she was driving at. "Nor is my aunt, nor any of my cousins. In fact, I have no other chaperone at Wold except the kitchen stove and a sense of my immense superiority."

The eyebrows of the red-haired girl went up to points.

"I don't think Ralph would like this——" she began.

"There are so many things that Ralph doesn't like"—it was Jim who stepped into the breach and saved Joan Carston from the humiliation of apologising for the things she undoubtedly would have said—"but I shouldn't bother to catalogue them. I don't think, Miss Hamon, that we need trouble Lady Joan with the old family feud."

He turned to the girl and held out his hand.

"I am extremely grateful to you," he said. "That is a very banal thing to say, but it expresses completely just how I feel."

He expected to find her embarrassed, but she was coolness itself, and he marvelled at her self-possession.

"I think you had better go in search of your housemaids," she said with a twinkle in her eyes, "and arrange for them to come to you to-morrow afternoon at two o'clock."

She emphasised the words, and a weight rolled from his heart, for he knew that Joan Carston would be there to breakfast.

Lydia watched the girl as she walked down the drive.

"Then it is true that Lady Joan is engaged to you?" she asked, and Jim's jaw dropped. "She told me so, but I thought she was being—well, annoying."

"Engaged to me?" he gasped. "Did—did she say so?"

Lydia smiled contemptuously.

"Of course, it wasn't true, though it might have been, judging by her indiscretion. She is a friend of yours?"

"A great friend," said Jim vaguely, "but only in the sense that Lady Bountiful is a friend of the bedridden villager."

"You, of course, being the bedridden villager?"

She forced a smile, but he saw in her face something of the emotion she was endeavouring to suppress, as the object of her visit came back to her.

"Seriously, Mr. Morlake," she drawled, "don't you think it is time that your stupid quarrel with Ralph came to an end?"

"Do I understand that you are an ambassador bearing olive branches?" he asked, a little amused. "Because, if you are, I suppose, like all ambassadors, you have something to offer me besides an intangible friendship, and that of a very doubtful quality."

She walked across to the door and closed it, and then, coming nearer, said in a low voice:

"Ralph said that you wanted something that he had—he no longer has it!"

Jim frowned down at her.

"Has he destroyed it?"

"He no longer has it," repeated the girl. "It is in other hands."

He stared at her incredulously.

"Do you seriously mean that?"

She nodded.

"Then how does it come about that your brother is at large?" he asked, and she flamed up at that.

"I don't know what you mean, Mr. Morlake. 'At large?' Do you mean that my brother should be in prison?"

"He should be in prison, anyway," said Jim calmly. "But if the document—and I take it you are referring to a certain document—has fallen into other hands, then most certainly, unless the finder is a thief and a blackmailer, your brother should be waiting his trial."

It was very evident to him that she had been speaking in the dark, and that she had no idea of the nature of the missing paper.

"What does he want me to do?" he went on.

"He particularly wants your friendship," she said. "He asked me to tell you that there is no difference between you which cannot be smoothed over."

"In other words, if the gentleman who has the statement in his hands brings it to light, your brother wishes me to testify in his favour?"

She hesitated.

"I don't know whether that is what he wishes—perhaps it is. He did not tell me any more than I have told you, that the something which you wanted had passed out of his hands, and he asked for your friendship."

Jim walked to the window and looked out, trying to solve the riddle she had set him; and all the time there ran through the web of his thoughts the more amazing discovery that Jane Smith was Joan Carston, the daughter of the Earl of Creith, and, from his standpoint, an unapproachable person.

That was the first of the many surprises that awaited James Morlake.

"I don't see what I can do," he said, turning back to Lydia. "The feud, as you prefer to call it, between your brother and myself is dependent upon his making reparation. You may tell him that."

"Then it is to be war?" she said, a little dramatically.

He smiled, and was serious again instantly.

"Yes, I'm afraid it is to be war."

She bit her lip, thinking quickly. Her instructions had been more or less vague, and Ralph Hamon had left to her the actual method by which she would carry his suggestions into effect. There was an alternative attitude for her to take, and she decided that the moment had come to initiate the new rôle.

"Do you know what this means to me, his only sister?" she asked with a little catch in her voice. "Do you realise what it means to lie awake night after night, thinking, worrying, terrified of what the morning will bring forth?"

"I'm sorry that I don't. Honestly, Miss Hamon, I am not sympathetic. If it is true that you feel these misgivings and emotions—well, that is unfortunate."

He walked up and stood squarely before her.

"You may take this message to your brother, Lydia Hamon—that I am in this to the very end. I have risked consequences more fearful than any you can picture, and I go on until my mission is completed."

"A burglar with a mission!" she sneered.

"Rather amusing, isn't it?" he said good-humouredly.

If he had any doubts as to her sincerity, those doubts were now dispelled. The woman was an actress and a bad one; she could not sustain the pose of distress at the continuance of the "feud," or hide the chagrin of her failure.

"You've had your chance, Morlake," she said, the venom in her coming out. "I don't know what this trouble is between you and Ralph, but he's too clever for you, and sooner or later you'll admit it. I'm sick of the whole business! If Ralph's a crook, what are you? Aren't there enough pickings in the world for both of you?"

"Spoken like a little lady," said Jim Morlake, as he showed her to the door.

CHAPTER XXV

The Cablegram

IN A week a remarkable change had come over Ralph Hamon. There were times when he appeared to his sister to be a little old man. He was greyer, new lines had appeared in his forbidding face, and he seemed to stoop more. Lydia, wise in her generation, did not attempt to probe too deeply into the cause. To her surprise, when she had reported the result of her interview with Morlake, he had not, to use her own expression, gone up in the air, but had accepted her account of the talk with the greatest calmness. Even her little titbit about Joan Carston's presence at Wold House had not aroused him.

She went to his office that day after her interview with Jim, her baggage at the station, her railway ticket and reservation in her handbag.

"I'm going back to Paris this afternoon," she said airily, "and I want a little money."

He looked up at her.

"Who told you you were going back to Paris?" he asked, and her simulated surprise did not impress him. "You're staying in London until I ask you to go. I told you that a week ago. It may be necessary for us to move, and move pretty quick."

"What is wrong?" she asked, realising for the first time the immense seriousness of the position. "Are things very bad?" she asked.

"As bad as they can be," said Hamon, and added: "for the moment. You see, Lydia," he went on in a kindlier tone, "I don't want to be left quite alone at this moment. You're part of the baggage. And besides"—he hesitated—"I promised Sadi that I would take you out to Tangier."

She did not speak until she had pulled a chair up to the table and sat down opposite him, her elbows on the desk, her eyes fixed on his.

"Have you promised Sadi anything more?" she asked.

He avoided her gaze.

"Five or six years ago you were very keen on my living at Tangier," she said. "Why? What have you promised Sadi?"

"Nothing, directly. You used to like him, Lydia."

She made a little face.

"He interested me, naturally. Any young girl would be interested in a picturesque Moor—and, from what you tell me, he isn't even picturesque any longer. Besides, I've got my values in order."

"Sadi is very useful to me—extremely useful. He belongs to one of the first Moorish families, he is a Christian—at least, he's supposed to be—and he's rich."

She smiled contemptuously.

"So rich that he draws a quarterly allowance from you! No, Ralph, you can't bluff me. I know all about Sadi, as much as I want to know. He's just a tricky Moor; and if you expect me to play Desdemona to him, you've got another guess coming. Othello was never a favourite play of mine. He is very amusing, I daresay, and he is quite a big person in Tangier, and he may be a Christian, though I doubt it. But I'm not going to be Number Twenty-three in his establishment, and the Lord didn't intend me to end my days in an unventilated harem, even though I become the pearl of great price and the principal wife of the Shereef Sadi Hafiz. I've been reading a few books on the subject lately," she went on, "and I understand that there's a whole lot of romance in the desert, but, to anybody who's sniffed the Near East, there's not enough romance to compensate for one bad smell. The last weeks I was in Paris I had several letters from you, Ralph, talking about the languorous joys of Morocco, and I've had it in my mind to ask you just what you were thinking about."

"Sadi is very fond of you," he said awkwardly. "And these

marriages often turn out well. He is a man well thought of by the Government, and he has more decorations than a general."

"If he was as well decorated as a Christmas tree, he wouldn't appeal to me," said she decisively, "so let us consider that matter settled finally."

She was secretly astonished that he accepted her very plain talk without protest.

"Have it your own way," he said, "but you'll have to stay in London, Lydia, until I'm through with this other business."

After she had gone, he made an effort to work, but without success. From time to time he glanced at the clock on his desk, as though he were expecting some visitor. A cable from Tangier had come that morning, and once or twice he took it from his pocket-book and read it over gravely. Sadi's impecuniosity was no new experience, but this last demand was interesting in view of possible contingencies.

A small and frugal lunch was served in his office, and after it was cleared away he rang for his clerk, and taking his cheque-book from the safe, wrote reluctantly.

"Take this to the bank and bring the money back in fives."

The well-trained clerk did not whistle when he saw the figures, for he was used to dealing with large sums, but seldom had Mr. Hamon drawn actual cash to that amount.

He returned in half-an-hour with three stout packages, which Hamon did not even trouble to count.

"I am expecting Mr. Marborne," he said, as he put the money away in a drawer. "Show him right in."

Marborne was due at half-past two. It was nearer three when he swaggered into the office, a marvellously transformed man, for he was dressed in what he conceived to be the height of fashion, and added to the outrage of a crimson tie a grey top-hat. He took the big cigar from his teeth and nodded jovially at the watchful man behind the desk.

"'Morning, Hamon! Sorry I'm a bit late, but I had one or two calls to make."

He had been drinking: Hamon was quick to notice this. On the whole, he preferred to deal with people who drank. One of his stock arguments against prohibition was that it put the habitually sober at a disadvantage with the occasionally drunk.

"Got the money, old man?"

Without a word, Hamon opened the drawer and threw the notes on to the table.

"Thanks," said Marborne, who invariably developed gentility in his cups. "How does it feel, having a family retainer, eh?"

Hamon leant his elbows on the table and glared across at the blackmailer.

"See here, Marborne, I'm willing to finance you up to the limit, but you've got to keep your promise."

"I don't remember having made any," said the other coolly. "I told you that your little secret was safe with me. You aren't going to kick about expenses again, are you?" he asked humorously. "I've got a position to keep up. Thanks to working for you, I've been kicked out of the police force without my pension, and so has Slone. You would have left us to starve if I hadn't had a bit of luck and a naturally prying disposition."

"Where have you left that—that paper? Suppose it falls into somebody else's hands?" asked Hamon, and Marborne laughed.

"Do you think I'm such a fool that I'd throw away a good living?" he asked contemptuously.

Unconsciously he pressed his hand to his left side. It was an involuntary movement, but it did not escape the attention of Hamon.

"It is in a safe," said Marborne loudly, "burglar-proof and fire-proof, and I am the only person that's got the key. See?"

"I see," said Hamon, and was almost cheerful when he opened the door to facilitate his visitor's departure.

He came back to his desk, and without hesitation took a cable form and addressed a message to "Colport, Hotel Cecil, Tangier." There was only one possible solution to the tyranny of Marborne. He must go the way of the unknown sailor whom a cyclist had found dying on the Portsmouth Road.

CHAPTER XXVI

Joan Called Jane

NOT since that night of storm had Joan seen the lodger at Mrs. Cornford's cottage. She had purposely avoided her visitor, and with that extraordinary determination which was part of her character, had ruled out her vision and knowledge as a bad dream, something hideous born of the storm.

Once in the middle of the night she woke up to the stark reality of fact. In the morning Jim had seen traces of the despair that had entered her heart, and had wondered, and, wondering, had been troubled.

On the morning that was to see her final visit to Wold House, her maid came into her room as she was dressing.

"Mrs. Cornford wishes to see you," she said, and Joan paled.

"You're a great coward," she said aloud.

"Me, my lady?" asked the astonished girl.

"No, me, Alice. I'll be down in a few minutes."

There are certain disadvantages about putting things out of your mind. The reactions are apt to be a little drastic, and Joan was inwardly quaking when she came into the presence of her guest.

"I heard that you were back, and I came to ask whether Lord Creith would grant me a lease of the cottage, Lady Joan."

"Is that all?" said Joan, immeasurably relieved. "Of course he will, Mrs. Cornford. Are you settling in Creith?"

Mrs. Cornford hesitated.

"I think so," she said. "Mr. Farringdon is doing so well that he wants me to stay. He has made me a very handsome offer, and I can afford to give up my music teaching."

"Mr. Farringdon?" Joan's voice trembled a little. "He is your lodger, isn't he? The young man who—who drinks. Where did he come from?"

"I don't know. He was on the West Coast of Africa for some time. He got into some scrape in England, and his people sent him abroad when he was very young—he was expelled from his school for an escapade."

"Did he tell you what it was?"

She waited, holding her breath.

"No—he just said that he did something pretty bad. He took to drink on the Coast, and drifted back to England. His father died and left him an annuity. Would you like to meet him?"

"No!"

The refusal was so abrupt and so emphatic that Joan saw she had hurt the woman.

"No, my dear—I don't want to meet him—my nerves are a little on edge with recent happenings in this neighbourhood."

"You mean Mr. Morlake. How very terrible that was! His servants have left him, they tell me. I almost volunteered to look after him. Mr. Farringdon saw him on the night of his arrival."

"I know he did," said the girl, and corrected herself hastily. "I'm told he did."

Mrs. Cornford left her a little thoughtful. She must go back to London and stay there, even though she left the American burglar to subsist on raw eggs!

. . . . .

There were two strange men in the village. Joan saw them long before the gossips of Creith told her that they were young business men spending a holiday in the country. She saw them as they rode into the village on the previous afternoon, two healthy-looking men who seemed to find time hanging on their hands.

When she came to Wold House to cook the breakfast (it was half-past nine when she appeared) she mentioned her discovery.

Jim Morlake nodded.

"Yes—Sergeant Finnigan and Detective Spooner from headquarters. I saw them arrive the night after I returned. They came by the last train and were driven over from the station in a car belonging to the local police."

He saw the concern in her face and laughed.

"You didn't imagine that the police would drop me as an unprofitable subject, did you? Welling sent them to make a study of my habits. They will be here for at least another week—I thought of asking them up to dinner one night. I guess the food they get at the Red Lion doesn't wholly satisfy them."

She made no reply, turning instantly to another matter.

"I shall not come again. I think you can gather your domestic staff. I saw Cleaver in the village yesterday and he was almost tearful at the thought of losing a good job."

"He's lost it," said Jim grimly. "He's fixed—permanently! He is the one man I'll never have."

"When he asks to return, you must take him back," she said. "Don't be feeble! Of course he must come back."

"Must he?—Well, if you say——"

"It isn't what I say. Don't shield your weaknesses behind me. You'll take him back because you can't quarrel with servants any more than you can quarrel with poor Mr. Colter."

She heard him chuckle, and frowned.

"Forgive my unseemly mirth, Lady Joan," he said penitently, "but I haven't been bullied for—oh, a long time! I'll take Cleaver or anybody else. Why did you tell Lydia——"

He stopped, and she paused, fry-pan in hand, to shoot a questioning glance at him.

"Tell her—what?"

"Oh, nothing . . . I suppose you said it to annoy her. She thinks so anyhow."

He found himself confused; he could feel the colour going to his face, and the more he tried to control this ridiculous display the more incoherent of speech and *gauche* of manner he became.

"You mean that I told her I was engaged to you?" she said calmly. "Yes, I did. I wanted to shock her, and yours was the first name that occurred to me—you don't mind?"

"Mind . . . ? Well, I should say not . . . !"

"I hoped you wouldn't. When I remembered, after I had left you, that I had confided my awful secret to Lydia Hamon, I had ten million fits."

Skilfully she lifted the eggs from the pan and laid them on the dish.

"I was afraid that I had hopelessly compromised you—*you're* married, of course?"

"I am *not* married," he said violently, "and have never been married."

"Most nice people are," she said with such indifference that his heart sank; "and I suppose you *are* nice . . . yes, I'm sure you are. Don't put your elbow on the egg—thank you!"

He had no mind for eggs. He hated eggs: the sight of a yolk made him shudder.

"I am sorry you are Lady Joan. I liked Jane . . . I like Joan too, immensely. There was a girl in Springfield, Connecticut, that I knew——"

"Is it necessary to tell me about your early love affairs?" she asked. "I am too young to be interested."

"This was not a love affair," he protested hotly. "Her name was Joan, and she called me Jim. Her father was an Alderman."

"My name is Joan, and if you wish to call me Joan don't let anything stand in your way," she said, seating herself at the kitchen table. "I may even call you Jim, but father has a pet Persian cat he calls Jim, and if I called you that I'd expect you to *mew!* I don't like Lexington—it is too much like the name of a railway station. And I don't like Morlake. I had better call you nothing. . . . About this engagement of ours. I wonder if you would mind if I did not break it off for a week or so? Mr. Hamon has views about me and my future."

"But suppose he carries this ridiculous story to your father?" he asked, aghast.

" 'Ridiculous story' would have come better from me," she said coldly, "but as you got in first, it is due to my father to say that he would be amused. I was worried at first for fear the story got into the newspapers."

"Why has Hamon such a pull in this part of the country?" he asked.

She told him very frankly just how Mr. Hamon's local interests had developed, and he whistled.

"So you see, our title is rather a hollow mockery. The real Lord of Creith is Hamon, and I am his handmaiden. He wants to marry me, just as all bad men in stories want to marry the daughter of the ruined earl. To make the story complete, I should be madly in love with the poor but honest farmer who is the real heir to the estate. But all the farmers round here are rich, and daddy says that there isn't one he'd trust with a waggon load of wurzels."

He could not keep his eyes from her as he listened, fascinated. It was not her beauty that held him, nor her breathtaking self-possession, nor the humour behind irony. A little of each perhaps, but something else. He remembered the morning—was it yesterday?—that she had come with the unmistakable evidence of tears in her eyes. This hard, practical side of her, this flippancy of comment, was not the real Joan Carston She puzzled him a lot, and frightened him too.

"Don't stare, James—that is better than Jim, but rather on the footman side—it is very rude to stare. I wanted to ask you something too . . . what was it? I know! Last night I borrowed a pair of night glasses from Peters. From my window I can see Wold House. At night there is a yellow blob of light which I couldn't identify. With the glasses I saw that it was the library window. And I saw your shadow passing and repassing across the white blind. Why do you have white shades, James? You need not answer that. You were still walking up and down when I went to bed at one o'clock. I watched you for an hour . . . why are you laughing?"

"Finnigan and Spooner watched for longer," he said between paroxysms. "They made a special report on my restlessness. I guess that."

"How do you know—that they were watching, I mean?"

"After it was dark I laid down 'trip wires,' only I used black thread," he said. "Every thread was broken this morning. So was the cotton I pegged across the gate, which I left unlocked. On the path under the window I laid down sheets of brown paper covered with bird lime—I found them on the road this morning."

Her eyes danced with joy.

"The boy who cleans the boots at the Red Lion is a friend of mine. I went down early this morning and found him scraping the sticky stuff off Finnigan's boots, and Spooner's pants were horrible to see—he must have sat down in it! They will watch me, of course—they would be fools if they didn't."

When the meal was over and they were washing the dishes together, she asked:

"What were you thinking about last night that you couldn't sleep?"

"My sins," he answered solemnly, and for some reason or other her attitude was a little frigid toward him for the remainder of the morning.

And to whatever error he had committed in the morning, he added what proved to be a crowning indiscretion. He came into the kitchen and found her at the table, bare-armed, kneading some pastry.

"That was a bad burn," he said.

He had never before seen the heart-shaped scar on the back of her hand.

To his surprise, she flushed red.

"It only shows sometimes," she said shortly.

She left soon after without saying good-bye.

In the afternoon came a humble Cleaver, with a rambling and unconvincing story of the causes that led to his resignation. Jim Morlake cut him short.

"You may come back," he said, "and you may reëngage any servants who wish to return. But there is a new routine in this household. Everybody must be in bed by ten, and under no circumstances may you or anybody else interrupt me when I am working in my room."

"If Mr. Hamon hadn't, so to speak, lured me away——" began Cleaver.

"I have known Mr. Hamon in many rôles," interrupted Jim, "but I confess that Hamon the siren is a new one on me."

The study was situated at that end of the building nearest Creith House. It was a long, rather narrow room, with two entrances, one leading to the hall, the other opening into a small lobby. Here was a narrow staircase leading directly into his bedroom, which was above the study. The bedroom, in a sense, ran at right angles to the room below, for whilst this ran lengthwise along the front of the house, the bedroom extended from the front to the back.

Whilst Cleaver was collecting his scattered staff, Jim went up the staircase to the bedroom, locked the door, and, taking up a corner of the carpet, opened a small trapdoor in the floor and took out a black tin box, which he carried to the table. From this he extracted his little leather hold-all of tools, a gun and the inevitable square of silk, and these he took down to the study, putting them into his drawer. Though all the detectives in the world were watching him, though the threat of life imprisonment hung over him like a cloud, The Black must again go about his furtive work. For the voice of the dead was whispering again, urgently, insistently, and Jim Morlake did not hesitate to obey.

CHAPTER XXVII

Mrs. Cornford's Lodger

JIM filled up the tank of his car, stacked a couple of tins in the dickey and drove the machine into the village, stopping first at the post office to send a wire to Binger, and then at the blacksmith's shop, which, since the demise of the garage, had served the rough needs of motorists. The complicated repairs which he described to the blacksmith could not be carried out at Creith, as he well knew.

"You had better take the car to Horsham, Mr. Morlake," said the blacksmith. "I don't know enough about these here machines to do the work you want."

The police watcher saw him drive off and strolled across to the blacksmith to discover what was the trouble.

"His steering apparatus has gone wrong," said the smith. "He has patched it up himself, but I told him it is dangerous to drive and he's taken it over to Bolley's at Horsham."

Satisfied, Detective Spooner went back to his chief and reported. Just as it was getting dark, Jim returned by the little motor omnibus which plied three times a day between Creith and Horsham. This also Spooner reported.

"I don't see what's the use of keeping us down here at all," said Sergeant Milligan. "It's a dead and alive hole, and it's not likely that Morlake is going to start anything just yet. The trial's shaken him up a bit."

"I wish he'd get in the habit of going to bed early," grumbled his subordinate. "I had a talk with the butler—who is going back to him, by the way—and he said that he'd never known his boss to have insomnia before."

"Perhaps it is his conscience," said Milligan hopefully.

Soon after Jim returned to the house, Binger arrived with a small handbag, containing all that was necessary for him in the matter of changes, and William Cleaver showed him into Jim's room.

"I've got a job for you that you'll like, Binger," said Jim. "It is to sit in a chair and do nothing for five or six hours every night. You will be able to sleep in the day and I've not the slightest doubt that you'll also put in a few short winks whilst on duty."

Binger, whose face had fallen at the suggestion of work, brightened up again.

"I'm not naturally a lazy man, sir," he said, "but I find at my time of life, after my military experience, that things tire me very hastily. I think it must be the fever I got in Hindia. It isn't that I'm lazy—ho no! Work I love. Are you having a hard time 'ere, sir?—I expect you hare! Naturally the gentry would be a bit put out, you being a burglar, sir. I'm sure the way the reporters came hafter me when you was in jug was disgraceful. They put my portrait in the papers, sir—maybe you saw it?" He fumbled in his pocket and took out a large, creased and somewhat idealised photograph of Mr. Binger. "Not that I court publicity, sir, to use a foreign hexpression, but if you're in the public heye, you're in the public heye, and there's no getting away from it. This Mommet" (he referred to Mahmet thus) "he doesn't mind at all. Being a Hafrican, he 'asn't got any sense. You've given it hup, I suppose, sir?"

"Given what hup?" asked Jim.

"Burglarising, sir."

He saw an unfamiliar object standing on a side table.

"Going in for music, sir?" he asked.

Jim looked across at the big gramophone that had been delivered to him a few days before.

"Yes, I've developed a pretty taste in jazz," he said. "Now listen to my instructions, Binger, and they are to be carried out to the letter. To-night at ten o'clock you will take up your post outside my door. You can have the most comfortable chair you can find, and I don't mind very much if you sleep. But nobody is to come into this room—you understand? And under no circumstances am I to be interrupted. If any detectives call——"

"Detectives?" said the startled Binger.

"There are two in Creith," said Jim coolly, "but I don't think they will worry you. But if they call, knock at the front door, or do anything after ten o'clock, they are not to be admitted unless they can produce a warrant signed by a magistrate, which is extremely unlikely. You understand?"

"Yes, sir. Do you want me to bring you in some coffee?"

"I want you to bring me in nothing," said Jim sharply. "If you attempt to come in or interrupt me, you'll be fired."

He had the best dinner he had had in weeks that night, for the majority of the staff were again on duty. At half-past nine he interviewed Cleaver, who was already making preparations to retire for the night.

Jim strolled into the grounds and walked to the gate. The road was deserted, but in the shadow of a hedge he saw a red spark of light that glowed and died with regularity. It was the cigar of the watcher, and he smiled to himself.

Going back to his study, he found that Binger, with a rug and a chair, had taken up his position in the hall.

"Good-night, Binger," he said and locked the door.

Though the house was equipped for electric lighting, the petrol engine which supplied the current had not been working since his return. On his study table was a shaded vapour lamp, which threw a powerful light on to the desk. The shade he had removed and the brilliance of the flame was almost blinding.

He picked up the gramophone and put it on the table in the middle of the room, wound it tight and regulated the turn-table until it moved at its slowest pace. Then, from his desk, he took a long steel rod, which he screwed into the end of the turn-table. To this he had fixed a tiny cardboard figure, the silhouette of a man with his hands behind him, clamped to a piece of stout wire. This he fastened to the end of the rod, and carrying the vapour lamp from his desk, placed it in the centre of the turn-table and released the catch. The disc turned slowly and with it the lamp and the cardboard figure. Presently the blurred shadow of the silhouette passed across the white window shade.

"There he goes again!" groaned Detective Spooner, as he saw the shadow pass. "How long is he going to keep that up?"

Apparently not for long, for Jim stopped the machine, and, passing upstairs to his room, changed into an old black suit. Over this he drew a tightly fitting ulster that reached almost to his heels, and this, with a soft black hat, completed his wardrobe. He put his tools and gun in his pocket, added a small but powerful electric torch and looked at his watch. It was half-past ten. The house was silent. He went back to the study and, going close to the door, called Binger.

"Are you all right?"

"Yes, sir."

"Remember I am not to be interrupted."

"No, sir, I quite understand."

From the voice he gathered that the watchful Binger was already half asleep.

He set the gramophone working again, watched it for a little while, regulating the speed, and then, passing up to his bedroom, crossed to the window at the back of the house, and, lifting the sash, stepped out upon a small balcony.

In a minute he was in the grounds, making his way furtively in the shadow of the bushes to the little footbridge that led to the Creith estate. Ten minutes' walk and he came to an isolated barn, approached by a cart track across a field which was his property, and here the car was waiting. . . .

"He's at it again," said Spooner to his sergeant who had strolled up to join the watcher. "There he goes," as a shadow crossed the window jerkily.

Spooner groaned.

"This means an all-night job," he said.

At that moment Jim's car was running up the Haymarket in a drizzle of rain. He turned into Wardour Street and, putting the machine at the tail of a long queue of cars that were waiting here to pick up the theatre traffic, he walked into Shaftesbury Avenue and hailed a taxi. As the car drew up, the door of a saloon bar was pushed open violently and a man stumbled out.

He fell against Jim, who caught and jerked him to his feet.

" 'Scuse me!" said the drunkard, "had a slight argument . . . on purely abstrac' question of metaphysics," he got the word out with difficulty.

Jim looked at him closely. It was the young man who had come to his house on the night of the storm.

"Hello, my friend, you're a long way from home," he said, before he remembered that he particularly did not wish to be recognised. But the man was incapable of recognition.

The taxicab was waiting, and, seeing the little crowd that was gathering, he pushed the sot into the car.

"Drive to Long Acre," he said.

At this hour of the night the street of wholesale fruit salesmen and motor-car depôts would be empty. Stopping the cab in the quietest part of the street, he guided his companion to the side-walk.

"Now, Mr. Soak, I advise you to go home."

"Home!" said the other bitterly. "Got no home! Got no friends, got no girl!"

"Perhaps that is not unfortunate—for the girl," said Jim, impatient to be gone.

"Is it? I dunno. I'd like to get hold of the girl who played the trick on me. I'd kill her—I would, I'd kill her!"

His weak face was distorted with sudden rage and then he burst into drunken tears.

"She ruined my life, damn her!" he sobbed, "and I don't know her, except her Christian name, don't know anything except that her father's a lord . . . she's got a little heart-shaped scar on the back of her hand."

"What is the name of this girl who—who ruined your life?" asked Jim huskily.

The young man wiped his eyes and gulped.

"Joan—that is her name, Joan . . . she played it low down on me and if I ever find her, I'll kill her!"

CHAPTER XXVIII

Mr. Welling Gives Advice

On the day that Ralph Hamon received an answer to his Moorish cablegram, Mr. Marborne dined well and expensively, for he had reached that blissful stage of conscious prosperity when money came natural.

His guest that night was Mr. Augustus Slone; and Sergeant Slone, from being an uninteresting, snub-nosed man with a vacuous face and an apologetic air, had developed into a man of fashion.

So they dined in the largest restaurant in Oxford Street, and it was a dinner of many courses.

"Another bottle," said Mr. Marborne grandly.

He pushed down the stiff front of his shirt, which bulged above the white waistcoat, and examined his cigar with a critical air.

"Well, Slone, this is more my idea of life than rousting round looking for little tea-leaves."*

"You've said it," said Slone simply.

He also was dressed in expensive raiments and if his black dress bow had an edging of purple, it was only because a certain gentlemen's outfitter had assured him that this was the latest and most recherche vagary of fashion.

"How long is it going on?" he asked, leaning back in his chair and regarding his companion with a glassy stare.

"For ever," said the other, and as he waved his hand the overhead lights were reflected brilliantly from the diamond in his new ring.

"What have you got on Hamon?"

"What do you mean—what have I got on him?"

"You've got something." Slone nodded with drunken wisdom. "You've put som'n on to him somehow. What have you found out about him?"

"Never mind what I've found out. All you've got to do is to be satisfied and ask no questions. Am I doing the right thing by you or am I not?"

"You're certainly doing the right thing by me," admitted Slone with warmth and they shook hands fervently across the table.

"I'll tell you—not everything, but a little. A certain document has come into my possession," said Marborne. "I won't say what it is or how I got it, but it is something which would do him a lot of no good. That fellow is worth a million, Slone, and he has a sister. . . . !" He kissed the tips of his fingers and waved them to the ceiling ecstatically.

"I know all about his sister," said Slone, "and she's not the sort of girl who would have anything to do with you, Marborne."

Marborne's face went a dull red. In his cups he was somewhat quarrelsome.

"What do you mean?" he demanded. "What was she before Hamon made his money? A barmaid! That's what she was.

*_In the argot of the London crook, a tea-leaf is a thief._

She served the drinks in a little dive off Glasshouse Street. She's no better than me—in fact, she is not so good."

Slone assented sycophantically.

"And there's no sense in talking about putting the black on Hamon," Marborne went on. "What is he—a thief, that's what he is and I can prove it."

"Is that what you know about him, Marborne?"

"Never mind what I know," retorted Marborne, beckoning the waiter as a resolve came to him.

"Let us have another drink," suggested Slone.

"You've had enough," said the other. "There's that old swine, Welling!"

The shock of the discovery that he had been under the observation of that grey-haired sleuth probably all the evening, sobered him. As he caught Marborne's eye Welling rose from the little table where he had been enjoying a protracted dinner and walked across to the two and instinctively Slone stood to attention.

"Sit down, you fool," said Marborne under his breath. "You're not in the police force now. Good evening, Captain Welling."

"Good evening, Marborne. Having a good time?" He sat down at the unoccupied end of the table and his mild eyes surveyed the former police officer with interest. "Doing well, eh? Making a lot of money? That's the thing to do, Marborne. Honest money brings happiness, crook money brings time."

"I'm not going to discuss with you, Captain Welling, whether my money's honest or dishonest. If you think——"

Welling stopped him with an almost humble gesture.

"You can't mean to suggest that you aren't making a fortune?" he said. "How is friend Hamon?"

"I don't know Mr. Hamon—at least not very well," protested Marborne loudly. "What are these innuendoes, Captain? I don't know why you should intrude yourself upon me. I've got nothing to thank you for."

"You've a lot to thank me for," said Welling, lighting the ragged stub of a cigar which he extracted with care from his waistcoat pocket. "The Commissioner wanted to prosecute you.

and I think you would have had nine months' hard labour as the result of certain indiscretions of yours, but I persuaded him, in the interests of the service, that it would be better if we let bygones be bygones. Hamon is well, you say?"

"I didn't say anything about Hamon."

"A nice man," mused Julius softly, "an extremely nice man. You're working for him?"

"I tell you, I've nothing to do with Mr. Hamon."

"You must be working for him," said the other with gentle insistence. "He drew a thousand pounds from the bank only a week ago and at least three of the notes have been passed by you. He would hardly pay you for nothing, would he, Marborne, because that is not the way of the world." He sighed heavily. "Our cruel employers get the last ounce out of us, and perhaps they're right. What are you now—a financier?"

Marborne was silent.

"I've been worrying about Hamon," Welling went on. "I saw him for a few minutes the other day and he looked ill. As if he had some trouble on his mind. He couldn't have lost anything from Grosvenor Place, or he would have reported the matter to the police, wouldn't he? Of course he would! Yes, I'm glad to see you're getting on, Marborne. And Slone too! They tell me he's living in a Bloomsbury hotel like a gentleman! You boys are making money." He shook a finger waggishly at the infuriated and a little frightened Marborne. "You're simply dragging it in, Inspector——It sounds better to call you Inspector, doesn't it? Somebody was telling me, you've had a safe put up in your apartments—a beautiful new, green, warranted-to-defy-fire-and-thieves safe."

"You've been tailing me up, Welling," said Marborne roughly. "You've no right to do that."

"Tailing you up?" Julius Welling seemed shocked at the charge. "That is the last thing in the world I should think of doing. But gossip gets around—you know how small London is. One man sees one thing, one man sees another, and they sort of pass on the information. And I think you are wise. If you've got a lot of loose money lying around, and you don't patronise banks, it is only an intelligent precaution to have a good safe."

"What do you mean by not using banks?" said Marborne hotly. "I've got a banking account in Holborn."

"But you never use it," said the gentle Julius, shaking his head, "and again I'm sure you are right. You never know when a bank will fail. On the other hand, if you've got a nice, big, green, fire proof safe, there's nothing to fear except burglars. And what are burglars? The Black wouldn't rob you, even if he hadn't gone out of the burglarly business for good —which of course he has."

He looked round quickly and then lowering his voice, he said:

"Marborne, have you ever tried to tie a tin can to the tail of a wildcat? I see by your expression that you haven't. It is less dangerous than 'tinning' Ralph Hamon. The Old Book says there's a time to make merry and a time to be sad, a time to sleep and a time to eat; and let me tell you that there is a time to quit, too! And that's very near at hand. I wish you no harm, Marborne. You're a bit of a bad lad, but there's a lot about you that I like. Your simplicity is one of the things and your transparent honesty is another. And I shouldn't feel right if I didn't pass on these few words of wisdom and guidance. Pack up your bundle and go while the going's good."

"Go where?" asked the puzzled Marborne.

Welling rose heavily from the table.

"They tell me Spain is a pretty useful place. But keep to the north. The south is too near to Morocco. Italy is another country where living is cheap and the climate is passable. I'll do what I can to protect you."

"Protect me!" gasped Marborne, and Welling nodded.

"Yes, sir, that is the word I used. I tell you I'll do my best for you, but I'm not superhuman. Keep away from wildcats."

To Marborne's intense irritation, the old man patted him on the shoulder.

"Remember that easy money stings. You don't feel the sting for a long time after, but when you do, it'll hurt like hell!"

CHAPTER XXIX

A Love Call

"HE IS a dithering old fool," said Marborne angrily, "and I can't stand here all night discussing Welling. Get me a taxi, commissionaire."

"Don't you make any mistake about Welling," said Slone, a greatly troubled man. "That man knows! If he says 'quit' you take my advice and quit."

"I don't even want your advice. I'll see you in the morning," said Marborne, bustling into the taxi.

He was more sober than he had been since the dinner started and his first impulse was to go home. Indeed, he gave instructions to this effect, but changed them and leaning from the window ordered the driver to take him to Grosvenor Place.

There was a light in the drawing-room and he smiled as he mounted the steps.

Lydia heard his voice in the hall and almost before the footman had announced his name—

"I am not at home," she said in a low voice.

This was the third evening visit Marborne had paid in a week and with each he had grown a little bolder. Before the servant could get out of the room, the door was pushed open and the ex-inspector appeared.

"Hullo, Lydia! Thought I would come and see how you were getting along."

It was the first time he had called her by her Christian name and for a second there was a gleam in her eye which boded ill for the adventurous man.

"Ralph is out, I suppose?"

"How long has he been 'Ralph' to you, Mr. Marborne?"

"Oh, for a long time," said Marborne lightly. "I'm not one of these sticklers for etiquette. If a man's name is Ralph, he should be called Ralph."

She checked the retort on her lips, having discovered that

the best method of wearying her visitor was to allow him to make all the conversation, for Marborne had not a great stock of small talk. But to-night she had not the patience to continue in her abstention and presently she was irritated into asking:

"What has happened lately, Mr. Marborne, that you have become so very familiar, both with my brother and myself? I'm not a snob, and I daresay you're as good as anybody else, but I tell you frankly that I do not like your calling me 'Lydia' and I will ask you not to call me so again."

"Why not?" he demanded with a tolerant smile. "Your name *is* Lydia. They used to call you Lydia in the dear old days when you shook cocktails for the thirsty boys!"

She was white with passion but had gained control over her speech.

"Come now, Lydia, what is the use of putting on side? I am a man, the same as other men you meet. Why can't we be good friends? Come and have a bit of luncheon with me to-morrow and we can go on to a matinée afterwards."

"I am thrilled," she said coldly. "Unfortunately I have a luncheon engagement."

"Put it off," said Marborne, his admiring eyes devouring her. "Lydia, why can't we be good friends?"

"Because I don't like you," she said. "After all, barmaids do not choose barmen for their companions; they like to get something a little above them, socially and intellectually. What you are intellectually, I have never had an opportunity of discovering; but I would as soon think of going to luncheon with one of my brother's footmen. Is that plain to you?"

By his purple face and the incoherent sounds that were escaping from his lips she gathered it was plain enough. Fortunately, her brother came in at that moment and gave her an excuse for leaving the room.

"What's the matter with you?" asked Ralph Hamon, glowering at the man.

"What's the matter with me?" spluttered Marborne. "I'll tell you what's the matter with me, Hamon. That sister of yours has got to apologise to me . . . throwing my manners up in my face . . . telling me I'm no better than a footman. . . ."

"I guess she's right," said Hamon, his lips curling at the man's hurt vanity and self-pity. "She didn't call you a blackmailer by any chance, did she? Because, if she did, she'd have been right again. Now see here," his voice was like a rasp. "I'm paying you money because you stole something from me, and you're using the threat of exposure to get it. I'll go on paying money just so long as I have to buy your silence. But you will confine all your business transactions to me. You will have nothing whatever to do with any member of my family, by which I mean my sister. You understand that?"

"I'll do as I dam' well please!" stormed Marborne.

"You're drunk," said Hamon calmly. "If you weren't drunk you wouldn't have made a fool of yourself. See me in the morning."

"I want Lydia to apologise to me," said the other and Hamon laughed sourly.

"Come to-morrow and maybe she will," he said. "I want to go to bed. Have you seen Welling?"

"Welling? Yes. What made you ask that?" asked Marborne in surprise.

"He was standing outside the house as I came in, that is all."

Marborne walked to the window and, drawing aside the blind, peered out. On the opposite side of the road he saw a man standing by the edge of the sidewalk.

"That's Welling," he agreed. "What does he want?"

"He has tailed me up," growled Marborne.

"I'm glad," said the other. "I was afraid for the minute he was tailing me. Have a drink?"

Marborne smiled and shook his head.

"No, thanks—if I'm going to be poisoned I'll have mine at home."

The watcher had disappeared when Marborne left the house. He walked to the corner to get a taxicab and though he looked back several times, he saw no sign of the shadow. He went through the side door of the shop which constituted the entrance to his flat, and waited for some time in the dark passage before he pulled the door open and stepped out. There was still no sign of Welling. Possibly Hamon had been mistaken, or else Welling's presence had been sheer coincidence.

His apartments occupied the whole of a floor above a shop and had been furnished by the landlord with those solid and useless articles which have been called "furniture" from time immemorial. A buffet that he did not use, a clock that did not go, a table at which it was impossible to write and a three-branch chandelier only one lamp of which was practicable. But on the buffet was a tantalus, and pouring himself out a stiff glass of whisky, he drank it down.

What was Welling driving at, he wondered. And what significance was there in his reference to the safe? It was perfectly true that Marborne kept his money in the flat; and he did this because he had sufficient intelligence to know that there might come a moment when his victim would make it necessary for his hasty departure. And to Marborne money was not real money unless it was visible. A balance at the bank meant nothing except figures that gave him no satisfaction whatsoever.

He stirred the fire into a blaze, took off his dress jacket and went into the bedroom. Switching on the light, he stood in the doorway and the first object on which his eyes rested was the safe. It stood in a corner of the room, supported by a stout wooden stand.

He looked at it dully, uncomprehendingly, and then with a shriek of rage he leapt into the room and began feeling wildly in its dark interior. For the door was hanging and the safe was empty!

When he had recovered from his rage, he made a rapid search of the apartment. The method of entrance was clear. The thief had come up the fire escape, broken through the window of the bedroom and had worked at his leisure.

He dashed downstairs to the street and threw open the door. Captain Welling, his hands clasped behind him, his head perched on one side, was standing on the sidewalk, gazing intently up at the lighted windows of the flat.

"Captain Welling, I want you!"

Marborne's voice betrayed his agitation.

"Anything wrong?" asked Welling as he came over. "Curious my being here."

"I've been robbed—robbed!" said Marborne. "Somebody's broken open my safe. . . ."

He led the way up the stairs, babbling incoherently, and kneeling before the rifled safe, Welling made a brief examination.

"He certainly did the job thoroughly," he said. "But burglar-proof safes are easy to a good cracksman. You'd better not touch it until this morning and we'll have it photographed for finger-prints."

He got out of the window on to the fire escape.

"Hullo! What's this?" he said and took something from the landing at his feet.

"One cotton glove. I suppose we'll find the other at the bottom. I don't think it is necessary to bother about looking for finger-prints."

He examined the glove under the light.

"And you couldn't trace these if you spent a week of Sundays. I'm afraid he's made a good getaway. How much money did you lose?"

"Between two and three thousand pounds, I think," whined Marborne.

"Anything else?"

The ex-inspector looked at him sharply.

"What else was there to lose?" he asked surlily. "Isn't it enough to lose two thousand?"

"Had you any books, any documents of any kind?"

"No, not in the safe," said Marborne and added quickly: "nor anywhere else for the matter of that."

"Looks like The Black's work to me," mused Welling, coming back again to the safe. "It certainly does look like The Black's work. And I don't see how it can be. Have you got a telephone here?"

"In the other room," said Marborne.

Welling put through a long-distance call and went back to make what he knew was doomed to be a fruitless and hopeless search for clues.

The thief had evidently not been satisfied with the money he had found in the safe. Every drawer had been ransacked, its contents thrown to the ground; the cupboard had been wrenched open; a trunk beneath the bed had been forced and its contents strewn about the floor. Even the bed had been dismantled, blanket by blanket, sheet by sheet, and the mattress lay half on the floor and half on the bedstead.

Welling went back to the dining-room. There were no cupboards here and no drawers, save three in the sideboard, which were empty. He looked round the walls. One of the pictures was hanging askew and he nodded.

"He was looking for something, this friend of ours. What was it?" he asked.

"How in hell do I know?" demanded Marborne savagely. "He didn't get it anyway."

"I don't know how you can say that, if you don't know what he was looking for," said Julius gently.

The telephone bell rang. It was the call which Welling had put through to Creith.

"Captain Welling speaking. Is that you, Milligan?"

"Yes, sir."

"Where is your man?"

"He's in his house—or he was five minutes ago."

"Are you sure?"

"Absolutely certain. I haven't seen him, but I've seen his shadow. He's here all right. Besides which, he hasn't got a car; it went to Horsham to-day for repair."

"Oh, it did, did it?" said Welling softly. "All right."

He hung up the telephone receiver and went back to Marborne, surveying the wreckage helplessly.

"You'd better 'phone the divisional police and ask them to send a man up, Marborne," said the old chief. "I don't think they'll be able to help you—too bad your losing all that money. Banks are safer."

Marborne said nothing.

CHAPTER XXX

Sadi

If the traveller passed up the narrow, hilly street which leads from the Mosque to Great *Sok* of Tangier, and turned abruptly to the right as though the *Kasbah* were his objective, he would have found on his left a high white wall pierced only by a massive gate with bronze-green hinges.

Behind the wall was an untidy garden and a broken stone fountain, sufficiently repaired by an unskilful European workman to allow a feeble jet of water to jerk spasmodically in the air before it fell into a black basin, where, amidst the rubbish of years, swam languid gold-fish.

The house of Sadi Hafiz stood at right angles to the wall, an ugly, lime-washed barn boasting a verandah and a stoep where, when the weather was warm, Sadi Hafiz himself sat in a faded drawing-room chair drinking mint tea and smoking. He was a tall, pale Moor with plump cheeks and a smear of beard, and he had the appearance at all times of being half-awake. He sat one morning, a cigarette drooping from his full underlip, his dull eyes fixed upon a wilted geranium in the centre of the court.

The Shereef Sadi Hafiz was a man who had held many positions of trust under many governments, but had not held them for long. He had served two sultans and four pretenders, had been the confidential agent of six European and one American consulates and in turn had robbed or betrayed them all. A linguist of ability, a known friend of the brown-legged men who carried their rifles into Tangier whenever they came shopping, his influence reached into strange and distant places, and he was a concession-monger without equal.

There came to him at the sunset hour a little man named Colport, who was the accredited agent in Tangier of Mr. Ralph Hamon's companies.

"Good evening—have a drink," grunted the shereef in English. "Did you get any reply to your cable?"

"He says the quarter's allowance is not due for a month," said Colport and the Moor spat contemptuously.

"Did he spend twenty pesetas to cable that? Allah! If it is not due for twenty months I need money now, Colport. Is he coming?"

"I don't know; he didn't say."

The Moor looked at him from under his tired eyelids.

"Is Lydia coming with him? Of course! For five years she has been coming, and for five years she cannot. I am tired of Hamon. He treats me worse than Israel Hassim the Jew. I give him companies, he makes millions and all I see is the allowance. Sha! What did I do for Hamon years ago? Ask him that!"

Colport listened philosophically. Sadi was for ever complaining, for ever hinting of mysterious services; he never went further than to hint.

"He would see me in the Kasbah, chained by the leg and dying for a centimo measure of water. And I have two new wonders for him—a trace of silver in the hills! Ah ha, that makes your eyes sparkle. There are fifty million pesetas in that concession alone. Who else could find such beauties but the Shereef? I am the most powerful man in Morocco—greater than a *basha*—greater than the Sultan. . . ."

He grumbled on and Colport waited for his opportunity. It came at last.

"Mr. Hamon says he will let you have your quarter's allowance and five hundred sterling. But you must send at once . . . wait."

He fished out the cablegram from his pocket and smoothed it on his knee.

" 'Tell Sadi I must have another Ali Hassan'—what does that mean, Sadi?"

Sadi's eyes were wide open now, his tobacco-stained fingers were caressing his hairy chin.

"He is in trouble," he said slowly. "I thought he was. Ali Hassans do not grow on every cactus bush, Colport."

He was silent for a long time, thinking, and his thoughts were not pleasant. After a while he said:

"Cable to him that it will cost a thousand," he said. "Bring the money to me in the evening of to-morrow. Even then . . . but I will see."

He clapped his hands lazily and to the slave girl who came:

"Bring tea, you black beast," he said pleasantly.

He paid Colport the unusual honour of walking with him to the gate, and then he went back to his dingy chair and sat, elbow on knee, chin in hand, until the call to prayer sent him to his perfunctory devotions.

He rose stiffly from his knees and called to the man who was his scribe and valet.

"Do you know Ahmet, the mule driver?"

"Yes, Excellency. He is the man that killed the money changer, and some say he robbed another Jew and threw him down a well. He is a bad man."

"Does he speak English?"

"Spanish and English, they say. He was a guide at Casa Blanca, but he stole from a woman and was flogged."

Sadi inclined his head.

"He must be my Ali Hassan," he said. "Go into the low houses by the beach. If he is drunk leave him, for I do not wish the French police to see him. If he is sober, let him come to me at the twelfth hour."

Tangier's one striking clock was chiming midnight when the servant admitted the burly figure of the mule man.

"Peace on this house and may God give you happy dreams!" he said, when the white-robed figure of the shereef confronted him in the moonlight.

"Ahmet, you have been to England?"

They stood in the centre of the courtyard, away from the ears that listened at three lattice-covered windows.

"Yes, Shereef, many times on the mule ships when the War was on."

"Go now, Ahmet. There is a man who needs you. Remember that I saved you from death twice. Twice, when the rope was round your neck, I, the Shereef Sadi of Ben-Aza, pleaded to the *basha* and saved you. There will be nobody to save you in England if you are a fool. Come to me to-morrow and I will give you a letter."

CHAPTER XXXI

Joan Tells the Truth

JIM MORLAKE returned home in the early hours of the morning. At half-past three, Spooner saw the white window shade go up and Jim appeared, silhouetted against the bright light of the room. In another second he opened the French windows and stepped out, crossing the lawn to the gate. The detective drew back to the shadows, but Jim's voice hailed him.

"Is that you, Finnigan, or is it Spooner?"

"Spooner," said the officer a little sheepishly, as he came forward.

"Come inside and have a large glass of ice water," said Jim, opening the gate. "Pretty cold waiting, wasn't it?"

"How did you know we were here?"

Jim laughed.

"Don't be silly," he said. "Of course I knew you were here. Say when."

The detective drank the potion that was offered him and smacked his lips.

"I think it is silly, too," he said, "wasting a good man's time——"

"Two good men," corrected Jim.

"Don't you ever get any sleep?" asked the detective, selecting a cigar from the box Jim handed him.

"Very rarely," replied his host gravely. "It freshens me up, walking up and down this room."

"How do you do it? I only notice you pass the window one way."

"I walk round the table as a rule. It is quite a good stretch," said the other carelessly. "What I principally wanted to speak to you about, Spooner, was to ask you whether you had heard anybody shouting, or whether insomnia is getting on my nerves?"

Mr. Spooner shook his head.

"I've heard nobody shout. It must be your imagination. From what direction did it come?"

"From the meadows on the other side of the river," said Jim. "But if you didn't hear it, it is not worth while investigating."

"Is there a bridge?" asked the detective, glad of any diversion. "What sort of a noise was it?"

"It sounded like a cry for help to me," said Jim. "If you think it is worth while, I'll get a lamp and we'll go and look."

He lit a storm lantern and they crossed the lawn to the little footbridge. He led the way over the bridge.

"It was from this field that the cry seemed to come," he said, and then the detective saw a figure lying on the ground and ran toward it.

"What is it?" asked Jim.

"Looks to me like a drunk. Here, wake up!"

He dragged the inanimate figure to its knees and shook it vigorously by the shoulder.

"Wake up, you! It is the young man who lives at Mrs. Cornford's cottage," said Spooner suddenly.

"I thought I recognised him," said Jim. "I wonder how the dickens he got here. Perhaps you'll see him home?"

After the detectives with their half-conscious burden had gone their staggering way to the village, Jim returned to the house. Not only the work of the night had been heavy—and Marborne's burglar-proof safe had been one of the hardest jobs he had ever tackled—but the responsibility of this half-crazy dipsomaniac had added a new tax on his strength. He had gone back for the car he had left near Shaftesbury Avenue and had deposited the drunkard in a corner just in time to save him from arrest. Mr. Ferdie Farringdon had slept in the car what time Jim went about his unlawful occasions. He had slept all the way down and in the end Jim had had to half-carry and half-walk him from the place where he had left the machine to Wold House. Here he had settled him comfortably in the meadow of Creith Hall before it occurred to him that he might utilise the detectives who were watching him, to save the sleeping man from the serious consequences of his folly.

He went up to his bedroom, counted the heap of notes that he took from an inside pocket, put them in an envelope and addressed them, before he placed the implements of his craft in the secret hole beneath the carpet.

He had failed, but his failure was less oppressive to him than the strange story that Farringdon had told. It could not be Joan—and yet, her father was a peer; she had the heart-shaped scar on the back of her hand, and her name was Joan.

"It's preposterous!" he muttered. "Preposterous! How could Joan ruin any man's life? Why, she's only a child . . ."

It was the mad babble of a drunken man, he tried to tell himself, but reason would not accept that explanation. He made a resolve. At whatever risk, he would call upon Mr. Ferdinand Farringdon in the morning and ask for an explanation.

He slept for four hours, and, waking, took a cold bath and dressed. His first thoughts on waking, as were his last thoughts on sleeping, revolved about the dipsomaniac and his strange statements.

After swallowing a cup of tea that Binger brought to him he mounted his horse and taking the side-road that misses the village came to the gardener's cottage. He had never seen Mrs. Cornford before and his first impression was a correct one. She was a lady, as he had expected her to be. He had heard, not from Joan, but from those prolific sources of gossip which existed in Creith, that she was a friend of the girl's.

"My name is Morlake," he said, watching her keenly. "I'm

glad to see that you do not faint at the approach of a member of the criminal classes," he added, as she smiled her recognition of his name. "I want to see your boarder."

"Mr. Farringdon?" Her face changed. "I'm afraid you can't see him; he's very ill. He is an invalid, you know, and he went out yesterday afternoon when I was shopping in the village and did not come home until late this morning. I have just sent for the doctor."

"Is he very ill?" asked Jim. "I mean, too ill to see me?"

She nodded.

"I'm afraid he has fever; his temperature is high and he is not normal in other ways. Do you know him very well?" she asked.

"Not very well. I know something about him, that is all."

She was evidently not prepared to discuss the eccentric young man who lodged with her, and Jim had to return. He turned his horse and rode across the fields to No Man's Hill, a ride of which he was particularly fond. He could learn no more until the man had recovered—if he ever did recover. That kind of person had nine and ninety lives, he reflected, and he could wait until he sought an explanation from a saner and a more convincing Mr. Farringdon.

It was freakish of him to turn from the well-known road to send his horse climbing the hill, threading a slow way between the pines and the rhododendrons, but he had a sudden desire for the solitude which hill-tops give to man. He could not see the crest for the surrounding trees, and until he rode clear to the flat top, he was unaware that there was another early morning rider. Suddenly he came face to face with Joan. She was sitting her horse, a quizzical smile in her eyes, and she laughed aloud at his look of surprise.

"Father came back to Creith last night," she said. "Our humdrum life has been resumed, and we expect the Hamon man at any moment."

"Congratulations!"

"And do you know there was a burglary in London last night? It looked very, very much like one of yours!"

Her eyes were fixed on him steadily.

"Base imitation," said Jim. "Will you make me responsible for every robbery——"

"Was it you?" she asked.

He swung from the saddle with a laugh.

"You're a most disconcerting young lady, and I shan't satisfy your curiosity."

"Will you tell me it wasn't you?" she bent down toward him, watching him closely.

"Mr. James Morlake refuses to make any statement; this is official," said Jim.

"It *was* you!" She caught her breath in a sigh. "I was afraid it was, though they are perfectly certain in the village that you didn't leave Wold House."

"As a matter of fact, I did leave Wold House, and I was in London last night. Whatever evil work I did, at least I performed one kindly action. I saved a young man from being arrested for drunkenness, and I brought him home to his good, kind Mrs. Cornford."

Her face went deathly white.

"That was kind of you," she said steadily.

"Do you know this man?"

She did not answer.

"Has he any reason to hate you?"

She shook her head.

"Joan, are you in some kind of trouble?"

"I'm always in trouble," she said lightly, "and have been since I was so high!"

"I see you won't answer me. Will you tell me this?" He found difficulty in framing the words. "Joan—if, if I were not—if I were a respectable member of society and could claim to be . . . of your own class—would you marry me?"

Her eyes, deep and sombre, held his as she shook her head.

"No," she said.

"Why not?" he asked.

"Because . . . you asked me about Ferdie Farringdon just now."

"Well?" as she paused.

He saw her lick her dry lips, and then:

"He is my husband," she said, and, pulling round her horse's head, she sent it at full gallop down the uneven path.

CHAPTER XXXII

Captain Welling Understands

HE WAS dreaming, he told himself mechanically. It couldn't be true; it was too absurd to think about. She had been shocking him as she had shocked Lydia Hamon. Of course it wasn't true. How could it be? She was only a child. . . .

He found himself with drawn reins before the Cornford cottage. He could go in there and learn the truth—could drag it from the drunkard. Then he saw the doctor coming out and the old man nodded to him cheerily.

"How is your patient?" Jim found voice to say.

"Pretty bad. I think he's got rheumatic fever. He has little or no resistance, so what will happen to him heaven only knows. You look a bit under the weather, Morlake. I haven't seen you since you came from your——"

"Since I came from Brixton Prison," smiled Jim. "No, I don't think we've met. You needn't worry about me, doctor. I'm as fit as the Derby favourite."

"My experience is that they are usually unfit," growled the doctor, "though you never discover it until after the race is won and you've lost your money."

He walked by Jim's side into the village.

"Queer fish, that man Farringdon," he said, breaking the silence. "A college man, I should think, but a queer fish. He is quite delirious to-day and the things he is saying would make your hair stand on end. Happily," he said after a moment's thought, "I am bald. Ever heard of the Midnight Monks?"

"Eh?" said Jim.

"Midnight Monks. I wonder if, in your wider knowledge

of the world, you may have heard of them. Some sort of secret society, I should think. He's been babbling about them all the time, though it is not my business to give away my patient's secrets. The only satisfaction you can get out of my unprofessional conduct is that I shall probably give away yours. Hm! The Midnight Monks and Joan," he mused. "I wonder what Joan it is?"

Jim did not answer and he rambled on.

"It is a common enough name. Have you ever noticed how names go in cycles? All the Marjories belong to '96; they're contemporary with the Doras and the Dorothys. And all the Joans are about twelve years old. Just now there is an epidemic of Margarets. It is a curious world," he added inconsequently, as, with a wave of his hand, he dived into his surgery.

Jim did not hear him.

That must be the explanation. She was shocking him in her impish way. He told himself this with a firmness that sought to mask his act of self-deception.

He was turning into Wold House when a big Italian car swept past. He caught a glimpse of a face, and turning his horse, watched the car out of sight. Hamon's presence would bring happiness to nobody, he reflected. It certainly gave him none.

"The hofficers of the law have been 'ere," hissed Binger melodramatically, coming half-way down the drive to meet him.

"Which particular hofficers? And, by-the-way, I'll have to be careful or I shall be talking like you."

"I was always considered a very classy talker in my military days," said Binger complacently. "I remember once my colonel telling me——"

"Shut up about your colonel. Let's get down to common busy fellows. Do you mean Spooner or Finnigan?"

"All of 'em," said Binger. "He saw William—it's funny his name being William and mine being William——"

"It is so funny that I'm screaming with laughter," said Jim impatiently. "What did he say to William?"

"He wanted to know whether you were out last night. It was the other fellow who asked the question. And William said that so far as he knew you were hindoors. And, of course, I knew that you were hindoors, so I gave my testimony hunsolicited, as it were."

"When did they go?"

"They're not gone. They're in the study," said Mr. Binger. "And the other gentleman—there was three—he said he felt faint and would like to sit down away from the glare of the sun."

"There has been no sun for a month. I gather the other gentleman's name is Welling. It sounds rather like him."

"That's right, sir—Mr. Welling. An old gentleman, not very right in his head, I should think—childish as a matter of fact. He's had that gramophone on the table and has been asking what the little holes in the side were for. It's hawful to see a man in the prime of life talk like that."

"Horrible," agreed Jim in all sincerity.

When he walked into the study, Welling was examining with an air of quiet, detached admiration a big etching that hung over the carved mantelpiece. He bent his head sideways, looking over his glasses as Jim came in.

"Here you are then, Morlake," he said. "I think you're looking remarkably well."

"The village doctor has just passed an opinion which is directly contrary, but I guess you know," said Jim as he shook hands.

"I thought I'd look you up," said Welling. He had a trick of thrusting his chin into the air and looking down at his *vis-à-vis*. The taller they were, the farther rose his chin. His face was almost turned to the ceiling as he regarded Jim with that queer pale stare which had broken down so many obdurate and uncommunicative criminals.

"I only discovered last night that, outside of all my knowledge, the Yard had sent two men down to shadow you. Now, that's not right," he said, shaking his head. "It isn't right at all. The moment I discovered this, I decided that I would come down personally and withdraw these officers. I can't have you annoyed; you must have your chance, Morlake."

Jim laughed aloud.

"I haven't the slightest doubt, Welling, that you were the gentleman who sent these sleuths to watch me," he said.

"And I have less doubt," said Welling frankly, "that I did send them! That is the worst of our business," he shook his head mournfully. "We have to lie! Such unnecessary lies. I sometimes shudder when I recall the stories I have to tell in the course of a day. That is a nice little gramophone of yours. Have you any records?"

"Plenty," said Jim promptly.

"Ah! I set it going just now."

He turned the switch as he spoke and the turn-table slowly revolved.

"Very slow, eh? Now, I've been thinking that, if you had a lamp on the top of that turn-table and a figure cut in the shape of a man, so placed that every time the dial turned the shadow fell across that blind—how's that for an idea? When I write my little text-book for burglars, that notion is going to be put very prominently—with illustrations."

Jim turned the regulator and the disc spun quickly.

"It only shows how even a clever plan can come unstuck for want of an elementary precaution," he said. "I should have turned that back to full speed if I had been a criminal and had been endeavouring to deceive the good, kind police. You mustn't forget to put those instructions in your text-book, Welling."

"No, I mustn't," agreed the other warmly. "Thank you very much."

He looked round at Spooner and his superior.

"All right, sergeant, I don't think you need wait. You can take Spooner back to town with you by the next train. I will join you at the station. In the meantime, I want just a little private talk with Mr. Morlake—just a little exchange of reminiscences, shall we say?" he beamed.

He walked to the window and watched the twc officers disappear.

"They're very good fellows," he said, turning, "but they have no brains. Beyond that, they are perfect policemen. In fact, they are the ideal of our force. Where were you last night, Morlake?" He asked the question curtly.

"Where do you think I was?" said Jim, taking down his pipe from the mantelshelf and loading it.

"I think you were at 302, Cambridge Circus, opening the safe of my friend Mr. Marborne. When I say 'I think' I mean I know. That isn't the game, Morlake," he shook his head reproachfully. "Dog does not eat dog, nor thief rob thief. And that Marborne was the biggest thief that ever wore a uniform jacket, heaven and the Commissioner know. You made a killing, but did you get what you wanted?"

"I did not get what I wanted," said Jim.

"Then why take the money?"

"What money?" asked Jim innocently.

"I see." Captain Welling settled himself down on a settee and pulled up the knees of his trousers as outward evidence that he intended making a long stay. "I see we shall have to bicker awhile, Morlake."

"Don't," begged Jim. "I only take money when the money I want belongs to the man I am after."

Welling nodded.

"I guessed that. But this was Marborne's own—money dishonestly earned, and therefore his by right. What is Marborne's pull with Hamon?"

"Blackmail, I should imagine—in fact, I am pretty certain. He has come into possession of a document which is very incriminating to Hamon, and he is bleeding that gentleman severely; that is my diagnosis."

Again Welling nodded.

"Now we come to the one mystery that intrigues me," he said. "There is a document, which you want to get, and which you say Marborne has got. It is a document, the publication of which, or should it fall into the hands of the law officers, would lead to very disastrous consequences to Hamon. Have I stated the matter right?"

"As nearly as possible," said Jim.

"Very well, then." Welling ticked off the points on his finger-tips. "First, we have a document, a letter, a statement, and anything you like, the publication of which will, let us say, put Hamon in a very awkward position. Now, tell me this: is there anything in that document which it is absolutely necessary Hamon should keep?"

"Nothing," said Jim.

"Then why on earth doesn't he destroy it?" asked Welling in amazement.

A slow smile dawned on Jim's face.

"Because he's a monkey," he said. "He's put his hand into the gourd and he has grasped the fruit; he cannot get his hand out without letting go his prize."

"But you say that there is nothing in the wording of this paper which can possibly advantage him, and yet he does not destroy it! That is incredible. I've heard he is a miser, somebody told me that he's got thirty pairs of boots that he's hoarded since his childhood. But why on earth does he hoard a thing which may——"

"Put his head in a noose," suggested Jim, and Welling's face went grave.

"As bad as that?" he asked quietly. "I had a feeling it might be. The man is mad—stark, staring, raving mad. To hold on to evidence that can convict him—why, there's no precedent in the history of jurisprudence. A man may keep a document through sheer carelessness, or forgetfulness, but deliberately to hoard it! Is it something he has written?"

Jim shook his head.

"It is something written by another, accusing him of conspiracy to defraud and attempted murder."

Captain Welling was a man who was not readily surprised, but now he sat speechless with amazement.

"I give it up," he said. "It is killing Hamon, anyway. I saw him yesterday and he looked like a man on the verge of a nervous breakdown."

"I should hate to see Hamon die—naturally," said Jim. "He's down here, by-the-way."

Welling nodded.

"Yes, he telegraphed to Lord Creith this morning, asking if he could put him up. He has sent his sister away to Paris." He scratched his chin. "One would like to get to the bottom of this," he said. "I have an idea that we should discover a little more than you know or guess."

"There is nothing bad about Hamon that I cannot guess," said Jim.

He liked Welling and would, in other circumstances, have gladly spent the day with him; but now he was not in the mood for company and was relieved when the old man took his departure. Jim was sick at heart, miserable beyond belief. The shock of Joan Carston's declaration had stunned him. She would not play with him; she must have spoken the truth. Twice that afternoon he found himself riding in the direction of Mrs. Cornford's cottage, and once he stopped and asked after the patient, and his enquiry was not wholly disinterested.

"He is very ill, but the doctor takes a more hopeful view," said the lady. "Lady Joan very kindly came and brought some wine for him."

A little pang shot through Jim Morlake's heart, but he was ashamed of himself the next minute.

"Of course she would," he said, and Mrs. Cornford smiled at him.

"You are a friend of hers—she spoke of you to-day."

"Do you know anything at all about Mr. Farringdon?" he asked her.

"Nothing, except that he has no friends. An allowance comes to him from a firm of lawyers in the city. I wish I knew where I could find his relations, they ought to be told. But he speaks of nobody except these 'Midnight Monks' anc the only name he mentions besides that of a girl is one whick seems very familiar to me—Bannockwaite. It has some sort of significance for me, but I can't tell what."

Jim had heard the name before and it was associated in his mind with something unsavoury. A thought struck him. He had passed Welling in the village street, and the old man hac told him that he was staying on for a day or two and Jim had asked him up to dinner. He rode back to the Red Lion where the detective was staying and found him in the public bar, the least conscious of its habitués, and he was drinking beer out of a shining tankard.

"Do you know anybody named Bannockwaite?"

"I knew a man named Bannockwaite," said Welling instantly, "and a rascal he was! You remember the case? A young parson who got into a scrape and was fired out of the church. There was nothing much wrong with him, except natural devilry and a greater mistake than choosing a clerical career I cannot imagine. Then he was mixed up with a West End gang of cardsharpers and came into our hands, but there was no case against him. When the War broke out he got a commission—in his own name, remarkably enough. He did magnificently, earned the V.C., and was killed on the Somme. You probably remember him in connection with one of those societies he started. He never actually came into our hands on that score——"

"What do you mean by societies?"

"He had a mania for forming secret societies. In fact, when he was at school, he initiated one which disorganised not only his own school but a dozen in the neighbourhood. He was something of a mystic, I think, but devilry was his long suit."

"What was his school? I suppose you wouldn't know that?"

"Curiously enough I do. It was Hulston—a big school in Berkshire."

Jim went back and wrote to the headmaster at Hulston, hoping most fervently that the schoolmaster would not recognise him as the hero of an Old Bailey trial. Late in the afternoon he saw Hamon's car flash past toward London and wondered what urgent business was taking the financier back to town. Long after midnight he heard the peculiar roar of the Italian engine, and, looking through the window, saw the car returning.

"He is a very busy fellow in these days," thought Jim, and he thought correctly, for Ralph Hamon had spent two hours in a profitable interview with a stranger, who had arrived in London and the conversation had been carried on exclusively in Arabic.

CHAPTER XXXIII

The Foreign Sailor

THERE was no man more sympathetic for a fellow in misfortune than ex-Sergeant Slone. But when he discovered that the misfortune extended to himself, Slone was inclined to be querulous.

"I don't mind you doing what you like with your own money, Marborne," he said, "but there was four hundred of mine in that safe of yours, and I've been asking you for a week to put it in your bank."

"You wouldn't have had the money if it wasn't for me," said Marborne. "Anyway, there's plenty more where that came from."

"But have you got plenty more?" asked the practical Slone.

"He sent five hundred this morning. It was like getting blood out of a stone," said Marborne. "Anyway, we shan't starve. Slone, I've been sitting up all night, thinking about things."

"I don't wonder," said Slone, his gloomy eyes surveying the empty safe. "That's The Black's work, nobody else could have done it so neatly."

"What did he come for?"

"Money," said Slone bitterly. "What do you think he came for—to pass the evening?"

"You needn't get fresh with me," said Marborne sharply. "You'll pay the same respect to me, Sergeant Slone, as you did in the old days, or you and I part company. I've told you that before."

"I meant no harm," growled Slone, "but it is a bit of a blow losing all that money."

"The Black didn't come for it. He took it, but that wasn't what he came for. He came for this." He tapped his side significantly. "And that is what The Black has been after ever since he started operations. He's been after *this!* I was looking up my scrap-book this morning. I've got every one of The Black's robberies pasted, and I'll tell you what I discovered —and, mind you, Slone, I haven't been a police officer for twenty-three years without being able to put two and two together."

"That's natural," agreed the obliging Slone. "And I'll say this of you, Marborne—there wasn't a better detective officer at the Yard than yourself—not even Welling."

"You're a fool," said Marborne. "Welling could give me or anybody else a mile start and lick 'em sick. Now listen; every bank that's been burgled has been a bank where Hamon has had an account. In all banks there is a strong room, where customers keep their private documents, and it invariably has been the strong room that was burgled. And if it wasn't a bank it was a safe deposit, where Ralph Hamon had a private box. And he's been after this." He tapped his side again.

"What is it?" asked Slone, consumed with curiosity, and the other man smiled contemptuously.

"Wouldn't you like to know?" he asked, and continued: "This fellow Morlake is a rich man. I've always suspected he was a rich man——"

"Naturally he's rich," put in Slone wrathfully.

"Wouldn't you be rich if you'd pulled off forty-two jobs and got away with thousands and thousands of pounds? He's richer by four hundred of mine——"

"Don't interrupt me. He is a rich man apart from that. And, besides, nobody knows that he *has* taken any money."

"I know he's taken ours," said Slone bitterly.

"Fix this in your nut, Slone. It is just as likely that he would pay me as well for this, as old Hamon would."

"He'd sooner pinch it," said Slone with conviction, "like he pinched my money. I wish I'd been somewhere handy!"

"You'd have been a dead man if you had, so what is the good of wishing? I'm going to think this over and if I have any trouble with Mr. Blinking Hamon to-morrow——" He snapped his fingers significantly.

Slone went home early. He had yet to recover from the shock of his loss, and Marborne was left alone. He had plenty to occupy his thoughts. The sting of Lydia Hamon's contempt still smarted. She seemed, at that moment, less the woman of his dreams than she had been, and he harboured no other emotion in his bosom than a desire to get even with her for her gratuitous insult.

That morning he had sent a peremptory demand to Hamon, and had received a paltry five hundred. He had instantly despatched a second message, to learn that Hamon had gone out of town, which Marborne regarded as the merest subterfuge, until he called himself and interviewed the butler. Miss Hamon had gone too, that official informed him; she had left by the eleven o'clock Continental train and was expected to be absent for a week.

Although the night was chilly, he threw open the windows to let in the light and sound of Cambridge Circus. Almost under his eyes were the gay lights of a theatre. He sat for some time watching the audience arrive, and trying to recognise them, for he had an extensive acquaintance with West End life.

He saw a tall, thick-set man cross the road at a run, although there was no fear of his intercepting the traffic. A foreigner, Marborne guessed. He watched him for some time, for the man did not seem quite sure of his destination. First he walked along one sector of the Circus, then he came back and stood undecidedly on one of the islands in the middle of the thoroughfare. By the light of the street standard Marborne thought he was a seafaring man. He wore a jersey up to his neck, a thick pea-jacket and a cheese-cutter cap. Turning his eyes away to watch a car drive up to the theatre, Marborne lost sight of the stranger and he passed out of his mind.

He closed the window and, taking a pack of cards from a drawer, began to play solitaire. He was nervous, jumpy;

he heard sounds and whispering voices which he knew were born in his imagination. At last, unable to bear the solitude any longer, he put on his hat and went out, wandering down Shaftesbury Avenue to Piccadilly Circus, where he stood for an hour watching the night signs. Here, to his surprise and relief, he came upon Slone.

"I've got the creeps," said that worthy. "Marborne, what do you say to making a big haul from this fellow and getting out of the country? You remember what Welling told you—that the north of Spain is healthy?"

Marborne nodded. Something of the same idea had occurred to him.

"I think you're right," he said. "I'll wire to Hamon in the morning, he's staying with Lord Creith; and I'll put the matter frankly before him. It will be Italy, not Spain."

"Hamon is in town," said Slone unexpectedly. "I saw his car passing along Coventry Street, and he was in it."

"Are you sure?"

"Well, you couldn't mistake him, could you?" said Slone scornfully.

"Wait a bit." Marborne went into a telephone booth and called up Hamon's house.

"It is no good lying," he said, when the butler protested that his master was not in. "Hamon was seen in Coventry Street an hour ago."

"I swear to you, Mr. Marborne, he has gone to the country. I know he came back to town to do some business because I forwarded a coded message on to him and he came back for ten minutes—not longer. He's gone away again."

"I wouldn't be surprised if he is telling the truth," said Marborne when he reported the conversation. "Anyway, we'll see him to-morrow."

He parted from his friend in Shaftesbury Avenue and walked back to Cambridge Circus, feeling a little more cheerful than he had been when he came out. And then he saw the tall, foreign-looking sailor, and the first thing that impressed him was his big pale face and his tiny black moustache. He was standing near the door of the apartment as Marborne inserted the key, watching the ex-inspector until the door opened. Then he came forward, cap in hand.

"Excuse me," he said, speaking with a guttural accent, "but are you Marborne?"

"That is my name," said the other.

"I have this for you." The stranger held up a large envelope. "It is from Mr. Hamon. But first I must be sure that you are Marborne."

"Come in," said Marborne quickly.

Hamon had relented, he thought joyously. That parcel meant money and Hamon employed curious messengers at times. He opened the door for the big man, who had come silently up the stairs behind him, and the messenger passed through. He looked hard at his host.

"You are Marborne?" he said. He spoke English with great difficulty.

"Yes, I am that gentleman," said Marborne almost jovially, and the man laid the package on the table.

"That is for you," he said. "Will you please open and give me a sign?"

"You mean signature."

"That's the word—signature."

Marborne wrenched the string from the package and tore open the envelope. For a second his back was to the visitor and Ahmet, the muleman, drew a curved knife from each pocket and struck inward and upward with a deep-throated "Huh!"

CHAPTER XXXIV

The Cord

WHAT made Marborne raise his eyes, he did not know. In the glass above the mantelpiece he saw the glitter of the knife and leapt forward, pushing the table with him. He had turned to confront the assassin and in that instant he lifted the edge of the table and flung it over against his assailant. His gun came into his hand and the lights went out simultaneously; for though Ahmet, the muleman, was a barbarian, he lived in a city that was lit by electric light, and he knew the value of a near-by switch.

Marborne heard the patter of his feet on the stairs and ran after him, tripping and falling over the table. By the time the lights were on, the stairs and passage were empty. There was no sign of the sailor in the street, and double-locking the door, he came back to his room and reached for a handy whisky bottle, and he did not trouble to dilute the fluid.

"The swine!" he breathed. He put down the bottle and examined the letter that the man had dropped.

It consisted of a package of old newspapers.

So that was it! He had, as Welling told him, tinned the wildcat and the cat had shown his claws.

He was cool now, in mind if not in body, for his forehead was streaming. So that was Hamon—the real Hamon, who would stick at nothing to get back the thing he had lost. He sat for half-an-hour, then, rising, took off his coat, his vest, his shirt, and then the silk singlet beneath. Fastened to his body with strips of sticking plaster was a small bag of oiled silk, through which he could read certain of the words which appeared on the document which Hamon, no less than Morlake, so greatly desired.

He fixed two fresh strips of sticking plaster, dressed himself, and, examining his revolver carefully, slipped it into his hip pocket. There was only one thing to be done, and that must be done immediately. He had a thought of calling on Slone, but Slone might easily complicate matters, and he decided on the whole that it would be best if he worked alone. He must go at once, before the would-be murderer recovered from his fright. He put on his overcoat, took a loaded cane from the hall stand, and went out.

Jim Morlake was the solution to his difficulties and the shield to his danger. He saw that with startling clearness. Closing the door behind him, he looked left and right, but, as he expected, there was no sign of the foreign-looking sailor.

A cab took him to Victoria, and he found he had half-an-hour to wait for a train to the nearest railway junction. Another whisky fortified him for the journey, and he ensconced himself in the corner of a first-class carriage which was occupied by two other men.

At eleven o'clock that night, Jim, who was genuinely working in his study, heard feet coming up the gravel drive, and, opening the door, was audience to a parley between Binger and some unknown person. Presently Binger came in in a state of great excitement.

"It's that damned Marborne," he whispered.

"Show him in," said Jim, after a moment's thought.

What would Marborne be wanting, he wondered? That he should suspect Jim of being The Black was natural, but he would hardly have taken a journey at that hour of the night, either to express his reproaches or to conduct a cross-examination.

"Bring him in here."

Marborne was looking very haggard and drawn, he thought. He expected trouble, but the man's attitude and manner were civility itself.

"I'm sorry to interrupt you at this time of night, Mr. Morlake," he said, "and I hope that you won't think I've come to see you about that little job last night."

Jim was silent.

"The fact of the matter is," said Marborne, dropping his voice, "I'm in——" Suddenly he spun round. "What's that?" he croaked.

There was a crunch of slow footsteps on the gravel outside.

"Who is it?" he asked hoarsely.

"I'll find out," said Jim.

He himself opened the door to the visitor.

"Come in, Welling. You're the second last person I expected to see."

"And who was the first?" asked Welling.

"An old friend of yours, who has just arrived—Marborne."

The white eyebrows of Captain Welling rose.

"Marborne! How interesting! Has he come down to get his money back?"

"I thought that at first," said Jim good-humouredly, "and of course, I couldn't very well refuse. No, I think it is something more serious than the loss of money that is bothering him."

Marborne's relief at seeing Jim's visitor was so evident that Jim was puzzled.

"Expecting a friend, Marborne?" said Julius genially.

"No—no, sir," stammered the man.

"I thought you weren't. You can put your gun away. Very bad business, carrying guns. I'm surprised at an old policeman like you thinking of such things. A good stick is all that a policeman needs—a good stick and the first blow!"

Something of Marborne's nerve had returned at the sight of the man who, more than any other, had been responsible for his ruin. He seemed suddenly to rid himself of the terror which had enveloped him like a cloud a few moments before.

"I won't trouble you about my business to-night, Mr. Morlake. Perhaps you could give me a few minutes in the morning?"

"If I'm in the way——" began Welling.

"No, sir. Where can I sleep to-night? I suppose there's an hotel here?"

"There is an inn," said Welling, "the Red Lion. I'm staying there myself. But I can wait; my business isn't very important. I merely wanted to ask Mr. Morlake a question or two."

"No, the morning will do," said Marborne.

He had come to a definite decision. Hamon should have his last chance. He was here, within a stone's throw. In the morning he would make his offer, and perhaps, with the accusation of an attempted murder hanging over his head, Hamon would pay more handsomely and more readily.

"You'll find two other friends of yours waiting outside—Milligan and Spooner," said Julius Welling. "Don't corrupt them, Marborne!"

"I thought you'd sent your bloodhounds back to town?" asked Jim when Marborne had gone.

"I did, but the man who was responsible for their being here sent them back to Creith by the next train. In our service, Mr. Morlake, it is a great mistake for one department to butt into the affairs of another. Messrs. Spooner and Milligan are not in my department."

He chuckled at this little comedy of inter-departmental dignity.

"But I'll shift them. I'll have them moved for you. I came up to-night to tell you that they were here—I shouldn't like you to think that I'd broken a promise. To-morrow I will apply humbly to the superintendent whom I asked to send these men, that he will be gracious enough to withdraw them, and they will be withdrawn. What is wrong with Marborne?"

"I don't know. He talked about being in something—I think he was going to say 'danger.' Maybe he has been drinking."

Welling shook his head.

"He wasn't drunk," he said. "I wonder what he means?" He was talking to himself. "We'll have him back, Morlake. He'll be talking with those fellows of mine."

They went out into the road together and the two detectives who were waiting for Welling's return came over to them.

"Is Marborne there?"

"No, sir," said Milligan.

"Has he gone?"

"I don't know what you mean, sir. I haven't seen him."

"You haven't what?" almost shouted Welling. "Didn't he come out of this gate two minutes ago?"

"No, sir," the two men spoke together. "Nobody came out of that gate until you came out."

There was a silence.

"Have either of you men got a lamp?"

For answer, Milligan's pocket torch shot a fan of light on to the ground, and, seizing the lamp, Welling walked back, sweeping the drive from left to right.

Half-way between the gates and the house he stopped and turned the light on to the bushes that bordered the drive.

Marborne lay face downward. There was a slight wound at the back of his head, but it was the knotted silk cord wound tightly around his throat that had killed him.

CHAPTER XXXV

The Letter That Came by Post

"HE's dead, I'm afraid," said Jim, at the end of half-an-hour's work on the still figure that lay on the floor of the study.

Stripped to his singlet, he had applied artificial respiration, but without effect. The man must have died a few seconds before they found him.

"Thorough!" said Welling, biting his lip thoughtfully, "very thorough and very quick. Searched to the skin, you notice."

The dead man's clothes had been torn open, so that his breast was exposed.

"That is where the mystery was hidden—fastened to his skin. It is an old dodge, which Marborne must have learnt in the course of his professional career."

Milligan returned from a search of the grounds, to report failure.

"We can do nothing till daylight, except warn the local police. Put a call through, Spooner. Turn out all the men you can find to search the meadows; the murderer must have gone that way because he could not have come out of the gate. He may make for one of the woods, but that is doubtful. You know the topography of the country, Morlake; which way would he have gone?"

"It depends entirely whether he knew it also," said Jim. "I suggest the footbridge across the river and the riverside path to the Amdon Road. But there are half-a-dozen ways that he may have gone if he can climb, and I should imagine that if you make an inspection of the walls, you will find that he has gone that way."

But here he was wrong.

Neither daylight nor beaters brought the murderer into their hands. The only discovery—and that was of first importance—was made by Spooner, who found, on the towpath, a long, curved knife which the assassin had dropped in his hurry.

"Moorish," said Jim. "That is to say, made in Birmingham and sold in Morocco. It is a type that is greatly favoured by the countryfolk, and unless it is a blind I think you can issue an order to pull in any Moor who is found within twenty miles of this place in the next few hours."

The only information that came to them was that a foreign-looking sailor had been seen on the Shoreham Road, but he was not black, added the report virtuously. Welling brought the wire to Jim.

"What do you think of the clever lads?" he groaned. "Not black! I suppose they expected to see a coal-black nigger. What colour would he be?"

"White, as likely as not," said Jim. "Many of the Moors are whiter than you or I."

The London police had searched Marborne's apartments, and his friend had been interviewed. Slone's evidence was that he had seen the dead man only the previous night. He had told him that he was nervous and mentioned the fact that he had seen a foreign sailor in Cambridge Circus who seemed to have lost himself.

"That is our man," said Welling. "He went to Marborne's flat and there was a fight. The dining-room was in disorder, tables and chairs overthrown, and they found a dummy letter addressed to Marborne, which is probably the excuse on which the man secured admission. Marborne must have fought him off and come down to you."

"Why?"

"Obviously because he wanted to sell you the document with which he was blackmailing Hamon. Therefore, he must have thought that Hamon employed the Moor to kill him. Therefore, again, Hamon must be privy to this murder, and."

he added in despair, "there is not enough evidence against Hamon even to justify a search warrant!"

Welling had made Wold House his headquarters—a singular choice, thought and said Ralph Hamon when he was summoned to meet Julius Welling in Jim's study.

"It may be amusing and it may be tragic," said Julius, no longer gentle, "but this place is good enough for me, and therefore I'm afraid it must be good enough for you. You know the news, Mr. Hamon?"

"That Marborne is killed? Yes, poor fellow!"

"A friend of yours?"

"I knew him. Yes, I could almost say that he was a friend of mine," said Hamon.

"When did you see him last?"

"I haven't seen him for several days."

"Was your interview a friendly one?"

"Very. He came to me to borrow some money to start a business."

"And you lent it to him, of course?" said Welling dryly. "And that is intended to explain the financial transactions between you and him?"

"What do you mean?" demanded Ralph Hamon. "Are you suggesting that I'm lying?"

"I'm *telling* you you're lying," said Welling shortly. "I suggest nothing when I'm investigating a charge of murder. I tell you again that you're lying. You gave him money for a purpose of your own. He had some document in his possession which you were anxious to recover, and since he would not return it to you, you paid him large sums of money by way of blackmail."

Hamon's face was grey.

"You're making a statement which may be investigated in a court of law."

"It certainly will, if I catch the murderer," said Welling grimly.

"Has it occurred to you," sneered Hamon, "that this man Harborne was an enemy of Morlake's, and that he was found dead in his grounds?"

"It has occurred to me many times in the night," said Welling. "Only, unfortunately for your theory, Morlake was with me when this man was killed, and the package, which was affixed to his body by strips of sticking plaster, was taken."

He saw the light come into Ralph Hamon's eyes and the drawn look of terror seemed instantly to disappear. It was the most wonderful facial transformation that he had seen in his long experience.

"You didn't know it, eh? Yes, your man got the package all right."

"My man?" said Hamon instantly. "What do you mean? You had better be careful, Welling. You're not so powerful a man at headquarters that you cannot be pulled down!"

"And you're not so wonderful a fellow that you couldn't be hanged," said Welling good-naturedly. "Come, come, Mr. Hamon, we don't want to quarrel; we want to get at the truth. Is it true that Marborne blackmailed you? I'll save you a lot of trouble by telling you that we have absolutely convincing proof that he did so blackmail you. Slone has told us."

Hamon shrugged his shoulders.

"What Slone told you is of no interest to me. I can only tell you that I lent money to this unfortunate man in order to start him in business, and if you have any proof to the contrary, you may produce it."

Nobody knew better than he that no such proof existed. Welling knew that his bluff had failed, but that did not greatly worry him. He tried a new tack.

"You have been sending a number of cables to Morocco recently, mainly in code, one especially in which you referred to Ali Hassan. Who is he?"

Again that look of anxiety came to Hamon's face, only to vanish instantly and leave him his cool, smiling self.

"Now I understand why they call detectives 'busies,'" he said. "You've had a very busy night! Ali Hassan is a brand of Moorish cigar!"

He looked at Jim and Jim nodded in confirmation.

"That is true. It is also the name of a notorious Moorish murderer who was hanged twenty-five years ago."

"Then take your choice," said Hamon with a quiet smile.

"This is your writing?" An envelope was suddenly produced from behind Welling's desk and thrust under the eyes of the other.

"No, it isn't my writing," said Hamon without hesitation. "What do you suggest, Inspector?"

"I suggest that Marborne was killed by a Moor, who was specially brought to this country for the purpose by you."

"In other words, that I am an accessory before and after this murder?"

Welling nodded.

"If the idea wasn't amusing, I should be very angry," said Hamon, "and in all the circumstances, I decline to give you any further information." He paused at the door carefully to fold the top of his soft felt hat. "And you cannot force me—nobody knows that better than you, Captain Welling. You understand—I will give you no further information."

Welling nodded.

"He has already given us more than he knows," he said when the door had closed upon the unwilling witness. "Who is Sadi Hafiz?"

"He is a poisonous rascal who lives in Tangier," said Jim without hesitation, "a man entirely without scruple but immensely useful to people like Hamon and other shady company promoters who want a plausible proposition to put before the public. He is an agent of Hamon's. I knew him years ago—in fact we had a slight shooting match—when I was employed on the survey of a suggested Fez railway. There were remarkable stories about him, some of them incredible. He is certainly the pensioner of half-a-dozen interests, and, I should imagine, has more serious crime or what passes for crime on his conscience than any other man in Morocco."

"Murder, for instance?" asked Welling.

Jim smiled.

"I said 'serious crimes.' Murder isn't a serious crime in the Rifi Hills."

Welling scratched his nose again.

"If we catch this Moorish fellow, he'll talk."

"He'll say nothing against Sadi Hafiz," said Jim promptly. "These shereefs are, in a sense, holy men. Sadi Hafiz could not pass through the streets of Tangier without having the hem of his garments frayed by kissing, and our murderer will die without saying a word to incriminate Sadi or any other person."

The story of the murder came to Joan through her agitated maid, and at first she was seized with a panic.

"In Mr. Morlake's garden? Are you sure?" she faltered.

"Yes, miss. Mr. Welling, a London gentleman, and Mr. Morlake found him, and it was only a minute or two after the poor man had left them that he was killed. Everybody is saying it is a judgment on the village for letting Mr. Morlake stay here."

"Then you can tell everybody they're fools," said Joan relieved.

"And they say that poor gentleman at Mrs. Cornford's is dying."

Joan did not make any reply to this. Later in the morning she went down to the cottage and learnt that the maid's fears were exaggerated.

At luncheon that day the murder was naturally the absorbing interest of conversation, but to Lord Creith alone.

"By gad!" he said with satisfaction. "The jolly old village is coming on! Haven't had a murder here for three hundred years. I was looking up the old records. A gypsy murdered another gypsy and was hanged at the top of No Man's Hill. They called it Gibbet Hill for a hundred years. What is your theory, Hamon? I understand you went down and saw the police?"

"I saw the police—yes," said Hamon shortly, "but what is the sense of discussing the matter with men of their limited intelligence? Welling is an old dotard, entirely under the thumb of that damned thief——"

"That thief," corrected Lord Creith with a bland smile. "We never damn anybody at this table unless my daughter is—er—not here. You were talking about Morlake, of course? So the police are under his thumb? Well, well, we are getting on! I thought Welling was an exceptionally bright man; and for his being old, he is two years younger than I, and nobody could call me old! Oh, by the way, Joan, that young man who is staying with Mrs. Cornford and is so ill—do you know who he is?"

Her lips moved, but she did not speak.

"He is young Farringdon—Sir Willoughby Farringdon's son. You remember old Farringdon? The boy was at Hulston College. You were at a school near Hulston of course! Yes, he is young Farringdon—a sad rascal. He got into some scrape at school and was kicked out. Old Willoughby never forgave him. I think he's been drinking too, but that is the old man's fault. All the Farringdons drank too much. I remember his grandfather . . ."

The girl sat rigid, listening without comment.

"Hulston turned out some queer birds," said the earl reminiscently. "There was that fellow Bannockwaite, the rascal! The fellow that started all those tomfool societies in the schools and demoralised them most devilishly. You remember him, Joan?"

"Yes, Father," she said, and something in her tone made Hamon look at her. She was white to the lips. Following the direction of his guest's eyes, Lord Creith jumped up and went to her side.

"Is anything wrong, Joan?" he asked anxiously.

"I feel a little faint—I don't know why. The day has been rather an exciting one. Will you excuse me, Daddy?"

He took her upstairs himself and did not leave her until he had brought half the household to her side.

Lord Creith went down to the village and in a frenzy of investigation found himself ringing the bell of Wold House. It was his first visit and Jim was flabbergasted to see him.

"Come in, Lord Creith," he said. "This is a very unexpected honour."

"If I didn't call now, I never should," said the earl with a twinkle in his eye. "I want to know all about this murder, and most of the police theories."

Jim was silent. He could not detail views which were unflattering to Lord Creith's guest. So he limited his narrative to a very full description of what happened on the night Marborne was killed, and the earl listened attentively. As chief of the local magistrates, it would be his duty to conduct the preliminary enquiry if a charge was brought.

"It is a most extraordinary happening," he said when Jim had finished, "wholly oriential in design and execution. I lived for some years in India and that type of murder is not new to me. Now what are the police theories?"

But here Jim excused himself, and, seeing through the window Welling engaged in directing the measurements which were being taken, he seized the opportunity of taking his lordship to the fountain-head.

"The curious thing is," said Lord Creith, "that I had a feeling that something unusual had happened. I woke an hour earlier than I ordinarily do. I should have heard about it at once from the postman, who is a great gossip, but for some reason or other, we had no early morning post to-day. In fact," Lord Creith meandered on, "only one letter came to Creith House to-day and that was at eleven o'clock and even that was not for me, but for my guest."

Welling spun round.

"For Mr. Hamon?" he asked quickly.

"Yes."

"From London?"

"No, curiously enough, it wasn't from London; it was from a little village about eight miles from here. I meant to ask Hamon who the dickens his correspondent was, but probably he is buying property in the neighbourhood—in fact, I know he is," he added grimly.

"What was the name of the village?"

"Little Lexham."

The detective frowned in an effort of concentration. If it came by the eleven o'clock mail, it would have been posted that morning.

"Was it a thick letter?"

"Yes. The first impression I had was that it had a pocket

handkerchief in it. Why do you ask these questions? Surely my guest's correspondence does not interest you, Captain Welling?"

"It interests me very much. You don't remember the handwriting?"

Lord Creith's brows met.

"I don't quite get the tendency of this inquiry," he said, "but I did notice the handwriting. It was addressed in printed characters."

"Was the envelope a thick one?"

"Yes, I should say it was. I remember it because it was covered with dirty finger-marks, and I asked the postman who had been handling the mail."

Welling made up his mind quickly.

"I am going to take you into my confidence, Lord Creith," he said. "I have reason to believe that Marborne was murdered because he had in his possession a document which Mr. Hamon was anxious to procure."

"Good God!" said Lord Creith aghast.

"If my theory is right—and the document was obviously taken from the body of Marborne—the murderer slipped whatever he found into an addressed envelope which had already been supplied to him. If he is a Moor, he would have enough intelligence to place the letter in the post."

"Do you know what you're saying?" asked Lord Creith breathlessly.

"I'm merely giving you my theory in confidence, and you're entitled to receive it in confidence, Lord Creith, since you are a magistrate in this county. Is it possible to get that envelope?"

Lord Creith thought for a little while.

"Come back to the house with me," he said. "I don't know whether I'm standing on my head or my heels—by the time we get to the Hall I shall be more certain of myself."

Hamon was out. He had followed Joan into the park, to her intense annoyance.

"I'm blessed if I know what to do," said his lordship helplessly. "I suppose I might as well be hanged for a sheep as for a lamb, so go ahead and look at his room."

Welling's search was thorough and rapid; it was also in part fruitless. There was a writing-table and a waste-paper basket, but the basket was empty—had been emptied in the early morning.

"Ah, there it is!" said Welling suddenly and pointed to the large open fireplace.

A scrap of burnt ash had blown into the corner and he picked it up tenderly.

"This is the envelope and something else." There were ashes which were not of paper.

He picked up a small portion and smelt.

"That isn't paper," he said. Welling looked up at the ceiling for inspiration. "No, I can't place it. Will you give me an envelope?"

He collected the ashes into two separate envelopes and put them in his pocket and got downstairs in time to see a weary Joan and her suitor coming up the broad stairs of the terrace before the house. She passed Welling with a little nod and took her father's arm.

"Daddy, can I speak to you?" she said. "Can I come to the library?"

"Certainly, my love," he said, looking at her closely. "You're still very pale; are you sure you ought to be out?"

She nodded.

"I'm quite all right," she said. "You mustn't worry. I wonder how pale you'll be when I—when I tell you what I have to tell you?"

He stopped and looked at her.

"And I wonder how disappointed in me you'll be?"

Here he shook his head.

"It is going to take a lot to make me disappointed in you, Joan," he said, and put his arm round her shoulder.

She tried hard not to cry, but the strain was terrific. Lord Creith closed the door and led her to a recessed window seat.

"Now, Joan," he said, and his kindly eyes were full of love and sympathy, "confess up."

Twice she tried to speak and failed, and then:

"Daddy, I married Ferdie Farringdon when I was at school," she said in a low voice.

His eyes did not waver.

"A jolly good family, the Farringdons, but addicted to drink," said his lordship, and she fell, sobbing, into her arms.

CHAPTER XXXVI

The Bannockwaite Bride

"Now let's hear all about it."

He held her at arm's length.

"And look up, Jean. There's nothing you'll ever do that is going to make any difference to me or my love for you. You're the only person in the world who isn't a bother and who couldn't be a bother."

Presently she told the story.

"Mr. Bannockwaite started it. It was a society called the Midnight Monks. The boys at Hulston used to come over the wall and we would sit around in the convent garden and eat things—pastry and pies, a sort of midnight picnic. It will sound strange to you that that could be innocent, but it was. All those queer societies of his started that way, however they developed. We were the Midnight Monks, and my dearest friend, Ada Lansing, was our 'prioress.' Of course, the sisters knew nothing—the sisters of the convent I mean. Poor dears! They'd have died if they had dreamt of such goings-on! And then somebody suggested that, in order that the two branches of the society should be everlastingly united there should be a wedding symbolical of our union—that and nothing more. You think all this is madly incredible, but things like that happen, and I think Bannockwaite was behind the suggestion. He had just come down from Oxford and had built the little chapel in the woods. He never lost touch with any of the societies he formed and he was very much interested in the Monks, which was the first he invented. I know he came down because he presided at one of our summer night feasts. We drew lots as to who should be the bride——"

"And the choice fell on you?" said Lord Creith gently.

She shook her head.

"No, it fell upon Ada, and she was enthusiastic—terribly enthusiastic until the day of the wedding. It was a holiday and the seniors were allowed out in twos. Mr. Bannockwaite arranged everything. The man was to dress like a monk, with his face cowled, and the girl was to be heavily veiled. Nobody was to know the other. We weren't even supposed to know who had drawn the lots. Can you imagine anything more mad? Mr. Bannockwaite was to perform the ceremony. We went to this dear little chapel in the woods near Ascot, and in the vestry poor Ada broke down. I think it was then that I first realised how terribly serious it was. I won't make a long story of it, Daddy—I took Ada's place."

"Then you never saw your husband's face?"

She nodded.

"Yes, the cowl fell back and I saw him, and when the ceremony was over and I signed the register, I saw his name. I don't think he saw mine, unless he has been back since."

"And you never saw him again?"

She shook her head.

"No, that was the plan. I never saw him until—until he came here. I heard he was dead. It seems a terribly wicked thing to say, but I was almost glad when poor Ada died."

Lord Creith filled his pipe with a hand that shook.

"It was damnable of Bannockwaite, and even his death doesn't absolve him. It might have been worse." He put his arm around her and squeezed her gently. "And it is hard on you, Joan, but it can be remedied."

"It is harder—than you think," she said.

The Lord of Creith was a very human man, and his knowledge of humanity did not stop short at guessing.

"What is wrong, girlie?" he asked. "Do you love somebody else?"

She nodded.

"That certainly is unfortunate." The old twinkle had come back to his eyes, and he pulled her up to her feet. "Come along and have tea," he said. "Feel better?"

She kissed him. The Creiths were not demonstrative, and to be kissed by his daughter was generally a source of embarrassment to his lordship. On this particular occasion he felt like crying.

Joan went up to her room, removed the traces of tears from her face, and his lordship strolled into the library. Hamon was there with his back to the fire, his face black as a thundercloud.

"My man tells me that you took the police up to my room—why?"

"Because I am the principal magistrate in this part of the world, and I cannot refuse a request when it is made to me by a responsible officer," said Lord Creith quietly.

"I suppose you remember occasionally that this house is mine?"

"I never forget it," said the earl, "but if this county was yours it would not make the slightest difference to me, Hamon. If you were under suspicion of murder——"

"Under suspicion? What do you mean? Have you taken up that crazy story? What did the police want? Why did they search my room? What did they expect to find?"

He fired off the questions in rapid succession.

"They expected to find a burnt envelope," said Lord Creith wearily, and he got a certain malicious satisfaction when he saw his guest start. "It was a letter that was delivered to you, posted at Little Lexham this morning."

"They didn't find it," said the other harshly.

"They found the ashes thereof," said Lord Creith, and then: "Do you mind switching off wilful murder? I find I'm not so fascinated by crime as I used to be. And, by the way, Hamon, what time shall I order your chauffeur?"

"Why order my chauffeur at all?"

"Because you're going back to town to-night," said his lordship, almost jauntily. "You're constantly reminding me that this house is yours. Let me remind you that I am a tenant for life, and that until my certain-to-be-regretted demise I have all the authority, legal and moral, to order you out of my house, which I do at this moment and in the plainest terms I can command!"

"This is a remarkable action on your part, Lord Creith," said the visitor in a milder tone.

"I don't know that it is remarkable, but it is certainly necessary," said his lordship, and, without any further conversation with his visitor, he ordered the car to be ready in an hour.

His valet brought the news to Ralph Hamon.

"We're not returning to London. Go down to the Red Lion and book me a bedroom and a sitting-room," he said.

This development had considerably altered his plans. Marborne's death and the safe recovery of the thing he had risked so much to hold, did not promise complete safety; and now that he was under suspicion, there was a double reason why he should not leave Creith until his mission was accomplished, and until he had made sure that disaster did not come from the least considered source.

Besides, he had told Ahmet to hurt but not to kill! It was no fault of his if the fool had exceeded his instructions. He had given similar orders to a certain Ali Hassan, with as unhappy consequences; but Ali Hassan was a smoker of hashish and an undependable man, or he might have carried out his orders to the letter.

Lord Creith heard that his guest had taken up his quarters at the Red Lion without feeling any sense of uneasiness.

"I don't know what the Red Lion is like nowadays," he said to his daughter. "In the days of my youth it was notoriously dirty and full of fleas, and I trust it has not changed. The air is cleaner now, my duck. This Hamon is a very nasty fellow."

And she was inclined to agree. She had not seen Jim since the meeting on the hill, and she purposely avoided contact with him. What would he think of her? How was he feeling? Was he hurt? She hoped most fervently that he was.

"Do you like Americans, Father?"

"I like some of them, and I detest some of them," said his lordship, without raising his eyes from the newspaper he was reading; "but that remark equally applies to almost any nation. Why?" He looked over the top of the paper. "You're thinking of Morlake?" he said.

"I was," she confessed.

"A very nice fellow. I never knew that a desperado could be so nice. He is a gentleman, too," he added, and returned to his newspaper.

CHAPTER XXXVII

The Letter

THE people of Creith wondered to see their lord's principal guest, and, if rumour did not lie, the future owner of the estate, moving his lodgings to the village inn; but Hamon had got to the point where he did not care what they thought. A week ago, such an affront to his dignity would have driven him desperate; but now something else was at stake. Unexpectedly his world was rocking dangerously.

He wired Lydia to meet him in London on the morrow, and, waiting until it was dark, he went out from his lodgings and bent his steps to the gardener's cottage. Mrs. Cornford opened the door to him, and at first she did not recognise him in the darkness.

"I want to see you, Mrs. Cornford," he said.

"Who is it?" she asked.

"Ralph Hamon."

She did not move, standing squarely in the narrow passage, and then, opening the door wider:

"Come in," she said, and followed him into the little parlour.

"You haven't changed very much, Mrs. Cornford," he said, at a loss how to approach the subject which had brought him there.

She made no reply. It was an awkward situation, and again he sought for an opening.

"I suppose you're still feeling sore with me?"

"No," she replied quietly, and then: "Won't you sit down, Mr. Hamon?"

"There is no reason why you should feel sore. I did everything I could for Johnny."

"Where is he?" she asked.

"I don't know—dead, I suppose," he said, and at the brutality of his words she winced a little.

"I think he is dead too," she breathed, nodding slowly. "You were equally sure that he was alive twelve years ago," she said quietly. "What happened to his money, Mr. Hamon?"

"He lost it: I told you that before," said Hamon impatiently.

Her eyes never left him.

"He wrote to me from Morocco, saying that he had seen the mine, and how splendid a property it was, and then a month later he wrote from London, saying that he was fixing everything with you, and I never heard from him again."

"He disappeared: that is all I know," said Hamon. "He was coming to my office to complete the purchase of shares, and he didn't turn up. I wired you, asking where he was, immediately."

His tone was a defiance.

"I only know that he drew a hundred thousand pounds from the bank, and that neither he nor the money was seen again," she said steadily. "I am not pretending, Mr. Hamon, that my husband and I were very happy. He was of too erratic a disposition, had too many friends of both sexes that I could not possibly approve; he was a drunkard too, but he was in some respects a good man. He would not have left me a beggar as he did."

He shrugged his shoulders.

"Why didn't you go to the police?" he asked blandly. "If you had any doubts about me——"

She looked down upon him, a contemptuous smile upon her tired face.

"You begged me not to go to the police," she said in a low voice. "I see now what a fool I was. You begged me, for my own sake and for the sake of my husband's people, not to advertise his absence."

"Didn't I put advertisements in every newspaper? Didn't I send agents to Monte Carlo, to Aix, to Deauville—to every gambling place where he might be?" he demanded with simulated indignation. "Really, Mrs. Cornford, I don't think you're treating me quite fairly."

It was useless to reply to him. He had put her off her search until the cleverest detective agencies in England found it impossible to pick up a clue, for she had delayed independent action until that independent action was futile. One day she had been a rich woman with a home and an independent income. The next, she was beggared.

If John Cornford had been the ordinary type of business man, there would have been no question as to her action. She would have notified the police immediately of his disappearance. But Johnny Cornford, prince of good fellows to all but his own, had a habit of making these mysterious disappearances. She had learnt, in the course of her life, the discretion of silence.

"Why have you come?" she asked.

"Because I wanted to settle up this matter of Johnny. I feel responsible, to the extent that I brought him to London. Will you show me the letter he sent you from town?"

She shook her head.

"You wanted to see that before, Mr. Hamon. It is the only evidence I have that he had returned to England at all. Some time ago, a man asked you what had become of my husband, and you said that he had been lost in the desert in Morocco. Hundreds of people who knew him are under the impression that he died there."

"What is that?" he asked suddenly. There was a low wail of sound.

"I have a young man staying with me who is very ill," she said, and hurried from the room.

He looked round the apartment. Where would a woman of that sort keep her letters? Not in an accessible dining-room, he thought. Somewhere in the bedroom, probably. The door connecting the rooms was open, and he looked in. A candle was burning on the table. He heard her footsteps and stepped back quickly to his seat.

"Now I'll tell you what I'm going to do, Mrs. Cornford. If you will let me see that letter, I will tell you the whole truth about Johnny's death."

"He is dead, then?" she asked huskily, and he nodded.

"He has been dead ten years."

She seemed to be struggling with herself. Presently she got up, went to the bedroom and closed the door behind her, returning in a few minutes with a small ebony box, which she opened.

"Here is the letter," she said. "You may read it."

Yes, it *was* blue! He knew that it was written on Critton Hotel notepaper—the Critton note was blue.

He read the scrawled writing. It was dated from a London hotel.

I am seeing Ralph Hamon to-day, and we are fixing the purchase of the shares. The only thing about which I am not certain—and this I must discover—is whether the property I saw was Hamon's mine, or a very prosperous concern which has no connection whatever with Ralph's company. Not that I think he would deceive me.

She watched him intently, ready to snatch at the letter if he attempted to pocket it, but he handed it back to her, and she replaced it in the box and closed the lid. She was about to speak when again there came that moaning sound from the next room. She hesitated a moment, locked the little ebony box and carried it back to her bedroom, turning the key on the bedroom door after her when she came out. He watched with a certain amount of amusement, and when she went into the invalid's room he followed her.

"Who is this man?" he asked, regarding curiously the gaunt face that lay on the pillows.

"He is my boarder," she said, troubled. "I'm afraid he is worse to-night.

Farringdon rose on his elbow and tried to get out of bed. It took all her strength to push him back. Again he tried to rise, and it took their united efforts to force him back.

"Will you stay here whilst I get the doctor?" she asked.

Ralph Hamon had no desire to act as nurse to a half-crazy patient, but in all the circumstances he thought it would be advisable. He pulled up a chair and watched the poor wretch who tossed from side to side, muttering and laughing in his delirium. Presently the sick man's voice grew clear.

"Joan—married? Yes, her father is Lord somebody or other," said the patient. "I never knew. You see, they found out that afternoon—the house-master heard me talking to Bannockwaite. We were married at the little church in the wood. I didn't want to marry, but the gang insisted. We drew lots. It was Bannockwaite's fault. He was never quite normal. You know Bannockwaite? He was ordained that year, and he thought it was a great joke. They chucked him out of the Church for something queer that happened, but I was abroad then and don't quite know what it was all about. Anyway, he was killed in the war. He ought never to have been a parson. Bannockwaite, I mean. He started the society, the Midnight Monks, when he was a kid at Hulston—that's my school. The girls at the convent next door used to sneak over the wall and we ate candies. . . . Joan, that was her name—Joan. Her father was Lord somebody and lived in Sussex. Bannockwaite told me that she was a peeress. I didn't want her. . . . Ban called her Ada something when we were married, but her name was Joan . . ."

Hamon listened, electrified. Joan! It must be Joan Carston. He bent over the sick man and asked eagerly:

"Where were you married?"

For a time the invalid said something that he could not catch.

"Where?" he asked sharply.

"Little church in a wood at Ascot," murmured Farringdon. "It is in the register."

Hamon knew the reputation of Bannockwaite, and guessed the rest of the story. Joan was married! He pursed his lips at the thought. It was at once a lever and a barrier. He heard the feet of Mrs. Cornford and the doctor, and drew back to the doorway. It was easy to take his farewells now, and, with a nod to the woman which she hardly saw, he went back to the hotel.

It was half-an-hour before the doctor left, and, in spite of the feverish condition of the patient, he reported a distinct improvement.

"I'll have a nurse in from the County Hospital to-night, Mrs. Cornford," he said, and she thanked him gratefully. She had had little sleep for forty-eight hours.

Why had Ralph Hamon called, she asked herself? And what could be the object of his wanting to see that letter? He had asked years before, but she had refused him access, feeling, in some way, that its possession retained for her a last grasp on the fortune which had slipped through her hands.

She had taken a great risk in letting him touch it, and she was thankful that there were no worse consequences to her folly. Before she went to bed that night she opened the drawer of her bureau, took out the box and unlocked it. There was the faded blue letter on the top. She was closing the lid down when it occurred to her to read this last message from her husband, and she opened the sheet. It was blank.

Ralph Hamon knew the colour of the letter, knew its shape and size. It had been easy to ring the changes.

What should she do? The hour was late. Should she go to the hall and invoke Lord Creith's assistance? She had only seen him once, and she was already in his debt. And then her mind turned to Jim—that quiet, capable man, and, putting on her hat and coat, she hurried to Wold House.

There are certain advantages and some disadvantages to an hotel. The disadvantage, from Ralph Hamon's point of view, was its accessibility to the outside public. He was sitting before a fire in his bedroom, for the night was chilly, smoking his last cigar, and ruminating upon the queerness of this latest development, when, without so much as a knock, the door opened and Jim Morlake walked in.

"I've got two pieces of news for you, Hamon. The first is

that your Moor is caught. The second is that you're going to give me a letter that you stole from Mrs. Cornford, and you're going to give it to me very, very quickly."

CHAPTER XXXVIII

A Yachting Trip

RALPH HAMON rose to his feet, his hands in his pockets, his jaw out-thrust.

"My Moor, as you call him, doesn't interest, and this yarn about a stolen letter doesn't even amuse me."

"I didn't come here at this hour of the night to make you laugh," said Jim. "I want that letter."

He took two strides across the room, and then, with an oath, Hamon sprang between him and the dressing-table.

"It's there, is it? Get out of my way!"

He brushed the man aside as though he were a child, and pulled open the drawer. On the top was a pocket-book, and this he took out.

"You thief!" howled Hamon, and leapt at him.

Again he reeled back from the outstretched hand.

"Here is the letter," said Jim. "Now, if——"

He did not finish his sentence. Grinning with rage, Hamon saw him make a rapid search of the pocket-book, but the thing he sought was not there.

"Found it?" he said exultantly.

"I've found the letter—that was enough," said Jim, as he slipped it into his pocket and dropped the case back into the drawer. "You can call the police if you like. I don't mind—I'm used to it. There's a fine charge for you—breaking and entering!"

Hamon said nothing.

"If your Moor talks, there will be some sad hearts on Wall

Street—nothing depreciates the stock of a Corporation more than the hanging of its president!"

Still Hamon made no reply. He flung open the window, and, leaning out, watched the tall man till he disappeared into the night, and then he went back to his interrupted reflections, but now they were on another plane. And invariably his thoughts came back to the starting point, which was Joan Carston—the married Joan. Joan, linked in some indefinable way with Jim Morlake. Lydia had told him they were engaged, and he had laughed at the idea. Was he the real barrier? If he could be sure . . . !

He left the next morning for London and went to Victoria to meet Lydia in the afternoon. She had read of the murder of Marborne in the Paris newspapers, and was a little frightened and nervous—he was amazed to note how the news had affected her.

"How did it happen, Ralph?" she asked in the car on the way home. "How dreadful! Was he really killed by a Moor? You know nothing about it, do you, Ralph?" She gripped his hand in both of hers and peered into his face. "You didn't, did you? It would be horrible if I thought otherwise. Of course you didn't!"

"You're getting hysterical, Lydia. Of course I know no more about this poor devil's death than you. It was a great shock to me. I don't pretend I liked the man, and I liked him less after he got so fresh with you."

"What are you going to do, Ralph?"

"I'm going to get away out of this country," he said. "I'm sick of it."

"To Morocco?"

He saw the corners of her mouth droop.

"Yes, to Morocco. We'll go there for Christmas: it is the best time of the year."

"Not for good?"

"Of course not. If you're bored you can run over to Gibraltar or Algeciras. You needn't stay in the place," he soothed her. "Maybe I won't go there at all. I ought to go to New York to finish off a business deal. You were telling me last week, when you were over here, about a swell French friend of yours who was hiring a yacht to take some people to the South Sea Islands. It fell through, didn't it?"

"Yes," she said, looking at him wonderingly.

"Do you think you could go along and charter the yacht for the winter?"

"Why not go by the usual route, Ralph? It is more comfortable," she said.

"I prefer the sea."

She did not answer him, knowing that he was a bad sailor.

"Will you see what you can do in this matter?" he asked impatiently.

"Yes, Ralph. Count Lagune is in London at this moment, I think. It could easily be arranged."

She came to him in the evening with a story of accomplishment. She had chartered the yacht provisionally, and the Count had telegraphed to Cherbourg to have the vessel sent to Southampton. She found her brother in a jubilant mood, for the Moor had escaped from the little Sussex lockup to which he had been taken, and had half-killed a policeman in the process.

"Your Moor will talk!" he mimicked Jim. "Let him. I guess he's talking!"

She was staring at him, wide-eyed with horror.

"Ralph!" she gasped. "It isn't true—you knew nothing about this?"

"Of course I didn't, you fool!" he said roughly. "They thought I did. That swine Morlake practically accused me—said the man was in my service, which was a lie. I've never heard of him."

That night he wrote a letter to the Earl of Creith, and it was both conciliatory and logical.

"I must say," said his lordship, wagging his head, "this fellow isn't as bad as he looks. He has written a most charming letter, and I'm rather sorry I was such a pig."

"The only man you could talk about so offensively is Mr. Hamon," said the girl with a smile.

She took the letter from her father's hand and read it.

I'm afraid I have been rather a boor these last few days [it ran] *but so many things have happened to get on my nerves and I know I have not been quite normal. I hope you will not think too badly of me, and that in a year or two's time we shall both be amused at the absurd suggestion that I was in any way responsible for poor Marborne's death. I have been called unexpectedly to America, which has changed my plans considerably, for I had contemplated a yachting cruise in the Mediterranean and I find myself with a yacht on my hands. I wonder if I can persuade you to take the trip? You would be quite alone, and I am sure you would have an enjoyable time. I only regret that neither myself nor my sister can be with you. The yacht is the "L'Esperance," and will be at Southampton on Tuesday. May I beg of you, as a very great favour, to use the yacht as if she were yours, and save me from what, to a financier, is a misery —a sense of having wasted my money.*

"H'm!" mused the Earl. "Of course, if he'd been going on a trip, I should have written him a very polite letter, telling him that in no circumstances should I share the voyage with him. But this is different, don't you think, my love?"

Again he shook his head at the letter.

"I'm not so sure that the trip wouldn't be good for us all," he said.

Knowing how strong were her prejudices against Hamon, he expected some opposition. He was therefore agreeably surprised when she fell in with his view. Creith was on her nerves too—Creith and the sick man at Mrs. Cornford's, and Jim, whom she never saw and ached to see.

The first news of the intended trip came, as usual, ex Binger, and the divers junctions of intelligence that met in the tap-room of the Red Lion.

"It appears that this yacht—it is hon loan to Hamon."

"What do you mean by 'on loan'—has it been chartered?"

"Yes, sir. If my information is haccurate."

"Which in all likelihood it isn't—where are they going?"

"To the Mediterranean, sir. Mr. Hamon and sister are hoff to America. Which they are welcome to."

"To the Mediterranean?"

Jim looked into the bowl of his pipe thoughtfully.

"That means . . . When do they go?"

"On Saturday, sir."

"Indeed!" said Jim.

For the Mediterranean meant Tangier, and Tangier stood in his mind for Sadi Hafiz and the beautiful hell in the Rifi Hills.

CHAPTER XXXIX

The Chapel in the Wood

THERE is a little chapel which stands back from the Bagshot Road. The beauty of its outlines is hidden by the jealous trees. An open gateway in a side road leads, apparently, into the cool depths of the wood, without any suggestion that anything more solid than the pines or more beautiful than the wild violets that grow here in spring is concealed there.

Ralph Hamon left his car on the Bagshot Road and proceeded afoot to his investigations. For a time he stood looking at the graceful lines of the little edifice, though in his mind there was no thought of its æsthetic beauty or the loveliness of its surroundings. He only wondered who could have been such a fool as to build a church miles from the nearest village. He also speculated as to what the collections were, and what it cost to build the chapel, and who was the lunatic who had endowed such a useless structure.

The door was open: he went into the tiny porch and pushed gingerly at the baize door. The interior, with its gorgeous stained-glass windows and its marble altar, looked bigger than it actually was. A man was sweeping the tessellated floor, and looked round as he heard the door close.

"Good-day to you," said Ralph. "Is the vicar about?"

The cleaner shook his head.

"No, sir, there's no vicar here. The curate of St. Barnabas' generally comes over to take the service. But usually we open it for marriages—there is one to-day."

"Why for marriages?" asked Ralph, surprised.

"Because it's romantic," said the man vaguely. "You know what young people are—they like a bit of romance in their lives. It was built for a marrying church by a rich young parson named—now, what was his name?"

"Bannockwaite?" suggested Ralph.

"That's the name." The verger shook his head. "He was a bad lot, according to what I've heard."

It was a marrying church! That was good news. There would be a register. He asked the question.

"Yes, sir, the register is kept here."

He looked round dubiously toward the vestry door.

"I don't know whether I'm supposed to show it to you. You have to pay a fee, don't you?"

"I'll pay your fee, my friend. You produce your register."

He followed the man through the little arched doorway into a small stone room furnished with a table and a few chairs. His fear was that the verger would not have either the authority for or the opportunity of showing him the book, but apparently there was no difficulty here, for the man unlocked the chest and laid a heavy volume on the table.

"What date would it be?"

"It would be five or six years ago," said Hamon.

"That's as long as the church has been built," said the verger doubtfully, and turned back to the first page to verify his statement.

And the first entry on the first page was the record of a marriage between Ferdinand Charles Farringdon and Joan Mary Carston!

With fingers that trembled he made a copy of the entry, tipped the verger lavishly, and hurried out into the open. He saw a man walking unconcernedly between the pines, but, in his excitement, scarcely noticed, let alone recognised him.

How was he to use his knowledge to the best advantage?

Should he go to the girl, tell her all he knew, and threaten her with exposure? He rejected this plan. What was there to expose? Still, he had the knowledge, and sooner or later it must be of value.

He went back to town in a more cheerful mood than he had been for days. Julius Welling watched his departure, and would have followed instantly, but he was anxious to know what business had brought the financier to Ascot. . . .

Lydia was superintending her packing when her brother arrived, and she was more amiable than usual.

"You're back, Ralph?" she said. "I wanted to see you about one or two things. You can't tell how glad I am you've decided to go to America. I've always wanted to see the United States. You'll go to Palm Beach, won't you——"

"Let us get this thing right before we go any farther," said Hamon. "We are not going to America!"

Her face fell.

"We're going to Morocco."

"Morocco!" she gasped. "But, Ralph, you've made the reservations."

He sighed wearily.

"It was necessary to make reservations, because I don't want anybody to know what my plans are."

"But you have loaned the yacht to Lord Creith. You said you hated the idea of a sea voyage——"

"We're going by train—as you suggested," said Hamon. "My business calls me there, and it is absolutely necessary that I should see Sadi before Christmas."

She was silent and resentful, and stood biting her lip and regarding him from under her lowered brows.

"I don't like this, Ralph," she said. "There is something wrong."

"There is more than one thing wrong, my dear," he said. "The whole universe is a little off its feet, and I am speaking more especially of *my* universe. I'll tell you this plainly: I want Joan Carston."

She looked up at him.

"You mean you want to marry her?"

"I want to marry her if it is possible," he said carefully. "There are certain obstacles in the way for the moment, but they won't remain obstacles very long."

"But if she doesn't like you——?"

"What married couple ever like one another?" said Ralph roughly. "They are infatuated—in love, as they call it. But liking is a matter of growth and a matter of respect. And you can make a woman respect you in half-a-dozen ways. The first essential to respect is fear. Puzzle that out, my girl."

"Is it necessary that I should come?"

"Very necessary," he said promptly.

She took a cigarette from a little jewelled case and lit it, watching him keenly.

"I suppose you'll want a whole lot of help from Sadi Hafiz?" she said carelessly.

"I certainly shall."

"And you think that Sadi will be more amenable—if I am there?"

His surprise did not deceive her.

"I have never thought of it in that light," he said.

"I hate the place!" She stamped her foot angrily. "That beastly old house and dingy garden, and those wretched women prying at me from behind the grilles——"

"It is a lovely house," he interrupted enthusiastically, "and the air is like wine——" He stopped suddenly.

"You're thinking of another house," she said quickly. "Has he another?"

"I believe he has, somewhere on the hills," he answered shortly, and refused to be drawn any further on the subject.

He locked himself in his study for the rest of the day, and she thought he was working; imagined him turning out drawers, destroying papers, and clearing up the correspondence that such a man allowed to fall into arrears. But, in truth, Ralph Hamon was dreaming. He sprawled in an easy chair, his eyes fixed on vacancy, conjuring a hundred situations in which he played a leading and a flattering part. He dreamt Jim Morlake into prison and Joan into his arms. He dreamt great financial coups and the straightening out of life's tangle. And so he passed from romance to reality, and his dreams became plans, just as Lady Joan Carston became Lady Joan Hamon.

At five o'clock he unlocked the door and lounged into his sister's room. She had a cup of tea, a novel and a cigarette, but she also had found occupation for her thoughts, and the book was unread and the cigarette was burning itself away in the jasper tray.

"You look pleased with yourself."

"I am," he said, his eyes shining, "I am!"

CHAPTER XL

The Lover

"PLEASE, sir, there's a lady to see you."

Cleaver spoke in hushed tones, and, by the air of awestricken wonder, Jim gathered somebody unusual had called.

"Who is the lady?" he asked, and knew before the man replied.

"Lady Joan."

Jim jumped up from his chair.

"Why didn't you ask her in?" he said.

"She wouldn't come in, sir. She is on the lawn: she asked if she could speak to you."

He hurried out into the garden. Joan was standing at the river bank, her hands behind her, looking down into the water, and, hearing the swish of his shoes on the grass, she turned.

"I wanted to see you," she said. "Shall we cross the river? I am on my way to the house, and you might take me as far as the coverts."

They walked in silence until they were beyond the inquisitive eyes of Cleaver.

"I left you rather abruptly on No Man's Hill," she said. "I think that it is due to you that I should finish my story."

And then she told him, in almost identical words, the story she had told her father and he listened, dumfounded.

"I am so sick of it all and I've had to make this confession twice; once to my father, because—well it was due to him, and once to you because——"

She did not finish her sentence nor did he press her.

"The marriage can be annulled, of course," he said.

She nodded.

"Father said that, and I suppose it seems very simple to you. But to me it means going into court and having this ghastly business thrashed out point by point." She shivered. "I don't think I shall ever do it," she said. "I'm a coward; did you know that?"

"I have never had that estimate of you," he laughed. "No, Joan. I don't believe that! One isn't a coward because one shirks the ugliness of life. You're going away, aren't you?"

She nodded.

"I don't want to make the trip, but I think it will be good for father. The winter climate here doesn't suit him and it will be a change for us both. I thought there was a catch in it somewhere," she half smiled, "but really Mr. Hamon is going to America. He is with father now, taking his farewells."

"And that is one of the reasons why I have the privilege of seeing you?" he chuckled, but she protested vigorously.

"No, I should have come anyway. I had to tell you about—about the marriage. And do you know, James, I have a feeling that Hamon knows."

"How could he?"

"He was at the house one night when Mr. Farringdon was unusually violent. It was the night Mrs. Cornford lost her letter, which you got back for her. And she said that Farringdon had been talking about the church in the wood at Ascot all the time. A man of Hamon's shrewdness would jump at the truth."

"Does it matter?" asked Jim quietly after a pause, "whether he knows or not? How is Farringdon, by the way?"

She shrugged her shoulders.

"He is better. It is wicked of me not to be thankful, but,

Jim, I can't be—I shall have to call you Jim, I suppose. I saw him to-day; he was walking in the plantation at the back of the cottage."

"Is he so far recovered as that?" asked Jim in surprise, "but would he recognise you?"

She nodded.

"I have a feeling that he did," she said. "Yes, he has recovered. The doctor told Mrs. Cornford that these cases get better with surprising rapidity. I didn't know he was in the wood. I was on my way to the cottage to ask after him, and suddenly we came face to face and he looked at me very oddly as I passed. What makes me think he knows is that Mrs. Cornford told me he had been asking who was Lady Joan and what rank was her father. And then he asked how far it was to Ascot."

Her voice trembled and she bit her lip to recover her self-possession.

"He may be guessing," she said after a while, "but even that may make it more difficult for me. What am I to do, Jim? What am I to do?"

He had to hold himself in, or he would have taken her into his arms. He loved her; he had not realised how intensely until that moment. To Jim Morlake she was the beginning and end of existence and all its desirability. He would have changed the plan of his life, and abandoned the quest that had occupied ten years of his life, to save her from one heart-ache.

Looking up, she dropped her eyes again, as though she read in his face something of the burning fire that was consuming him. He laid his hand on her shoulders and his touch was a caress. Slowly they paced toward the wood, and instinctively she leaned more and more upon him, until his arm was about her and her cheek brushed the home-spun of his sleeve.

Ralph Hamon had said good-bye to the Earl of Creith and was searching the grounds for the girl when he saw the two and stopped dead. Even at that distance, there was no mistaking the athletic figure and the clean-moulded face of Jim Morlake. Still more impossible was it to misunderstand the relationship of these two.

They disappeared into the straggling plantation and he stood for some time biting his nails, his heart hot with impotent rage. There *was* something between them, after all! He had pooh-poohed the suggestion when Lydia had made it, but here was a demonstration beyond all doubt. He broke into a run down the grassy slope toward the strip of wood, not knowing what he would do, or what he would say when he saw them. All he wanted was to meet them face to face and release upon them the fury which burnt within him.

Blundering across the grass-land, he reached the wood breathless. He stopped to listen, heard footsteps and went toward the sound. Moving forward stealthily from tree to tree, he saw the walker and stopped. It was Farringdon, the man he had seen at Mrs. Cornford's cottage!

His appearance took Hamon by surprise. He thought the walker was bedridden. The man came nearer and Hamon took cover and watched. Farringdon was a wild-looking figure with his week's growth of beard, his pale face and his untidy dress. He was talking to himself as he slouched along, and Hamon strained his ears, without being able to distinguish what he was saying. The man passed and, coming from his hiding place, the watcher followed at a distance, guessing that the course he was taking would intercept the lovers.

To Jim those were the most precious moments of his life. The burden of life had slipped from him; all other causes and ambitions were lost in his new-found happiness. In silence they walked into the wood, oblivious to all the world that lay outside their hearts. Presently she stopped and sat down on a fallen tree trunk.

"Where are we going?" she asked, and he knew that she did not refer to their immediate destination.

"We're going to happiness, sooner or later," he said, as he sat by her side and drew her to him. "We will disentangle all the knots, big and little, and straighten out all the paths, however crooked and uneven they may be."

She smiled and lifted her lips to his. And then, in that moment of pure ecstasy, Jim heard a low, chuckling laugh, and gently putting her away from him, turned.

"A forest idyll! That's a fine sight for a husband—to see his wife in another man's arms!"

Farringdon stood tensely before them, his arms folded, his dark eyes glistening feverishly. The girl sprang up with a cry of distress and clutched at Jim Morlake's arm.

"He knows!" she whispered in terror.

The man's keen ears heard the words.

"He knows . . . !" he mocked. "You bet he knows! So you're my Joan, are you? If I hadn't been a lazy brute I'd have found that out years ago."

He took off his hat with a sweep.

"Glad to met you, Mrs. Farringdon!" he said. "It is a long time since you and I were joined together in the holy bonds of matrimony. So you're my Joan! Well, I've dreamt about you for all these years, but I never dreamt anything so pretty. Do you know this . . ." he pointed at her with a shaking finger. "There was a girl I could have married, and would have married if it hadn't been for that cursed folly! You've been a stumbling block in my road, a handicap that nothing but booze could overcome!"

He took a step toward her and suddenly, gripping her, jerked her toward him.

"You're coming home," he said, and laughed.

In another instant he was thrust backward and, stumbling, fell. Jim stooped to pick him to his feet, but he struck the hand aside, and, with a scream of rage, sprang at the tall man.

"You dog!" he howled. But he was a child in the hands that held him.

"You're ill, Farringdon," said Jim gently. "I'm sorry if I hurt you."

"Let me go! Let me go!" screamed Ferdie Farringdon. "She is my wife. I'm going to tell the village . . . she is my wife! You're coming with me, Joan Carston—do you hear! You're my wife till death do us part. And you can't divorce me without bringing him into it."

He wrenched himself from Jim's grip and staggered back. He was breathing painfully, his face, distorted with rage, was demoniacal.

"I've got something to live for now—you! You came to see me, didn't you? And he came too . . . you're coming again, Joan—alone!"

And then he spun round and, running like a person demented, flew down the woodland path and was lost to view. Jim turned to the girl. She was trying to smile at him.

"Oh, Jim!"

It hurt him to feel the quivering, trembling agony of her soul as he held her.

"I'm all right now," she said after a while. "You'll have to see me home part of the way, Jim. What am I to do? Thank God we're going away on Saturday!"

He nodded.

"And I was regretting it!" he said. "The man has been at the bottle again, or else he's gone mad."

"Do you think he will come to the house?" she asked fearfully, and then, with a surprising effort, she put him at arm's length and smiled through her unshed tears. "I told you I was a coward and I am. Matrimony doesn't suit me. Jim, I'm beginning to sympathise with wives who murder their husbands. That is a terrible thing to say, isn't it? But I am! He won't come up to the Hall—I don't care if he does," she said, with something of her old spirit. "Father knows. Who could have told him—Mr. Farringdon, I mean?"

"He guessed," said Jim decisively, "and why he hadn't guessed before, I don't know. Probably it was the accident which brought him to Creith, and the opportunity he had of seeing you and hearing your name, which made the discovery possible."

Conversation was difficult; they were each too full of their own thoughts to find speech anything but an effort. But when they came in sight of Creith House, the girl asked unexpectedly:

"Jim, what were you before you were a burglar?"

"Eh?" he replied, startled. "Before I was a burglar? Oh, I was a respectable member of society."

"But what were you? Were you in the Army?"

He shook his head.

"In any public service?"

"What makes you ask that?" he demanded, looking at her in amazement.

"I don't know—I guessed."

"I was in the diplomatic service for a while—which doesn't mean that I was an ambassador or a consul. I was a sort of hanger-on to embassies and ministries . . ."

"In Morocco?" she asked when he did not go on.

"In Morocco and Turkey and other Asiatic countries. I gave it up because—well, because I had sufficient money and because I found a new avenue to adventure."

She nodded.

"I thought it was something like that," she said. "You mustn't go any further. Will you write to me?"

He hesitated and, quick to notice such things, she said:

"Poor man! You don't know where to write! Daddy is having all his correspondence addressed to the English Club at Cadiz—will you remember that? Good-bye!"

She held out both her hands and he took them.

"I don't think you'd better kiss me again. I want to keep as near to normality as I can—I've got to face the lynx-eyed Mr. Hamon."

The lynx-eyed Mr. Hamon was watching the parting from a distance, and he ground his teeth as her companion, disregarding her wishes, put his arm about her and kissed her.

CHAPTER XLI

A Photograph

JIM MORLAKE had one predominant habit of behaviour. It was to clear up as he went along. Before the girl was out of sight he had decided on his line of action, and without hesitation turned off from the field path, and crossing the field, reached the by-lane which led to the village, and incidentally, to Mrs. Cornford's cottage.

Farringdon must give the girl her freedom and he must disabuse that young man's mind of any queer ideas which had crept into his crazy brain.

Mrs. Cornford opened the door to him, and he saw at a glance that something out of the ordinary had happened to trouble her.

"I hope I haven't come at an inconvenient moment."

She shook her head.

"I'm glad to see you, Mr. Morlake," she said, and showed him into her little sitting-room.

It was not hard to guess where the trouble lay, for the sound of ravings came to him distinctly.

"I've come to the end of my dreams," she smiled, "a little suddenly."

"That is a tragic place to reach, Mrs. Cornford," said Jim. "What is wrong?"

"I was hoping to stay on at Creith, but everything depended upon my keeping Mr. Farringdon with me."

"Is he going?" he asked.

She shook her head.

"Not of his own will, but I must ask him to leave. He is like a maniac to-day. A few minutes ago he came in, so beside himself that I was terrified."

Jim thought for a moment.

"I want to see him," he said, and her face grew grave.

"I wish you wouldn't," she begged. "Perhaps to-morrow, or later in the day. He has locked his door. I tried to take him a cup of tea just now, and he would not open it. I am growing frightened."

Jim felt sorry for the woman, for he had guessed that some tragedy had come to her which had altered the whole course of her life. She had the air of one who was used to good living and comfortable surroundings; and it was a pain to him to realise what this drab life must mean to her.

"Will you forgive me if I ask you what you do for a living?" he asked. "Perhaps I might be able to help you?"

She shook her head.

"Unless you wanted music lessons, I'm afraid you can't be of much assistance to me," she said, and he laughed softly.

"Music isn't my long suit," he said, "but I may be able to help you in other directions."

The raving became louder and he looked round and half-rose from the chair to which she had invited him, but she put out a restraining hand.

"Leave him alone," she said. "I will get the district nurse. I think he is ill again."

"Will you forgive me if I ask you a very personal and very impertinent question?"

She did not reply, but her eyes gave him encouragement.

"You have——" he hesitated, not knowing how to frame the question—"you have lost a great deal of money at some time or other?"

"You mean I have come down in the world?" she smiled. "Yes, I'm afraid I have. My husband disappeared some years ago and when his affairs were settled it was found that he, who I thought was a very rich man, was practically penniless. That is my whole story in the smallest compass," she said frankly. "John Cornford was rather a law to himself and did eccentric things which made tracing him a very difficult matter. Perhaps I was ill-advised at the time, for I did not attempt to make enquiries. I trusted Mr. Hamon——"

"Hamon?" he said quickly. "Was it Hamon who gave you the advice not to trace him? When did your husband disappear?"

"Nearly eleven years ago," she said.

He made a rapid mental calculation.

"In what month?"

"In May. May was the last time I heard from him. It was his last letter that you so kindly recovered from Mr. Hamon."

"May I see it?" he asked.

She brought it to him and he read it through twice.

"Your husband's name was John Cornford?"

"Why?" she asked eagerly. "Did you know him?"

He shook his head.

"No, only—years ago I had a very singular adventure. It happened a week after your husband disappeared, but it is absurd to associate the two things. Have you his portrait?"

She nodded, and went into her bedroom and was gone some time.

"I had to search for it," she apologised. "I put it away in a place of safety.

He took the photograph from her hand and he did not betray by so much as a twitching muscle the shock he received.

It was the portrait of a good-looking man of forty, clean-shaven and obviously satisfied with himself.

But it was something else: it was the face of the dying sailor whom he had picked up from the Portsmouth Road, and who, before his death, had told him the strangest story that James Morlake had ever heard.

John Cornford was the unknown sailor who slept in a nameless grave at Hindhead! For ten years he had trailed the man responsible for his death, seeking the evidence that would bring him to justice.

"Do you know him?" asked Mrs. Cornford anxiously.

He handed the portrait back to her.

"I have seen him," he said simply, and something in his tone told her the truth.

"He is dead?"

Jim nodded gravely.

"Yes, he is dead, Mrs. Cornford," and she sank down into a chair and covered her face with her hands.

Jim thought she was weeping, but presently she looked up.

"I have always felt that he was dead," she said, "but this is the first definite news I have received. Where did he die?"

"He died in England."

Again she nodded.

"I knew he had died in England. Hamon said he was lost in the desert. Can you tell me anything about it?"

"I'd rather not," said Jim reluctantly, "not just yet. Will you be patient for a little while?"

She smiled

"I've been patient for so long that I can endure for a little while longer. Please understand, Mr. Morlake, that, though this is a great shock, my husband and I were not," she hesitated, "were not very great friends. I don't think the blame is mine. I am almost ready to accept it all, though it is very difficult to analyse where the blame lies after so many years."

"Can I have that portrait?" he asked.

She handed it to him without a word.

"There is one more thing. Before your husband died, he handed me a sum of money to give to his wife——" And then, seeing the look of surprise and doubt in her face: "You will understand, Mrs. Cornford, that I did not know his name."

"You didn't know his name?" she asked in amazement. "Then how——?"

"It is too long a story to tell, but you will have to trust me."

Then suddenly she remembered Jim's antecedents and the proved charge against him.

"Was he mixed up in any—any——" She was at a loss how to put the matter politely.

"In any crooked business?" smiled Jim. "No, so far as I am concerned, he was a perfect stranger to me when I saw him. I tell you I do not even know his name."

He was gone before she began to ask herself how John Cornford could have given him a thousand pounds without telling him the name of the wife to whom it was to be delivered.

He had not left half-an-hour before Binger came to the door with an envelope. It contained ten notes for a hundred pounds, and a scrap of writing on a visiting-card.

"Please trust me," it said, and for some reason she felt no embarrassment when she locked the money away in her box.

"Did you wait?" asked Jim.

"Yes, sir, and she said there was no hanswer."

"I suppose it sounded like that," said Jim with a sigh of relief.

"Have you any plans, sir?"

"About what?"

"About the future, about going back to town. To tell you the truth, sir," said Binger, "the country don't agree with me.

The hair isn't like what it is in London. Some like country hair; personally I prefer the hair of the Barking Road."

Jim thought awhile.

"You may go back by the next train. Get me on the telephone and ask Mahmet to speak."

Telephones Mahmet under no circumstances would touch. All other conveniences of civilisation he could employ familiarly, but there was something about that forbidding machine which terrified him.

Binger left by the next train with the greatest alacrity. He was a Cockney, to whom the quiet and unsociability of the country was anathema. And Jim was not sorry to see him go, for the regularity which Binger imposed upon life was repugnant to him at the moment. Binger was the spirit of the stereotyped. He did things in a regular way at regular hours. He brought morning tea as the clock struck seven; set the bath tap running at a quarter past; at a quarter to eight Jim's shoes fell with a clatter outside his bedroom door. The Cockney valet was a constant reminder that time was flying.

Jim Morlake needed the solitude, for a new factor had appeared, a new leader from the main stream of his mystery. It was one of those coincidences which appear in every branch of investigation, that, on the day that Mrs. Cornford revealed the identity of the dead sailor, Mr. Julius Welling took hold of a thread that was to lead him to the same discovery.

CHAPTER XLII

Captain Welling: Investigator

JULIUS WELLING appeared in the record office at headquarters, and the officer on duty hurried to discover his wishes, for this white-haired man seldom made a personal call, and if he did, there was big trouble on the way for somebody or other.

"Just tell me if my memory is failing. It was ten years ago when The Black robberies started, wasn't it, Sergeant?"

A drawer was opened, a procession of cards flickered under the Sergeant's nimble fingers, and:

"Yes, sir—ten years this month."

"Good! Now give me a list of all the murders that were committed for a year before."

Another drawer shot out noiselessly.

"Shall I make a list, sir, or will you see the cards—they have a précis of the crimes."

"The cards will do."

A package of fifty large cards was put before him, and he turned them over, speaking to himself all the time.

"Adams, John, hanged; Bonfield, Charles, insane; Brasfield, Dennis, hanged—all these are 'knowns,' Sergeant."

"The unknowns are at the bottom, sir."

These Welling read without comment until he came to the last.

"Man unknown, believed murder. Assailant unknown——"

His eyes opened wide.

"Got it!" he cried exultantly, and now he read aloud.

"Man, apparently sailor, was found on the edge of the Punch Bowl, Hindhead, unconscious. Lacerated wounds and contusion of scalp. No identity established. Deceased was found by a cyclist, whose name is not available (U.S.D.I.6. (See F.O.) Foreign Intelligence Officers' Regulation, c. 970). Decreased died soon after admission to cottage hospital. All stations notified and portrait published. No identification."

Welling looked up over his glasses.

"What is U.S.D.I.6?" he asked.

"United States Diplomatic Intelligence—6 is the number of the department," said the officer promptly. "The F.O. Regulation deals with the treatment offered to Foreign Intelligence officers in this country. I was looking it up the other day, sir."

"And what is the regulation?"

"If they are acting on behalf of their Government, with the knowledge of our people, they are not to be interfered with unless there is a suspicion that they are engaged in espionage."

Captain Julius Welling rubbed his nose.

"Then it comes to this; the cyclist was an intelligence officer of a foreign Government. When he was questioned as to the identity of the dead man, I presume he produced his card to the local police inspector, and the local police inspector, in accordance with the regulations, did not put his name in the report."

"That's about what it is, sir."

"Then obviously, the person to see is the local police inspector," said Welling.

Late in the afternoon he arrived at Hindhead and interviewed the chief of police.

"The Inspector who took that report has left the service some years ago, Captain Welling," said the official. "We've got our own record, but the name of the man would not be there."

"Who was the inspector at the time?"

"Inspector Sennett. He lives at Basingstoke now. I remember the day when the sailor was found; I was acting-sergeant at the time, and was the first man to report at the hospital, but he was dead by then."

The hospital authorities gave Welling all the technical details he required, together with a description of the clothing the man had worn when he was brought into the hospital unconscious. Welling read the entry very carefully. No money was in his pocket, no books or papers of any kind to identify him.

"I think," said Welling as they left the hospital, "I should like to see the place where the body was found if you know where it is?"

"I can point to the exact spot," said the local inspector.

They entered the officer's car and drove until they came to a lonely stretch of road that bordered that deep depression which is known locally as the Devil's Punch Bowl.

"It was here," said the officer, stopping the car, and pointed to a grassy stretch by the side of the road.

Welling got down and stared for a long time at the scene of the tragedy.

"Did you personally visit this place after the man was found?" he asked.

"Yes," nodded the other.

"Was there any sign of struggle, any weapon?"

"None whatever. The impression I had at the time was that he had been brought to this place after the assault was committed and thrown on to the grass."

"Ah!" said Welling, a gleam in his eye. "That sounds to me like an intelligent hypothesis."

He scanned the countryside, beginning with the hollow and ending with the hill that sloped up from the road on the opposite side.

"Whose house is that?"

The Inspector told him; it was the property of a local doctor.

"How long has he been living there?"

"Fifteen or twenty years. He built the house himself."

Again the detective's eyes roved.

"Whose cottage is that? It seems to be empty."

"Oh, that is a little bungalow that belongs to a lawyer who died two or three years ago. It hasn't been occupied since '14."

"How long did he have it?"

"A few years."

"And before then?" asked Welling, continuing his inspection of the country.

"Before then——" The Inspector frowned in an effort to recall the name of its previous proprietor. "I know; it used to belong to a man named Hamon."

"What! Ralph Hamon?"

"Yes, he's a millionaire now. He wasn't so rich then, and he used to live here in the summer."

"Oh, he did, did he?" said Welling softly. "I'd like to see that cottage."

The path up the hillside was overgrown with weeds, though at one time it had been well kept, for it was gravelled and in places steps had been made to facilitate the owner's progress. The house bore a lifeless appearance; the windows were shuttered, spiders had spun their webs in the angles of the doorposts.

"How long did the lawyer live here, you say?"

"He never lived here. He owned the place, but I think it has been unoccupied since Mr. Hamon left—in fact I'm sure it has

Mr. Hamon sold it to him as it stood, furniture and all. . . . I'm sure of that because Mr. Steele—that was the lawyer's name—told me he intended letting it furnished."

Welling tried to pry open one of the shutters and after a while succeeded. The windows were grimed with dust and it was impossible to see the interior.

"I intend going into this cottage," said Welling and brought his stick down with a crash upon one of the window-panes.

Inserting his hand, he drew back the window-bolt and lifted the sash. There was nothing unusual about the appearance of the room. It was a simply furnished bedroom, and though dust lay thick upon every article, there was a certain neatness about the character and arrangement of the furniture which defied the dishevelling results of neglect. Nor was there anything remarkable about the other rooms. The furniture was good and the carpets, which had been rolled up, were almost new.

But the furnishing of the room did not seem to interest Welling. His attention was devoted to the walls, all of which were distempered in pink. At the back of the house was a fairly large kitchen, the windows being heavily barred.

"Would you like me to search the bureau——"

Welling shook his head.

"You will find nothing there," he said. "What I am looking for is——"

He opened the window and pushed out the shutter.

"Now I think I can find what I want," he said, and pointed. "Do you see that patch?"

"I see nothing," said the puzzled officer.

"Can't you see that a portion of the wall here has been repainted?"

The kitchen was distempered white, and the irregular patch of new paint was distinct.

"Here is another," said Welling suddenly.

He took a knife from his pocket and began to scrape the wash carefully.

"Murder will out," he said, speaking to himself.

"Murder?" said the other in surprise.

For answer, Welling pointed to a pear-shaped stain that his knife had uncovered.

"That is blood, I think," he said simply.

With his pocket handkerchief he cleared the dust from the table and examined the top inch by inch.

"It has been scraped here. Do you feel that?"

He felt tenderly along the surface of the pine wood.

"Yes, it has been scraped."

"Do you suggest——?"

"I suggest that your unknown sailor was hammered to death in this very room," said Welling.

"But Mr. Hamon would have known."

"He probably wasn't in residence," said Welling, and his companion accepted this as completely exonerating the former owner of the bungalow.

"Naturally you wouldn't think of searching a near-by house to discover how some poor sailor had met his death," mused Welling. "I think that is all I want to know, Inspector. You had better nail up the shutters and give instructions that whoever comes to take possession must first interview me because I want this house empty for a week or two."

He came down the hill path and paced the distance between the spot where the path joined the road and the place where the dying man was found, and made a few notes.

"Now, Inspector, if you will lend me your car to go to Basingstoke, I don't think I will trouble you any further."

He found the pensioned policeman without any difficulty—he was a well-known local character—but it was less easy to induce him to talk, even to a high official of Scotland Yard—or possibly because of that, for the jealousy between the country police and police headquarters is proverbial.

But Captain Welling had a way of his own; a fund of anecdotes calculated to soften the sourest of pensioned officers with a grievance against headquarters.

"It's against all regulations," he said, mollified at last, "but I can tell you all you want to know, because I kept his card as a curio. These highbrow intelligence people had never come my way before and naturally I was interested."

The finding of the card involved an hour's search amongst such oddments as an old man, with a passion for hoarding old race cards, old dance programmes and other mementoes of a cheerful life will accumulate through the years. Watching him, Welling wondered whether the same spirit guided Ralph Hamon and whether it was just the innate craving of the miser for holding on to useless scraps of paper that conduced to the folly of keeping in his possession a document which might hang him.

"Here it is," said the pensioner in triumph and handed a stained card to his guest.

Captain Welling fixed his glasses and read:

"Major James L. Morlake, U. S. Consulate, Tangier."

He handed back the card with a beatific smile.

All the mysteries but one were solved, and that one defied solution. It was the mystery of Ralph Hamon's passion for clinging to his own death warrant.

CHAPTER XLIII

The Man in the Night

CREITH HOUSE was in that turmoil which comes to every house, big or little, when the family is on the point of leaving for a holiday. Lord Creith was looking forward to his voyage with the zest and enthusiasm of a schoolboy.

"Young people are not what they used to be," he said. "Now, when I was your age, Joan, I'd have been dancing round at the prospect of a real holiday free from bother. We shan't see Hamon for two months. That ought to be enough to make you cheerful."

"I'm bubbling over with cheer, Daddy," she said wearily, "only I'm rather tired."

If she had said she was exhausted, she would have been

nearer the truth. The events of the day had taken their toll, she realised, as she dragged herself to her room, undecided as to whether she should go to bed or try to find, in the pages of a book, the quietness of mind that was so desirable. Oscillating between the two alternatives, she took the course which was least profitable. She thought. She thought of Jim and the haggard man at the cottage, and of Hamon a little. It was curious how he had receded into the background.

Her maid came to pack her clothes, but she sent her away. How was Farringdon, she wondered? Was that outburst of his part of his disease . . . was he mad? She wished there were a telephone at the cottage, so that she could ring up Mrs. Cornford and ask her. On the spur of the moment she went to her writing-table and wrote a note, but when her maid came, in answer to her ring, she had changed her mind. She would go down to the cottage herself and see the man, reason with him, if he was in a reasonable frame of mind. She must know just where she stood.

Lord Creith saw her coming down the stairs.

"Going out?" he asked in consternation. "My dear old girl, you can't go out to-night. It is blowing great guns!"

"I'm only going to walk as far as the lodge gates, Daddy," she said.

She hated lying to him.

"I'll come with you."

"No, no, please don't. I want to be by myself."

"Can't you take your maid?" he insisted. "I don't like you roaming around alone. By gad! I haven't forgotten the fright you gave me on the night of the storm."

But, with a reassuring smile, she went out through the big doors on to the terrace and he stood uncertainly, half-inclined to follow her. She followed the drive almost to the lodge gates, then turned off by what was known as the wall path, that would bring her within a few yards of the cottage. Half a gale was blowing, and the trees creaked and groaned, and the bare branches rattled harshly above her. But she was for the moment oblivious to the elements and to any storm but that which raged in her own heart.

Mrs. Cornford had had a very uneasy evening with her patient, and the doctor, hastily summoned, now took a graver view of the disorder.

"You'll have to keep nurses here," he said. "I am afraid this man is certifiable. I'll bring in Dr. Truman from Little Lexham to-morrow to examine him."

"Do you mean he is insane?" she asked in horror.

"I am afraid so," said the doctor. "These dipsomania cases generally end that way. Has he had a shock?"

"No, nothing that I know about. He was up this morning, walking in the garden and was quite rational. Then this afternoon," she pointed to an empty whisky bottle, "I found it in the garden. I don't know how he got it, but probably he sent one of the villagers to the Red Lion."

The doctor glared at the bottle.

"That is the cause," he said. "I don't think our friend will drink again for a very long time. I would have him moved to-night, but I cannot get in touch with the hospital authorities. Hark at him!"

The patient was yelling at the top of his voice, but it was quite impossible to distinguish any consecutive sentence.

"Joan," occurred at intervals.

"That Joan is certainly on his nerves," said the doctor. "Have you any idea who she is?"

"None," said Mrs. Cornford.

In her heart of hearts she harboured a faint suspicion, which she had dismissed as being disloyal to the girl who had done so much for her.

"It may be an hallucination, but the chances are that there is a Joan somewhere in the world who could fix matters for him."

As he went out, he saw a girl on the garden path.

"Is that you, Nurse?" he asked.

"No, Doctor, it is Joan Carston."

"Lady Joan!" he gasped. "Whatever are you doing out to-night?"

"I've come to see Mrs. Cornford," said Joan.

"Well, well, you're a brave girl. I wouldn't turn out to-night for anything but dire necessity."

"How is your patient?" she asked.

He shook his head.

"Very bad, very bad. Don't you go anywhere near him."

She did not answer him. Mrs. Cornford, hearing the voices, had hurried to the door and was as much surprised as the doctor to see who the visitor was.

"You must not see him," she said, shaking her head vigorously when Joan, in the privacy of the sitting-room, told her why she had come.

"But I must, I must! I must talk to him."

Her heart sank as the sound of the raving voice came to her.

"Is he so bad?" she asked in a whisper.

"He is very bad," said the puzzled Mrs. Cornford.

"You can't understand why I want to talk to him, can you?" said Joan, smiling faintly. "I see that you can't! Perhaps one day I will tell you."

She waited awhile, listening with knit brows at the animal sounds that came from the other room.

"He'll not be quiet all night," said Mrs. Cornford. "The nurses are coming at any moment now; the doctor has sent for them."

"Aren't you afraid?" asked Joan wonderingly.

Mrs. Cornford shook her head.

"No, I—I once had a case almost as bad," she said, and Joan did not ask her any more.

Her journey had been a folly and this end to it was a fitting finish.

"It was silly of me to come," she confessed, as she grasped her cloak. "No, no, don't come with me. I can find my way back to the house. And please don't even come to the door."

She went out, closing the front door behind her. To the left was a lighted window—Farringdon's bedroom. She crept nearer and could hear, and shuddered as she heard, the wild sound that came forth. Then, wrapping her cloak about her, she stole down the path.

She heard the click of the gate and stepped behind the big elm that grew before the house, not wishing to be seen. Was it the doctor? The nurse, she supposed. But it was a man's figure she saw dimly in the darkness. There was something remarkable in his gait; he was moving stealthily, noiselessly, as though he did not wish his presence to be known. She could have reached out and touched him, he passed so close. Who was he, she wondered, and waited in curiosity to discover Mrs. Cornford's visitor.

But he did not knock at the door. Instead, he moved towards the window of the sick man's room. Then she heard him fumbling with the window-latch. It was a casement window, and as he pulled it opened. The window-shade began flapping, and he lifted it with one hand, while the girl stood, frozen with horror. She could not move, she could not scream. She saw the glitter of the man's pistol, but her eyes were on the black-masked face.

"Jim!" she gasped feebly.

At that moment the intruder fired twice, and Ferdinand Farringdon screamed and rolled over on to the floor, dead.

CHAPTER XLIV

Murder

SHE heard a terrified cry in the house, and her first impulse was to run to Mrs. Cornford's help. But somebody else had heard the shot. There came the noise of running feet, a police whistle was blown and a man dashed through the gates and ran up the path as the door opened.

"What was that?" he asked sharply.

"I don't know," said Mrs. Cornford's agitated voice. "Something dreadful has happened. I think Mr. Farringdon has shot himself."

The girl waited, trembling with terror. What should she do? If she said that she had been a witness of the shooting, she must also describe the assailant. As the visitor disappeared through the door, she crept to the garden gate and slipped out.

There were flying footsteps on the road. They must not see her; the presence of these strangers decided her. In another minute she was racing along the wall path. Her heel caught in a soft path and she all but fell. Before she realised what she was doing, she was running up the stairs of Creith House. Happily, there was nobody in the hall. Lord Creith, who was in his room, heard the slam of her door and came along to ask a question about his collars. He found the door locked.

"Have you gone to bed, my dear?" he called.

"Yes, Daddy," she gasped.

The room was in darkness. She staggered to the bed and flung herself upon it.

"Jim, Jim!" she sobbed in her anguish of soul. "Why did you? Why did you?"

She must have fallen asleep, for she came to consciousness to the insistent knocking on her door. It was her father's voice:

"Are you asleep, Joan?"

"Yes, Daddy. Do you want me?"

"Can you come down? Something dreadful has happened."

Her heart sank. She knew what that "something dreadful" was.

"Can I come in?"

She opened the door.

"Haven't you got a light?" he asked and was reaching for the switch but she stopped him.

"Don't put the light on, Daddy; I've got a headache. What is it, dear?"

"Farringdon has met with an accident," said Lord Creith, who lacked something in diplomacy. "In fact, he's shot. Some people think that he shot himself, but Welling is not of that opinion."

"Is Mr. Welling here?" she asked, her heart sinking.

Of a sudden she feared that shrewd old man.

"Yes, he came back from town to-night. He is downstairs. He wanted to see you."

"He wants to see me, Daddy?" she said in consternation, seized with a momentary panic.

"Yes, he tells me that you had only left Mrs. Cornford's house a few minutes before the shooting occurred."

He heard her little gasp in the dark.

"Oh, is that why?" she said softly. "I will come down."

Welling had returned to Creith that night and had had time to take his baggage to the Red Lion. He was, in fact, on his way to Wold House when he had heard the shot and the scream. The Red Lion was less than fifty yards from the gardener's cottage and the wind had been blowing in his direction.

"There is no doubt about it being murder," he explained to Lord Creith. "The window was open and no weapon has been found. The only clue I have is footprints on the garden bed outside."

"Was he dead when you found him?"

"Quite dead," replied Welling. "Shot through the heart. Two shots were fired in such rapid succession that it sounded to me like one, which means that an automatic pistol was used. You have no idea why Lady Joan went to Mrs. Cornford's?"

"I haven't. Mrs. Cornford is a great friend of hers, and probably she went down to enquire after Farringdon. She has been there before on that errand," said Lord Creith quietly and Welling nodded.

"That is what Mrs. Cornford told me," he said.

"Then why the dickens did you ask me?" demanded Lord Creith wrathfully.

"Because it is a detective's business to ask twice," said Julius at his gentlest, and his lordship apologised for his display of temper.

"Here is my daughter," he said. As Joan came into the library he shot a quick, searching glance at her. The pale face and shadowed eyes might mean anything. Mr. Welling was one of the few people who knew the secret of the church in the forest and could forgive her emotion.

"His Lordship has told you that Farringdon has been killed?" he said.

She inclined her head slowly.

"You must have been very near the house when the shot was fired. Did you hear anything?"

"Nothing."

"Or see anybody?"

She shook her head.

"Not in the garden or in the road?" persisted Welling. "Mrs. Cornford tells me that you had not left the house a minute when the shot was fired."

"I heard nothing and saw nobody," she said, and he looked thoughtfully at the carpet.

"The wind would be blowing in the opposite direction," he mused, "so it is quite possible you did not hear the shot. Is there any place in the garden where a man could conceal himself?"

"I don't know the garden well enough," she answered quickly.

"Hm!" He scratched his nose with an air of irritation. "You don't know this man Farringdon, of course?" he said, and when she did not answer, he went on: "Perhaps it is better that you didn't know him. It would save a lot of unnecessary pain to many people and your knowledge of him will not help the cause of justice."

Walking down the dark drive, he tried to piece together the puzzle which this new outrage made. Who had shot Farringdon? Who had reason to shoot him? "Find the motive and you find the criminal," is an old axiom of police work. Who had a motive for destroying that useless life? Only one person in the world—Joan Carston.

"Pshaw!" he said with a shrug. "Why not Lord Creith? His motive was certainly as obvious."

He had come back to the village singlehanded, and had to depend upon the local constabulary, represented for the moment by a sergeant of police.

Nothing had been found in the preliminary search and Welling decided to put into execution his original plan, which was to call on Jim Morlake. When he got to Wold House no light showed from any of the windows; the garden gate was wide open and that was unusual. Welling had found his way along the road by the aid of a torch and he was using this to guide him up the drive, when he saw what were evidently fresh wheel tracks. The garage stood at the side of the house, and, acting on the impulse of the moment, he turned his steps toward this building. He came abreast of it and put the light on the garage. The doors were wide open and the little shed was empty.

Welling knew that Jim had got his car back—where was it?

Cleaver opened the door to him.

"Do you want to see Mr. Morlake?" he said. "I'm afraid he's out."

"How long has he been out?" asked Welling.

"He's been gone about half-an-hour. I was rather surprised to see him go, because he'd already made arrangements for me to call him early in the morning—Binger has gone back to town."

"Did he tell you he was going?"

Cleaver shook his head.

"No, sir, the first intimation I had was when I saw the lights of Mr. Morlake's car going through the gates. He went away in a great hurry, because he left his pipe and tobacco pouch behind and he doesn't usually do that. Not only that, but he went by the window. I hadn't any idea he was out of the house until I saw the machine."

The French window in the study was still unfastened. Pushing open the door, Welling looked carefully on the floor.

"So he went in a hurry, did he?" said Welling softly. "Went half-an-hour ago? Will you leave me, Mr. Cleaver? I want to use the telephone."

His first call was to Horsham police headquarters.

"Hold a two-seater car, painted black. The driver's name is Morlake. I want you to hold him—not arrest him, you understand, but hold him."

"What is the charge, Captain Welling?"

"Murder," said Welling laconically.

CHAPTER XLV

Wanted

Jim Morlake had disappeared. He had been seen neither at his flat nor at the restaurant he affected when he was in London. His car had been found outside the door of the garage where it was usually kept when in London. It was covered with mud, for the night had been wet, and showed evidence of hard driving, but there was no note nor any word of instructions as to its disposal.

Binger had not seen him, and Mahmet the Moor presented a stolid unintelligent face to the questioners who came to him, and disclaimed all knowledge of his master. The afternoon newspapers printed prominently a request to Mr. James Morlake to report himself to the nearest police station, but this produced no result.

"Always in trouble, always in trouble!" groaned Binger. "I can't understand why Mr. Morlake don't take helementary precautions."

Mahmet did not answer. If his knowledge of English was slight, his understanding of Binger's English was negligible.

"You're a man of the world, Mahmet!" continued Binger, who liked nothing better than to address an audience that could not under any circumstances protest or interrupt him, "and I'm a man of the world, Mahmet. We know young gentlemen are a bit eccentric, but this is going beyond a joke. Of course, Mr. Morlake is a foreigner, so to speak, but he's a Hanglo-Saxon, Mahmet, and Hanglo-Saxons, like you and me, don't go dodging off to nowhere without telling nobody."

That great Anglo-Saxon, Mahmet Ali, concealed a yawn politely and listened with stolid patience to a further exposition on the thoughtlessness of employers. When Mr. Binger had talked himself to a standstill, Mahmet said:

"I go way a bit."

"What you are trying to say is: 'I'm going hout,' " said Binger. "I wonder you don't try to learn the English language. I'm willing to give you an hour a day for heducational purposes."

"I go now?" said Mahmet, and Binger, in his lordly way, gave him leave.

Mahmet went to the little room where he slept, took off his white jallab and dressed himself in a ready-made European suit, which turned him from something that was picturesque to a nondescript weed. He travelled on the top of a bus eastward, and did not descend until he had reached dockland. Up a side street was a small, dingy-looking establishment that had once been a bar, which had lost its licence owing to the misguided efforts of the proprietor, who augmented his income by conducting a betting business. It was now a home, in the sense that here strange coloured folk stranded in London could buy indifferent coffee and could sleep in a cell a little bigger than an egg-box on payment of a sum which would sustain them in comfort in their own countries for a week.

Mahmet went into the smoky room which served as lounge and card-room. Half-a-dozen dusky-skinned men were playing cards, and near one of these Mahmet saw a compatriot and, beckoning to him, they retired to an empty alcove at the far end of the room.

"My good man has gone," said Mahmet without preliminary. "Will you write to your uncle in Casa Blanca and tell him to buy four mules, also that he send a message to the Shereef El Zuy at Tetuan, telling him to be with the mules near the lighthouse at El Spartel on the twelfth day of this month? You have heard no more?"

His companion, a tall, loose-made Moor, his face disfigured by the ravages of smallpox, had indeed much to tell.

"There is trouble in the Angera country, and there has been fighting. I think the Sultan's soldiers will be defeated. Sadi Hafiz is supposed to be with the Angera people, and it is true that they are making great preparations at his house in the hills. He is sending serving women there. Now that is strange, for Sadi has never taken servants to this place."

Mahmet interrupted him.

"You're an old man," he said contemptuously. "You have told me that story twice, and that is the way of old men."

There were other items of gossip to be picked up, but Mahmet did not stop either to hear the latest scandal about the Basha's favourite wife, or the peculations of the Grand Wazir. He hurried back to the flat, made a bundle of his clothes, tying his complete wardrobe in a pillow case. When Binger came the next morning there was no sign of Mahmet, and though the indignant valet made a complete inventory of the contents of the flat, he discovered, to his annoyance, that nothing was missing.

CHAPTER XLVI

Pointed Shoes

A GREAT change had come over Joan Carston in the last few days. She was the first to be sensible of the difference, and had wondered at herself. For now every remnant of the old Joan had been annihilated in the terrific shock of this supreme tragedy. She did not sleep that night, but sat at the window, her hands clasped on the broad sill, her eyes everlastingly turned in the direction of Wold House. If Jim's light would only appear! If she could hear the sound of his voice in those dark and stormy hours of night! Her heart yearned toward him. How happy she had been! She had not realised her blessings.

Daylight found her pale and hollow-eyed, an ache in her heart, depressed by a sense of utter weariness and despair. With a start she realised that she was leaving Creith that day! She could not go away now; she must wait to be at hand in case Jim wanted her. She did not judge him, for that was beyond human judgment. Nor did she attempt to analyse the condition of mind which drove him to that terrible act. She could only set the facts of the deed badly, with a numb sense of resignation to the inevitable.

There came a knock at the door. She dragged her weary limbs across the floor to turn the key. It was her maid with the morning coffee.

"Put it down," she said.

"You haven't slept in your bed, m'lady!" said the girl, aghast.

"No, I shall have plenty of time to sleep on the yacht," she said.

She drank the coffee gratefully and felt refreshed enough to go downstairs into the open. A sky grey with hurrying clouds was above her; the wind was keen and cold; pools of water stood in the little hollows of the drive. The dreary scene was in tune with her heart. Unconsciously she walked down the drive until she came to the lodge gates and stood there, her hands holding the bars, looking through—at nothing.

Then her eyes turned toward the cottage and she shuddered, and, turning, she walked quickly back the way she had come. She had not gone a few paces when somebody called her, and, looking back, she saw Welling in a dingy yellow ulster and nondescript hat pulled down over his head.

"You've been up all night too, Captain Welling?" she said. His chin was silvery with bristles, his boots thick with mud, and the hand he raised to lift his hat was inexpressibly grimy.

"I gather from that, young lady," he said, "that you've not had a great deal of sleep, and I don't blame you. The wind has been most disturbing. Is his Lordship up?"

"I don't know: I expect so. Father doesn't usually rise till nine, but I think to-day he has made some sort of arrangement with his valet to get up at the unnatural hour of eight." She smiled faintly.

"You've had your share of trouble in this village, I think," said the detective, walking at her side; but she did not make any rejoinder to that most obvious statement. "Queer case, that—very queer! Have you ever noticed that Morlake wears broad-toed shoes, the American type?"

"No, I haven't noticed anything about him," she said quickly, lest she should be an unwilling agent to his hurt.

"Well, he *does*," said Welling. "He never wears any other kind. I've been searching his house——"

"He is gone, then? The maid told me last night—he has gone?"

"Vanished," said Welling. "There is no other word, he has vanished. That is the worst of these clever fellows—when they disappear they do it thoroughly. An ordinary criminal would leave his visiting card on every mile-post."

He waited, but she did not speak, till:

"What is the significance of the broad-toed shoes?" she plucked up courage to ask.

"Well, it was a pointed toe that killed Farringdon."

At his words she spun round.

"You mean—you mean—that Jim Morlake did not kill him?" she asked unsteadily. "You mean that, Captain Welling? You are not trying to trap me into saying something about him, are you? You wouldn't do that?"

"I'm capable of doing even that," confessed Julius with a mournful shake of his head. "There is no depth of depravity to which I wouldn't sink, and that is the truth, Lady Joan. But on this particular occasion I'm being perfectly sincere. The feet under the window are the feet of a man who wears French boots with pointed toes. Also, the gun he used was of much heavier calibre than any Morlake owns. I know the whole Morlake armoury, and I'll swear he never owned the gun that threw those two bullets. Jim Morlake has three: the one he carries and two Service Colts. You seemed pretty sure it was Morlake?" he said, eyeing her intently.

"Yes, I was," and then, following her impulse: "I saw Mr. Farringdon killed."

She expected he would be staggered by this revelation, but he only guffawed.

"I know you did," he said calmly, "you were hiding behind the tree. It was easy to pick up your footmarks. You came back to the house by way of the wall path—I found the heel of one of your shoes there and guessed you were in a hurry. If you'd lost it in daylight you would have picked it up. If you'd lost it by night and had plenty of time on your hands, you'd have looked for it. Anyway, you wouldn't have lost it, if you hadn't been running at such a speed. Do you think Pointed

Toes knew you were there?—by the way, you didn't see his face?"

"How do you know?"

"Because you weren't sure whether it was Morlake or not; therefore, you couldn't have seen his face. And once more, therefore, he must have been masked. Black?"

She nodded.

"From head to foot, eh? In that style which Mr. James Morlake has made popular. I guessed that, too," he said as she nodded. "It may have been a coincidence, of course, but probably wasn't."

He stopped, and she followed his example. He was looking down at her with his head thrown back, and his eyes seemed to possess an hypnotic power.

"Now perhaps you can give me a little information that will be really useful," he said. "Who else wears pointed French boots in Creith besides your father?"

CHAPTER XLVII

The Yacht

SHE stared at him for a minute, and then burst into a fit of uncontrollable laughter.

"Oh, Mr. Welling, for a moment you scared me. Daddy wouldn't kill anybody: it would be too much bother!"

The detective was unruffled.

"I am not suggesting that your father did shoot this man. I am merely saying that Lord Creith is the only man within ten miles who wears pointed shoes."

"How silly!" she scoffed. "Why, lots of people wear pointed shoes. Mr. Hamon wears pointed——"

She checked herself suddenly.

"That is what I wanted to know," said Julius gently, "that

is all I wanted to know! Does Mr. Hamon wear pointed shoes? I know Lord Creith does, because I've interviewed the village cobbler, and the village cobbler knows the secret history of every pair of boots in your house."

"Mr. Hamon is so rich that he doesn't need to have his shoes repaired," said the girl, and then, seriously: "You don't suspect Mr. Hamon? He wasn't in Creith last night."

"If he shot Farringdon, then he certainly was in Creith. If he didn't shoot Farringdon, I don't care where he was," said Welling.

The reaction after that night of terror and anxiety was so great that she felt hysterical. She could have flung her arms round the neck of this interesting old man and hugged him in her joy and relief.

"Are you sure—absolutely sure?"

"About Morlake?" he asked, sensing the cause of her anxiety. "I don't think there is any doubt about that. He is one of those big-hoofed fellows. He could not have got his feet into the shoes that left the marks. Though," he added cautiously, "it is by no means certain that the owner of the shoes was also the murderer. What makes it look so queer against Morlake is that Pointed Shoes was in the grounds of Wold House last night. We've got a cast of his feet leading toward the river, and at the bottom of the river it is any odds on finding the pistol with which the crime was committed."

"Why do you say that?" she asked.

"What is more," he went on, "I guess we're going to get a letter from some person unknown, telling us exactly where to look for that gun. I love anonymous letters, especially when I'm expecting 'em. The letter will be in printed characters and will be posted"—he looked up to the dull sky and considered—"will be posted . . . now where will it be posted? Yes, I have it," he said brightly. "It will be posted at the G. P. O."

"You're a prophet," she smiled.

"I'm a student," he replied.

When they got to the house, Lord Creith was superintending the labelling of the baggage, which meant that every package had been labelled wrongly.

"Hullo, Welling!" he said. "Who have you arrested this morning?"

"I never arrest people on Saturdays: it spoils their week-end," said Welling. "You've had a telephone message from Mr. Hamon?"

"Yes," said the Earl in surprise. "How do you know?"

"It came last night, didn't it?"

"About midnight. How on earth do you know that? If the exchange was in the village I could quite understand, but my calls are put through from Lexham."

"It was about something he'd left behind, asking you to forward it?"

"No. As a matter of fact, he wanted to know what time I would be leaving this morning."

"Why, of course," nodded Welling, "that was the natural thing to do. About twelve o'clock?"

"A little before, I should imagine. You've been listening in," accused Lord Creith.

When he went away to discover the whereabouts of a sporting rifle which had mysteriously disappeared at the last moment, Joan asked:

"How do you know all this, Captain Welling?"

"I guessed," said the old man. "It is natural that, if Pointed Toes was friend Hamon, he should seize the earliest opportunity of establishing the fact that he was in town." He shook his head sadly. "Telephonic alibis are terribly numerous," he said.

Her mind was occupied by one pressing thought, and after a while she expressed the question that was in her mind.

"Why did Mr. Morlake go away?" she asked.

She had asked Welling to breakfast with them, which meant breakfasting with her, for the choler of Lord Creith was rising rapidly. Some fishing rods had joined the rifle, and his favourite tennis racquet had suddenly disappeared from the face of the earth.

"I don't know," said Welling helplessly. "That fellow is beyond the understanding of normal people. Something is wrong

—I don't know where, I don't know how. But all I know is that he's left in a hurry."

"You don't think . . . ?" she asked quickly, and he smiled at her.

"These fellows are in danger and out of danger all the time," he said carelessly. "Probably he is carrying out some quiet little burglary——"

"Don't be horrid, Captain Welling," she said hotly. "You know Mr. Morlake is not a burglar."

"If there is one thing I know," said Welling, "it is that he *is* a burglar! I don't care what noble incentive he has, but that doesn't make him less a burglar. What is more, he is the cleverest safe-breaker in this country."

"Has he stolen much money?" she asked.

"Thousands, but it has all been Hamon's. That is the rum thing about this burglar, although it isn't so rum to me as it was. He's broken into other safes and other boxes, but not one of the people who have suffered from his curiosity have complained that they lost money. Hamon has complained about nothing else. And the crowning queerness of his action is that it isn't money he is after."

If she was hoping, as she was, for a miracle to happen and for Jim to reappear at the last moment, she was doomed to disappointment. The car which took her and her father to Southampton passed Wold House, and she craned out of the window in the hope that she might catch one glimpse of him. When the machine had passed the entrance she looked back through the window of the hood.

"Expecting anybody, dear?" asked Lord Creith drily. "Missed anything?"

"Yes, Daddy, I have," she said, with some spirit.

"You can buy almost anything you want at Cadiz," said His Lordship, wilfully dense. "Cadiz is my favourite city. Unfortunately, it is rather late for the bull fights."

"I never dreamt you were so bloodthirsty, Father," she said.

"Bulls' blood, yes, but human blood, no," he said with a shiver. "By gad, I'm glad to be out of Creith! I was scared that they'd hold me for a witness. Happily, I was drinking the waters of Lethe in the presence of the impeccable Peters when the murder was committed. In fact, I heard the shot through the window."

"The waters of Lethe" was Lord Creith's synonym for his normal whisky and soda.

The first emotion which Joan experienced when she saw the yacht lying out in Southampton Water was one of pleasurable surprise. She had expected to see a very small ship, and, when she had time to think about such matters, had felt a little uneasy at the prospect of a voyage across the Bay of Biscay in a tiny craft. *L'Esperance* had the appearance of a small cruiser, and was unusually large even for an ocean-going yacht: the same idea seemed to strike Lord Creith.

"That must have cost friend Hamon a pretty penny," he said. "Why, the infernal thing is as big as a liner!"

The captain, an Englishman, welcomed them at the gangway, and apparently every preparation had been made to leave as soon as the party was on board.

"Mr. Hamon is not coming, I understand?" said Captain Green, a typical teak-faced sailorman. "If you like, my Lord, we'll get under way. There is a moderate sea in the Channel, and with any kind of luck we ought to get through the Bay without so much as a roll."

"Let her go, Captain," said Lord Creith gaily.

The girl's cabin was beautifully appointed and smothered with hothouse flowers. She did not trouble to ask who had sent them. Mr. Hamon would not lose an opportunity of emphasising his devotion. She was too fond of flowers to throw them out of the porthole, but the knowledge that he had sent them robbed them of at least one attraction.

Lord Creith and she dined alone that evening. The captain was on the bridge, for they were steaming down the crowded Channel, and fog banks were reported by wireless between Portland Bill and Brest.

"A jolly good dinner," said his lordship with satisfaction. "You've got an excellent cook, Steward."

"Yes, sir," said the chief steward, a Frenchman who spoke

English much better than his lordship spoke French, "we have two."

"All the crew are French, I suppose, as this is a French yacht?"

The steward shook his head.

"No, my Lord," he said, "most of the hands are English and Scottish. The owner of the yacht prefers an English crew. We have a few Frenchmen on board—in fact, we've almost every nationality, including a man who I think is either a Turk or a Moor. He came on board at the last moment to work in the pantry, and he's been ill ever since we came out of the Solent. I believe he is a servant of the owner's; we are dropping him at Casablanca."

He served the coffee, and Lord Creith took a gulp and made a wry face.

"I praised your dinner too soon, Steward," he said good-humouredly. "That coffee is execrable."

The steward snatched up the cup and disappeared into the mysterious regions at the back of the saloon. When he returned, it was with apologies.

"The chef will send you in some more coffee, my Lord. We've got a new assistant cook who isn't quite up to his job."

After dinner, Joan strolled on to the deck. It was a calm night, with a sea that was absolutely still. Through the mist she could see the stars twinkling overhead, and on the starboard beam a bright light flickered at irregular intervals.

"That is Portland Bill," explained one of the officers who had come down from the bridge, "and the last of the lights of England you'll see until you return."

"Will it be foggy?" she asked, looking ahead.

"Not very. I think you're going to have an ideal voyage for this time of the year. If we can get abreast of Cherbourg without slackening speed, we shall be quit of the fog for good."

She stood, leaning over the taffrail, talking to the officer, until Lord Creith joined her, smoking a long cigar and at peace with the world. He brought with him an acceptable coat, which she was glad to put on, for the night was very cold—a fact she had not noticed until she came on deck.

They stood side by side, her father and she, watching in silence the faint phosphorescence of the waters; and then:

"Happy, old girl?"

"Very happy, Daddy."

"Whom were you sighing about just now?"

He heard her low laugh, and grinned to himself in the darkness.

"I didn't know that I was sighing. I was thinking about Jim Morlake."

"A very nice fellow," said his lordship heartily. "An American, but a very nice fellow. I don't want a burglar in the family—naturally. But I'd just as soon have a burglar as a moneylender. In fact, I should prefer one. I don't know whether that is particularly generous to our beloved host, but there is something in the sea air that makes me candid."

The days that followed were, for Joan, days of almost perfect peace. The yacht was a delightful sea boat; the comfort and luxury of the appointments, and a glimpse of a scarcely remembered sun, added to her happiness. If, by some miracle . . . the waving of a magic wand, or the muttering of some potent incantation, she could have brought Jim into that deep, red-cushioned armchair—Jim, in white flannels, Jim, with his classical face and a patch of grey at his temples. . . . She sighed.

CHAPTER XLVIII

Mutiny

THE voyage passed without event until the morning of the day they reached Cadiz. Something aroused Joan from deepest sleep to most complete wakefulness. There was no sound but the sough of wind and sea, and the peculiar monotony of the "creak-creak" at intervals which is a ship's own noise. The grey light showed against the porthole and faintly illuminated the cabin. Sitting up in bed, she looked around.

A movement by the door attracted her attention; it was slowly closing, and, jumping to the floor, she ran and pulled it open. She caught a glimpse of a big figure disappearing in the gloom of the alleyway, and then a strange thing happened. He had almost reached the end of this narrow passage when something rose from under his feet and tripped him. Even amidst the sea noises she heard the thud as he struck the hard deck. He was on his feet in an instant and then, for some reason, he fell again. Straining her eyes, Joan saw a man stand over him and pull him upright. In another instant they were out of sight.

She locked her door and went back to bed, but not to sleep. It may have been an accident; it may have been that one of the crew was a thief—few crews, even a yacht's crew, but may include one of those pests of the sea. Perhaps the thief had been detected by a watchful quartermaster, and that was the explanation of the little fight she had witnessed. She did not wish to worry her father, but as soon as she was up and dressed, she went in search of the chief steward and reported what had happened. He was genuinely concerned.

"I don't know who it could have been, Miss. The watch were on deck, scrubbing down, at daybreak, and there's a night steward on duty in the alleyway. What was the man like?"

"As far as I could see, he wore a white singlet and a pair of blue trousers."

"Was he tall or short?"

"He was very big," she said, and the man passed the crew under review.

"I'll speak to the chief officer," he said.

"I don't want to make any trouble."

"Your Ladyship will probably make more trouble if you don't report this," he retorted.

Lord Creith, who generally found the most comfortable explanation, suggested that she had been dreaming—a suggestion which she indignantly rejected.

"Then, my dear," he said, "probably the *man* was walking in his sleep! You should have locked your cabin door."

She spent two full and delightful days at Cadiz, that city of languid, beautiful women and unshaven men; drove out to Jerez to see the wine pressed, and learnt—though she had a dim idea that she had already learnt this at school—that Jerez had been corrupted into English as "sherry" and had given its name to a wine. The bad weather had passed; the sky was a delightful blue, and if the wind that blew down from the sierras had a nip that made the men of Cadiz wear their high-collared blue cloaks, it was to the girl a tonic and a stimulant.

They left Cadiz at midnight on the third day, and at daybreak the stopping of the engines woke her. She heard the rattle of a hawser and splash as the anchor fell into the water, and, looking out of her porthole, saw a twinkle of lights near at hand. It was her first glimpse of Africa, and the mystery and wonder of it thrilled her. In daylight, much of the enchantment was gone. She saw a straggle of white houses fringing a lemon-coloured beach; beyond, the blue of hills. In the cold, cheerless light of morning the mystery had gone. She shivered.

The stewardess came in answer to her ring of the bell.

"Where are we?" she asked.

"At Suba, a little coast village."

At that moment a lowered boat came into view through the porthole and disappeared. She heard the splash of it as it struck the water.

"The crew are going ashore to bring out some cases of curios that Mr. Hamon wishes to be brought home," explained the stewardess, and through the porthole Joan watched the boat draw away.

Lord Creith knocked at the door at that moment and came in in his dressing-gown.

"This is Suba," he explained unnecessarily. "Put your coat on and come up on deck, Joan."

She slipped into her fur coat and followed him up the companion-way. Except for one sailor, the deck was deserted. On the bridge was a solitary officer, leaning over the bridge and regarding the retreating boat without interest.

"There aren't many people left on the ship," she said, glancing round.

Lord Creith looked up at the clouds with a nautical eye.

"A man and a boy could navigate this ship on a day like this," he said. "There is no wind."

And then, looking across to the port side, he saw a tall, white, billowing sail moving slowly toward them.

"There is wind enough," she smiled. "Aren't they coming rather close?"

"Bless you no!" said his lordship cheerfully. "These fellows can handle a boat better than any Europeans. Moors are born seamen, and by the cut of his sail I should think it is a Moorish craft. This coast is the home of the Barbary pirates."

She glanced nervously round at the approaching sail, but he went on, oblivious to the impression he was creating.

"For hundreds of years they levied a tax on every ship that passed. Why, the word 'tariff' comes from Tarifa, a little village on the other side of the Straits——"

He stopped as the girl turned quickly. They had both heard that deep "oh!" of pain.

"What was that?" asked Lord Creith. "It sounded like somebody hurt."

There was nobody in sight, and he went forward to the bridge. As he did so, a big man crept up the companion ladder, and Joan immediately recognised the figure she had seen in the alleyway. Barefooted, the man approached the unconscious officer leaning over the taffrail.

"Look out!" yelled Lord Creith.

The officer spun round and the blow just missed his head, but caught him on the shoulder and he fell with a cry of pain. In another instant the big man had turned, and the girl saw with horror that in his hand he carried a huge hammer.

That diversion saved the officer's life. Injured as he was, he thrust himself forward and tobogganed down the steep ladder, falling on to the deck. In an instant he was on his feet and climbed down the companion-way, the big, white-faced Moor in pursuit.

"Down the companion, quick!" cried Lord Creith, and she obeyed.

As she flew down the ladder, she saw over her shoulder the high white sail of the dhow rising sheer above the ship's side, and heard the jabber of excited, guttural voices.

"Run along the alleyway into my cabin," cried Lord Creith.

She sat panting on the sofa, whilst her father shot the bolt in the door. He opened his bag and made a search.

"My revolver is gone," he said.

"What is wrong?" she asked. She was calm now.

"It looks precious like mutiny," said his lordship grimly.

She heard a patter of feet on the deck above, and again a babble of talk.

"They've boarded us from the dhow," said her father quietly, and the sound of somebody swearing softly came to them from the next cabin.

"Is anybody there?" Lord Creith called.

The partition dividing the cabins did not extend to the upper deck, and a space of three or four inches made conversation possible. It was the wounded officer, they discovered. No bones were broken, he told them, but he was in considerable pain.

"Have you any kind of firearm on your side?" he asked anxiously.

Lord Creith had to confess sadly that he was unarmed.

"What has happened?" he asked.

"I don't know," was the reply. "Most of the crew are ashore. The Captain and the first and second officers have gone to collect some packing-cases."

"How many of the crew are left on the ship?"

There was a silence as the officer calculated, and then:

"Six, including the steward. One deckhand, two chefs and a cook's mate, and, of course, the Moor we took on at Southampton. He is the fellow who bowled me over. I think they must have got the deckhands, and the chef wouldn't fight. That leaves us with the cook's mate."

He laughed bitterly.

"And the cook's mate is going to have a bad time," he said after a pause. "He beat up the Moor a few days ago. I only heard about it in the early watch. You remember your daughter complained—she is with you, I suppose?"

"Yes," said Lord Creith. "Was it the Moor who opened the door?"

"That's the man. I suppose he was looking for loose guns," said the officer. "The cook's mate happened to be on duty and saw the fellow, and there was trouble! And there's worse trouble ahead—here they come."

There was a patter of bare feet in the alleyway, and somebody hammered on the cabin door.

"You come out, you not be hurt, mister," said a husky voice.

Lord Creith made no reply.

Crash! The door shivered under the blow, but it was obvious that the narrow alleyway did not give sufficient play to the hammer, for the lock remained intact. Again the blow fell, and a long crack appeared in one of the panels of the door.

Lord Creith looked round helplessly.

"There is no kind of weapon here," he said in a slow voice to the girl. "Even my wretched razor is a safety!"

He looked at the porthole.

"Do you think you could squeeze through that?"

She shook her head.

"I won't leave you, Daddy," she said, and he patted her shoulder.

"I don't think you could get through," he said, eyeing the porthole dubiously.

Crack! Bang! The panel broke, but it was not the sound of its smashing they heard. Outside in the alleyway there was a quick scurry of feet, a shot was fired, and another. Then, from the other end of the alleyway came three shots in quick succession. Somebody fell heavily against the wall with a hideous howl, and then there was a momentary silence.

"What was that?"

It was the officer's voice from the next cabin.

"I think it was somebody shooting," said Lord Creith. He peered through the splintered panel. The man on the floor was still howling dismally, but there was no other sound.

"Look, Daddy," cried the girl excitedly. "The boat is returning."

She pointed through the porthole, and over her shoulder he saw the two boats rowing furiously toward the yacht.

And now the alleyway pandemonium broke out. Again came the rush of feet and the deafening staccato of the automatic.

"Who is it? It must be one of the deckhands. Where did he get his gun?"

The questions were fired across the top of the partition, but Lord Creith was too intent upon the struggle outside. The firing had ceased, but the screaming fury of the fighters went on. Presently there was an exultant yell and somebody was dragged along the alleyway.

"They've got him," said Lord Creith, a little hoarsely. "I wonder who he is."

Then, as the leader of the mob came parallel with the door, a voice hailed them in English.

"Don't open your door until the crew come aboard. They are returning."

The girl stood petrified at the sound of the voice, and pushing her father aside she stooped to peer through the broken panel. She saw a man struggling in the hands of his white-robed captors; a tall man in the soiled white garb of a cook. It was Jim Morlake!

CHAPTER XLIX

The Man on the Beach

JOAN screamed and tugged at the door.

"The key, the key, Father!" she said wildly. "It is Jim!"

But he dragged her back.

"My dear, you're not going to help Jim Morlake or yourself by putting yourself in the hands of these beasts," he said, and presently her struggles ceased and she hung heavily in his arms.

He laid her on the settee and ran to the porthole. The boats were nearing the yacht, and he could see, by the attitude of the Captain, who stood in the stern, revolver in hand, that news of the mutiny had reached him. There was no noise from the alleyway nor overhead on the deck; only the whining of the wounded man outside the door broke the complete stillness. In another minute they heard the boats bump against the side of the ship, and the rattle of booted feet above them. And then came the Captain's voice.

"Is anybody here?" he called.

Lord Creith unlocked the cabin door and stepped out over the prostrate figure.

"Thank God you're safe!" said Captain Green fervently. "The young lady, is she all right?"

Joan had recovered, and though she lay without movement she was conscious. Then realising that she alone knew the secret of the "cook's" identity, she staggered to her feet.

"Jim! They have taken Jim!" she said wildly.

"Your cook." Lord Creith supplied the startling information.

"My cook!'" said the puzzled captain, and then a light dawned on him. "You mean the assistant cook—the man I took on at Southampton? Is he the fellow who did this?" He looked down at the motionless figure in the alleyway. "If they have taken him, he is on the dhow," said the Captain. "It pushed off as we came on board."

He ran up to the deck, and the girl did her best to imitate his alacrity, but her limbs were shaking and she was curiously weak. The dhow was already a dozen yards from the ship, and was heeling over under the fresh land breeze, her big leg-o'-mutton sail filling.

"Are you sure they've taken him on board?" asked the Captain. "He may be amongst the——" He did not finish the sentence.

One of the crew was dead, another so badly injured that his life was despaired of, and search parties were sent to discover other casualties, but no sign of Jim was reported.

"We can overtake them," said Lord Creith, and the Captain nodded.

"I'll get up anchor, but it is by no means certain we can do much unless they are fools enough to keep to the open sea. I think they'll run round the point, and there I shan't be able to follow them, except with boat crews."

The dhow was gaining way every minute. The white wake at her stern was significant.

The wireless operator, in his little cabin on the upper deck, had been overlooked by the boarders, and it was he who had signalled the Captain back. He had done something more: he had got in touch with an American destroyer that was cruising some twenty miles away, and a blur of smoke showed on the horizon.

"Whether she can come up before the dhow gets to safety is a question," said the Captain.

At that moment the white-sailed vessel changed her course, and the Captain grunted.

"She is going inshore round the point. I thought she would," he said.

"What will they do with him?" asked the girl, and for a moment he did not know to whom she referred.

"Oh, the cook? I don't suppose he'll come to much harm. If they thought he was a man of substance they would hold him to ransom. As it is, he'll probably be fairly well treated. The Moor isn't particularly vindictive to the enemies he takes in fair fight."

The wind had freshened and was blowing strongly when the yacht's bow turned in pursuit of the Moorish craft, but by this time he was rounding the promontory that ran out to sea for two miles, and by his tactics the Captain guessed what plan was being followed.

"We shall never get up to them," he said, "and if we do, we shan't find the man we want."

"Why?" asked Joan, but he did not supply the gruesome information.

In his days he had been a member of the Royal Navy, engaged in the suppression of slave traffic on the East Coast of Africa, and he had seen slaves dropped overboard, with a bar of iron about their necks, in order that the incriminating evidence against the captors should be removed. And he did not doubt that the skipper of the dhow would follow the same procedure.

When they rounded the point, the dhow was so close inshore that it seemed to have grounded.

"They're landing," said Captain Green, watching the boat through his glasses, "and there goes my cook!"

The girl almost snatched the binoculars from him and focussed them on the beach. Her hand trembled so violently that all she saw was a blur of white figures and yellow sand, but presently she mastered her emotion and held the glasses upon the tall, dark form that walked leisurely up the beach.

"That is he," she whispered. "Oh, Jim, Jim!"

"Do you know him?"

She nodded.

"Then there is no need for me to pretend ignorance," said the Captain, "and I will ask you to keep this matter from my owners. Captain Morlake and I are old acquaintances. I knew him when he was at Tangier. He came to me in a great hurry on the Friday night before we sailed, and begged me to ship him on board the yacht as an extra hand. Knowing that he has always been mixed up in queer adventures—he was an intelligence officer, and may be still, for all I know—I took him on as a cook. He warned me of what would happen, and, like a fool, I thought he was romancing."

"He warned you of this attack?" said Lord Creith in astonishment. "How could he know?"

The Captain shook his head.

"That I can't tell you, but he did know, though I imagine he wasn't sure where the attempt would be made, because he said nothing before I went ashore to pick up those darned packing-cases—which were not there!"

The destroyer was now visible to the naked eye.

"She is useless to us," said the Captain, shaking his head. "Before she can land a party, these fellows will be well away into the desert." He bit his lip thoughtfully. "They won't hurt Captain Morlake. He speaks the language, and there is hardly a big man in Morocco who doesn't know him. I should imagine that at this moment the captain of the dhow is scared to death to find who is his prisoner."

He focussed his glasses again.

"Two Europeans!" he gasped. "What other man have they taken? Do you know, Johnson?" He turned to his second officer.

"I've been looking at him and I can't make him out," he said.

He steadied his telescope against a stanchion and looked again.

"He is certainly a European, and he is certainly not a sailor. He is wearing a civilian overcoat."

"May I look?"

Assisted by the officer, the girl brought the telescope to bear upon the figure that was walking with a white-gowned Moor. Jim had disappeared over the crest of a sandhill, and these two walked alone, the Moor gesticulating, the other emphasising some point with his clenched fist.

She shook her head.

"I don't know him," she said. "I never expected I would."

It was a humiliating confession for her to make, did she but know it, for she had once boasted that she would know Ralph Hamon anywhere and in any garb! And it was Ralph Hamon who strode angrily side by side with the master of the dhow.

CHAPTER L

The Play

RALPH HAMON, shivering in his light suit, despite the heavy overcoat he wore, growled his imprecations as he toiled painfully up the steep slope of the sandhill and Arabic is a language which was specially designed for cursing.

"You're a fool!" he stormed. "Did I not tell you a hundred times what to do?"

The black-bearded captain of the dhow shrugged his shoulders.

"It was the fault of my officer, who now roasts in hell, for I told him first to silence all the members of the crew that were left on board, but they forgot this sailor with a pistol."

"Why didn't you knock him on the head? Why did you bring him on board?" growled Hamon.

"Because the men desired to settle with him in their own way. He has killed Yussef, whom the men loved. I think he will be sorry he did not die," said the Captain ominously, and Ralph Hamon snorted.

"What he will be sorry for and what he will be happy about doesn't concern me," he growled. "You had the woman in your hands and you did not take her."

"If this sailor with a pistol——" began the Captain again, and Ralph Hamon shouted him down.

"Curse the sailor with a pistol!" he shouted. "Do you think I've been lying ill in your foul boat for two days in order to capture a sailor?"

"If you will see him——" pleaded the Moor.

"I don't want to see him, and I don't want him to see me. If you allowed the woman to escape, you are fools enough to let him go also. And do you think I want him to carry the news to Tangier that I was with you on your dhow? Do what you like with him."

He saw the prisoner at a distance—a tall man whose face was unrecognisable under the mask of grime and blood, but he did not venture near to him. Mules were waiting for them at a little village and at the sight of one, more richly caparisoned than the rest, with a saddle of soft red leather, and tinkling bells about its neck, Ralph Hamon bit his lip until the blood came. It was the palfrey that he had designed for the girl.

With no delay the party mounted and soon a string of a dozen mules was crossing the wild land. They halted for two hours in the afternoon and resumed the journey, halting for the night in the vicinity of a little village of charcoal burners.

"You will not come to the play?" said the Captain interrogatively. "This man is of your race and it would give you unhappiness to see them whip him."

"It would not make me unhappy at all," said Ralph savagely, "but I'm tired."

They pitched a tent for him next to the chief, and he was on the point of retiring, though the sun had scarcely touched the western horizon, when a diversion came. There was an excited stir amongst the men of the caravan; the drone of conversation rose to a higher pitch and he enquired the cause.

"El Zafouri," was the laconic answer.

Ralph knew the name of this insurgent chief, though he had never met him.

"Is he here?"

"He is coming," said the other indifferently, "but I am a good friend of his and there is nothing to fear."

A cloud of dust on the hill-road was evidence of the size and importance of El Zafouri's retinue; and when, half-an-hour later, he pitched his camp near by, Ralph Hamon was glad in his heart that the rebel was likely to prove a friend.

He went in person to greet the notorious shereef, and found him sitting before his tent, a squat and burly man, distinctly negroid of countenance, and black.

"Peace on your house, Zafouri!" he said conventionally.

"And on you peace," said Zafouri, looking up straightly at the stranger. "I think I know you. You are Hamon."

"That is my name," said Ralph, gratified that his fame had extended so far.

"You are a friend of the Shereef Sadi Hafiz?"

Here Ralph Hamon was on more delicate ground. So rapidly did Sadi change his friendships and his allegiances that, for all he knew, he might at the moment be a deadly enemy of the man who was watching him.

"Sadi is my agent," he said carefully, "but who knows whether he is my man now? For Sadi is a man who serves the sun that shines."

He was perfectly safe in saying this, for the reputation of Sadi Hafiz was common property and he was secretly relieved to see the twinkle that came in Zafouri's dark eyes.

"That is true," he said. "Where are you going, *haj?*" He addressed the captain of the dhow, who had stood by Ralph during the interview.

"To the Rifi Hills, Shereef," he said and the little Moor stroked his chin.

"You are coming the longest way," he said significantly. "You have a prisoner?"

The dhow captain nodded.

"My men told me of him. He dies, they say? Well, that is best for him and for all. When a man is asleep he harms nobody and is happy. I will come to your play."

Ralph would have been present, but nature forbade the exertion. For forty-eight hours he had been without sleep, and no sooner had he lain on the matting that his servant had spread for him in the tent, than he was asleep.

The play had been fixed for an hour after sunset, and it was of a kind that was novel to Zafouri. Two lines of men arranged themselves at a few paces' interval, leaving a narrow lane through which the prisoner was to pass, ostensibly to safety, for, if he reached the end of the lane and was sufficiently agile to escape the two swordsmen placed there to give him his quietus, he was free. It was the old, bad punishment of running the gauntlet, and Jim, who in his experience had heard of this method of settling accounts with malefactors and political enemies, faced the certainty that, swift as he might run, he could not hope to survive the hail of blows which would fall on him, for each man in the two lines was armed with a wooden stave.

His captors brought him fruit and water.

"Be swift and you will be happy," said one with a chuckle, and was taken aback when Jim answered in the Moorish Arabic quoting a familiar tag.

"Justice is faster than birds and more terrible than lions."

"Oh!" said his gaoler in surprise. "You speak the language of God! Now, friend, speak well for me to the djinn, for tonight you will live amongst ghosts!"

They brought him out for the final condemnation and the dhow captain, squatting in state on a silken carpet, gave judgment.

"Death for Death. Who kills shall be killed," he recited in a monotonous sing-song.

"Remember that, man," said Jim sternly, and Zafouri, who shared the silken carpet with his host, shot a quick glance at the bearded prisoner.

They brought the Captain a glass of water and he ceremoniously washed his hands of the prisoner.

"Listen, man without a name," said Jim in fluent Arabic. "If I die, people will talk and the consequence will come to you wherever you are, and you will hand in the *sok,* and your soul will go down to Gehenna and meet my soul——"

"Take him away," said the Captain huskily.

"Let him stay."

It was Zafouri who spoke.

"Peace on you, Milaka." It was the old Moorish name for him and Jim's eyes kindled.

"And on you peace, Zafouri," said Jim, recognising the man.

And then Zafouri drew his squat bulk erect, and, putting his arms about the prisoner, kissed him on the shoulder.

"If any man says death to my friend, let him say it now," he said, and his left hand closed over the hilt of his curved sword.

The Captain did not speak.

CHAPTER LI

The Courtyard

TANGIER lay bathed in the early morning sunlight, a vast mosaic of white and green, and Joan Carston gazed spellbound at the beauty of the city as the yacht moved slowly into the bay. Overhead was a cloudless blue sky; and a shore wind brought in its lap a faint, pungent and yet indescribable aroma.

"That is the East," sniffed Lord Creith.

Joan had thrown off the effects of her terrible experience,

but the change which Lord Creith had noticed in her before they had left England was more marked than ever.

"Do you feel equal to going ashore?"

She nodded.

"You're a wonderful girl, Joan," he said admiringly. "You have had more knock-down blows in the past few weeks than come to most people in the course of their lives."

She laughed.

"You can become inured even to knock-down blows. I think it would take a human earthquake to disturb me now."

He shot a furtive glance in her direction.

"You're not worrying any more about—about Morlake?"

She seemed to be examining her own mind before she replied.

"It is difficult to tell how I feel. I have such faith in him and this feeling—that if anything terrible had happened I should know."

Lord Creith was only too happy to agree. He had a weakness for agreeing to all cheerful, and for dissenting violently from all dismal, predictions.

"The Captain says he has arranged to stay here a week and I think we can well afford the time."

He had booked rooms at the big white hotel that overlooked the beach and, later in the day, from the broad terrace, she could gaze in wonder at the confused jumble of buildings, which made modern Tangier.

"Rather like the Old Testament lit by electricity," said his lordship. "I don't know whether I've read that or whether I've invented it. If I've invented it, it is jolly good. I hope you're not being disappointed, Joan. These Eastern cities are never quite so pleasant near at hand as they are from three miles out at sea. And the smell—phew!" He dabbed his nose with his handkerchief and pulled an unpleasant face.

"Jim lived here for years," she said.

"Even that doesn't make it smell like Attar of Roses," said her practical father. "What was he doing here?"

"Captain Green says he was in the diplomatic service. I am going to enquire."

The next day she threaded the tortuous street in which the various consulates were situated. The news she secured about Jim Morlake was, however, of the most fragmentary character. By very reason of his profession, the officials at the consulates and embassies were reticent. She was, however, able to confirm the Captain's statement, which had been news to her, that for some years Jim Morlake had been something of a power in this city. Lord Creith knew the British Minister and they went to tea at the Residency and Joan listened without hearing to the talk of concessions, of representations, of the enormities of the sanitary council and the hideous injustice which was inflicted by the native *basha* upon the unfortunate subjects of the Sultan.

She did not accompany her father in his visit to the prison and she was glad afterwards, when he brought back a highly coloured narrative of his experience.

"A hell upon earth," he described it tersely, and she felt a little sinking of heart. If the method of the *Kasbah* was the standard of the Moorish treatment of prisoners, then it would go hard with Jim.

It was the third day of their visit and already Joan had almost wearied of the town. She had seen the great market-place, and wandered amidst the charcoal sellers and the kneeling camels, had watched the native jugglers and the professional holy men, and chaffered with the sellers of brass in the bazaar.

"The prettiest part of Tangier one doesn't see. Do you remember that ugly street we passed through at the back of the mosque?" she asked. "A very old door opened and I caught a glimpse of the most gorgeous garden and there were two veiled women on a balcony, feeding the pigeons. It was so lovely a picture that I nearly went in."

Lord Creith said something about the insanitary conditions of the houses and went on to discuss the hotel bill. That afternoon, they walked up the hill to see a gun play. A number of tribesmen had come in from the hills to celebrate the anniversary of a local saint's death and at her request he turned aside from the market place to show her the exterior of the prison.

She shuddered as a horrible face leered out at her from behind the bars.

"Do you want to have a look inside?"

"No thank you, Daddy," she said hastily, and they turned their steps toward the bazaar.

Lord Creith opened his lawn umbrella and put it up, for the sun's rays were unpleasantly hot.

"East is East and West is West," he chanted. "What always interests me about these fellows is, what are they thinking about? You don't really get into the East until you understand its psychology."

The girl, who had been walking behind him, did not answer, but he was used to that.

"Now, if you were to ask me——" he began and turned his head to emphasise his remarks.

Joan was not there!

He strode back along the street. A begging man stood at the corner of a court, demanding alms in the name of Allah; a stout veiled woman was waddling away from him carrying a basket of native work; but there was no sign of Joan. He looked up at the high walls on either side, as though he expected to find her perched miraculously on the top.

And then the seriousness of possibilities struck him and he ran along the uneven cobbled street to the end. He looked left and right, but there was no sign of Joan. In one street he saw four men carrying a wooden case, chanting as they went, and he came back to the beggar and was about to ask him if he had seen a lady, when he saw that the man had been blinded.

"Joan!" he roared.

There was no answer. A man who was asleep in the shadow of a doorway woke with a start, stared at the pallid old man, then, cursing all foreigners who disturb the rest of the faithful, curled up and went to sleep again.

Lord Creith saw in the distance a French officer of gendarmes and ran up to him.

"Have you seen a European lady—my daughter——?" he began incoherently.

Rapidly he told the story of the girl's disappearance.

"Probably she has gone into one of the houses. Have you any Moorish friends?" asked the officer.

"None," said Lord Creith emphatically.

"Where was she when you saw her last?" and Lord Creith pointed.

"There is a short cut to the *sok* near here," suggested the officer and led the way.

But Joan was not in the big market place and Lord Creith hurried back to the hotel. The lady had not returned, the manager told him. She was not on the terrace. The only person on the terrace was a tall man in grey, who was fanning himself gently with his broad-brimmed sombrero.

He looked round at the sound of Lord Creith's voice and jumping to his feet, hurried toward him.

"Morlake!" gasped Creith. "Joan . . . !"

"What has happened to her?" asked Jim quickly.

"She has disappeared! My God, I'm afraid—I'm afraid!"

CHAPTER LII

The House of Sadi

Jim had a brief consultation with the chief of police before Lord Creith guided him to the spot where Joan had disappeared.

"I thought it was here!"

He said something in a low voice to the police chief and Lord Creith saw the officer shake his head and heard him say:

"I can't help you there. It may lead to serious trouble for me. The only thing I can do is to be on hand if you want me."

"That will do," said Jim.

There was a small door in the wall and to this he went and knocked. After a time the wicket opened and a black face appeared in the opening.

"The Shereef is not in the house," said the slave in guttural accents.

Jim looked round. The police officer had withdrawn to a discreet distance.

"Open the door, my rose of Sharon," he breathed. "I am from the *basha,* with news for the Shereef."

The woman hesitated and shook her head.

"I must not open," she said, but there was an indecision in her tone of which Jim took immediate advantage.

"This message is from Hamon," he said in a low voice. "Go to the Shereef and tell him."

The wicket closed. Jim glanced round at the troubled Lord Creith.

"You had better join our friend," he said under his breath.

"But if she is there, I can insist——"

Jim shook his head.

"The only form of insistence is the one I shall employ," he said grimly. "You would help me greatly, Lord Creith, if you did not interfere."

Soon after his lordship had walked reluctantly to the unhappy police chief, Jim heard the sound of bolts being drawn, a key squeaked in the rusty lock, and the gate was opened a few inches to admit him to a familiar quadrangle. He glanced at the ancient fountain, and the untidy verandah and its faded chairs, and then, as a man appeared in the doorway, he walked swiftly across the untidy space and went up the steps of the verandah in one bound.

"Sadi Hafiz, I want you," he said, and at the sound of his voice the man started back.

"God of Gods!" he gasped. "I did not know that you were in Tangier, Milaka!"

It seemed that his pale face had gone a shade whiter.

"Now what can I do for you, my dear Captain Morlake?" he said in his excellent English. "Really this is a surprise—a pleasant surprise. Why did you not send your name——"

"Because you would not have admitted me," said Jim. "Where is Lady Joan Carston?"

The man's face was a blank.

"Lady Joan Carston? I don't seem to remember that name," he said. "Is she a lady at the British Embassy?"

"Where is the girl who was lured into this place half-an-hour ago?" asked Jim. "And I warn you, Sadi Hafiz, that I will not leave this house without her."

"As God lives," protested the fat man vigorously, "I do not know the lady and I have not seen her. Why should she be here, in my poor house, for she is evidently of the English nobility."

"Where is Lady Joan Carston?" asked Jim deliberately. "By God, you had better answer me, Sadi, or there will be a dead man for me to explain."

He jerked his gun from his pocket, and the gleam of it seemed to blind the Moor, for he half closed his eyes and blinked.

"This is an outrage," he said, and, as he grew more and more excited, his English suffered. "I will report this matter to the Consulate——"

Jim pushed him aside and strode into the flagged hall. A door was on the left; he kicked it open. It was evidently Sadi's smoking-room, for it reeked with a scent of hashish and tobacco. At one end was an iron circular staircase leading to an upper floor, an incongruous object in that primitive Oriental setting. Without hesitation he flew up the stairs, and, with a scream, a girl who was lolling on a lounge jumped up and pulled her veil across her face.

"Where is the English lady?" asked Jim quickly.

"Lord," said the trembling girl, "I have seen no English woman."

"Who else is here?"

He ran across the half-darkened room, pulling aside the curtains of its three sleeping places, but Joan was not there. He came down the stairs to confront the outraged Sadi Hafiz.

Jim knew what was going to happen before Sadi fired, for he had committed the unpardonable sin of invading the women's apartments of an Oriental magnate.

"Drop your gun, Sadi," he said sternly, "or you die. I've got you covered."

Sadi fired at the place where Jim had disappeared, and then, unexpectedly, the intruder came into view from behind a pillar, and Sadi put up his hands. In another instant Jim was upon him and had snatched his pistol away.

"Now," he said, breathing through his nose. "Where is Joan Carston?"

"I tell you I don't know."

Outside the door was a small knot of frightened servants, and Jim slammed the heavy open doors into their place and shot the bars.

"Where is Joan Carston?'

"She's gone," said the man sullenly.

"You lie. She hasn't had time to go."

"She was here only for a minute, then she went into the Street of the School—there is another door in the yard."

"With whom?"

"I don't know," was the defiant reply.

Jim towered over him, his hands on his hips, his eyes scarcely visible.

"Sadi," he said softly, "do you know Zafouri? Last night he told me that he will have your head because you betrayed him to the Government, took money from him to buy rifles, and used it for yourself. I will save your life."

"I have been threatened before, Mr. Morlake," said Sadi Hafiz, recovering a little of his audacity, "and what has happened? I am still alive. I tell you I know nothing about this lady."

"You told me just now she was in the courtyard and had been taken out of the door into the Street of the Schools. Who took her?"

"As Allah lives, I do not know," cried the man in Arabic, and Jim struck him across the face with the back of his hand.

"You will keep, Sadi Hafiz."

Jim turned as he unbarred the doors and flung them open, and he pointed to his throat with a long forefinger.

"Zafouri will get you—that is certain. But more certain than that is, that, if any harm comes to this lady, I will find you and kill you inch by inch."

He slammed the doors behind him and strode out of the house and into the courtyard.

A brief examination showed him that the man had spoken the truth to this extent, that there was another door leading to the narrow street which Lord Creith had searched.

And then he remembered that Joan's father had seen four men carrying a heavy case. He strode into the street and beckoned the policeman.

"I want your people to trace four men who were carrying a heavy case up the Street of The Schools. They must have crossed the *sok*."

The movements of the party were easy to follow. A native policeman had seen them crossing to the Fez Road and load the case upon a light car which had been waiting there all the morning. A camel driver, who had been resting by the side of the road near the car, confirmed this, and said that something inside the box had moved, and he had asked the man in charge of the carrying party what it was, and had been told it was a crate of chickens.

"Wait here," said Jim.

He ran back through the crowd that had gathered in the market, and disappeared in their midst. Ten minutes later Lord Creith saw a big car come flying along the road, and Jim was at the wheel.

"I found it outside the Hotel d'Angleterre," he said breathlessly. "God knows who is the owner."

Lord Creith jumped into the car.

"I'm afraid I can't come with you," said the police officer, who was a Frenchman and regarded all regulations as inelastic. "Beyond here is outside my jurisdiction."

Jim nodded curtly and sent the car flying along the Fez Road. The tracks of the motor-van were visible for a long way, but ten miles out of Tangier . . .

"There's the car!" said Jim.

It was abandoned by the side of the road, and the case was still intact. Suppose he were wrong, and they were on the wrong track? His heart grew heavy at the thought.

He pulled the car up at the tail of the trolley and leapt on to the float. And then he saw that the box was empty, the lid having been thrown into the undergrowth on the side of the road.

Not wholly empty, for in the bottom lay a little white shoe, and, as he lifted it out, Lord Creith groaned.

"That was Joan's," he said.

CHAPTER LIII

The House in the Hollow

JOAN CARSTON was sauntering behind her father, and had come opposite to the door in the wall, when it opened and she paused to look into the courtyard. The first view was disappointing, but the smiling black woman who held the door invitingly open pointed, as though it was something worth seeing, and Joan, her curiosity aroused, stepped through the doorway. Instantly the door was slammed behind her, a big, black hand covered her mouth, and she was drawn backward against the gate-woman, who whispered something fiercely in her ear. It was unintelligible, but there was no mistaking the threat.

Before she realised what had happened, four men, who had appeared from nowhere, closed on her, and a scarf was knotted tightly round her ankles, a great wad of cottonwool was thrust into her face, blinding and stifling her, and she felt herself lifted up from her feet.

She struggled, kicking furiously, but it was futile to struggle against those odds, and, her terror subsiding, she lay passive on the stone-flagged ground whilst her hands were bound tightly together. Then she was lifted and she sniffed the scent of clean wood. The wool was pulled from her face and another silken scarf bound tightly round her mouth by an expressionless negro, who pulled the edges of the scarf away so that she could breathe. In another minute the lid of the case was fastened on, and she was lifted irregularly into the air. She dared not struggle for fear of throwing the bearers off their balance.

The air in the box was stifling: she felt she would suffocate and tried to raise the lid with her head, but it had been fastened from the outside. For an eternity she seemed to be swaying dizzily on the shoulders of the bearers, and then there was a little bump, and the box was slid on to a flat surface. What it was she knew, for she could feel the throb and pulsation of the engine beneath her. The car moved on, gathering speed, and evidently the driver was in a hurry, for he did not slow even over the irregular country road. Soon she was aching in every limb and ready to swoon.

She must have lost consciousness for a while, for she woke suddenly to find herself lying on the side of the road. The trolley and the box had disappeared, and her four captors, whose heads were swathed in scarves, were looking down at her. Presently one stooped and lifted her to her feet, saying something in Arabic which she did not understand. She shook her head to signify her ignorance of the language, and then she saw the waiting mules. Carrying her in his arms, the big negro sat the girl on a mule, and led it down a steep slope at right angles to the road, his companions following.

Her head was in a whirl, she was feeling dizzy and sick. To add to her torment, her thirst was almost unbearable, but they had not far to go. She saw one of the men, evidently the leader, looking back anxiously, and wondered what he feared. If there was a pursuit she must be rescued, and her heart leapt at the thought. The end of her journey, however, was near at hand. In a hollow was a low-roofed house, surrounded by a high, white wall, through the low gate of which the man led her mule.

The courtyard was a blaze of autumnal flowers; the inevitable fountain played in the centre. She waited while they closed the gates, and then her attendant signalled her to dismount, and leading the way to the house, knocked at the door. It was opened immediately, and he pushed her into the hall. At first it was so dark that she could see nothing and then there developed from the darkness the figure of a Moorish woman. She was pretty, Joan thought, in spite of the unhealthy pallor of her complexion. Guided by the girl she passed through another door into a long room, the floor of which was covered with shabby rugs, which, with a divan, constituted its furnishing.

Light was admitted from windows set high up in the wall, and she recognised the place, from the descriptions she had read, as the harem of a Moorish house. No other woman was in the room, and the girl who had conducted her there disappeared almost immediately, closing the door behind her.

Joan sat down on the edge of the settee and dropped her face in her hands. She must face the danger bravely, she told herself, terrible as that danger was. She had no illusions as to what these two attempts on her liberty signified. The first had failed, but now she realised, as she had suspected all along, that the attack upon the yacht at Suba had been designed for her capture, and was not, as the Captain had asserted and Lord Creith had believed, the haphazard attack of pirates in search of treasure.

The abduction had been carried out so smoothly that it must have been planned. How did they knew she would pass that door? They must have been waiting for days to carry their plot into execution. And who were "they"?

Her head ached; she felt at the end of her resources; and then she sprang up as the door opened and a girl came in, bearing a large brass tray containing native bread, fruit, and a large brown carafe of water. With this was a chipped cup.

"Do you speak English?" asked Joan.

The girl shook her head. The prisoner tried in French, with no better result.

"I can speak Spanish a little," said the Moorish girl, but though Joan recognised the language, her knowledge was too slight to carry on a conversation.

When she had gone, Joan poured out a cupful of water and drank feverishly. She regarded the food with an air of suspicion, and then resolutely broke the bread and ate a little.

"Joan Carston," she said, shaking her head, "you're in a very unhappy situation. You have been kidnapped by Moors! That sounds as though you're dreaming, because those things do not happen outside of books. You're not dreaming, Joan Carston. And you may eat the food. I don't suppose they will try to poison you—yet! And if they do, perhaps it will be better for you."

"I doubt it," said a voice behind her, and she turned with a cry.

A man had come into the room from the far end, and had been watching her for a long time before he made his presence known.

"You!" she said.

Ralph Hamon smiled crookedly.

"This is an unexpected pleasure," he said.

The appearance of the man momentarily stunned her, and then there dawned slowly upon her the true meaning of his appearance.

"So it was you all the time?" she said slowly. "And that was why you sent us on this voyage? You were the other man, on the beach? I ought to have known that. Where is Jim Morlake?"

She saw his jaw drop.

"Jim Morlake? What are you talking about? He is in England, I suppose, under arrest for murder, if there is any justice in the country. You probably know that your husband was killed the night before you left, and that Morlake shot him."

She shook her head, and he was amazed to see her smile.

"You killed Farringdon," she said. "Captain Welling told me before I left. Not in so many words, but he found your footprints on the garden bed."

If she wished to frighten him, she had succeeded. That old look she had seen before came into his grey face.

"You're trying to scare me," he said huskily.

"Where is Jim Morlake?" she asked again.

"I don't know, I tell you. Dead, I hope, the damned Yankee crook!"

"He is not dead, unless you killed him when you found you had him in your hands."

His blank astonishment was eloquent.

"In my hands? I don't understand you. When was he in my hands?"

"He was the sailor you took from the yacht," she said; "the cook."

"Hell!" breathed Hamon, and took a step backward. "You're fooling me. That wasn't Morlake. It was a sailor—a cook."

She nodded.

"It was Mr. Morlake. What did you do to him?"

"Damn him!" he snarled. "That swine Zafouri took him away——" He stopped and changed his tone. "He is dead," he said. "He was executed by the crew of the dhow——"

"You're not telling the truth. You told it at first. Mr. Morlake got away!"

He did not speak. Fingering his quivering lips, he glared at her.

"Morlake here! He can't be here: it is impossible!" he said. "You've invented that, Joan. I thought he was miles away. And what did Welling say? That is an invention too. What reason had I to shoot that soak?"

"Captain Welling practically told me that you were the murderer," said the girl with calm malice.

He took out his handkerchief and wiped his streaming forehead.

"I'm a murderer, eh?" he said dully. "Well, they can only hang me, whatever I do," and his glance fell upon her. "I was going to tell you something, but you've upset my programme, Joan. It is easy to find out whether Morlake is in Tangier."

"I didn't say he was in Tangier. I don't know that he is," she said, and for a second his face cleared.

"He will come to Tangier," he said, frowning again. "He is not likely to lose much time if he knows you're there. Bit keen on him, aren't you? Lovers! I saw him kissing you in the wood. I hope he taught you how. Most of you cold white women haven't learnt the trick."

He bit his lip, and evidently his mind was elsewhere than in that tawdry room.

"I'll soon find out if he is in Tangier," he said, and went out the way he had come, through the little door behind the curtain which she had overlooked.

A few minutes after he had gone, the Moorish girl returned, and led her to a room at the back of the house. A brick bath had been sunk in the floor, and the girl signalled to her to undress. Thrown across the back of a rickety chair, Joan saw some garments which she guessed were the costume of a Moorish woman, and at first she refused, but the girl pointed significantly at the door; and guessing that if she offered any resistance force would be applied, Joan undressed under the watchful eye of the girl and stepped down into the bath.

When she came out and was enveloped in the warm towel that the girl had put for her, she saw that her clothes had been moved.

"You want me to wear these?" she asked in lame Spanish.

"Si, señorita," said the Moorish girl, and Joan dressed herself slowly.

The costume was curiously unlike any she had seen (and had worn) at amateur theatricals. There was no tinsel, no glitter of sequins . . . her first feeling was one of comfort. Only one article of her old attire she was allowed to retain—her stockings. Fortunately, she had not far to walk, for she had lost her shoe, and though the stocking sole was brown with the dust of the Fez Road, it was not worn through. When she had finished, the girl led her back to the room where she had first been imprisoned, and left her there.

It was growing dark when Ralph Hamon returned to her.

"Your unofficial fiancé is in trouble with the Moorish authorities," he said, "but he asked for it! A man with his knowledge of the country should have thought twice before attempting to raid the women's apartments of a Moorish noble. You will be interested to learn that he was the gentleman who trailed you this afternoon."

"Anything you tell me about him interests me," she said, and his scowl rewarded her.

"I think you'd better get into a new frame of mind, Joan, and readjust your values," he said. "Big changes are coming into your life and into mine."

He seated himself beside her on the settee and she edged away from him, and finally rose.

"I'm going to enjoy the existence that I've always wanted," he said. "The *dolce far niente* of Morocco is a real thing: in Italy it is a phrase."

"You don't imagine that you are beyond the reach of the law?" she asked.

"The law!" he scoffed. "There is no law in the hills, but the law of the rifle and the chieftain who happens to be reigning in that particular district. Don't you realise that there is a man in this country called Raisuli, who has been the law in his own province for twenty years? My dear Joan," he said blandly, "no country is going to war in order to save you from a little inconvenience. I am probably rendering you a very great service," he went on. "You are going to know life—the life that is worth the living."

"In what capacity?" she asked, looking at him gravely.

"As my wife," he replied. "There will be some difficulty about marrying for a year or two, but Moorish marriages are arranged much more easily. You shall learn Arabic: I will be your teacher, and we will read the poems of Hafiz together. You will look back pityingly upon the old Joan Carston, and wonder what attractions she found in life that were comparable with the happiness——"

"You talk quite well," she interrupted him. "Nobody would guess that a man of your age, and with your curious face, would ever speak of poetry."

She looked down at him, her hands clasped behind her, an obvious interest in her eyes.

"You *are* a remarkable man," she said emphatically. "I don't know how many murders you have committed, but you have certainly committed one; and probably the whole of your fortune is founded upon some horrible crime of that description. It doesn't seem possible, does it, that we have that type of person living in the twentieth century? And yet there must be—oh, a whole lot of people who have committed undetected murders for their own profit."

He was speechless with fear and rage. This, to him, was the tremendous fact—that she was presenting him as he was, and as now, for the first time, he knew he was. For a man may lie to himself and screen his own actions from himself; so veil his motives, and the sordidness of those motives, that, when they are faithfully described, he stands aghast at the revelation.

"I am not a murderer," he croaked, his face working convulsively, "I'm not a murderer, do you hear? I—I am many things, but I'm not a murderer."

"Who killed Ferdie Farringdon?" she asked quietly, and he screwed up his eyes with an expression of pain.

"I don't know—I did, perhaps. I didn't mean to kill him . . . I meant to—I don't know what I meant. I thought I'd get Morlake. I drove my machine to within three miles of the village and came the rest of the journey on foot."

He covered his eyes with his arm as though shutting out some horrible sight.

"Damn you, how dare you say these things?" he nearly sobbed in his rage. "I'll make you so interested in yourself that you won't talk about me, Joan, understand that!"

He was about to say something else, but changed his mind, and, turning, walked quickly out of the room. She did not see him again that night, but just as she was dozing on the divan, she heard the door open and sitting up, saw the Moorish girl carrying a long blue cloak over her arm. Without a word she put it about Joan's shoulders, and she knew that the second stage of her journey had begun.

Whither would it lead? In her faith that it would lead to Jim Morlake, she went out, impatient to resume the journey.

CHAPTER LIV

A Visit to the Basha

HAMON had spoken no more than the truth when he had said that Jim was in serious trouble with the authorities. But it was that kind of serious trouble which he could handle. The *basha* of Tangier, governor and overlord of the faithful, was at coffee when Jim was announced by the great man's majordomo. The *basha* pulled his beard and frowned horribly.

"Tell the Excellency that I cannot see him. There has been a complaint by the Shereef Sadi Hafiz which must go before the Consulate Board to-morrow."

The servant disappeared, to return almost immediately.

"Lord," he said, "Morlaki sends you one word and waits your answer."

"You're a fool," said the *basha* angrily. "I tell you I will not see him. What is the word?"

"The word, Lord, is 'sugar.' "

It was an innocent enough word, but the official's hand came straight to his beard and plucked at it nervously.

"Bring him to me," he said after a while, and Jim came into the presence unabashed.

"Peace on your house, Tewfik Pasha!" he said.

"And on you peace!" gabbled the other, and, with a wave of his hand, dismissed the servant from the room. "Now I tell you, Excellency, that there is serious trouble in Tangier. The Shereef Sadi Hafiz has brought charges against you of breaking into"—he lowered his voice fearfully—"his harem."

"O la la!" said Jim contemptuously. "Do I come here to talk of harems, Tewfik? I come here to talk sugar—great cases of sugar that came to you in the spring of the year of the rising, and in those cases of sugar were rifles, which went out to the pretender."

"God give you grace!" groaned the *basha*. "What can I do? If Sadi makes a complaint I must listen to him, or my authority is gone. As to the sugar——"

"We will not talk about sugar," said Jim, sitting down on a cushion in front of the *basha's* divan. "We will talk about a lady who has been taken from this town through the agency of Sadi Hafiz."

"If you can prove this——"

"What proof is there in Tangier?" said Jim scornfully. "Where you may buy a thousand witnesses for ten pesetas on either side! You know Sadi, Tewfik: he has been your enemy——"

"He has also been my friend," said Tewfik uneasily.

"He is your enemy now. A week ago he sent word to the Sultan that you had been plotting with the Spaniards to sell a railway concession."

"May he die!" exploded the *basha*. "I did no more than give a feast to a distinguished Spanish Excellency——"

Again Jim stopped him.

"This much I tell you, that you may know how you stand with Sadi. Now give me authority to deal with him."

The *basha* hesitated.

"He is a very powerful man, and the Angera people are friends of his. They say that he is also a friend of Raisuli, though I doubt this, for Raisuli has no friends. If I do not take action——"

"How can you take action if Sadi Hafiz is in prison?" asked Jim quietly, and the *basha* jumped.

"Prison? Bismallah! Could I put a man of his importance in the *kasbah?* You're mad, Morlake! What crime?"

"Find me a crime at the right moment," said Jim. He took from his pocket a thick bundle of thousand-peseta notes and threw them into the lap of the governor of Tangier, "God give you peace!" he said as he rose.

"And may he give you many happy dreams!" replied the *basha* mechanically, as he touched the notes lovingly.

Jim went back to the hotel and saw Lord Creith, and for once that nobleman did not object to being bothered.

"It is going to be difficult to search the houses where she may be hidden," said Jim. "I've got into bad trouble already. The only searches we can make are purely unauthorised. Of one thing I'm certain—that they have not gone along the Fez Road. I've gone twenty miles beyond the place where we found the trolley, and nobody had seen such a party. They must be in the vicinity, and to-night I am going out to conduct my investigations alone."

He was impatient to be gone, the more so as Lord Creith expressed a desire to accompany him. The old man went up to his room to get an authority he had procured that afternoon from the international consulates, and whilst he was waiting Jim stepped out on to the balcony. The night was chill, but a full moon rode serenely in the unclouded heavens, and he stood spellbound for a moment by the beauty of the scene. The broad terrace was deserted except for one man who sat with his coat collar turned about his ears, his feet raised to the stone parapet.

American or English, thought Jim. Nobody else would be mad enough to risk the ills which are supposed to attend the night air.

The stranger was smoking a cigar, and Jim sniffed its fragrance and found it good, but Creith appeared at that moment with the authorisation.

"I'm afraid it is not going to help you much, Morlake," he said, "but in such places as acknowledge the Sultan you will find it of assistance with the local authorities." He held out his hand. "Good luck to you!" he said simply. "Bring back my girl—I want her, and I think you want her too."

Jim pressed the hand of the old man in his, his heart too full for words. Dropping his hand on Creith's shoulder, he nodded, and then gently pushed him through the glass door into the lobby of the hotel. He needed solitude at that moment.

He stood for a moment, his eyes on the old man, as, with bowed shoulders, he walked up the carpeted corridor; then, turning abruptly, Jim made for the steps that led to the Beach Road. He was on the point of descending when a voice hailed him:

"Hi!"

It was the smoker of cigars. Thinking that he had made a mistake, he was going on.

"Hi! Come here, Morlake!"

Astounded, he turned, and went toward the lounger.

"As you know me well enough to call me by name, I feel no diffidence in telling you that I'm in a great hurry," he said.

"I suppose you are," drawled the man on the seat, crossing his legs comfortably. "What I want to know is this: have you seen anything of my friend Hamon?"

Jim stooped to get a better view of the man's face. It was Captain Welling!

CHAPTER LV

The Lady from Lisbon

"WHAT on earth are you doing here?"

"Inviting an attack of rheumatism," grunted Welling. "You're in a hurry: anything wrong?"

"Lady Joan has disappeared," said Jim, and briefly told as much of the story of the girl's abduction as he knew.

The old man listened thoughtfully.

"That is bad," he said. "I heard there'd been a shindy in the town, but didn't get the hang of it. My Spanish is very rusty, and my Arabic is nil. Not that Arabic is ever necessary to a traveller in Morocco," he said. "Lady Joan. By gosh, that's bad! Where are you off to?"

"I'm going to look for her," said Jim briefly.

"I won't stop you. No sign of Hamon?"

Jim shook his head.

"He is in Morocco, of course. You know that? I trailed him down as far as Cadiz. He came across on the *Peleago* to Gibraltar. There I missed him. He flitted from Gibraltar, leaving no trace."

The news took Jim's breath away. He had not seen Hamon on the dhow or subsequently, and he made a quick calculation.

"He may have got here," he said, "but I haven't seen him. I've gone on the supposition that Sadi Hafiz has been responsible for all the arrangements made to date, but it is quite possible that Hamon is somewhere in the background, putting in the fine touches."

He was turning away when a thought struck him.

"I wish you'd go in and see Lord Creith. He is rather under the weather. He will be able to tell you what happened at Suba," and, with a hasty word of farewell, he ran down the steps and hurried toward the gates of the city.

Near the Street of the Mosque is a small and unpretentious

house, the door of which is reached by a flight of stone steps flush with the house. He mounted the steps, knocked at the door and was instantly admitted. Nodding to the Moorish tailor who sat cross-legged at his craft, he went into the inner room, taking off his coat as he went. Presently he appeared in the doorway.

"You have made all the arrangements?" he asked.

"Yes," said the tailor, not looking up from his work or ceasing to ply his busy needle. "They will wait for you on the road near the English doctor's."

Jim was stripping off his waistcoat when he heard a snore that seemed to shake the ancient house. He looked up to the square opening against which the top of a worn ladder rested.

"Who is there?" he asked from the doorway.

The tailor threaded a needle near-sightedly, but with extraordinary quickness, before he answered.

"A man lives there," he said unconcernedly. "He has the roof which the water-seller had. Yassin the Jew could not find a tenant because the water-seller had smallpox, so he gave it to the Inglezi for six pesetas a month. I pay fifty, but Yassin knows that I can find no other shop, and my fathers lived here since the days of Suliman."

There was a stir up above and the sound of a grumbling voice.

"He smokes," said the tailor. "He will go now to a café where the *hashish* pipe costs ten centimos."

Jim wondered whether it was the characteristic of all lodgers to be addicted to unnatural cravings, and as he wondered, a ragged shoe felt tremulously for the top rung of the ladder. The ankle above the shoe was bare, the ragged trouser leg reached half-way down the calf. Slowly the man descended, and Jim paused, taking stock of him. His hair was a dirty grey and hung over the collar of his shiny coat; the nose thick and red; the mouth a slit that drooped at each end.

He wore a stubbly and uneven red beard as though he had trimmed it himself, and he turned his pale blue eyes upon the visitor with an insolent stare.

"Good evening," he said wheezily.

"English?" said Jim in surprise, and disgusted by the unwholesome appearance of the man.

"Britannic—don't look so infernally sick, my good man. *Honesta mors turpi vita potior!* I can see that noble sentiment in your eyes! By your damnable accent you are either a Colonial or an American, and what the devil you're doing here I don't know. Lend me five pesetas, dear old boy; I'm getting a remittance from home to-morrow."

Jim dropped a Spanish *doura* into the outstretched paw and watched him hobble out into the night.

"Faugh!" said Jim Morlake. "How long has he been here?"

"Five years," said the tailor, "and he owes me five pesetas."

"What is his name?"

"I don't know—what does it matter?"

Jim agreed.

The dingy man had scarcely left the shop when a woman came slowly up the road, guided by a native boy in a narrow brown jellab. He carried a candle lantern in his hand, and if this method of illumination was unnecessary in the main streets, it became vitally essential when they struck the labyrinth of narrow alleys and crooked streets which lay at the back of the post office.

Behind her a porter carried two large grips, for Lydia Hamon had come ashore from the Portuguese West African packet that occasionally sets down passengers at Tangier. Presently they came to the well-lighted guests' entrance of the Continental Hotel, and she dismissed her guide and porter and, after a second's hesitation, wrote her name in the register.

"There is a letter for you, Miss Hamon," said the reception clerk, and took down an envelope from the rack.

It was in Ralph's handwriting, and she dreaded to read the message. In the seclusion of the writing-room she tore open the envelope and took out the sheet of paper it contained.

If you get this before registering, you had better sign the book by an assumed name [it ran]. *The moment you arrive, come up to the house of Sadi Hafiz. I wish to see you urgently. Under no circumstances will you tell anybody that I am here.*

She read the letter and, walking across to the fire, dropped it into the blazing coal and watched it till it was consumed. Then, with a sigh, she went back to the reception clerk.

"I want a boy to guide me up to the Sok," she said.

"Has madam had dinner?"

She nodded.

"Yes, I dined on the ship."

He bustled out into the street. Presently he returned with a diminutive boy, carrying a lantern. Apparently the clerk had told the boy where she wanted to go, for he asked no questions, leading her back to the little market place where the bread sellers sat like sheeted mummies, a candle advertising their wares.

"I want the house of Sadi Hafiz," she said when they were nearing the top of the hill, and without a word he turned off and, coming to a stop before the forbidding door, hammered with his clenched fists.

It was a long time before the call was answered.

"Wait for me here," she said in Spanish. "I shall be returning."

He grunted, blew out his candle, being of an economical turn of mind, and squatted down, pulling his ragged hood over his head.

The door opened, and the keeper of the door scrutinised her for a moment by the light of her lantern, and then shuffled in front of her to the house. Before she could reach the door, Sadi, resplendent in a blue silk robe, was coming down to meet her.

"This is a great honour you have done to my poor house, Miss Hamon," he said in English.

"Is Ralph here?" she asked, cutting short the complimentary flow.

"No, he has been called out of Tangier, but I expect him back very soon."

He led her into the room where Jim Morlake had searched, and clapped his hands vigorously. Half-a-dozen servants came running to obey the summons.

"Sweetmeats for the lady and English tea," he said. "Also bring cigarettes, quickly!"

The room was very dimly illuminated. One electric lamp, heavily shaded in a pseudo-oriental lantern, supplied all the light, and more than half of the apartment was in shadow.

"You will sit down and refresh yourself after your long journey?" he said. "Your brother will be with us soon."

"Are you sure he is coming?" she asked suspiciously. "I'm not staying here—you understand that?"

"Naturally," he said with a touch of asperity in his voice. "My wretched home is not good enough for your ladyship."

"It isn't that, only I prefer the hotel," she said shortly.

Was he deceiving her, she wondered? And then she caught her breath, for she heard Ralph's voice outside. She looked at him in amazement. She had never seen him in Moorish costume before. He kicked off his yellow slippers and came toward her, pulling back the hood of his jellab.

"You got here, then?" he said surlily. "I thought you were arriving yesterday?"

"We were held up at Lisbon. There has been some political trouble there. What did you want?" she said.

At the last minute Ralph had changed his plans and had gone on ahead of her, leaving her to come overland to Lisbon, whilst he went on to Gibraltar.

At a signal from Hamon, Sadi Hafiz withdrew noiselessly, pulling the curtains to hide the ugliness of the prison-like door before he made his exit.

"Lydia, you've got to know I'm in bad," said Hamon. "If what this girl tells me is true, I've made a very bad mistake."

"This girl?" she asked quickly.

"I'm talking about Joan."

"Joan? Is she here? Where?"

"Never mind where she is—she is here."

"Oh, yes!" The tension in her face relaxed. "How you frightened me, Ralph! Of course, the yacht is in the bay: they pointed it out to me as we came in. You have seen her?"

"She is not on the yacht, if that is what you mean," said Ralph roughly. "She is in one of Sadi's houses, twenty miles from here. She is doubly necessary to me now. She is my hostage, for one thing. Morlake is in Tangier."

She did not speak; she was staring wildly at him as though she could not believe her ears.

"You have Joan Carston! What do you mean—have you taken her—by force?"

He nodded.

"Oh, my God! Ralph, are you mad?"

"I'm very sane," said Hamon. He fumbled in the pocket of his clothes and, finding his case, lit a cigarette. "Yes, I'm very sane."

"You—you haven't hurt her?"

"Don't be a fool," he said roughly. "Why should I hurt her? She is going to be my wife."

"But, Ralph, how can you hope to escape punishment?" she almost wailed.

"It isn't so much hope as knowledge," he said. "There is no law in Morocco: fix that in your mind. The country is chronically at war, and the European governments have no more power than that." He snapped his finger. "They're so jealous that they will not move for fear of giving one another an ad vantage. You needn't worry about me. And, Lydia, I'm here for good."

"In Morocco?" she said in horror.

He nodded.

"I'm friends with most of the big clansmen," he said, "and after a while, when matters have blown over and Joan has settled down to the new life, I might think of moving, but for the moment I'm here."

"You want me to go back, of course?" she said nervously. "Somebody must settle your affairs in London."

"They're settled," he said. "I sold the house before I left. In fact, I sold everything except Creith. I want to keep that for my children."

"But I have affairs that need settling, Ralph," she said desperately "I can't stay here. I'll come back if you wish me to——"

"You are not going," he said. "Now listen, Lydia." He

sprang to her side as she reeled, and shook her violently. "I want none of that nonsense," he growled. "The success of my scheme depends on Sadi Hafiz. It is absolutely vital that I should retain his friendship and his support. My life may depend upon it—get that! I don't know how much Welling knows and how much was bluff on Joan's part, but if he knows half as much as she says he does, I'm booked for the drop."

"You—you haven't killed anybody?" she whispered.

"I've been responsible for at least two deaths," he said, and she sank under the shock. "You've been living your artistic life in Paris, getting acquainted with Count this and Countess that—on my money. Did it worry you how it came, or where I got it from? Not that I ever gained a penny from Cornford's death," he said moodily, "but I shall—I shall! That is what decided me to stay here. It doesn't matter what they know then."

She got up unsteadily.

"Ralph, I'm going home," she said ."I can't stand any more."

She held out her hand, but he did not take it, and then, with a little sigh, she walked to the curtains and pulled them back, turning the handle of the door. It did not move.

"Locked," said her brother laconically. "You're going home, are you? Well, this is your home, Lydia—this and Sadi's house in the hills. I've made a good match for you."

She stared at him incredulously.

"You mean . . . you want me to marry a Moor? Ralph, you don't mean that?"

"Well, I don't know what else I mean," he said. "Lydia, you've got to make the best of things. This house is rotten, I admit, but the other place in the hills is wonderful. And it'll be good for Joan to have a woman handy like you." He chuckled. "That'll swamp a little of her pride, having Sadi Hafiz as a brother-in-law."

The thought seemed to please him, for he chuckled.

She was trapped—as much trapped as Joan Carston. She knew that it was useless to make any appeal to him. Ralph Hamon had never shrunk from the sacrifice of his relatives, and would not do so now.

She was about to speak when the door was unlocked and flung open, and Sadi Hafiz ran in.

"Quick!" he cried earnestly. "Get out—through the little gate! The house is surrounded by the *basha's* soldiers. They may be coming to arrest me: I shall know soon, but nothing can happen to me. Take her away!"

Ralph seized her by the arm and led her at a run into the courtyard. He seemed to know his way without guidance, for he came to the little gate that led to the Street of Schools. The door had already been unlocked. As they passed through, the door was slammed on them by Hafiz himself, and they were a long way from the house before the sound of the heavy knocking on the front gates died away.

The sight of a Moorish man and a European woman excited no comment. Ralph, his face shaded by his hood, shuffled along by her side, never once relaxing his hold of her arm. They came to the Sok, deserted at this hour of the night, and she turned instinctively to the hill which would take her back to the Continental.

"Oh no, you don't," he said between his teeth. "I know a little place where you can stay the night."

"Ralph, for God's sake let me go!" she begged.

And then, out of the shadows, came a man who was wearing a long fur-lined coat. The collar was turned up to his ears, and between its ends protruded the stump of a glowing cigar.

"Can I be of any assistance, madam?"

Ralph heard the voice and, dropping the girl's arm, turned and ran into the night.

There were many people he expected to meet in Tangier, but Julius Welling was not one of them.

Hamon raced across the dark market place and along a narrow, twisting lane, hedged with cactus, and was slowing to a walk when he saw somebody coming toward him and stepped aside to avoid the passer. Unfortunately, the unknown made a similar movement and they came into violent collision.

"Curse you!" snapped Ralph in English. "Look where you are going!"

He was startled when the reply came in the same language.

"Blundering hound! Have you eyes, oaf? To barge against a gentleman—you're drunk, sir!"

Arrested by the tone of the man's voice, Ralph struck a match and nearly dropped it again when he saw the blotched face and the red beard.

"E tenebris oritur lux," murmured the smoker of hashish. "Forgive me if my language was a little unrefined—excuse me!"

He threw back his head and searched the moonlit heavens.

"Would it be too much to ask you to point out the Gemma in the Constellation of Orion? I live somewhere underneath. In a foul den, sir, above a beastly Moorish tailor's shop. And what am I, dear friend? A gentleman of the cloth! No unfrocked priest—but a gentleman of the cloth—a reverend gentleman! And an officer holding the supreme decoration of the world, the Victoria Cross, sir! Aylmer Bernando Bannockwaite, sir—could you of your amazing kindness lend me five pesetas . . . my remittance arrives to-morrow . . ."

Like a man in a dream Ralph Hamon pushed a note into the man's hand.

Bannockwaite—the man who had made Joan and Ferdie Farringdon husband and wife!

CHAPTER LVI

Captain Welling Adds a Postscript

At the corner of the hilly street, Julius Welling waited for the girl to grow calmer.

"Thank you, thank you!" she was sobbing hysterically. "Will you please see me to my hotel? I'm so grateful!"

"Was that man molesting you?" he asked.

"Yes—no—he was a friend. It was my brother."

He stopped dead.

"Your brother?"

"And then, in the light of a standard, she saw his face.

"Captain Welling!" she gasped.

"That is my name. You must be Miss Lydia Hamon. I've been looking for you all over town. Was that your brother?"

She swallowed something.

"No," she said.

"I see it was," said the imperturbable detective. "Curiously enough, I never thought of his wearing Moorish costume. Why I shouldn't have expected that little piece of theatricality I don't know. It is very becoming; I'm thinking of buying a jellab to take back to London," he mused, and even the incongruous picture of Captain Julius Welling in a white, loose-sleeved wrap did not give her any amusement.

He walked all the way back to the hotel, and she was glad. It gave her an opportunity of making her plans. They were walking up the narrow lane in which the Continental is situated, when she said suddenly:

"Captain Welling, I am afraid of my brother."

"I don't wonder," he murmured. "I am a little afraid of him myself—in a way."

"Would it be possible," she asked, "to put somebody to guard me? That sounds very stupid, but——"

"I think I understand," said the detective. "That is simply arranged. What is the number of your room?"

"I don't even know," she said despairingly, and then: "Are you staying at the Continental?"

He nodded.

"I think I can arrange to have my room moved next to yours," he said, but on examination of the register he found that was unnecessary. She occupied a room at the end of the second floor corridor; and, by a coincidence, Captain Welling was in the next room.

At half-past eleven, when the hotel door was closing, there came a Moor with a letter addressed to Lydia, and Welling took it up to her. She opened the door to him, opened the envelope and read; then, without a word, she handed the letter to the old man.

Everything was all right [it ran]. *It was only the basha's bluff. Sadi Hafiz says that Morlake saw the basha this evening, and the raid was the result. Come up for a few minutes and be civil to Sadi. I will bring you back to the hotel myself.*

"May I answer this?" said Welling, a twinkle in his eye.

When she nodded, he found his fountain pen, and, writing at the bottom:

Come down and have a talk.—J. W.

he enclosed it in an envelope and took it back to the waiting messenger.

"I don't think he will come," he said, when he returned to the girl. "For your sake I hope he doesn't."

Welling went to bed that night without any fear of being disturbed. Hamon would not run the risk of putting himself in the detective's way, for, although the evidence that the police had against him was scrappy and not sufficient to justify the hope even of a committal, let alone a conviction, Ralph Hamon would be ignorant of its incompleteness, and his conscience would occupy the gaps which Welling was trying to fill.

He was a light sleeper, and the first pebble that struck his window pane woke him. He did not put on the light, but, getting noiselessly out of bed, he opened half of his window and looked out cautiously.

Two men, one carrying a lantern, were standing in the lane below. He saw one raise his hand and throw a stone. This time it struck Lydia's window, and he heard her walk across the room.

"Is that Miss Hamon?" asked a low voice.

"Yes?" she replied. "Who is that?"

"It is Sadi Hafiz. Your brother has shot himself!"

Welling heard her cry of distress, but did not move.

"Will you come down?" urgently, and then: "I am afraid

he cannot live, and he has given me something for you, something he wants you to give to Mr. Morlake."

"Wait—I will come immediately," she said hurriedly.

Welling waited to hear no more, but pulled on his slippers and his overcoat. She must have been fully dressed, for she was out of sight by the time he was in the corridor, and he heard her fumbling with the locks and chains of the front door. She opened it at last, and, peering over the stairway, he saw the Moor enter.

"When did this happen?"

Her voice was trembling.

"It happened last night. Apparently your brother had seen a police officer he knew, and he came back to my house in a state of great trouble. I left him for a little while to get coffee, and I had hardly turned my back before I heard a shot, and, running in, found him lying on the divan."

"He is not dead?"

Sadi Hafiz shook his head.

"For a moment, no. You have nothing to fear because the house is in possession of the *basha's* soldier's," he said, "and Captain Morlake is there. Will you come?"

"You said you had something for me."

He put his hand into his breast and took out a little package, which he handed to her. In another instant she had followed him through the door into the dark street.

Welling, old as he was, jumped the last six stairs, and, flying across the hallway, reached her just as she put her foot on the street step.

"One minute," he said, and jerked her through the door.

And then, with amazing agility, he leapt aside to avoid the bludgeon stroke that was aimed at him by a man concealed in the deep doorway. In another second he was in the house, the doors locked, and he had switched on the hall light.

"Fooled 'em!" he said breathlessly.

"But, Mr. Welling—my brother——"

"Your brother has not shot himself. That kind of guy never does."

He took the envelope from her hand.

"They were killing two birds with one stone, young lady, but I was the real burnt-offering. This wonderful something is, of course, a blank sheet of paper."

He took her back to her room, bewildered and dazed by the happening.

"You don't think that it is true?"

"I know it is not true," he said. "The stone that was thrown at my window was intended to wake me, and it was intended that I should overhear your conversation. And the general idea, as they say in military circles, was that, as soon as I put my foot outside the street door, I was to get it in the neck—and I nearly did! On the whole, I think I have taken too unflattering a view of the Oriental mind. They are clever!"

CHAPTER LVII

The Ride to the Hills

THAT night held for Joan Carston an unbelievable experience. For four hours she sat on an ambling mule, passing through a country which she could not see, and the very character of which was a mystery to her. They were following, so far as she could tell, no beaten tracks, and from time to time her feet were caught by thorn-like bushes that clung to the soft white wrap she wore.

At daybreak she saw that they were in a wild and apparently uninhabited country. The party consisted of six men and the girl who had looked after her at her resting place. One of the men lit a fire and put on a pot of water, whilst another took the mules to a stream which must have been near but which was not visible to her.

She looked around, trying in vain to recall such physical features of Morocco as she had learnt at school, that would enable her to identify the spot. Blue mountains bordered half the horizon, and far away in the distance she saw an isolated mountain of peculiar shape, which she recognised as the crest of Gibraltar. One of the men found a little bower in the bushes and spread a blanket, signing to her to sleep. But Joan had never felt more wide awake, and though she retired to such privacy as the "bower" offered, it was only to lie and think and think, and then to think again.

The Moorish girl brought her a large tumblerful of coffee and an oaten cake, and she was glad of this refreshment, for she had had nothing to eat since her lunch on the previous day.

"Have we far to go?" she asked in halting Spanish.

The Moorish girl shook her head, but volunteered no information.

After two hours' rest the cavalcade got in movement again, and it puzzled her why such isolated travellers as they met with did not show any surprise at the appearance of a European woman, until she remembered that she was wearing Moorish dress. If they stared at her at all, it was because she did not veil her face when she passed them.

The hills were growing nearer, and she saw a little white patch on the slope, without realising that that was their objective. The patch grew to a definite shape as the way began to lead uphill, and she could not but admire the beautiful setting of the house. It looked like a white jewel, and even from that distance she could guess the glory of the gardens laid out on terraces above and below.

Here the country was undulating, and they were threading their way between the bushes down a gentle slope, when she saw a man sitting on a sorry-looking horse a little distance to their right. The rest of the members of the party paid him no attention, but the Moorish girl, who was now riding by her side, used a word that Joan understood.

"A mendicant?" she said in surprise, and might have been amused in other circumstances at the spectacle of a beggar on horseback.

He was an elderly man with a beard in which grey predominated. His face looked as if it had never known soap and water. The tarboosh at the back of his head was old and greasy He stared at the party as it passed, and the Moorish gir dropped her veil and signed to her companion to follow he example.

Joan was too interested. She took stock of the man as they passed, noted the ragged jellab that covered his stooping frame the discoloured shirt that showed at his throat, and though that she had never seen anything quite so repulsive.

"Alms!" he bawled when they were level with him. "Alms in the name of God the Compassionate!"

One of the party flung him a copper coin and he caught i dexterously in his uncleanly hands.

"Alms, O my beautiful rose, in the name of the Compas-sionate and Merciful, pity the poor!"

His voice sank away to a drone.

The girl was ready to drop from weariness before they reached the open gates that took them through the gardens to the house. Near at hand, the white house was even more beau-tiful than it had appeared from the distance. It was nearly new, yet its walls were smothered with begonias.

"It must be beautiful in the summer," she said in English before she realised that the girl at her side could not under-stand her.

Before the door stood a big pillared porch, so much out of architectural harmony that she wondered what freak had in-duced the owner to add this European finish to a building which, in its graceful, simple lines, was wholly satisfying.

As she walked into the house, the girl, who seemed to be as much a stranger to the place as she, ran forward to ask a question in a whisper of the women who were curiously re-garding the arrival. One of these came forward, a stout woman with a heavy face, disfigured at the moment with a scowl which made her forbidding. She said something in a sharp tone, and when Joan shook her head to signify that she did not under-stand, she clicked her lips impatiently. Pointing to a door, the Moorish girl, who seemed in awe of the stout lady, opened it and beckoned Joan forward.

The room was exquisitely furnished and reminded her of

an English drawing-room, except that the windows, like those in most of the Moorish houses, were barred. She looked round curiously, and then asked in Spanish:

"Who is that fat woman?"

The Moorish girl giggled shrilly.

"That is the Señora Hamon," she said, and Joan sat down suddenly on the nearest divan and shook with helpless laughter.

She might become the principal, but she certainly would not be the first wife of Mr. Ralph Hamon!

CHAPTER LVIII

At the White House

"WHO are the other women? Are they his wives also?" she asked drily.

The little Moor shook her head.

"There is only one wife here," she said, and Joan managed to follow her Spanish without difficulty. "The others are women of attendance. The wife does not live here; she came a little time ago. She has not seen her husband for many years."

She spoke slowly, repeating her words when Joan failed to grasp the meaning.

"Thank you," said the girl.

"*Claro?*" asked the little Moor, whose name was Zuleika.

"Perfectly *claro,*" said Joan with a smile.

Why she should be so extraordinarily cheerful at this, which promised to be the most tragic moment of her life, puzzled her. It might have been the tang of the fresh mountain air that induced the strange exhilaration in her heart; or was it the consciousness that the future could hold no surprises for her, that enabled her to draw a line under her misfortunes and seek for some balance on the credit side of life's ledger? The ceiling reminded her of Jim's room: it was made of thick white plaster, in which Moorish workmen, with their sharp knives had cut so delicate a tracery that it almost seemed that the ceiling was made of frothing lace.

European houses must have supplied the furniture and the panelling. The big blue carpet, bordered with arabesques of gold and brown, had been woven in one piece on the looms of Persia. She saw the European touch in the white marble fireplace, with its green pillars and its crouching lions. Ralph Hamon must have had this retreat in his mind all his life, for she detected at a glance the care which had been exercised in choosing every single article in the room.

Beautiful it was, but a prison! It might be something worse

At the far end of the chamber a wide window was covered on the outside by a hand-worked grille of wrought iron. She opened the window and leant out, taking in the beauty of the wide valley. From here she caught the distant sparkle of the sea, and, turning her head, saw that the bulk of Gibraltar was in view.

She noticed something moving in the valley, and shaded her eyes from the glare of the setting sun. It was the beggar, and he was riding back on the Tangier Road. For one second her poise was disturbed.

"Joan, Joan," she said breathlessly, "you are not going to weep or faint or do anything equally feminine, are you?" and she shook her head.

Closing the window, she walked back to the door and turned the silver handle. She did not expect it to open as it did. The hall was empty; the swing doors were not fastened Apparently she was to be given a certain amount of liberty, and for that at least she was grateful.

But once she was in the garden, she saw how hopeless any thought of escape must be. The wall about the property was unusually high, even for a Moorish house, and was crowned at the top by spears of broken glass that glittered in the sunlight, as though to remind her that escape that way was futile.

The gate was equally impossible. There was a little brick lean-to built against the wall, in which the gatekeeper slept, and she was reminded (and again she felt that pang of poignant sorrow) of Creith and the empty lodge which Lord Creith could never afford to fill.

Tired and sickened against her fierce determination to keep all thoughts of home, of father and of someone else out of her mind, she went back to the big room, which was evidently reserved for her, since nobody else came to relieve her solitude.

News had been brought to Ralph Hamon of the successful ending of the flight, and he rode across the uneven country, a fierce song of triumph in his soul, his eyes glued upon the white house in the hills.

At last! Joan Carston was his, in every possessive sense. He had had a secret interview with a red-bearded man in Tangier, and now his happiness was complete. Sadi Hafiz, who rode by his side, was in a less cheerful frame of mind. He had seen his cup of joy shattered whilst it was almost at his lips, and Ralph Hamon had found him a sulky and uncompanionable fellow-passenger.

"We shall get there soon after sunset," said Ralph.

"Why I go there at all, Heaven knows," said Sadi pettishly. He invariably spoke in English, priding himself, with reason, not only upon his extraordinary knowledge of the language but his acquaintance with the rich classics of that tongue. "You've made a bungling mess of my affairs, Hamon!"

Ralph Hamon laughed coarsely, not being in the mood to feel angry, even at so unjust an accusation.

"Who was it came flying into the room and saying that the *basha* and his soldiers were at the door? Who practically turned her out of the house when he had her safe? Whose plan was it to wake up the detective so that he might be quietened, when it would have been a simple matter, as was proved, to have brought Lydia to your house? I haven't bungled it, Sadi. You must have patience. Lydia is still in Tangier, and will probably remain there for a few days, and it should not be difficult, if I could bring my lady to this place——"

"If *you* could bring!" sneered the other. "Inshallah! Who brought her but me, the Shereef Sadi Hafiz?"

"She is lovely," said the unthinking Hamon with enthusiasm.

"Why else should I be making this journey?" said Sadi

coldly, and something in his tone made Ralph Hamon look round.

"You may satisfy your curiosity and then you may go," he said curtly, "and bestow your attentions where they are most likely to be acceptable. Let there be no mistake about this, Sadi: this girl is to marry me."

The shereef shrugged his broad shoulders.

"Women are as many as beggars," he quoted, and jerked his head to the nondescript figure that was ambling toward them.

"Alms, in the name of Allah the Compassionate and Merciful!" moaned the beggar, and Ralph looked at him without interest. He had seen such sights too often.

"A toothless old devil," he said, and in the manner of the East flung him a coin.

"God grant you happy dreams," whined the mendicant, and urged his horse after him. "Gain joy in heaven and the pleasure of the prophets," he moaned, "by giving me one little house to sleep in to-night, for I am an old man . . . !"

Sadi, being what he was, could bear this appeal philosophically. Ralph turned with a smile and glared into the red-rimmed eyes.

"Get away, you dog!" he roared, but the old man followed on, continuing his supplications in a monotonous whine.

"Let me sleep in the shadow of your house, O my beautiful bird of paradise! Give me a blanket and a little roof, for the nights are cold and I am a very ancient man."

"Let him alone," said Sadi. "Why do you argue with beggars, and you so long in Morocco?"

So they suffered the old man to follow them at a distance, until the door slammed in the long face of his horse, and he went, grumbling and complaining, down the hillside, and later Ralph saw him, his horse hobbled by the leg grazing in the coarse grass, and a blue line of smoke rising from the bushes where the ancient beggar ate his dinner.

Ralph Hamon had an unpleasant task, and he was not particularly anxious to go to it. He dined with Sadi in a small room off the hall.

"You're not a very ardent lover," said the Moor. "Have you seen her?"

"She can wait," replied Hamon.

"Then I will meet her," said Sadi blandly. And seeing the other's hesitation: "After all, you're not a Mussulman, and I think the young lady might be reassured to meet a Moorish gentleman and to learn that we are not wholly without good breeding."

"I'll take you in to her later, but I have something else to do," said Ralph shortly.

The "something else" was to interview a woman whom he had not seen for eight years. As he walked into her room, it seemed impossible that this stout, scowling female was once a Moorish lady of considerable beauty, slim and wholly delectable.

"So you have come, Hamon?" she said harshly. "All these years I have not heard from you or seen you."

"Have you been hungry?" asked Hamon coolly. "Have you been without a roof or a bed?"

"Who is this girl you have brought here?" asked the woman suspiciously.

"She will soon be my wife," replied Hamon, and the woman leapt up, quivering with anger.

"Then why did you bring me here?" she stormed. "To make me look a fool before my servants? Why did you not leave me at Mogador? At least I have friends there. Here I am buried alive in the wilderness. And why? That I should be a slave to your new wife? I will not do it, Hamon!"

Hamon felt sure of himself now.

"You can go back to Mogador next week. You are here for a purpose of my own."

She brooded awhile.

"Does she know?" she asked.

"I told the girl to tell her, so I suppose she does," said Hamon carelessly.

He had indeed a very excellent purpose to serve. His Moorish "wife" had been brought post haste to the house in the hills that Joan might see her, and, seeing her, understand. The subtle mind of Ralph Hamon was never better illustrated than in this act of his.

He went back to Sadi Hafiz.

"I'm going to see my lady," he said, "and afterwards I will bring you in."

He tapped at the door of the drawing-room, and as there was no answer, he turned the handle and walked in. Joan was on a music-stool before the grand piano, her hands folded on her lap. All the evening she had been trying to work up an inclination to play, and she had at last brought herself to the piano when Hamon made his appearance.

"Are you comfortable?" he asked.

She did not reply. He stood for a while, admiring the straight figure and the calm, imperturbable face. A lesser breed would have shown the hatred and loathing she felt, but not a line of her face changed, and he might have been a servant of Creith who had come at her summons, so unmoved and unemotional was her reception.

"It is a beautiful place, eh? One of the loveliest in Morocco," he went on. "A girl could be happy here for a year or two. Have you seen Number One?"

He sat down, uninvited, and lit a cigar.

"By Number One I presume you mean Mrs. Hamon?"

He nodded. She had never seen Ralph Hamon look quite so cheerful as he did at that moment. It was as though all the trouble in the world had rolled away from him and left him care-free and buoyant of heart.

"When I say 'first,'" said Joan carefully, "I of course expose my ignorance of Moorish customs. At any rate, she is the first I have seen."

"And the last you'll see, Joan," he said with a laugh. "Marriages, they say, are made in heaven. Pleasant alliances can be made in Morocco, but Number One, first, last and all the time, will be Lady Joan Hamon."

A shadow of a smile came and went.

"It sounds beastly, doesn't it?" she said frankly.

She had a trick of irritating him more than any other human

being. She could get under his skin and drag on the raw places. For a second his eyes blazed, and then, swallowing his rage, he forced a laugh. Secretly he admired her cool insolence, and would gladly have imitated her if it were possible.

"It may sound bad, but it is a good enough name for me," he said.

"Is that a Moorish custom too?" she asked coolly. "That a girl takes the name of the man who abducts her? You must instruct me in the Moorish marriage laws; I'm afraid I'm totally ignorant on the subject."

He crossed to where she was sitting, pulling his chair with him.

"Now listen, Joan," he said quietly. "There is to be no Moorish marriage. There is to be an honest-to-God marriage, conducted by a fully ordained minister of the Episcopalian Church, with wedding ring and the usual paraphernalia. I asked you just now, had you seen my Moorish wife, and I guess you have. What do you think of her?"

Joan did not speak. She was trying to discover what he was aiming at.

"What do you think of her?" he asked again.

"I feel extremely sorry for her. She wasn't particularly pleasant to me, but I have every sympathy with her."

"You have, eh? Fat, isn't she? Pasty-faced and over-fed. They go like that in Morocco. It is the dark of the harem, the absence of liberty and exercise. It is being treated like cattle, locked up in a hothouse atmosphere day and night, and exercised for half-an-hour a day under the eyes of slaves. Why, it is worse than being in prison. That is what it means to be a Moorish wife. Joan, do you want to be a Moorish wife?"

She met his eyes straightly.

"I don't want to be any kind of wife to you," she said.

"Do you want to be a Moorish wife?" he asked her. "Or do you want to be married, and have children who can bear your name and inherit your father's title?"

She rose abruptly from the stool and walked to the end of the room, her back toward him.

"We won't go any farther into this question for the moment," said Ralph rising. "I'd like you to meet a very dear friend of mine, Sadi Hafiz, and be civil to him, do you hear, but not too civil."

Something in his tone made her turn.

"Why?" she asked.

"Because he is feeling sore with me just now. He is very keen on Lydia, and Lydia has slipped him. I don't want him to have ideas about you."

He left her to meditate upon this warning, and went out, to return with the silk-robed Sadi, and a new factor came immediately into play. One glance Joan gave, and she knew that this man was as great a danger as Ralph Hamon. Greater, for if he was as remorseless, he was less susceptible, since he had not that brand of human vanity which made Ralph Hamon so easy to handle. She hated him, with his fat, expressionless face and his dark, unblinking eyes that looked at her through and through, appraising her as though she were cattle. She hated him for the veneer of his civilisation, his polite English, his ready smile.

Here, then, was the danger: this she recognised instantly.

Sadi Hafiz did not remain very long—just long enough to create an impression. In Joan's case he would have been surprised if he had read her heart and mind, for he rather flattered himself upon his flair for imposing his personality upon women.

"What do you think of him?" asked Ralph when he had gone.

"I haven't thought," she said untruthfully.

"A good friend and a bad enemy," said Hamon sententiously. "I wish Lydia had had a little more sense. She owes me something."

Joan thought it was possible that he might owe Lydia something too, but was not in the mood for conversation. Unexpectedly he rose.

"I'm going now. You'll find your sleeping room, I suppose? Pleasant dreams!"

She said nothing.

At the door he turned.

"A Christian wife has a better time than a Moorish wife. I guess you've noticed that already."

Still she did not speak.

"We'll be married in two days," he said, and, with a crooked smile: "Would you like anybody else to come to the wedding?"

"You dare not," she was taunted into saying. "You dare not produce an English clergyman!"

"Oh, daren't I?" he said. "I'll not only produce him, but he'll marry us whatever you say, and whatever protests you make. You're going to meet an old friend, Joan."

"An old friend?" She was for the moment taken aback.

"An old clerical friend," said Hamon. "The Reverend Mr. Bannockwaite," and with this parting shot he left her, and she heard the key turn in the lock.

CHAPTER LIX

The Face at the Window

Sadi was waiting for him in the smoking-room, and so absorbed was the Moor in his thoughts that he did not hear Hamon until his name was called.

"Eh?" he said, looking up. "Allah, you frightened me. Yes, yes, she is a pretty woman—not the Moorish kind, and too thin for my liking. But you Aryans prefer them that way; I have never understood why."

Hamon was not deceived; the girl had made a tremendous impression upon the Moor and he was watchful and alert.

"Do you like her better than Lydia?" he asked humorously, as he poured out a drink from the decanter.

The Moor shrugged his shoulders.

"In some ways Lydia is impossible," he said.

That was a bad sign and Hamon knew it. The thought of Lydia had absorbed this man to the exclusion of all else, and now he could talk of her critically and without heat—a very bad sign.

"Shall you go back to Tangier to-morrow?" he asked, and his eyes narrowed when the Moor shook his head.

"No, I have decided to stay on for a little while. I need the change. It has been a nervous time for me."

"But you promised to bring Bannockwaite?"

"He will come without any assistance from me. I've told one of my men. Besides, your English agent could arrange to bring him. He'll come if you pay him."

"Do you know him very well?" asked Hamon.

"I've seen him. He has become quite a character in Tangier," said Sadi Hafiz. "He arrived during the war and the story I have heard is that he got drunk on the eve of the Battle of the Somme and deserted. He is a man entirely without principle, surely he could not perform the marriage ceremony? You told me he was unfrocked."

Ralph shook his head.

"His name appeared in the official list of clergymen of the Established Church until he was reported missing on the Somme. I have an idea it is still in the list; but even if it isn't, that would not invalidate the marriage."

"Why marry at all?" asked the Moor, looking up suddenly. "You are a stickler for the conventions, my friend."

Ralph smiled.

"Not so much as you think," he said. "I've a reason. The Creith title will descend through my wife to her children."

Again the Moor shrugged.

"It is a freakish idea," he said, "but then, freakishness has been responsible for your downfall, Hamon."

"I have not fallen yet," snarled Hamon.

"But you will," said the other, "unless," he went on quickly, seeing the look of distrust and suspicion in the man's eyes, "unless you elect to remain here in Morocco, outside the jurisdiction of the embassies."

He stretched his arms and yawned.

"I'm going to bed," he said. "You will be pleased to learn that I've decided to go back to Tangier in the morning."

He saw the look of relief in the other's face and smiled inwardly.

"And I will send along your Bannockwaite under escort."

When Hamon woke the next morning, he learnt that the Shereef had departed, and was thankful. He did not go in to Joan, though he saw her, from his room, walking in the garden.

Hamon's plan was not wholly dictated by a desire to break into the peerage. As Creith's son-in-law he would be possessed of powerful influence. It was not likely that the Earl would kick once the girl was married; and he knew her well enough to be satisfied that, if she bore his name, she would at least be outwardly loyal.

He mounted a horse and went down the hillside, and his way took him past the camp of the old beggar. The scarecrow horse raised his head to view him for a moment, and resumed its grazing, but the old man was not in sight. A fantastic idea came to him and he grinned at the thought. There was something about Ralph Hamon that was not quite normal.

In the evening his servant reported that a party was approaching the house, and, taking his glasses, he inspected the three men who were riding across the wild country in his direction. Two were Moors; the third, who rolled about on his horse like somebody drunk, he recognised, though he had never seen him except by match light, and, hastily running from the house, he was waiting at the open gates when the Rev. Aylmer Bannockwaite arrived.

The man almost fell from his horse, but recovered himself with the aid of the Moor who was with him and who evidently expected some such accident, for he had sprung off his horse the moment the party halted and run to the clergyman's side.

Bannockwaite turned his bloated face to his host, but, ignoring the outstretched hand, he fumbled in his dilapidated waistcoat and produced a glass, which he fixed in his eye.

"Who are you and what are you?" he said irritably. "You have brought me across this wretched country, you have interfered with my proper and pleasant recreations—now what the devil do you mean by it?"

"I'm sorry if I have inconvenienced you, Mr. Bannockwaite," said Ralph, humouring the man.

"Handsomely said."

A big, flabby paw gripped Ralph Hamon's feebly.

"Handsomely said, my boy. Now if you can give me a little time to rest, and a pipe of that seductive hemp to steady my nerves and stimulate my imagination I'm your friend for life. And if you will add a glass of the priceless Marsala and a scented cigarette, I am your slave body and soul!"

Watching from her window, Joan saw the obscene figure, and immediately guessed his identity. Could that be Bannockwaite, the tall, dapper ascetic? She had only seen him twice, and yet . . . there was a likeness; something in his walk, in the roll of his head. She stared open-mouthed until he had passed out of view, then sat, her head in her hands, trying to bring into order that confusion of her thoughts.

It was Bannockwaite. Then he was not dead: Bannockwaite, the fastidious, half-mad parson, the idol of Hulston, the inventor of bizarre secret societies was this gross and uncleanly creature whose rags and dirt were an offence to the eye.

How had Ralph Hamon found him, she wondered, and changed the current of her thoughts as she realised the unprofit of speculation.

Bannockwaite would marry her, whatever were her protests; that she knew instinctively. Even if he had been his old, sane self—if he ever were sane—the queer situation would have so appealed to him that he would not have hesitated.

Ralph made no appearance that night, although she expected him to bring the besotted parson to meet her. The bedroom led from the principal apartment, a large room, furnished in the Empire style. The window here was barred, with less elegance but as effectively as the bigger room. She waited until twelve, and then, undressing, she put over the night attire that the Moorish girl had brought her a long fleecy cloak, and, pulling a chair to the window and having extinguished the light, pulled back the curtain. As she did, she screamed and almost dropped with fright. A face was staring at her through the bars, long-bearded, hook-nosed, red-eyed, hideous! It was the wandering mendicant and in his teeth he held a long knife that glittered in the moonlight.

CHAPTER LX

The Marriage

He heard the scream and dropped quickly out of sight and she stood, holding on to the window-ledge, her heart thumping painfully. Who was he, and what did he want? How did he come into the garden? In the house complete silence reigned. Nobody had heard the scream, for the walls were thick.

It took an effort to thrust open the window and look out as far as the bars would allow her. The little garden looked peaceful and mysterious in the moon's rays. Long shadows ran across the ground; strange shapes seemed to appear and disappear. And then she saw him, moving cautiously toward the wall. In another instant he was beyond her view.

Why did she associate this midnight prowler in her mind with Sadi Hafiz? And yet she did. Was he some agent of this cunning Moor? The knife had not been intended for her; of that she was sure.

It was daylight before she went to bed and she was sleeping heavily when Zuleika brought in coffee and fruit and drew aside the curtains.

"Zuleika," she said in her halting Spanish, which had improved since she had had an opportunity of talking to the girl, "do you remember the old beggar we saw, the mendicant on the horse?"

"Yes, Lady," said the girl, nodding.

"Who is he?"

The girl smiled.

"There are many in Morocco. Some say they are the spies of the chieftains."

A spy of Sadi Hafiz! Put there to watch her arrival—why? Again that fear of the Moor swept through her, but she was left little time that morning to meditate, either upon her terrifying experience of the night or the intentions of Sadi. She had hardly dressed and finished her breakfast when Ralph came in. He was brisk and gave her a cheerful and smiling good-morning.

"Joan, I want you to meet the Rev. Aylmer Bannockwaite," he said. "I think you've met him before. Anyway, you'll find him changed. This gentleman has consented to perform the necessary ceremony that will mark, I hope, the beginning of a happier and a brighter time for both of us."

She did not reply.

"Are you going to be sensible, Joan? I'm trying to do the right thing by you. You're absolutely alone here, and there is nobody within a hundred miles who'd raise their hand if I killed you."

"When do you wish——" she hesitated.

"To-day, immediately," he said.

She was panic-stricken.

"You must give me time to think this matter over, Mr. Hamon," she said. "To-morrow——"

"To-day," he insisted. "I'm not going to let another day pass. I think I know my friend Sadi Hafiz. Sadi has enough respect for the law and the sanctity of married life," he sneered, "to leave you alone if you're married. But if I wait until to-morrow——" He shrugged his shoulders.

But there was no yielding in her determined face.

"I absolutely refuse to marry you." she said, "and if Mr. Bannockwaite has a lingering remnant of decency he will refuse to perform the ceremony."

"You can make up your mind on one point," said Hamon, "that he hasn't even the dregs of decency. You'd better meet him. He is more or less exhilarated now and is more bearable than he will be."

In the morning sunlight, Aylmer Bannockwaite looked even more horrible than he had in the kindly blue of the dusk. She shuddered. It seemed as though some horrible incarnation of evil had come into the room as he strutted forward with his plump hand outstretched.

"It is my dear little Carston girl!" he said jovially. "Well, this is the most amazing coincidence—that I should marry you twice is an especial privilege!"

One glance she gave at his face and shuddered. Thereafter, she never looked beyond the second button of his stained waistcoat.

"I am not going to be married, Mr. Bannockwaite. I want you to understand that distinctly; if you marry me, it is against my will."

"Tut, tut!" said Bannockwaite loudly. "This will never do. A shy bride! 'Standing with reluctant feet where the brook and river meet,' eh? God bless my life! Marriage is the natural state of mankind. It has ever been a matter for regret to me——"

"I won't marry him, I won't, I won't," she flamed. "If I am to be married, I'll be married decently by a clean man to a clean man!"

She stood erect, her eyes blazing, her finger outstretched in accusation.

"I know you now. You look what you are, what you always have been, and all your posturing and posing does not disguise you. You are corruption in human form—Ada called you 'The Beast with the silver tongue,' and she was right."

That was her curious and hateful gift—to touch the raw places of human vanity. The man's thick underlip stuck out; there was an insane fury in his eyes that momentarily frightened her.

"You Jezebel!" he boomed. "I'll marry you, if they hang me for it! And it will be legal and binding on you, woman! I posture, do I? I pose? You, you——"

Hamon gripped his arm.

"Steady," he whispered, and then, to the girl: "Now, Joan, what is the use of this foolishness? He was good enough a parson to marry you before."

"I won't marry you, I won't!" She stamped her foot. "I would sooner marry the beggar I saw on the roadside. I'd sooner marry the meanest slave in your household than marry you, a thief and a murderer—a man to whom no crime is too mean. I'd rather marry——"

"A burglar?" he said, white with passion.

"Ten thousand times yes—if you mean Jim Morlake. I love him, Hamon. I'll go on loving him till I die!"

"You will, will you?" he muttered. And then, turning, he ran out of the room, leaving her alone with the clergyman.

"How can you, Mr. Bannockwaite? How have you brought yourself to this low level?" she asked sternly. "Is there nothing in you that is wholesome to which a woman could appeal?"

"I don't want the heads of a sermon from you," he growled. "I will have you understand that I am intellectually your superior, socially your equal——"

"And morally the mud under my feet," she said scornfully.

For a moment she thought he would strike her. His bloated face grew first purple with passion, then faded to a pasty white.

"Intellectually your superior and socially your equal," he muttered again. "I am superior to your insults. *Telum imbelle sine ictu!*"

And then came a half-mad Hamon, dragging behind him a man, at the sight of whom Joan reeled backward. It was the beggar, a grinning, fawning toothless old man, horrible to look upon as he came cringing into this lovely room.

"Here is your husband!" almost shrieked the demented man. "Look at him! You'd sooner marry a beggar, would you, damn you! Well, you shall marry him and you shall have the desert for your honeymoon!"

She looked from the beggar to Bannockwaite and, even in her distress, she could not help thinking that she had never seen two more hideous men in her life.

"Get your book, Bannockwaite!" yelled Hamon. He was frothing at the mouth, so utterly beside himself that he seemed inhuman.

From his pocket, Bannockwaite produced a small book and opened it.

"You'll want witnesses," he said, and again Hamon dashed out, returning with half-a-dozen servants.

And there, under the curious eyes of the tittering Moors

Lady Joan Carston was married to Abdul Azim. Hamon muttered something in Arabic to the man, and then the girl felt herself caught by the arm and pulled and led through the hall into the garden.

Hamon dragged her to the open gates and flung her out with such violence that she nearly fell.

"Take your husband back to Creith!" he howled. "By God, you'll be glad to come back to me!"

CHAPTER LXI

The Beggar Husband

HAMON pushed the beggar out after his bride and slammed the gate on him.

Joan tried to walk, stumbled, recovered again, and then she knew no more. She recovered from her faint, lying under the shadow of a big juniper bush. Her face and neck were wet; a bowl of water was by her side. The old beggar had disappeared, and, raising herself on her elbow, she saw him unhobbling his sorry-looking horse. What should she do? She came unsteadily to her feet and looked round wildly. Escape was impossible.

And then she saw, far away in the valley, a cloud of dust. A party was approaching, and, straining her eyes, she caught sight of white *jellabs* and the glint of steel. It was a party of Moors, probably Sadi Hafiz returning—there would be no help there.

She looked again at her husband. The old man was wrapping his face and head in voluminous scarves, until only his iron-grey beard and the tip of his red hooked nose were visible.

He saw her and came toward her, leading the horse, and she obeyed his signal without a word, and mounted. Walking ahead he kept his hand on the bridle and she noticed that he took a path that was at right angles to the main road to Tangier.

Once or twice he looked back, first at the house and then the swift-moving party of horsemen which were now in view. It was Sadi—Joan recognised the figure riding at the head of the party. And she saw, too, that each man carried a rifle.

Suddenly the beggar changed direction, moved parallel with the cavalcade, as far as she could guess, for they were now out of sight and mounting the hill toward a point which would bring them clear of the gardens. From the anxious glances he shot backward, she guessed that he was in some fear lest Hamon, in a saner moment, had relented his mad folly. He walked the horse down to the bed of a hill stream and followed its tortuous windings, keeping the horse in the shallow waters. Suddenly she heard a shot, and then another. The sound re-echoed from the hills, and she looked down at the old man anxiously.

"What was that?" she asked in Spanish.

He shook his head without looking round.

Again came a shot, and then she guessed the reason. The shots were to attract the attention of the beggar and to recall him, and he evidently had the same view, for he jerked the reins of the horse and the animal broke into a trot, the beggar running nimbly by his animal's head.

They came to a little wood of pines and he brought the horse up the steep slope into its cover, and, signalling her to wait, he went back on foot. It was nearly half-an-hour before he returned, and then, holding up his hand, he lifted her from the saddle and she closed her eyes that she might not see his face. After a time he brought her water from the stream, and opening a little bundle, displayed food, but she was too tired to do any more than drink the cold, refreshing liquid. So tired, that, when she lay down upon the rug he spread, she forgot her terrible danger, forgot the trick of fate that had made her the wife of a beggar and fell instantly into a sound and dreamless sleep.

Ralph Hamon sat, crouched in his bedroom, his nails at his teeth, feeling weak and ill. The mad gust of temper that had driven him to such an act of lunacy had passed, leaving him shaking in every limb. From his window he could see the beggar carrying the girl down the hill, and at the sight he started to his feet with a hoarse cry of rage. That folly could be remedied and quickly.

There was a man amongst his servants who had been his pensioner for years, an old man, grizzled and grey, and he sent for him.

"Ahab," he said, "you know the beggar who rides the horse?"

"Yes, lord."

"He has taken with him at this moment the lady of my heart. Go bring her back and give the old man this money." He took a handful of notes from his pocket and put them into the eager palm of his servitor. "If he gives you trouble—kill him."

Ralph went up to his bedroom to watch his emissary go through the gates, and then for the first time he saw the party of mounted men winding their way up the hillside.

"Sadi," he said under his breath and guessed what that visit signified.

It was too late to recall his messenger and he ran down to the gates to welcome his some-time agent. Sadi Hafiz threw himself from his horse and his tone and mien were changed. He was no longer the polite and polished product of the mission school. He was the Moorish chieftain, insolent, overbearing, unsmiling.

"You know why I've come, Hamon," he said, his hands on his hips, his feet apart, his big head thrust forward. "Where is the girl? I want her. I presume you are not married, but, if you are, it makes very little difference."

"I am not married," said Hamon, "but she is!"

"What do you mean?"

He was not left long in doubt.

"My lady expressed a preference for a beggar. She said she would rather marry the old man who asked for alms than marry me—her wish has been fulfilled."

Sadi's eyes were slits.

"They were married half-an-hour ago and are there." He took in the country with a gesture.

"You're lying, Hamon," said the other steadily. "That story doesn't deceive me. I shall search your house as Morlake searched mine."

Hamon said nothing. There were twenty armed men behind Sadi and at a word from their leader he was a dead man.

"You're at liberty to search the house from harem to kitchen," he said coolly, and the Moor strode past him.

He could not have had time to make a very complete inspection, for he was back again almost immediately.

"I've spoken to your servants, who tell me that what you have said is true. Which way did she go?"

Hamon pointed and the Moor gave an order to his men. One of the horsemen fired in the air. A second and a third shot followed.

"If that does not bring him back we will go and look for him," said Sadi grimly.

"So far as I am concerned," Ralph shrugged his shoulders—"you may do as you wish. My interest in the lady has evaporated."

He was not speaking the truth, but his manner deceived the Moor.

"You were a fool to let her go," he said more mildly.

"If I hadn't let her go, you would probably have persuaded me," said Hamon, and Sadi's slow smile confirmed his suspicion.

A minute later the party was riding down the hill, scattering left and right in an endeavour to pick up the trail of the beggar and his wife. Hamon watched them before he returned to the house, to gather the pieces of his scattered dreams and discover which of the fragments had a solid value.

From an inside pocket he took a black leather case and, emptying the contents, laid them on the table and examined them one by one. The last of these possessions was an oblong document, covered with fine writing. Hindhead seemed far away—Hindhead and Jim Morlake and the prying Welling, and Creith, with its avenues and meadowlands. He knew the document by heart, but he read it again:

Believing that Ralph Hamon, who I thought was my friend, designs my death, I wish to explain the circumstances under which I find myself a prisoner in a little house overlooking Hindhead. Acting on the representations and on the advice of Hamon, I went to Morocco to inspect a mine, which I believed to be his property. We returned to London secretly, again on his advice, for he said it would be fatal to his plans if it were known that he was transferring any of his interests in the mine. Having a suspicion that the property, which he stated was his, had in reality nothing whatever to do with his company, I went to Hindhead, determined not to part with my money, until he could assure me that I was mistaken. I took a precaution which I believed and still believe is effective. At Hindhead my suspicions were confirmed and I refused to part with the money. He locked me up in the kitchen under the guardianship of a Moor whom he had brought back from Tangier with him. An attempt has already been made, and I fear the next——

Here the writing ended abruptly. He rolled up the damning charge and, returning it to his pocket-book with the other contents, slipped it into his inside pocket again. And, as he did so, he recalled Jim Morlake's description. The monkey's hand was in the gourd and he had come to the place where he could not release the fruit.

In the meantime, one of Sadi's men had picked up the track of footprints, and Sadi and two of the party had reached the edge of the stream.

"Leave your horses and come on foot," he ordered.

They followed the course of the stream downward until it was clear to the shereef that they could not have gone in that direction. From thereon, he had a view of the country. Moreover, they passed a particularly shallow stretch with a sandy bottom and there were no marks of hoofs.

"We will go back," he said, and led the way.

An hour's walk brought them to a place where the stream ran between high banks, and here the Moor's quick eyes saw the new marks of horse's feet, and he signalled his men to silence. With remarkable agility he ran up the bank and crept forward . . .

Joan woke from her sleep to meet the dark eyes of Sadi Hafiz looking down at her.

"Where is your friend?" asked Sadi, stooping to assist her to her feet.

She looked round, still dazed with sleep.

"My friend? You mean Abdul?"

"So you know his name," said Sadi pleasantly.

"What do you want with me?" she asked.

"I am taking you with me to Tangier, to your friends," he said, but she knew he was lying.

Looking round, she saw no sign of the beggar. His horse still grazed beneath a tree, but the old man had disappeared. Sadi sent one of his people to bring in the animal, and helped her to mount.

"I was terribly worried," he said in his excellent English, "when our friend Hamon told me the stupid thing he had done. There are times when Hamon is crazy and I am very angry with him. You like Morocco, Lady Joan?"

"Not very much," she said, and he chuckled.

"I don't suppose you do." He looked up at her admiringly. "How well the Moorish costume suits you! It might have been designed for your adornment."

A trick he had of using pretentious words that would at any other time have amused her. He walked by her side, one of his riflemen leading the horse, and after a while they came to a place where they had taken the stream. The remainder of his party were waiting for him, sitting on the bank, and at a signal they mounted.

"Perhaps it is as well I did not meet your husband," said Sadi ominously. "I trust he has not given you any trouble?"

She was not in the mood for conversation and she answered curtly enough and he seemed amused. No time was lost. She was lifted from the beggar's horse to a beautiful roan that had evidently been brought specially for her and she could not help reflecting on the certainty that, even if Ralph had married her, she would still have ridden on that horse before the day was through. Sadi Hafiz had come to take her back with him to his little house in the hollow, married or unmarried.

He rode by her side most of the day, talking pleasantly of people and things, and she was surprised at the wideness and catholicity of his knowledge.

"I was agent for Hamon in Tangier, and I suppose you have an idea that I was a sort of superior servant," he said. "But it suited me to act for him. He is a man without scruple or gratitude."

That was a sentiment which she thought came ill from Sadi Hafiz.

Before sunset they halted and made a camp. In spite of the coldness of the night, the men prepared to sleep in the open, wrapped in their woollen cloaks, but for the girl a tent was taken from the pack-horse and pitched in the most sheltered position Sadi could find.

"We will rest here until midnight," he said. "I must reach my destination before daybreak."

She lay wide awake, listening to the talk and watching the shadow of the smoking fires that the sunset threw on the thin walls of the tent, and then the talk gradually died down. There was no sound but an occasional whinny from a horse. She looked at the watch on her wrist, the one article of jewellery she had retained. It was nine o'clock. She had three hours left in which she could make her escape.

She drew aside the curtain of the little tent and, looking out, saw a dark figure—a sentry, she guessed. Escape was impossible that way. She tried to lift the curtain at the back of the tent, but it was pegged down tightly. Working her hand through under the curtain she groped around for the peg and presently found it. It took all her power to loosen it, but after a while, with a supreme effort, she pulled it from the earth and, exerting all her strength, she lifted the curtain a little farther and got her head beneath, and, by dint of perseverance, wriggled clear.

Ahead of her were impenetrable thorn bushes. She crept round the outside of the tent, conscious that her white dress would be detected if the sentry turned his head. And then she found an opening in the undergrowth and wriggled through. At the sound of cracking twigs the sentry turned and shouted something in Arabic. And now, desperate, the girl rose to her feet and ran. She could hardly see a yard before her; once she ran into a dwarf tree and fell momentarily stunned, but was on her feet again immediately. The moon was just rising and showed her a sparsely wooded stretch of plain; but it also revealed her to her pursuers.

The camp was now in an uproar. She heard shouts and the bellowing voice of Sadi Hafiz, and the clatter of horses' hoofs. It was Sadi himself who was coming after her. She knew it was he without seeing him, and, terrified, she increased her speed. But she could not hope to outpace the horse. Nearer and nearer he came, and then with a thunder of hoofs the horseman swept past her and turned.

"Oh no, my little rose!" he said exultantly. "That is not the way to happiness!"

He reached over and caught at her cloak and, swinging himself from the saddle, he caught her in his arms.

"This night I live!" he cried hoarsely.

"This night you die!"

He turned in a flash to confront the aged beggar and dropped his hand to the folds of his *jellab*.

Joan Carston stood, rooted to the spot, staring at the newcomer. She looked at the hideous face of Abdul Azim, but it was the voice of Jim Morlake that had spoken!

CHAPTER LXII

The Escape

Two shots rang out together, and Sadi Hafiz went to his knees with a groan and fell sideways.

"Get on to that horse, quick," said Jim, and almost threw her into the saddle.

He was up behind her in a second.

"Jim!" she whispered, and the arm that encircled her increased its pressure.

Burdened as he was, the big horse strode out freely, and Jim, looking over his shoulder, saw that the white figures that had followed Sadi from the camp had halted to succour their fallen chief.

"We've got ten minutes' start of them, anyway," he said, "and with any luck we ought to miss them."

Wisely, he left the direction to the horse, who would know the country, and whose eyes would detect the pitfalls and barriers in which the plain abounded. There was no sign now of pursuers, but Jim was without illusions. If Sadi Hafiz was capable of issuing orders, there would be no dropping of the pursuit. After an hour's travelling the horse gave evidence of his weariness, and Jim dropped from the saddle and went to his head.

"There used to be a guard house on the coast," he said, "though I don't know that a Moorish guard is much more companionable than the gentleman we have left behind."

She was looking down at him, trying to recognise, in the unpleasant face, one vestige of the Jim she knew.

"It *is* you?"

"Oh yes, it is I," he laughed. "The make-up is good? It is an old character of mine, and if Sadi had had the sense of a rabbit, he would have remembered the fact. The nose is the difficulty," he added ruefully. "The wax gets warm in the sun and has to be remodelled, but the rest is easy."

"But you have no teeth," she said, catching a glimpse of the black cavity of his mouth.

"They're there, somewhere," he said carelessly. "A toothbrush and a cake of soap will make a whole lot of difference to me, Joan."

He heard her gasp.

"What is the matter?" he asked quickly.

"Nothing," she said, and then: "How funny!"

"If your sense of humour is returning, my young friend, you're on the high road to safety!"

Before daybreak they halted near a spring and unsaddled and watered the horse.

"I'm afraid I can give you nothing to eat," said Jim. "Th only thing I can do——"

He stripped off his jellab and unfastened his ragged shir and produced from a pocket a small waterproof bag and car ried it to the stream.

He went down a hideous old man; he came back Jim Mor lake, and she could only sit and look at him.

"This is a dream," she said decidedly. "I shall wake u presently and find myself——" she shuddered.

"You'll hardly be any more awake than you are at this mo ment," said Jim. "We are within two miles of the coast, an unless friend Sadi has given very emphatic orders, his me will not follow us to the guard-house."

His estimate proved to be correct; they did not see a whit cloak again, and reached the guard-house to find it in charge as Jim had suspected, of a Spanish officer; for they ha reached that territory which Spain regarded as within th sphere of her influence.

"From here, we shall have to follow the coast-line and tak a chance," said Jim, after interviewing the officer. "The Spar iards can't give us an escort to Tangier for political reason —the French are rather jealous of their neighbours crossin the line, but I don't think we shall be molested."

They made camp that night almost within view of the light of Tangier. Jim had borrowed blankets from the Spanish ou post and spread them for the girl under the ruin of an ol Moorish post.

"By the way," he said, as he bade her good-night, befor retiring himself to the windy side of the wall, "this mornin you said something was very funny—what was it?"

"I'm not going to tell you," said Joan firmly.

As she settled down to sleep, she wondered whether the cere mony of the morning had been legal and binding—and ferv ently hoped that it had.

CHAPTER LXIII

The End of Sadi

THEY brought Sadi Hafiz to the house on the hill and the journey was a long one for a man with a bullet in his shoulder. The first news Ralph had of the happening was a thundering knock at the gates which roused him from a fitful sleep and sent him to his window.

The gates were locked and barred and could not be opened without his permission. He saw the gleam of lanterns outside, and presently a shrill voice called him by name and he knew it was Sadi. Hurrying downstairs, he joined the suspicious gatekeeper, who was parleying through the barred wicket.

"Let them enter," he said, and himself lifted one of the bars.

A glance at Sadi told him that something serious had happened and he assisted the wounded man into the house.

"Allah, I am finished!" groaned Sadi. "That pig. If that pistol had not caught in the folds of my cloak he would have been in hell to-night!"

Hamon sent for a woman and in the meantime examined the wound.

"It is nothing," said Sadi roughly. "The last time he shot me was more serious."

"The last time he shot you?" repeated Hamon dully.

Sadi had noticed a peculiar development in the man, which was not altogether explained in his changed appearance. He seemed to be thinking of something so intently that he had no time to interest himself in the events of the moment.

"What is the matter with you?"

"Nothing," said Hamon, coming out of his reverie. "You were saying . . . ?"

"I was saying that the last time he shot me was more serious."

"Who shot you, anyway?" asked Hamon. "Not the beggar?"

"The beggar," repeated the other grimly.

Here conversation was interrupted by the arrival of the woman whom the Moorish girl had called Señora Hamon. She carried a large bowl of water and cloths and Hamon watched her unseeingly while she dressed the wound. When she had gone, he took up the thread of the conversation.

"I never thought he would do you much harm," he said, "he is very old and feeble—you did not tell me that you knew him."

"I did not know that I knew him," replied the Moor, "or that you knew him. But Mr. Morlake is an old enemy of mine!"

With a start Hamon came to himself.

"You were speaking about the beggar, weren't you?" he said, frowning. "I'm so rattled and muddled to-night. You were talking of the old beggar man, Abdul."

"I'm talking about Mr. Morlake," said the other between his teeth. "The gentleman you so considerately married to your woman this morning!"

"Oh!" said Hamon blankly.

The tidings were too tremendous for him to take in. He passed his hand wearily before his eyes.

"I don't get it," he said haltingly. "The beggar was Morlake, you say? But how could he be? He was an old man——"

"If I'd had the eyes of a mole," said the other bitterly, "I'd have known it was Morlake. It was his favourite disguise when he was in the Intelligence Service in Morocco."

Hamon sat down on the divan where the man was lying.

"The beggar was Morlake," he said stupidly. "Let me get that in my mind. And I married them!"

He burst into a fit of laughter and Sadi, with his knowledge of men, saw how near his host was to a breakdown. Presently he calmed himself.

"Did he get her? Of course he did. He took her from you and shot you. Oh God! What a fool I was!"

"He hates you," said the Moor after a long interval of silence. "What is behind it?"

"He wants something I have—that is behind it." The flushed face and the slurred voice aroused Sadi's suspicion. Had the man been drinking?"

As though he read Sadi's mind, Hamon said:

"You think I'm drunk, don't you, but I'm not. I was never more sober. I'm just——" he hesitated to find a word, "well, I feel differently, that is all."

He made one of his abrupt exits, leaving Sadi to nurse his wound and to ponder on a development which brought almost as much unease to his mind as did his wound to his body. Hamon must go, he decided coldbloodedly. If it was true that there was an English police officer looking for him in Tangier, then the policeman must have his prey. Only in that way could Sadi be rehabilitated in the eyes of his many employers. Hamon had ceased to be profitable; was nearing the end of his financial tether. The shrewd Moor weighed up the situation with unerring judgment. He did not sleep, his shoulder was too painful; and soon after sunrise he went in search of his host.

Hamon was in the room that the girl had occupied. He at any rate had found forgetfulness, and on the table, where his head rested on folded arms, was an open pocket-book and a scatter of papers. Sadi examined them furtively.

There were half a dozen negotiable bank drafts, made out to "Mr. Jackson Brown," and there was also a white paper folded in four . . .

Hamon awakened and lifted his head slowly. The Moor was reading, and:

"That is mine, when you've done with it," said Hamon.

In no way disconcerted, Sadi dropped the papers on the table.

"So that is it? I wondered what you were scared of. You're a fool; that paper would hang you. Why don't you burn it?"

"Who told you to read it?" asked the other and his eyes were like live coals. "Who asked you to sneak in here and spy on me, Sadi?"

"You're a fool. I'm in pain and bored. I came in to talk to you, expecting to find you in bed."

Ralph was slowly gathering his property together.

"It was my fault, for leaving it around," he said. "Now you know."

Sadi nodded.

"Why don't vou destroy it?" he asked.

"Because I won't, I won't!" snarled the other, and pushed the case savagely into his pocket.

He followed Sadi with his eyes as the Moor strolled out of the room and sat motionless, staring at the door and fingering his lip.

Toward the evening, he saw one of Sadi's men mount his horse, and, leading another, go down the hillside. That could only mean one thing: the messenger was riding to Tangier without drawing rein except to change his horse. And he could only be riding to Tangier on one errand. Ralph Hamon chuckled. For some reason the discovery afforded him intense amusement. Sadi Hafiz was saving his own skin at his expense. In two days—to-morrow perhaps—authorisation would come through from the Sultan's representative, and he, Ralph Hamon, would be seized by the man whom he had befriended, and carried into Tangier, there to be extradited to stand his trial for—what?

He drew a long whistling breath. His hand unconsciously touched the case in his pocket. There were no safes to hide it there, no strong boxes, and yet a match, one of a hundred from a ten-centimos box, would relieve him of all danger. And he did not, would not, could not burn the accursed thing. He was well enough acquainted with himself to know that he was physically incapable of that last drastic act.

At the back of the house were his own stables, and the grooms' quarters. He strolled round casually and called the head groom to him.

"I'm going on a journey to-night, but it is secret. You will bring your horse and mine to the river where the road crosses—we'll go to the coast and afterward into Spanish territory. There is a thousand pesetas for you and yet another thousand if you are a discreet man."

"Lord, you have sewn up my mouth with threads of gold," said the man poetically.

Hamon went into Sadi's room to take dinner with him and was unusually cheerful.

"Do you think they will reach Tangier?" he asked.

"That is certain," said Sadi, "but I have as good a tale as any.

I told her I was taking her back to her friends. I did not harm her in any way and I think I will be able to satisfy the consulate that the young lady was alarmed for no good reason. The beggar I shot at—why? Because I do not know that he is Mr. Morlake. To me he is an evil old thief from whom I am rescuing the lady. Yes, the consulates will accept my story."

"And do you think *I* shall be able to satisfy the consulates?" asked Hamon, fixing his blazing eyes on the wounded man.

Sadi shrugged his shoulder and winced with the pain of it.

"You are a rich man and powerful," he said diplomatically. "I am a poor Moor, at the mercy of foreigners. To-morrow I will go back to Tangier," he said, "and you?"

"To-morrow I also may go to Tangier," said Hamon, not moving his eyes from the other, and he saw him shift uncomfortably.

"These things are with God," said the philosophical Sadi.

The household went to bed early. Sadi's men had been accommodated within the walls—a course which satisfied their chieftain. Midnight was striking on the little clock in the drawing-room when Hamon, dressed for riding, and wearing a thick coat that reached to his knees, came down the stone stairs to the hall. He wore rubbers over his shoes and made no sound as, creeping to the door of the room where Sadi was sleeping, he turned the handle softly. Only a candle burnt to give light to the sick man and Hamon stood, listening in the open doorway, till he heard the regular breathing of the sleeper. Then he drew a long, straight knife from his pocket and went into the room. He was only there a few minutes, and then the candle was extinguished and he came out.

He rode hard for two hours and halted whilst his groom heated some water and prepared a meal, and in the light of the dancing fire, the man said in alarm:

"Lord, there is blood on your sleeve and on your hands."

"That is nothing," said Hamon calmly. "This morning a dog of my house would have bitten me, so I killed him."

CHAPTER LXIV

A Moorish Woman's Return

SUNLIGHT bathed Tangier in a yellow flood, the surface of the bay was a mass of glittering gold; and all that could please the eye was there for their admiration; but the two elderly men who leant over the balustrade of the terrace saw no beauty in the scene; for the heart of one was breaking, and Welling's ached in sympathy.

The Cadiz mail was in the bay, a black, long-funnelled steamer, that at that moment was taking on the passengers who had been rowed out from the quay.

"I told her I couldn't come down to see her off, so she won't be very much disappointed," said Welling.

"Who? Lydia Hamon?"

Welling nodded.

"She'll be glad to see the last of Tangier." A pause. "That girl has the makings of a good woman."

"All women have," said Lord Creith quietly. "At least, that has been my experience."

Welling sniffed sceptically.

"There is no news, I suppose?"

Lord Creith shook his head. His eyes wandered to the stately yacht that lay at anchor in the bay.

"You'll wait here until you hear something?" suggested Welling.

"I suppose so," listlessly. "And you?"

"My work is practically done," said Welling, pulling thoughtfully at his cigar. "I came out to get the beginnings of Hamon, and I've pretty well cleaned up the obscurity of his start. He was a floater of fake companies, and was moderately successful until he brought a strange Englishman out here, a man of some wealth. They lived at the house of Sadi Hafiz and were here together for about a fortnight, when the Englishman and Hamon left together. I have discovered that the stranger paid him a very considerable sum of money—I have been round to the Credit Lyonnais, who have turned up the records. The transaction is very clear; the sum paid was fifty thousand pounds on account."

"On account of what?" asked Lord Creith, interested in spite of his trouble.

"That is what I want to know. Apparently a still larger sum was to be paid, but it certainly did not go into Hamon's account here."

"You don't know the name of this mysterious Englishman?"

The old man shook his head.

"I don't, but I guess the money was paid. I should say the final payment was made in the vicinity of Hindhead—if I could only be sure of that, Hamon would not show his nose in Tangier again."

"He won't anyway," said Creith bitterly. "By heavens, Welling, if the government of this infernal country doesn't do something by to-morrow, I'm going to raise an expedition and go into the interior to find my girl! And the day I meet Ralph Hamon will be his last!"

Welling sucked at his cigar, his eyes fixed upon the sunlit waters.

"If Jim Morlake can't find her, you won't," he said.

"Where has he gone?" wailed Creith. "It is the uncertainty about him that is holding me back."

"Nobody knows. That English dope-fiend that lives at the tailor's where, I have discovered, Morlake has a room, has been away from Tangier for two days. He came back last night. I've got a feeling that he's in the business, but when I tried to talk with him, he was too sleepy to snore!"

Two people were riding along the beach toward the town. They were less than half-a-mile away, but were conspicuous by reason of their unseemly animation.

"You don't often see a Moorish man and woman carrying on a bright conversation in public, do you?" said Welling, watching.

"Is the smaller one a woman?" asked Creith.

"I guess so; she is sitting side-saddle."

Lord Creith fixed his glass and peered at the two, and then the woman raised a hand and waved, and it seemed that the greeting was for him.

"Are they signalling to us?"

"It looks like it," said Welling.

Lord Creith's face had gone suddenly pale.

"It can't be," he said in a tremulous voice. Then, turning, he ran down the steps across the beach road on to the sands, and the two riders turned their steeds in the direction and kicked them into a gallop.

Welling watched the scene dumfounded. He saw the Moorish woman suddenly leap from the saddle into the arms of the bareheaded old man and then the bigger Moor got down, to be greeted warmly.

"If that is not Jim Morlake, I'm a Dutchman," said Welling.

In another instant he was flying across the sands to meet them. A crowd of Moors had watched the unseemly behaviour of the unveiled woman and stared painfully at her outrageous conduct.

"I don't care," said Joan hilariously. "I feel drunk with happiness."

In an hour four happy people sat down to the first square meal two of them had taken in days. Welling went away after lunch and came back in an hour with the news that the *basha* had sent a posse to arrest Hamon on information laid by Sadi Hafiz.

"Which means that Sadi, having saved his life, is now rapidly saving his skin," said Jim. "In a sense I'm glad I didn't kill him." He turned to Lord Creith. "You are going to get Lady Joan out of this very quickly, aren't you?"

"We sail this evening," said his lordship fervently, "and if there is a gale in the channel and the seas of the Bay of Biscay are mountains high, I'm heading straight for Southampton. I would go home by the nearest route," he added, "and let the yacht find its way back without my assistance, but the real owner is a personal friend of mine. You're coming too, Morlake?"

Jim shook his head.

"Not yet," he said quietly. "I came out here with two objects. One is to a great extent fulfilled; the other remains."

"You mean Hamon?"

He nodded.

"I'm certainly not going to leave you here, my good man," said Joan with spirit. "I have an especial right to demand that you will return with us!"

But on this point Jim was obdurate. The day after the yacht sailed, he received news of the death of Sadi Hafiz and the murderer's flight, and cursed himself for not following his heart. He flew over to Cadiz by military aeroplane, in the hope of picking up the yacht at that port, but even as the aeroplane was crossing the coast line, he saw the *L'Esperance* steaming out. He caught the afternoon train to Madrid, and was on the quay at Southampton to welcome them. And Joan did not see the man she loved until another month had passed, for Jim Morlake had been seized with a sudden shyness and a doubt had come to his mind which had developed into an obsession.

CHAPTER LXV

The Reverend Gentleman

"HANIMALS are hanimals," said the aggrieved Binger. "They 'ave their places, the same as everything helse."

"They may have their places, but if you kick my dog," said Jim Morlake, "I shall kick you!"

"If you kick me, sir," said Binger with dignity, "I shall hoffer my resignation."

Jim laughed and caressed the lame terrier who was showing his teeth at the valet.

"A hanimal's place is in the country, sir, if you'll excuse me."

"I won't excuse you, Binger," said Jim good-humouredly. "Get out."

He filled his pipe and sat back in the deep chair, scanning the evening newspaper and the terrier, who had resented the gentle kick which Binger had delivered because of a certain missing mutton-bone, put his head between his paws and went to sleep.

Presently Jim put down his newspaper, went to the bookshelf in his bedroom and brought back a large atlas. He turned the pages until he came to the coast line of Morocco and with a pencil he traced the possible avenues of escape that might lie open to a hunted murderer. He was in the midst of this occupation when Welling came.

"Planning out a honeymoon trip?" he asked pleasantly and Jim flushed.

"I am not contemplating a honeymoon trip," he said a little stiffly.

"Then you're wasting a perfectly good atlas," said the calm detective, laying his hat carefully over the head of the sleeping dog. "Your man is alive."

"Hamon?" asked Jim quickly.

The detective nodded.

"Two bank drafts have been cashed, both in Tangier, for a considerable sum. They were made payable to Hamon in a fictitious name—I only discovered the fact yesterday when I went to one of his banks. Hamon had several accounts running, and it was rather difficult to discover them all; but when I did get on to the right track I made that discovery. The drafts have been honoured—in fact, they're back in England."

Jim looked serious.

"Then he got to Tangier?"

"Undoubtedly, but that would be easy. I am willing to accept your theory that he got through to the Spanish territory. From Tetuan to Tangier is only a step. I think one of the Gibraltar steamers calls at both ports."

"He'll stay there if he is wise."

"But he isn't wise," said Welling. "It is dangerous enough for him in Tangier. He'll be tried for the murder of Sadi Hafiz if he is detected. The mere fact that he has drawn this money seems to me to be pretty convincing proof that he's shaking Tangier at the earliest opportunity—probably he is away by now. It is rather curious to see you fiddling with that atlas. I was doing exactly the same thing this morning, guessing the lines he took——"

"Which would be——?"

"Gibraltar-Genoa, or Gibraltar-Naples. Genoa or Naples to New York or New Orleans. New York or New Orleans to London, or maybe Cadiz and a banana boat to Thames River—*that's* more likely."

"You think he'll come here!" asked Jim in surprise.

"Certainly," said the other. "And what is more, we shall never take him."

Jim put down his atlas and leant back in his chair.

"You mean you'll never capture him?" he asked in surprise.

The detective shook his head.

"We may capture him, though at present we've no evidence worth the gum on a penny stamp," he said, "but he'll never hang. Because he is mad, Morlake! I've seen the report of the doctor who examined Sadi Hafiz after he was found, and I can tell you, as a student of medical jurisprudence, that Ralph Hamon is the third lunatic I've met in this case."

Jim lit his pipe again.

"Am I one?" he asked ironically.

"No, there have been three, but you haven't been one. The first was Farringdon, who was undoubtedly mad; the second was Bannockwaite, who is also mad but not dangerous; the third is Hamon, who is the worst of the lot."

Jim Morlake pondered as he recalled the characteristics of the men.

"Bannockwaite is the maddest of the lot," he said at last.

"He has left Tangier," nodded Welling. "The British Minister gave him twenty-four hours to quit, for some reason, which I haven't discovered, but which was probably due to your representation. He went over to Algeciras, but the Spanish people sent him packing. He was in Paris until yesterday. He is in London to-night."

"How do you know?" asked Jim in surprise.

"I had him tailed from the station. He is living in a little lodging in Stamford Street, Blackfriars."

Jim was not sufficiently curious to enquire much about the decadent minister, but now he learnt for the first time that Bannockwaite was practically penniless at the time when he was supposed to have died. He had run through a large fortune, scattering his money lavishly. His only income was from a group of houses the rents of which had been left to him by a maternal aunt in the days when he was so wealthy that he had regarded the legacy with something like contempt. These had been overlooked by him in the final squandering of his patrimony, and when he would have sold them the estate was fortunately in bankruptcy. Enough had been realised to clear his debts, but the administration of this little property remained in the trustee's hands.

"A remarkable fellow," said Welling, shaking his head. "He built three churches, endowed an orphanage, and brought more souls to the verge of hell than any living man."

Welling was on his way home. He had lately got into the habit of calling at the flat in Bond Street.

"Why don't you go back to Wold House?" he asked.

"I prefer this place for the time being. It is rather cold in the country," Jim excused himself lamely.

"What are you afraid of?" asked the detective contemptuously. "A bit of a girl!"

"I'm afraid of nothing," said Jim, going red.

"You're afraid of Joan Carston, my lad," and he spoke the truth.

Jim saw him out and went back to his pipe and his atlas, but now he had no interest in tracing possible routes, and closing the book returned it to the shelf.

Yes, he was afraid of Joan Carston—afraid of what she might feel and think; afraid that, in her less emotional moments, she would feel he had taken advantage of his disguise and sneaked into matrimony—that was his own expression. He was afraid that the marriage was not legal—equally afraid that it was. He might have accepted one of Joan's invitations, that grew colder and colder with repetition, and gone down to

Creith House and talked it over with her, but he had shirked the meeting. He heard the front door bell ring and Binger came in.

"There's a man wants to see you, sir."

"What sort of a man?"

"Well, to tell you the truth, my hown impression is that he's hintoxicated."

"What sort of a man?" asked Jim again.

"He's what I call the himage of a chronic boozer."

Jim looked at him and past him.

"Did he give his name?"

"Bannockburn is his name," said Binger impressively. "In my opinion it is a put-up job. Shall I say you're hout?"

"No," said Jim, "he might misunderstand you. Ask your Mr. Bannockburn to come in—by the way, his name is Bannockwaite."

"It sounds like a piece of hartfulness to me," said Binger and showed the man into the room.

There was very little improvement in the appearance of the marrying clergyman. He carried himself a little more jauntily, his manner was perhaps less aggressive. He wore a collar and a tie, the former of which had probably been in use since his return to London.

"Good evening, Morlake," he said with a sprightly wave of his hand. "I think we have met before."

"Won't you sit down," said Jim gravely. "Put a chair for Mr. Bannockwaite."

Binger obeyed with a grimace of distaste.

"And close the door tight," said Jim significantly, and Binger bridled as he went out.

"I got your address from a mutual friend."

"In other words, a telephone directory," said Jim. "I do not know that we have any mutual friends except Abdullah the tailor of Tangier. An excellent fellow!"

The wreck of a man fixed his glass in his eye and beamed benevolently on Jim.

"A limited but an excellent fellow. The industry of the Moor is a constant source of wonder to me." He stroked his uneven red beard and looked approvingly round the apartment. "It is delightful, perfectly delightful," he murmured. "A touch of old Morocco! I specially admire the ceiling."

Jim was wondering what was the object of the visit, but was not long left in doubt.

"I performed a little service for you, Mr. Morlake," said Bannockwaite with an airy wave of his swollen hand. "A mere trifle, but in these hard times, *necessitas non habet legem.* At the moment I was not aware that we had such a distinguished —er—client, but it has since transpired, though I have not advertised the fact, that the unprepossessing bridegroom was none other than the very interesting and—if I may be excused the impertinence—the very good-looking gentleman who is sitting before me.

"To turn my sacred calling into commerce is repugnant to all my finer feelings, but a man of your financial standing will not object to a mere trifle of five guineas. I could make an even larger sum if I wrote a little account, one of those frothy, epigrammatical soufflés of literature with which my name was associated at Oxford, and through the good offices of my friend of the editor of the *Megaphone*——"

"In other words, if I don't pay your fee of five guineas, you're going to broadcast the fact that I married Lady Joan Carston?"

"That would be blackmail," murmured the other and smiled jovially. "No, no, I will tell you candidly, *intra muros,* that I am too lazy to write. My dear fellow, I will be perfectly candid with you—I have no intention of writing," and again he beamed.

Jim took a note from his pocket and passed it across the table.

"Mr. Bannockwaite, I often wonder whether you think?"

"I beg your pardon?" The man leant forward with an exaggerated gesture of politeness, his hand to his ear.

"Whether I think?" he repeated. "My dear fellow, why should I think? I ask you, in the name of heaven, why I *should* think? I live for the moment. If the moment is good, I am happy; if it is bad, I sorrow. I have lived that way all my life."

"You have no regrets?" asked Jim wonderingly.

The man pocketed the note, smacked his lips and smiled.

"I shall see you again," he said, rising.

"If you call again, I will have you thrown out," said Jim without heat. "I hate to say it to a man of your surpassing intellect, but you are altogether horrible."

The visitor threw back his head and laughed, with such heartiness that Binger opened the door and stared in.

"My dear fellow," he said, "you lack something in philosophy. I wish you a very good evening."

When the door closed upon him, Jim rang the bell for Binger.

"Open the windows and air the room," he said.

"I should jolly well say so," said the indignant Binger.

"Then jolly well don't," snapped Jim.

He looked at his watch. It was eight o'clock and he was conscious that he had not dined. Binger was a bad cook and Mahmet had not returned from Casa Bianca. To avoid starvation or indigestion, Jim patronised a little restaurant in Soho, but to-night he craved for dishes that were home-made, and the very thought of the rich fare that awaited him in Soho made him feel ill. Home dishes, served in a big old-fashioned dining-room, with a fire crackling on the hearth, the rustle of bare boughs in the garden outside, a frozen lawn, and a river where little fishes leapt. He rang the bell.

"Telephone through to Cleaver and say I'm coming down to-night. Let him get me a large joint of juicy beef, with a mountainous pie to follow. And beer."

"To-night, sir?" said Binger incredulously. "It's height o'clock."

"I don't care if it is heighty," said Jim. "Get me my coat."

Soon he was speeding through the night, the cold wind rasping his cheeks. This was better than Tangier; better than warm breezes and sunny skies were these scurrying clouds that showed glimpses of the moon. There was a smell of snow in the air; a speck fell against his wind-screen and on the south side of Horsham it was snowing fast. The hedges were patched with white and the road revealed by his headlamps began to disappear under a fleecy carpet. His heart leapt at the sight of it. It could not be too cold, too snowy, too rainy, too anything—the country was the only place. There was something wrong about people who wanted to live in town all the year round, and especially in winter. Amongst the attractions of the country he did not think of Joan; yet, if he had thought of the country without her, it would have been drear indeed.

Cleaver greeted him with just that amount of pompousness that Jim enjoyed and took his wet coat from him.

"Dinner is ready, sir. Shall I serve?"

"If you please, Cleaver," said Jim. "Everything quiet here?"

"Everything, sir. A hayrick caught fire at Sunning Farm——"

"Oh, blow the hayrick!" said Jim. "Is that all the excitement you've had here since I've been away?"

"I think so, sir," said Cleaver gravely. "The tortoise-shell cat has given birth to four kittens and the price of coal has risen owing to the strike, but, beyond that, very little has happened. The country is very dull."

"Are you another of those dull-country people, my man?" said Jim gaily, as he rubbed his hands before the log fire. "Well, get that out of your head! It came on me to-night, Cleaver, that the country is the only place where a man can live. I'll have a fire in my bedroom, and turn on every light in the study, let up the shades and open the shutters."

Joan, going to bed, looked out of the window as was her practice, and saw the illumination.

"Oh, you have come back, have you!" she said softly, and kissed her finger-tips to the lights.

CHAPTER LXVI

A Luncheon Party

"WHAT is worrying me," said Lord Creith at breakfast, "is the future of this wretched estate."

"Why, Daddy?" she asked.

"What is going to happen, supposing this horrible scoundrel is arrested and tried and hanged, as very probably he will be? Who inherits Creith House?"

That had not occurred to her.

"His sister, I suppose," she said, after a moment's thought.

"Exactly," said Lord Creith, "and we're as badly off as ever we were! I'm jiggered in this matter, my dear, absolutely jiggered!"

"Have you actually sold the property?"

"N-no," said his lordship. "What I gave Hamon was a sort of extravagant mortgage."

"What kind of mortgage is that?" she asked, smiling.

"Well, he gave me a sum which it is humanly impossible that I could ever pay back, so that foreclosure sooner or later is inevitable, in exchange for which I received the tenancy for life."

He mentioned a sum which took her breath away.

"Did he pay you all that money?" she said in awe. "Why, Daddy, what did you do with it?"

Lord Creith tactfully changed the subject.

"I gather Jim Morlake is back," he said. "Why the dickens he hasn't come down before, I do not know. Really young men have changed since my day. Not that Morlake is a chick, I suppose he's fifty."

"Fifty!" she said scornfully. "He may be thirty but he's not much more."

"There is very little difference between thirty and fifty, as you will discover when you are my age," said his lordship. "I sent him a note asking him to come over to breakfast, but I don't suppose he is up."

"He is up every morning at six, Daddy," she corrected him severely, "hours before you dream of coming down."

"I dream of it," he murmured, "but I don't do it. How do you know?"

"He told me a whole lot about himself in Morocco," she said, and the subiect of their discussion was ushered in at that moment.

All his fears had come back to him, and her attitude did not make matters any better. She seemed scarcely interested in his recital of what he had been doing since he came to London, a recital called for by Lord Creith's persistent question:

"But why on earth haven't you been down?" demanded his lordship. "Joan——"

"Will you please leave me out of it?" said Joan immediately. "Mr. Morlake isn't at all interested in my views."

"On the contrary," said Jim hastily, "I am very much interested, and as I say I had a tremendous lot of work to do."

"And I hope you did it," said Joan briskly, "and now I'm going to the dairy. And don't come with me," she said as he half rose, "because I shall be very busy for the next two hours."

"You're staying to lunch, Morlake?"

"How absurd, Daddy," she said. "One would think Mr. Morlake had come down from London for the day! We're upsetting all his household arrangements and the admirable Mr. Cleaver will never forgive you."

Lord Creith stared glumly at the visitor after the girl had gone.

"That cuts out lunch so far as you're concerned, my boy," he said. "You're going to stay over for the hunting, of course?"

"I don't think so." Jim was annoyed, though he made an effort not to show it. "The country doesn't appeal to me very much. I came down to get my house in order. I've only paid one visit to Wold House since I returned from Morocco. I'm going to America next week," he added.

"It is a nice country," said his lordship, oblivious to the fact that he was called upon to show some regret or surprise.

Jim went home feeling particularly foolish and was irritated at himself that he had been guilty of such childishness.

The visitor was gone when Joan came back to lunch.

"Where is Mr. Morlake?" she asked.

"He's gone home, where you sent him," said Lord Creith, unfolding a serviette with care.

"But I thought he was staying to lunch?"

Lord Creith raised his pained eyes at this shocking piece of inconsistency.

"You knew jolly well he was not staying to lunch, Joan!" he said severely. "How could the poor man stay to lunch when you sent him home? I'm going to London to-morrow to see him off."

"Where?" she gasped.

"He's going to America," said his lordship, "South America, probably. And," he added, "he will be away ten years."

"Did he tell you that?" she demanded, staring at him.

"He didn't mention the period," he answered carefully, "but I gathered from his general outlook on things that he finds Creith dull and that a few healthy quibbles with a boa-constrictor on the banks of the perfectly horrible Amazon would bring amusement into his life. Anyway, he's going. Not that I intended seeing him off. I can't be bothered."

"But seriously, Daddy, is he leaving Creith?"

His lordship raised his eyes wearily and sighed.

"I've told you twice that he's going to America. That is the truth." He pulled out a chair and sat down.

"I don't want anything, thank you, Peters."

"Aren't you eating? You've been drinking milk," accused his lordship. "There's nothing like milk for putting you off your food. And it will make you fat," he added.

"I haven't been drinking milk. I'm just simply not hungry."

"Then you'd better see the doctor."

She dropped her head on her hands, her white teeth biting at her underlip. Lunch promised to be a silent meal until she said:

"I don't believe he is going!"

"Who?"

"Who were we talking about?"

"We haven't talked about anybody for a quarter of an hour," said his lordship in despair. "You're the most unsociable woman I've ever dined with. Usually people do their best to amuse me. And believe me I pay for amusing! He's going!"

She raised her eyebrows to signify her indifference.

"I don't believe he is going," she said. "I'm hungry and there isn't anything to eat. I hate lamb!"

Her parent sighed patiently.

"Go and lunch with him, my dear, for heaven's sake! Take a message from me that you're growing more and more unbearable every day. I wonder, by the way, if you'll ever develop into an old maid? We had an aunt in our family—you remember Aunt Jemima—she was taken that way. She bred rabbits, if I remember aright. . . ."

But Joan did not want to discuss her Aunt Jemima and flounced up to her room.

His lordship was in his study when he saw her walking across the meadows in the direction of Wold House and shook his head. Joan could be very trying. . . .

"Thank you, Cleaver," said Jim. "I don't think I want any lunch."

"It is a woodcock, sir," said Cleaver anxiously. "You told me last night you could enjoy a woodcock."

Jim shuddered.

"Take it away, it seems almost human! Why do they serve woodcocks with their heads on? It isn't decent."

"Shall I get you a chop, sir?"

"No, thanks, a glass of water, and bring me some cheese—no, I don't think I'll have any cheese—oh, I don't want anything," he said, and got up and poked the fire savagely.

"Jane Smith," said a voice from the doorway. "I've announced myself."

She took off her coat and handed it to Cleaver and threw her hat on to a chair.

"Have you had any lunch?"

"I haven't; I'm not hungry."

"What have you got for lunch?" she asked.

"We have a woodcock," said Jim dismally. "It isn't enough for two."

"Then you can have something else," said Joan, and rang the bell. "Jim, are you going to America?"

"I don't know. I'm going somewhere out of this infernal place," he said gloomily. "The country gives me the creeps;

snowing all the morning and the sound of the wind howling round the house makes my hair stand up."

"You're not going anywhere, you are staying in Creith; I've decided that," said Joan.

She was eating bread and butter hungrily.

"Don't they feed you at home?" asked Jim looking at her in wonder.

"What are you going to do about us?" was her reply.

"What do you mean—us?" he asked, inwardly quaking.

"About our marriage. I've taken legal advice and there is not the slightest doubt that we're married. At the same time there's not the least doubt that we're not. You see I've been to two sets of lawyers."

"Have you really?"

She nodded.

"I haven't been to lawyers exactly, but I've written to two newspapers that give free advice and one says one thing and one says the other. Now what are we to do?"

"What do you want to do?" he countered.

"I want to get a divorce," she said calmly, "except for the publicity. I shall base my petition on incompatibility of temperament."

"That isn't a good cause in this country."

"We shall see."

Jim drew a long face.

"There's another way out of the trouble, Mrs. Morlake," he said.

"Don't call me Mrs. Morlake. At the worst, I am Lady Joan Morlake. Jim, are you really going to America?"

"I've had very serious thoughts about it," he said. "But honestly, what are we to do, Joan? My lawyer says that it is no marriage because the necessary licence is not issued, and the mere fact that a clergyman performed the ceremony does not legalise it."

Consternation was in her face when he looked at her.

"Do you mean that?" she said.

"Are you sorry?"

"No, I'm not exactly sorry. I'm annoyed. That means that

we've got to get married all over again. And, Jim, that will take an awful time. . . ."

Cleaver, coming in at that moment, turned round and went out again very quickly, and it seemed almost as if the woodcock winked.

CHAPTER LXVII

The Return

IT HAD snowed all night. The roads were ankle-deep but the man who tramped doggedly through the mean streets of East London hardly noticed the weather. It was too early to get a cab. The little ship had come in with the tide and was moored near Tower Bridge and he had had some difficulty in persuading the man at the docks to let him pass, but as he carried no luggage, that difficulty had been overcome, and now he was heading for the city.

He passed Billingsgate, crowded even at that early hour, and turning up Monument Hill, came to the Mansion House. Here he found a wandering taxi which set him down at the end of Grosvenor Place. There was nobody in sight. The snow was falling again and a fierce wind had driven the policeman to cover. The blinds of the house were drawn, he noticed, and wondered whether it was empty. Taking a key from his pocket, he opened the door.

Nothing had been moved. He had sold the house and the new tenant had told him he would not wish to take possession for a year. He muttered his satisfaction. Looking into the drawing-room, he saw it was untouched. On one of the tables was an embroidery frame, the needle showed in the fabric and he nodded. Lydia was here then, she had not returned to Paris, and she was wise. On the way upstairs he met a servant coming down and the woman stared at him as though he were a ghost. Fortunately he knew her.

"You needn't tell anybody I'm back," he said gruffly and went on to his room.

It looked very desolate with its sheeted furniture. The floors were bare and the bed innocent of clothing. He took off his overcoat and looked at himself in the glass with a queer smile, and he heard a rustle of feet on the landing outside. The door opened suddenly and Lydia came in in her dresisng-gown.

"Ralph!" she gasped. "Millie told me that she had seen you."

"Well, she told the truth," he said, looking at her strangely. "So you're here, are you?"

"Yes, Ralph, I came straight back."

"After telling the police as much as you could about me?"

"I told them nothing," she said.

He grunted his disbelief.

"Ralph, there's a story about Sadi Hafiz. He was murdered in Morocco and you were—you were in the house."

"Well?" he asked.

"Is that true?"

"I didn't know he was dead," he said, not meeting her eyes. "Besides, what happened in Morocco is nothing to do with us here. They can't extradite me for a murder committed in a foreign country. And if they do who's to prove I did it? Sadi Hafiz got what was coming to him," he said cunningly. "I killed him because he insulted you."

She knew he was not speaking the truth but did not argue with him.

"The police have been here," she began.

"Of course they've been here. Haven't you been running round with old Welling? I heard about it in Tangier. As to the police, I'm going to Welling this morning."

"Ralph, you're not!" She laid her hand on his arm but he shook it off.

"I'm going to Welling this morning, I tell you. I've been thinking things over on the ship and I'm sick of living like a hunted dog. If they've got anything on me, let them produce it. If it is a question of trial, why I'll stand my trial! Get me something to eat."

She hurried away, coming back to tell him that she had laid a tray in his study.

"I suppose the police have looked there too, haven't they?"

"They didn't look anywhere, Ralph," she said, "they merely called. They had no warrant——"

"Hadn't they?" He turned on her quickly, a gleam in his eyes. "That means that they're not sure of themselves," he added. "I'll see old Welling to-day and he will be a very surprised man. Then I'm going down to Creith, my property," he said emphatically.

"Ralph, you're mad to go to the police," she said tremulously, "couldn't you go abroad somewhere?"

"I've had too much of abroad already. I tell you I'm going to surprise old man Welling."

Inspector Welling was not easily shocked, but when a policeman came into his office that morning and laid a card on his table he almost jumped from his chair.

"Is he here?" he asked incredulously.

"Yes, sir, in the waiting-room."

"He himself?" He could not believe his ears.

"Yes, sir."

"Bring him along," and even then he did not expect to see Ralph Hamon.

Yet it was the Ralph of old, with his immaculate silk hat and his well-fitting morning coat, who walked into the office and laid his cane upon the officer's table and smiled down into his astonished face.

"Good-morning, Welling," he said cheerfully. "I understand that you have been looking for me?"

"I certainly have," said Welling, recovering from the shock of surprise.

"Well, here I am," said Hamon, and found a chair for himself.

He looked ten years older than he had when Welling saw him last, and the frothy little locks that covered the top of his head had completely disappeared, leaving him bald.

"I want you to account for what you did—or, at any rate, for your movements—in Morocco," said Welling, beginning cautiously. Anything further that he might have said was interrupted by his visitor's laughter.

"You can't ask me anything, Welling, or make any enquiries, unless you are requested to do so by the police authorities of that district in which Sadi Hafiz died. You see, I am making no disguise of the fact that I know it is Sadi Hafiz's murder you are thinking about. My sister tells me you also require certain information concerning Farringdon and his untimely end. I can only tell you that, at the time of his murder, I was in London, and if you can prove to the contrary you are welcome to take any steps which you may think necessary."

The detective looked at him from under his bushy eyebrows.

"And what of the murder in the little cottage overlooking the Devil's Punch Bowl?" he asked.

Not a muscle of Ralph Hamon's face moved.

"That is a new one to me," he said, "though the locality sounds familiar. I had a bungalow there—or in that region."

"It is about the bungalow I am speaking," said Welling. "A man was killed there, stripped and put into a sailor's suit, and left for dead on the Portsmouth Road. He was picked up, as you probably know, by Mr. James Lexington Morlake, and conveyed to the Cottage Hospital, where he died. I have examined the premises, and I find bloodstains on the wall of the kitchen."

Ralph Hamon smiled slowly.

"Have you also found that I put them there?" he asked drily. "Really, Captain Welling, I am not prepared to discuss these crimes in detail. What I do ask you plainly is this." He got up and walked across to the table, and stood leaning upon its edge, looking down into Welling's upturned face.

"Have you any charge to make against me? Because, if you have, I am here to answer that charge."

Welling did not reply. The enemy had carried the war into his country, and had established a very favourable point for himself. He was practically demanding an enquiry into rumour and a precipitation of suspicion. There was no warrant for the man, no definite charge against him. Even Scotland Yard would hesitate to arrest Ralph Hamon on the information it possessed; and he knew that the man was on safe ground when he said that no charge could follow the murder of Sadi Hafiz unless representations had been made by the Moorish Government—and none had been made.

"Most of the charges are those which you are bringing yourself," he drawled. "I do not even ask you to produce your pocket-case and show me its contents."

He watched the man narrowly as he spoke. If Hamon had shown the slightest uneasiness, if he had turned the conversation elsewhere, if he had protested against the suggestion, he would have arrested the man on the spot and have searched him, on any charge that came into his head. But the answer of Ralph Hamon was characteristic. He dived his hand into his pocket and flung the case on to the table.

"Look for yourself," he said, "and if you wish to search me . . ." he flung out his arms—"you are at liberty."

Welling opened the case and examined the papers it contained with a professional eye. Then he handed the leather pouch back to its owner.

"Thank you," he said. "I will not detain you, Mr. Hamon."

Hamon picked up his hat and stick, pulled on his gloves and walked leisurely to the door.

"If you want me, you know where you will find me—either at my house in Grosvenor Place, or at my country residence, Creith House."

Welling smiled.

"I never find anybody except in the place I put them," he said.

Ralph Hamon strolled down the long corridor, twirling his stick, and out on to the Thames Embankment, where a hired car was awaiting him. On his way through the Park he looked back wondering which of the taxicabs which were bowling along behind contained the shadow that Welling had affixed to him.

He found Lydia waiting in a state of nervous tension.

"What did they say, Ralph?" she asked, almost before he was in the room.

"What could they say?" he smiled contemptuously.

He went to her writing bureau, pulled out a cheque book and sat down.

"Since you are so infernally nervous, you had better go off to Paris this afternoon," he said, and, writing a cheque, tore it out and handed it to her.

She looked at the amount and gasped; then, from the cheque, her eyes went back to her brother.

"Have you this amount in the bank?" she asked, and he swung round to stare at her.

"Of course I have," he said.

He turned again to the table, wrote another cheque and, enclosing it in an envelope, added a card: "With Compliments," and, having addressed the envelope, rang the bell.

"We have no butler now, Ralph," she said nervously. "Would you like me to take the letter to the post? Are you staying in?" she added.

"No," he answered curtly, "I am going to my wife."

Her hand went up to her mouth.

"Your wife, Ralph?" she faltered. "I did not know you were married."

"I am referring to Joan," he said gravely, and went out, and up to his room.

She sat motionless, twisting a torn handkerchief in her hand, and after a while she heard him come down again and the street door close. She went to the window and looked out, to see him enter his car and drive off. He had changed his attire, and wore the suit he had been wearing when he arrived that morning. Before the car was out of sight, she was flying up to her room to dress, for she knew that the moment of crisis was at hand.

CHAPTER LXVIII

The End of Hamon

WELLING was going out to lunch when she arrived, and he met her literally on the doorstep.

"I must see you, Captain Welling, at once," she said. "It is vitally important."

"Come back to my room," he said kindly. "You look ill, Lydia."

"I am distracted. I don't know what I shall do," she said, her voice trembling.

In his room he poured her a glass of water, and waited until she was sufficiently composed to tell him the object of her visit.

"It is about Ralph," she said. "He was here this morning?"

The old man nodded with a rueful smile.

"He was here, and he emerged with flying colours," he said. "If it was a bluff, it was the cleverest bluff I've met with. You have seen him since?"

She nodded.

"He came back to the house, and I haven't seen him so buoyant in years. He asked me if I would like to go to Paris, and gave me a cheque. Here it is."

She handed him the cheque and the detective took it and read, and when he had read, he whistled. For the sum which Ralph Hamon had drawn was a million pounds!

"What is that?" he asked, seeing the envelope in the girl's hand. It was addressed to him, he saw. "From your brother?" he asked with a frown.

She nodded, and, tearing open the envelope, he extracted a second cheque, which was also for a million pounds.

Welling bit his lip.

"That looks pretty bad to me," he said. "Where is he now?"

"He's gone off to see Joan. He called her his wife," said the girl.

She was crying softly, and he put his arm around her shoul-er and patted her cheek.

"You're going to have a bad time for a while, Lydia," he aid, "and I am going to help you all I know how. You must ay at an hotel to-night, and not your maid or any of your ervants must know where you are. Come and lunch."

She protested that she had no appetite, but he insisted, and id not leave her until he had carried her bag into the vestibule f the Grand Central and handed her over to the especial care f the hotel detective.

He had come so far in a taxicab, but a big police car was vaiting for him, with three men from police headquarters.

Jim was practising with a golf club on the lawn when the ar arrived.

"A queer occupation," said Welling, for the snow lay thick everywhere.

"If you dip a gold ball in ink——" began Jim lightly, when he caught sight of the car's three half-frozen men who were huddled in its depths. "Come inside, Welling," he said. "What is the trouble?"

"There is trouble for somebody, and I'm not quite sure who it is going to be," said Welling.

He told all he knew, related the incident of the cheques, and Jim listened in silence.

"I am putting two men at Creith House. You had better put up the other here."

Jim shook his head.

"Let the three go to Creith House," he said. "I can look after myself. Has he left London?"

Welling nodded.

"He had a car in a garage—a public garage—near by. Unfortunately, I was not able to trace that until it was too late. This afternoon he took it out, and since then he has not been seen."

Snow was falling heavily when the police car turned through the gates of Creith House and made a slow and noisy way up the drive. Lord Creith watched the arrival from the dining-room window, and came to the door to meet them. At the first sight of Welling his face fell.

"There is going to be bother," he said fretfully. "You stormy old petrel!"

They were glad to get into the warmth and cosiness of the library, for it was bitterly cold and the snow was freezing as it fell.

"Who are you after?" asked Creith anxiously. "Not Hamon?"

Welling nodded.

"Hamon it is. He is in England, and probably not four miles from Creith," he said, and his lordship looked serious.

"Where is Joan?" asked Welling.

"She is out," said Creith. "Mrs. Cornford asked her to go down to lunch at the cottage."

Welling shook his head reprovingly.

"From now on, until this man is under lock and key, she must not be allowed out alone," he said. "Somebody ought to go and bring her back."

But Jim was already on his way. He ploughed knee-deep through the icy covering, and, finding that the short cut to the cottage would in the end be the longest way, he struggled back to the drive and followed the wall path. Here he found the tracks of Joan; the impress of her rubber boots was plain, and he felt a little thrill of satisfaction in this evidence of her nearness.

Then, for no apparent reason, the footprints turned to the right, entering the deeper snow that had drifted about a clump of bushes. With an exclamation of surprise, he followed them. They led him deeper and deeper into the snow, until they turned again and disappeared.

He peered into the bushes but could see no sign of her. Crushing his way between the snow-covered boughs, he found a comparatively clear space where the grass showed. But there was no sign of Joan. She must have gone out somewhere, and he pushed his way clear of the bushes, to find her tracks leading to the path again.

He stood with a frown on his forehead, puzzling out her eccentric movements. And then he saw another set of footprints which were obviously recent, for the falling snow had not yet obliterated them. They were fairly small, and the toes were pointed. He gasped—Hamon! The girl must have seen him coming along the path, and then flown on to her destination.

He turned back, this time following Hamon's tracks. There were two sets: one going toward Creith House and the other returning; and presently he found the place where the man had turned. Jim unbuttoned his overcoat and took from his pocket the little black automatic, and slipped it into his overcoat; and then, hurrying as fast as the snow would allow him, he made for the gardener's cottage, all the time keeping his eyes upon the footprints.

At the end of the path the two sets branched off—Joan's toward the cottage. He ran up the cottage path, and a glance at the house told him that something unusual had happened. The shutters were drawn in every room. He knocked at the door, and, receiving no answer, knocked again more loudly.

"Are you there, Mrs. Cornford?" he called, and he thought he heard a creaking sound inside, and flung himself against the door.

It shook under his weight, and an agonised voice called:

"If you open the door, I will shoot you."

It was the voice of Joan!

"It is I, Joan," he called eagerly. "Look through the keyhole—it is Jim!"

He walked back half-a-dozen paces in order to give her a clear view, and, as he did so, he felt his hat jerked violently from his head. That and the crack of the explosion came together, and he spun round to face the danger. Nobody was in sight.

And then the door of the cottage opened.

"Keep inside," he cried. "For God's sake don't come out."

Ping!

The bullet struck the wall of the cottage with a snap, and, running, he gained the shelter of the passage and slammed the door.

"Oh, I'm so glad!" sobbed the girl distraitly. "Oh, Jim, I'm frightened—frightened! I saw him in the grounds," she went on, when he had soothed her.

"And you hid in the bushes—I followed your tracks. He didn't see you?"

She shook her head.

"Not until I was nearly at the cottage, and then he ran after me. Mrs. Cornford had seen him, and had put up her shutters. It is Hamon, isn't it?"

Jim nodded.

The shutters operated from inside the house, and he gently raised the lower half of one and peered out. He had hardly done so before a bullet smashed the window, tore a long, jagged hole in the wooden shutter, and temporarily numbed his hand with the shock.

"I think we had better wait," he said. "Welling will have heard the shots. Our only hope is that friend Hamon guesses, by my hasty retreat, that I am unarmed, and comes to close quarters."

"Have you no weapon?" she asked anxiously.

He produced a little pistol.

"Only this," he said, "which is comparatively useless except at short range. It is, in fact," he smiled, "the weapon with which I have terrified night watchmen and unfortunate banking officials these ten years past."

He had rightly estimated the effect of his precipitate flight upon the cunning madman who was glaring at the house from behind the cover of a wood pile. Hamon knew that Jim Morlake would not fly into the house if he had a gun handy; and he knew, too, that the sound of the shooting must soon bring assistance. Already a curious and fearful knot of children had gathered in the middle of the street at a respectful distance, and if he were to accomplish his great revenge, and bring to fruition a plan that had occupied his mind for the past three months, he must move quickly.

He sprang from his place of concealment and ran across the cottage garden; and, as he expected, he drew no fire from the house. He looked round for something he could use as a battering-ram, and his eyes returned to the wood pile, and, going back, he picked up a heavy branch and brought it to the door. The whole cottage seemed to shake under the impact of the ram, and Jim, watching from the passage, knew that the lock would not stand another blow.

"Keep back," he warned the girl in a whisper, and slipped through the door which led from the passage into the room where Farringdon had lost his life.

Again Hamon struck, and the lock broke with a crash. In another second, Hamon had pushed open the door, and, gun in hand, had stepped in. He saw the open doorway and guessed who stood there.

"Come out, Morlake!" he screamed. "Come out, you dog!"

He fired at the lintel, and the bullet ricochetted past Jim's face. Jim was waiting for the second shot, and when it came he leapt out, his little black pistol levelled.

Before Hamon could fire, Jim pressed the trigger. There was no explosion. Only from the muzzle of the black "gun" shot with terrific force a white spray of noxious vapour. It struck the would-be murderer in the face, and with a choking gasp he fell heavily to the floor.

Jim's eyes were watering, he himself found it difficult to breathe, and he came back for a moment to the girl, who held her handkerchief to her mouth.

"Open the windows," he ordered quickly, and then went back to the unconscious man, just as Welling and his men came flying up the path.

"It isn't pleasant, is it?" said Jim, eyeing his stubby gun with a smile. "It has never carried a cartridge, because it isn't built that way. It throws a spray of pure ammonia vapour, and throws it a considerable distance."

It was necessary to put the maniac into a strait-jacket before he could be moved to the nearest lock-up, and they did not see Welling again until he came to Creith House late that afternoon, weary and bedraggled, but with a look of triumph in his eyes.

"Well," he said, speaking to the company in general but addressing Jim, "I have discovered the mystery is not such a mystery after all. And why I did not hit upon the solution as soon as I heard and knew that you were burgling banks and strong rooms in order to secure a document which would incriminate Ralph Hamon, I cannot for the life of me understand. Maybe I am getting old and dull."

"I am too," said the girl, "for it certainly puzzles me."

Lord Creith stretched his hands to the blazing warmth, rubbed them together and ruminated profoundly.

"I give it up too—our American friend must explain. But perhaps you have the document, Welling?"

Captain Welling smiled.

"It is here," he said, and produced Ralph Hamon's pocket-book. "It seemed incredible to me that Hamon should carry about with him a statement written by his victim that would most inevitably bring him to the gallows if it ever was produced in a court of law."

"Then why the devil didn't he burn it?" asked Lord Creith irritably, and for answer Welling produced the document.

Lord Creith read it through with a frown.

"He could have burnt this——" he began.

"Turn it over," said Welling quietly, and Creith obeyed. He stared for a moment at the engraved letters on the other side.

"Good God!" he said.

The statement was written on the back of a Bank of England note for £100,000.

"He could have burnt it," said Jim, "but his natural cupidity would not allow him to destroy so much money. He dared not pay it into the bank; he could not bring himself to do away with the evidence of his guilt. When I found John Cornford, he was dying, and the first name I heard was that of Ralph Hamon, whom I had met once in Tangier and knew to be a shady customer. And then I recognised in the sailor the mysterious visitor that Hamon had had some months before. Little by little, I learnt from the half-sane man the story of Hamon's villainy. In order that he might not be wronged, Cornford had changed all his money into one note of a hundred thousand pounds. I was able to trace that at the bank, and even if Hamon had presented it for payment, it would have been stopped. The monkey and the gourd," he mused; "he could not let go of his treasure and he was caught."

. . . .

On a bitterly cold day in January, when the whole country was ice-bound, and rivers which had never known obstruction were frozen from bank to bank, Jim Morlake and Joan Carston came out of Creith parish church, man and wife. They left that afternoon by car for London, and it was Joan's wish that they should make a détour through Ascot.

"You are sure you don't mind. Jim?" she asked for the tenth time, as the car was rolling swiftly along the frozen Bagshot Road.

"Why, of course not, honey. It is very dear of you."

"He was a boy, just a silly, romantic boy, who had held such promise of a big career, and I feel that this—this ruined him."

She was thinking of Ferdinand Farringdon, and Jim understood. They halted near the place where the black pines hid the little church in the wood, and she handed a great bunch of lilies to Jim as he got out of the car.

"Lay them on the altar, Jim," she said, and he nodded and slammed the door tight.

The cold was phenomenal: it struck through his fur-lined coat and made his fingers tingle. How different it was in winter, he thought! And yet the chapel in the wood had a beauty of its own, even on this drear day. As he turned to cross, he stood looking, and then he saw the figure crouched against the steps—a bundle of rags that bore no semblance to anything human. He ran forward and looked down into the cold, grey face, strangely beautiful in death. What freak impulse brought Bannockwaite to the door of the church he had built, there to die in the cold night?

Jim looked round: there was nobody in sight, and, stooping, he laid the lilies on the dead man's stiffened hands, and, bareheaded, walked back to the car.

Lightning Source UK Ltd.
Milton Keynes UK
UKHW011146010822
406675UK00003B/929